The Third Cadfael Omnibus

Ellis Peters

The Third Cadfael Omnibus

The Sanctuary Sparrow
The Devil's Novice
Dead Man's Ransom

Brother
CADFAEL

WARNER FUTURA

A *Warner Futura* Book

First published in this omnibus edition in Great Britain in 1992 by
Warner Futura

Reprinted 1995, 1996, 1997

THE SANCTUARY SPARROW first published by Macmillan London in
1983 and by Futura in paperback in 1984
Copyright © Ellis Peters 1983

THE DEVIL'S NOVICE first published by Macmillan London in 1983 and
by Futura in paperback in 1985
Copyright © Ellis Peters 1983

DEAD MAN'S RANSOM first published by Macmillan London in 1984 and
by Futura in paper in 1985
Copyright © Ellis Peters 1984

This omnibus edition copyright © Ellis Peters 1992

The moral right of the author has been asserted.

A CIP catalogue record for this book
is available from the British Library.

ISBN 0 7515 0111 5

Photoset in North Wales by
Derek Doyle & Associates, Mold, Clwyd.
Printed in England by Clays Ltd, St Ives plc

Warner Futura
A Division of
Little, Brown and Company (UK)
Brettenham House
Lancaster Place
London WC2E 7EN

Contents

The Third Cadfael Omnibus

The Sanctuary Sparrow

Chapter One

Friday midnight to Saturday morning

T BEGAN, as the greatest of storms do begin, as a mere tremor in the air, a thread of sound so distant and faint, yet so ominous, that the ear that was sharp enough to catch it instantly pricked and shut out present sounds to strain after it again, and interpret the warning. Brother Cadfael had a hare's hearing, readily alerted and sharply focused. He caught the quiver and bay, at this point surely still on the far side of the bridge that crossed Severn from the town, and stiffened into responsive stillness, braced to listen.

It could have been an innocent sound enough, or if not innocent of murderous intent, at any rate natural, the distant voices of hunting owls, and the predatory bark of a dog-fox prowling his nocturnal barony. Certainly the ferocious note of the hunt sounded clearly in it to Cadfael's ear. And even Brother Anselm the precentor, wholly absorbed into his chanting of the office, wavered and slipped off-key for an instant, and took up the cadence jealously, composing his mind sternly to duty.

For there could not be anything in it to trouble the midnight rite of Matins, here in this kindly spring, barely four weeks past Easter of the year of Our Lord 1140, with Shrewsbury and all this region secure within the king's peace, whatever contentions raged farther south between king and empress,

3

cousins at odds for the throne. The winter had been hard indeed, but was blessedly over, the sun had shone on Easter Day, and continued shining ever since, with only light scattered showers to confirm the blessing. Only westward in Wales had there been heavy spring rains, swelling the river level. The season promised well, the town enjoyed fair rule under a dour but just sheriff, and defended stoutly by a sensible provost and council. In a time of civil war, Shrewsbury and its shire had good cause to thank God and King Stephen for relative order. Not here, surely, should the conventual peace of Matins fear any disruption. And yet Brother Anselm, for one instant, had faltered.

In the dim space of the choir, partially shut off from the nave of the church by the parish altar and lit only by the constant lamp and the candles on the high altar, the brothers in their stalls showed like carven copies in this twilight, without age or youth, comeliness or homeliness, so many matched shadows. The height of the vault, the solid stone of the pillars and walls, took up the sound of Brother Anselm's voice, and made of it a disembodied magic, high in air. Beyond where the candle-light reached and shadows ended, there was darkness, the night within, the night without. A benign night, mild, still and silent.

Not quite silent. The tremor on the air became a faint, persistent murmur. In the dimness under the rood loft, to the right of the entrance to the choir, Abbot Radulfus stirred in his stall. To the left, Prior Robert's habit rustled briefly, with an effect of displeasure and reproof rather than uneasiness. The merest ripple of disquiet shivered along the ranks of the brothers, and again subsided.

But the sound was drawing nearer. Even before it grew so loud as to compel notice there was no mistaking the anger in it, the menace and the dangerous excitement, all the marks of the hunt. It sounded as if the pursuit had reached the point where the van chasseours had run the quarry to exhaustion, and the parfytours were closing in for the kill. Even at this distance it was clear that some creature's life was in peril.

The sound drew nearer now very rapidly, hard to ignore, though the precentor continued valiantly leading his flock in the office, and raised his voice and quickened his tempo to ride over the challenge. The younger brothers and novices were shifting uneasily, even whispering, half stimulated, half affrighted. The murmur had become a ferocious, muted howl, as if gigantic bees were in swarm after an intruder. Even abbot

4

and prior had leaned forward ready to rise from their stalls, and were exchanging questioning looks in the dimness.

With obstinate devotion Brother Anselm lifted the first phrase of Lauds. He got no farther. At the west end of the church the unlatched leaf of the great parish door was suddenly hurled open to crash against the wall, and something unseen came hurtling and scrabbling and gasping down the length of the nave, reeling and fumbling and fending itself off from wall and pillar, heaving at breath as though run to death already.

They were on their feet, every man. The younger ones broke out in frightened exclamation and wonder, nudging and wavering in doubt what to do. Abbot Radulfus in his own domain was hampered by no such hesitation. He moved with speed and force, plucked a candle from the nearest sconce, and went striding out round the parish altar in great, loping strides that sent his gown billowing out behind him. After him went Prior Robert, more tender of his dignity, and therefore slower to reach the scene of need, and after Robert all the brothers in jostling agitation. Before they reached the nave they were met by a great, exultant bellow of triumph, and a rushing and scrambling of dozens of frenzied bodies, as the hunt burst in at the west door after its prey.

Brother Cadfael, once well accustomed to night alarms by land and by sea, had surged out of his stall as soon as the abbot moved, but took time to grasp a double candelabrum to light his way. Prior Robert in full sail was already blocking the right-hand way round the parish altar, too patrician to make enough haste to ruffle his silvery beauty. Cadfael doubled round to the left and emerged into the nave before him, with his light thrust out ahead, as much weapon as illumination.

The hounds were streaming in by then, a quarter of the town, and not the best quarter, though not necessarily the worst either; decent craftsmen, merchants, traders jostled with the riff-raff always ready for any brawl, and all of them beyond themselves either with drink or excitement or both together, howling for blood. And blood there was, slippery on the tiles of the floor. On the three steps to the parish altar lay sprawled some poor wretch flattened beneath a surge of trampling, battering foes, all hacking away with fist and boot, happily in such a tangle that comparatively few of their kicks and blows got home. All Cadfael could see of the quarry was a thin arm and a fist hardly bigger than a child's, that reached out of the chaos to grip the edge of the altar-cloth with life-and-death desperation.

Abbot Radulfus, all the long, lean, muscular length of him, with his gaunt, authoritative lantern head blazing atop, sailed round the altar, smoky candle in hand, slashed the skirts of his habit like a whip across the stooping beast-faces of the foremost attackers, and with a long bony leg bestrode the fallen creature that clawed at the fringes of the altar.

'Rabble, stand off! Blasphemers, quit this holy place, and be ashamed. Back, before I blast your souls eternally!'

He had no need to raise his voice to a shout, he had only to unsheathe it like a knife, and it sliced through the babble as through cheese. They recoiled as though his nearness seared, but they did not go far, only out of range of the burning. They hopped and hovered and clamoured, indignant, aggrieved, but wary of tempting Heaven. They drew off from a miserable fragment of a man, flat on his face up the altar steps, soiled and crumpled and bloodied, and no bigger than a boy fifteen years old. In the brief, daunted silence before they screamed their charge against him, every soul present could hear how his breath heaved and laboured and clapped in his ribs, toiling for dear life, threatening to break his meagre frame apart. Flaxen hair dabbled with dust and blood spilled against the fringes of the altar-cloth he gripped so frantically. Skinny arms and legs hugged the stone as if his life depended upon the contact. If he could speak, or lift his head, he had too much sense left in him to venture the attempt.

'How dare you so affront the house of God?' demanded the abbot, darkly smouldering. He had not missed the steely flash of reflected light in the hand of one squat fellow who was sliding roundabout to get at his victim privily. 'Put up that knife or court your soul's damnation!'

The hunters recovered breath and rage together. A dozen at least gave tongue, crying their own justification and the hunted man's offences, so variously that barely a word conveyed any meaning. Radulfus brandished a daunting arm, and their clamour subsided into muttering. Cadfael, observing that the armed man had done no more than slide his weapon out of sight, took his stand firmly between, and advanced his candles with a flourish in the direction of a fine bushy beard.

'Speak one, if you have anything of worth to say,' ordered the abbot. 'The rest be silent. You, young man, you would seem to put yourself forward ...'

The young man who had taken a pace ahead of his supporters, and whose prior right they seemed to acknowledge, stood forth flushed and important, an unexpected figure enough to be out man-hunting at midnight. He was tall and well-made and assured of manner, a little too well aware of a handsome face, and he was very elegant in festival finery, even if his best cotte was now somewhat crumpled and disordered from the turmoil of pursuit, and his countenance red and slack from the effects of a good deal of wine drunk. Without that induced courage, he would not have faced the lord abbot with quite so much impudence.

'My lord, I will speak for all, I have the right. We mean no disrespect to the abbey or your lordship, but we want that man for murder and robbery done tonight. I accuse him! All here will bear me out. He has struck down my father and plundered his strong-box, and we are come to take him. So if your lordship will allow, we'll rid you of him.'

So they would, never a doubt of it. Radulfus kept his place, the brothers crowding close to complete the barrier.

'I had thought to hear you make some amend,' said the abbot sharply, 'for this intrusion. Whatever this fellow may or may not have done, it is not he who has shed blood and drawn steel here within the church on the very steps of the altar. Violence he may have done elsewhere, but here none, he does but suffer it. The crime of sacrilege is yours, all of you here breaking our peace. You had best be considering on the health of your own souls. And if you have a lawful complaint against this person, where is the law? I see no sergeant here among you. I see no provost, who could at least make a case for the town. I see a rabble, as far at fault in law as robber and murderer can be. Now get hence, and pray that your offence may be pardoned. Whatever charges you have to make, take them to the law.'

Some among them were drawing back stealthily by then, sobering and thinking better of their invasion, and only too anxious to sneak away to their homes and bed. But the vaga-bonds, always ready for mischief, stood their ground with sullen, sly faces, and had no intention of going far, and the more respectable, if they abated their noisy ardour, kept their bitter indignation. Cadfael knew most of them. Perhaps Radulfus himself, though no Shrewsbury man by birth, was better-read in them than they supposed. He kept his place and bent his steady, menacing brow against them, forbidding action.

'My lord abbot,' ventured the fine young man, 'if you will let us take him hence we will deliver him up to the law.'

To the nearest tree, thought Cadfael. And there were trees in plenty between here and the river. He snipped at the wicks of his candles and let them flare afresh. The beard was still hovering in the shadows.

'That I cannot do,' said the abbot crisply. 'If the law itself were here, there is no power can now take away this man from the sanctuary he has sought. You should know the right of it as well as I, and the peril, body and soul, to any who dares to breach that sanctuary. Go, take the pollution of your violence out of this holy place. We have duties here which your presence in hatred defiles. Go! Out!'

'But my lord,' bleated the angry young man, tossing his curled head but keeping his distance, 'you have not heard us as to the crime ...'

'I will hear you,' said Radulfus with a snap, 'by daylight, when you come with sheriff or sergeant to discuss this matter calmly, and in proper form. But I warn you, this man has claimed sanctuary, and the rights of sanctuary are his, according to custom, and neither you nor any other shall force him away out of these walls until the time of his respite is over.'

'And I warn you, my lord,' flared the youth, blazing red, 'that should he venture a step outside, we shall be waiting for him, and what falls out of your lordship's lordship will be no concern of yours, or the church's.' Yes, unquestionably he was moderately drunk, or he would never have gone so far, an ordinary young burgess of the town, if a wealthy one. Even with an evening's wine in him, he blenched at his own daring, and shuffled back a pace or two.

'Or God's?' said the abbot coldly. 'Go hence in peace, before his bolt strike you.'

They went, shadows edging backwards into shadow, through the open west door and out into the night, but always with their faces turned towards the miserable bundle prostrate clutching the altar-cloth. Mob madness is not so easily subdued, and even if their grievance proved less than justified, it was real enough to them. Murder and robbery were mortal crimes. No, they would not all go away. They would set a watch on the parish door and the gatehouse with a rope ready.

'Brother Prior,' said Radulfus, running an eye over his shaken flock, 'and Brother Precentor, will you again begin Lauds? Let the office proceed, and the brothers return to their beds according to the order. The affairs of men require our attention, but the affairs of God may not be subordinated.' He looked down at the motionless fugitive, too tensely still not to be aware of everything that passed above him, and again looked up to catch Brother Cadfael's concerned and thoughtful eye. 'We two, I think, are enough to take what confession this guest of ours wills to make, and tend his needs. They are gone,' said the abbot dispassionately to the prone figure at his feet. 'You may get up.'

The thin body stirred uneasily, keeping one hand firmly on the fringe of the altar-cloth. He moved as if every flinching movement hurt, as well it might, but it seemed that he had at least escaped broken bones, for he used his free arm to help him up to his knees on the steps, and raised to the light a gaunt, bruised face smeared with blood and sweat and the slime of running nose. Before their eyes he seemed to dwindle both in years and size. They might have been gazing at some unlucky urchin of the Foregate who had been set upon by a dozen or more of his capricious fellows for some trivial offence, and left howling in a ditch, but for the desperation of fear that emanated from him, and the memory of the pack that had been beaten off from his heels just in time.

A poor little wretch enough to be credited with murder and robbery. On his feet he might perhaps be about as tall as Cadfael, who was below the middle height, but width-ways Cadfael would have made three of him. His cotte and hose were ragged and threadbare, and had several new rents in them now from clawing hands and trampling feet, besides the dust and stains of long use, but originally they had been brightly-coloured in crude red and blue. He had a decent width of shoulder, better feeding might have made a well-proportioned man of him, but as he moved stiffly to look up at them he seemed all gangling limbs, large of elbow and knee, and very low in flesh to cover them. Seventeen or eighteen years old, Cadfael guessed. The eyes raised to them in such desolate entreaty were hollow and evasive, and one of them half-closed and swelling, but in the light of the candles they flared darkly and brilliantly blue as periwinkle flowers.

'Son,' said Radulfus, with chill detachment, for murderers come in all shapes, ages and kinds, 'you hear what is charged against you by those who surely sought your life. Here you have committed body and soul to the care of the church, and I and all here are bound to keep and succour you. On that you may rely. As at this moment, I offer you only one channel to grace, and ask of you but one question. Whatever the answer, here you are safe as long as the right of sanctuary lasts. I promise it.'

9

The wretch crouched on his knees, watching the abbot's face as though he numbered him among his enemies, and said no word.

'How do you answer to this charge?' asked Radulfus. 'Have you this day murdered and robbed?'

Distorted lips parted painfully to loose a light, high, wary voice like a frightened child's. 'No, Father Abbot, I swear it!'

'Get up,' said the abbot, neither trusting nor judging. 'Stand close, and lay your hand upon this casket on the altar. Do you know what it contains? Here within are the bones of the blessed Saint Elerius, the friend and director of Saint Winifred. On these holy relics, consider and answer me once again, as God hears you: are you guilty of that with which they charge you?'

With all the obstinate, despairing fervour so slight a body could contain, and without hesitation, the light voice shrilled: 'As God sees me, I am not! I have done no wrong.'

Radulfus considered in weighty silence an unnerving while. Just so would a man answer who had nothing to hide and nothing to fear from being heard in Heaven. But no less, so would a godless vagabond answer for his hide's sake, having no faith in Heaven, and no fear of anything beyond the terrors of this world. Hard to decide between the two. The abbot suspended judgement.

'Well, you have given a solemn word, and whether it be true or no, you have the protection of this house, according to law, and time to think on your soul, if there is need.' He looked at Cadfael, and eye to eye they considered the needs that came before all. 'He had best keep to the church itself, I think, until we have spoken with the officers of law, and agreed on terms.'

'So I think, also,' said Cadfael.

'Should he be left alone?' They were both thinking of the pack recently expelled from this place, still hungry and ripe for mischief, and surely not gone far.

The brothers had withdrawn, led back to the dortoir by Prior Robert, very erect and deeply displeased. The choir had grown silent and dark. Whether the brethren, particularly the younger and more restless, would sleep, was another matter. The smell of the dangerous outer world was in their nostrils, and the tremor of excitement quivering like an itch along their skins.

'I shall have work with him a while,' said Cadfael, eyeing the smears of blood that marked brow and cheek, and the painful list with which the man stood. A young, willowy body,

10

accustomed to going lightly and lissomely. 'If you permit, Father, I will stay here with him, and take his care upon me. Should there be need, I can call.'

'Very well, do so, brother. You may take whatever is necessary for his provision.' The weather was mild enough, but the hours of the night would be cold, in this sanctified but stony place. 'Do you need a helper to fetch and carry for you? Our guest should not be left unfellowed.'

'If I may borrow Brother Oswin, he knows where to find all the things I may need,' said Cadfael.

'I will send him to you. And should this man wish to tell his own side of this unhappy story, mark it well. Tomorrow, no doubt, we shall have his accusers here in proper form, with one of the sheriff's officers, and both parties will have to render account.'

Cadfael understood the force of that. A small discrepancy in the accused youth's story between midnight and morning could be revealing indeed. But by morning the voluble accusers might also have cooled their heads, and come with a slightly modified tale, for Cadfael, who knew most of the inhabitants of the town, had by this time recalled the reason for their being up so late in their best clothes, and well gone in drink. The young cockerel in the festival finery should by rights have been bedding a bride rather than pursuing a wretched wisp of manhood over the bridge with hunting cries of murder and robbery. Nothing less than the marriage of the heir could have unloosed the purse-strings of the Aurifaber household enough to provide such a supply of wine.

'I leave the watch to you,' said Radulfus, and departed to hale out Brother Oswin from his cell, and send him down to join the vigil. He came so blithely that it was plain he had been hoping for just such a recall. Who but Brother Cadfael's apprentice should be admitted to his nocturnal ministrations? Oswin came all wide eyes and eager curiosity, as excited as a truant schoolboy at being foot-loose at midnight, and attendant on the fringes of a sensational villainy. He hung over the shivering stranger, between fascinated horror at viewing a murderer close, and surprised pity at seeing so miserable a human being, where a brutal monster should have been.

Cadfael gave him no time to marvel. 'I want water, clean linen, the ointment of centaury and cleavers, and a good measure of wine. Hop to it, sharp! Better light the lamp in the workshop, we may need more things yet.'

11

Brother Oswin plucked out a candle from its socket, and departed in such a gust of dutiful enthusiasm that it was a marvel his light was not blown out in the doorway. But the night was still, and the flame recovered, streaming smokily across the great court towards the gardens.

'Light the brazier!' called Cadfael after him, hearing his wretched charge's teeth begin to chatter. A close brush with death is apt to leave a man collapsing like a pricked bladder, and this one had little flesh or strength about him to withstand the shock. Cadfael got an arm about him before he folded like an empty coat, and slid to the stones.

'Here, come ... Let's get you into a stall.' The weight was slight as a child's, he hoisted it bodily, and made to withdraw round the parish altar to the somewhat less draughty confines of the choir, but the skinny fist that had all this time held fast to the altar-cloth would not let go. The thin body jerked in his arms.

'If I loose, they'll kill me ...'

'Not while I have hands or voice,' said Cadfael. 'Our abbot has held his hand over you, they'll make no further move tonight. Leave go of the cloth and come within. There are relics enough there, trust me, holier even than this.'

The grubby fingers, with black and bitten nails, released the cloth reluctantly, the flaxen head drooped resignedly on Cadfael's shoulder. Cadfael bore him round into the choir and laid him in the nearest and most commodious stall, which was that of Prior Robert. The usurpation was not unpleasing. The young man was shivering violently from head to toe, but relaxed into the stall with a huge sigh, and was still.

'They've hunted you into the ground,' Cadfael allowed, settling him into shelter, 'but at least into the right earth. Abbot Radulfus won't give you. up, never think it. You can draw breath, you have a home here for some days to come. Take heart! Nor are that pack out there so bad as you suppose, once the drink's out of them they'll cool. I know them.'

'They meant to kill me,' said the youth, trembling.

No denying that. So they would have done, had they got their hands on him out of this enclave. And there was a note of simple bewilderment in the high voice, of terror utterly at a loss, that caught Cadfael's leaning ear. The lad was far gone in weakness, and relief from fear, and truly it sounded as if he did not know why he had ever been threatened. So the fox must feel, acting innocently after his kind, and hearing the hounds give tongue.

Brother Oswin came, burdened with a scrip full of wine-flask and unguent-jar, a roll of clean linen under one arm, and a bowl of water in both hands. His lighted candle he must have stuck to the bench in the porch, where a tiny, flickering light played. He arrived abrupt, urgent and glowing, the light-brown curls round his tonsure erected like a thorn-hedge. He laid down his bowl, laid out his linen, and leaned eagerly to support the patient as Cadfael drew him to the light.

'Be thankful for small mercies, I see no sign of broken bones in you. You've been trampled and hacked, and I make no doubt you're a lump of bruises, but that we can deal with. Lean here your head – so! That's a nasty welt across your temple and cheek. A cudgel did that. Hold still, now!'

The fair head leaned submissively into his hands. The weal grazed the crest of the left cheekbone, and broke the skin along the left side of his head, oozing blood into the pale hair. As Cadfael bathed it, stroking back the tangled locks, the skin quivered under the cold water, and the muck of dust and drying blood drained away. This was not the newest of his injuries. The smoothing of the linen over brow, cheek and chin uncovered a thin, pure, youthful face.

'What's your name, child?' said Cadfael.

'Liliwin,' said the young man, still eyeing him warily.

'Saxon. So are your eyes, and your hair. Where born? Not here along the borders.'

'How should I know?' said the youth, listless. 'In a ditch, and left there. The first I know is being taught to tumble, as soon as I walked.'

He was past fending for himself; perhaps he was even past lying. As well to get out of him whatever he was willing to tell, now, while he was forced to surrender himself to the hands of others, with his own helplessness like a weight of black despair on him.

'Is that how you've lived? Travelling the road, cutting capers at fairs, doing a little juggling and singing for your supper? It's a hard life, with more kicks than kindness, I dare say. And from a child?' He could guess at the manner of training that went to school a childish body to the sort of contortions a fairground crowd would gape at. There were ways of hurting, by way of punishment, without spoiling the agility of growing limbs. 'And solitary now? They're gone, are they, that picked you out of your ditch and bent you to their uses?'

'I ran from them as soon as I was half-grown,' said the soft, weary voice. 'Three mummers padding the road, a lad come by

13

for nothing was a gift to them, they had their worth out of me. All I owed them was kicks and blows. I work for myself now.'

'At the same craft?'

'It's all I know. But that I know well,' said Liliwin, suddenly raising his head proudly, and not wincing from the sting of the lotion bathing his grazed cheek.

'And that's what brought you to Walter Aurifaber's house last night,' said Cadfael mildly, stripping back a torn sleeve from a thin, sinewy forearm marked by a long slash from a knife. 'To play at his son's wedding-feast.'

One dark blue eye peered up at him sidelong. 'You know them?'

'There are few people in the town that I don't know. I tend many folk within the walls, the old Aurifaber dame among them. Yes, I know that household. But it had slipped my mind that the goldsmith was marrying his son yesterday.' Knowing them as well as he did, he was sure that for all their wish to make an impressive show, they would not pay out money enough to attract the better sort of musicians, such as the nobility welcomed as guests. But a poor vagrant jongleur trying his unpromising luck in the town, that they might consider. All the more if his performance outdid his appearance, and genuine music could be had dead cheap. 'So you heard of the celebration, and got yourself hired to entertain the guests. Then what befell, to bring the jollity to such a grim ending? Reach me here a pad of cloth, Oswin, and hold the candle nearer.'

'They promised me three pence for the evening,' said Liliwin, trembling now as much with indignation as fear and cold, 'and they cheated me. It was none of my fault! I played and sang my best, did all my tricks ... The house was full of people, they crowded me, and the young fellows, they were drunk and lungeous, they hustled me! A juggler needs room! It was not my fault the pitcher was broken. One of the youngsters jumped to catch the balls I was spinning, he knocked me flying, and the pitcher went over from the table, and smashed. She said it was her best ... the old beldame ... she screeched at me, and hit out with her stick ...'

'She did this?' questioned Cadfael gently, touching the swathed wound on the jongleur's temple.

'She did! Lashed out like a fury, and swore the thing was worth more than I'd earned, and I must pay for it. And when I complained, she threw me a penny, and told them to put me out!'

14

So she would, thought Cadfael ruefully, seeing her life-blood spilled if a prized possession was broken, she who hoarded every groat that was not spent on her perverse tenderness for her soul, which brought alms flowing to the abbey altars, and rendered Prior Robert her cautious friend.

'And they did it?' It would not have been a gentle ejection, they would all have been inflamed and boisterous by then. 'How late was that? An hour before midnight?'

'More. None of them had left, then. They tossed me out of door, and wouldn't let me in again.' He had long experience of his own helplessness in similar circumstances, his voice sagged despondently. 'I couldn't even pick up my juggling balls, I've lost them all.'

'And you were left chill in the night, thrown out of the burgage. Then how came this hunt after you?' Cadfael smoothed a turn of his linen roll round the thin arm that jerked in his hands with frustrated rage. 'Hold still, child, that's right! I want this slit well closed, it will knit clean if you take ease. What did you do?'

'Crept away,' said Liliwin bitterly. 'What else could I do? The watch let me out of the wicket in the town gate, and I crossed the bridge and slipped into the bushes this side, meaning to make off from this town in the morning, and make for Lichfield. There's a decent grove above the path down to the river, the other side of the highroad from the abbey here, I went in there and found me a good place in the grass to sleep the night out.' But with his grievance boiling and festering in him, and his helplessness over and above, if what he told was truth. And long acquaintance with injustice and despite does not reconcile the heart.

'Then how comes it the whole pack of them should be hunting you an hour or so later, and crying murder and theft on you.'

'As God sees me,' blurted the youth, quaking, 'I know no more than you! I was near to sleeping when I heard them come howling across the bridge. I'd no call to suppose it was aught to do with me, not until they were streaming down into the Foregate, but it was a noise to make any man afraid, whether he'd anything on his conscience or not. And then I could hear them yelling murder and vengeance, and crying it was the mummer who did it, and baying for my blood. They spread out and began to beat the bushes, and I ran for my life, being sure they'd find me. And all the pack of them came roaring after.

15

They were all but plucking at my hair when I stumbled in here at the door. But God strike me blind if I know what I'm held to have done – and dead if I'm lying to you now!'

Cadfael completed his bandage, and drew the tattered sleeve down over it. 'According to young Daniel, it seems his father's been struck down and his strong-box emptied. A poor way of rounding off a wedding night! Do you tell me all this can have happened after you were put out without your pay? On the face of it, that might turn their minds to you and your grievance, if they were casting about for a likely felon.'

'I swear to you,' insisted the young man vehemently, 'the goldsmith was hale and well the last time I set eyes on him. There was no quarrelling, no violence but what they used on me, they were laughing and drinking and singing still. What's happened since I know no more than you. I left the place – what use was there in staying? Brother, for God's sake believe me! I've touched neither the man nor his money.'

'Then so it will be found,' said Cadfael sturdily. 'Here you're safe enough in the meantime, and you must needs put your trust in justice and Abbot Radulfus, and tell your tale as you've told it to me when they question you. We have time, and given time, truth will out. You heard Father Abbot – stay here within the church tonight, but if they come to a decent agreement tomorrow you may have the run of the household.' Liliwin was very cold to the touch, with fear and shock, and still trembling. 'Oswin,' said Cadfael briskly, 'go and fetch me a couple of brychans from the store, and then warm me up another good measure of wine on the brazier, and spice it well. Let's get some warmth into him.'

Oswin, who had held his tongue admirably while his eyes devoured the stranger, departed in a flurry of zeal to do his errands. Liliwin watched him go, and then turned to watch Cadfael no less warily. Small wonder if he felt little trust in anyone just now.

'You won't leave me? They'll be peering in at the door again before the night's out.'

'I won't leave you. Be easy!'

Advice difficult to follow, he admitted wryly, in Liliwin's situation. But with enough mulled wine in him he might sleep. Oswin came again glowing with haste and the flush of bending over the brazier, and brought two thick, rough blankets, in which Liliwin thankfully wound himself. The spiced draught went down gratefully. A little colour came back to the gaunt, bruised face.

'You go to your bed, lad,' said Cadfael, leading Oswin towards the night stairs. 'You can now, he'll do till morning. Then we shall see.'

Brother Oswin looked back in some wonder at the swaddled body almost swallowed up in Prior Robert's capacious stall, and asked in a whisper: 'Do you think he can really be a murderer, though?'

'Child,' said Cadfael, sighing, 'until we get some sensible account of what's happened in Walter Aurifaber's burgage tonight, I doubt if there's been murder done at all. With enough drink in them, the fists may well have started flying, and a few noses been bloodied, and some fool may very well have started a panic, with other fools ready enough to take up the cry. You go to your bed, and wait and see.'

And so must I wait and see, he thought, watching Oswin obediently climb the stair. It was all very well distrusting the alarms of the moment, but for all that, not all those voluble accusers had been drunk. And something unforeseen had certainly happened in the goldsmith's house, to put a violent end to the celebrations of young Daniel's marriage. How if Walter Aurifaber had really been struck dead? And his treasury robbed? By that woebegone scrap of humanity huddled in his brychans, half-drunk with the wine they had poured into him, half asleep but held alert by terror? Would he dare, even with a bitter grievance? Could he have managed the affair, even if he had dared? One thing was certain, if he had robbed he must have disposed of his gains in short order in the dark, in a town surely none too well known to him. In those scanty garments of his, that threadbare motley, there was barely room to conceal the single penny the old dame had thrown at him, much less the contents of a goldsmith's coffer.

When he approached the stall, however quietly, the bruised eyelids rolled wide from the dark blue eyes, and they fixed on him in instant dread.

'Never shrink, it's I. No one else will trouble you this night. And my name, if you need it, is Cadfael. And yours is Liliwin.' A name strangely right for a vagabond player, very young and solitary and poor, and yet proud of his proficiency in his craft, tumbler, contortionist, singer, juggler, dancer, purveying merriment for others while he found little cause to be merry himself. 'How old are you, Liliwin?'

Half asleep and afraid to give way and sleep in earnest, he

17

looked ever younger, dwindling into a swaddled child, reassuringly flushed now as the chill ebbed out of him. But he himself did not know the answer. He could only knit his fair brows and hazard doubtfully, 'I think I may be turned twenty. It could be more. The mummers may have said I was less than I was – children draw more alms.'

So they would, and the boy was lightly built, spare and small. He might be as much as two and twenty, perhaps, surely no more.

'Well, Liliwin, if you can sleep do so, it will be aid and comfort, and you have need of it. You need not watch, I shall be doing that.'

Cadfael sat down in the abbot's stall, and trimmed the attendant candles, so that he might have a fair view of his charge. The quiet came in, on the heels of their silence, very consolingly. The night without might well have its disquiets, but here the vault of the choir was like linked hands sheltering their threatened and precarious peace. It was strange to Cadfael to see, after prolonged calm, two great tears welling from beneath Liliwin's closed eyelids, and rolling slowly over the jut of his gaunt cheek-bone, to fall into the brychan.

'What is it? What troubles you?' For himself he had shivered, argued, burned but not wept.

'My rebec – I had it with me in the bushes, in a linen bag for my shoulder. When they flushed me out – I don't know how, a branch caught in the string, and plucked it away. And I dared not stop to grope for it in the dark … And now I can't go forth! I've lost it!'

'In the bushes, this side the bridge – across the highway from here?' It was a grief Cadfael could comprehend. 'You cannot go forth lad, no, not yet, true enough. But *I* can. I'll look for it. Those who hunted you would not go aside once they had you in view. Your rebec may be lying safe enough among the bushes. Go to sleep and leave grieving,' said Cadfael. 'It's too early to despair. For despair,' he said vigorously, 'it is always too early. Remember that, and keep up your heart.'

One startled blue eye opened at him, he caught the gleam of the candles in it before it closed again. There was silence. Cadfael lay back in the abbot's stall, and resigned himself to a long watch. Before Prime he must rouse himself to remove the interloper to a less privileged place, or Prior Robert would be rigid with offence. Until then, let God and his saints take charge, there was nothing more mere man could do.

18

As soon as the first light of dawn began to pluck colours out of the dark, on this clear May morning, Griffin, the locksmith's boy who slept in the shop as a watchman, got up from his pallet and went to draw water from the well in the rear yard. Griffin was always the first up, from either household of the two that shared the yard, and had usually kindled the fire and made all ready for the day's work before his master's journeyman came in from his home two streets away. On this day in particular Griffin took it for granted that all those who had kept it up late at the wedding would be in no condition to rise early about their work. Griffin himself had not been invited to the feast, though Mistress Susanna had sent Rannilt across to bring him a platter of meats and bread, a morsel of cake and a draught of small ale, and he had eaten his fill, and slept innocently through whatever uproar had followed at midnight.

Griffin was thirteen years old, offspring of a maidservant and a passing tinker. He was well-grown, comely, of contented nature and good with his hands, but he was a simpleton. Baldwin Peche the locksmith preened himself on his goodness in giving house-room to such an innocent, but the truth was that Griffin, for all his dimness of wit, had a gift for picking up practical skills, and far more than earned his keep.

The great wooden bucket, its old boards worn and fretted within and without from long use, came up out of the depths sparkling in the first slanting ray of the rising sun. Griffin filled his two pails, and was slinging the bucket back over the shaft when the gleam caught a flash of silver between two of the boards, lodged edgeways in the crevice. He balanced the bucket on the stone rim of the well, and leaned and fished out the shining thing, tugging it free between finger and thumb, and shaking off a frayed shred of blue cloth that came away with it. It lay in his palm shining, a round disc of silver prettily engraved with a head, and some strange signs he did not know for letters. On the reverse side there was a round border and a short cross within it, and more of the mysterious signs. Griffin was charmed. He took his prize back with him to the workshop, and when Baldwin Peche finally arose from his bed and came forth blear-eyed and cross-grained, the boy presented him proudly with what he had found. Whatever belonged here belonged to his master.

The locksmith clapped eyes on it and kindled like a lighted

lamp, head and eyes clearing marvellously. He turned it in his fingers, examining both sides closely, and looked up with a curious, private grin and a cautious question:

'Where did you find this, boy? Have you shown it to anyone else?'

'No, master. I brought it straight in for you. It was in the bucket of the well,' said Griffin, and told him how it had lodged between the boards.

'Good, good! No need to let others know I have such. Stuck fast in the boards, was it?' mused Baldwin, brooding gleefully over his treasure. 'You're a good lad! A good lad! You did right to bring it straight to me, I set a great value on this! A great value!' He was grinning to himself with immense satisfaction, and Griffin reflected his content proudly. 'I'll give you some sweetmeats to your dinner I got from last night's feast. You shall see I can be grateful to a dutiful boy.'

Chapter Two

Saturday, from Prime to noon

ROTHER CADFAEL had Liliwin awake and made as presentable as possible before the brothers came down to Prime. He had risked helping him out at first light to the necessary offices, where he might at least wash his battered face and relieve himself, and return to stand up before the assembled convent at Prime with some sad dignity. Not to speak of the urgent need to have Prior Robert's stall vacant and ready for him, for Robert's rigid disapproval of the intrusion and the intruder was already sufficiently clear, and there was no need to aggravate his hostility. The accused had enough enemies already.

And in they came at the gatehouse, just as the brothers emerged from Prime, a solid phalanx of citizens intent on lodging their accusations this time in due and irreproachable form. Sheriff Prestcote had deputed the enquiry and negotiations to his own sergeant, having more important items of the king's business on his hands than a passing assault and robbery in a town dwelling. He was newly back from his Easter attendance at King Stephen's court and the delivery of the shire accounts and revenues, and his early summer survey of the county's royal defences was about to begin. Already Hugh Beringar, his deputy, was in the north of the shire about the same necessary business, though Cadfael, who relied on Hugh's good sense in all matters of poor souls fetched up hard

21

against the law, hoped fervently that he would soon be back in Shrewsbury to lend a shrewd eye and willing ear to both sides in the dispute. The accusers had always the advantage without a healthy sceptic in attendance.

Meantime, here was the sergeant, large, experienced and sharp enough, but disposed to the accusers rather than the accused, and with a formidable array of townsmen behind him, led by the provost, Geoffrey Corviser. A decent, stout, patient man, and in no hurry to condemn without conscientious probing, but already primed with the complaints of several equally solid citizens, in addition to the aggrieved family. A wedding party provides at once large numbers of witnesses, and a powerful argument for doubting the half of their evidence.

Behind the authorities of shire and town came young Daniel Aurifaber, slightly the worse for wear after his hectic and unorthodox wedding night, and in his working clothes this time, but still belligerent. Surely, however, not so disturbed as a young man should be at his father's untimely slaying? Even slightly sheepish, and all the surlier because of it.

Cadfael withdrew to the rear of the brothers, between the citizen army and the church, and prepared to block the doorway if any of the witnesses should again lose his head and dare the abbot's thunder. It did not seem likely, with the sergeant there in control, and well aware of the necessity of dealing civilly and amicably with a mitred abbot. But in any dozen men there may well be one incorrigible idiot capable of any folly. Cadfael cast a glance over his shoulder, and glimpsed a pallid, scared face, but a body still, silent and intent, whether trusting in his ecclesiastical shelter, or simply resigned, there was no knowing.

'Keep within, out of sight, lad,' said Cadfael over his shoulder, 'unless you're called for. Leave all to the lord abbot.'

Radulfus greeted the sergeant composedly, and after him the provost.

'I expected your visit, after the night's alarm. I am acquainted with the charges then made against a man who has appealed to sanctuary within our church, and been received according to our duty. But the charges have no force until made in due form, through the sheriff's authority. You are very welcome, sergeant, I look to you to inform me truly how this matter stands.'

He had no intention, Cadfael thought, watching, of inviting

22

them within doors into the chapter-house or hall. The morning was fine and sunny, and the matter might be agreed more briskly here, standing. And the sergeant had already recognised that he had no power to take the fugitive out of the hands of the church, and was intent only on agreeing terms, and hunting his proofs elsewhere.

'There is a charge lodged with me,' he said practically, 'that the jongleur Liliwin, who was employed last night to play at a wedding in the house of Master Walter Aurifaber, struck down the said Walter in his workshop, where he was then laying away certain valuable wedding gifts in his strong-box, and robbed the strong-box of a treasure in coins and goldsmith's work to a great value. This is sworn to by the goldsmith's son, here present, and by ten of the guests who were at the feast.'

Daniel braced his feet, stiffened his neck, and nodded emphatic confirmation. Several of the neighbours at his back murmured and nodded with him.

'And you have satisfied yourself,' said Radulfus briskly, 'that the charges are justified? At least, whoever did them, that these deeds were done?'

'I have viewed the workshop and the strong-box. The box is emptied of all but heavy items of silverware that would be ill to carry undetected. I have taken sworn witness that it held a great sum in silver pence and small, fine works of jewellery. All are gone. And as to the act of violence against Master Aurifaber, I have seen the marks of his blood close to the coffer, where he was found, and I have seen how he lies still out of his senses.'

'But *not* dead?' said Radulfus sharply. 'It was murder was cried here at midnight.'

'Dead?' The sergeant, an honest man, gaped at the suggestion. 'Not he! He's knocked clean out of his wits, but it was not so desperate a blow as all that. If he hadn't had a fair wash of drink in him he might have been fit to speak up for himself by now, but he's still addled. It was a fair dunt someone gave him, but with a good hard head ... No, he's well alive, and will live his proper span if I'm a judge.'

The witnesses, solid and sullen at his back, shifted their feet and looked elsewhere, but covertly came back to eyeing the abbot and the church door, and if they were discomfited at having their largest claims refuted, nonetheless held fast to their mortal grievance, and wanted a neck stretched for it.

'It seems, then,' said the abbot composedly, 'that the man

we have in sanctuary is accused of wounding and robbing, but not of murder.'

'So it stands. The evidence is that he was docked of his full fee because he broke a pitcher in his juggling, and complained bitterly when he was put out. And some time after that, this assault upon Master Aurifaber was made, while most of those invited were still there in the house, and vouched for.'

'I well understand,' said the abbot, 'that on such a charge you must enquire, and may justice be done. But I think you also know well the sacredness of sanctuary. It is not shelter against sin, it is the provision of a time of calm, when the guilty may examine his soul, and the innocent confide in his salvation. But it may not be violated. It has a period, but until that time is spent it is holy. For forty days the man you seek on this charge is ours – no, he belongs to God! – and he may not be haled forth, nor persuaded forth, nor any way removed against his will from these premises. He is ours to feed, to care for and to shelter, for those forty days.'

'That I grant,' said the sergeant. 'But there are conditions. He came of his own will within, he may enjoy only the allowance of food those within here enjoy.' Less than he did, by his lusty bulk, but surely more than Liliwin had ever enjoyed as his regular provision. 'And when the respite is over, he may not again be supplied with food, but must come forth and submit himself to trial.'

He was as iron-sure of his case here as was Radulfus in the days of grace, he voiced his mandate coldly. There would be no extension of the time allowed, after that they would make sure he starved until he came forth. It was fair. Forty days is consideration enough.

'Then during that time,' said the abbot, 'you agree that the man may rest here and study on his soul. My concern for justice is no less than yours, you know I will keep to terms, and neither make nor allow others to make any offer to help the man away out of hold and out of your reach. But it would be seemly to agree that he need not confine himself to the church, but have the freedom of the whole enclosure here, so that he may make use of the lavatorium and necessarium, take some exercise in the open air, and keep himself decent among us.'

To that the sergeant agreed without demur. 'Inside your pale, my lord, he may make free. But if he step one pace outside, my men will be ready and waiting for him.'

'That is understood. Now, if you so wish, you may speak

24

with the accused youth, in my presence, but without these witnesses. Those who charge him have told their story, it is fair that he should also tell his just as freely. After that, the matter must wait for trial and judgement hereafter.'

Daniel opened his mouth as if to make furious protest, caught the abbot's cold eye, and thought better of it. The henchmen at his back shuffled and muttered, but did not venture to be clearly heard. Only the provost spoke up, in the interests of the town in general.

'My lord, I was not a guest at yesterday's marriage, I have no direct knowlege of what befell. I stand here for the fair mind of Shrewsbury, and with your leave I would wish to hear what the young man may say for himself.'

The abbot agreed to that willingly. 'Come, then, into the church. And you, good people, may disperse in peace.' So they did, still with some reluctance at not getting their hands immediately on their prey. Only Daniel, instead of withdrawing, stepped forward hastily to arrest the abbot's attention, his manner now anxious and ingratiating, his grievance put away in favour of a different errand.

'Father Abbot, if you please! It's true we all ran wild last night, finding my poor father laid flat as he was, and bleeding. Truly we did believe him murdered, and cried it too soon, but even now there's no knowing how badly he's hurt. And my old grandmother, when she heard it, fell in a seizure, as she has once before, and though she's better of it now, she's none too well. And from the last fit she had, she puts more faith in Brother Cadfael's remedies than in all the physicians. And she bid me ask if he may come back with me and medicine her, for he knows what's needed when this breathlessness takes her, and the pains in her breast.'

The abbot looked round for Cadfael, who had come forth from the shadow of the cloister at hearing this plea. There was no denying he felt a distinct quiver of anticipation. After the night he had spent beside Liliwin, he could not help being consumed with curiosity as to what had really happened at Daniel Aurifaber's wedding supper.

'You may go with him, Brother Cadfael, and do what you can for the woman. Take whatever time you need.

'I will, Father,' said Cadfael heartily, and went off briskly into the garden, to fetch what he thought might be required from his workshop.

25

The goldsmith's burgage was situated on the street leading to
the gateway of the castle, where the neck of land narrowed, so
that the rear plots of the houses on either side the street ran
down to the town wall, while the great rondel of Shrewsbury
lay snug to the south-west in the loop of the Severn. It was one
of the largest plots in the town, as its owner was thought to be
one of the wealthiest men; a right-angled house with a wing on
the street, and the hall and main dwelling running lengthwise
behind. Aurifaber, ever on the lookout for another means of
making money, had divided off the wing and let it as a shop
and dwelling to the locksmith Baldwin Peche, a middle-aged
widower without children, who found it convenient and
adequate to his needs. A narrow passage led through between
the two shops to the open yard behind, with its well, and the
separate kitchens, byres and privies. Rumour said of
Walter Aurifaber that he had even had his cesspit stone-lined,
which many considered to be arrogating to himself the
privileges of minor nobility. Beyond the yard the ground fell
away gradually in a long vegetable-garden and fowl-run to the
town wall, and the family holding extended even beyond,
through an arched doorway to an open stretch of smooth grass
going down to the riverside.

Cadfael had paid several visits to the house at the old
woman's insistence, for she was now turned eighty years old,
and held that her gifts to the abbey entitled her to medical care
in this world, as well as purchasing sanctity for the next. At
eighty there is always something ailing the body, and Dame
Juliana was given to ulcers of the leg if she suffered any slight
wound or scratch, and stirred very little from her own
chamber, which was one of the two over the hall. If she had
presided at Daniel's wedding supper, as clearly she had, it must
have been with her walking-stick ready to hand – unluckily for
Liliwin! She was known to be willing to lash out with it readily
if anything displeased her.

The only person on whom she doted, people said, was this
young sprig of a grandson of hers, and even he had never yet
found a way to get her to loose her purse-strings. Her son
Walter was made in her own image, as parsimonious as the
dame, but either surer of his own virtue as admitting him by
right to salvation, or else not yet so old as to be worrying about
the after-life, for the abbey altars owed no great benefits to

26

him. There would have been an impressive show for the heir's wedding, but the pence that paid for it would be screwed out of the housekeeping for the next few months. It was a sour joke among those who did not like the goldsmith that his wife had died of starvation as soon as she had borne him a son, spending on her keep being no longer necessary.

Cadfael followed a glum and taciturn Daniel through the passage between the shops. The hall door stood wide open on the yard, at this hour in long shadow, but with a pale blue sky radiant overhead. Within, timber-scented gloom closed on them. There was a chamber door on the right, the daughter's room, and beyond that the household stores over which she presided. Beyond that doorway the stairs went up to the upper floor. Cadfael climbed the broad, unguarded wooden steps, needing no guidance here. Juliana's chamber was the first door off the narrow gallery that ran along the side of the wall. Daniel, without a word, had slouched back out of the hall below, and made for the shop. For a few days, at least, he was the goldsmith. A good workman, too, they said, when he chose, or when his elders could hold him to it.

A woman came out of the room as Cadfael approached it. Tall, like her young brother, of the same rich brown colouring, past thirty years old and mistress of this household for the last fifteen of those years, Walter's daughter Susanna had a cool dignity about her that went very ill with violence and crime. She had stepped into the shoes of her mother, whom she was said to resemble, as soon as Dame Juliana began to ail. The keys were hers, the stores were hers, the pillars and the roof of the house were held up by her, calmly and competently. A good girl, people said. Except that her girlhood was gone.

She smiled at Brother Cadfael, though even her smile was distant and cool. She had a pale, clear oval face with wide-set grey eyes, that went very strangely with her wealth of russet hair, braided and bound austerely on her head. Her housewifely gown was neat, dark and plain. The keys at her waist were her only jewellery.

They were old acquaintances. Cadfael could not claim more or better than that.

'No call to fret,' said the girl briskly. 'She's over it already, though frightened. In good case to take advice, I hope. Margery is in there with her.'

Margery? Of course, the bride! Strange office for a bride, the day after the wedding, to be nursing her bridegroom's

27

grandam. Margery Bele, Cadfael recalled, daughter to the cloth-merchant Edred Bele, had a very nice little fortune in line for her some day, since she had no brother, and brought with her a very proper dowry even now. Well worth a miserly family's purchase for their heir. But was she, then, so bereft of suitors that this one offer must buy her? Or had she already seen and wanted that curly-haired, spoiled, handsome brat now no doubt frowning and fretting over his losses in the shop here?

'I must leave her to you and God,' said Susanna. 'She takes no notice of anyone else. And I have the dinner to prepare.'

'And what of your father?'

'He'll do well enough,' she said practically. 'He was very mellow, it did him good service, he fell soft as a cushion. Go along and see him, when *she's* done with you.' She gave him her wry smile and slipped away silently down the stairs.

If Dame Juliana's attack had affected her speech at all on this occasion, she had made a remarkable recovery. Flat on her pillows she might be, and indeed had better remain for a day or so, but her tongue wagged remorselessly all the time Cadfael was feeling her forehead and the beat of her heart, and drawing back an eyelid from a fierce grey eye to look closely at the pupil. He let her run on without response or encouragement, though he missed nothing of what she had to say.

'And I expected better of the lord abbot,' she said, curling thin bluish lips, 'than to take the part of a vagabond footpad, murderer and thief as he is, against honest craftsmen who pay their dues and their devotions like Christians. It's great shame to you all to shelter such a rogue.'

'Your son, I'm told,' said Cadfael mildly, rummaging in his scrip for the little flask of powder dried from oak mistletoe, 'is not dead, nor like to be yet, though the pack of your guests went baying off through the night yelling murder.'

'He well might have been a corpse,' she snapped. 'And dead or no, either way this is a hanging matter, as well you know. And how if I had died, eh? Whose fault would that have been? There could have been two of us to bury, and the family left ruined into the bargain. Mischief enough for one wretched little minstrel to wreak in one night. But he'll pay for it! Forty days or no, we shall be waiting for him, he won't escape us.'

'If he ran from here loaded with your goods,' said Cadfael,

28

shaking out a little powder into his palm, 'he certainly brought none of them into the church with him. If he has your one miserly penny on him, that's all.' He turned to the young woman who stood anxiously beside the head of the bed. 'Have you wine there, or milk? Either does. Stir this into a cup of it.'

She was a small, round, homely girl, this Margery, perhaps twenty years old, with fresh, rosy colouring and a great untidy mass of yellow hair. Her eyes were round and wary, no wonder if she felt lost in this unfamiliar and disrupted household, but she moved quietly and sensibly, and her hands were steady on pitcher and cup.

'He had time to hide his plunder somewhere,' the old woman insisted grimly. 'Walter was gone above half an hour before Susanna began to wonder, and went to look for him. The wretch could have been over the bridge and into the bushes by then.'

She accepted the drink that was presented to her lips, and swallowed it down readily. Whatever her dissatisfaction with abbot and abbey, she trusted Cadfael's remedies. The two of them were unlikely to agree on any subject under the sun, but for all that they respected each other. Even this avaricious, formidable old woman, tyrant of her family and terror of her servants, had certain virtues of courage, spirit and honesty that were not to be despised.

'He swears he never touched your son or your gold,' said Cadfael. 'As I grant he may be lying, so you had better grant that you and yours may be mistaken.'

She was contemptuous. She pushed away from under her wrinkled neck the skimpy braid of brittle grey hair that irritated her skin. 'Who else could it have been? The only stranger, and with a grudge because I docked him the value of what he broke …'

'Of what he says some boisterous young fellow hustled him and caused him to break.'

'He must take a company as he finds it, wherever he hires himself out. And now I recall,' she said, 'we put him out without those painted toys of his, wooden rings and balls. I want nothing of his, and what he's taken of mine I'll have back before the end. Susanna will give you the playthings for him, and welcome. He shall not be able to say we've matched his thievery.'

She would give him, scrupulously, what was his, but she would see his neck wrung without a qualm.

29

'Be content, you've already broken his head for him. One more blow like that, and you might have had the law crying murder on *you*. And you'd best listen to me soberly now! One more rage like that, and you'll be your own death. Learn to take life gently and keep your temper, or there'll be a third and worse seizure, and it may well be the last.'

She looked, for once, seriously thoughtful. Perhaps she had been saying as much to herself, even without his warning. 'I am as I am,' she said, rather admitting than boasting.

'Be so as long as you may, and leave it to the young to fly into frenzies over upsets that will all pass, given time. Now here I'm leaving you this flask – it's the decoction of heart trefoil, the best thing I know to strengthen the heart. Take it as I taught you before, and keep your bed today, and I'll take another look at you tomorrow. And now,' said Cadfael, 'I'm going along to see how Master Walter fares.'

The goldsmith, his balding head swathed and his long, suspicious face fallen slack in sleep, was snoring heavily, and it seemed the best treatment to let him continue sleeping. Cadfael went down thoughtfully to find Susanna, who was out in the kitchen at the rear of the house. A skinny little girl laboured at feeding a sluggish fire and heaving a great pot to the hook over it. Cadfael had caught a glimpse of the child once before, all great dark eyes in a pale, grubby face, and a tangle of dark hair. Some poor maidservant's by-blow by her master, or her master's son, or a passing guest. For all the parsimony in this household, the girl could have fallen into worse hands. She was at least fed, and handed down cast-off clothing, and if the old matriarch was grim and frightening, Susanna was quiet and calm, no scold and no tyrant.

Cadfael reported on his patient, and Susanna watched his face steadily, nodded comprehension, and asked no questions.

'And your father is asleep. I left him so. What better could anyone do for him?'

'I fetched his own physician to him last night,' she said, 'when we found him. She'll have none but you now, but father relies on Master Arnald, and he's close. He says the blow is not dangerous, though it was enough to lay him senseless some hours. Though it may be the drink had something to do with that, too.'

'He hasn't yet been able to tell you what happened? Whether he saw who the man was who struck him?'

'Not a word. When he comes to, his head aches so he can remember nothing. It may come back to him later.'

For the saving or the damning of Liliwin! But whichever way that went, and whatever else he might be, Walter Aurifaber was not a liar. Meantime, there was nothing to be learned from him, but from the rest of the household there might be, and this girl was the gravest and most reasonable of the tribe.

'I've heard the general cry against this young fellow, but not the way the thing happened. I know there was some horse-play with the lads, nothing surprising at a wedding feast, and the pitcher got broken. I know your grandmother lashed out at him with her stick, and had him cast out with only one penny of his fee. His story is that he made off then, knowing it was hopeless to protest further, and he knew nothing of what followed until he heard the hunters baying after him, and ran to us for shelter.'

'He would say so,' she agreed reasonably.

'Every man's saying may as well be true as untrue,' said Cadfael sententiously. 'How long after his going was it when Master Walter went to his workshop?'

'Nearly an hour it must have been. Some of the guests were leaving then, but the more lively lads would stay to see Margery bedded, a good dozen of them were up the stair to the chamber. The wedding gifts were on the table to be admired, but seeing the night was ending, father took them and went to lock them away safely in his strong-box in the workshop. And it must have been about half an hour later, with all the merriment above, that I began to wonder that he hadn't come back. There was a gold chain and rings that Margery's father gave her, and a purse of silver links, and a breast ornament of silver and enamel – fine things. I went out by the hall door and round to the shop, and there he was, lying on his face by the coffer, and the lid open, and all but the heavy pieces of plate gone.'

'So the singing lad had been gone a full hour before this happened. Did anyone see him lurking after he was put out?'

She smiled, shaking a rueful head. 'There was darkness enough to hide a hundred loiterers. And he did not go so tamely as you suppose. He knows how to curse, too, he cried us names I'd never heard before, I promise you, and he howled that he'd have his own back for the wrong we did him. And I won't say but he was hard done by, for that matter. But who else should it be? People we've known lifelong, neighbours

31

here in the street? No, you may be sure he hung about the yard in the dark until he saw my father go along to the shop, and he stole in there, and saw what wealth there was in the open coffer. Enough to tempt a poor man, I grant you. But even poor men must needs resist temptation.'

'You are very sure,' said Cadfael.

'I am sure. He owes a life for it.'

The little maidservant turned her head sharply, gazing with lips parted. Such eyes, huge and grieved. She made a very small sound like a kitten's whimper.

'Rannilt is daft about the boy,' said Susanna simply, scornfully tolerant of folly. 'He ate with her in the kitchen, and played and sang for her. She's sorry for him. But what's done is done.'

'And when you found your father lying so, of course you ran back here to call help for him?'

'I couldn't lift him alone. I cried out what had happened, and those guests who were still here came running, and Iestyn, our journeyman, came rushing up the stairs from the undercroft where he sleeps – he'd gone to bed an hour or more earlier, knowing he'd have to man the shop alone this morning ...' Of course, in expectation of the goldsmith's thick head and his son's late tarrying with his bride. 'We carried father up to his bed, and someone – I don't know who was the first – cried out that this was the jongleur's doing, and that he couldn't be far, and out they all went streaming, every man, to hunt for him. And I left Margery to watch my father, while I ran off to fetch Master Arnald.'

'You did what was possible,' Cadfael allowed. 'Then when was it Dame Juliana took her fit?'

'While I was gone. She'd gone to her chamber, she may even have been asleep, though with the larking and laughing in the gallery I should doubt it. But I was hardly out of the door when she hobbled along to father's room, and saw him lying, with his bloody head, and senseless. She clutched at her heart, Margery says, and fell down. But it was not such a bad fit this time. She was already wake and talking,' said Susanna, 'when I came back with the physician. We had help then for both of them.'

'Well, they've both escaped the worst,' said Cadfael, brooding, 'for this time. Your father is a strong, hale man, and should live his time out without harm. But for the dame, more shocks of the kind could be the death of her, and so I've told her.'

32

'The loss of her treasury,' said Susana drily, 'was shock enough to kill her. If she lives through that, she's proof against all else until her full time comes. We are a durable kind, Brother Cadfael, very durable.'

Cadfael turned aside from leaving by the passage to the street, and entered Walter Aurifaber's workshop by the side door. Here Walter would have let himself in, when he came burdened with several choice items in gold and silver, enamel and fine stones, to lock them up with his other wealth in the strong-box; from which, in all likelihood, Mistress Margery would have had much ado to get them out again for her wearing. Unless, of course, that soft and self-effacing shape concealed a spirit of unsuspected toughness. Women can be very deceptive.

As he entered the shop from the passage, the street door was on his left, there was a trestled show-table, cloth-covered, and the rear part of the room was all narrow shelving, the small furnace, cold, and the work-benches, at which Daniel was working on a setting for a clouded moss-agate, brows locked in a gloomy knot. But his fingers were deft enough with the fine tools, for all his preoccupation with the family misfortunes. The journeyman was bent over a scale on the bench beside the furnace, weighing small tablets of silver. A sturdy, compact person, this Iestyn, by the look of him about twenty-seven or twenty-eight years old, with cropped, straight dark hair in a thick cap. He turned his head, hearing someone entering, and his face was broad but bony, dark-skinned, thick-browed, deep-eyed, wholly Welsh. A better-humoured man than his master, though not so comely.

At sight of Cadfael, Daniel put his tools aside. 'You've seen them both? How is it with them?'

'The pair of them will do well enough for this time,' said Cadfael. 'Master Walter is under his own physician, and held to be out of any danger, if his memory is shaken. Dame Juliana is over this fit, but any further shock could be mortal, it's only to be expected. Few reach such an age.'

By the young man's face, he was pondering whether any ever should. But for all that, he knew she favoured him, and had a use for her indulgence. He might even be fond of her, after his fashion, and as far as affection was possible between sour age and impatient youth. He did not seem altogether a callous person, only spoiled. Sole heirs of merchant houses can be as deformed by their privilege as those of baronies.

33

In the far corner of the shop, Walter's pillaged strong-box stood, a big, iron-banded wooden coffer, securely bolted to floor and wall. Intent on impressing the magnitude of the crime upon any representative of the abbey that insisted on sheltering the felon, Daniel unlocked the double locks and heaved up the lid to display what was left within, a few heavy dishes of plate, too cumbersome to be concealed about the person. The tale he told, and would tell and retell indignantly as often as he found a listener, matched Susanna's account. Iestyn, called to bear witness at every other aggrieved sentence, could only nod his black head solemnly, and confirm every word.

'And you are all sure,' said Cadfael, 'that the jongleur must be the guilty man? No thought of any other possible thief? Master Walter is known to be a wealthy man. Would a stranger know how wealthy? I daresay there are some here in the town may well envy a craftsman better-off than themselves.'

'That's a true word,' agreed Daniel darkly. 'And there's one no farther away than the width of the yard that I might have wondered about, if he had not been there in my eye every minute of the time. But he was, and there's an end. I fancy he was the first to hit on it that it was the jongleur we wanted.'

'What, your tenant the locksmith? A harmless soul enough, I should have thought. Pays his rent and minds his shop, like the rest.'

'His man John Boneth minds the shop,' said Daniel, with a snort of laughter, 'and the daft lad helps him. Peche is more often out poking his long nose into other people's business, and carrying the gossip round the ale-houses than tending to his craft. A smiling, sneaking toady of a man to your face, and back-biting as soon as you turn away. There's no sneak-thievery I'd put past him, if you want to know. But he was there in the hall the whole time, so it was not he. No, make no mistake, we were on the right trail when we set the pack after the rogue Liliwin, and so it will be proved in the end.'

They were all in the same story, and the story might well be true. There was but one point to be put to them counter: where would a stranger to the town, and out in the dark, stow away so valuable a booty safely enough and secretly enough to hide it from all others, and yet be able to recover it himself? The aggrieved family might brush that aside. Cadfael found it a serious obstacle to belief.

He was withdrawing by the same door at which he had

34

entered, and drawing it closed after him by the iron latch, when the draught of the movement and the lengthening shaft of sunlight piercing the passage fluttered and illuminated a single primrose-coloured thread, waving at the level of his eyes from the doorpost. The doorpost now on his right, on his left when he entered, but then out of range of the sun's rays. Pale as flax, and long and shining. He took it between finger and thumb, and plucked it gently from the wood, and a little blotch of dark, brownish red which had gummed it to the post came away with it, a second, shorter hair coiled and stuck in the blot. Cadfael stared at it for an instant, and cast one glance back over his shoulder before he closed the door. From here the coffer in the far corner was plainly in view, and so would a man be, bending over it.

A small thing, to make so huge a hole in the defence a man put up for his life. Someone had stood pressed against that doorpost, looking in, someone about Cadfael's own height – a small man with flaxen hair, and a bloodied graze on the left side of his head.

Chapter Three

Saturday, from noon to night

ADFAEL WAS still standing with the tiny, ominous speck in his palm when he heard his name called from the hall door, and in the same moment a freshening puff of wind took the floating hairs and carried them away. He let them go. Why not? They had already spoken all too eloquently, they had nothing to add. He turned to see Susanna withdrawing into the hall, and the little maidservant scurrying towards him, with a knotted bundle of cloth held out before her.

'Mistress Susanna says Dame Juliana wants these out of the house.' She opened the twist of cloth, and showed a glimpse of painted wood, scarred from much use. 'They belong to Liliwin. She said you would take them to him.' The great dark eyes that dwelt unwaveringly on Cadfael's face dilated even more. 'Is it true?' she asked, low and urgently. 'He's safe, there in the church? And you'll protect him? You won't let them fetch him away?'

'He's with us, and safe enough,' said Cadfael. 'No one dare touch him now.'

'And they haven't hurt him?' she questioned earnestly.

'No worse than will mend now, in peace. No need to fret for a while. He has forty days grace. I think', he said, studying the thin face, the delicate, staring cheekbones under the wide-set eyes, 'you like this young man.'

36

'He made such lovely music,' said the child wistfully. 'And he spoke me gently, and was glad of being with me in the kitchen. It was the best hour I ever spent. And now I'm frightened for him. What will happen to him when the forty days are up?'

'Why, if it goes so far – for forty days is time enough to change many things – but even if it goes so far, and he must come forth, it will be into the hands of the law, not into the hands of his accusers. Law is grim enough, but tries to be fair. And by then those who accuse him will have forgotten their zeal, but even if they have not, they cannot touch him. If you want to help him, keep eyes and ears open, and if you learn of anything to the purpose, then speak out.' Clearly the very thought terrified her. Who ever listened to anything she might say? 'To me you may speak freely,' he said. 'Do you know anything of what went on here last night?'

She shook her head, casting wary glances over her shoulder. 'Mistress Susanna sent me away to my bed. I sleep in the kitchen, I never even heard ... I was very tired.' The kitchen was set well apart from the house for fear of fire, as was customary with these close-set and timber-framed town houses, she might well sleep through all the alarm after her long hours of labour. 'But I do know this,' she said, and lifted her chin gallantly, and he saw that for all her youth and frailty it was a good chin, with a set to it that he approved. 'I know Liliwin never harmed anyone, not my master nor any other man. What they say of him is not true.'

'Nor ever stole?' asked Cadfael gently.

She was no way put down, she held him steadily in her great lamps of eyes. 'To eat, yes, perhaps, when he was hungry, an egg from under a hen somewhere, a partridge in the woods, even a loaf ... that may be. He has been hungry all his life.' She knew, for much of her life so had she. 'But steal more than that? For money, for gold? What good would that do him? And he is not like that ... never!'

Cadfael was aware of the head emerging from the door before Rannilt was, and warned her softly, 'There, run! Say I kept you with questions, and you knew no answers.'

She was very quick, she had whirled and was speeding back when Susanna's voice pealed impatiently, 'Rannilt!'

Cadfael did not wait to see her vanish within on the heels of her mistress, but turned at once to resume his way along the passage to the street.

Baldwin Peche was sitting with a pot of ale on the steps of his shop. The fact that the street was narrow, and the frontages here faced north-west and were in deep shadow, suggested that he had a reason beyond idleness and ease for being where he was at this hour. No doubt all those townsmen who had been guests at the Aurifaber wedding were up and alert this morning, as soon as they could shake off the effects of their entertainment, roused and restored by the sensational gossip they had to spread, and the possibility of further revelations.

The locksmith was a man in his fifties; short, sturdy, but beginning to grow a round paunch, a noted fisherman along the Severn, but a weak swimmer, unusually for this river-circled town. He had, truly enough, a long nose that quivered to every breath of scandal, though he was cautious in the use he made of it, as though he enjoyed mischief for its own sake rather than for any personal profit. A cold, inquisitive merriment twinkled in his pale-blue eyes, set in a round, ruddy and smiling face. Cadfael knew him well enough to pass the time of day, and gave him good morrow as though making the approach himself, whereas he was well apprised Peche had been waiting to make it.

'Well, Brother Cadfael,' said the locksmith heartily, 'you'll have been tending these unlucky neighbours of mine. I trust you find them bearing up under their griefs? The lad tells me they'll make good recoveries, the both of them.'

Cadfael said what was required of him, which was rather enquiry than response, and kept his mouth shut and his ears open to listen to the tale all over again, with more and richer detail, since this was Peche's chosen craft. The journeyman locksmith, a fine-looking young man who lived with his widowed mother a street or two away in the town, looked out once from the shop doorway, cast a knowledgeable eye on his master, and withdrew, assured of having work to himself, as he preferred it. By this time John Boneth knew everything his skilled but idle tutor could teach him, and was quite capable of running the business single-handed. There was no son to inherit it, he was trusted and depended on, and he could wait.

'A lucky match, mark,' said Peche, prodding a knowing finger into Brother Cadfael's shoulder, 'especially if this treasury of Walter's is really lost, and can't be recovered. Edred Bele's girl has money enough coming to her to make up

38

the half, at least. Walter's worked hard to get her for his lad, and the old dame's done her share, too. Trust them!' He rubbed finger and thumb together suggestively, and nudged and winked. 'And the girl no beauty and without graces – neither sings nor dances well, and dumb in company. No monster, though, she'll pass well enough, or that youngster would never have been brought to … not with what he has in hand!'

'He's a fine-looking lad,' said Cadfael mildly, 'and they say not unskilled. And a good inheritance waiting for him.'

'Ah, but short *now*!' whispered Baldwin, leaning closer still and stabbing with a stiff forefinger, his knowing face gleeful. 'It's the waiting is hard to bear. Young folk live now, not tomorrow, and this side marriage – you take my meaning? – not t'other. Oh, the old dame may dote on him, the sun shines out of his tail for her, but she keeps her hold on the purse and doles out sweets very sparingly. Not enough for the sort *he* fancies!'

It occurred to Cadfael, rather belatedly, that it was hardly becoming behaviour in one of his habit to listen avidly to local scandal, but if he did nothing to encourage confidences, he certainly did not stop listening. Encouragement, in any case, was unnecessary. Peche had every intention of making the most of his probings.

'I wouldn't say,' he breathed into Cadfael's ear, 'but he's had his fingers in her purse a time or two, for all her sharpness. His present fancy comes expensive, not to speak of the game there'll be if ever her husband gets to know of their cantrips. It's a fair guess the bride's dowry, as much of it as he can get his hands on, will go to deck out another wench's neck. Not that he had any objections to this match – not he, he likes the girl well enough, and he likes her money a good deal better. But he likes somebody else best of all. No names, no revenges! But you should have seen her as a guest last night! Bold as a royal whore, and the old man puffed up beside her, proud of owning the handsomest thing in the hall, and she and the bridegroom eyeing each other fit to laugh out loud at the old fool. As well I was the only one there had sharp enough eyes to see the sparks pass!'

'As well, indeed!' said Cadfael almost absently, for he was busy reflecting how understandable it was that Daniel should view his father's tenant with such ill-will. No need to doubt Peche's information, really devoted pryers make sure of their

39

facts. Doubtless, though never a word need have been said, certain quiverings of that inquisitive nose and knowing glances from those coldly merry eyes had warned Daniel, evidently not quite a fool, that his gallivantings were no secret.

And the other, the old fool, welcome guest at the wedding – of consequence, therefore, among the merchants of Shrewsbury and with a young, bold, handsome wife ... A second marriage, then, on the man's part? The town was not so great that Cadfael had to look very far. Ailwin Corde, widowed a few years ago and married again, against his grown son's wishes, to a fine, flaunting beauty a third of his age, called Cecily ...

'I'd keep your tongue within your teeth,' he advised amiably. 'Wool merchants are a power in this town, and not every husband will thank you for opening his eyes.'

'What, I? Speak out of turn?' The merry eyes sparkled with all the cordiality of ice, and the long nose twitched. 'Not I! I have a decent landlord and a snug corner, and no call to overturn what suits me well. I take my fun where I find it, Brother, but quietly and privately. No harm in what does none.'

'None in the world,' agreed Cadfael, and took his leave peaceably, and went on towards the winding descent of the Wyle, very thoughtful, but none too sure of what he should be thinking. For what had he learned? That Daniel Aurifaber was paddling palms, and probably more, with mistress Cecily Corde, whose wool-merchant husband collected fleeces from the bordering district of Wales, and traded them into England, and therefore was often absent for some days at a time, and that the lady, however fond, was accustomed to gifts, and did not come cheaply, whereas the young man was baulked by equally parsimonious father and grandmother, and was reputed already to be filching such small sums as he could get his fingers on. And no easy matter, either! And had his father not gone to lock up at least half of the bride's dowry out of reach? Out of reach now in good earnest – or had last night's events snugged it away well *within* reach? Such things can happen in families.

What else! That Daniel held no good opinion, reasonably enough, of the tenant who spent his leisure so inconveniently, and claimed he would have held him to be a prime suspect, if he had not been in full view throughout the time when the deed was done.

Well, time would show. They had forty days in hand.

High Mass was over when Cadfael had crossed the bridge and

made his way back to the gatehouse and the great court. Prior Robert's shadow, Brother Jerome, was hovering in the cloister to intercept him when he came.

'The lord abbot asks that you will wait upon him before dinner.' Jerome's pinched, narrow nose quivered with a suggestion of depreciation and distaste which Cadfael found more offensive than Baldwin Peche's full-blooded enjoyment of his own mischief. 'I trust, Brother, that you mean to let time and law take their course, and not involve our house beyond the legal obligations of sanctuary, in so sordid a matter. It is not for you to take upon yourself the burdens that belong to justice.'

Jerome, if he had not explicit orders, had received his charge from Prior Robert's knotted brow and quivering nostril. So low and ragged and miserable a manifestation of humanity as Liliwin, lodged here within the pale, irked Robert like a burr working through his habit and fretting his aristocratic skin. He would have no peace while the alien body remained, he wanted it removed, and the symmetry of his life restored. To be fair, not merely his own life, but the life of this house, which fretted and itched with the infection thus hurled in from the world without. The presence of terror and pain is disruptive indeed.

'All the abbot wants from me is an account of how my patients fare,' said Cadfael, with unwonted magnanimity towards the narrow preoccupations of creatures so uncongenial to him as Robert and his clerk. For their distress, however strange to him, was still comprehensible. The walls did, indeed, tremble, the sheltered souls did quake. 'And I have burdens enough with them, and am hardly looking for any others. Is that lad fed and doctored? That's all my business with him.'

'Brother Oswin has taken care of him,' said Jerome.

'That's well! Then I'll go pay my respects to the lord abbot, and get to my dinner, for I missed breakfast, and those up there in the town are too distraught to think of offering a morsel.'

He wondered, however, as he crossed the court to the abbot's lodging, how much of what he had gleaned he was about to impart. Salacious gossip can be of no interest to abbatial ears, nor was there much to be said about a tiny plaque of dried blood tethering a couple of flaxen hairs; not, at least, until the vagabond, with every hand against him and his life at stake, had exercised the right to answer for himself.

41

Abbot Radulfus received without surprise the news that the entire wedding party was united in insisting on the jongleur's guilt. He was not, however, quite convinced that Daniel, or any other of those attending could be certain who had, or had not, been in full view throughout.

'With a hall full of so many people, so much being drunk, and over so many hours of celebration, who can say how any man came and went? Yet so many voices all in one tale cannot be disregarded. Well, we must do our part, and leave the law to deal with the rest. The sergeant tells me his master the sheriff is gone to arbitrate in a dispute between neighbour knights in the east of the shire, but his deputy is due in the town before night.'

That was good news in Cadfael's ear. Hugh Beringar would see to it that the search for truth and justice should not go sliding down the easiest way, and erase such minor details as failed to fit the pattern. Meantime, Cadfael had just such a detail to take up with Liliwin, besides restoring him the tools of his juggling trade. After dinner he went to look for him, and found him sitting in the cloister, with borrowed needle and thread, trying to cobble together the rents in his coat. Beneath the bandaged brow he had washed his face scrupulously, it showed pale and thin but clear-skinned, with good, even delicate features. And if he could not yet wash the dust and mire from his fair hair, at least he had combed it into decent order.

The sop first, perhaps, and then the switch! Cadfael sat down beside him, and dumped the cloth bundle in his lap. 'Here's a part of your property restored you, for an earnest. There, open it!'

But Liliwin already knew the faded wrapping. He sat gazing down for a moment in wonder and disbelief, and then untied the knotted cloth and sank his hand among his modest treasures with affection and pleasure, faintly flushing and brightening, as though for the first time recovering faith that some small comforts and kindnesses existed for him in the world.

'But how did you get them? I never thought I should see them again. And you thought to ask for them ... for me ... That was kind!'

'I did not even have to ask. That old dame who struck you, terror though she may be, is honest. She won't keep what is not hers, if she won't forgo a groat of what is. She sends them back

42

to you.' Not graciously, but no need to go into that. 'There, take it for a good sign. And how do you find yourself today? Have they fed you?'

'Very well! I'm to fetch my food from the kitchen at breakfast, dinner and supper.' He sounded almost incredulous, naming three meals a day. 'And they've given me a pallet in the porch here. I'm afraid to be away from the church at night.' He said it simply and humbly. 'They don't all like it that I'm here. I stick in their craw like a husk.'

'They're accustomed to calm,' said Cadfael sympathetically. 'It is not calm you bring. You must make allowances, as they must. At least from tonight you may sleep secure. The deputy sheriff should be in town by this evening. In his authority, I promise you, you can trust.'

Trust would still come very hardly to Liliwin, after all he had experienced in a short life, but the toys he had tucked away so tenderly under his pallet were a promise. He bent his head over his patient stitching, and said no word.

'And therefore,' said Cadfael briskly, 'You'd best consider on the half-tale you told me, and own to the part you left out. For you did not creep away so docilely as you let us all think, did you? What were you doing, hugging the door-post of Master Walter's workshop, long after you claim you had made off into the night? With the door open, and your head against the post, and the goldsmith's coffer in full view … and also open? And he bending over it?'

Liliwin's needle had started in his fingers and pricked his left hand. He dropped the needle, thread and coat, and sat sucking his pierced thumb, and staring at Brother Cadfael with immense, frightened eyes. He began to protest shrilly, 'I never went there … I know nothing about it …' Voice and eyes sank together. He blinked down at his open hands, lashes long and thick as a well-bred cow's brushing his staring cheekbones.

'Child,' said Cadfael, sighing, 'you were there in the doorway, peering in. You left your mark there. A lad your size, with a bloodied head, leaned long enough against that door-post to leave a little clot of his blood, and two flax-white hairs gummed into it. No, no other has seen it, it's gone, blown away on the wind, but I saw it, and I know. Now tell me truth. What passed between you and him?'

He did not ask why Liliwin had lied in omitting this part of his story, there was no need. What, place himself there on the spot, there where the blow had been struck? Innocence would have

43

avoided admission every bit as desperately as guilt.

Liliwin sat and shivered, fluttering like a leaf in that same wind which had carried off his stray hairs. Here in the cloister the air was still chilly, and he had only a patched shirt and hose on him, the half-mended coat lying on his knees. He swallowed hard and sighed.

'It's true, I did wait … It was not fair!' he blurted, shaking. 'I stayed there in the dark. They were not all as hard as she, I thought I might plead … I saw him go to the shop with a light and I followed. He was not so furious when the pitcher was broken, he did try to calm her, I dared approach him. I went in and pleaded for the fee I was promised, and he gave me a second penny. He gave it to me and I went. I swear it!'

He had sworn the other version, too. But fear does so, the fear bred of a lifetime's hounding and battering.

'And then you left? And you saw no more of him? More to the point still, did you see aught of any other who may have been lurking as you did, and entered to him afterwards?'

'No, there was no one. I went, I was glad to go, it was all over. If he lives, he'll tell you he gave me the second penny.'

'He lives, and will,' said Cadfael. 'It was not a fatal blow. But he's said nothing yet.'

'But he will, he will, he'll tell you how I begged him, and how he took pity on me. I was afraid,' he said quivering, 'I was afraid! If I'd said I went there, it would have been all over with me.'

'Well, but consider,' said Cadfael reasonably, 'when Walter is his own man again, and comes forth with that very tale, how would it look if he brought it out when you had said no word of it? And besides, when his wits settle and he recalls what befell, it may well be that he'll be able to name his attacker, and clear you of all blame.'

He was watching closely as he said it, for to an innocent man that notion would come as powerful comfort, but to a guilty one as the ultimate terror; and Liliwin's troubled countenance gradually cleared and brightened into timid hope. It was the first truly significant indication of how far he should be believed.

'I never thought of that. They said murdered. A murdered man can't accuse or deliver. If I'd known then he was well alive I would have told the whole truth. What must I do now? It will look bad to have to own I lied.'

'What you should do for the best,' Cadfael said after some

44

thought, 'is let me take this word myself to the lord abbot, not as my discovery – for the evidence is gone with a puff of wind – but as your confession. And if Hugh Beringar comes tonight, as I hope and hear he may, then you may tell the tale over again to him in full, yourself. Whatever follows then, you may rest out your days of grace here with a clear conscience and truth will speak on your side.'

Hugh Beringar of Maesbury, deputy sheriff of the shire, reached the abbey for Vespers, after a long conference with the sergeant concerning the lost treasury. In search of it, every yard of ground between the goldsmith's house and the bushes from which Liliwin had been flushed at midnight had been scoured without result. Every voice in the town declared confidently that the jongleur was the guilty man, and had successfully hidden his plunder before he was sighted and pursued.

'But you, I think,' said Beringar, walking back towards the gatehouse with Cadfael beside him and twitching a thin dark eyebrow at his friend, 'do not agree. And not wholly because this enforced guest of yours is young and hungry and in need of protection. What is it convinces you? For I do believe you are convinced he's wronged.'

'You've heard his story,' said Cadfael. 'But you did not see his face when I put it into his head that the goldsmith may get back his memory of the night in full, and be able to put a name or a face to his assailant. He took that hope to him like a blessed promise. The guilty man would hardly do so.'

Hugh considered that gravely and nodded agreement. 'But the fellow is a player, and has learned hard to keep command of his face in all circumstances. No blame to him, he has no other armour. To appear innocent of all harm must now be his whole endeavour.'

'And you think I am easily fooled,' said Cadfael drily.

'Far from it. Yet it is well to remember and admit the possibility.' And that was also true, and Hugh's dark smile, slanted along his shoulder, did nothing to blunt the point. 'Though I grant it would be nothing new for you to be the only creature who holds against the grain, and makes his wager good.'

'Not the only one,' said Cadfael almost absently, with Rannilt's wan, elfin face before his mind's eye. 'There's one other more certain than I.' They had reached the arch of the gatehouse, the broad highway of the Foregate crossed beyond, and the evening was just greening and dimming towards twilight. 'You say you found the place where the lad bedded down for the night? Shall we take a look there together?'

They passed through the arch, an odd pair to move so congenially side by side, the monk squat and square and sturdy, rolling in his gait like a seaman, and well launched into his sixtieth year, the sheriff's deputy more than thirty years younger and half a head taller, but still a small man, of graceful, nimble movements and darkly saturnine features. Cadfael had seen this young man win his appointment fairly, and a wife to go with it, and had witnessed the christening of their first son only a few months ago. They understood each other better than most men ever do, but they could still take opposing sides in a matter of the king's justice.

They turned towards the bridge that led into the town, but turned aside again on the right, a little way short of the riverside, into the belt of trees that fringed the road. Beyond, towards the evening gleam of the Severn, the ground declined to the lush level of the main abbey gardens, along the meadows called the Gaye. They could see the green, clear light through the branches as they came to the place where Liliwin had settled down sadly to sleep before leaving this unfriendly town. And it was a nest indeed, rounded and coiled into the slope of thick new grass, and so small, like the haunt of a dormouse.

'He started up in alarm, in one leap clear of his form, like a flushed hare,' said Hugh soberly. 'There are young shoots broken here – do you see? – where he crashed through. This is unquestionably the place.' He looked round curiously, for Cadfael was casting about among the bushes, which grew thickly here for cover. 'What are you seeking?'

'He had his rebec in a linen bag on his shoulder,' said Cadfael. 'In the dark a branch caught the string and jerked it away, and he dared not stop to grope after it. So he told me, like a man bereaved. I am sure that was the truth. I wonder what became of it?'

He found the answer that same evening, but not until he had parted from Hugh and was on his way back to the gatehouse. It was a luminous evening and Cadfael was in no hurry to go in, and had plenty of time before Compline. He stood to watch the leisurely evening walk of the Foregate worthies, and the prolonged games of the urchins of the parish of Holy Cross

46

reluctant to go home to their beds, just as he was. A dozen or so of them swept by in a flurry of yelling and laughter, shrill as starlings, some still half-naked from the river, but not yet so cold that they must make for the home hearth. They were kicking a shapeless rag ball among them, and some of them swiping at it with sticks, and one with something broader and shorter. Cadfael heard the impact of hollow wood, and the thrumming reverberation of one surviving string. A lamentable sound, like a cry for help with little expectation that the plea would be heard.

The imp with this weapon loitered, dragging his implement in the dust. Cadfael pursued, and drew alongside like a companion ship keeping station rather than a pirate boarding. The brat looked up and grinned, knowing him. He had but a short way to go home, and was tired of his plaything.

'Now what in the world have you found there?' said Cadfael amicably. 'And where did you happen on such an odd thing?'

The child waved a hand airily back towards the trees that screened the Gaye. 'It was lying in there, in a cloth bag, but I lost that down by the water. I don't know what it is. I never saw a thing like it. But it's no use that I can see.'

'Did you find,' asked Cadfael, eyeing the wreckage, 'a stick with fine hairs stretched along it, that went with this queer thing?'

The child yawned, halted, and abandoned his hold on his toy, letting it drop into the dust. 'I hit Davey with that when he tripped me in the water, but it broke. I threw it away.' So he would, having proved its uselessness, just as he walked away from this discarded weapon, leaving it lying, and went off scrubbing at sleepy eyes with the knuckles of a grimy fist.

Brother Cadfael picked up the sorry remnant and examined ruefully its stove-in ribs and trailing, tangled strings. No help for it, this was all that remained of the lost rebec. He took it back with him, only too well aware of the grief he was about to cause its luckless owner. Say that Liliwin came alive in the end out of his present trouble, still he must emerge penniless, and deprived now even of his chief means of livelihood. But there was more in it even than that. He knew it even before he presented the broken instrument to Liliwin's appalled hands, and watched the anguish and despair mantle like bleak twilight over his face. The boy took the ruin in his hands and fondled it, rocked it in his arms, bowed his head to its splintered frame, and burst into tears. It was not the loss of a possession so much as the death of a sweetheart.

47

Cadfael sat down apart, in the nearest carrel of the scriptorium, and kept decently silent until the storm passed, and Liliwin sat drained and motionless, hugging his broken darling, his thin shoulders hunched against the world.

'There are men,' said Cadfael then mildly, 'who understand such arts as repairing instruments of music. I am not one of them, but Brother Anselm, our precentor, is. Why should we not ask him to look at your fiddle and see what can be done to make it sing again?'

'*This?*' Liliwin turned on him passionately, holding out the pathetic wreck in both hands. 'Look at it – no better than firewood. How could anyone restore it?'

'Do you know that? What's lost by asking the man who may? And if this is past saving, Brother Anselm can make one new.'

Bitter disbelief stared back at him. Why should he credit that anyone would go out of his way to do a kindness to so despised and unprofitable a creature as himself? Those within here held that they owed him shelter and food, but nothing more, and even that as a duty. And no one without had ever offered him any benefit that cost more than a crust.

'As if I could ever pay for a new one! Don't mock me!'

'You forget, we do not buy and sell, we have no use for money. But show Brother Anselm a good instrument damaged, and he'll want to heal it. Show him a good musician lost for want of an instrument, and he'll be anxious to provide him a new voice. Are you a good musician?'

Liliwin said: 'Yes!' with abrupt and spirited pride. In one respect, at least, he knew his worth.

'Then show him you are, and he'll give you your due.'

'You mean it?' wondered Liliwin, shaken between hope and doubt. 'You will truly ask him? If he would teach me, perhaps I could learn the art.' He faltered there, losing his momentary brightness with a suddenness that was all too eloquent. Whenever he took heart for the future, the bleak realisation came flooding over him afresh that he might have no future. Cadfael cast about hurriedly in his mind for some crumb of distraction to ward off the recurrent despair.

'Never suppose that you're friendless, that's black ingratitude when you have forty days of grace, a fair-minded man like Hugh Beringar enquiring into your case, and one creature at least who stands by you stoutly and won't hear a word against you.' Liliwin kindled a little at that, still doubtfully, but at least it had put the gallows and the noose out of his mind for the moment. 'You'll remember her – a girl named Rannilt.'

Liliwin's face at once paled and brightened. It was the first smile Cadfael had yet seen from him, and even now tentative, humble, frightened to reach for anything desired, for fear it should vanish like melting snow as he clutched it.

'You've seen her? Talked to her? And she does not believe what they all say of me?'

'Not a word of it! She affirms – she *knows* – you never did violence nor theft in that house. If all the tongues in Shrewsbury cried out against you, she would still stand her ground and speak for you.'

Liliwin sat cradling his broken rebec, as gently and shyly as if he clasped a sweetheart indeed. His faint, frightened smile shone in the dimming light within the cloister.

'She is the first girl who ever looked kindly at me. You won't have heard her sing – such a small, sweet voice, like a reed. We ate in the kitchen together. It was the best hour of my life, I never thought ... And it's true? Rannilt believes in me?'

Chapter Four

Sunday

ILIWIN FOLDED away his brychans and made himself presentable before Prime on the sabbath, determined to cause as little disruption as possible in the orderly regime within these walls. In his wandering life he had had little opportunity to become familiar with the offices of the day, and Latin was a closed book to him, but at least he could attend and pay his reverences, if that would make him more acceptable.

After breakfast Cadfael dressed the gash in the young man's arm again, and unwound the bandage from the graze on his head. 'This is healing well,' he said approvingly. 'We'd best leave it uncovered, and let in the air to it now. Good clean flesh you have, boy, if something too little of it. And you've lost that limp that had you going sidewise. How is it with all those bruises.'

Liliwin owned with some surprise that most of his aches and pains were all but gone, and performed a few startling contortions to prove it. He had not lost his skills. His fingers itched for the coloured rings and balls he used for his juggling, safely tucked away in their knotted cloth under his bed, but he feared they would be frowned on here. The ruin of his rebec also reposed in the corner of the porch next the cloister. He returned there after his breakfast to find Brother Anselm turning the wreck thoughfully in his hands, and running a questing finger along the worst of the cracks.

The precentor was past fifty, a vague, slender, short-sighted person who peered beneath an untidy brown tonsure and bristling brows to match, and smiled amiably and encouragingly at the owner of this disastrous relic.

'This is yours? Brother Cadfael told me how it had suffered. This has been a fine instrument. You did not make it?'

'No. I had it from an old man who taught me. He gave it to me before he died. I don't know,' said Liliwin, 'how to make them.'

It was the first time Brother Anselm had heard him speak since the shrill terror of the first invasion. He looked up alertly, tilting his head to listen. 'You have the upper voice, very true and clear. I could use you, if you sing? But you must sing! You have not thought of taking the cowl, here among us?' He recalled with a sigh why that was hardly likely under present circumstances. 'Well, this poor thing has been villainously used, but it is not beyond help. We may try. And the bow is lost, you say.' Liliwin had said no such thing, he was mute with wonder. Evidently Brother Cadfael had given precise information to a retentive enthusiast. 'The bow, I must say, is almost harder to perfect than the fiddle, but I have had my successes. Have you skills on other instruments?'

'I can get a tune out of most things,' said Liliwin, charmed into eagerness.

'Come,' said Brother Anselm, taking him firmly by the arm, 'I will show you my workshop and you and I between us, after High Mass, will try what can best be done for this rebec of yours. I shall need a helper to tend my resins and gums. But this will be slow and careful work, mind, and matter for prayer, not to be hastened for any cause. Music is study for a lifetime, son – a lifetime however long.'

He blew so like a warm gale that Liliwin went with him in a dream, forgetting how short a lifetime could also be.

Walter Aurifaber woke up that morning with a lingering headache, but also with a protesting stiffness in his limbs and restless animation in his mind that made him want to get up and stretch, and stamp, and move about briskly until the dullness went out of him. He growled at his patient, silent daughter, enquired after his journeyman, who had had the sense to make sure of his Sunday rest by vanishing from both shop and town for the day, and sat down to eat a substantial breakfast and stare his losses in the face.

51

Things were coming back to him, however foggily, including one incident he would just as soon his mother should not hear about. Money was money, of course, the old woman had the right of it there, but it's not every day a man marries off his heir, and marries him, moreover, to a most respectable further amount of money. A little flourish towards a miserable menial might surely be forgiven a man, in the circumstances. But would she think so? He regretted it bitterly himself now, reflecting on the disastrous result of his rare impulse of generosity. No, she must not hear of it!

Walter nursed his thick head and vain regrets, and took some small comfort in seeing his son and his new daughter-in-law off to church at Saint Mary's, in their best clothes and properly linked, Margery's hand primly on Daniel's arm. The money Margery had brought with her, and would eventually bring, mattered now more than anything else until the lost contents of his strong-box could be recovered. His head ached again fiercely when he thought of it. Whoever had done that to the house of Aurifaber should and must hang, if there was any justice in this world.

When Hugh Beringar came, with a sergeant in attendance, to hear for himself what the aggrieved victim had to tell, Walter was ready and voluble. But he was none too pleased when Dame Juliana, awaiting Brother Cadfael's visit, and foreseeing more strictures as to her behaviour if she wanted to live long, took it into her head to forestall the lecture by being downstairs when her mentor came and stumped her way down, cane in hand, prodding every tread before her and scolding Susanna away from attempting to check her. She was firmly settled on her bench in the corner, propped with cushions, when Cadfael came, and challenged him with a bold, provocative stare. Cadfael chose not to gratify her with homilies, but delivered the ointment he had brought for her, and reassured himself of the evenness of her breathing and heart, before turning to a Walter grown unaccountably short of words.

'I'm glad to see you so far restored. The tales they told of you were twenty years too soon. But I'm sorry for your loss. I hope it may yet be recovered.'

'Faith, so do I,' said Walter sourly. 'You tell me that rogue you have in sanctuary has no part of it on him, and while you hold him fast within there he can hardly unearth and make off with it. For it must be somewhere, and I trust the Sheriff's men here to find it.'

'You're very certain of your man, then?' Hugh had got him to the point where he had taken his valuables and gone to stow them away in the shop, and there he had suddenly grown less communicative. 'But he had already been expelled some time earlier, as I understand it, and no one has yet testified to seeing him lurking around your house after that.'

Walter cast a glance at his mother, whose ancient ears were pricked and her faded but sharp eyes alert. 'Ah, but he could well have stayed in hiding, all the same. What was there to prevent it in the dark of the night?'

'So he could,' agreed Hugh unhelpfully, 'but there's no man so far claims he did. Unless you've recalled something no one else knows? Did *you* see anything of him after he was thrown out?'

Walter shifted uneasily, looked ready to blurt out a whole indictment, and thought better of it in Juliana's hearing. Brother Cadfael took pity on him.

'It might be well,' he said guilessly, 'to take a look at the place where this assault was made. Master Walter will show us his workshop, I am sure.'

Walter rose to it thankfully, and ushered them away with alacrity, along the passage and in again at the door of his shop. The street door was fast, the day being Sunday, and he closed the other door carefully behind them, and drew breath in relief.

'Not that I've anything to conceal from you, my lord, but I'd as lief my mother should not have more to worrit her than she has already.' Plausible cover, at any rate, for the awe of her in which he still went. 'For this is where the thing happened, and you see from this door how the coffer lies in the opposite corner. And there was I, with the key in the lock and the lid laid back against the wall, wide open, and my candle here on the shelf close by. The light shining straight down into the coffer – you see? – and what was within in plain view. And suddenly I hear a sound behind me, and there's this minstrel, this Liliwin, creeping in at the door.'

'Threateningly?' asked Hugh, straight-faced. If he did not wink at Cadfael, his eyebrow was eloquent. 'Armed with a cudgel?'

'No,' admitted Walter, 'rather humbly, to all appearance. But then I'd heard him and turned. He was barely into the doorway, he could have dropped his weapon outside when he saw I was ware of him.'

53

'But you did not hear it fall? Nor see any sign of such?'

'No, that I own.'

'Then what had he to say to you?'

'He begged me to do him right, for he said he had been cheated of two thirds of his promised fee. He said it was hard on a poor man to be so blamed and docked of his money, and pleaded with me to make it good as promised.'

'And did you?' asked Hugh.

'I tell you honestly, my lord, I could not say he had been hardly used, considering the worth of the pitcher, but I did think him a poor, sad creature who had to live, whatever the rights or wrongs of it. And I gave him another penny – good silver, minted in this town. But not a word of this to Dame Juliana, if you'll be so good. She'll have to know, now it's all come back to me, that he dared creep in and ask, but no need for her to know I gave him anything. She would be affronted, seeing she had denied him.'

'Your thought for her does you credit,' said Hugh gravely. 'What then? He took your bounty and slunk out?'

'He did. But I wager *he* has not told you anything of this begging visit. A poor return I got for the favour!' Walter was sourly vengeful still.

'You mistake, for he has. He has told us this very same tale that you now tell. And confided to the abbey's keeping, while he remains there, the two silver pence which is all he has on him. Tell me, had you closed the lid of the coffer as soon as you found yourself observed?'

'I did!' said Walter fervently. 'And quickly! But he had seen. I never gave him another thought at the time but – see here, my lord, how it follows! As soon as he was gone, or I thought he was gone, I opened the coffer again, and was bending over it laying Margery's dowry away, when I was clouted hard from behind, and that's the last I knew till I opened an eye in my own bed, hours later. If it was two minutes after that fellow crept out of the door, when someone laid me flat, it was not a moment more. So who else could it be?'

'But you did not actually *see* who struck you?' Hugh pressed. 'Not so much as a glimpse? No shadow cast, to give him a shape or size? No sense of a bulk heaving up behind you?'

'Never a chance.' Walter might be vindictive, but he was honest. 'See, I was stooping over the coffer when it seemed the wall fell on me, and I pitched asprawl, head-down into the box, clean out of the world. I heard nothing and saw nothing, not even a shadow, no – the last thing I recall was the candle flickering, but what is there in that? No, depend on it, that rogue had seen what I had in my store before I clapped down the lid. Was he going tamely away with his penny, with all that money there to take? Not he! Nor hide nor hair of any other did I see in here that night. You may be certain of it, the jongleur is your man.'

'And it may still be so,' admitted Hugh, parting from Cadfael on the bridge some twenty minutes later. 'Enough to tempt any poor wretch with but two coins to rub together. Whether he had any such thought in his head before the candle shone on our friend's hoard or no. Equally, I grant the lad may not even have realised what lay beneath his hand, or seen anything but his own need and the thin chance of getting a kinder reception from the goldsmith than from that ferocious mother of his. He may have crept away thanking God for his penny and never a thought of wrong. Or he may have picked up a stone or a stave and turned back.'

At about that time, in the street outside Saint Mary's church, which was the common ground for exchanging civilities and observing fashions on a fine Sunday morning after Mass, Daniel and Margery Aurifaber in their ceremonial progression, intercepted by alternate well-wishers and commiserators – wedding and robbery being equally relished subjects of comment and speculation in Shrewsbury – came face to face with Master Ailwin Corde, the wool-merchant, and his wife, Cecily, and halted by general consent to pass the time of day as befitted friends and neighbours.

This Mistress Cecily looked more like a daughter to the merchant, or even a granddaughter, than a wife. She was twenty-three years old to his sixty, and though small and slender of stature, was so opulent in colouring, curvature and gait, and everything that could engage the eye, that she managed to loom large as a goddess and dominate whatever scene she graced with her presence. And her elderly husband took pleasure in decking out with sumptuous fabrics and fashions the gem he should rather have shrouded in secretive, plain linens. A gilt net gathered on her head its weight of auburn hair, and a great ornament of enamel and gemstones jutted before her, calling attention to a resplendent bosom.

Faced with this richness, Margery faded, and knew that she

faded. Her smile became fixed and false as a mask, and her voice tended to sharpen like a singer forced off-key. She tightened her clasp on Daniel's arm, but it was like trying to hold a fish that slid through her fingers without even being aware of restraint.

Master Corde enquired solicitously after Walter's health, was relieved to hear that he was making a good recovery, was sad, nonetheless, to know that so far nothing had been found of all that had been so vilely stolen. He sent his condolences, while thanking God for life and health spared. His wife echoed all that he said, modest eyes lowered, and voice like distant wood-doves.

Daniel, his eyes wandering more often to Mistress Cecily's milk-and-roses face than to the old man's flabby and self-satisfied countenance, issued a hearty invitation to Master Corde to bring his wife and take a meal with the goldsmith as soon as might be, and cheer him by his company. The wool-merchant thanked him, and wished it no less, but must put off the pleasure for a week or more, though he sent his sympathetic greetings and promised his prayers.

'You don't know,' confided Mistress Cecily, advancing a small hand to touch Margery's arm, 'how fortunate you are in having a husband whose trade is rooted fast at home. This man of mine is for ever running off with his mules and his wagon and his men, either west into Wales or east into England, over business with these fleeces and cloths of his, and I'm left lonely days at a time. Now tomorrow early he's off again, if you please, as far as Oxford, and I shall lack him for three or four days.'

Twice she had raised her creamy eyelids during this complaint, once ruefully at her husband, and once, with a miraculously fleeting effect which should have eluded Margery, but did not, at Daniel, eyes blindingly bright in the one flash that shot from them, but instantly veiled and serene.

'Now, now, sweet,' said the wool-merchant indulgently, 'you know how I shall hurry back to you.'

'And how long it will take,' she retorted, pouting. 'Three or four nights solitary. And you'd better bring me something nice to sweeten me for it when you return.'

As she knew he would. He never came back from any journey but he brought her a gift to keep her sweet. He had bought her, but there was enough of cold sense in him, below his doting, to know that he had to buy her over and over again if he wanted to keep her. The day he acknowledged it, and examined the implications, she might well go in fear for her slender throat, for he was an arrogant and possessive man.

'You say very truly, madam!' said Margery, stiff-lipped. 'I do know, indeed, how fortunate I am.'

Only too well! But every man's fortune, and every woman's too, can be changed given a little thought, perseverance and cunning.

Liliwin had spent his day in so unexpected and pleasant a fashion that for an hour and more at a time he had forgotten the threat hanging over him. As soon as High Mass was over, the precentor had hustled him briskly away to the corner of the cloister where he had already begun to pick apart, with a surgeon's delicacy and ruthlessness, the fractured shards of the rebec. Slow, devoted work that demanded every particle of the pupil's attention, if he was to assist at a resurrection. And excellent therapy against the very idea of death.

'We shall put together what is here broken,' said Brother Anselm, intent and happy, 'for an avowal on our part. No matter if the product, when achieved, turns out to be flawed, yet it shall speak again. If it speaks with a stammering voice, then we shall make another, as one generation follows its progenitor and takes up the former music. There is no absolute loss. Hand me here that sheet of vellum, son, and mark in what order I lay these fragments down.' Mere splinters, a few of them, but he set them carefully in the shape they should taken when restored. 'Do you believe you will play again upon this instrument?'

'Yes,' said Liliwin, fascinated, 'I do believe.'

'That's well, for faith is necessary. Without faith nothing is accomplished.' He mentioned this rare tool as he would have mentioned any other among those laid out to his hand. He set aside the fretted bridge. 'Good workmanship, and old. This rebec had more than one master before it came to you. It will not take kindly to silence.'

Neither did he. His brisk, gentle voice flowed like a placid stream while he worked, and its music lulled like the purling of water. And when he had picked apart and set out in order all the fragments of the rebec, and placed the vellum that held them in a safe corner, covered with a linen cloth, to await full light next day, he confronted Liliwin at once with his own small portative organ, and demanded he should try his hand with that. He had no need to demonstrate its use, Liliwin had seen one played, but never yet had the chance to test it out for himself.

He essayed the fingering nimbly enough at his first attempt, but concentrated so totally on the tune he was playing that he forgot to work the little bellows with his left hand, and the air ran out with a sigh into silence. He caught himself up with a startled laugh, and tried again, too vigorously, his playing hand slow on the keys. At the third try he had it. He played with it, entranced, picked out air after air, getting the feel to it, balancing hand against hand, growing ambitious, attempting embellishments. Five fingers can do only so much.

Brother Anselm presented to him a curious, figured array of signs upon vellum, matched by written symbols which he knew to be words. He could not read them, since he could not read in any tongue. To him this meant nothing more than a pleasing pattern, such as a woman might draw for her embroidery.

'You never learned this mystery? Yet I think you would pick it up readily. This is music, set down so that the eye, no less than the ear, may master it. See here, this line of neums here! Give me the organ.'

He took it and played a long line of melody. 'That – what you have heard – that is written down here. Listen again!' And again he plucked it jubilantly forth. 'There, now sing me that!'

Liliwin flung up his head and paid him back the phrase.

'Now, follow me still ... answer as I go.'

It was an intoxication, line after line of music to copy and toss back. Within minutes Liliwin had begun to embellish, to vary, to return a higher echo that chorded with the original.

'I could make of you a singer,' said Brother Anselm, sitting back in high content.'

'I *am* a singer,' said Liliwin. He had never before understood fully how proud he was of being able to say so.

'I do believe it. Your music and mine go different ways, but both of them are made up of these same small signs here, and the sounds they stand for. If you stay a little, I shall teach you how to read them,' promised Anselm, pleased with his pupil. 'Now, take this, practise some song of your own with it, and then sing it to me.'

Liliwin reviewed his songs, and was somewhat abashed to discover how many of them must be suppressed here as lewd and offensive. But not all were so. He had a favourite, concerned with the first revelation of young love, and recalling

58

it now, he recalled Rannilt, as poor as himself, as unconsidered, in her smoky kitchen and coarse gown, with her cloud of black hair and pale, oval face lit by radiant eyes. He fingered out the tune, feeling his way, his left hand now deft and certain on the bellows. He played and sang it, and grew so intent upon the singing that he scarcely noticed how busily Brother Anselm was penning signs upon his parchment.

'Will you believe,' said Anselm, delightedly proffering the leaf, 'that what you have just sung to me is written down here? Ah, not the words, but the air. This I will explain to you hereafter, you shall learn both how to inscribe and how to decypher. That's a very pleasant tune you have there. It could be used for the ground of a Mass. Well, now, that's enough for now, I must go and prepare for Vespers. Let be until tomorrow.'

Liliwin set the organetto tenderly back on its shelf, and went out, dazed, into the early evening. A limpid, pale-blue day was drifting away into a deeper blue twilight. He felt drained and gentle and fulfilled, like the day itself, silently and hopefully alive. He thought of his battered wooden juggling rings and balls, tucked away under his folded brychans in the church porch. They represented another of his skills which, if not practised, would rust and be damaged. He was so far buoyed up by his day that he went to fetch them, and carried them away hopefully into the garden, which opened out level below level to the pease-fields that ran down to the Meole brook. There was no one there at this hour, work was over for the day. He untied the cloth, took out the six wooden balls and the rings after them, and began to spin them from hand to hand, testing his wrists and the quickness of his eye.

He was still stiff from bruises and fumbled at first, but after a while the old ease began to return to him, and his pleasure in accomplishment. This might be a very humble skill, but it was still an achievement, and his, and he cherished it. Encouraged, he put the balls and rings away, and began to try out the suppleness of his thin, wiry body, twisting himself into grotesque knots. That cost him some pain from muscles trampled and beaten, but he persisted, determined not to give up. Finally he turned cartwheels all along the headland across the top of the pease-fields, coiled himself into a ring and rolled down the slope to the banks of the brook, and made his way up again, the slope being gentle enough, in a series of somersaults.

Arrived again at the level where the vegetable gardens and the enclosed herbarium began, he uncurled himself, flushed and pleased, to find himself gazing up at a couple of yards distance into the scandalised countenance of a sour-faced brother almost as meagre as himself. He stared, abashed, into eyes rounded and ferocious with outrage.

'Is this how you reverence this holy enclave?' demanded Brother Jerome, genuinely incensed. 'Is such foolery and lightmindedness fit for our abbey? And have you, fellow, so little gratitude for the shelter afforded you here? You do not deserve sanctuary, if you value it so lightly. How dared you so affront God's enclosure?'

Liliwin shrank and stammered, out of breath and abased to the ground. 'I meant no offence. I am grateful, I do hold the abbey in reverence. I only wanted to see if I could still master my craft. It is my living, I must practise it! Pardon if I've done wrong!' He was easily intimidated, here where he was in debt, and in doubt how to comport himself in a strange world. All his brief gaiety, all the pleasure of the music, ebbed out of him. He got to his feet almost clumsily, who had been so lissome only moments ago, and stood trembling, shoulders bowed and eyes lowered.

Brother Jerome, who seldom had business in the gardens, being the prior's clerk and having no taste for manual labour, had heard from the great court the small sound, strange in these precincts, of wooden balls clicking together in mid-air, and had come to investigate in relative innocence. But once in view of the performance, and himself screened by bushes fringing Brother Cadfael's herb-garden, he had not called a halt at once and warned the offender of his offence, but remained in hiding, storing up a cumulative fund of indignation until the culprit uncoiled at his feet. It may be that a degree of guilt on his own part rendered more extreme the reproaches he loosed upon the tumbler.

'Your *living*,' he said mercilessly, 'ought to engage you rather in prayers and self-searchings than in these follies. A man who has such charges hanging over him as you have must concern himself first with his soul's welfare, for whether he has a living to make hereafter or none, he has a soul to save when his debt in this world is paid. Think on that, and go put your trumpery away, as long as you are sheltered here. It is not fitting! It is blasphemy! Have you not enough already unpaid on your account?'

Liliwin felt the terror of the outer world close in on him: it could not be long evaded. As some within here wore hovering haloes, so he wore a noose, invisible but ever-present.

'I meant no harm,' he whispered hopelessly and turned, half-blind with misery, to grope for his poor bundle of toys and blunder hastily away.

'Tumbling and juggling, there in our gardens,' Jerome reported, still burning with offence, 'like a vagabond player at a fair. How can it be excused? Sanctuary is lawful for those who come in proper deference, but this ... I reproved him, of course. I told him he should be thinking rather of his eternal part, having so mortal a charge against him. "My living," he says! And he with a life owing!'

Prior Robert looked down his patrician nose, and maintained the fastidious and grieved calm of his noble countenance. 'Father Abbot is right to observe the sanctity of sanctuary, it may not be discarded. We are not to blame, and need not be concerned for the guilt or innocence of those who lay claim to it. But we are, indeed, concerned for the good order and good name of our house, and I grant you this present guest is little honour to us. I should be happier if he took himself off and submitted himself to the law, that is true. But unless he does so, we must bear with him. To reprove where he offends is not only our due, but our duty. To use any effort to influence or eject him is far beyond either. Unless he leaves of his own will,' said Prior Robert, 'both you and I, Brother Jerome, must succour, shelter and pray for him.'

How sincerely, how resolutely. But how reluctantly!

Chapter Five

Monday, from dawn to Compline

 UNDAY PASSED, clear and fine, and Monday came up no less sunnily, a splendid washing day, with a warm air and a light breeze, and bushes and turf dry and springy. The Aurifaber household was always up and active early on washing days, which were saved up two or three weeks at a time, to make but one upheaval of the heating of so much water, and such labour of scrubbing and knuckling with ash and lye. Rannilt was up first, to kindle the fire under the brick and clay boiler and hump the water from the well. She was stronger than she looked and used to the weight. What burdened her far more, and to that she was not used, was the terror she felt for Liliwin.

It was with her every moment. If she slept, she dreamed of him, and awoke sweating with fear that he might be hunted out already and taken and she none the wiser. And while she was awake and working, his image was ever in her mind, and a great stone of anxiety hot and heavy in her breast. Fear for yourself crushes and compresses you from without, but fear for another is a monster, a ravenous rat gnawing within, eating out your heart.

What they said of him was false, could not under any circumstances be true. And it was his life at stake! She could not help hearing all that was said of him among them, how they all united to accuse him, and promised themselves he should hang for what he had done. What she was certain in her heart and soul he had *not* done! It was not in him to strike down any man, or rob any man's coffers.

The locksmith, up early for him, heard her drawing up the bucket from the well, and came out from his back door to stroll down into the garden in the sunlight and pass the time of day. Rannilt did not think he would have troubled if he had known it was only the maidservant. He made a point of being attentive to his landlord's family, and never missed the common neighbourly courtesies, but his notice seldom extended to Rannilt. Nor did he linger on this fine morning, but took a short turn about the yard and returned to his own door. There he looked back, eyeing for a moment the obvious preparations at the goldsmith's house, the great mound of washing in hand, and the normal bustle just beginning.

Susanna came down with her arms full of linen, and went to work with her usual brisk, silent competence. Daniel ate his breakfast and went to his workshop, leaving Margery solitary and irresolute in the hall. Too much had happened on her wedding night, she had had no time to grow used to house and household, or consider her own place in it. Wherever she turned to make herself useful, Susanna had been before her. Walter lay late, nursing his sore head, and Dame Juliana kept her own chamber, but Margery was too late to carry food and drink to either, it was already done. There was no need yet to think of cooking, and in any case all the household keys were on Susanna's girdle. Margery turned her attention to the one place where she felt herself and her own wishes to be dominant, and set to work to rearrange Daniel's bachelor chamber to her own taste, and clear out the chest and press which must now make room for her own clothes and stores of linen. In the process she discovered much evidence of Dame Juliana's noted parsimony. There were garments which must have belonged to Daniel as a growing boy, and could certainly never again be worn by him. Neatly mended again and again, they had all been made to last as long as possible, and even when finally outgrown, had still been folded away and kept. Well, she was now Daniel's wife, she would have this chamber as she wanted it, and be rid of these useless and miserly reminders of the past. Today the household might still be running on its customary wheels, as though she had no part to play, but it would not always be so. She was in no haste, she had a great deal of thinking to do before she took action.

On her knees in the yard, Rannilt scrubbed and pummelled, her hands sore from the lye. By mid-morning the last of the washing was wrung and folded and piled into a great wicker basket. Susanna hoisted it on her hip and bore it away down the slope of the garden, and through the deep arch in the town wall, to spread it out on the bushes and the smooth plain of grass that faced almost due south to the sun. Rannilt cleared away the tub and mopped the floor, and went in to tend the fire and set the salt beef simmering for dinner.

Here quiet and alone, she was suddenly so full of her pain on Liliwin's account that her eyes spilled abrupt tears into the pot, and once the flow began she could not dam it. She groped blindly about the kitchen, working by touch, and shedding helpless tears for the first man who had caught her fancy, and the first who had ever fancied her.

Absorbed into her misery, she did not hear Susanna come quietly into the doorway behind her, and halt there at gaze, watching the fumbling hands feeling their way, and the half-blind eyes still streaming.

'In God's name, girl, what is it with you now?'

Rannilt started and turned guiltily, stammering that it was nothing, that she was sorry, that she was getting on with her work, but Susanna cut her off sharply:

'It is not nothing! I'm sick of seeing you thus moping and useless. You've been limp as a sick kitten this two days past, and I know why. You have that miserable little thief on your mind – I know! I know he wound about you with his soft voice and his creeping ways, I've watched you. Must you be fool enough to fret over a guilty wretch the like of that?'

She was not angry; she was never angry. She sounded impatient, even exasperated, but still contemptuously kind, and her voice was level and controlled as ever. Rannilt swallowed the choking residue of tears, shook the mist from her eyes, and began to be very busy with her pots and pans, looking hurriedly about her for a distraction which would turn attention from herself at any cost. 'It came over me just for a minute: I'm past it now. Why, you've got your feet and the hem of your gown wet,' she exclaimed, seizing gratefully on the first thing that offered. 'You should change your shoes.'

Susanna shrugged the diversion scornfully aside. 'Never mind my wet feet. The river's up a little, I was not noticing until I went too near the edge, leaning to hang a shirt on the bushes. What of your wet eyes? That's more to the point. Oh, fool girl, you're wasting your fancy! This is a common rogue of the roads, with many a smaller deed of the kind behind him, and he'll get nothing but his due in the noose that's waiting for him. Get sense, and put him out of your mind.'

'He is not a rogue,' said Rannilt, despairingly brave. 'He did not do it, I know it, I know *him*, he could not. It isn't in him to do violence. And I do fret for him, I can't help it.'

'So I see,' said Susanna resignedly. 'So I've seen ever since they ran him to ground. I tire of him and of you. I want you in your wits again. God's truth, must I carry this household on my back without even your small help?' She gnawed a thoughtful lip, and demanded abruptly, 'Will it cure you if I let you go see for yourself that the tumbler is alive and whole, and out of our reach for a while, more's the pity. Yes, and likely to worm his way out of even this tangle in the end!'

She had spoken magical words. Rannilt was staring up at her dry-eyed, bright as a candle-flame. 'See? See him? You mean I could go there?'

'You have legs,' said Susanna tartly. 'It's no distance. They don't close their gates against anyone. You may even come back in your right senses, when you see how little store he sets by *you*, while you're breaking your fool heart for him. You may get to know him for what he is, and the better for you. Yes, go. Go, and be done wth it! This once I'll manage without you. Let Daniel's wife start making herself useful. Good practice for her.'

'You mean it? whispered Rannilt, stricken by such generosity. 'I may go? But who will see to the broth here, and the meat?'

'I will. I have often enough, God knows! I tell you, go, go quickly, before I change my mind, stay away all day long, if that will send you back cured. I can very well do without you this once. But wash your face, girl, and comb your hair, and do yourself and us credit. You can take some of those oat-cakes in a basket, if you wish, and whatever scraps were left from yesterday. If he felled my father,' said Susanna roughly, turning away to pick up the ladle and stir the pot simmering on the hob, 'there's worse waiting for him in the end, no need to grudge him a mouthful while he is man alive.' She looked back over a straight shoulder at Rannilt, who still hovered in a daze. 'Go and visit your minstrel, I mean it, you have leave. I doubt if he even remembers your face! Go and learn sense.'

Lost in wonder, and only half believing in such mercies, Rannilt washed her face and tidied her tangle of dark hair with trembling hands, seized a basket and filled it with whatever morsels were brusquely shoved her way, and went out through the hall like a child walking in its sleep. It was wholly by chance that Margery was coming down the stairs, with a pile of discarded garments on her arm. She marked the small, furtive figure flitting past below, and in surprised goodwill, since this waif was alien and lonely here as she was, asked, 'Where are you sent off to in such a hurry, child?'

Rannilt halted submissively, and looked up into Margery's rounded, fresh countenance. 'Mistress Susanna gave me leave. I'm going to the abbey, to take this provision to Liliwin.' The name, so profoundly significant to her, meant nothing to Margery. 'The minstrel. The one they say struck down Master Walter. But I'm sure he did not! She said I may go, see for myself how he's faring – because I was crying ...'

'I remember him,' said Margery. 'A little man, very young. They're sure he's the guilty one, and you are sure he is not?' Her blue eyes were demure. She hunted through the pile of garments on her arm, and very faintly and fleetingly she smiled. 'He was not too well clothed, I recall. There is a cotte here that was my husband's some years ago, and a capuchon. The little man could wear them, I think. Take them with you. It would be a pity to waste them. And charity is approved of in Heaven, even to sinners.'

She sorted them out gravely, a good dark-blue coat outgrown while it was still barely patched, and a much-mended caped hood in russet brown. 'Take them! They're of no use here.' None, except for the satisfaction it gave her to despatch them to the insignificant soul condemned by every member of her new family. It was her gesture of independence.

Rannilt, every moment more dazed, took the offerings and tucked them into her basket, made a mute reverence, and fled before this unprecedented and hardly credible vein of good will should run out, and food, clothing, holiday and all fall to ruin round her.

Susanna cooked, served, scoured and went about her circumscribed realm with a somewhat grim smile on her lips. The provisioning of the house under her governance was

discreetly more generous than ever it had been under Dame
Juliana, and on this day there was enough and to spare, even
after she had carried his usual portion to Iestyn in the workshop,
and sat with him for company while he ate, to bring back the dish
to the kitchen afterwards. What remained was not worth
keeping to use up another day, but there was enough for one.
She shredded the remains of the boiled salt beef into it, and took
it across to the locksmith's shop, as she had sometimes done
before when there was plenty.

John Boneth was at work at his bench, and looked up as she
entered, bowl in hand. She looked about her, and saw everything in placid order, but no sigh of Baldwin Peche, or the boy
Griffin, probably out on some errand.

'We have a surfeit, and I know your master's no great cook. I
brought him his dinner, if he hasn't eaten already.'

John had come civilly to his feet, with a deferential smile for
her. They had known each other five years, but always at this
same discreet distance. The landlord's daughter, the rich
master-craftsman's girl, was no meat for a mere journeyman.

'That's kind, mistress, but the master's not here. I've not seen
him since the middle of the morning, he's left me two or three
keys to cut. I fancy he's off for the day. He said something about
the fish rising.'

There was nothing strange in that. Baldwin Peche relied on
his man to take charge of the business every bit as competently
as he could have done himself, and was prone to taking holidays
whenever it suited his pleasure. He might be merely making the
round of the ale-houses to barter his own news for whatever
fresh scandal was being whispered, or he might be at the butts by
the riverside, betting on a good marksman, or out in his boat,
which he kept in a yard near the watergate, only a few minutes
down-river. The young salmon must be coming up the Severn by
this time. A fisherman might well be tempted out to try his luck.

'And you don't know if he'll be back?' Susanna read his face,
shrugged and smiled. 'I know! Well, if he's not here to eat it … I
daresay you have still room to put this away, John?' He brought
with him, usually, a hunk of bread and a strip of salt bacon or a
piece of cheese, meat was festival fare in his mother's house.
Susanna set down her bowl before him on the bench, and sat
down on the customer's stool opposite, spreading her elbows
comfortably along the boards. 'It's his loss. In an ale-house he'll
pay more for poorer fare. I'll sit with you, John, and take back
the bowl.'

67

*

Rannilt came down the Wyle to the open gate of the town, and passed through its shadowed arch to the glitter of sunlight on the bridge. She had fled in haste from the house, for fear of being called back, but she had lingered on the way through the town for fear of what lay before her. For the course was fearful, to one unschooled, half-wild, rejected by Wales and never welcomed in England but as a pair of labouring hands. She knew nothing of monks or monasteries, and none too much even of Christianity. But there inside the abbey was Liliwin, and thither she would go. The gates, Susanna had said, were never closed against any.

On the far side of the bridge she passed close by the copse where Liliwin had curled up to sleep, and been hunted out at midnight. On the other side of the Foregate lay the mill pool, and the houses in the abbey's grant, and beyond, the wall of the enclave began, and the roofs of infirmary and school and guest-hall within, and the tall bulk of the gatehouse. The great west door of the church, outside the gates, confronted her in majesty. But once timidly entering the great court, she found reassurance. Even at this hour, perhaps the quietest of the day, there was a considerable bustle of coming and going within there, guests arriving and departing, servants ambling about on casual errands, petitioners begging, packmen taking a mid-day rest, a whole small world of people, some of them as humble as herself. She could walk in there among them, and never be noticed. But still she had to find Liliwin, and she cast about her for the most sympathetic source of information.

She was not blessed in her choice. A small man, in the habit of the house, scurrying across the court; she chose him because he was as small and slight as Liliwin, and his shoulders had a discouraged droop which reminded her of Liliwin, and because someone who looked so modest and disregarded must surely feel for others as insignificant as himself. Brother Jerome would have been deeply offended if he had known. As it was, he was not displeased at the low reverence this suppliant girl made to him, and the shy whisper in which she addressed him.

'Please, sir, I am sent by my lady with alms for the young man who is here in sanctuary. If you would kindly teach me where I may find him.'

She had not spoken his name because it was a private thing, to be kept jealously apart. Jerome, however he might regret

68

that any lady should be so misguided as to send alms to the offender, was somewhat disarmed by the approach. A maid on an errand was not to be blamed for her mistress's errors.

'You will find him there, in the cloister, with Brother Anselm.' He indicated the direction grudgingly, disapproving of Brother Anselm's complacent usage with an accused man, but not censuring Rannilt, until he noted the brightening of her face and the lightness of her foot as she sprang to follow where he pointed. Not merely an errand-girl, far too blithe! 'Take heed, child, what message you have to give him must be done decorously. He is on probation of a most grave charge. You may have half an hour with him, you may and you should exhort him to consider on his soul. Do your errand and go!'

She looked back at him with great eyes, and was very still for one instant in her flight. She faltered some words of submission, while her eyes flamed unreadably, with a most disquieting brilliance. She made a further deep reverence, to the very ground, but sprang from it like an angel soaring, and flew to the cloister whither he had pointed her.

It seemed vast to her, four-sided in stony corridors about an open garden, where spring flowers burst out in gold and white and purple on a grassy ground. She flitted the length of one walk between terror and delight, turned along the second in awe of the alcove cells furnished with slanted tables and benches, empty but for one absorbed scholar copying wonders, who never lifted his head as she passed by. At the end of this walk, echoing from such another cell, she heard music. She had never before heard an organ played, it was a magical sound to her, until she heard a sweet, lofty voice soar happily with it, and knew it for Liliwin's.

He was bending over the instrument, and did not hear her come. Neither did Brother Anselm, equally absorbed in fitting together the fragments of the rebec's back. She stood timidly in the opening of the carrel, and only when the song ended did she venture speech. At this vital moment she did not know what her welcome would be. What proof had she that he had thought of her, since that hour they had spent together, as she had thought ceaselessly of him? It might well be that she was fooling herself, as Susanna had said.

'If you please ...' began Rannilt humbly and hesitantly.

Then they both looked up. The old man viewed her with mildly curious eyes, unastonished and benign. The young one stared, gaped and blazed, in incredulous joy, set aside his

69

strange instrument of music blindly on the bench beside him, and came to his feet slowly, warily, all his movements soft almost to stealth, as though any sudden start might cause her to quiver and dissolve into light, vanishing like morning mist.

'Rannilt ... It *is* you?'

If this was indeed foolery, then she was not the only fool. She looked rather at Brother Anselm, whose devoted fingers were held poised, not to divert by the least degree the touch he had suspended on his delicate operations.

'If you please, I should like to speak with Liliwin. I have brought him some gifts.'

'By all means,' said Brother Anselm amiably. 'You hear, boy? You have a visitor. There, go along and be glad of her. I shall not need you now for some hours. I'll hear your lesson later.'

They moved towards each other in a dream, wordless, took hands and stole away.

'I swear to you, Rannilt, I never struck him, I never stole from him, I never did him wrong.' He had said it at least a dozen times, here in the shadowy porch where his brychans were folded up, and his thin pallet spread, and the poor tools of his craft hidden away in a corner of the stone bench as though some shame attached to them. And there had never been any need to say it even once, as she a dozen times had answered him.

'I know, I know! I never believed for a moment. How could you doubt it? I know you are good. They will find out, they will have to own it.'

They trembled together and kept fast hold of hands in a desperate clasp, and the touch set their unpractised bodies quivering in an excitement neither of them understood.

'Oh, Rannilt, if you knew! That was the worst of all, that you might shrink from me and believe me so vile ... *They* believe it, all of them. Only you ...'

'No,' she said stoutly, 'I'm not so sure. The brother who comes to physic Dame Juliana, the one who brought back your things ... And that kind brother who is teaching you ... Oh, no, you are not abandoned. You must not think it!'

'No!' he owned thankfully. 'Now I do believe, I do trust, if *you* are with me ...' He was lost in wonder that anyone in that hostile household should send her to him. 'She was good, your lady! I'm so beholden to her ...'

70

Not for the gifts of food, orts to her, delicacies to him. No, but for this nearness that clouded his senses in a fevered warmth and delight and disquiet he had never before experienced, and which could only be love, the love he had sung by rote for years, while his body and mind were quite without understanding.

Brother Jerome, true to what he felt to be his duty, had marked the passing of time, and loomed behind them, approaching inexorably along the walk from the great court. His sandals silent on the flagstones, he observed as he came the shoulders pressed close, the two heads, the flaxen and the black, inclined together with temples almost touching. certainly it was time to part them, this was no place for such embraces.

'It will all be well in the end,' said Rannilt, whispering. 'You'll see! Mistress Susanna – she says as they say, and yet she let me come. I think she doesn't really believe ... She said I might stay away all day long ...'

'Oh, Rannilt ... Oh, Rannilt, I do love you ...'

'Maiden,' said Brother Jerome, harshly censorious behind them, 'you have had time enough to discharge your mistress's errand. There can be no further stay. You must take your basket and depart.'

A shadow no bigger than Liliwin's, there behind them black against the slanting sun of mid-afternoon, and yet he cast such a darkness over them as they could hardly bear. They had only just linked hands, barely realised the possibilities that lie within such slender bodies, and they must be torn apart. The monk had authority, he spoke for the abbey, and there was no denying him. Liliwin had been granted shelter, how could he then resist the restrictions laid upon him?

They rose, tremulous. Her hand in his clung convulsively, and her touch ran through him like a stiffening fire, drawn by a great, upward wind that was his own desperation and anger.

'She is going,' said Liliwin. 'Only give us, for pity's sake, some moments in the church together for prayer.'

Brother Jerome found that becoming, even disarming, and stood back from them as Liliwin drew her with him, the basket in his free hand, in through the porch to the dark interior of the church. Silence and dimness closed on them. Brother Jerome had respected their privacy and remained without, though he would not go far until he saw one of them emerge alone.

And it might be the last time he would ever see her! He

71

could not bear it that she should go so soon, perhaps to be lost for ever, when she had leave to be absent all day long. He closed his hand possessively on her arm, drawing her deep into the shadowy, stony recesses of the transept chapel beyond the parish altar. She should not go like this! They were not followed, there was no one else here within at this moment, and Liliwin was well acquainted now with every corner and cranny of this church, having prowled it restlessly and fearfully on his first night here alone, when his ears were still pricked for sounds of pursuit, and he was afraid to sleep on his pallet in the porch.

'Don't go, don't go!' His arms were clasped tightly about her as they pressed together into the darkest corner, and his lips were whispering agitatedly against her cheek. 'Stay with me! You can, you can, I'll show you a place … No one will know, no one will find us.'

The chapel was narrow, the altar wide, all but filling the space between its containing columns, and stood out somewhat from the niche that tapered behind it. There was a little cavern there, into which only creatures as small and thin as they could creep. Liliwin had marked it down as a place to which he might retreat if the hunters broke in, and he knew his own body could negotiate the passage, so for her it would be no barrier. And within there was darkness, privacy, invisibility.

'Here, slip in here! No one will see. When he's satisfied, when he goes away, I'll come to you. We can be together until Vespers.'

Rannilt went where he urged her; she would have done anything he asked, her hunger was as desperate as his. The empty basket was drawn through the narrow space after her. Her wild whisper breathed back from the darkness: 'You will come? Soon?'

'I'll come! Wait for me …'

Invisible and still, she made no murmur nor rustle. Liliwin turned, trembling, and went back past the parish altar, and out at the south porch into the east walk of the cloisters. Brother Jerome had had the grace to withdraw into the garth, to keep his jealous watch a little less blatantly, but his sharp eyes were still on the doorway, and the emergence of the solitary figure, head drooping and shoulders despondent, appeared to satisfy him. Liliwin did not have to feign dejection, he was already in tears of excitement, compounded of joy and grief together. He did not turn along the scriptorium to go back to Brother

72

Anselm, but went straight past the bench in the porch, where the gifts of food and clothing lay on his folded brychans, and out into the court and the garden beyond. But not far, only into cover among the first bushes, where he could look back and see Brother Jerome give over his vigil, and depart briskly in the direction of the grange court. The girl was gone, from the west door of the church; the disturbing presence was removed, monastic order restored, and Brother Jerome's authority had been properly respected.

Liliwin flew back to his pallet in the porch, rolled up food and clothing in his blankets, and looked round carefully to make sure there was now no one paying any attention to him, either within or without the church. When he was certain, he slipped in with his bundle under his arm, darted into the chapel, and slid as nimbly as an eel between altar and pillar into the dark haven behind. Rannilt's hands reached out for him, her cheek was pressed against his, they shook together, almost invisible even to each other, and by that very mystery suddenly loosed from all the restraints of the outer world, able to speak without speech, delivered from shyness and shame, avowed lovers. This was something quite different even from sitting together in the porch, before Jerome's serpent hissed into their Eden. There they had never got beyond clasping hands, and even those clasped hands hidden between them, as if a matter for modesty and shame. Here there was neither, only a vindicated candour that expanded in darkness, giving and receiving passionate, inexpert caresses.

There was room there to make a nest, with the blankets and the basket and Daniel's outgrown clothes, and if the stone floor was thick with a generation or more of soft, fine dust, that only helped to cushion the couch they laid down for themselves. They sat huddled together with their backs against the stone wall, sharing their warmth, and the morsels Susanna had discarded, and holding fast to each other for reassurance, until they drifted into a dreamlike illusion of safety where reassurance was unnecessary.

They talked, but in a few whispered words.

'Are you cold?'

'No.'

'Yes, you're trembling.' He shifted and drew her into his arm, close against his breast, and with his free hand plucked up a corner of the blanket over her shoulder, binding her to him. She stretched up her arm within the rough wool, slipped her hand about his neck, and embraced him with lips and cheek and nestling forehead, drawing him down with her until they lay breast to breast, heaving as one to great, deep-drawn sighs.

There was some manner of lightning-stroke, as it seemed, that convulsed them both, and fused them into one without any coherent action on their part. They were equally innocent, equally knowing. Knowing by rote is one thing. What they experienced bore no resemblance to what they had thought they knew. Afterwards, shifting a little only to entwine more closely and warmly, they fell asleep in each other's arms, to quicken an hour or more later to the same compulsion, and love again without ever fully awaking. Then they slept again, so deeply, in such an exhaustion of wonder and fulfilment, that even the chanting of Vespers in the choir did not disturb them.

'Shall I fetch in the linen for you?' Margery offered in the afternoon, making a conciliatory foray into Susanna's domain, and finding that composed housekeeper busy with preparations for the evening's supper.

'Thank you,' said Susanna, hardly looking up from her work, 'but I'll do that myself.' Not one step is she going to advance towards me, thought Margery, damped. *Her* linen, *her* stores, *her* kitchen! And at that Susanna did look up, even smiled; her usual, wry smile, but not unfriendly. 'If you wish me well, do take charge of my grandmother. You are new to her, she'll take more kindly to you, and be more biddable. I have had this some years, she and I wear out each other. We are too like. You come fresh. It would be a kindness.'

Margery was silenced and disarmed. 'I will,' she said heartily, and went away to do her best with the old woman, who, true enough, undoubtedly curbed her malevolence with the newcomer.

Only later in the evening, viewing Daniel across the trestle table, mute, inattentive and smugly glowing with some private satisfaction, did she return to brooding on her lack of status here, and reflecting at whose girdle the keys were hung, and whose voice bound or loosed the maidservant who was still absent.

'I marvel,' said Brother Anselm, coming out from the refectory after supper, 'where my pupil can have got to. He's been so eager, since I showed him the written notes. An angel's ear, true as a bird, and a voice the same. And he has not been to the kitchen for his supper.'

'Nor come to have his arm dressed,' agreed Brother Cadfael, who had spent the whole afternoon busily planting, brewing and compounding in his herbarium. 'Though Oswin did look at it earlier, and found it healing very well.'

'There was a maidservant here bringing him a basket of dainties from her mistress's table,' said Jerome, one ear pricked in their direction. 'No doubt he felt no appetite for our simple fare. I had occasion to admonish them. He may have taken some grief, and be moping solitary.'

It had not occurred to him, until then, that he had not seen the unwanted guest since the boy had come out of the church alone; now it seemed, moreover, that Brother Anselm, who had had more reason to expect to spend time with his pupil, had not seen hide or hair of him, either. The abbey enclave was extensive, but not so great that a man virtually a prisoner should disappear in it. If, that is, he was still within it?

Jerome said no word more to his fellows, but spent the final half-hour before Compline making a rapid search of every part of the enclave, and ended at the south porch. The pallet on the stone bench was bare and unpressed, the brychans unaccountably missing. He did not notice the small cloth bundle tucked under a corner of the straw. As far as he could see, there was no sign left of Liliwin's presence.

He reported as much to Prior Robert, returning breathless just before Compline was due to begin. Robert did not exactly smile, his ascetic face remained benign and bland as ever, but he did somehow radiate an air of relief and cautious pleasure.

'Well, well!' said Robert 'If the misguided youth has been so foolish as to quit his place of safety on account of a woman, it is his own choice. A sad business, but no blame lights upon any within here. No man can be wise for another.' And he led the procession into the choir with his usual impressive gait and saintly visage, and breathed the more easily now that the alien burr had been dislodged from his skin. He did not warn Jerome to say no word yet to anyone else within here; there was no need, they understood each other very well.

75

Chapter Six

Monday night to Tuesday afternoon

ILIWIN AWOKE with a jolting shock to darkness, the unmistakable sound of Brother Anselm's voice leading the chanting in the choir, a wild sense of fear, and the total remembrance of the wonderful and terrible thing he and Rannilt had done together, that revelation of bliss that was at the same time so appalling and unforgivable a blasphemy. Here, behind the altar, in the presence of relics so holy, the sin of the flesh, natural and human as it might be out in some meadow or coppice, became mortal and damning. But the immediate terror was worse than the distant smell of hellfire. He remembered where he was, and everything that had passed, and his senses, sharpened by terror and dismay, recognised the office. Not Vespers! Compline! They had slept for hours. Even the evening was spent, the night closing in.

He groped with frantic gentleness along the brychan, to lay a hand over Rannilt's lips, and kissed her cheek to awaken her. She started instantly and fully out of the depths of sleep. He felt her lips move, smiling, against his palm. She remembered, but not as he did; she felt no guilt and she was not afraid. Not yet! That was still to come.

With his lips close to her ear, in the tangle of her black hair, he breathed, 'We've slept too long … it's night, they're singing Compline.'

She sat up abruptly, braced and listening with him. She whispered, 'Oh mercy! What have we done? I must go ... I shall be so late ...'

'No, not alone ... you can't. All that way in the dark!'

'I'm not afraid.'

'But I won't let you! There are thieves and villains in the night. You shan't go alone, I'm coming with you.'

She put him off from her with a hand flattened against his breast, her fluttering whisper agitated but still soft on his cheek: 'You can't! You can't, you mustn't leave here, they're watching outside, they'd take you.'

'Wait ... wait here a moment, let me look.' The faint light from the choir, shut off by stone walls from their cranny, but feebly reflected into the chapel, had begun to show in a pallid outline the shape of the altar behind which they crouched. Liliwin slipped round it, and padded across to peer round a sheltering column into the nave. There were a number of elderly women of the Foregate who attended even non-parochial services regularly, having their souls in mind, their homes only a few paces distant, and nothing more interesting to do with their evenings in these declining years. Five of them were present on this fine, mild night, kneeling in the dimness just within Liliwin's view, and one of them must have brought a young grandson with her, while another, fragile enough to need or demand a prop, had a young man in his twenties attendant on her. Enough of them to provide a measure of cover, if God, or fate, or whatever held the dice, added the requisite measure of luck.

Liliwin fled back into the dark chapel, and reached a hand to draw Rannilt out from their secret nest.

'Quick, leave the brychans,' he whispered feverishly, 'but give me the clothes – the cotte and capuchon. No one has ever seen me but in these rags ...'

Daniel's old coat was ample for him, and worn over his own clothes gave him added bulk, as well as respectability. The nave was lit by only two flares close to the west door, and the rust-brown capuchon, with its deep shoulder-cape, widened his build and hid his face to some extent even before he could hoist it over his head on quitting the church.

Rannilt clung to his arm, trembling and pleading. 'No, don't ... stay here, I'm afraid for you ...'

'Don't be afraid! We shall go out with all those people, no one will notice us.' And whether in terror or no, they would be together still a while longer, arms linked, hands clasped.

'But how will you get in again?' she breathed, lips against his cheek.

'I will. I'll follow someone else through the gate.' The office was ending, in a moment the brothers would be moving in procession down the opposite aisle to the night stairs. 'Come, now, close to the people there ...'

The ancient, holy women of the Foregate waited on their knees, faces turned towards the file of monks as they passed, shadowy, towards their beds. Then they rose and began their leisurely shuffle towards the west door, and after them, emerging unquestioned from shadow, went Liliwin and Rannilt, close and quiet, as though they belonged.

And it was unbelievably easy. The sheriff's officers had a guard of two men constantly outside the gatehouse, where they could cover both the gate itself and the west door of the church, and they had torches burning, but rather for their own pleasure and convenience than as a means of noting Liliwin's movements, since they had to while away the hours somehow on their watch, and you cannot play either dice or cards in the dark. By this time they did not believe that the refugee would make any attempt to leave his shelter, but they knew their duty and kept their watch faithfully enough. They stood to watch in silence as the worshippers left the church, but they had no orders to scrutinise those who went in, and so had not either counted them or observed them closely, and noted no discrepancy in the numbers leaving. Nor was there any sign here of the jongleur's faded and threadbare motley, but neat, plain burgess clothing. Having no knowledge that a young girl had made her way in, intent on seeing the accused man, they thought nothing of watching her make her way out in his company. Two insignificant young people passed and dwindled into the night on the heels of the old women. What was there in that?

They were out, they were past, the lights of the torches dimmed behind them, the cool darkness closed round them, and the hearts that had fluttered up wildly into their throats, like terrified birds shut into a narrow room, settled back gradually into their breasts, still beating heavily. By luck two of the old women, and the young man who supported the elder, inhabited two of the small houses by the mill, as pensioners of the abbey, and so had to turn towards the town, and Liliwin and Rannilt did not have to go that way alone from the gate, or they might have been more conspicuous. When the women had turned aside to their own doors, and they two alone were stealing silently betweeen mill-pool on one hand and the copses above the Gaye on the other, and the stone rise of the bridge showed very faintly before them, Rannilt halted abruptly, drawing him round face to face with her in the edge of the trees.

'Don't come into the town! Don't! Turn here, to the left, this side the river, there's a track goes south, they won't be watching there. Don't come through the gate! And don't go back! You're out now, and none of them know. They won't, not until tomorrow. Go, go, while you can! You're free, you can leave this place ...' Her whisper was urgent, resolute with hope for him, desolate with dismay on her own account. Liliwin heard the one as clearly as the other, and for a moment he, too, was torn.

He drew her deeper into the trees, and shut his arms about her fiercely. 'No! I'm coming with you, it isn't safe for you alone. You don't know what things can happen by night in a dark alley. I'll see you to your own yard. I must, I will!'

'But don't you see ...' She beat a small fist against his shoulder in desperation. 'You could go now, escape, put this town behind you. A whole night to get well away. There'll be no second chance like this.'

'And put you behind me, too? And make myself seem what they say I am?' He put a shaking hand under her chin, and turned up to him none too gently the face he saw only as a pale oval in the darkness. 'Do you *want* me to go? Do you want never to see me again? If that's what you want, say it, and I'll go. But say truth! Don't lie to me!'

She heaved a huge sigh, and embraced him in passionate silence. In a moment she breathed, 'No! no ... I want you safe ... But *I want you!*'

She wept briefly, while he held her and made soft, inarticulate sounds of comfort and dismay; and then they went on, for that was settled, and would not lightly be raised again. Over the bridge, with lambent light flickering up from the Severn's dimpling surface on either side, and the torches burning down redly in the side-pillars of the town gate before them. The watchmen at the gate were easy, bestirring themselves only when brawlers or obstreperous drunks rolled in upon them. Two humble but respectable young people hurrying home got only a glance from them, and an amiable goodnight.

'You see,' said Liliwin, on their way up the dark slope and curve of the Wyle, 'it was not so hard.'

Very softly she said, 'No.'

'I shall go in again just as simply. Late travellers come, I shall tread in on their heels. If there are none, I can sleep rough over the night, and in these clothes I can slip in when the morning traffic begins.'

'You could still go from here,' she said, 'when you leave me.'

'But I will not leave you. When I go from here, you will go with me.'

He was flying his small pennon of defiance against the wind, and knew it, but he meant it with all his heart. It might all end ignominiously, he might still fall like the heron to the fowler, but he had had until now a name, however humble, never traduced with accusation of theft and violence, and it was worth a venture to keep that; and now he had a still dearer stake to win or lose. He would not go. He would abide to win or lose all.

At the High Cross they turned to the right, and were in narrower and darker places, and once, at least, something furtive and swift turned aside from their path, perhaps wary of two, where one might cry out loud enough to rouse others, even if the second could be laid out with the first blow. Shrewsbury was well served in its watchmen, but every solitary out at night is at the mercy of those without scruples, and the watch cannot be everywhere. Rannilt did not notice. Her fear for Liliwin was not of any immediate danger to him here.

'Will they be angry with you?' he wondered anxiously, as they drew nearer to Walter Aurifaber's shop-front, and the narrow passage through into the yard.

'She said I might stay all day, if it would cure me.' She smiled invisibly in the night, far from cured, but armed against any questioning. 'She was kind, I'm not afraid of her, she'll stand by me.'

In the deep darkness of a doorway opposite he drew her to him, and she turned and clung. It came upon them both alike that this might be the last time, but they clung, and kissed and would not believe it.

'Now go, go quickly! I shall watch until you're within.' They stood where he could gaze deep into the passage, and mark the faint glow from an unshuttered window within. He put her away from him, turned her about, and gave her a push to start her on her way. 'Run!'

She was gone, across the street and into the passage, scurrying obediently, blotting out for a moment the inner glow. Then she was into the yard, and the small light picked out the shape of her for one instant as she flew past the hall door and was gone indeed.

Liliwin stood motionless in the dark doorway, staring after her for a long time. The night was very still and quiet about him. He did not want to move away. Even when the dull spark within the yard was quenched, he still stood there, straining blindly after the way she had gone.

But he was wrong, the spark had not been quenched, only blotted out from sight for the minute or so it took for a man's form to thread the passage silently and emerge into the street. A tall, well-built man, young by his step, in a hurry by the way he hurtled out of the passage, and about some private and nefarious business by the agility and stealth with which he slid in and out of the deepest shadows as he made off along the lane, with his capuchon drawn well forward and his head lowered.

There were but two young men who habited within that burgage at night, and a man who had played and sung and tumbled a long evening away in their company had no difficulty in distinguishing between them. In any case, the fine new coat marked him out, for all his furtive procedure. Only three days married, where was Daniel Aurifaber off in such a hurry, late at night?

Liliwin left his station at last, and went back along the narrow street towards the High Cross. He saw no more of that flitting figure. Somewhere in this maze of by-streets Daniel had vanished, about what secret business there was no knowing. Liliwin made his way down the Wyle to the gate, and was hardly shaken at being halted by a guard wider awake than his fellows.

'Well, well, lad, you're back soon. Wanting out again at this hour? You're back and forth like a dog at a fair.'

'I was seeing my girl safe home,' said Liliwin, truth coming both welcome and easy. 'I'm away back to the abbey now. I'm working there.' And so he was, and would work the harder the next day for having deserted Brother Anselm on this one.

'Oh, you're in their service, are you?' The guard was benevolent. 'Take no unwary vows, lad, or you'll lose that girl of yours. Off you go then, and goodnight to you.'

The cavern of the gateway, reflecting torchlight from its stony vault, fell behind him, the arch of the bridge, with liquid silver on either side, opened before him, and above there was a light veil of cloud pierced here and there by a stray star. Liliwin crossed, and slipped again into the bushes that fringed the roadway. The silence was daunting. When he drew nearer to the abbey gatehouse he was afraid to stir out of cover, and cross the empty street to brave the scrutiny beyond. Both the west door of the church and the open wicker of the gate seemed equally inaccessible.

He stood deep in cover, watching the Foregate, and it came back to him suddenly and temptingly that he was, indeed, out of sanctuary undetected, and the whole of the night before him to put as many miles as possible between himself and Shrewsbury, and hide himself as deeply as possible among men to whom he was unknown. He was small and weak and fearful, and very greedy for life, and the ache to escape this overhanging peril was acute. But all the time he knew he would not go. Therefore he must get back to the one place where for thirty-seven more days he was safe, here within reach of the house where Rannilt slaved and waited and prayed for him.

He had luck in the end, and not even long to wait. One of the lay servants of the abbey had had his new son christened that day, and opened his house to the assembly of his relatives and friends to celebrate the occasion. The abbey stewards, shepherds and herdsmen who had been his guests came back along the Foregate in a flock, well-fed and merry, to return to their quarters in the grange court. Liliwin saw them come, spanning the street with their loose-knit chain, and when they drew near enough, and closed at leisure on the gatehouse, those bound within taking spacious leave of those living without, so that he was sure of the destination of perhaps a third of their number, he slipped out of the bushes and mingled with the fringes of the group. One more in the dimness made no matter. He went in unquestioned by any, and in the unhurried dispersal within he slipped away silently into the cloister, and so to his deserted bed in the south porch.

He was within the fold, and it was over. He sidled thankfully into the empty church – a good hour yet before Matins – and went to retrieve his blankets from behind the altar in the chancel chapel. He was very tired, but so agonisingly awake that sleep seemed very far off. Yet when he had spread his bedding again on his pallet, tucked away under the straw his new capuchon and cotte, and stretched himself out, still trembling, along the broad stone bench, sleep came to him so abruptly that all he knew of it was the descent, fathoms deep, into a well of darkness and peace.

Brother Cadfael rose well before Prime to go to his workshop, where he had left a batch of troches drying overnight. The bushes in the garden, the herbs in the enclosed herbarium, all glimmered softly with the lingering dew of a brief shower, and reflected back the dawn sunlight from thousands of tiny facets of silver. Another fine, fresh day beginning. Excellent for planting, moist, mild, the soil finely crumbled after the intense frosts of the hard winter. There could be no better auguries for germination and growth.

He heard the bell rousing the dortoir for Prime, and went directly to the church as soon as he had put his troches safely away. And there in the porch was Liliwin, his bedding already folded tidily away, his ill-cobbled motley exchanged for his new blue cotte, and his pale hair damp and flattened from being plunged in the bowl where he had washed. Cadfael took pleasure in observing him from a distance, himself unobserved. So wherever he had been hiding himself yesterday, he was still here in safety, and, moreover, developing a wholly creditable self-respect, with which guilt, or so it seemed to Cadfael, must be incompatible.

Brother Anselm, detecting the presence of his truant in church only when a high, hesitant voice joined in the singing, was similarly reassured and comforted. Prior Robert heard the same voice, looked round in incredulous displeasure, and frowned upon a dismayed Brother Jerome, who had so misled him. They still had the thorn in the flesh, thanksgiving had been premature.

The lay brothers were planting out more seedlings in a large patch along the Gaye that day, and sowing a later field of pease for succession, to follow when those by the Meole brook were harvested. Cadfael went out after dinner to view the work. After the night's soft shower the day was brilliant, sunlit and serene, but the earlier rains were still coming down the river from the mountains of Wales in their own good time, and the water was lapping into the grass where the meadow sloped smoothly down, and gnawing gently under the lip of the bank where it could not reach the turf. The length of a man's hand higher since two days ago, but always with this sunlit innocence upon it, as if it would be ashamed to endanger the swimming urchins, and could not possibly be thought capable of drowning

83

any man. And this as perilous a river as any in the land, as treacherous and as lovely.

It was a pleasure to walk along the trodden path that was only a paler line in the turf, following the fast, quiet flood downstream. Cadfael went with his eyes on the half-turgid, half-clear eddies that span and murmured under the lip of green, a strong current here hugging this shore. Across the stream, so silent and so fast, the walls of Shrewsbury loomed, at the crest of a steep green slope of gardens, orchards and vineyard, and further downstream fused into the solid bulk of the king's castle, guarding the narrow neck of land that broke Shrewsbury's girdle of water.

On this near shore Cadfael had reached the limit of the abbey orchards, where lush copses began, fringing the abbey's last wheat-field, and the old disused mill jutted over the river. He passed, threading the trees and bushes, and went on a short way, to where the level of land dipped to water-level in a little cove, shallowly covered by clear water now, the driving current spinning in and out again just clear of disturbing the gravel bottom. Things tended to come in here and be cast ashore if the Severn was in spate, and enclosing shoulders of woodland screened whatever came.

And something wholly unforeseen had come, and was lying here in uneasy repose, sprawled face-down, head butted into the gravelly calm of the bank. A solid body in good homespun cloth, shortish and sturdy, a round bullish head with floating, grizzled brown hair, thinning at the crown. Splayed arms, languidly moving in the gentle stir of the shallows, clear of the deadly purposeful central flow, fingered and fumbled vaguely at the fine gravel. Squat legs, but drawn out by the hungry current tugging at their toes, stretched towards open water. Cast up dead, all four limbs stirred and strained to prove him living.

Brother Cadfael kilted his habit to the knee, plunged down the gentle slope into the water, took the body by the bunched capuchon swaying at his neck and the leather belt at his wrist, and hoisted him gradually clear of the surface, to disturb as little as possible the position in which he had been swept ashore, and whatever traces the river had spared in his clothing, hair and shoes. No haste to feel for any life here, it had been gone for some time. Yet he might have something to tell even in his final silence.

The dead weight sagged from Cadfael's hands. He drew it,

streaming, up the first plain of grass, and there let it sink in the same shape it had had in the river. Who knew where it had entered the water and how?

As for naming him, there was no need to turn up that sodden face to the light of day, not yet. Cadfael recognised the russet broadcloth, the sturdy build, the round, turnip head with its thinning crown and bushy brown hedge of hair all round the shiny island of bone. Only two mornings ago he had passed the time of day with this same silenced tongue, very fluent and roguish then, enjoying its mischief without any great malice.

Baldwin Peche had done with toothsome scandal, and lost his last tussle with the river that had provided him with so many fishing sorties, and hooked him to his death in the end.

Cadfael hoisted him by the middle, marked the derisory flow from his mouth, barely moistening the grass, and let him down carefully in the same form. He was a little puzzled to find so meagre a flow, since even the dead may give back the water they have swallowed, for at least a brief while after their death. This one had left a shallow shape scooped in the gravel of the cove, which was hardly disturbed by currents. His outlines in the grass now duplicated the outline he had abandoned there.

Now how had Baldwin Peche come to be beached here like a landed fish? Drunk and careless along the riverside at night? Spilled out of a boat while fishing? Or fallen foul of a footpad in one of the dark alleys and tipped into the water for the contents of his purse? Such things did occasionally happen even in a well-regulated town on dark enough nights, and there did seem to be a thicker and darker moisture in the grizzled hair behind Peche's right ear, as though the skin beneath was broken. Scalp wounds tend to bleed copiously, and even after some hours in the water or cast up here traces might linger. He was native-born, he knew the river well enough to respect it, all the more as he acknowledged he was a weak swimmer.

Cadfael threaded the belt of bushes to have a clear view over the Severn, upstream and down, and was rewarded by the sight of a coracle making its way against the current, turning and twisting to make use of every eddy, bobbing and dancing like a shed leaf, but always making progress. There was only one man who could handle the paddle and read the river with such ease and skill, and even at some distance the squat, dark figure was easily recognisable. Madog of the Dead-Boat was as Welsh as Cadfael himself, and the best-known waterman in twenty miles of the Severn's course, and had got his name as result of the cargo he most often had to carry, by reason of his knowledge of all the places where missing persons, thought to have been taken by the river whether in flood or by felony, were likely to fetch up. This time he had no mute passenger aboard; his natural quarry was here waiting for him.

Cadfael knew him well and for no ascertainable reason, except the customary association of Madog with drowned men, took for granted that even in this case the connection must hold good. He raised a hail and waved an arm as the coracle drew nearer, picking its feathery way across the mid-stream current where it was diffused and moderate. Madog looked up, knew the man who beckoned him in, and with a sweep of his paddle brought his boat inshore, clear of the deceitfully silent and rapid thrust that sped down-river, leaving this cove so placid and clear. Cadfael waded into the shallows to meet him, laying a hand to the rim of hide as Madog hopped out nimbly to join him, his brown feet bare.

'I thought I knew that shaven sconce of yours,' he said heartily, and hoisted his cockle-shell of withies and hide on to his shoulder to heft it ashore. 'What is it with you? When you call me, I take it there's a sound reason.'

'Sound enough,' said Cadfael. 'I think I may have found what you were looking for.' He jerked his head towards the plain of grass above, and led the way up without more words. They stood together over the prone body in thoughtful silence for some moments. Madog had taken note in one glance of the position of the head, and looked back to the gravelled shore under its liquid skin of water. He saw the shadowy shape left in the fine shale, and the mute, contained violence of the current that swept past only a man's length away from that strange calm.

'Yes. I see. He went into the water above. Perhaps not far above. There's a strong tow under that bank, upstream from here a piece, under the castle. Then it could have brought him across and thrown him up here just as he lies. A good, solid weight, head-first into the bank. And left him stranded.'

'So I thought,' said Cadfael. 'You were looking for him?' People along the waterside who had kin go missing usually sought out Madog before they notified the provost or the sheriff's sergeant.

'That journeyman of his sent after me this morning. It seems his master went off yesterday before noon, but nobody wondered, he did the like whenever he chose, they were used to it. But this morning he'd never been back. There's a boy sleeps in his shop, he was fretting over it, so when Boneth came to work and no locksmith he sent the lad to me. This one here liked his bed, even if he sometimes came to it about dawn. Not the man to go hungry or dry, either, and the alehouse he favoured hadn't seen him.'

'He has a boat,' said Cadfael. 'A known fisherman.'

'So I hear. His boat was not where he keeps it.'

'But you've found it,' said Cadfael with conviction.

'A half-mile down-river, caught in the branches where the willows overhang. And his rod snagged by the hook and trailing. The boat had overturned. He ran a coracle, like me. I've left it beached where I found it. A tricky boat,' said Madog dispassionately, 'if he hooked a lusty young salmon. The spring ones are coming. But he knew his craft and his sport.'

'So do many and take the one chance that undoes them.'

'We'd best get him back,' said Madog, minding his business like any good master-craftsman. 'To the abbey? It's nearest. And Hugh Beringar will have to know. No need to mark this place, you and I both know it well, and his marks will last long enough.'

Cadfael considered and decided. 'You'll get him home best afloat, and it's your right. I'll follow ashore and meet you below the bridge, we shall make much the same time of it. Keep him as he lies, Madog, face-down, and note what signs he leaves aboard.'

Madog had at least as extensive a knowledge of the ways of drowned men as Cadfael. He gave his friend a long, thoughtful look, but kept his thoughts to himself, and stooped to lift the shoulders of the dead man, leaving Cadfael the knees. They got him decently disposed into the light craft. There was a fee for every Christian body Madog brought out of the river, he had indeed a right to it. The duty had edged its way in on him long ago, almost unaware, but other men's dying was the better part of his living now. And an honest, useful, decent art, for which many a family had been thankful.

Madog's paddle dipped and swung him across the contrary flow, to use the counter-eddies in moving up-river. Cadfael took a last look at the cove and the level of grass above it, memorised as much of the scene as he could, and set off briskly up the path to meet the boat at the bridge.

The river was fast and self-willed, and by hurrying, Cadfael won the race, and had time to recruit three or four novices and lay brothers by the time Madog brought his coracle into the ordered fringes of the Gaye. They had an improvised litter ready, they lifted Baldwin Peche on to it, and bore him away up the path to the Foregate and across to the gatehouse of the abbey. A nimble and very young novice had been sent in haste to carry word to the deputy-sheriff to come to the abbey at Brother Cadfael's entreaty.

But for all that, no one knew how, somehow the word had gone round. By the time Madog arrived, so had a dozen idle observers, draped over the downstream parapet of the bridge. By the time the bearers had got their burden to the level of the Foregate and turned towards the abbey, the dozen had become a score, and drifted in ominous quietness towards the end of the bridge, and there were a dozen more gradually gathering behind them, emerging from the town gate. When they reached the abbey gatehouse, which could not well be closed against any who came in decorous silence and apparent peace, they had between forty and fifty souls hovering at their heels and following them within. The weight of their foreboding, accusation and self-righteousness lay heavy on the nape of Cadfael's neck as the litter was set down in the great court. When he turned to view the enemy, for no question but they were the enemy, the first face he saw, the first levelled brow and vengeful eye, was that of Daniel Aurifaber.

Chapter Seven

Tuesday, from afternoon to night

HEY CAME crowding close, peering round Madog and Cadfael to confirm what they already knew. They passed the word back to those behind, in ominous murmurs that swelled into excited speculation in a matter of moments. Cadfael caught at the sleeve of the first novice who came curiously to see what was happening.

'Get Prior Robert and sharp about it. We're likely to need some other authority before Hugh Beringar gets here.' And to the litter-bearers, before they could be completely surrounded: 'Into the cloister with him, while you can, and stand ready to fend off any who try to follow.'

The sorry cortège obediently made off into cover in some haste, and though one or two of the younger fellows from the town were drawn after by gaping curiosity to the threshold of the cloister, they did not venture further, but turned back to rejoin their friends. An inqusitive ring drew in about Cadfael and Madog.

'That was Baldwin Peche the locksmith you had there,' said Daniel, not asking, stating. 'Our tenant. He never came home last night. John Boneth has been hunting high and low for him.'

'So have I,' said Madog, 'at that same John's urging. And between the two of us here we've found both the man and his boat.'

'Dead.' That was not a question either.

'Dead, sure enough.'

By that time Prior Robert had been found, and came in haste with his dutiful shadow at his heels. Of the interruptions to his ordered, well-tuned life within here, it seemed, there was to be no end. He had caught an unpleasant murmur of 'Murder!' as he approached, and demanded in dismay and displeasure what had happened to bring this inflamed mob into the great court. A dozen voices volunteered to tell him, disregarding how little they themselves knew about it.

'Father Prior, we saw our fellow-townsman carried in here, dead ...'

'No one had seen him since yesterday ...'

'My neighbour and tenant, the locksmith,' cried Daniel. 'Father robbed and assaulted, and now Master Peche fetched in dead!'

The prior held up a silencing hand, frowning them down. 'Let one speak. Brother Cadfael, do you know what this is all about?'

Cadfael saw fit to tell the bare facts, without mention of any speculations that might be going on in his own mind. He took care to be audible to them all, though he doubted if they would be setting any limits to their own speculations, however careful he might be. 'Madog here has found the man's boat overturned, down-river past the castle,' he concluded. 'And we have sent to notify the deputy-sheriff, the matter will be in his hands now. He should be here very soon.'

That was for the more excitable ears. There were some wild youngsters among them, the kind who are always at leisure to follow up every sensation, who might well lose their heads if they sighted their scapegoat. For the implication was already there, present in the very air. Walter robbed and battered, now his tenant dead, and all evil must light upon the same head.

'If the unfortunate man drowned in the river, having fallen from his boat,' said Robert firmly, 'there can be no possibility of murder. That is a foolish and wicked saying.'

They began to bay from several directions. 'Father Prior, Master Peche was not a foolhardy man ...' 'He knew the Severn from his childhood ...'

'So do many,' said Robert crisply, 'who fall victim to it in the end, men no more foolhardy than he. You must not attribute evil to what is natural misfortune.'

'And why should natural misfortune crowd so on one

90

house?' demanded an excited voice from the rear. 'Baldwin was a guest the night Walter was struck down and his coffer emptied.'

'And next-door neighbour, and liked to nose out whatever was hidden. And who's to say he didn't stumble on some proof that would be very bad news to the villain that did the deed, and lurks here swearing to his innocence?'

It was out, they took it up on all sides. 'That's how it was! Baldwin found out something the wretch wouldn't have been able to deny!'

'And he's killed the poor man to stop his mouth ...'

'A knock on the head and souse into the river ...'

'No trick to turn his boat loose for the river to take down after him ...'

Cadfael was relieved to see Hugh Beringar riding briskly in at the gatehouse then with a couple of officers behind him. This was getting all too predictable. When men have elected a villain, and one from comfortably outside their own ranks, without roots or kin, they need feel nothing for him, he is hardly a man, has no blood to be shed or heart to be broken, and whatever else needs a scapegoat will be laid on him heartily and in the conviction of righteousness. Nor will reason have much say in the matter. But he raised his voice powerfully to shout them down: 'The man you accuse is absolutely clear of this, even if it were murder. He is in sanctuary here, dare not leave the precinct, and has not left it. The king's officers wait for him outside, as you all know. Be ashamed to make such senseless charges!'

He said afterwards, rather resignedly than bitterly, that it was a precise measure of Liliwin's luck that he should appear innocently from the cloister at that moment, bewildered and shocked by the incursion of a dead body into the pale, and coming anxiously to enquire about it, but utterly ignorant of any connection it might be thought to have with him. He came hastening out of the west walk, solitary, apart, marked at once by two or three of the crowd. A howl went up, hideously triumphant. Liliwin took it like a great blast of cold wind in his face, shrank and faltered, and his countenance, healing into smooth comeliness these last two days, collapsed suddenly into the disintegration of terror.

The wildest of the young bloods moved fast, hallooing, but Hugh Beringar moved faster. The raw-boned grey horse, his favourite familiar, clattered nimbly between quarry and hounds, and Hugh was out of the saddle with a hand on Liliwin's shoulder, in a grip that could have been ambiguously arrest or protection, and his neat, dark, saturnine visage turned blandly towards the threatening assault. The foremost hunters froze discreetly, and thawed again only to draw back by delicate inches from challenging his command.

The nimble young novice had acquitted himself well, and shown an excellent grasp of his charge, for Hugh had the half of it clear in his mind already and understood its perilous application here. He kept his hold – let them read it however they would – on Liliwin throughout the questioning that followed, and listened as narrowly to Daniel Aurifaber's heated witness as to Cadfael's account.

'Very well! Father Prior, it would be as well if you yourself would convey this in due course to the lord abbot. The drowned man I must examine, as also the place where he was cast ashore and that where his boat came to rest. I must call upon the help of those who found out these matters. For the rest of you, if you have anything to say, say it now.'

Say it they did, intimidated but still smouldering, and determined to pour out their heat. For this was no chance death in the river, of that they were certain. This was the killing of a witness, close, curious, likely of all men to uncover some irrefutable evidence. He had found proof of the jongleur's strenuously denied guilt, and he had been slipped into the Severn to drown before he could open his mouth. They began by uttering it, they ended by howling it. Hugh let them rave. He knew they were no such monsters as they made themselves out to be, but knew, too, that given a following wind and a rash impulse, they could be, to their own damage and that of every other man.

They ran themselves out of words at length, and dwindled like sails bereft of wind.

'My men have been camped outside the gates here,' said Hugh then, calmly, 'all this while and have seen no sign of this man you accuse. To my knowledge he has not set foot outside these walls. How, then, can he have had any hand in any man's death?'

They had no answer ready to that, though they sidled and exchanged glances and shook their heads as though they knew beyond doubt that there must be an answer if they could only light on it. But out of the prior's shadow the insinuating voice of Brother Jerome spoke up mildly, 'Pardon, Father Prior, but is it certain that the young man has been every moment within here? Only recall, last night Brother Anselm was enquiring after him and had not seen him since just after noon, and remarked, moreover, that he did not come to the kitchen for his supper as is customary. And being concerned for any guest of our house, I felt it my duty to look for him and did so everywhere. That was just when twilight was falling. I found no trace of him anywhere within the walls.'

They took it up gleefully on the instant and Liliwin, as Cadfael observed with a sigh, shook and swallowed hard, and could not get out a word, and drops of sweat gathered on his upper lip and ran down, to be licked off feverishly.

'You see, the good brother says it! He was not here! He was out about his foul business!'

'Say rather,' Prior Robert reproached gently, 'that he could not be found.' But he was not altogether displeased.

'And go without his supper? A half-starved rat scorn his food unless he had urgent business elsewhere?' cried Daniel fiercely.

'Very urgent! He took his life in his hands to make sure Baldwin should not live to speak against him.'

'Speak up!' said Hugh drily, shaking Liliwin by the shoulder. 'You have a tongue, too. Did you leave the abbey enclave at any time?'

Liliwin gulped down gall, hung in anguished silence a moment, and got out in a great groan: 'No!'

'You were within here yesterday, when you were sought and could not be found?'

'I didn't want to be found. I hid myself.' His voice was firmer when he had at least a morsel of truth to utter. But Hugh pressed him still.

'You have not once set foot outside this pale since you took refuge here?'

'No, never!' he gasped, and dragged in breath as though he had run a great way.

'You hear?' said Hugh crisply, putting Liliwin aside and behind him. 'You have your answer. A man penned securely here cannot have committed murder outside, even if this proves to be murder, as at this moment there is no proof whatsoever. Now go, get back to your own crafts, and leave to the law what is the law's business. If you doubt my thoroughness, try crossing me.' And to his officers he said simply, 'Clear the court of those who have no business here. I will speak with the provost later.'

In the mortuary chapel Baldwin Peche lay stripped naked, stretched now on his back, while Brother Cadfael, Hugh Beringar, Madog of the Dead-Boat and Abbot Radulfus gathered about him attentively. In the corners of his eyes, now closed, traces of ingrained mud lingered, drying, like the pigments vain women use to darken and brighten their eyes. From his thick tangle of grizzled brown hair Cadfael had coaxed out two or three strands of water crowfoot, cobweb-fine stems with frail white flowers withering into veined brown filaments as they died, and a broken twig of alder leaves. There was nothing strange in either of those. Alders clustered in many places along the riverside, and this was the season when delicate rafts of crowfoot swayed and trembled wherever there were shallows or slower water.

'Though the water where I found him,' said Cadfael, 'runs fast, and will not anchor these flowers. The opposite bank I fancy, harbours them better. That is reasonable – if he launched his boat to go fishing it would be from that bank. And now see what more he has to show us.'

He cupped a palm under the dead man's cheek, turned his face to the light, and hoisted the bearded chin. The light falling into the stretched cavities of the nostrils showed them only as shallow hollows silted solid with river mud. Cadfael inserted the stem of the alder twig into one of them, and scooped out a smooth, thick slime of fine gravel and a wisp of crowfoot embedded within it.

'So I thought, when I hefted him to empty out the water from him and got only a miserable drop or two. The drainings of mud and weed, not of a drowned man.' He inserted his fingers between the parted lips, and showed the teeth also parted, as if in a grimace of pain or a cry. Carefully he drew them wider. Tendrils of crowfoot clung in the large, crooked teeth. Those peering close could see that the mouth within was clogged completely with the debris of the river.

'Give me a small bowl,' said Cadfael, intent, and Hugh was before Madog in obeying. There was a silver saucer under the unlighted lamp on the altar, the nearest receptacle, and Abbot Radulfus made no move to demur. Cadfael eased the stiffening jaw wider, and with a probing finger drew out into the bowl a thick wad of mud and gravel, tinted with minute fragments of vegetation. 'Having drawn in this, he could not draw in water.

94

No wonder I got none out of him.' He felt gently about the dead mouth, probing out the last threads of crowfoot, fine as hairs, and set the bowl aside.

'What you are saying,' said Hugh, closely following, 'is that he did not drown.'

'No, he did not drown.'

'But he did die in the river. Why else these river weeds deep in his throat?'

'True. So he died. Bear with me, I am treading as blindly as you. I need to know, like you, and like you, I must examine what we have.' Cadfael looked up at Madog, who surely knew all these signs at least as well as any other man living. 'Are you with me so far?'

'I am before you,' said Madog simply. 'But tread on. For a blind man you have not gone far astray.'

'Then, Father, may we now turn him again on his face, as I found him?'

Radulfus himself set his two long, muscular hands either side of the head, to steady the dead man over, and settled him gently on one cheekbone.

For all his self-indulgent habits of life, Baldwin Peche showed a strong, hale body, broad-shouldered, with thick, muscular thighs and arms. The discolorations of death were beginning to appear on him now, and they were curious enough. The broken graze behind his right ear, that was plain and eloquent, but the rest were matter for speculation.

'That was never got from any floating branch,' said Madog with certainty, 'nor from being swept against a stone, either, not in that stretch of water. Up here among the islands I wouldn't say but it might be possible, though not likely. No, that was a blow from behind, before he went into the water.'

'You are saying,' said Radulfus gravely, 'that the charge of murder is justified.'

'Against someone,' said Cadfael, 'yes.'

'And this man was indeed next-door neighbour to the household that was robbed, and may truly have found out something, whether he understood its meaning or not, that could shed light on that robbery?'

'It is possible. He took an interest in other men's business,' agreed Cadfael cautiously.

'And that would certainly be a strong motive for his removal, if the guilty man got to know of it,' said the abbot, reflecting. 'Then since this cannot be the work of one who was here within our walls throughout, it is strong argument in favour of the minstrel's innocence of the first offence. And somewhere at large is the true culprit.'

If Hugh had already perceived and accepted the same logical consequence, he made no comment on it. He stood looking down at the prone body in frowning concentration. 'So it would seem he was hit on the head and tossed into the river. And yet he did not drown. What he drew in, in his fight for breath – in his senses or out – was mud, gravel, weed.'

'You have seen,' said Cadfael. 'He was smothered. Held down somewhere in the shallows, with his face pressed into the mud. And set afloat in the river afterwards, with the intent he should be reckoned as one more among the many drowned in Severn. A mistake! The current cast him up before the river had time to wash away all these evidences of another manner of death.'

He doubted, in fact, if they would ever have been completely washed away, however long the body had been adrift. The stems of crowfoot were very tenacious. The fine silt clung tightly where it had been inhaled in the struggle for breath. But what was more mysterious was the diffused area of bruising that spread over Peche's back at the shoulder-blades, and the two or three deep indentations in the swollen flesh there. In the deepest the skin was broken, only a tiny lesion, as though something sharp and jagged had pierced him. Cadfael could make nothing of these marks. He memorised them and wondered.

There remained the contents of the silver bowl. Cadfael took it out to the stone basin in the middle of the garth and carefully sluiced away the fine silt, drawing aside and retaining the fragments of weed. Fine threads of crowfoot, a tiny, draggled flower, a morsel of an alder leaf. And something else, a sudden speck of colour. He picked it out and dipped it into the water to wash away the dirt that clouded it, and there it lay glistening in the palm of his hand, a mere scrap, two tiny florets, the tip of a head of flowers of a reddish purple colour, speckled at the lip with a darker purple and a torn remnant of one narrow leaf, just large enough to show a blackish spot on its green.

They had followed him out and gathered curiously to gaze. 'Fox-stones, we call this,' said Cadfael, 'for the two swellings at its root like pebbles. The commonest of its kind, and the earliest, but I don't recall seeing it much here. This, like the broken twig of alder, he took down with him when he was pushed into the water. It might be possible to find that place somewhere on the town bank – where crowfoot and alder and fox-stones all grow together.'

The place where Baldwin Peche had been cast ashore had little to tell beyond what it had already told. The spot where Madog had turned down the dead man's coracle on the meadow grass was well down-river, and so feather-light a boat, loose without a man's weight aboard, might well have gone on bobbing gaily downstream a mile or more beyond, before the first strong curve and encroaching sandbank would inevitably have arrested it. They would have to comb the town bank, Madog reckoned, from below the water-gate, to establish where he had been assaulted and killed. A place where crowfoot grew inshore under alders, and fox-stones were in flower close to the very edge of the water.

The first two could be found together all along the reach. The third might occur in only one place.

Madog would search the riverside, Hugh would question the Aurifaber household and the immediate neighbours, as well as the tavern-keepers of the town, for everything they knew about the recent movements of Baldwin Peche: where he had last been seen, who had spoken with him, what he had had to say. For someone, surely, must have seen him after he left his shop about mid-morning of the previous day, which was the last John Boneth knew of him.

Meantime, Cadfael had business of his own, and much to think about. He came back from the riverside too late for Vespers, but in time to visit his workshop and make sure all was in order there before supper. Brother Oswin, left in charge alone, was developing a deft touch and a proprietorial pride. He had not broken or burned anything for several weeks.

After supper Cadfael went in search of Liliwin, and found him sitting in deep shadow in the darkest corner of the porch, drawn up defensively against the stone with his arms locked about his knees. At this hour the light was too far gone for work to proceed on the mending of his rebec, or his new studies under Brother Anselm, and it seemed that the day's alarms had driven him back into distrust and despair, so that he hunched himself as small as possible into his corner and kept a wary face against the world. Certainly he gave Cadfael a bright, nervous, sidelong flash of his eyes as the monk hitched his habit comfortably and sat down beside him.

97

'Well, young man, have you fetched your supper tonight?' said Cadfael placidly.

Liliwin acknowledged that with a silent nod, watching him warily.

'It seems you did not yesterday, and Brother Jerome tells us that a maidservant came to visit you in the afternoon and brought you a basket of food from her lady's table. He had, he said, occasion to admonish you both.' The silence beside him was charged and uneasy. 'Now, granted Brother Jerome is uncommonly good at finding grounds for admonishment, yet I fancy there is but one maidservant whose presence here would have caused him qualms for the propriety of your conduct – let alone the well-being of your soul.' It was said with a smile in his voice, but he did not miss the slight shudder that convulsed the thin body beside him or the stiffening of the hands that were clasped so tightly round Liliwin's knees. Now why in the world should the lad quake at the mention of his soul's health, just when Cadfael was becoming more and more convinced that he had no guilt whatever upon his conscience, bar an understandable lie or two.

'Was it Rannilt?'

'Yes,' said Liliwin, just audibly.

'She came with good leave? Or of her own accord?'

Liliwin told him, in as few words as possible.

'So that was how it befell. And Jerome bade her do her errand and go, and stood over you to make sure she obeyed. And it was from that hour, as I understand – after he had witnessed her going – that no one saw *you* again until Prime this morning. Yet you say you were here within the pale and what you say, that I accept. Did you speak?'

'No,' said Liliwin, none too happily. Not speech, exactly, but a small, shamed sound hurriedly suppressed.

'You let her go somewhat tamely, did you not?' remarked Cadfael critically. 'Seeing the magnitude of the step she had taken for you.'

The evening was closing down tranquilly all round them, there was no one else to hear, and Liliwin had spent much of the day wrestling alone with the belated conviction of his mortal sin. Terror of men was surely enough to bear, without being suddenly visited by the terror of damnation, let alone the awful sense of having brought about the damnation of another person as dear to him as himself. He uncurled abruptly from his dark corner, slid his legs over the edge of the stone bench, and

98

clutched Cadfael impulsively by the arm.

'Brother Cadfael, I want to tell you … I must tell someone! I did – *we* did, but the fault was mine! – we did a terrible thing. I never meant it, but she was going away from me, and I might never see her again, and so it happened. A mortal sin and I've caused her to share in it!' The words spurted out like blood from a new wound, but the first flow eased him. From incoherent he grew quiet, and his shaking subsided and was gone. 'Let me tell you, and then do whatever you think is just. I couldn't bear it that she must go so soon, and it might be for ever. We went through the church, and I hid her within there, behind the altar in the transept chapel. There's a space behind there, I found it when I came new here and was afraid they might come for me in the night. I knew I could creep in there, and she is smaller than I. And when that brother had gone away, I went back to her there. I took my blankets in with me, and the new clothes she brought me – it's hard and chill on the stone. All I wanted,' said Liliwin simply, 'was to be with her as long as we dared. We did not even talk very much. But then we forgot where we were and what was due …'

Brother Cadfael said no word either to help or check him, but waited in silence.

'I couldn't think of anything but that she would go away, and I might never be with her again,' blurted Liliwin miserably, 'and I knew she was in the selfsame pain. We never intended evil, but we committed a terrible sacrilege. Here in the church, behind one of the holy altars – We couldn't bear it … We lay together as lovers do!'

He had said it, it was out, the very worst of it. He sat humbly waiting for condemnation, resigned to whatever might come, even relieved at having shifted the burden to other shoulders. There was no exclamation of horror, but this brother was not so given to prodigal admonishment as that sour one who had frowned on Rannilt.

'You love this girl?' asked Cadfael after some thought, and very placidly.

'Yes, I *do* love her! With all my heart I want her for my wife. But what is there for her if I am brought out of here to trial and the matter goes blackly for me? As they mean it should! Don't let it be known that she had been with me. Her hopes of marriage are wretched enough, a poor servant-girl without folk of her own. I don't want to damage them further. She may still get a decent man, if I …' he let that die away unfinished. It was no comforting thought.

'I think,' said Cadfael, 'she would rather have the man she has already chosen. Where mutual love is, I find it hard to consider any place too holy to house it. Our Lady, according to the miracles they tell of her, has been known to protect even the guilty who sinned out of love. You might try a few prayers to her, that will do no harm. Don't trouble too much for what was done under such strong compulsion and pure of any evil intent. And how long, then,' enquired Cadfael, eyeing his penitent tolerantly, 'did you remain hidden there? Brother Anselm was worried about you.'

'We fell asleep, both of us.' Liliwin shook again at the memory. 'When we roused, it was late and dark, they were singing Compline. And she had to go back all that way into the town in the night!'

'And you let her go alone?' demanded Cadfael with deceitful indignation.

'I did not. What do you take me for?' Liliwin had flared and fallen into the snare before he stopped to think, and it was too late to take it back. He sat back with a deflated sigh, stooping his face into deeper shadow.

'What do I take you for?' Cadfael's smile was hidden by the dusk. 'A bit of a rogue, perhaps, but no worse than the most of us. A bit of a liar when the need's great enough, but who isn't? So you did slip out of here to take the child home. Well, I think the better of you for it, it must have cost you some terrors.' And provided a salutary stiffening of self-respect, he thought but did not say.

In a small and perversely resentful voice Liliwin asked: 'How did you know?'

'By the effort it cost you to get the denial out. For you will never make a really *good* liar, lad, and the more you hate doing it, the worse you'll manage, and it seems to me you've taken strongly against lying these last few days. How did you contrive to get out and in again?'

Liliwin took heart and told him, how the new clothes had got him past the guards on the heels of the worshippers, and how he had taken Rannilt to her very doorway, and made his way back under cover of the returning lay servants. What had passed between himself and Rannilt on the way he kept to himself, and it did not enter his mind to say any word of what else he had noticed, until Cadfael took him up alertly on that very subject.

100

'So you were there, ouside the shop, about an hour after Compline?' Night is the favoured time for ridding oneself of enemies, and this was the one night that had passed since Baldwin Peche was last seen alive.

'Yes, I watched her safe into the courtyard. Only I fret,' said Liliwin, 'over what sort of welcome she may have found. Though her lady did say she might stay the day out. I hope no one was angry with her.'

'Well, since you were there, did you see aught of anything or anyone stirring about the place?'

'I did see one man who was out and about,' said Liliwin, remembering. 'It was after Rannilt had gone in. I was standing opposite, in a dark doorway, and Daniel Aurifaber came out through the passage, and went away to the left along the lane. He can't have gone far without turning aside, for when I went back to the Cross and down the Wyle he was gone already, I never saw sign of him after.'

'Daniel? You're sure it was he?' That young man had been prompt and present this afternoon, as soon as the usual idlers saw a body being lifted ashore under the bridge. Very prompt and very forward to lead the accusers who made haste to fling this, like the other offences, on the stranger's head, reason or no reason, sanctuary or no sanctuary.

'Oh, yes, there's no mistaking him.' He was surprised that such a point should be made of it. 'Is it important?'

'It may be. But no matter now. One thing you haven't said,' pointed out Cadfael gravely, 'and yet I'm sure you are not so dull but you must have thought on it. Once you were out of here and no alarm, and the night before you, you might have made off many miles from here, and got clean away from your accusers. Were you not tempted?'

'So *she* prompted me, too,' said Liliwin, remembering, and smiled. 'She urged me to go while I could.'

'Why did you not?'

Because she did not truly want me to, thought Liliwin, with a joyful lift of the heart for all his burdens. And because if ever she does come to me, it shall not be to an accused felon, but to a man acknowledged honest before the world. Aloud he voiced only the heart of that revelationary truth, 'Because now I won't go without her. When I leave – *if* I leave – I shall take Rannilt with me.'

Chapter Eight

Wednesday

 UGH SOUGHT out Cadfael after chapter the next morning for a brief conference in his workshop in the herbarium. 'They're all in a tale,' said Hugh, leaning back with a cup of Cadfael's latest-broached wine under the rustling bunches of last year's harvest of herbs. 'All insistent that this death must be linked to what happened at the young fellow's wedding feast. But since they're all of them obsessed with money, *their* money – except, perhaps, the daughter, who curls her lip very expressively but says little, and certainly nothing against her kin – they can think of nothing but their grievance and every other man must be as intent on it as they are. Yet there's profit and profit, and this locksmith's business does very nicely for itself, and now there's no kith nor kin to take it over, and it seems to be common knowledge the man had commended his journeyman to take the shop over after him. This young Boneth has been doing most of the work now above two years, he deserves he should get the credit. As right and virtuous a young man as ever I saw, to all appearances, but who's to be sure he didn't get tired of waiting? And we'd best bear in mind another truth – it was Baldwin Peche made the lock and keys for that strong-box of Aurifaber's.'

'There's a boy runs errands and sleeps there in the shop,' said Cadfael. 'Has he aught to say?'

'The dark boy, the simpleton? I wouldn't say his memory goes back farther than a day or so, but he's positive his master did not come back to his shop after he looked in at mid-morning, the day before he was fished out of the Severn. They were used to his absences by day, but the boy was anxious when there was no return at twilight. He didn't sleep. I would take his word for it there was no disturbance, no prowling about the burgage during the night. Nor are we the nearer knowing just when the man died, though the night would seem to be when he was set adrift, and the boat, too. There was no overturned coracle sighted down the Severn during the day – either day.'

'You'll be going back there, I suppose,' said Cadfael. There had been very little time the previous day for hunting out all the neighbours to testify. 'I've an errand there myself to the old dame tomorrow, but no occasion to go that way today. Give an eye for me to the little Welsh girl, will you, see in what spirits she is, and whether they're being rough or smooth with her.'

Hugh cocked a smiling eye at him. 'Your countrywoman, is she? To judge by the way I heard her singing away about her pot-scouring, last night, she's in good enough heart.'

'Singing, was she?' That would come as very welcome news to that draggled sparrow in his sanctuary cage here. Evidently no hardship more than normal had fallen upon Rannilt for her day of freedom. 'Good, that answers me very properly. And, Hugh, if you'll take a nudge from me without asking any questions as to where I picked up the scent – probe around as to whether anyone on that street saw Daniel Aurifaber slipping out in the dark an hour past Compline, when he should have been snug in bed with his bride.'

Hugh turned his black head sharply, and gave his friend a long and quizzical look. '*That* night?'

'That night.'

'Three days married!' Hugh grimaced and laughed. 'I'd heard the young man has the name for it. But I take your meaning. There may be other reasons for leaving a new wife to lie cold.'

'When I spoke with him,' said Cadfael, 'he made no secret of it that he heartily disliked the locksmith. Though had his dislike had a solid core, and gone as far as congealing into hate, I think he might have been less voluble about it.'

'I'll bear that in mind, too. Tell me, Cadfael,' said Hugh, eyeing him shrewdly, 'how strong is the scent you got wind of?

Say I find no such witness – no *second* such witness, ought I to say? – shall I be justifed in wagering on the accuracy of your nose?'

'In your shoes,' said Cadfael cheerfully, '*I* would.'

'You seem to have found your witness in very short order,' remarked Hugh drily, 'and without leaving the precinct. So you got it out of him – whatever it was that had him choking on a simple lie. I thought you would.' He rose, grinning, and set down his cup. 'I'll take your confession later, I'm away now to see what I can get out of the new wife.' He clouted Cadfael amiably on the shoulder in passing, and looked back from the doorway. 'No need to fret for that weedy lad of yours, I'm coming round to your opinion. I doubt if he ever did worse in his life than sneak a few apples from an orchard.'

The journeyman, Iestyn, was working alone in the shop, repairing the broken clasp of a bracelet, when Hugh came to the Aurifaber burgage. It was the first time Hugh had spoken with this man alone, and in company Iestyn kept himself silent and apart. Either he was taciturn by nature, thought Hugh, or the family had taken care to make his status clear to him, and it was not theirs, and there should be no stepping over the line that divided them.

In answer to Hugh's question he shook his head, smiling and hoisting impassive shoulders.

'How would I see what goes on in the street after dark or who's on the prowl when decent folks are in bed? I sleep in the back part of the undercroft, beneath the rear of the hall, my lord. Those outside stairs go down to my bed, as far from the lane as you can get. I neither see nor hear anything from there.'

Hugh had already noted the stairs that dived below the house at the rear, a shallow flight, since the ground dropped steadily away from the street level, and the undercroft, completely below-ground at the street end, was half above-ground at the back. From there, certainly, a man would be cut off from the world outside.

'At what hour did you go there, two nights ago?'

Iestyn knotted his thick black brows and considered. 'I'm always early, having to rise early. I reckon about eight that night, as soon as my supper had settled.'

'You had no late errands to do? Nothing that took you out again after that?'

104

'No, my lord.'

'Tell me, Iestyn,' said Hugh on impulse, 'are you content in your work here? With Master Walter and his family? You have fair treatment, and a good relationship?'

'One that suits me well enough,' said Iestyn cautiously. 'My wants are simple, I make no complaint. I never doubt time will bring me my due. First to earn it.'

Susanna met Hugh in the hall doorway, and bade him in with the same practical composure she would have used with any other. Questioned, she shrugged away all knowledge with a rueful smile.

'My chamber is here, my lord, between hall and store, the length of the house away from the street. Baldwin's boy did not come to us with his trouble, though he well could have done. At least he would have had company. But he didn't come, so we knew nothing of his master being still astray until the morning, when John came. I was sorry poor Griffin worried out the night alone.'

'And you had not seen Master Peche during the day?'

'Not since morning, when we were all about the yard and the well. I went across to his shop at dinner with a bowl of broth, having plenty to spare, and it was then John told me he'd gone out. Gone since mid-morning and said something about the fish rising. To the best I know, that's the last known word of him.'

'So Boneth has told me. And no report of him from any shop or ale-house or friend's house since. In a town where every man knows every man, that's strange. He steps over his door-sill and is gone.' He looked up the broad, unguarded stairs that led up from beyond her door to the gallery and the rooms above. 'How are these chambers arranged? Who has the one on the street, above the shop?'

'My father. But he sleeps heavily. Yet ask him, who knows but he may have heard or seen something. Next to him my brother and his wife. Daniel is away to Frankwell, but Margery you'll find in the garden with my father. And then my grand-mother has the nearest chamber. She keeps her room today, she's old and has had some trying seizures, perilous at her age. But she'll be pleased if you care to visit her,' said Susanna, with a brief, flashing smile, 'for all the rest of us grow very tedious to her, she's worn us out long ago, we no longer amuse her. I doubt if she can tell you anything that will help you, my lord, but the change would do marvels for her.'

105

She had wide eyes at once distant and brilliant, fringed with lashes russet as her coil of lustrous hair. A pity there should be grey strands in the russet, and fine wrinkles, whether of laughter or long-sighted pain, at the corners of the grey eyes, and drawn lines, like cobweb, about her full, firm mouth. She was, Hugh judged, at least six or seven years older than he, and seemed more. A fine thing spoiled for want of a little spending. Hugh had come by what was his as an only child, but he did not think a sister of his would have been left thus used and unprovided, to furnish a brother richly forth.

'I'll gladly present myself to Dame Juliana,' he said, 'when I have spoken with Master Walter and Mistress Margery.'

'That would be kind,' she said. 'And I could bring you wine, and that would give me the chance to bring her, with it, a dose she might otherwise refuse to take, even though Brother Cadfael comes tomorrow and she minds him more than any of us. Go down this way, then, my lord. I'll look for you returning.'

Either the goldsmith had nothing to tell, or else could not bring himself to spend even words. The one thing that haunted him day and night was his lost treasury, of which he had rendered an inventory piece by piece, almost coin by coin, in loving and grieving detail. The coins in particular were notable. He had silver pieces from before Duke William even became King William, fine mintage not to be matched now. His father and grandfather, and perhaps one progenitor more, must have been of the same mind as himself, and lived for their fine-struck wealth. Walter's head might be healed now without, but his loss might well have done untold harm to the mind within.

Hugh stood patiently under the apple and pear trees of the orchard, pressing his few questions concerning the vanishing of Baldwin Peche. Almost it seemed to him that the name no longer struck any spark, that Walter had to blink and shake himself and think hard before he could recall the name or the face of his dead tenant. He could not see the one or remember the other for brooding on his voided coffer.

One thing was certain, if he knew of anything that could help to recover his goods, he would pour it out in a hurry. Another man's death, by comparison, meant little to him. Nor did it seem that he had yet hit upon one possibility that was hovering in Hugh's mind. If there was indeed a connection between the

106

robbery and this death, need it be the one to which the town had jumped so nimbly? Robbers can also be robbed, and may even be killed in the robbing. Baldwin Peche had been a guest at the wedding, he had made the locks and keys for the strong-box, and who knew the house and shop better than he?

Margery had been feeding the fowls that scratched in a narrow run under the town wall, at the bottom of the garden. Until a year previously Walter had even kept his two horses here within the town, but recently he had acquired a pasture and an old stable across the river, westward from Frankwell, where Iestyn was regularly sent to see that they were fed and watered and groomed, and exercise them if they were short of work. The girl was coming up the slope of the garden with the morning's eggs in a basket, the bulk of the wall in shadow behind her, and the narrow door in it closed. A short, rounded, insignificant young person to the view, with an untidy mass of fair hair. She made Hugh a wary reverence, and raised to him a pair of round, unwavering eyes.

'My husband is out on an errand, sir, I'm sorry. In half an hour or so he may be back.'

'No matter,' said Hugh truly, 'I can speak with him later. And you may well be able to speak for both, and save the time. You know on what business I'm engaged. Master Peche's death seems likely to prove no accident, and though he was missing most of the day, yet the night is the most favourable time for villainies such as murder. We need to know what every man was doing two nights ago, and whether he saw or heard anything that may help us lay hands on the culprit. I understand your chamber is the second one, back from the street, yet you may have looked out and seen someone lurking in the alley between the houses, or heard some sound that may have meant little to you then. Did you so?'

She said at once, 'No, It was a quiet night, like any other.'

'And your husband made no mention of noticing anything out of the way? No one out and about on the roads when law-abiding people are fast at home? Had he occasion to be in the shop late? Or any errand ouside?'

Her rose and white countenance flushed very slowly a deeper rose, but her eyes did not waver, and she found a ready excuse for her colour. 'No, we retired in good time. Your lordship will understand – we are only a few days married.'

'I understand very well!' said Hugh heartily. 'Then I need hardly ask you if your husband so much as left your side.'

107

'Never for a moment,' she agreed, and voice and flush were eloquent, whether they told the truth or no.

'The idea would never have entered my mind,' Hugh assured her urbanely, 'if we had not the testimony of a witness who says he saw your husband creeping out of the house and making off in haste about an hour after Compline that night. But of course, more's the unwisdom, not all witnesses tell the truth.'

He made her a civil bow, and turned and left her then, neither lingering nor hurrying, and strolled back up the garden path to the house. Margery stood staring after him with her underlip caught between her teeth, and the basket of eggs dangling forgotten from her hand.

She was waiting and watching for Daniel when he came back from Frankwell. She drew him aside into a corner of the yard, where they could not be overheard, and the set of her chin and brows stopped his mouth when he began to blurt out loud, incautious wonder at being thus waylaid. Instead, he questioned in an uneasy undertone, impressed by her evident gravity, 'What is it? What's the matter with you?'

'The sheriff's deputy has been here asking questions. Of all of us!'

'Well, so he must, what is there in that? And what, of all people, could you tell him?' The implied scorn did not escape her; that would change, and soon.

'I *could* have told what he asked me,' she spat, bitter and low, 'where you were all night on Monday. But could I? Do I even know? I know what I believed then, but why should I go on believing it? A man who was out of his bed and loose in the town that night may not have been bustling to another woman's bed after all – he *could* have been battering Baldwin Peche over the head and throwing him into the river! That's what *they* are thinking. And now what am I to believe? Bad enough if you left me to go to that woman while her husband's away – oh, yes, I was there, do you remember, when she told you, all nods and winks, the shameless whore! – that he was bound away for several days! But how do I know now that that's what you were about?'

Daniel was gaping at her, white-faced and aghast, and gripping her hand as if his senses at that moment had no other anchor. 'Dear God, they can't think that. *You* can't believe that of me? You know me better ...'

'I don't know you at all! You pay me no attention, you're nothing but a stranger to me, you steal out at night and leave me in tears, and what do you care?'

'Oh, God!' babbled Daniel in a frantic whisper, 'What am I to do? And you told him? You told him I went out – the whole night?'

'No, I did not. I'm a loyal wife, if you're no proper husband to me. I told him you were with me, that you never left my side.'

Daniel drew breath deep, gawping at her in idiot relief, and began to smile, and jerk out praise and thanks incoherently while he wrung her hand, but Margery measured out her moment like a fencer, and struck the grin ruthlessly from his face.

'But he knows it is not true.'

'What?' He collapsed again in terror. 'But how can he? If you told him I was with you …'

'I did. I've perjured myself for you and all to no purpose. *I* gave nothing away, though God knows I owe you nothing. I put my soul in peril to save you from trouble! And then he tells me smoothly that there's a witness who saw you sneak out that night and has the hour right, too, so never think this was a trick. There *is* such a witness. You're known to have been out roving in the dark the night that man was murdered.'

'I never had aught to do with it,' he wailed softly. 'I told you truth …'

'You told me you had things to do that were no concern of mine. And everybody knows you had no love for the locksmith.'

'Oh, God!' moaned Daniel, gnawing his knuckles. 'Why did I ever go near the girl? I was mad! But I swear to you, Margery, that was all, it was to Cecily I went … and never again, never! Oh, girl, help me … what am I to do?'

'There's only one thing you can do,' she said forcefully. 'If that's truly where you were, you must go to this woman, and get her to speak up for you, as she ought. Surely she'll tell the truth, for your sake, and then the sheriff's men will let you alone. And I'll confess that I lied. I'll say it was for shame of being slighted, though it was truly for love of you – however little you deserve it.'

'I will!' breathed Daniel, weak with fear and hope and gratitude all mingled, and stroking and caressing her hand as he had never done before. 'I'll go to her and ask her. And never see her again, I promise you, I swear to you, Margery.'

'Go after dinner,' said Margery, securely in the ascendancy, 'for you must come and eat and put a good face on it. You can, you must. No one else knows of this, no one but I, and I'll stand by you whatever it cost me.'

Mistress Cecily Corde did not brighten or bridle at the sight of her lover creeping in at the back door of her house early in the afternoon. She scowled as blackly as so golden a young woman could, hauled him hastily into a closed chamber where they could not possibly be overlooked by her maidservant, and demanded of him, before he had even got his breath back, what he thought he was doing there in broad daylight, and with the sheriff's men about the town as well as the usual loiterers and gossips. In a great, gasping outpour Daniel told her what he was about, and why, and what he needed, entreated, must have from her, avowal that he had spent Monday night with her from nine of the evening until half an hour before dawn. His peace of mind, his safety, perhaps his life, hung on her witness. She could not deny him, after all they had meant to each other, all he had given her, all they had shared.

Once she had grasped what he was asking of her, Cecily disengaged violently from the embrace she had permitted as soon as the door was closed, and heaved him off in a passion of indignation.

'Are you mad? Throw my good name to the four winds to save your skin? I'll do no such thing, the very idea of asking it of me! You should be ashamed! Tomorrow or the next day my man will be home, and very well you know it. You would not have come near me now, if you had any thought for me. And like this, in daylight, with the streets full! You'd better go, quickly, get away from here.'

Daniel clung, aghast, unable to believe in such a reception. 'Cecily, it may be my life! I *must* tell them …'

'If you dare,' she hissed, backing violently out of his desperate attempt at an embrace, 'I shall deny it. I shall swear that you lie, that you've pestered me, and I've never encouraged you. I mean it! Dare mention my name and I'll brand you liar, and bring witness enough to bear me out. Now go, go, I never want to see you again!'

Daniel fled back to Margery. She had the shrewd sense to be watching for him, having known very well what his reception must be, and spirited him competently away to their own chamber where, if they kept their voices down, they could not be heard. Dame Juliana, next door, slept in the afternoon and

110

slept soundly. Their private business was safe from her.

In agitated whispers he poured out everything though he was telling her nothing she did not already know. She judged it time to soften against his shoulder, while keeping the mastery firmly in her own hands. He had been shocked out of his male complacency, and almost out of his skin, she felt pity and affection for him, but that was a luxury she could not yet afford.

'Listen, we'll go together. You have a confession to make, but so have I. We'll not wait for the Lord Beringar to come to us, we'll go to him. I'll own that I lied to him, that you left me alone all tht night, knowing you were gone to a paramour. You'll tell him the same. I shall not know her name. And you will refuse to give it. You must say she is a married woman, and it would be her ruin. He'll respect you for it. And we'll say that we start anew, from this hour.'

She had him in her hand. He would go with her, he would swear to whatever she said. They would start anew from that hour; and she would be holding the reins.

In bed that night she clasped a devout, grateful husband, who could not fawn on her enough. Whether Hugh Beringar had believed their testimony or not, he had received it with gravity, and sent them away solemnly admonished but feeling themselves delivered. A Daniel eased of all fear that the eye of the law was turned ominously upon him would sit still where a hand could be laid on him at any moment.

'It's over,' Margery assured him, fast in his arms, and surprisingly contented there, considering all things. 'I'm sure you need not trouble any more. No one believes you ever harmed the man. I'll stand with you, and we have nothing to fear.'

'Oh, Margery, what should I have done without you?' He was drifting blissfully towards sleep, after extreme fear and the release of correspondingly great pleasure. Never before had he felt such devotional fervour, even to his mistress. This might have been said to be his true wedding night. 'You're a good girl, loyal and true ...'

'I'm your wife, who loves you,' she said, and more than half believed it, to her own mild surprise. 'And loyal you'll find me, whenever you call upon me. *I* shall not fail you. But you must also stand by me, for as your wife I have rights.' It was well to have him so complacent, but not to let him fall asleep, not yet.

111

She took steps to rouse him; she had learned a great deal in one unsatisfactory week. While he was still glowing, she pursued very softly and sweetly: 'I am your wife now – wife to the heir, there's a status belongs to me. How can I live in a house and have no place, no duties that are mine by right?'

'Surely you have your place,' he protested tenderly. 'The place of honour, mistress of the house. What else? We all bear with my grandmother, she's old and set in her ways, but she doesn't meddle with the housekeeping.'

'No, I don't complain of her, of course we must reverence the elders. But your wife should be granted her due in responsibilities as well as privilege. If your mother still lived it would be different. But Dame Juliana has given up her direction of the household, being so old, to our generation. I am sure your sister has done her duty nobly by you all these years ...'

Daniel hugged her close, his thick curls against her brow. 'Yes, so she has, and you can keep your hands white and take your ease, and be the lady of the house, why should you not?'

'That is not what I want,' said Margery firmly, gazing up into the dark with wide-open eyes. 'You're a man, you don't understand. Susanna works hard, no one could complain of her, she keeps a good table without waste, and all the linen and goods and provisions in fine order, I know. I give her all credit. But that is the *wife's* work, Daniel. Your mother, if she had lived. Your wife, now you have a wife.'

'Love, why should you not work together? Half the load is lighter to bear, and I don't want my wife worn out with cares,' he murmured smugly into the tangle of her hair. And thought himself very cunning, no doubt, wanting peace as men always want it, far before justice or propriety; but she would not let him get away with that sop.

'She won't give up any part of the load, she has had her place so long, she stands off any approach. Only on Monday I offered to fetch in the washing for her, and she cut me off sharply, *that* she would do herself. Trust me, my love, there cannot be two mistresses in one house, it never prospers. *She* has the keys at her girdle, *she* sees the store-bins kept supplied, and the linen mended and replaced, *she* gives the orders to the maid, *she* chooses the meats and sees them cooked as *she* wishes. *She* comes forth as hostess when the visitors appear. All *my* rights, Daniel, and I want them. It is not fitting that the wife should be so put aside. What will our neighbours say of us?'

'Whatever you want,' he said with sleepy fervour, 'you shall have. I do see that my sister ought now to give up her office to you, and should have done so willingly, of her own accord. But she has held the reins here so long, she has not yet considered that I'm now a married man. Susanna is a sensible woman, she'll see reason.'

'It is not easy for a woman to give up her place,' Margery pointed out sternly. 'I shall need your support, for it's your status as well as mine in question. Promise me you will stand with me to get my rights.'

He promised readily, as he would have promised her anything that night. Of the two of them, she had certainly been the greater gainer from the day's crises and recoveries. She fell asleep knowing it, and already marshalling her skills to build on it.

Chapter Nine

Thursday, from morning to late evening

AME JULIANA tapped her way down the broad wooden treads of the stairs to the hall in good time on the following morning, determined to greet Brother Cadfael when he came after breakfast with all the presence and assurance of a healthy old lady in full command of her household, even if she had to prepare her seat and surroundings in advance and keep her walking-stick handy. He knew that she was no such matter, and she knew that he knew it. She had a foot in the grave, and sometimes felt it sinking under her and drawing her in. But this was a final game they played together, in respect and admiration if not in love or even liking.

Walter was off to his workshop with his son this morning. Juliana sat enthroned in her corner by the stairs, cushioned against the wall, eyeing them all, tolerant of all, content with none. Her long life, longer than any woman should be called upon to sustain, trailed behind her like a heavy bridal train dragging at the shoulders of a child bride, holding her back, weighing her down, making every step a burden.

As soon as Rannilt had washed the few platters and set the bread-dough to rise, she brought some sewing to a stool in the hall doorway, to have the full light. A decent, drab brown gown, with a jagged tear above its hem. The girl was making a neat job of mending it. Her eyes were young. Juliana's were

114

very old, but one part of her that had not mouldered. She could see the very stitches the maid put in, small and precise as they were.

'Susanna's gown?' she said sharply. 'How did she come to get a rent like that? And the hems washed out too! In my day we made things last until they wore thin as cobweb before we thought of discarding them. No such husbandry these days. Rend and mend and throw away to the beggars! Spendthrifts all!'

Plainly nothing was going to be right for the old woman today, she was determined to make her carping authority felt by everyone. It was better, on such days, to say nothing, or if answers were demanded, make them as short and submissive as possible.

Rannilt was glad when Brother Cadfael came in through the passage with dressings in his scrip for the ulcer that was again threatening to erupt on the old woman's ankle. The thin, eroded skin parted at the least touch or graze. He found his patient reared erect and still in her corner, waiting for him, silent and thoughtful for once, but at his coming she roused herself to maintain, in the presence of this friendly enemy, her reputation for tartness, obstinacy and grim wit, and for taking always, with all her kin, the contrary way. Whoever said black, Juliana would say white.

'You should keep this foot up,' said Cadfael, cleaning the small but ugly lesion with a pad of linen, and applying a new dressing. 'As you know very well, and have been told all too often. I wonder if I should not rather be telling you to stamp about upon it day-long – then you might do the opposite and let it heal.'

'I kept my room yesterday,' she said shortly, 'and am heartily sick of it now. How do I know what they get up to behind my back while I'm shut away up there? Here at least I can see what goes on and speak up if I see cause – as I will, to the end of my days.'

'Small doubt!' agreed Cadfael, rolling his bandage over the wound and finishing it neatly. 'I've never known you baulk your fancy yet, and never expect to. Now, how is it with your breathing? No more chest pains? No giddiness?'

She would not have considered she had had her full dues unless she had indulged a few sharp complaints of a pain here, or a cramp there, and she did not grudge it that most of them he brushed away no less bluntly. It was all a means of beguiling

115

the endless hours of the day that seemed so long in passing, but once past, rushed away out of mind like water slipping through the fingers.

Rannilt finished her mending, and carried off the gown into Susanna's chamber, to put it away in the press; and presently Susanna came in from the kitchen and stopped to pass the time of day civilly with Cadfael, and enquire of him how he thought the old woman did, and whether she should continue to take the draught he had prescribed for her after her seizure.

They were thus occupied when Daniel and Margery came in together from the shop. Side by side they entered, and there was something ceremonious in their approach, particularly in their silence, when they had certainly been talking together in low, intent tones on the threshold. They barely greeted Cadfael, not with any incivility, but rather as if their minds were fixed on something else, and their concentration on it must not be allowed to flag for a moment. Cadfael caught the tension and so, he thought, did Juliana. Only Susanna seemed to notice nothing strange, and did not stiffen in response.

The presence of someone not belonging to the clan was possibly an inconvenience, but Margery did not intend to be deflected or to put off what she was braced to say.

'We have been discussing matters, Daniel and I,' she announced, and for a person who looked so soft and pliable her voice was remarkably firm and resolute. 'You'll understand, Susanna, that with Daniel's marriage there are sure to be changes in the order here. You have borne the burden of the house nobly all these years ...' That was unwise, perhaps; it was all those years that had dried and faded what must once have been close to beauty, their signature was all too plain in Susanna's face. 'But now you can resign it and take your leisure and no reproach to you, it's well earned. I begin to know my way about the house, I shall soon get used to the order of the day here, and I am ready to take my proper place as Daniel's wife. I think, and he thinks too, that I should take charge of the keys now.'

The shock was absolute. Perhaps Margery had known that it would be. Every trace of colour drained out of Susanna's face, leaving her dull and opaque as clay, and then as swiftly the burning red flooded back, rising into her very brow. The wide grey eyes stared hard and flat as steel. For long moments she did not speak; Cadfael thought she could not. He might have stolen silently away and left them to their fight, if he had not

116

been concerned for its possible effect on Dame Juliana. She was sitting quite still and mute, but two small, sharp points of high colour had appeared on her cheek bones, and her eyes were unusually bright. Or again, he might in any case have stayed, unobtrusive in the shadows, having more than his fair share of human curiosity.

Susanna had recovered her breath and the blood to man her tongue. Fire kindled behind her eyes, like a vivid sunset through a pane of horn.

'You are very kind, sister, but I do not choose to quit my charge so lightly. I have done nothing to be displaced, and I do not give way. Am I a slave, to be put to work as long as I'm needed, and then thrown out at the door? With nothing? *Nothing*! This house is my home, *I* have kept it, I *will* keep it: my stores, my kitchen, my linen-presses, all are *mine*. You are welcome here as my brother's bride,' she said, cooling formidably, 'but you come new into an old rule, in which *I* bear the keys.'

The quarrels of women are at all times liable to be bitter, ferocious and waged without quarter, especially when they bear upon the matriarchal prerogative. Yet Cadfael found it surprising that Susanna should have been so shaken out of her normal daunting calm. Perhaps this challenge had come earlier than she had expected, but surely she could have foreseen it and need not, for that one long moment, have stood so mute and stricken. She was ablaze now, claws bared and eyes sharp as daggers.

'I understand your reluctance,' said Margery, growing sweet as her opponent grew bitter. 'Never think here is any implied complaint, oh, no, I know you have set me an exemplary excellence to match. But see, a wife without a function is a vain thing, but a daughter who has borne her share of the burden already may relinquish it with all honour, and leave it to younger hands. I have been used to working, I cannot go idle. Daniel and I have talked this over, and he agrees with me. It is my right!' If she did not nudge him in the ribs, the effect was the same.

'So we have talked it over and I stand by Margery,' he said stoutly. 'She is my wife, it's right she should have the managing of this house which will be hers and mine. I'm my father's heir, shop and business come to me, and this household comes to Margery just as surely, and the sooner she can take it upon her, the better for us all. Good God, sister, you must have known it. Why should you object?'

'Why should I object? To be dismissed all in a moment like a

117

thieving servant? I, who have carried you all, fed you, mended for you, saved for you, held up the house over you, if you had but the wit to know it or the grace to admit it. And my thanks is to be shoved aside into a corner to moulder, is it, or to fetch and carry and scrub and scour at the orders of a newcomer? No, that I won't do! Let your wife clerk and count for you, as she claims she did for her father, and leave my stores, my kitchen, my keys to me. Do you think I'll surrender tamely the only reason for living left to me? This family has denied me any other.'

Walter, if he had anticipated any of this, had been wise to keep well away from it, safe in his shop. But the likelihood was that he had never been warned or consulted, and was expendable until this dispute was settled.

'But you knew,' cried Daniel, impatiently brushing aside her lifelong grievance, seldom if ever mentioned so plainly before, 'you knew I should be marrying, and surely you had the sense to know my wife would expect her proper place in the house. You've had your day, you've no complaint. Of course the wife has precedence and requires the keys. And shall have them, too!'

Susanna turned her shoulder on him and appealed with flashing eyes to her grandmother, who had sat silent this while, but followed every word and every look. Her face was grim and controlled as ever, but her breathing was rapid and shallow, and Cadfael had closed his fingers on her wrist to feel the beat of her blood there, but it remained firm and measured. Her thin grey lips were set in a somewhat bitter smile.

'Madam grandmother, do you speak up! Your word still counts here as mine, it seems, cannot. Have I been so useless to you that you, also, want to discard me? Have I not done well by you all, all this while?'

'No one has found fault with you,' said Juliana shortly. 'That is not the issue. I doubt if this chit of Daniel's can match you, or do the half as well, but I suppose she has the goodwill and the perseverance to learn, if it has to be by her errors. What she has, and so I tell you, girl, is the right of the argument. The household rule is owing to her, and she will have to have it. I can say no other, like it or lump it. You may as well make it short and final, for it must happen.' And she rapped her stick sharply on the floor to make a period to the judgment.

Susanna stood gnawing at her lips and looking from face to

face of all these three who were united against her. She was calm now, the anger that filled her had cooled into bitter scorn.

'Very well,' she said abruptly. 'Under protest I'll do what's required of me. But not today. I have been the mistress here for years, I will not be turned out in the middle of my day's work, without time to make up my accounts. She shall not be able to pick flies here and there, and say, this was left unfinished, or, she never told me there was a new pan needed, or, here's a sheet was left wanting mending. No! Margery shall have a full inventory tomorrow, when I'll hand over my charge. She shall have it listed what stocks she inherits, to the last salt fish in the last barrel. She shall start with a fair, clean leaf before her. I have my pride, even if no other regards it.' She turned fully to Margery, whose round fair face seemed distracted between satisfied complacency and discomfort, as if she did not quite know, at this moment, whether to be glad or sorry of her victory. 'Tomorrow morning you shall have the keys. Since the store-room is entered through my chamber, you may also wish to have me move from there, and take that room yourself. Then you may. From tomorrow I won't stand in your way.'

She turned and walked away out of the hall door and round towards the kitchen, and the bunch of keys at her waist rang as if she had deliberately set them jangling in a last derisive spurt of defiance. She left a charged silence behind her, which Juliana was the first one bold enough to break.

'Well, children, make yourselves content,' she said, eyeing her grandson and his bride sardonically. 'You have what you wanted, make the most of it. There's hard work and much thought goes into running a household.'

Margery hastened to ingratiate herself with thanks and promises. The old woman listened tolerantly, but with that chill smile so unnervingly like Susanna's still on her lips. 'There, be off now, and let Daniel get back to his work. Brother Cadfael, I can see, is none too pleased with seeing me roused. I'm likely to be getting some fresh potion poured into me to settle me down, through the three of you and your squabbles.'

They went gladly enough, they had much to say to each other privately. Cadfael saw the spreading grey pallor round Juliana's mouth as soon as she relaxed her obstinate self-control and lay back against her cushions. He fetched water from the cooling jar, and shook out a dose of the

119

powdered oak mistletoe for her to take. She looked up at him over the cup with a sour grin.

'Well, say it! Tell me my granddaughter has been shabbily used!'

'There is no need for me to say it,' said Cadfael, standing back to study her the better and finding her hands steady, her breath even, and her countenance as hardy as ever, 'since you know it yourself.'

'And too late to mend it. But I've allowed her the one day she wanted. I could have denied her even that. When I gave her the keys, years ago, you don't think they were the only ones? What, leave myself unfurnished? No, I can still poke into corners, if I choose. And I do, sometimes.'

Cadfael was packing his dressings and unguents back into his scrip, but with an eye still intent on her. 'And do you mean to give up both bunches to Daniel's wife now? If you had meant mischief, you could have handed them to her before your granddaughter's face.'

'My mischief is almost over,' said Juliana, suddenly sombre. 'All keys will be wrested from me soon, if I don't give them up willingly. But these I'll keep yet a day or two. I still have a use for them.'

This was her house, her family. Whatever boiled within it, ripe for eruption, was hers to deal with. No outsider need come near.

In the middle of the morning, when Susanna and Rannilt were both busy in the kitchen, and would certainly be occupied for some time, and the men were at work in the shop, Juliana sent the only remaining witness, Margery, to fetch her a measure of a strong wine she favoured for mulling from a vintner's a satisfactory distance away across the town. When she had the hall to herself, she rose, bearing down heavily on her stick, and felt beneath her full skirt for the keys she kept hidden in a bag-pocket there.

Susanna's chamber door was open. A narrow rear door gave quick access here to the strip of yard which separated the kitchen from the house. Faintly Juliana could hear the voices of the two women, their words indistinguishable, their tones revealing. Susanna was cool, short and dry as always. The girl sounded anxious, grieved, solicitous. Juliana knew well enough about that truant day when the chit had come home hastily and in the dark. No one had told her, but she knew. The sharpness of her senses neither denied nor spared her anything. Shabbily used, and too late to mend! The girl had been listening, appalled, to the quarrel in the hall, and felt for the mistress who had shown her kindness. Young things are easily moved to generous indignation and sympathy. the old have no such easy grace.

The store-room, with its heavy vats of salted food, jars of oil, crocks of flour and oatmeal and dry goods, tubs of fat, bunches of dried herbs, shared the width of the hall with Susanna's chamber, and opened out of it. This door was locked. Juliana fitted the key Baldwin Peche had cut for her before ever she gave up the original, and opened the door and went in, into the myriad fat, spicy, aromatic, salt smells of the pantry.

She was within for perhaps ten minutes, hardly more. She was ensconced in her cushioned corner under the staircase and the door locked again securely by the time Margery came back with her wine, and the spices needed to mull it to her liking for her indulgence at bedtime.

'I have been telling this youngster,' said Brother Anselm, fitting together curved shards of wood with the adroit delicacy appropriate to the handling of beloved flesh wounded, 'that should he consider taking vows as a novice here, his tenure would be assured. A life of dedication to the music of worship – what better could he seek, gifted as he is? And the world would withdraw its hand from him, and leave him in peace.'

Liliwin kept his fair head bent discreetly over the small mortar in which he was industriously grinding resins for the precentor's gum, and said never a word, but the colour rose in his neck and mounted his cheek and brow to the hairline. What was offered might be a life secured and at peace, but it was not the life he wanted. Whatever went on inside that vulnerable and anxious head of his, there was not the ghost of a vocation for the monastic life there. Even if he escaped his present peril, even if he won his Rannilt and took her away with him, after more of the world's battering he might end as a small vagrant rogue, and she as what? His partner in some enforced thievery, picking pockets at fair and market in order to keep them both alive? Or worse, as his breadwinner by dubious means when all else failed? We have more to answer for here, thought Brother Cadfael, watching the work in silence, than the rights and wrongs of one local charge of robbery and assault. What we send out from here, in the end, must be armed against fate in

121

something better than motley.

'A fast learner, too,' said Anselm critically, 'and very biddable.'

'Where he's busy with what he loves, no doubt,' agreed Cadfael, and grinned at seeing Liliwin's brief, flashing glance, which met his eyes and instantly avoided them, returning dutifully to the work in hand. 'Try teaching him his letters instead of the neums, and he may be less ardent.'

'No, you mistake, he has an appetite for either. I could teach him the elements of Latin if I had him for one year.'

Liliwin kept his head down and his mouth shut, grateful enough, and from the heart, for such praise, greedy to benefit by such generous teaching, enlarged and comforted by such simple kindness, and desirous of gratifying his tutor in return, if only he could. Now that his innocence began to be accepted as a probability, however uncertain as yet, these good people began also to make plans for his future. But his place was not here, but with his little dark girl, wherever their joint wanderings might take them about the world. Either that or out of the world, if the forty days of grace ebbed out without true vindication.

When the light faded too far to allow the fine work to continue, Brother Anselm bade him take the organetto and play and sing by ear to show off his skills to Brother Cadfael. And when Liliwin somewhat forgot himself and launched into a love song, innocent enough but disturbing within these walls, Anselm showed no sign of perturbation, but praised the melody and the verses, but the melody above all, and noted it down briskly to be translated to the glory of God.

The Vesper bell silenced their private pleasure. Liliwin put away the organetto with hasty gentleness, and followed to pluck Cadfael by the sleeve.

'Did you see her? Rannilt? She came to no harm by me?'

'I saw her. She was mending a gown, altogether composed and in no trouble. You did her no harm. Yesterday, I hear, she was singing at her work.'

Liliwin released him with a thankful sigh and a whisper of gratitude for such news. And Cadfael went into Vespers reflecting that he had told but the more welcome half of truth, and wondering if Rannilt felt much like singing this evening. For she had overheard the battle that sent Susanna away defeated, displaced, robbed of the only realm a parsimonious grandmother and sire had left her. And Susanna was the mistress who, if she had never shown her much warmth, had nevertheless kept her from cold, hunger and blows and, above all, had sent her to her strange marriage, so heretically blessed, and witnessed only by the saints whose relics sanctified her marriage bed. Tomorrow Susanna would give up the keys of her realm to a young rival. The little Welsh girl had a partisan heart, quicker to grief even than to joy. No, she would not feel like singing until tomorrow was over.

Rannilt crouched unsleeping on her pallet in the kitchen until all the house lights had been put out, except one, on which her attention was fixed. A miserly household goes early to bed to save lights and fuel, banking down the hearth-fire in the hall under small rubble, and snuffing all the candles and lamps. It was barely Compline, only just dark, but the young pair, quite full of each other now and cooing like doves, were happy enough to withdraw to their bed, and the others habitually fell asleep with the sun and awoke with it. Only in the store-room, showing a narrow chink of light downhill towards the kitchen, was there a candle still burning.

Rannilt had taken off neither shoes nor gown, but sat hugging herself for warmth and watching that meagre slit of light. When it was the only waking sign remaining, she got up and stole out across the few yards of hard-stamped earth between, and pressed herself against the narrow door that led into Susanna's chamber.

Her lady was there within awake, tireless, proud, going between her chamber and the store, hard at work as she had sworn, resolute to render account of every jar of honey, every grain of flour, every drop of oil or flake of fat. Rannilt burned and bled for her, but also she went in awe of her, she dared not go in and cry aloud her grief and indignation.

The steps that moved about within were soft, brisk and purposeful. All Susanna's movements were so, she did everything quickly, nothing in apparent haste, but now it did seem to Rannilt's anxious ear that there was something of bridled desperation about the way she took those few sharp paces here and there, about her last housewifely survey in this burgage. The slight went deep with her, as well it might.

The faint gleam of light vanished from the slit window of the store-room, and reappeared at the chink of the shutter of the bed-chamber. Rannilt heard the door between closed, and the key turned in the lock. Even on this last night Susanna would not sleep without first securing the safety of her charge. But surely now she had finished, and would go to her bed and take what rest she could.

The light went out. Rannilt froze into stillness in the listening silence, and after a long moment heard the inner door into the hall opened.

On the instant there was a sharp, brief sound, a subdued cry that was barely audible, but so charged with dismay and anger that Rannilt put a hand to the latch of the door against which she stood pressed, half in the desire to hold fast to something solid and familiar, half wishful to go in and see what could have provoked so desolate and frustrated a sound. The door gave to her touch. Distant within the hall she heard a voice, the words indistinguishable, but the grim tones unmistakably those of Dame Juliana. And Susanna's voice replying bitter and low. Two muted murmurs, full of resentment and conflict, but private as pillow confidences between man and wife.

Trembling, Rannilt pushed open the door, and crept across towards the open door into the hall, feeling her way in the dark. There was a feeble gleam of light high within the hall, it seemed to her to be shining from the head of the stairs. The old woman would not let anything happen in this house without prying and scolding. As though she had not done enough already, discarding her granddaughter and siding with the newcomer!

Susanna had half-closed the door of her room behind her, and Rannilt could see only the shadowy outline of her left side, from shoulder to hems, where she stood some three or four paces into the hall. But the voices had words now.

'Hush, speak low!' hissed the old woman, fiercely peremptory. 'No need to wake the sleepers. You and I are enough to be watching out the night.'

She must be standing at the head of the stairs, with her small night-lamp in one hand and shielded by the other, Rannilt judged. She did not want to rouse any other member of the household.

'One more, madam, than is needed!'

'Should I leave you lone to your task, and you still hard at work so late? Such diligence! So strict in your accounting, and so careful in your providing!'

'Neither you nor she, grandmother, shall be able to claim that I left one measure of flour or one drop of honey unaccounted for,' said Susanna bitingly.

'Nor one grain of oatmeal?' there was a small, almost stealthy quiver of laughter from the head of the stairs. 'Excellent housewifery, my girl, to find your crock still above half-full, and Easter already past! I give you your due, you have managed your affairs well.'

'I learned from you, grandmother.' Susanna had vanished from the chink of the door, taking a step towards the foot of the staircase. It seemed to Rannilt that she was now standing quite still, looking up at the old woman above her, and spitting her soft, bitter protest directly into the ancient face peering down at her in the dimness. What light the small lamp gave cast her shadow along the boards of the floor, a wide black barrier across the doorway. By the shape of the shadow, Susanna had wrapped her cloak about her, as well she might, working late in the chill of the night. 'It is at your orders, grandmother,' she said, low and clearly, 'that I am surrendering my affairs. What did you mean to do with me now? Had you still a place prepared for me? A nunnery, perhaps?'

The shadow across the door was suddenly convulsed, as though she had flung out her arms and spread the cloak wide.

After those bitterly discreet exchanges the screech that tore the silence was so terrifying that Rannilt forgot herself, and started forward, hurling the inner door wide and bursting into the hall. She saw Dame Juliana, at the head of the stairs, shaken and convulsed as the black shadow had been, the lamp tilting and dripping oil in her left hand, her right clutching and clawing at her breast. The mouth that had just uttered that dreadful shriek was wrenched sidelong, the cheek above drawn out of shape. All this Rannilt saw in one brief glimpse, before the old woman lurched forward and fell headlong down the stairs, to crash to the floor below, and the lamp, flying from her hand, spat a jet of burning oil along the boards at Susanna's feet, and went out.

Chapter Ten

Thursday night to Friday dawn

ANNILT SPRANG to smother the little serpent of fire that had caught something burnable and sent up a spurt of flame. Blindly, fumbling, her hands found the hard corner of a cloth-wrapped bundle, there on the floor near the wall, and beat out the fire that had caught at the fraying end of the cord that bound it. A few sparks floated and found splinters of wood, and she followed on her knees and quenched them with the hem of her skirt, and then it was quite dark. Not for long, for everyone in the house must be awake now; but for this moment, utterly dark. Rannilt groped about her blindly on the floor, trying to find where the old woman lay.

'Stay still,' and Susanna, in the gloom behind her. 'I'll make light.'

She was gone, quick and competent again as ever, back into her own room, where she could lay her hands instantly on flint and tinder, always ready by her bed. She came with a candle, and lit the oil-lamp in its bracket on the wall. Rannilt got up from her knees and darted to where Juliana lay on her face at the foot of the stairs. But Susanna was before her, kneeling beside her grandmother and running rapid hands over her in search of broken bones from her fall, before venturing to lift her over on to her back. Old bones are brittle, but it had not been a sheer fall, rather a rolling tumble from stair to stair.

126

Then they were all coming, clutching candles, gaping, crying questions, Daniel and Margery with one gown thrown hastily round the two of them, Walter bleared and querulous with sleep, Iestyn scurrying up the outdoor stairs from the undercroft and in by the rear door of Susanna's chamber, which Rannilt had left standing open. Light on light sprang up, the usual frugal rule forgotten.

They came crowding, demanding, incoherent with sleep, and alarm and bewilderment. The smoky flames and flickering shadows filled the hall with changing shapes that danced about the two figures quiet on the floorboards. What had happened? What was all the noise? What was the old woman doing out of her bed? Why the smell of burning? Who had done this?

Susanna slid an arm under her grandmother's body, cradled the grey head with her other palm, and turned her face-upward. She cast up at the clamouring circle of her kin one cold, glittering glance in which Rannilt saw, as none of them did, the scorn in which she held all the members of her family but this spent and broken one on her arm.

'Hold your noise, and make yourselves useful. Can you not see? She came out with her light to see how I was faring, and she took another seizure like the last, and fell, and the last it may very well be. Rannilt can tell you. Rannilt saw her fall.'

'I did,' said Rannilt, quivering. 'She dropped the lamp and caught at her breast, and then she fell. The oil spilled and took fire, I put it out ...' She looked towards the wall for the bundle, whatever it had been, that had offered an end of tow to the spark, but there was nothing there now. 'She's not dead ... look, she's breathing ... Listen!'

Certainly she was, for as soon as they hushed their clamour the air shook to her shallow-drawn, rattling breath. All one side of her face was dragged askew, the mouth grossly twisted, the eyes half-open and glaring whitely; and all her body on that side lay stiff as a board, the fingers of her hand contorted and rigid.

Susanna looked round them all, and made her dispositions, and no one now challenged her right. 'Father and Daniel, carry her to her bed. She has no broken bones, she feels nothing. We cannot give her any of her draught, she could not swallow it. Margery, feed the little brazier in the room. I will get a wine to mull for when she revives – if she does revive.'

She looked over Rannilt's shoulder to Iestyn, standing dumb and at a loss in the shadows. Her face was as set as marble and

127

as cold, but her eyes shone clear. 'Run to the abbey,' she said. 'Ask for Brother Cadfael to come to her. Sometimes he works late, if he has medicines making. But even if he has gone to his cell, the porter will call him. He said he would come if he was needed. He is needed now.'

Iestyn looked back at her without a word, and then turned as silently as he had come and ran as she had bade him.

It was not so late as all that. At the abbey the dortoir was still half awake, an uneasy stirring in certain cells, where the brothers found sleep difficult or remembrance all too strong. Brother Cadfael, having stayed late in his workshop to pound herbs for a decoction to be made next day, was just at his private prayers before sleep when the porter came edging along the passage between the cells to find him. He rose at once, and went silently down the night stairs and through the church to confer with the messenger at the gatehouse.

'The old dame, is it?' He had no need to fetch anything from the herbarium, the best of what he could give her was already supplied and Susanna knew how to use it, if its use was still of any avail. 'We'd best hurry, then, if it's so grave.'

He set a sharp pace along the Foregate and over the bridge, and asked such questions as were necessary as they went.

'How did she come to be up and active at this hour? And how did this fit come on?'

Iestyn kept station at his side and answered shortly. He had never many words to spare. 'Mistress Susanna was up late seeing to her stores, for she's forced to give up her keys. And Dame Juliana rose up, belike, to see what she was still about. The fit took her at the top of the stairs and she fell.'

'But the seizure came first? And caused the fall?'

'So the women say.'

'The women?'

'The maid was there and saw it.'

'What's her state now, then? The old dame? Has she bones broken? Can she move freely?'

'The mistress says nothing broken, but one side of her is stiff as a tree, and her face drawn all on a skew.'

They were let in at the town gate without question. Cadfael occasionally had much later errands and was well known. They climbed the steep curve of the Wyle in silence, the gradient making demands on their breath.

'I warned her the last time,' said Cadfael, when the slope

128

eased, 'that if she did not keep her rages in check the next fit might be the last. She was well in command of herself and all about her this morning, for all the mischief that was brewing in the house, but I had my doubts … What can have upset her tonight?'

But if Iestyn had any answer to that, he kept it to himself. A taciturn man, who did his work and kept his own counsel.

Walter was hopping about uneasily at the entrance to the passage, watching for them with a horn lantern in his hand. Daniel was huddled into his gown in the hall, with the spendthrift candles still burning unheeded around him, until Walter entered with the newcomers, and having seen them within, suddenly became aware of gross waste, and began to go round and pinch out two out of three, leaving the smell of their hot wicks on the air.

'We carried her up to bed,' said Daniel, restless and wretched in this upheaval that disrupted his new content. 'The women are there with her. Go up, they're anxious for you.' And he followed, drawn to a trouble that must be resolved before he could take any comfort, and hovered in the doorway of the sick-chamber, but did not step within. Iestyn remained at the foot of the stairs. In all the years of service here, most likely, he had never climbed them.

A brazier burned in an iron basket set upon a wide stone, and a small lamp on a shelf jutting out from the wall. Here in the upper rooms there were no ceilings, the rooms went up into the vault of the roof, dark wood on all sides and above. On one side of the narrow bed Margery, mute and pale, drew hastily back into the shadows to let Brother Cadfael come close. On the other, Susanna stood erect and still, and her head turned only momentarily to ascertain who it was who came.

Cadfael sank to his knees beside the bed. Juliana was alive, and if one sense had been snatched from her, the others she still had, at least for a brief while. In the contorted face the ancient eyes were alive, alert and resigned. They met Cadfael's and knew him. The grimace could almost have been her old, sour smile. 'Send Daniel for her priest,' said Cadfael after one look at her, and without conceal. 'His errand here is more now than mine.' She would appreciate that. She knew she was dying.

He looked up at Susanna. No question now who held the mastery here; no matter how they tore each other, she of all these was Juliana's blood, kin and match. 'Has she spoken?'

'No. Not a word.' Yes, she even looked as this woman must have looked fifty years ago as a comely, resolute, able matron, married to a man of lesser fibre than her own. Her voice was low, steady and cool. She had done what could be done for the dying woman, and stood waiting for whatever broken words might fall from that broken mouth. She even leaned to wipe away the spittle that ran from its deformed lips at the downward corner.

'Have the priest come, for I am none. She is already promised our prayers, that she knows.' And that was for her, to ensure that she was alive within this dead body, and need not regret all her gifts to the abbey, doled out so watchfully. Her faded eyes had still a flash within them; she understood. Wherever she was gone, she knew what was said and done about her. But she had said no word, not even attempted speech.

Margery had stolen thankfully out of the room, to send her husband for the priest. She did not come back. Walter was below, pinching out candles and fretting over the few that must remain. Only Cadfael on one side of the bed and Susanna on the other kept watch still by Dame Juliana's death.

The old woman's live eyes in her dead carcase clung to Cadfael's face, yet not, he thought, trying to convey to him anything but her defiant reliance on her own resources. When had she not been mistress of her own household? And these were still her family, no business of any other judge. Those outside must stay outside. This monk whom she had grown to respect and value, for all their differences, she admitted half-way, close enough to know and acknowledge her rights of possession. Her twisted mouth suddenly worked, emitted an audible sound, looked for a moment like a mouth that might speak memorable things. Cadfael stooped his ear close to her lips.

A laborious murmur, indistinguishable, and then: 'It was I bred them ...' she said thickly, and again struggled with incommunicable thoughts, and rested with a rattling sigh. A tremor passed through her rigid body. A thread of utterance emerged almost clearly: 'But for all that ... I should have liked to hold ... my great-grandchild ...'

Cadfael had barely raised his head when she closed her eyes. No question but it was by her will they closed, no crippling weakness. But for the priest, she had done.

Even with the priest she did not speak again. She bore with his

130

urgings, and made the effort to respond with her eyelids when he made his required probings into her sense of sin and need and hope for absolution. She died as soon as he had pronounced it, or only moments later.

Susanna stood by her to the end and never uttered a word. When all was done, she stooped and kissed the leather cheek and chilling brow somewhat better than dutifully, and still with that face of marble calm. Then she went down to see Brother Cadfael courteously out of the house, and thank him for all his attentions to the dead.

'She gave you, I know, more work than ever she repaid you for,' said Susanna, with the slight, bitter curl to her lips and the wry serenity in her voice.

'And is it you who tells me so?' he said, and watched the hollows at the corners of her lips deepen. 'I came to have a certain reverence for her, short of affection. Not that she ever required that of me. And you?'

Susanna stepped from the bottom stair, close to where Rannilt huddled against the wall, afraid to trespass, unwilling to abandon her devoted watch. Since Susanna had emerged from her room with the light, her cloak shed within now there was work to do, Rannilt had hovered attentive, waiting to be used.

'I doubt,' said Brother Cadfael, considering, 'whether there was any here who loved her half so well as you.'

'Or hated her half so well,' said Susanna, lifting her head with one measured flash of grey eyes.

'The two are often bed-fellows,' he said, unperturbed. 'You need not question either.'

'I will not. Now I must go back to her. She is my charge, I'll pay her what's due.' She looked round and said quite gently: 'Rannilt, take Master Walter's lantern, and light Brother Cadfael out. Then go to your bed, there is no more for you to do here.'

'I'd rather stay and watch with you,' said Rannilt timidly. 'You'll need hot water and cloths, and a hand to lift her, and to run errands for you.' As if there were not enough of them, up there now about the bed, son, grandson, and grandson's woman, and how much grief among the lot of them? For Dame Juliana had outstayed her time by a number of years and was one mouth less to feed once her burial was accomplished; not to speak of the whiplash tongue and the too-sharp eye removed from vexing.

'So you may, then,' said Susanna, gazing long upon the small, childlike figure regarding her with great eyes from the shadows, where Walter had quenched all but one candle, but inadvertently left his lantern burning. 'You shall sleep tomorrow in the day, you'll be ready then for your bed and your mind quiet. Come up, when you've shown Brother Cadfael out to the lane. You and I will care for her together.'

'You were there?' asked Cadfael mildly, walking on the girl's heels along the pitch-dark passage. 'You saw what happened?'

'Yes, sir. I couldn't sleep. You were there this morning when they all turned against her, and even the old woman said she must yield her place ... You know ...'

'I know, yes. And you were aggrieved for her.'

'She – was never unkind to me ...' How was it possible to say that Susanna had been kind, where the chill forbade any such word? 'It was not fair that they should turn and elbow her out, like that.'

'And you were watching and listening, and grieving. And you went in. When was that?'

She told him, as plainly as if she lived it again. She told him, as far as she could recall it, and that was almost word for word, what she had heard pass between grandmother and grandchild, and how she had heard the shriek that heralded the old woman's seizure, and burst in to see her panting and swaying and clutching her bosom, the lamp tilting out of her hand, before she rolled headlong down the stairs.

'And there was no other soul stirring then? No one within hand's-touch of her, there above?'

'Oh no, no one. She dropped the lamp just as she fell.' The little snake of fire, spitting sparks and sudden leaping flame as it found the end of tow, seemed to Rannilt to have nothing to do with what happened. 'And then it was dark, and the mistress said keep still, and went for a light.'

Certain, then, yes, quite certain she fell. No one was there to help her fall, the only witnesses were below. And if they had not gone to her aid at once, and sent as promptly for him, he would never have arrived here in time to see Dame Juliana die. Let alone hear the only words she had spoken before dying. For what they were worth! 'I bred them all ... For all that, I should have liked to hold my great-grandchild ...'

Well, her grandson, the only being she was reported to dote upon was now a husband, her proud old mind might well strain

132

forward to embrace a future generation.

'No, don't come out into the lane, child, time for you to be withindoors, and I know my way.'

She went, shy, wild and silent. And Cadfael made his way back thoughtfully to his own cell in the dortoir and took what comfort he might, and what enlightenment, but it was not much. In this death, at least, there was no question of foul play. Juliana had fallen when no other person was near by, and in an unquestionable seizure such as she had suffered twice before. The dissensions within the house, moreover, had broken out in a disturbing form that same day, cause enough for an old woman's body and heart and irascible nature to fail her. The wonder was this had not happened earlier. Yet for all he could do, Cadfael's mind could not separate this death from the first, nor that from the felony of which Liliwin stood accused. There was, there must be, a thread that linked them all together. Not by freakish chance was an ordinary burgess household thus suddenly stricken with blow after blow. A human hand had set off the chain; from that act all these later events stemmed, and where the impetus would finally run out and the sequence of fatalities end was a speculation that kept Cadfael awake half the night.

In Dame Juliana's death chamber the single lamp burned, a steady eye of fire, at the head of the bed. The night hung deep and silent over the town, past the mid-point between dusk and dawn. On a stool on one side Susanna sat, her own hands folded in her lap, quiet at last. Rannilt crouched at the foot of the bed, very weary but unwilling to go to her humble place, and certain that sleep would not come to her if she did. The lofty timbers of the roof soared above them into deep darkness. The three women, two living and one dead, were drawn together into a close, mute intimacy, for these few hours islanded from the world.

Juliana lay straight and austere, her grey hair combed into smooth order, her face uncovered, the sheet folded at her chin. Already the contortion was beginning to ease out of her features, and leave her at peace.

Neither of the two who watched beside her had spoken a word since their work was finished. Susanna had made no bones about dismissing Margery's reluctant offer of help, and had no difficulty in getting rid of all three of her kin. They were not sorry to return to their beds and leave all to her. Mistress and maid had the vigil to themselves.

'You're cold,' said Rannilt, breaking the silence very softly as she saw Susanna shiver. 'Shall I fetch up your cloak? You felt the want of it even about the store, when you were on the move, and now we sit here, and the night chiller than then. I'll creep down for it.'

'No,' said Susanna absently. 'It was a goose walking over my grave. I'm warm enough.' She turned her head and gave the girl a long, sombre stare. 'Were you so vexed for me that you must wake and watch into the night with me? I thought you came very quickly. Did you see and hear all?'

Rannilt trembled at the thought of having intruded uninvited, but Susanna's voice was equable and her face calm. 'No. I wasn't listening, but some part I couldn't help hearing. She praised your providing. Perhaps she was sorry then ... It was strange she should take to thinking on such things, and suddenly take pride that you should still have the oatmeal crock above half-full ... That I heard. Surely she was sorry in the end that you should be so misprised. She thought better of you than of any other.'

'She was returning to the days when she ruled all,' said Susanna, 'and had all on her shoulders, as I have had. The old go back, before the end.' Her eyes, large and intent upon Rannilt's face, gleamed in the dim, reflected light from the lamp. 'You've burned your hand,' she said. 'I'm sorry.'

'It's nothing,' said Rannilt, removing her hands hurriedly from sight into her lap. 'I was clumsy. The tow flared. It doesn't hurt.'

'The tow...?'

'Tied round the bundle that was lying there. It had a frayed end and took the flame before I was aware.'

'A pity!' said Susanna, and sat silent for some moments, watching her grandmother's dead face. The corners of her lips curved briefly in what hardly had time to become a smile. 'There was a bundle there, was there? And I was wearing my cloak ... yes! You noticed much, considering the fright we must have given you, between us.'

In the prolonged silence Rannilt watched her lady's face and went in great awe, having trodden where she had no right to go, and feeling herself detected in a trespass she had never intended.

'And now you are wondering what was in that bundle, and where it vanished to before ever we began lighting candles. Along with my cloak!' Susanna fixed her austere, half-smiling

134

regard upon Rannilt's daunted face. 'It is only natural you should wonder.'

'Are you angry with me?' ventured Rannilt in a whisper.

'No. Why should I be angry? I believe, I do believe, you have sometimes felt for me as a woman for a woman. Is that true, Rannilt?'

'This morning ...' faltered Rannilt, half-afraid, 'I could not choose but grieve ...'

'I know. You have seen how I am despised here.' She went very gently and quietly, a woman speaking with a child, but a child whose understanding she valued. 'How I have always been despised. My mother died, my grandmother grew old, I was of value until my brother should take a wife. Yes, but barely a day longer. All those years gone for nothing, and I am left here husbandless and barren and out of office.'

There was another silence, for though Rannilt felt her breast bursting with indignant sympathy, her tongue was frozen into silence. In the lofty darkness of the roof-beams the faint, soft light quivered in a passing draught.

'Rannilt,' said Susanna gravely and softly, 'can you keep a secret?'

'Your secret I surely can,' whispered Rannilt.

'Swear never to breathe a word to any other, and I'll tell you what no one else knows.'

Rannilt breathed her vow devotedly, flattered and warmed at having such trust placed in her.

'And will you help me in what I mean to undertake? For I should welcome your help ... I need your help!

'I'll do anything in my power for you.' No one had ever expected or required of her such loyalty, no one had ever considered her as better than menial and impotent, no wonder her heart responded.

'I believe and trust you.' Susanna leaned forward into the light. 'My bundle and my cloak I made away out of sight before I brought the candle, and hid them in my bedchamber. Tonight, Rannilt, but for this mortal stay, I meant to leave this place, to quit this house that has never done me right, and this town in which I have no honourable place. Tonight God prevented. But tomorrow night ... tomorrow night I am going! If you will help me I can take with me more of my poor possessions than I can carry the first short piece of the way alone. Come nearer, child, and I'll tell you.' Her voice was very low and soft, a confiding breath in Rannilt's ear. 'Across

135

the bridge, at my father's stable beyond Frankwell, someone who sets a truer value on me will be waiting ...'

Chapter Eleven

Friday, from morning to late evening

USANNA CAME to the table as the subdued household assembled next morning, with the keys at her girdle, and with deliberation unfastened the fine chain that held them, and laid them before Margery.

'These are now yours, sister, as you wished. From today the management of this house belongs to you, and I will not meddle.'

She was pale and heavy-eyed from a sleepless night, though none of them were in much better case. They would all be glad to make an early night of it as soon as the day's light failed, to make up for lost rest.

'I'll come round kitchen and store with you this morning, and show you what you have in hand, and the linen, and everything I'm handing over to you. And I wish you well,' she said.

Margery was almost out of countenance at such magnanimity, and took pains to be conciliatory as she was conducted remorselessly round her new domain.

'And now,' said Susanna, shaking off that duty briskly from her shoulders, 'I must go and bring Martin Bellecote to see about her coffin, and father will be off to visit the priest at Saint Mary's. But then – you'll hold me excused – I should like to get a little sleep, and so must the girl there, for neither of us has closed an eye.'

137

'I'll manage well enough alone,' said Margery, 'and take care not to disturb you in that chamber today. If I may take out what's needed for the dinner now, then you can get your rest.' She was torn between humility and exultation. Having death in the house was no pleasure, but the gloom would lie heavy for only a few days, and then she was rid of all barriers to her own plans, free of the old, censorious eyes watching and disparaging her best efforts, free of this ageing virgin, who would surely absent herself from all participation in the running of the house hereafter, and mistress of a tamed husband who would dance henceforth to her piping.

Brother Cadfael spent the early part of that afternoon in the herb-garden, and having seen everything left in order there, went out to view the work along the Gaye. The weather continued sunny and warm, and the urchins of the town and the Foregate, born and bred by the water and swimmers almost before they could walk, were in and out of the shallows, and the bolder and stronger among them even venturing across where the Severn ran smoothly. The spring spate from the mountains was over now, the river showed a bland face, but these water-children knew its tricks, and seldom trusted it too far.

Cadfael walked through the flowering orchard, very uneasy in his mind after the night's alarms, and continued downstream until he stood somewhere opposite the gardens of the burgages along the approach to the castle. Halfway up the slope the tall stone barrier of the town wall crossed, its crest crumbled into disrepair in places, not yet restored after the rigours of the siege two years ago. Within his vision it was pierced by two narrow, arched doorways, easily barred in dangerous times. One of the two must be in the Aurifaber grounds, but he could not be sure which. Below the wall the greensward shone fresh and vivid, and the trees were in pale young leaf and snowy flower. The alders leaned over the shallows lissome and rosy with catkins. Willow withies shone gold and silver with the fur-soft flowers. So sweet and hopeful a time to be threatening a poor young man with hanging or bludgeoning a single household with loss and death.

The boys of the Foregate and the boys of the town were rivals by tradition, carrying into casual warfare the strong local feeling of their sires. Their water-games sometimes became rough, though seldom dangerous, and if one rash spirit

138

overstepped the mark, there was usually an older and wiser ally close by, to clout him off and haul his victim to safety. There was some horseplay going on in the shallows opposite as Cadfael watched. An imp of the Foregate had ventured the crossing, plunged into a frolic of town children before they were aware, and ducked one of them spluttering below the surface. The whole incensed rout closed on him and pursued him some way downstream, until he splashed ashore up a slope of grass to escape them, falling flat in the shallows in his haste, and clawing and scrambling clear in a flurry of spray. From a smooth greensward where he certainly had no right to be, he capered and crowed at them as they drew off and abandoned the chase.

It seemed that he had fished something up with him out of the shallow water and gravel under the bushes. He sat down and scrubbed at it in his palm, intent and curious. He was still busy with it when another boy hardly older than himself came naked out of the orchard above, dropping his shirt into the grass, and trotting down towards the water. He saw the intruder, and checked at gaze, staring.

The distance was not so great but Cadfael knew him, and knew, in consequence, at whose extended burgage he was looking. Thirteen years old, well-grown and personable; Baldwin Peche's simpleton boy, Griffin, let loose from his labours for an hour to run down through the wicket in the wall, and swim in the river like other boys.

Griffin had seen, far better than Cadfael across the river could hope to see, whatever manner of trophy the impudent invader from the Foregate had discovered in the shallows. He let out an indignant cry, and came running down the grass to snatch at the cupped hand. Something dropped, briefly glinting, into the turf, and Griffin fell upon it like a hawk swooping and caught it up jealously. The other boy, startled, leaped to his feet and made to grab at it in his turn, but gave back before a taller challenger. He was not greatly disturbed at losing his toy. There was some exchange, light-hearted on his side, slow and sober on Griffin's. The two youthful voices floated light, excited sounds across the water. The Foregate urchin shrilled some parting insult, dancing backwards towards the river, jumped in with a deliberate splash, and struck out for his home waters, sudden and silvery as a trout.

Cadfael moved alertly to where the child must come ashore, but kept one eye on the slope opposite also, and saw how

139

Griffin, instead of plunging in after his repulsed rival, went back to lay his trophy carefully in the folds of the shirt he had discarded by the bushes. Then he slid down the bank and waded out into the water, and lay face-down upon the current in so expert and easy a fashion that it was plain he had been a swimmer from infancy. He was rolling and playing in the eddies when the other boy hauled himself ashore into the grass of Cadfael's bank, shedding water and glowing from his play, and began to caper and clap his arms about his slender body in the sunny air. Grown men would hardly be trying that water for a month or so yet, but the young have energy enough to keep them warm, and as old men tend to say tolerantly, where there's no sense there's no feeling.

'Well, troutling,' said Cadfael, knowing this imp as soon as he drew close, 'what was that you fished out of the mud over yonder? I saw you take to the land. Not many yards ahead of the vengeance, either! You picked the wrong haven.'

The boy had aimed expertly for the place where he had left his clothes. He darted for his cotte, and slung it round his nakedness, grinning. 'I'm not afeared of all the town hobbledehoys. Nor of that big booby of the locksmith's, neither, but he's welcome to his bit of trumpery. Knew it for his master's, he said! Just a little round piece, with a man's head on it with a beard and a pointed hat. Nothing to fall out over.'

'Besides, that Griffin is bigger than you,' said Cadfael.

The imp made a scornful face, and having scrubbed his feet and ankles through the soft grass, and slapped his thighs dry, set to work to wriggle into his hose. 'But slow, and hasn't all his wits. What was the thing doing drifted under the gravel in the water there, if there was any good in it? He can have it for me!'

And he was off at an energetic run to rejoin his friends, leaving Cadfael very thoughtful. A coin silted into the gravel under the bank there, where the river made a shallow cove, and clawed up in the fist of a scrambling urchin who happened to sprawl on his face there in evading pursuit. Nothing so very strange in that. All manner of things might turn up in the waters of Severn, queerer things than a lost coin. All that made it notable was that this one should turn up in that particular place. Too many cobweb threads were tangling around the Aurifaber burgage, nothing that occurred there could any longer be taken as ordinary or happening by chance. And what to make of all these unrelated strands was more than Cadfael could yet see.

140

He went back to his seedlings, which at least were innocent of any mystery, and worked out the rest of the afternoon until it drew near the time to return for Vespers; but there was still a good half-hour in hand when he was hailed from the river, and looked round to see Madog rowing upstream, and crossing the main current to come to shore where Cadfael was standing. He had abandoned his coracle for a light skiff, quite capable, as Cadfael reflected with a sudden inspiration, of ferrying an inquisitive brother across to take a look for himself at that placid inlet where the boy had dredged up the coin of which he thought so poorly.

Madog brought his boat alongside, and held it by an oar dug into the soft turf of the bank. 'Well, Brother Cadfael, I hear the old dame's gone, then. Trouble broods round that house. They tell me you were there to see her set out.'

Cadfael owned it. 'After fourscore years I wonder if death should be accounted troublous. But yes, she's gone. Before midnight she left them.' Whether with a blessing or a curse, or only a grim assertion of her dominance over them and defence of them, loved or unloved, was something he had been debating in his own mind. For she could have spoken, but had said only what she thought fit to say, nothing to the point. The disputes of the day, surely relevant, she had put clean away. They were her people. Whatever needed judgement and penance among them was her business, no concern of the world outside. And yet those few enigmatic words she had deliberately let him hear. Him, her opponent, physician and – was friend too strong a word? To her priest she had responded only with the suggested movements of her eyelids saying yea and nay, confessing to frailties, agreeing to penitence, desiring absolution. But no words.

'Left them at odds,' said Madog shrewdly, his seamed oak face breaking into a wry smile. 'When have they been anything else? Avarice is a destroying thing, Cadfael, and she bred them all in her own shape, all get and precious little give.'

'I bred them all,' she had said, as though she admitted a guilt to which her eyelids had said neither yea nor nay for the priest.

'Madog,' said Cadfael, 'row me over to the bank under their garden, and as we go I'll tell you why. They hold the strip outside the wall down to the waterside. I'd be glad to have a look there.'

'Willingly!' Madog drew the skiff close. 'For I've been up and down this river from the water-gate, where Peche kept his boat, trying to find any man who can give me word of seeing it or him after the morning of last Monday, and never a glimpse anywhere. And I doubt Hugh Beringar has done better enquiring in the town after every fellow who knew the locksmith, and every tavern he ever entered. Come inboard, then, and sit yourself down steady, she rides a bit deeper and clumsier with two aboard.'

Cadfael slid down the overhanging slope of grass, stepped nimbly upon the thwart, and sat. Madog thrust off and turned into the current. 'Tell, then! What is there over there to draw you?'

Cadfael told him what he had witnessed, and in the telling it did not seem much. But Madog listened attentively enough, one eye on the surface eddies of the river, running bland and playful now, the other, as it seemed, on some inward vision of the Aurifaber household from old matriarch to new bride.

'So that's what's caught your fancy! Well, whatever it may mean, here's the place. That Foregate lad left his marks, look where he hauled his toes up after him, and the turf so moist and tender.'

A quiet and almost private place it was, once the skiff was drawn in until its shallow draught gravelled. A little inlet where the water lay placid, clean speckled gravel under it, and even in that clear bottom the boy's clutching hands had left small indentations. Out of one of those hollows – the right hand, Cadfael recalled – the small coin had come, and he had brought it ashore with him to examine at leisure. Withies of both willow and alder grew out from the very edge of the water on either side of the plane of grass which opened out above into a broad green slope, steep enough to drain readily, smooth enough to provide an airy cushion for bleaching linen. Only from across the river could this ground be viewed, on this town shore it was screened both ways by the bushes. Clean, washed, white pebbles, some of considerable size, had been piled inshore of the bushes for weighting down the linens spread here to dry on washing days when the weather was favourable. Cadfael eyed them and noted the one larger stone, certainly fallen from the town wall, which had not their water-smoothed polish, but showed sharp corners and clots of mortar still adhering. Left here as it had rolled from the crest, perhaps used sometimes for tying up boats in the shallows.

'D'you see aught of use to you?' asked Madog, holding his skiff motionless with an oar braced into the gravel. The boy

Griffin had long since enjoyed his bathe, dried and clothed himself, and carried away his reclaimed coin to the locksmith's shop where John Boneth now presided. He had known John for a long time as second only to his master; for him John was now his master in succession.

'All too much!' said Cadfael.

There were the boy' traces, clutching hands under the clear water, scrabbling toes above in the grass. Down here he had found his trophy, above he had sat to burnish and examine it, and had it snatched from him by Griffin, who knew it as his master's, and was honest as only the simple can be. Here all round the boat the withies crowded, there above in the sward lay the pile of heavy pebbles and the fallen stone. Here swaying alongside danced the little rafts of water-crowfoot, under the leaning alders. And most ominous of all, here in the sloping grass verge, within reach of his hand, not one, but three small heads of reddish purple blossoms stood up bravely in the grass, the fox-stones for which they had hunted in vain downstream.

The piled pebbles and the one rough stone meant nothing as yet to Madog, but the little spires of purple blossoms certainly held his eyes. He looked from them to Cadfael's face, and back to the sparkling shallow where a man could not well drown, if he was in his senses.

'Is *this* the place?'

The fragile, shivering white rafts of crowfoot danced under the alders, delicately anchored. The little grooves left by the boy's fingers very gradually shifted and filled, the motes of sand and gravel sliding down in the quiver of water to fill them. 'Here at the foot of their own land?' said Madog, shaking his head. 'Is it certain? I've found no other place where this third witness joins the other two.'

'Under the certainty of Heaven,' said Cadfael soberly, 'Nothing is ever quite certain, but this is as near as a man can aim. Had he stolen and been found out? Or had he found out too much about the one who *had* stolen, and was fool enough to let it be known what he knew? God sort all! Ferry me back now, Madog, I must hurry back to Vespers.'

Madog took him, unquestioning, except that he kept his deep-browed and sharp-sighted old eyes fixed on Cadfael's face all the way across to the Gaye.

'You're going now to render account to Hugh Beringar at the castle?' asked Cadfael.

'At his own house, rather. Though I doubt if he'll be there yet to expect me.'

'Tell him all that we have seen there,' said Cadfael very earnestly. 'Let him look for himself, and make what he can of it. Tell him of the coin – for so I am sure it was – that was dredged up out of the cove there, and how Griffin claimed it for his master's property. Let Hugh question him on that.'

'I'll tell him all,' said Madog, 'and more than I understand.'

'Or I, either, as yet. But ask him, if his time serves for it, to come down and speak with me, when he has made what he may of all this coil. For I shall be worrying from this moment at the same tangle and may, who knows? – God aiding! – may arrive at some understanding before night.'

Hugh came late home from his dogged enquiries round the town which had brought him no new knowledge, unless their cumulative effect turned probability into certainty, and it could now be called knowledge that no one, in his familiar haunts or out of them, had set eyes on Baldwin Peche since Monday noon. News of Dame Juliana's death added nothing, she being so old, and yet there was always the uncomfortable feeling that misfortune could not of itself have concentrated such a volley of malice against one household. What Madog had to tell him powerfully augmented this pervading unease.

'There within call of his own shop? Is it possible? And all present, the alders, the crowfoot, the purple flower ... Everything comes back, everything comes home, to that burgage. Begin wherever we may, we end there.'

'That is truth,' said Madog. 'And Brother Cadfael is cudgelling his wits over the same tangle, and would be glad to consider it along with you, my lord, if you can spare him the needed hour tonight, however late.'

'I'll do that thankfully,' said Hugh, 'for God knows it wants more cunning that I have alone, and sharper vision, to see through this murk. Do you go home and get your rest, Madog, for you've done well by us. And I'll go knock up Peche's lad, and have out of him whatever he can tell us about this coin he claims for his master's.'

By this same hour Brother Cadfael had eased his own mind by imparting, after supper, all that he had discovered to Abbot Radulfus, who received it with thoughtful gravity.

'And you have sent word already to Hugh Beringar? You

144

think he may wish to take counsel with you further in the matter?' He was well aware that there was a particular understanding between them, originating in events before he himself took office at Shrewsbury. 'You may take whatever time you need if he comes tonight. Certainly this affair must be concluded as soon as possible, and it does increasingly appear that our guest in sanctuary may have very little to do with any of these offences. He is within here, but the evil continues without. If he is innocent of all, in justice that must be shown to the world.'

Cadfael left the abbot's lodging with time still for hard thought, and the twilight just falling. He went faithfully to Compline and then, turning his back on the dortoir, went out to the porch where Liliwin spread his blankets and made his bed. The young man was still wide awake, sitting with his knees drawn up and his back braced comfortably into the corner of the stone bench, a small, hunched shadow in the darkness, singing over to himself the air of a song he was making and had not yet completed to his satisfaction. He broke off when Cadfael appeared, and made room beside him on his blankets.

'A good tune, that,' said Cadfael, settling himself with a sigh. 'Yours? You'd best keep it to yourself, or Anselm will be stealing it for the ground of a Mass.'

'It is not ready yet,' said Liliwin. 'There lacks a proper soft fall for the ending. It is a love song for Rannilt.' He turned his head to look his companion earnestly in the eyes. 'I *do* love her. I'll brave it out here and hang rather than go elsewhere without her.'

'She would hardly be grateful to you for that,' said Cadfael. 'But God willing you shall not have to make any such choice.' The boy himself, though he still went in suspense and some fear, was well aware that every day now cast further doubt upon the case against him. 'Things move there without, if in impenetrable ways. To tell truth, the law is coming round very sensibly to my opinion of you.'

'Well, maybe ... But what if they found that I did leave here that night? They wouldn't believe my story as you did ...' He cast a doubtful glance at Brother Cadfael, and saw something in the bland stare that met him that caused him to demand in alarm: 'You haven't told the sheriff's deputy? You promised ... for Rannilt's sake ...'

'Never fret, Rannilt's good name is as safe with Hugh

145

Beringar as with me. He has not even called on her as a witness for you, nor will not unless the affair goes to the length of trial. Tell him? Well, so I did, but only after he had made it plain he guessed the half. His nose for a reluctant liar is at least as keen as mine, he never believed that "No" he wrung out of you. So the rest of it he wrung out of me. He found you more convincing telling truth than lying. And then there is always Rannilt, if ever you need her witness, and the watchmen who saw you pass in and out. No need to trouble too much about *your* doings that night. I wish I knew as much about everyone else's.' He pondered, conscious of Liliwin's intent and trusting regard. 'There's nothing more you've recalled? The smallest detail concerning that house may be of help.'

Hesitantly Liliwin cast his mind back, and told over again the brief story of his connection with the goldsmith's house. The host at a tavern where he had played and sung for his supper had told him of the marriage to be celebrated next day, he had gone there hopefully, and been engaged for the occasion, he had done his best to earn his money and been cast out, and hunted as a thief and murderer here into the church. All of it known already.

'How much of that burgage did you ever see? For you went first in daylight.'

'I went to the shop and they sent me in through the passage to the hall door, to the women. It was they who hired me, the old woman and the young one.'

'And in the evening?'

'Why, as soon as I came there they sent me to eat with Rannilt in the kitchen, and I was there with her until they sent out for me to come and play and sing while they feasted, and afterwards I played for dancing, and did my acrobatics, and juggled – and you know how it ended.'

'So you never saw more than the passage and the yard. You never were down the length of the garden, or through the town wall there to the waterside?'

Liliwin shook his head firmly. 'I didn't even know it went beyond the wall until the day Rannilt came here. I could see as far as the wall when I went through to the hall in the morning, but I thought it ended there. It was Rannilt told me the drying-ground was beyond there. It was their washing day, you see, she'd done all the scrubbing and rinsing, and had it all ready to go out by mid-morning. But usually she has the dinner to prepare as well, and watches the weather, and fetches the

146

clothes in before evening. But that day Mistress Susanna had said she would see to everything, and let Rannilt come here to visit me. That was truly kind!'

Strange how sitting here listening to the boy's recollections brought up clearly the picture of that drying-ground he had never seen but through Rannilt's eyes, the slope of grass, the pebbles for anchors, the alders screening the riverside, the town wall shielding the sward from the north and leaving it open to the south ...

'And I remember she said Mistress Susanna had her shoes and hems of her skirts wet when she came in from putting out the washing and found Rannilt crying. But still she took note first for my girl being so sad ... Never mind my wet feet, she said, what of your wet eyes? Rannilt told me so!'

All ready to go out by mid-morning ... As Baldwin Peche had gone out in mid-morning for the last time. The fish rising ... Cadfael, away pursuing his own thoughts, suddenly baulked, realising, belatedly, what he had heard.

'What was that you said? She had her feet and skirts wet?'

'The river was a little high then,' explained Liliwin, undisturbed. 'She'd slipped on the smooth grass into the shallows. Hanging out a shirt on the alders ...'

And she came in calmly, and sent the maidservant away so that none other but herself should go to bring in the linen. What other reason would any have for passing through the wicket in the wall? And only yesterday Rannilt had been sitting in the doorway to have the light on her work, mending a rent in the skirt of a gown. And the brown at the hem had been mottled and faded, leaving a tide-mark of dark colour round the pallor ...

'Brother Cadfael,' called the porter softly from the archway into the cloister, 'Hugh Beringar is here for you. He said you would be expecting him.'

'I am expecting him,' said Cadfael, recalling himself with an effort from the Aurifaber hall. 'Bid him come through here. I think we have word for each other.'

It was not quite dark, the sky being so clear, and Hugh knew his way everywhere within these walls. He came briskly, made no objection to Liliwin's presence, and sat down at once in the porch to show the silver coin in his palm.

'I've already viewed it in a better light. It's a silver penny of the sainted Edward, king before the Normans came, a

147

beautiful piece minted in this town. The moneyer was one Godesbrond, there are a few of his pieces to be found, but few indeed in the town where they were struck. Aurifaber's inventory listed three such. And this was stuck between the boards of the bucket in their well the morning after the theft. A scrap of coarse blue cloth, the lad says, was caught in with it, but he thought nothing of that. But it seems to me that whoever emptied Aurifaber's coffer tipped all into a blue cloth bag and dropped it into that bucket – the work of a mere few moments – to be retrieved later at leisure in the dark hours, before the earliest riser went to draw water.'

'And whoever hoisted it out again,' said Cadfael, 'snagged a corner of the bag on a splinter ... a small tear, just enough to let through one of the smaller coins. It could be so. And Peche's boy had found this?'

'He *was* the earliest riser. He went to draw water and lit on this. He took it to his master, and was rewarded, and told not to let it out to any other ears that the locksmith possessed any such. A great value, Peche said, he set on this.'

So he well might, if it meant to him that someone there in that very household must be the thief, and could be milked of the half of his gains in return for silence. The fish were rising! Now Cadfael began gradually to comprehend all that had happened. He forgot the young man hugging his knees and stretching his amazed ears in the corner of the bench close to them. Hugh had hardly given the boy a thought, so silent and so still he was.

'I think,' said Cadfael, picking his way without too much haste, for there might yet be pitfalls, 'that when he saw this he knew, or could divine with very fair certainty, which of that household must be the robber. He foresaw good pickings. What would he ask? A half-share in the booty? But it would not have made any difference had he been far more modest than that, for the one he approached had the force and the passion and the ruthlessness to act at once and waste no time on parley. Listen to me, Hugh, and remember that night. They sought Master Walter, found him stunned in his shop, and carried him up to his bed. And then someone – no one seems certain who – cried that it must be the jongleur who had done this, and sent the whole mob haring out after him, as we here witnessed. Who, then, was left there to tend the stricken man, and the old woman threatened by her fit?'

'The women,' said Hugh.

148

'The women. Of whom the bride was left to care for the victims upstairs in their own chambers. It was Susanna who ran for the physician. Very well, so she did. But did she run for him at once, or take but a few moments to run first to the well and place what she found there in safer hiding?'

In a brief and awed silence they sat staring at each other.

'Is it possible?' said Hugh marvelling. '*His daughter.*'

'Among humankind all things are possible. Consider! The locksmith had the key to the mystery put into his hands. If he had been honest he would have gone straight to Walter or to Daniel and showed it, and told what he knew. He did not, for he was not honest. He meant to gain by what he had found out. If he did not approach the one he believed guilty until the Monday, it was because he had no chance until then of doing so in private. He was able as we to remember how all the menfolk had gone baying after Liliwin here, and to reason that it was a woman who reclaimed the treasury from the well and put it safely away until all the hue and cry should be over, and a stray lad, with luck, hanged for the deed. And who kept the keys of the house and had the best command over all its hiding-places? He chose Susanna. And on Monday his time came, when she took her basket of linen and went down through the wall to spread it out in the drying-ground. About mid-morning Baldwin Peche was last seen in his shop, and went off with some remark about the fish rising. No one saw him, living, ever again.'

Liliwin, hitherto mute in his corner, leaned forward with a soft, protesting cry: 'You can't mean it! She ... But she was the only one, the only one who showed Rannilt some kindness. She let her come to me for her comfort ... She did not truly believe that *I* ...' He saw in time where he was headed, and halted with a great groan.

'She had good reason to *know* that you never harmed her father's person or stole his goods. The best! And a sound reason, also, for sending Rannilt away out of the house so that she herself, and none but she, should fetch in the washing, or have any other occasion to go down to the riverside, where she had left the extortioner dead.'

'I cannot believe,' whispered Liliwin, shaking, 'that she could, even if she would, do such a thing. A woman ... kill?'

'You underrate Susanna,' said Cadfael grimly. 'So did all her kin. And women have killed, many a time.'

'Granted, then, that he followed her down to the river,' said

Hugh. 'You had better go on. Tell us what you believe happened there, and how this thing came about.'

'I think he came down after her to the brink, showed her the coin, and demanded a share in her gains to pay for his silence. I think he, of all people, had worst underestimated her. A mere woman! He expected prevarication, lies, delay, perhaps pleading, some labour to convince her he knew what he knew and meant what he said. He had greatly mistaken her. He had not bargained for a woman who could accept danger instantly, with no outcry, make up her mind, and act, stamping out the threat as soon as it arose. I think she spoke him fair while she went on laying out the washing, and as he stood by the water's edge with the coin in his hand she so arranged that she passed behind him with a stone in her hand, reaching to a corner of linen, and struck him down.'

'Go on,' said Hugh, 'you cannot leave it there. There was more done than that.'

'I think you already know. Whether the blow quite stunned him or not, it flung him face-down into the shallow water. I think she did not wait to give him time to recover his wits and try to rise, but went on acting instantly. Her skirt and shoes were wet! I have only just learned it. And remember the bruises on his back. I think she stepped upon him in the water, almost as he fell, and held him down until he was dead.'

Hugh sat silent. It was Liliwin who uttered a small whimper of horror at hearing it, and shook as if the night had turned cold.

'And then considered calmly the possibility that the river might find force enough to float him away, and took steps to pin him down where he was, under the alders, under the water, until he could be conveyed away by night, to be discovered elsewhere, a drowned man. Do you recall the pitted bruise on his shoulders? There is a jagged stone fallen from the town wall, beside the pebbles there. As for the coin, it was under his body, she did not try to recover it.'

Hugh drew deep breath. 'It could be so! But it was *not* she who followed her father to his shop and struck him down, for she is one person who *is* vouched for fully, all that time that he was gone, until she went to look for him. And then she cried out at once for help. There was no time at all when she could have struck the blow or made off with the booty. She may have removed it from the well later, she certainly did not put it there. You are arguing, I take it, that there were two who planned this between them?'

150

'Two are implied. One to strike and steal and hide, the other to retrieve the goods by night and secrete them in a safer place. One to destroy the extortioner as soon as he declared himself, and the other to take away the body and dispose of it by night. Yes, surely two.'

'Then who is the second? Certainly brother and sister who suffered from such parsimonious elders might compound together to get their hands on what was withheld from them, and certainly Daniel was abroad that night and furtive about it. And for all his tale of a married woman's bed rings likely enough, I have still had an eye on him. Even shallow men can learn to lie.'

'I have not forgotten Daniel. But you may, for of all men living, her brother is the least likely to have had any part in Susanna's plans.' Cadfael was recalling, as in a storm-flash of illumination, small, unremarkable, unremarked things, Rannilt repeating the words she had overheard, Juliana's improbable praise of her granddaughter's excellent house-wifery, in preserving her oatmeal crock half-full past Easter, and Susanna's bitter taunt: 'Had you still a place prepared for me? A nunnery, perhaps?' And then the old woman shrieked and fell down ...

No, wait! There was more to it, he saw it now. The old woman at the head of the stairs, the only light that of the little lamp she carried, a falling light, pricking Susanna's form and features into sharpest light and shade, every curve or hollow magnified ... Yes! She saw what she saw, she shrieked and clutched her breast, and then fell, letting fall the revealing lamp from her hand. Somehow she had known the half of it, and come forth by night to confront her only, her best antagonist. She, too, must have seen the torn skirt, the stained hem, and made her own connections. And she had still, she had said, a use for those concealed keys of hers before she surrendered them at last. Yes, and the last words she ever spoke: 'For all that, I should have liked to hold my great-grandchild ...' Words better understood now than when first he had heard them.

'No, now I see! Nothing now could have held her back. The man who compounded with her to steal was no kinsman, nor one they would ever have admitted as kin. They made their plans perforce, those two, to vanish from here together at the first favourable time, and make a life somewhere far away from town. Her father grudged her a dowry, she has taken it for herself. Whatever his name may be, this man, we know now *what* he is. He is her lover. More, he is the man who has got her with child.'

Chapter Twelve

Friday night

UGH WAS on his feet before the last words were spoken. 'If you're right, after what has happened they won't wait for a better time. They've left it late as it is and so, by God, have I.'

'You're going there now? I am coming with you.' Cadfael was not quite easy about Rannilt. In all innocence she had spoken out things that meant nothing evil to her, but might uncover much evil to those who listened. Far better to have her away before she could further threaten Susanna's purposes. And it seemed that the same fear had fallen upon Liliwin, for he scrambled hastily out of the shadows to catch at Hugh's arm before they could leave the cloister.

'Sir, am I free now? I need not hide here any longer? Then take me with you! I want to fetch my girl away out of that house. I want her with me. How if they take fright at her too much knowledge? How if they do her harm? I'm coming to bring her away, whether or no it's safe for me!'

Hugh clapped him heartily on the shoulder. 'Come, and welcome. Free as a bird, and I'll ensure my men shall know it and hold you safe enough. Tomorrow the town shall know it, too.'

There were no lights in the Aurifaber house when Hugh's sergeant hammered at the hall door. The household was

153

already abed, and it took some time to rouse any of the family. No doubt Dame Juliana, by this time, was shrouded and ready for her coffin.

It was Margery who at last came down to enquire quaveringly through the closed door who was without, and what was the matter at this time of night. At Hugh's order she opened and let them in, herself surprised and vexed that Susanna, who slept downstairs, had not saved her the trouble. But it soon became clear that Susanna was not there to hear any knocking. Her room was empty, the bed undisturbed, the chest that had held her clothes now contained only a few discarded and well-worn garments.

The arrival of the sheriff's deputy and others, with several officers of the law, very soon brought out all the inhabitants, Walter coming down blear-eyed and suspicious, Daniel hurrying solicitously to his wife's side, the boy Griffin peering uncertainly from the other side of the yard. A curiously shrunken and unimpressive gathering, without its two dominant members, and every one of these few who remained utterly at a loss, staring about and at one another in consternation, as though somewhere among the shadows of the hall they might still discover Susanna.

'My daughter?' croaked Walter, looking about him helplessly. 'But is she not here? She must be … she was here as always, she put out the lights as she always does, the last to her bed. Not an hour since! She cannot be gone!'

But she was gone. And so, as Cadfael found when he took a lantern and slipped away by the outdoor stairs at the rear of the house and into the undercroft, was Iestyn. Iestyn the Welshman, without money or family or standing, who would never for a moment have been considered as fit for his master's daughter, even now she had ceased to be necessary to the running of his master's house, and was of no further value.

The undercroft ran under stone-vaulted ceilings the length of the house. On impulse Cadfael left the cold, abandoned bed, and lit himself through to the front, where a narrow stair ran up to a door into the shop. Directly opposite to him, as he opened it, stood the pillaged coffer where Walter had kept his wealth. There had been no shadow that night, no sound, only the candle had flickered as the door was silently opened.

A few yards away, when Cadfael retraced his steps and again climbed the outdoor stair, lay the well. And on his right hand, the door into Susanna's chamber, by which she could pass quickly between hall and kitchen, and a young man from below-stairs could as well enter when all was dark.

They were gone, as they had surely planned to go one night earlier and been detained by death. Acting on another thought, Cadfael went in by Susanna's door, and asked Margery to open for him the locked door of the store. The big stone crock in which Susanna had kept her stock of oatmeal stood in one corner. Cadfael lifted the lid, and held his lantern over it. There was still a respectable quantity of grain left in the bottom of it, enough to hide quite a large bundle, suitably disposed, but bereft of that padding it showed much less than a quarter full. Juliana with her keys had been before him, and left what she found there, intending, as always, to manage the fortunes of her own clan with no interference from any other. She had known, and she had held her peace when she could have spoken. And that stark girl, her nearest kin, all desperation and all iron calm, had tended her scrupulously, and waited to learn her fate without fear or complaint. The one as strong as the other, for good or for evil, neither giving nor asking quarter.

Cadfael replaced the lid, went out and relocked the door. In the hall they were fluttering and bleating, anxious to insist on their own innocence and respectability at all costs, distracted at the thought that a kinswoman should be suspect of such an enormity as robbing her own family. Walter stammered out his answers, aghast at such treachery, almost incoherent with grief for his lost money, lost to his own child. Hugh turned rather to Daniel.

'If she intended a long journey tonight, to take her out of our writ, or at least out of our hold, where would she run? They would need horses. Have you horses they may have taken?'

'Not here in the town,' said Daniel, pale-faced and tousled from bed, his comeliness looking almost idiot at this pass, 'but over the river we have a pasture and a stable. Father keeps two horses there.'

'Which way? In Frankwell?'

'Through Frankwell and along the westward road.'

'And the westward road may well be our road,' said Cadfael, coming in from the store, 'for there's a Welshman missing from under here, and what little he had gone with him, and once well into Wales he can thumb his nose at the sheriff of Shropshire. Whatever he may have taken with him.'

He had barely got it out, to indignant and disbelieving protests from Walter, outraged at the mere suggestion of such a

155

depraved alliance, when Liliwin came bursting in from the rear quarters, his small person stiff and quivering with alarm.

'I've been to the kitchen – Rannilt is not there. Her bed's cold, she's left her things just as they are, nothing taken ...' How little she must have to take, but he knew the value, to one with virtually nothing, of the poor possessions she had left behind. 'They've taken her with them – they're afraid of what she knows and may tell. That woman has taken her,' he cried, challenging the household, the law and all, 'and she has killed and will kill again if she sees need. Where will they have gone? For I am going after them.'

'So are we all,' said Hugh, and turned on Walter Aurifaber. Let the father sweat for his own, as the lover did for his love. For his own by blood or by greed. 'You, sir, come with us. You say she had but an hour's start of us and on foot. Come, then, let's be after them mounted. I sent for horses from the castle, they'll be in the lane by now. You best know the way to your own stable, bring us there fast.'

The night was dark, clear and still young, so that light lingered in unexpected places, won from a smooth plane of the river, a house-front of pale stone, a flowering bush, or scattered stars of windflowers under the trees. The two women had passed through the Welsh gate and over the bridge without question. Owain Gwynedd, the formidable lord of much of Wales, with-held his hand courteously from interfering in England's fratri-cidal war, and very cannily looked after his own interests, host to whoever fled his enemy, friend to whoever brought him useful information. The borders of Shrewsbury he did not threaten. He had far more to gain by holding aloof. But his own firm border he maintained with every severity. It was a good night, and a good time of night, for fugitives to ride to the west, if their tribal references were good.

Through the dark streets of the suburb of Frankwell they passed like shadows, and Susanna turned westward, keeping the river still in view, along a path between fields. The smaller bundle, but the heavier, Susanna carried. The large and unwieldy one that held all her good clothes they carried beween them. It would have been too clumsy for one to manage alone. If I had not your help, she had said, I must have left half my belongings behind, and I shall have need of them.

'Shall you get far tonight?' wondered Rannilt, hesitant but anxious for assurance.

156

'Out of this land, I hope. Iestyn, who is nobody here, has a kinship of his own, and a place of his own, in his own country. There we shall be safe enough together. After tonight, if we make good speed, we cannot be pursued. You are not afraid, Rannilt, coming all this way with me in the dark?'

'No,' said Rannilt sturdily, 'I'm not afraid. I wish you well, I wish you happy, I'm glad to carry your goods for you, and to know that you don't go unprovided.'

'No,' agreed Susanna, with a curious twist to her voice that suggested laughter, 'not quite penniless. I have earned my future, have I not? Look back now,' she said, 'over your left shoulder, at that mole-hill of the town.' It showed as a hunched shadow in the shadowy night, stray flickers of light cast up the pale stone of the wall from the silver of the river in between. 'A last glimpse,' said Susanna, 'for we have not far now to go. Has the load been heavy? You shall soon lay it down.'

'Not heavy at all,' said Rannilt. 'I would do more for you if I could.'

The track along the headlands was rough and rutted, but Susanna knew it well, and stepped securely. On their right the ground rose, its darkness furred and fragrant with trees. On their left the smooth green meadows swept down to the lambent, murmuring Severn. Ahead, a roof heaved dimly out of the night, bushes banked about it, rough ground sheltering it to northwards, the pasture opening serenely to the south.

'We are there,' said Susanna, and hastened her step, so that Rannilt hurried to keep up with her and balance their burden.

Not a large building, this one that loomed out of the night, but stout in its timbers, and tall enough to show that above the stable it had a loft for hay and fodder. There was a double door set wide upon deep darkness, out of which the scent of horseflesh and hay and grainy, dusty warmth came to meet them. A man emerged, a dark shape, tensed to listen for any approaching foot. Susanna's step he knew at once and he came with spread arms; she dropped her end of the bundle and opened her arms to him. Not a word, not a sound had passed between them. Rannilt stood clutching her end of the load, and shook as though the earth had trembled under her, as they came together in that silent, exultant embrace, laced arms straining. Once at least, if never again, she had experienced a small spark of this devouring flame. She closed her eyes, and stood quivering.

Their breaking apart was as abrupt and silent as their coming

157

together. Iestyn looked over Susanna's shoulder, and fixed his black glance on Rannilt. 'Why did you bring the girl? What do we want with her?'

'Come within,' said Susanna, 'and I'll tell you. Have you saddled up? We should get away quickly.'

'I was about it when I heard you.' He picked up the roll of clothing, and drew her with him into the warm darkness of the stable and Rannilt followed timidly, only too aware how little need they now had of her. Iestyn closed the doors, but did not fasten them. 'Who knows, there may still be some soul awake along the river, no need to let them see any movement here until we're away.'

She heard and felt them embrace again in the dark, even in this brief contact becoming one by passionate consent. She knew then that they had lain together as she and Liliwin had lain, but many times and with no better hope. She remembered the rear door of Susanna's chamber and the stair to the undercroft not many yards distant. Every temptation lavishly offered, and all countenance denied.

'This child here,' said Iestyn softly, 'what's your intent with her? Why did you bring her all this way?'

'She sees too clear and notices too much,' said Susanna shortly. 'She has said to me, poor fool innocent, things she had better not have said, and had better not say to any other, for if they understood more than she by it, they might yet be the death of us. So I brought her. She can go with us – a part of the way.'

Iestyn demanded, after a brief, deep silence: 'What do you mean by that?'

'What do you suppose? There are woods enough and wild places your side the border. Who's to look for her? A kinless kitchen slave.' The voice was so calmly and reasonably Susanna's voice that Rannilt could not take in what it was saying, and stood utterly lost and feeling herself forgotten, even while they spoke of her.

A horse stamped and shifted in the dark, the warmth of its body tempering the night air. Shapes began to emerge faintly, shadow separating itself from shadow, while Iestyn breathed long and deeply, and suddenly shuddered. Rannilt felt him quake, and still did not understand.

'No!' he said in a muted cry just below his breath. 'No, that we cannot, that I will not. Good God, what harm has she ever done us, a poor soul even less happy than we?'

'You need not,' said Susanna simply. 'I can! There is nothing now I cannot do to have you mine, to belong to you, to go by your side through this world. After what I've done already, what is there I dare not do?'

'No, not this! Not this offence, not if you love me. The other was forced on you, what loss was he, as mean as your kin! But not this child! I will not let you! Nor's there no need,' he said, turning from ordering to persuading. 'Here are we, well out of town, leave her here and go, you and I together, what else matters here? Let her make her way back by daylight. Where shall we be? Far past pursuit, over the border into Welsh land, safe. What harm can she do us, who has never done any yet, nor ever willed any?'

'They *will* pursue! If ever my father gets to know ... You know him! He would not stir step for me, but for this – this ...' She spurned with her foot the bundle she had brought with her, and it rang faintly in the dark. 'There could be barriers on the way into Wales, accidents, delays ... Far better be sure.'

'No, no, no! You shall not so despoil my love, I will not have you so changed. I want you as you are now ...'

The horses shifted and blew, uneasy at having disturbing company at this hour, yet wakeful and ready. Then there was a silence, brief and fathoms deep, and ending in a long-drawn sigh.

'My heart, my love,' Susanna said in a melting whisper, 'as you will, as you order ... Have it your way, then ... Yes, let her be! What if we are hunted? There's nothing I can refuse you – not my life ...'

And whatever it had been between them, and concerning her, it was over. Rannilt stood helpless in the corner of the stable, trying to understand, willing them away, westwards into Wales, where Iestyn was a man and a kinsman instead of a menial, and Susanna might be an honourable wife, who had been hitherto a household servant, baulked of her rights, grudged her dowry, a discard woman.

Iestyn plucked up the clothing roll, and by the stirring and trampling of one of the horses, he was busy strapping it into balance behind the saddle. The other bundle, the heavy one, gave forth again its soft, metallic sound as Susanna hoisted it, to be stowed behind the second mount. They were still barely visible, those horses. An occasional splinter of light glanced from their coats and was lost again; their warmth breathed on the air with every movement.

159

A hand swung wide the half of the double door, and a sector of sky peered in, lighter than the darkness, bluer than the blackness, growing luminous with the rising of a half-moon. One of the horses stirred into motion, led towards that paler interstice.

There was a short, sharp cry, so soft and desolate that the air ached with it. The opened half-door slammed to again, and Rannilt heard hasty hands fumbling with heavy bars, hoisting and dropping them into solid sockets. Two such beams guarding the door had the force and asurance of a fortress.

'What is it?' Susanna's voice pealed sharply out of the dusk within. She was holding the bridle, the abrupt halt made the horse stamp and snort.

'Men, a good number, coming down from the headland! There are horses, led behind! They're coming here – they know!'

'They cannot know!' she cried.

'They do know. They're spreading, to ring us round, I saw the ranks part. Get up the ladder! Take her with you. She may be worth all to us yet. What else,' he cried, suddenly raging, 'have we between ourselves and the judgement?'

Rannilt, bewildered and frightened, stood trembling in the darkness, stunned by the confusing turmoil of hooves stamping round her, and bodies in violent, blind motion, warm stable smells eddying on the air and pricking her nostrils as the stirrings of terror prickled her skin. The doors were barred, and Iestyn between her and that way out, even if she could have lifted the beams. And still she could not believe, could not take in what was happening to her, or relate these two desperate people with the Susanna and the Iestyn she had known. When a hand gripped her wrist and tugged her towards the rear corner of the stable, she went helplessly with the urgent compulsion. What else could she do? Her ankle struck against the lowest rung of a ladder, the hand dragged her upwards. Fumbling and panting, she went where she was hauled, and was tossed face-down into a pile of hay that enveloped her in dust and dry sweetness. Dimly she was aware of punctures of sky shining through the hay, distinguishably paler in the timber darkness before her, where whoever built this stable and loft had placed a ventilation lattice to air his store.

Somewhere behind her, at the door end of the loft, a larger square of sky looked in, the hatch by which the hay harvest was forked in here for storage, high above the barred doors below. She heard the rungs of the ladder creak at Iestyn's weight as he climbed in haste, and ran to fling himself on his knees beside that outlet, to watch his enemies close about his refuge. She heard, and suddenly was able to comprehend what she heard. The thud of fists hammering on the barred doors, the challenge of the law without.

'Open and come forth, or we'll hack you out with axes. We know you there within and know what you have to answer for!'

Not a voice she knew, for an eager sergeant had outrun his lord and his fellows when he heard the bars slam home, and had come well first to the doors. But she knew the import of what he bellowed to the night, and understood fully at last into what peril she had been brought.

'Stand back!' Iestyn's voice rang loud and hard. 'Or answer to God for a life, you also! Well away from those doors, and don't venture back, for I see you clearly. And I'll speak no more with you, underling, but only with your master. Tell him I have a girl here between my hands, and a knife at my belt, and so sure as axe strikes at these timbers, my knife slits her throat. Now bring me here someone with whom I can parley.'

There was a sharp command without and then silence. Rannilt drew herself back as far as she dared into the remaining store of hay, towards the faint pattern of stars. Between here and the head of the ladder by which she had climbed there was a silent, motionless presence which she knew for Susanna, on guard over her lover's only weapon.

'What did I ever do to you?' said Rannilt, without rancour or hope.

'You fell foul,' said Susanna, with unblaming bitterness. 'Your misfortune and ours.'

'And will you truly kill me?' She asked it in pure wonder, even her terror momentarily forgotten.

'If we must.'

'But dead,' said Rannilt, in a moment of desperately clear vision putting her finger on the one disastrous weakness in the holding of hostages, 'I am of no more use to you. It's only *living* that I can get you what you want. If you kill me you've lost everything. And you don't *want* to kill me, what pleasure would that be to you? Why, *I'm no use to you at all?*'

'If I must pull the roof down upon myself,' said Susanna with cold ferocity, 'I'll pull it down also upon as many of the innocent as I can contrive to crush with me and not go alone into the dark.'

Chapter Thirteen

Friday night to Saturday morning

UGH HAD halted his men instantly at Iestyn's challenge, drawn back those who had reached the stable doors, and enjoined silence, which is more unnerving than violent assault or loud outcry. Moving men could be detected, stillness made them only dubiously visible. The rising ground to the headland bore several small clumps of trees and a hedge of bushes, cover enough for men to make their way halfway round the stable, and the rest of the circle they closed at a greater distance, completing a ring all round the building. The sergeant came back from his survey, shadowy from tree to tree down the slope to the meadow, to report the stable surrounded.

'There's no other way out, unless he has the means to hew a way through a wall, and small good that would do him. And if he boasts of a knife, I take it he has no other weapon. What would a common workman carry but his knife for all purposes?'

'And we have archers,' mused Hugh, 'if they have no light to show them a target as yet. Wait – nothing in haste! If we have them securely, it's we who can afford to wait, not they. No need to drive them to madness.'

'But they have Rannilt in there – they're threatening her life,' whispered Liliwin, quivering at Brother Cadfael's shoulder.

162

'They're offering to spend her for their own ends,' said Hugh, 'therefore all the more they'll keep her safe to bargain with, short of the last despair, and I'll take good care not to drive them over the edge. Keep still a while, and let's see if we can tire them out or talk them out. But you, Alcher, find yourself the best place in cover to command that hatch above the doors, and keep it in your eye and a shaft always ready, in case of the worst. I'll try to hold the fellow there in the frame for you.' The loading door where Iestyn knelt to watch them was no more than a faint shape darker still in the dark timber wall and the deep-blue light, but like the doors it faced due east, and the first pre-dawn light, however many hours away yet, would find it early. 'No shooting unless I bid. Let's see what patience can do.'

He went forward alone, fixing the square of darkness with intent eyes, and stood some twenty paces distant from the stable. Behind him in the bushes Liliwin held his breath, and Brother Cadfael felt the boy's slight body quivering and taut, like a leashed hound, and laid a cautioning hand on his arm in case he slipped his leash and went baying after his quarry. But he need not have feared. Liliwin turned a white face and nodded him stiff reassurance. 'I know. I trust him, I must. He knows his business.'

At their backs, unable to be still, Walter Aurifaber sidled and writhed about the tree that sheltered him, biting his nails and agonising over his losses, and saying never a word to any but himself, and that in a soft, whining undertone that was half malediction and half prayer. At least all was not yet lost. The malefactors had not escaped, and could not and must not break loose now and run for it westward.

'Iestyn!' called Hugh, gazing steadily upwards. 'Here am I, Hugh Beringar, the sheriff's deputy. You know me, you know why I am here, you best know I am about what it is my duty to do. My men are all around you, you have no way of escape. Be wise, come down from there and give yourself – yourselves – into my hands, without more damage and worse offence, and look for what mercy such good sense can buy you. It's your best course. You must know it and take heed.'

'No!' said Iestyn's voice harshly. 'We have not come so far to go tamely to judgement now. I tell you, we have the girl, Rannilt, here within. If any man of yours comes too near these doors, I swear I will kill her. Bid them keep back. That's my first word.'

'Do you see any man but myself moving within fifty paces of your doors?' Hugh's voice was calm, equable and clear. 'You have, then, a girl at your mercy. What then? With her you have no quarrel. What can you gain by harming her but a hotter place in hell? If you could reach my throat, I grant you it might possibly avail you, but it can neither help you nor give you satisfaction to slit hers. Nor does it suit with what has been known of you heretofore. You have no blood-guilt on your hands thus far, why soil them now?'

'You may talk sweet reason from where you stand,' cried Iestyn bitterly, 'but we have all to lose, and see no let to making use of what weapons we have. And I tell you, if you press me, I will kill her, and if then you break in here after me by force, I will kill and kill as many as I can before the end. But if you mean such soft, wise talk, yes, you may have the girl, safe and sound – at a price!'

'Name your price,' said Hugh.

'A life for a life is fair. Rannilt's life for my woman's. Let my woman go free from here, with her horse and goods and gear and all that is hers, unpursued, and I well send out the girl to you unharmed.'

'And you would take my word there should be no pursuit?' Hugh pressed, angling after at least a small advantage.

'You're known for a man of your word.'

Two voices had let out sharp gasps at the mention of such terms, and two voices cried out, 'No!' in the same breath. Walter, frantic for his gold and silver, darted out a few steps towards where Hugh stood, until Cadfael caught him by the arm and plucked him back. He wriggled and babbled indignantly: 'No, no such infamous bargain! *Her* goods and gear? Mine, not hers, stolen from me. You cannot strike such a bargain. Is the slut to make off into Wales with her ill-gotten gains? Never! I won't have it!'

There was a shadowy flurry of movement in the hatch above, and Susanna's voice pealed sharply: 'What, have you my loving father there? He wants his money, and my neck wrung, like that of any other who dared lay hands on his money. Poor judgement in you, if you expected *him* to be willing to pay out a penny to save a servant-girl's life, or a daughter's either. Never fear, my fond father, I say no just as loudly as you. I will not accept such a bargain. Even in peril of death I would not go one step away from my man here. You hear that? My man, my lover, the father of my child! But on terms I'll part from him, yes! Let Iestyn take the horse, and go back unmolested into his own country, and I'll go freely, to my death or my wretched life, whichever falls on me. *I* am the one you want. Not he. I *have* killed, I tell you so open ...'

'She's lying,' cried Iestyn hoarsely. 'I am the guilty man. Whatever she did she did only for me ...'

'Hush, love, they know better! They know which of us two planned and acted. Me they may do as they like with – you they shall not have!'

'Oh, fool girl, my dearest, do you think I would leave you? Not for all the world's treasures ...'

Those below were forgotten in this wild contention above. Nothing was to be seen but the agitated tremor of certain pallors within the dark frame, that might have been faces and hands, faces pressed despairingly cheek to cheek, hands embracing and caressing. Next moment Iestyn's voice lifted sharply: 'Stop her! Quickly, stir! Mind your fawn!' And the shadowy embrace broke apart, and a faint, frustrated cry from deep within made Liliwin shiver and start against Cadfael's arm.

'That was Rannilt. Oh, God, if I could but reach her ...' But he spoke only in a whisper, aware of a tension that ought not to be broken, that was spun out here like the threatened thread of Rannilt's young life, and his own hope of happiness. His desperation and pain was something he must bear, and keep silent.

'Since she cries out,' whispered Cadfael firmly into his ear, 'she is alive. Since she made a bid to slip away out of reach while they were beset, she is unharmed and unbound. Keep that in mind.'

'Yes, true! And they don't, they can't hate her or want to harm her ...' But still he heard the extreme anger and pain of those two voices crying defiance, and knew, as Cadfael knew, that two so driven might do terrible things even against their own natures. More, he understood their suffering, and was wrung with it as though it matched his own.

'No comfort for you,' shouted Iestyn from his lair. 'We have her still. Now I offer you another choice. Take back the girl and the gold and silver, give us the two horses and this night free of pursuit, together.'

Walter Aurifaber broke free with a whimper of half-eager, half-doubtful hope and approval, and darted some yards into the open. 'My lord! My lord, that might be acceptable. If they restore my treasury ...' Even his lawful revenge did not count for much by comparison.

'There is a life they cannot restore,' said Hugh curtly, and motioned him back so sternly that the goldsmith recoiled, chastened.

'Are you listening, Iestyn?' called Hugh, raising his eyes once again to the dark hatch. 'You mistake my office. I stand here for the king's law. I am willing to stand here all night long. Take thought again, and better, and come down with unbloodied hands. There is no better thing you can do.'

'I am here. I am listening. I have not changed,' Iestyn responded grimly from above. 'If you want my woman and me, come and fetch us forth, and fetch away first this little carcase – *your* prey, not ours.'

'Have I raised a hand?' said Hugh reasonably. 'Or loosened my sword in the scabbard? You see me, clearer than I see you. We have the night before us. Whenever you have aught to say, speak up, I shall be here.'

The night dragged with fearful slowness over besiegers and besieged, for the most part in mourn silence, though if silence continued too long Hugh would deliberately break it, to test whether Iestyn remained awake and watchful, though with care not to alarm him, for fear he should be driven to panic action in expectation of an attack. There was no remedy but to outwait and outendure the enemy. In all likelihood they had very little food or water with them. They could as easily be deprived of rest. Even in such tactics there was the danger of sudden and utter despair, which might bring on a massacre, but if all was done very gradually and softly that might yet be avoided. Weariness has sometimes broken down spirits braced implacably to defy torture, and inaction sucked away all the resolution armed for action.

'Try if you can do better,' said Hugh softly to Cadfael, some time well past midnight. 'They cannot know you're here, not yet, you may find a chink in their mail that's proof against me.'

In those small hours when the heart is low, the least surprise may prick home as it could not do by day, in the noon of the body's vigour. Cadfael's very voice, deeper and rougher than Hugh's, startled Iestyn into leaning out from his watch-tower for one incautious stare at this new visitant.

'Who's that? What trick are you playing now?'

'No trick, Iestyn. I am Brother Cadfael of the abbey, who

166

came sometimes to the house with medicines. You know me, I dare not say well enough to trust me. Let me speak with Susanna, who knows me better.'

He had thought that she might refuse either to speak or to hear him. When she had set her mind upon one course, she might well be stone to any who sought to divert her or stand in her way. But she did come to the hatch, and she did listen. At least that was a further respite. Those two lovers changed places in the loft. Cadfael felt them pass, and now they passed without touching or caressing, for there was no need. They were two halves of one whole, living or dead. One of them, it was clear from the earlier outcry, must keep an eye on their prisoner. They could not bind her, then, or else they had not thought it needful. Perhaps they had not the means. They were trapped in the instant of flight. Was it unpardonable to wish they had ridden away half an hour earlier?

'Susanna, it is not too late to make restitution. I know your wrongs, my voice shall speak for you. But murder is murder. Never think there is any escape. Though you elude the judgement here, there is another you cannot avoid. Better far to make what amends can be made and be at peace.'

'What peace?' she said, bitter and chill. 'There is none for me. I am a stunted tree, denied the ground to grow, and now, when I am in fruit, in despite of this world, do you think I will abate one particle of my hate or love? Leave me be, Brother Cadfael,' she said more gently. 'Your concern is with my soul, mine is all with my body, the only heaven I've ever known or ever hope to know.'

'Come down and bring Iestyn with you,' said Cadfael simply, 'and I take it upon myself to promise you, as I must answer to God, that your child and his shall be born and cared for as befits every human soul brought innocent into the world. I will invoke the lord abbot to ensure it.'

She laughed. It was a fresh, wild and yet desolate sound. 'This is not Holy Church's child, Brother Cadfael. It belongs to me, and to Iestyn, my man, and there is none other shall ever cradle or care for it. Yet I do thank you for your goodwill to my son. And after all,' she said, with bitter derision in her voice, 'how do we know the creature would ever be brought forth living and whole? I am old, Brother Cadfael, old for childbirth. The thing may be dead before me.'

'Make the assay,' said Cadfael stoutly. 'He is not wholly yours, he is his own, your maybe child. Do him justice! Why

167

should he pay for your sins? It was not he trampled Baldwin Peche into the gravel of Severn.'

She made a dreadful, muted sound, as if she had choked upon her own rage and grief, and then she was calm and resolved again, and immovable. 'Three are here together and made one,' she said, 'the only trinity I acknowledge now. No fourth has any part in us. What do we owe to any man living?'

'You forget there is a fourth,' said Cadfael strongly, 'and you are making shameful use of her. One who is none of yours and has never done you wrong. She also loves – I think you know it. Why destroy another pair as little blessed as you?'

'Why not?' said Susanna. 'I am all destruction. What else is left to me now?'

Cadfael persisted, but after a while, talking away doggedly there past the mid of the night, he knew that she had risen and left him, unconvinced, unreconciled, and that it was Iestyn who now leaned in the hatch. He waited a considerable while, and then took up his pleading for this perhaps more vulnerable ear. A Welshman, less aggrieved than the woman, for all his hardships; and all Welsh are kin, even if they slit one another's throats now and then, and manure their sparse and stony fields with fratricidal dead in tribal wars. But he knew he had little hope. He had already spoken with the domina of that pair. There was no appeal to this one now that she could not wipe out with a gesture of her hand.

He was eased, if not verily glad, when Hugh came back to relieve him of his watch.

He sat slack and discouraged in the spring grass under the hedge of bushes, and Liliwin came plucking softly but urgently at his sleeve. 'Brother Cadfael, come with me! Come!' The whisper was excited and hopeful, where hope was in no very lavish supply.

'What is it? Come with you where?'

'He said there's no other way out,' whispered Liliwin, tugging at the sleeve he held, 'and by that token none in, but there is … there could be. Come and see!'

Cadfael went where he was led, up through the bushes on the headland, and along the slope in cover, just below the level of the stable roof and at no great distance from it, to the western end of the building. The timbers of the roof projected above the low gable, the fellow to the eastern one in which Iestyn crouched on watch. 'See there – the starlight shows dappling. They let in a lattice there for air.'

Peering narrowly, Cadfael could just discern a square shape that might well be what Liliwin described, but measured barely the span of hand and forearm either way, as close as he could estimate. The interstices between the slats, which the straining eye could either discern or imagine for a moment, only to lose them again, were surely too small even to admit a fist. Nor was there any way of reaching them, short of a ladder or the light weight and claws of a cat, even though the timbers of the wall below were rough and uneven.

'That?' breathed Cadfael, aghast. 'Child, a spider might get up there and get in, but scarcely a man.'

'Ah, but I've been down there, I know. There are toe-holds enough. And I think one of the slats is hanging loose already, and there'll be others ready to give way. If a man could get in there, while you hold them busy at the other end ... She is up there, I know it! You heard, when they ran to hold her, how far it was to run.'

It was true. Moreover, if she had any choice she would be huddled as far away from her captors as she could get.

'But, boy, even if you stripped away two or three of the boards – could you do more, unheard? I doubt it! There's not a man among us could get through that keyhole to her. No, not if you had time to strip the whole square.'

'Yes, *I can*! You forget,' whispered Liliwin eagerly, 'I'm small and light and I'm an acrobat, bred to it from three or four years old. It's my craft. I *can* reach her. Where a cat can go I can go. And she's even smaller than I, though she may not be trained as a tumbler. If I had a rope, I could make it fast there, and take my time opening up the way for her. Oh, surely, surely it's worth the attempt! We've no other way. And I *can* do it, and I *will*!'

'Wait!' said Cadfael. 'Sit you here in cover, and I'll go broach it to Hugh Beringar and get you your rope, and make ready to hold them fast in talk, as far as may be away from you. Not a word, not even a movement until I come back.'

'No madder than whatever else we may do to break this dam,' said Hugh when he had listened and considered. 'If you put some trust in it, I'll go with you. Can he really creep in there, do you think? Is it possible?'

'I've seen him tie himself in a knot a serpent might be proud of,' said Cadfael, 'and if he says there's room enough there for

169

him to pass, I say he's the better judge of that than I. It's his profession, he takes pride in it. Yes, I put my trust in him.'

'We'll send to fetch him his rope, and a chisel, too, to pry loose the slats, but he must wait for them. We'll make good certain they stay wakeful and watchful at this end, and try a feint or two, if need be, short of driving them to panic. And let him take his time, for I think we might be advised to wait for the first light, to give Alcher a clear view of that hatch and whatever body fills it, and a shaft fitted and aimed in case of need. If we must let a decent poor lad risk his life, at least we'll stand ready with all the cover we can give him.'

'I had rather,' said Cadfael sadly, 'there should be no killing at all.'

'So would I,' agreed Hugh grimly, 'but if there must be, rather the guilty than the innocent.'

The dawn was still more than an hour and a half away when they brought the rope Liliwin needed, but already the eastern sky had changed, turned from deepest blue to paler blue-green, and a faint line of green paler still outlined the curves of the fields behind them, and the towered hill of the town.

'Rather round my waist than my neck,' whispered Liliwin hardily, as Cadfael fastened the rope about him among the bushes.

'There, I see you have the true spirit in you. God keep you, the pair of you! But can she come down the rope, even if you reach her? Girls are not such acrobats as you.'

'I can guide her. She's so light and small, she can hold by the rope and walk backwards down the wall ... Only keep them busy there at the far end.'

'But go slowly and quietly, no haste,' cautioned Cadfael, anxious as for a son going into battle. 'I shall be running messenger between. And daylight will be on our side, not on theirs.'

Liliwin kicked off his shoes. He had holes in the toes of both feet of his hose, Cadfael saw. Perhaps none the worse for this enterprise, but when he came to be sent out into the world – God so willing, as surely God must – he must go better provided.

The boy slid silently down from the headland to the foot of the stable wall, felt with stretched arms above his head, found grips a heavier man would never have considered, set a toe to a first hold, and drew himself up like a squirrel on to the timbers.

Cadfael waited and watched until he had seen the rope

170

slipped through the firmest boards of the lattice and made fast, and the first rotten slat prised free, slowly and carefully, and let fall silently at arm's-length into the thick grass below. More than half an hour had passed by then. From time to time he caught the sound of voices in weary but alert exchanges to eastward. The criss-cross of boards at the air-vent showed perceptibly now. The removal of one board had uncovered a space big enough to let a cat in and out, but surely nothing larger or less agile. The vault of the sky lightened very gradually before there was any visible source of light.

Liliwin worked with a bight of the tethered rope fast round him, and half-naked toes braced into the timbers of the wall. He had begun patiently prising loose the second slat, when Cadfael made his way back in cover to report what he knew.

'God knows it looks impossible, but the lad knows his business, and if he is sure he can pass, as a cat knows by its whiskers, then I take his word for it. But for God's sake keep this parley alive.'

'Take it over for me,' said Hugh, drawing back with eyes still fixed on the hatch. 'Only some few moments ... A fresh voice causes them to prick their ears afresh.'

Cadfael took up the vain pleas he had used before. The voice that answered him was hoarse with weariness, but still defiant.

'We shall not go from here,' said Cadfael, roused out of his own weariness by a double anxiety, 'until all these troubled here, body and soul, have freedom and quiet, whether in this world or another. And who so prevents to the last, on him the judgement fall! Nevertheless, God's mercy is infinite to those who seek it, however late, however feebly.'

'The light will not be long,' Hugh was saying at that same moment to Alcher, who was the finest marksman in the castle garrison, and had long since chosen his ground with the dawn in view, and found no reason to change it. 'Be ready, the instant I shall call, to put an arrow clean into that hatch, and through whoever lurks there. But no shooting unless I do call. And pray God I am not forced to it.'

'That's understood,' said Alcher, nursing his strung bow and fitted shaft, and never shifting his eyes from their aim, dead-centre of the dark opening, now growing clearly visible above the stable doors.

When Cadfael again made his way along the headland, the lattice was a lattice no longer, but a small square opening under the eaves, and the dislodged slats lay cushioned in the thick grass below. Liliwin had one arm stretched within, to ease aside the hay cautiously, with as little sound as possible, and make room to creep within. Now if only Rannilt could keep from starting or crying out when she found herself approached thus from behind! It was high time to make as much and as menacing ado before the stable doors as possible. Yet Cadfael could not help standing with held breath to watch, until Liliwin slid head and shoulders through the space that seemed barely passable even for his slenderness, and drew the rest of himself after in one coiling, rapid movement, vanishing in a smooth somersault, and without a sound.

Cadfael made his way back in haste to a point still out of sight from the hatch, and signalled urgently to Hugh that the time of greatest danger was come. Alcher saw the waving arm before Hugh did, and drew his bow halfway to the ear, narrowing his eyes upon the moving blurs of drab brown coat and paler face that showed as his target. Behind him the sun was just showing a rim over the horizon, and its first ray gleamed along the ridge of the roof. In a quarter of an hour it would be high enough for the light to reach the hatch, and the shot would be an easy matter.

'Iestyn,' called Hugh sharply, mustering those of his men nearest him into plain sight, though not too near to the doors, 'you have had a night's grace to consider, now show decent sense, and come forth of your will, for you see you cannot escape us, and you are mortal like others, and must eat to live. You are not in sanctuary there, there are no forty days of respite for you.'

'There's nothing but a halter for us,' shouted Iestyn savagely, 'and well we know it. But if that's our end, I swear to you the girl shall go before us, and her blood be on your head.'

'So you say, big talk from a small man! Your woman may not be so ready either to kill or to die. Have you asked her? Or have you the only voice in the matter? Here, master goldsmith,' called Hugh, beckoning, 'come and speak to your daughter. However late in the day, she may still listen to you.'

He was bidding to sting her, to bring them both flying to the hatch to spit their joint defiance and leave their prisoner unwatched. But oh, not too fast, not too fast, prayed Cadfael, gnawing his knuckles on the headland. The boy needs a few more minutes yet ...

Liliwin tunnelled stealthily through the stored hay, as much in

172

terror of sneezing, as the odorous dust tickled his nostrils, as he was of making too audible a rustling and betraying himself all too soon. Somewhere before him, very close now, he could hear the faint stirrings Rannilt made in her nest, and prayed that they would cover whatever sound he was making. After a while, pausing to peer through the thinning screen, he caught the shape of her shrinking shoulders and head against the dim morning light. Carefully he enlarged the passage he had hollowed out, so that he might have room to draw to one side of her, and have her creep past him, to come first to the frame of the lattice. Iestyn was leaning out at the far end of the loft, shouting angry curses now at those without, threatening still but not looking this way.

There was a woman to fear, for wherever she was now, she was silent. But surely if those without were pressing, half at least of her care must be with her lover. And here in the loft it was still blessedly dark.

His hand, probing delicately ahead, found and touched Rannilt's bare forearm. She flinched sharply, but made no sound at all, and in a moment he slid his hand down to find hers, and clung. Then she knew. All he heard was a faint, long sigh, and her fingers closed on his. He drew her gently, and by slow inches she shifted and drew nearer, into the cavity he opened for her. She was beside him, the fragile screen of hay hiding him and already half shielding her, and still no outcry. He urged her on past him with the pressure of his hand, to come first to the lattice and the rope as he covered her going. Outside the stable doors, the circling voices were raised and peremptory, and Iestyn, wild with weariness and anger, roared back at them incoherent defiance. Then, blessedly, Susanna's voice, surely close there at her lover's shoulder, soared above the clamour.

'Fools, do you think there's any power can separate us now? I hold as Iestyn holds, I despise your promises and your threats as he does. Bring my father to plead with me, would you? Let him hear, then, what I owe him, and what I wish him. Of all men on earth, I hate him! As he has made me of no worth, so I set no value on him. Dare he say I am no longer his daughter? He is no longer my father, he never was a father to me. May he be fed molten gold in hell until belly and throat burn to furnace ashes ...'

Under the fury of that raging voice, clear and steely as a sword, Liliwin hustled Rannilt past him and thrust her bodily

173

through his dusty tunnel towards the lattice and the rope, all caution cast to the winds, for if this moment escaped them, there might be no other.

It was Iestyn's quick ear that caught, even through Susanna's malediction, the sudden frenzied rustling of hay. He swung round with a great cry of rage at what he saw, and lunged away to prevent it. The first ray of light entering caught the flash of the naked knife.

Hugh was quick to understand and act. 'Shoot!' he cried, and Alcher, who had that first finger of sunlight now bright on Iestyn's body, loosed his shaft. Meant for the breast, it would have been no less mortal in the back, if Susanna, for all her bitter passion, had not taken in all these signs in one breath. She uttered a shriek rather of rage than fear, and flung herself into the opening of the hatch, arms spread and braced to ward off her lover's death.

At the first cry Liliwin had thrust Rannilt towards the way of escape, and sprung erect out of the hay to put his slight body between her and harm. Iestyn bore down on him, the brandished dagger caught the levelled ray of the sun and sent splinters of light dancing about the roof. The blade hung over Liliwin's heart when Susanna's shriek caused Iestyn to baulk and shudder where he stood, straining backwards like a horse suddenly reined in, and the point of the knife slid wildly down, slicing along the boy's parrying forearm, and drawing a fine spray of blood in the hay.

She was melting, she was dissolving into herself, as a man of snow folds into himself gradually when the thaw comes. The impact of the arrow, striking full into her left breast, had spun her round. She sank slowly with her hands clutching the shaft where it had pierced her, and her eyes fixed, huge and clouded, upon Iestyn, for whom the death had been intended. Liliwin, dazedly watching as the man sprang back to clasp her, said afterwards that she was smiling. But his recollections were confused and wild, what he chiefly recalled was a terrible howl of grief and despair that filled and echoed through the loft. The knife was flung aside, and stuck quivering in the boards of the floor. Iestyn embraced his love, moaning, and sank with her in his arms. Round the fearful barrier of the arrow she essayed to lift her failing arms to clasp him. Their kiss was a contortion the trained contortionist in Liliwin remembered lifelong with pity and pain.

Liliwin came to himself soon, because he must. He drew

174

Rannilt up by the hand, away from the lattice of which they had no more need, and coaxed her after him down the ladder to the stable floor where the loaded horses stamped and shifted uneasily after all these nightlong alarms. He hoisted the heavy bars that held the doors, and it took all the strength he had left to lift them. The eastern light reached his face but no lower, as he pushed open both heavy doors, and led Rannilt out into the green meadow.

They were aware of men flowing in as they came gladly out. Their part was done. Brother Cadfael, breathing prayers of gratitude, took them both in his arms, and swept them aside to a grassy knoll at the foot of the headland, where they dropped together thankfully into the spring turf, and drew in the May air and the morning light, and gradually turned and stared and smiled, like creatures in a dream, waking to be glad of each other.

Hugh was up the ladder and into the loft, the sergeant hard on his heels. In the shaft of sunlight, bolder and broader now, and blindingly bright above the lingering dimness of the hay-strewn floor, Iestyn knelt with Susanna in his arms, tenderly holding her up from the boards, for the shaft had pierced clean through her, and jutted at her shoulder. Her eyes were already filmed over as though with sleep, but still kept their fixed regard upon her lover's face, a mask of grief and despair. When the sergeant made to lay a hand on Iestyn's shoulder, Hugh waved him away.

'Let him alone,' he said quietly, 'he will not run.' There was no future left to run for, nowhere to run to, no one to run with. Everything he cared for was in his arms, and would not be with him long.

Her blood was on his hands, on the lips and cheek that had caressed her frantically for a moment, as though caresses could make all whole again. He had given over that now, he only crouched and clasped her, and watched her lips trying to form words to take all upon herself, and deliver him but making no sound, and presently ceasing to attempt it. He saw the light go out behind the glassy grey of her eyes.

Not until then did Hugh touch him. 'She is gone, Iestyn. Lay her down now and come with us. I promise you she shall be brought home decently.'

Iestyn laid her in the piled hay, and got to his feet slowly. The climbing sun fingered the knotted binding of the one bundle they had brought up here with them. His dulled eyes fell upon it and flamed. He plucked it from the floor, and hurled it out through the hatch, to burst asunder in the grass of the meadow, scattering its contents in a shower of sparks as the level beams crept across the pasture.

A great howl of desolation and loss welled up out of Iestyn's throat to bay at the cloudless and untroubled sky: 'And I would have taken her barefoot in her shift!'

Outside in the pasture another aggrieved wail arose like an echo, as Walter Aurifaber grovelled in the grass on his hands and knees, frantically clawing up from among the tussocks his despised gold and silver.

Chapter Fourteen

Afterwards

THEY TOOK back the living and the dead alike into Shrewsbury in the radiant, slanting light of morning. Iestyn, mute now and indifferent to his fate, to a lodging in the castle; Susanna, safe from any penalty in this world, to the depeopled household from which three generations together would shortly be carried to the grave. Walter Aurifaber followed dazedly, hugging his recovered wealth, and regarding his daughter's body with a faint frown of bewilderment, as though, tugged between his loss and his gain, he could not yet determine what he should be feeling. For after all, she had robbed him and vilified him at the end, and if he had been deprived of a competent housekeeper, that was his sole serious loss, and there was another woman at home now to take her place. And with Daniel surely maturing and taking a pride in his own craftsmanship, he might very well manage without having to pay a journeyman. Whatever conflict disrupted Walter would soon be resolved in favour of satisfaction.

As for the two delivered lovers, bereft of words, unable to unlock eyes or hands, Cadfael took them in charge, and mindful of the proprieties, of Prior Robert's chaste disapproval and Abbot Radulfus' shrewd regard for the ordered peace of the rule, thought well to speak a word in Hugh's ear and enlist the ready sympathy of Hugh's lady. Aline welcomed Rannilt into her care with delight, and undertook to provide and instruct her in everything a bride should possess and know, to feed her plump and rosy, and coax into full light those beauties in her which hitherto had gone veiled and unregarded.

'For if you intend to take her away with you,' said Cadfael, propelling the half-reluctant Liliwin back over the bridge towards the abbey gatehouse, 'you'd best marry her here, where there'll be shame-faced folk enough anxious to set you up with small favours, to pay for their misuse of you earlier. No need to despise the gifts of this world when they come honestly. And you'll be doing the givers a kindness, they'll have made their peace with their consciences. You come back to us, and don't grudge a week's waiting to make ready for your marriage. You could hardly bring your girl back to share your bed in the porch.' Or behind an altar, he thought but did not say. 'She'll be safe there with Hugh's lady, and come to you with every man's goodwill.'

Cadfael was right. Shrewsbury had a bad conscience about Liliwin, as soon as word of the scandalous truth was being passed round over market-stalls and shop counters and traded along the streets. All those who had been too hasty in hunting him took care to proffer small favours by way of redress. The provost, who had taken no part, noted the sad state of the young man's only pair of shoes, and set an example by making him a fine new pair in which to resume his travels. Other members of the guild merchant took the hint. The tailors combined to clothe him decently. He bade fair to emerge better provided than ever before in his life.

But the best gift of all came from Brother Anselm.

'Well, since you won't stay and be celibate here among us,' said the precentor cheerfully, 'here is your own rebec ready for playing, and a good leather bag to carry it in. I'm pleased with my work, it came out better than I dared hope, and you'll find it still has a very sweet voice, after all its misadventures.' And he added sternly, while Liliwin embraced his recovered treasure with a joy far more profound than if it had been gold and silver, 'Now bear in mind what you've learned here concerning the reading and writing of music. Never lose your skills. Let me not be ashamed of my pupil when you come this way and visit us again.'

And Liliwin poured out fervent thanks, and promises he might never be able to keep, though he meant them with all his heart.

They were married at the parish altar, where Liliwin had first taken refuge, by Father Adam, priest of the Foregate parish, in the presence of Hugh and Aline Beringar, Brother Cadfael, Brother Oswin, Brother Anselm, and several more of the brothers who felt a sympathetic interest in their departing guest. Abbot Radulfus himself gave them his blessing.

Afterwards, when they had packed up their wedding clothes and put on the everyday homespun in which they meant to set out together, they sought out Hugh Beringar, who was sitting with Brother Cadfael in the ante-chamber of the guest-hall.

'We should be off soon,' said Liliwin, speaking for both, 'to get the best of the day on the road to Lichfield. But we wanted to ask, before we go ... His trial must be weeks away, we might never hear. He won't hang, will he?'

So little they had, those two, even if it was more than ever they had possessed before, and yet they had so much that they could afford pity. 'You don't want him to hang?' said Hugh. 'He would have killed you, Rannilt. Or do you not believe that, now it's all past?'

'Yes,' she said simply, 'I do believe it. I think he would have done it. I know she would. But I don't want his death. I never wanted hers. He won't hang, will he?'

'Not if my voice is heard. Whatever he may have done, he did not kill, and all that he stole has been restored. Whatever he did was done at her wish. I think you may set out with quiet minds,' said Hugh gently. 'He'll live. He's younger than she. He may yet take another, even if it must be a second-best.'

For whatever else might be called in question about those two unhappy sinners, Rannilt had been a witness to the devoted and desperate love between them.

'He may end as a decent craftsman, settled with wife and children,' said Hugh. Children who would be born in peace, not buried still in the womb, like Susanna's child. Three months gone, was the physician's estimate. Even if she had not seized the opportunity of her brother's wedding feast, she would have had to make her bid for freedom very soon.

'He would have given himself up for her sake,' said Liliwin seriously, 'and so would she for him. And she did die for him. I saw. We both saw. She knew what she did. Surely that must count?'

So it might, and so, surely, must the pity and prayers of two young creatures so misused and so magnanimous. Who should more certainly prevail?

'Come,' said Brother Cadfael, 'we'll bring you through the gate and see you on your way. And God go with you!'

And forth they went, hopefully and happily, the new leather bag slung proudly on Liliwin's shoulder. To a life that could never be less than hard and insecure, he the wandering entertainer at fairs and markets and small manors, she, no doubt, soon just as adept with that pure, small voice of hers, and a dance or two to her husband's playing. In all weathers, at all seasons, but with luck finding a decent patron for the winter, and a good fire. And at the very worst, together.

'Do you truly believe,' asked Cadfael, when the two little figures had vanished along the Foregate, 'that Iestyn also may have a life before him?'

'If he can make the effort. No one is going to press for his death. He is coming back to life, not willingly, but because he must. There is a vigour in him he can't shift all on to the past. It will be a minor love, but he'll marry and breed yet.'

'And forget her?'

'Have I said so?' said Hugh, and smiled.

'Whatever she did of worst,' said Cadfael soberly, 'came of that in her that might have been best, if it had not been maimed. She was much wronged.'

'Old friend,' said Hugh, shaking his head with rueful affection, 'I doubt if even you can get Susanna into the fold among the lambs. She chose her way, and it's taken her far out of reach of man's mercy, if ever she'd lived to face trial. And now, I suppose,' he said, seeing his friend's face still thoughtful and undismayed, 'you will tell me roundly that God's reach is longer than man's.'

'It had better be,' said Brother Cadfael very solemnly, 'otherwise we are all lost.'

180

The Devil's Novice

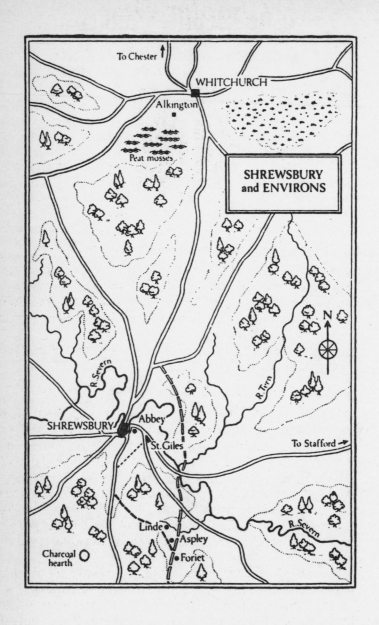

To Chester

WHITCHURCH

Alkington

Peat mosses

SHREWSBURY
and ENVIRONS

N

R. Severn

R. Tern

SHREWSBURY

Abbey

St. Giles

To Stafford

R. Severn

Linde

Aspley

Foriet

Charcoal
hearth

Chapter One

N THE middle of September of that year of Our
Lord, 1140, two lords of Shropshire manors, one
north of the town of Shrewsbury, the other south,
sent envoys to the abbey of Saint Peter and Saint
Paul on the same day, desiring the entry of younger sons of
their houses to the Order.

One was accepted, the other rejected. For which different
treatment there were weighty reasons.

'I have called you few together,' said Abbot Radulfus, 'before
making any decision in this matter, or opening it to
consideration in chapter, since the principle here involved is at
question among the masters of our order at this time. You,
Brother Prior and Brother Sub-Prior, as bearing the daily
weight of the household and family, Brother Paul as master of
the boys and novices, Brother Edmund as an obedientiary and
a child of the cloister from infancy, to advise upon the one
hand, and Brother Cadfael, as a conversus come to the life at a
ripe age and after wide venturings, to speak his mind upon the
other.'

So, thought Brother Cadfael, mute and passive on his stool
in the corner of the abbot's bare, wood-scented parlour, I am
to be the devil's lawman, the voice of the outer world.
Mellowed through seventeen years or so of a vocation, but still
sharpish in the cloistered ear. Well, we serve according to our
skills, and in the degrees allotted to us, and this may be as good

183

a way as any. He was more than a little sleepy, for he had been outdoors between the orchards of the Gaye and his own herb garden within the pale ever since morning, between the obligatory sessions of office and prayer, and was slightly drunk with the rich air of a fine, fat September, and ready for his bed as soon as Compline was over. But not yet so sleepy that he could not prick a ready ear when Abbot Radulfus declared himself in need of counsel, or even desirous of hearing counsel he yet would not hesitate to reject if his own incisive mind pointed him in another direction.

'Brother Paul,' said the abbot, casting an authoritative eye round the circle, 'has received requests to accept into our house two new devotionaries, in God's time to receive the habit and the tonsure. The one we have to consider here is from a good family, and his sire a patron of our church. Of what age, Brother Paul, did you report him?'

'He is an infant, not yet five years old,' said Paul.

'And that is the ground of my hesitation. We have now only four boys of tender age among us, two of them not committed to the cloistral life, but here to be educated. True, they may well choose to remain with us and join the community in due time, but that is left to them to decide, when they are of an age to make such a choice. The other two, infant oblates given to God by their parents, are already twelve and ten years old, and are settled and happy among us, it would be ill-done to disturb their tranquillity. But I am not easy in my mind about accepting any more such oblates, when they can have no conception of what they are being offered or, indeed, of what they are being deprived. It is joy,' said Radulfus, 'to open the doors to a truly committed heart and mind, but the mind of a child barely out of nurse belongs with his toys, and the comfort of his mother's lap.'

Prior Robert arched his silver eyebrows and looked dubiously down his thin, patrician nose. 'The custom of offering children as oblates has been approved for centuries. The Rule sanctions it. Any change which departs from the Rule must be undertaken only after grave reflection. Have we the right to deny what a father wishes for his child?'

'Have we – has the father – the right to determine the course of a life, before the unwitting innocent has a voice to speak for himself? The practice, I know, is long established, and never before questioned, but it is being questioned now.'

'In abandoning it,' persisted Robert, 'we may be depriving

184

some tender soul of its best way to blessedness. Even in the years of childhood a wrong turning may be taken, and the way to divine grace lost.'

'I grant the possibility,' agreed the abbot, 'but also I fear the reverse may be true, and many such children, better suited to another life and another way of serving God, may be shut into what must be for them a prison. On this matter I know only my own mind. Here we have Brother Edmund, a child of the cloister from his fourth year, and Brother Cadfael, conversus after an active and adventurous life and at a mature age. And both, as I hope and believe, secure in commitment. Tell us, Edmund, how do you look upon this matter? Have you regretted ever that you were denied experience of the world outside these walls?'

Brother Edmund the infirmarer, only eight years short of Cadfael's robust sixty, and a grave, handsome, thoughtful creature who might have looked equally well on horseback and in arms, or farming a manor and keeping a patron's eye on his tenants, considered the question seriously, and was not disturbed. 'No, I have had no regrets. But neither did I know what there might be worth regretting. And I have known those who did rebel, even wanting that knowledge. It may be they imagined a better world without than is possible in this life, and it may be that I lack that gift of imagination. Or it may be only that I was fortunate in finding work here within to my liking and within my scope, and have been too busy to repine. I would not change. But my choice would have been the same if I had grown to puberty here, and made my vows only when I was grown. I have cause to know that others would have chosen differently, had they been free.'

'That is fairly spoken,' said Radulfus, 'Brother Cadfael, what of you? You have ranged over much of the world, as far as the Holy Land, and borne arms. Your choice was made late and freely, and I do not think you have looked back. Was that gain, to have seen so much, and yet chosen this small hermitage?'

Cadfael found himself compelled to think before he spoke, and beneath the comfortable weight of a whole day's sunlight and labour thought was an effort. He was by no means certain what the abbot wanted from him, but had no doubt whatever of his own indignant discomfort at the notion of a babe in arms being swaddled willy-nilly in the habit he himself had assumed willingly.

185

'I think it was gain,' he said at length, 'and moreover, a better gift I brought, flawed and dinted though it might be, than if I had come in my innocence. For I own freely that I had loved my life, and valued high the warriors I had known, and the noble places and great actions I had seen, and if I chose in my prime to renounce all these, and embrace this life of the cloister in preference to all other, then truly I think I paid the best compliment and homage I had to pay. And I cannot believe that anything I hold in my remembrance makes me less fit to profess this allegiance, but rather better fits me to serve as well as I may. Had I been given in infancy, I should have rebelled in manhood, wanting my rights. Free from childhood, I could well afford to sacrifice my rights when I came to wisdom.'

'Yet you would not deny,' said the abbot, his lean face lit briefly by a smile, 'the fitness of certain others, by nature and grace, to come in early youth to the life you discovered in maturity?'

'By no means would I deny it! I think those who do so, and with certainty, are the best we have. So they make the choice of their own will, and by their own light.'

'Well, well!' said Radulfus, and mused with his chin in his hand, and his deep-set eyes shadowed. 'Paul, have you any view to lay before us? You have the boys in charge, and I am well aware they seldom complain of you.' For Brother Paul, middle-aged, conscientious and anxious, like a hen with a wayward brood, was known for his indulgence to the youngest, for ever in defence of mischief, but a good teacher for all that, instilling Latin without pain on either part.

'It would be no burden to me,' said Paul slowly, 'to care for a little lad of four, but it is of no merit that I should take pleasure in such a charge, or that he should be content. That is not what the Rule requires, or so it seems to me. A good father could do as much for a little son. Better if he come in knowledge of what he does, and with some inkling of what he may be leaving behind him. At fifteen or sixteen years, well taught ...'

Prior Robert drew back his head and kept his austere countenance, leaving his superior to make up his own mind as he would. Brother Richard the sub-prior had held his tongue throughout, being a good man at managing day-to-day affairs, but indolent at attempting decisions.

'It has been in my mind, since studying the reasonings of Archbishop Lanfranc,' said the abbot, 'that there must be a change in our thoughts on this matter of child dedication, and I am now convinced that it is better to refuse all oblates until they are able to consider for themselves what manner of life they desire. Therefore, Brother Paul, it is my view that you must decline the offer of this boy, upon the terms desired. Let his father know that in a few years' time the boy will be welcome, as a pupil in our school, but not as an oblate entering the order. At a suitable age, should he so wish, he may enter. So tell his parent.' He drew breath and stirred delicately in his chair, to indicate that the conference was over. 'And you have, as I understand, another request for admission?'

Brother Paul was already on his feet, relieved and smiling. 'There will be no difficulty there, Father. Leoric Aspley of Aspley desires to bring to us his younger son Meriet. But the young man is past his nineteenth birthday, and he comes at his own earnest wish. In his case, Father, we need have no qualms at all.'

'Not that these are favourable times for recruitment,' owned Brother Paul, crossing the great court to Compline with Cadfael at his side, 'that we can afford to turn postulants away. But for all that, I'm glad Father Abbot decided as he did. I have never been quite happy about the young children. Certainly in most cases they may be offered out of true love and fervour. But sometimes a man must wonder ... With lands to keep together, and one or two stout sons already, it's a way of disposing profitably of the third.'

'That can happen,' said Cadfael drily, 'even where the third is a grown man.'

'Then usually with his full consent, for the cloister can be a promising career, too. But the babes in arms – no, that way is too easily abused.'

'Do you think we shall get this one in a few years, on Father Abbot's terms?' wondered Cadfael.

'I doubt it. If he's placed here to school, his sire will have to pay for him.' Brother Paul, who could discover an angel within every imp he taught, was nevertheless a sceptic concerning their elders. 'Had we accepted the boy as an oblate, his keep and all else would be for us to bear. I know the father. A decent enough man, but parsimonious. But his wife, I fancy, will be glad enough to keep her youngest.'

They were at the entrance to the cloister, and the mild green twilight of trees and bushes, tinted with the first tinge of gold, hung still and sweet-scented on the air. 'And the other?' said

187

Cadfael. 'Aspley – that should be somewhere south, towards the fringes of the Long Forest. I've heard the name, but no more. Do you know the family?

'Only by repute, but that stands well. It was the manor steward who came with the word, a solid old countryman, Saxon by his name – Fremund. He reports the young man lettered, healthy and well taught. Every way a gain to us.'

A conclusion with which no one had then any reason to quarrel. The anarchy of a country distracted by civil war between cousins had constricted monastic revenues, kept pilgrims huddled cautiously at home, and sadly diminished the number of genuine postulants seeking the cloister, while frequently greatly increasing the numbers of indigent fugitives seeking shelter there. The promise of a mature entrant already literate, and eager to begin his novitiate, was excellent news for the abbey.

Afterwards, of course, there were plenty of wiseacres pregnant with hindsight, listing portents, talking darkly of omens, brazenly asserting that they had told everyone so. After every shock and reverse, such late experts proliferate.

It was only by chance that Brother Cadfael witnessed the arrival of the new entrant, two days later. After several days of clear skies and sunshine for harvesting the early apples and carting the new-milled flour, it was a day of miserable downpour, turning the roads to mud, and every hollow in the great court into a treacherous puddle. In the carrels of the scriptorium copiers and craftsmen worked thankfully at their desks. The boys kicked their heels discontentedly indoors, baulked of their playtime, and the few invalids in the infirmary felt their spirits sink as the daylight dimmed and went into mourning. Of guests there were few at that time. There was a breathing-space in the civil war, while earnest clerics tried to bring both sides together in agreement, but most of England preferred to stay at home and wait with held breath, and only those who had no option rode the roads and took shelter in the abbey guest-halls.

Cadfael had spent the first part of the afternoon in his workshop in the herbarium. Not only had he a number of concoctions working there, fruit of his autumn harvest of leaves, roots and berries, but he had also got hold of a copy of Aelfric's list of herbs and trees from the England of a century and a half earlier, and wanted peace and quiet in which to

188

study it. Brother Oswin, whose youthful ardour was Cadfael's sometime comfort and frequent anxiety in this his private domain, had been excused attendance, and gone to pursue his studies in the liturgy, for the time of his final vows was approaching, and he needed to be word-perfect.

The rain, though welcome to the earth, was disturbing and depressing to the mind of man. The light lowered; the leaf Cadfael studied darkened before his eyes. He gave up his reading. Literate in English, he had learned his Latin laboriously in maturity, and though he had mastered it, it remained unfamiliar, an alien tongue. He went the round of his brews, stirred here and there, added an ingredient in a mortar and ground until it blended into the cream within, and went back in scurrying haste through the wet gardens to the great court, with his precious parchment in the breast of his habit.

He had reached the shelter of the guest-hall porch, and was drawing breath before splashing through the puddles to the cloister, when three horsemen rode in from the Foregate, and halted under the archway of the gatehouse to shake off the rain from their cloaks. The porter came out in haste to greet them, slipping sidelong in the shelter of the wall, and a groom came running from the stable-yard, splashing through the rain with a sack over his head.

So that must be Leoric Aspley of Aspley, thought Cadfael, and the son who desires to take the cowl here among us. And he stood to gaze a moment, partly out of curiosity, partly out of a vain hope that the downpour would ease, and let him cross to the scriptorium without getting wetter than he need.

A tall, erect, elderly man in a thick cloak led the arrivals, riding a big grey horse. When he shook off his hood he uncovered a head of bushy, grizzled hair and a face long, austere and bearded. Even at that distance, across the wide court, he showed handsome, unsmiling, unbending, with a high-ridged, arrogant nose and a grimly proud set to his mouth and jaw, but his manner to porter and groom, as he dismounted, was gravely courteous. No easy man, probably no easy parent to please. Did he approve his son's resolve, or was he accepting it only under protest and with displeasure? Cadfael judged him to be in the mid-fifties, and thought of him, in all innocence, as an old man, forgetting that his own age, to which he never gave much thought, was past sixty.

He gave rather closer attention to the young man who had followed decorously a few respectful yards behind his father,

189

and lighted down from his black pony quickly to hold his father's stirrup. Almost excessively dutiful, and yet there was something in his bearing reminiscent of the older man's stiff self-awareness, like sire, like son. Meriet Aspley, nineteen years old, was almost a head shorter than Leoric when they stood together on the ground; a well-made, neat, compact young man, with almost nothing to remark about him at first sight. Dark-haired, with his forelocks plastered to his wet forehead, and rain streaking his smooth cheeks like tears. He stood a little apart, his head submissively bent, his eyelids lowered, attentive like a servant awaiting his lord's orders; and when they moved away into the shelter of the gatehouse he followed at heel like a well-trained hound. And yet there was something about him complete, solitary and very much his own, as though he paid observance to these formalities without giving away anything more, an outward and scrupulous observance that touched no part of what he carried within. And such distant glimpses as Cadfael had caught of his face had shown it set and composed as austerely as his sire's and deep, firm hollows at the corners of a mouth at first sight full-lipped and passionate.

No, thought Cadfael, those two are not in harmony, that's certain. And the only way he could account satisfactorily for the chill and stiffness was by returning to his first notion, that the father did not approve his son's decision, probably had tried to turn him from it, and held it against him grievously that he would not be deterred. Obstinacy on the one hand and frustration and disappointment on the other held them apart. Not the best of beginnings for a vocation, to have to resist a father's will. But those who have been blinded by too great a light do not see, cannot afford to see, the pain they cause. It was not the way Cadfael had come into the cloister, but he had known it happen to one or two, and understood its compulsion.

They were gone, into the gatehouse to await Brother Paul, and their formal reception by the abbot. The groom who had ridden in at their heels on a shaggy forest pony trotted down with their mounts to the stables, and the great court was empty again under the steady rain. Brother Cadfael tucked up his habit and ran for the shelter of the cloister, there to shake off the water from his sleeves and cowl, and make himself comfortable to continue his reading in the scriptorium. Within minutes he was absorbed in the problem of whether the 'dittanders' of Aelfric was, or was not, the same as his own 'dittany'. He gave no more thought then to Meriet Aspley, who was so immovably bent on becoming a monk.

The young man was introduced at chapter next day, to make his formal profession and be made welcome by those who were to be his brothers. During their probation novices took no part in the discussions in chapter, but might be admitted to listen and learn on occasions, and Abbot Radulfus held that they were entitled to be received with brotherly courtesy from their entry.

In the habit, newly donned, Meriet moved a little awkwardly, and looked strangely smaller than in his own secular clothes, Cadfael reflected, watching him thoughtfully. There was no father beside him now to freeze him into hostility, and no need to be wary of those who were glad to accept him among them; but still there was a rigidity about him, and he stood with eyes cast down and hands tightly clasped, perhaps over-awed by the step he was taking. He answered questions in a low, level voice, quickly and submissively. A face naturally ivory-pale, but tanned deep gold by the summer sun, the flush of blood beneath his smooth skin quick to mantle on high cheekbones. A thin, straight nose, with fastidious nostrils that quivered nervously, and that full, proud mouth that had so rigorous a set to it in repose, and looked so vulnerable in speech. And the eyes he hid in humility, large-lidded under clear, arched brows blacker than his hair.

'You have considered well,' said the abbot, 'and now have time to consider yet again, without blame from any. Is it your wish to enter the cloistered life here among us? A wish truly conceived and firmly maintained? You may speak out whatever is in your heart.'

The low voice said, rather fiercely than firmly, 'It is my wish, Father.' He seemed almost to start at his own vehemence, and added more warily, 'I beg that you will let me in, and I promise obedience.'

'That vow comes later,' said Radulfus with a faint smile. 'For this while, Brother Paul will be your instructor, and you will submit yourself to him. For those who come into the Order in mature years a full year's probation is customary. You have time both to promise and to fulfil.'

The submissively bowed head reared suddenly at hearing

191

this, the large eyelids rolled back from wide, clear eyes of a dark hazel flecked with green. So seldom had he looked up full into the light that their brightness was startling and disquieting. And his voice was higher and sharper, almost dismayed, as he asked, 'Father, is that needful? Cannot the time be cut short, if I study to deserve? The waiting is hard to bear.'

The abbot regarded him steadily, and drew his level brows together in a frown, rather of speculation and wonder than of displeasure. 'The period can be shortened, if such a move seems good to us. But impatience is not the best counsellor, nor haste the best advocate. It will be made plain if you are ready earlier. Do not strain after a perfection.'

It was clear that the young man Meriet was sensitive to all the implications of both words and tone. He lowered his lids again like shutters over the brightness, and regarded his folded hands. 'Father, I will be guided. But I do desire with all my heart to have the fullness of my commitment, and be at peace.' Cadfael thought that the guarded voice shook for an instant. In all probability that did the boy no harm with Radulfus, who had experience both of passionate enthusiasts and those gradually drawn like lambs to the slaughter of dedication.

'That can be earned,' said the abbot gently.

'Father, it shall!' Yes, the level utterance did quiver, however briefly. He kept the startling eyes veiled.

Radulfus dismissed him with somewhat careful kindness, and closed the chapter after his departure. A model entry? Or was it a shade too close to the feverish fervour an abbot as shrewd as Radulfus must suspect and deplore, and watch very warily hereafter? Yet a high-mettled, earnest youth, coming to his desired haven, might well be over-eager and in too much of a hurry. Cadfael, whose two broad feet had always been solidly planted on earth, even when he took his convinced decision to come into harbour for the rest of a long life, had considerable sympathy with the ardent young, who overdo everything, and take wing at a line of verse or a snatch of music. Some who thus take fire burn to the day of their death, and set light to many others, leaving a trail of radiance to generations to come. Other fires sink for want of fuel, but do no harm to any. Time would discover what young Meriet's small, desperate flame portended.

Hugh Beringar, deputy-sheriff of Shropshire, came down from his manor of Maesbury to take charge in Shrewsbury, for his superior, Gilbert Prestcote, had departed to join King Stephen at Westminster for his half-yearly visit at Michaelmas, to render account of his shire and its revenues. Between the two of them they had held the county staunch and well-defended, reasonably free from the disorders that racked most of the country, and the abbey had good cause to be grateful to them, for many of its sister houses along the Welsh marches had been sacked, pillaged, evacuated, turned into fortresses for war, some more than once, and no remedy offered. Worse than the armies of King Stephen on the one hand and his cousin the empress on the other – and in all conscience they were bad enough – the land was crawling with private armies, predators large and small, devouring everything wherever they were safe from any force of law strong enough to contain them. In Shropshire the law had been strong enough, thus far, and loyal enough to care for its own.

When he had seen his wife and baby son installed comfortably in his town house near St Mary's church, and satisfied himself of the good order kept in the castle garrison, Hugh's first visit was always to pay his respects to the abbot. By the same token, he never left the enclave without seeking Brother Cadfael in his workshop in the garden. They were old friends, closer than father and son, having not only that easy and tolerant relationship of two generations, but shared experiences that made of them contemporaries. They sharpened minds, one upon the other, for the better protection of values and institutions that needed defence with every passing day in a land so shaken and disrupted.

Cadfael asked after Aline, and smiled with pleasure even in speaking her name. He had seen her won by combat, along with high office for so young a man as his friend, and he felt almost a grandsire's fond pride in their firstborn son, to whom he had stood godfather at his baptism in the first days of this same year.

'Radiant,' said Hugh with high content, 'and asking after you. When time serves I'll make occasion to carry you off, and you shall see for yourself how she's blossomed.'

'The bud was rare enough,' said Cadfael. 'And the imp Giles? Dear life, nine months old, he'll be quartering your floors like a hound-pup! They're on their feet almost before they're out of your arms.'

'He's as fast on four legs,' said Hugh proudly, 'as his slave Constance is on two. And has a grip on him like a swordsman born. But God keep that time well away from him many years yet, his childhood will be all too short for me. And God willing, we shall be clear of this shattered time before ever he comes to manhood. There was a time when England enjoyed a settled rule, there must be another such to come.'

He was a balanced and resilient creature, but the times cast their shadow on him when he thought on his office and his allegiance.

'What's the word from the south?' asked Cadfael, observing the momentary cloud. 'It seems Bishop Henry's conference came to precious little in the end.'

Henry of Blois, bishop of Winchester and papal legate, was the king's younger brother, and had been his staunch adherent until Stephen had affronted, attacked and gravely offended the church in the persons of certain of its bishops. Where Bishop Henry's personal allegiance now rested was matter for some speculation, since his cousin the Empress Maud had actually arrived in England and ensconced herself securely with her faction in the west, based upon the city of Gloucester. An exceedingly able, ambitious and practical cleric might well feel some sympathy upon both sides, and a great deal more exasperation with both sides; and it was consistent with his situation, torn between kin, that he should have spent all the spring and summer months of this year trying his best to get them to come together sensibly, and make some arrangement for the future that should appease, if not satisfy, both claims, and give England a credible government and some prospect of the restoration of law. He had done his best, and even managed to bring representatives of both parties to meet near Bath only a month or so ago. But nothing had come of it.

'Though it stopped the fighting,' said Hugh wryly, 'at least for a while. But no, there's no fruit to gather.'

'As we heard it,' said Cadfael, 'the empress was willing to have her claim laid before the church as judge, and Stephen was not.'

'No marvel!' said Hugh, and grinned briefly at the thought. 'He is in possession, she is not. In any submission to trial, he has all to lose, she has nothing at stake, and something to gain. Even a hung judgement would reflect she is no fool. And my king, God give him better sense, has affronted the church, which is not slow to avenge itself. No, there was nothing to be hoped for there. Bishop Henry is bound away into France at this moment, he hasn't given up hope, he's after the backing of the French King and Count Theobald of Normandy. He'll be

194

busy these next weeks, working out some propositions for peace with them, and come back armed to accost both these enemies again. To tell truth, he hoped for more backing here than ever he got, from the north above all. But they held their tongues and stayed at home.'

'Chester?' hazarded Cadfael.

Earl Ranulf of Chester was an independent-minded demi-king in a strong northern palatine, and married to a daughter of the earl of Gloucester, the empress's half-brother and chief champion in this fight, but he had grudges against both factions, and had kept a cautious peace in his own realm so far, without committing himself to arms for either party.

'He and his half-brother, William of Roumare. Roumare has large holdings in Lincolnshire, and the two between them are a force to be reckoned with. They've held the balance, up there, granted, but they could have done more. Well, we can be grateful even for a passing truce. And we can hope.'

Hope was in no very generous supply in England during these hard years, Cadfael reflected ruefully. But do him justice, Henry of Blois was trying his best to bring order out of chaos. Henry was proof positive that there is a grand career to be made in the world by early assumption of the cowl. Monk of Cluny, abbot of Glastonbury, bishop of Winchester, papal legate – a rise as abrupt and spectacular as a rainbow. True, he was a king's nephew to start with, and owed his rapid advancement to the old king Henry. Able younger sons from lesser families, choosing the cloister and the habit could not all expect the mitre, within or without their abbeys. That brittle youngster with the passionate mouth and the green-flecked eyes, for instance – how far was he likely to get on the road to power?

'Hugh,' said Cadfael, damping down his brazier with a turf to keep it live but sleepy, in case he should want it later, 'what do you know of the Aspleys of Aspley? Down the fringe of the Long Forest, I fancy, no great way from the town, but solitary.'

'Not so solitary,' said Hugh, mildly surprised by the query. 'There are three neighbour manors there, all grown from what began as one assart. They all held from the great earl, they all hold from the crown now. He's taken the name Aspley. His grandsire was Saxon to the finger-ends, but a solid man, and Earl Roger took him into favour and left him his land. They're Saxon still, but they'd taken his salt, and were loyal to it and went with the earldom when it came to the crown. This lord

195

took a Norman wife and she brought him a manor somewhere to the north, beyond Nottingham, but Aspley is still the head of his honour. Why, what's Aspley to you?'

'A shape on a horse in the rain,' said Cadfael simply. 'He's brought us his younger son, heaven-bent or hell-bent on the cloistered life. I wondered why, that's the truth of it.'

'Why?' Hugh shrugged and smiled. 'A small honour, and an elder brother. There'll be no land for him, unless he has the martial bent and sets out to carve some for himself. And cloister and church are no bad prospects. A sharp lad could get farther that way than hiring out a sword. Where's the mystery?'

And there, vivid in Cadfael's mind, was the still young and vigorous figure of Henry of Blois to point the judgement. But was that stiff and quivering boy the stuff of government?

'What like is the father?' he asked, sitting down beside his friend on the broad bench against the wall of his workshop.

'From a family older than Ethelred, and proud as the devil himself, for all he has but two manors to his name. Princes kept their own local courts in content, then. There are such houses still, in the hill lands and the forests. I suppose he must be some years past fifty,' said Hugh, pondering placidly enough over his dutiful studies of the lands and lords under his vigilance in these uneasy times. 'His reputation and word stand high. I never saw the sons. There'd be five or six years between them, I fancy. Your sprig would be what age?'

'Nineteen, so he's reported.'

'What frets you about him?' asked Hugh, undisturbed though perceptive; and he slanted a brief glance along his shoulder at Brother Cadfael's blunt profile, and waited without impatience.

'His tameness,' said Cadfael, and checked himself at finding his imagination, rather than his tongue, so unguarded. 'Since by nature he is wild,' he went on firmly, 'with a staring eye on him like a falcon or a pheasant, and a brow like an overhanging rock. And folds his hands and clips his lids like a maidservant scolded!'

'He practises his craft,' said Hugh easily, 'and studies his abbot. So they do, the sharp lads. You've seen them come and go.'

'So I have.' Ineptly enough, some of them, ambitious young fellows gifted with the means to go so far and no farther, and bidding far beyond their abilities. He had no such feeling about this one. That hunger and thirst after acceptance, beyond rescue, seemed to him an end in itself, a measure of desperation. He doubted if the falcon-eyes looked beyond at all, or saw any horizon outside the enclosing wall of the enclave. 'Those who want a door to close behind them, Hugh, must be either escaping into the world within or from the world without. There is a difference. But do you know a way of telling one from the other?'

Chapter Two

HERE WAS a fair crop of October apples that year in the orchards along the Gaye, and since the weather had briefly turned unpredictable, they had to take advantage of three fine days in succession that came in the middle of the week, and harvest the fruit while it was dry. Accordingly they mustered all hands to the work, choir monks and servants, and all the novices except the schoolboys. Pleasant work enough, especially for the youngsters who were allowed to climb trees with approval, and kilt their habits to the knee, in a brief return to boyhood.

One of the tradesmen of the town had a hut close to the corner of the abbey lands along the Gaye, where he kept goats and bees, and he had leave to cut fodder for his beasts under the orchard trees, his own grazing being somewhat limited. He was out there that day with a sickle, brushing the longer grass, last cut of the year, from round the boles, where the scythe could not be safely used. Cadfael passed the time of day with him pleasantly, and sat down with him under an apple tree to exchange the leisured civilities proper to such a meeting. There were very few burgesses in Shrewsbury he did not know, and this good man had a flock of children to ask after.

Cadfael had it on his conscience afterwards that it might well have been his neighbourly attentions that caused his companion to lay down his sickle under the tree, and forget to pick it up again when his youngest son, a frogling knee-high, came hopping to call his father to his midday bread and ale.

However that might be, leave it he did, in the tussocky grass braced against the bole. And Cadfael rose a little stiffly, and went to the picking of apples, while his fellow-gossip hoisted his youngest by standing leaps back to the hut, and listened to his chatter all the way.

The straw baskets were filling merrily by then. Not the largest harvest Cadfael had known from this orchard, but a welcome one all the same. A mellow, half-misty, half-sunlit day, the river running demure and still between them and the high, turreted silhouette of the town, and the ripe scent of harvest, compounded of fruit, dry grasses, seeding plants and summer-warmed trees growing sleepy towards their rest, heavy and sweet on the air and in the nose; no marvel if constraints were lifted and hearts lightened. The hands laboured and the minds were eased. Cadfael caught sight of Brother Meriet working eagerly, heavy sleeves turned back from round, brown, shapely young arms, skirts kilted to smooth brown knees, the cowl shaken low on his shoulders, and his untonsured head shaggy and dark and vivid against the sky. His profile shone clear, the hazel eyes wide and unveiled. He was smiling. No shared, confiding smile, only a witness to his own content, and that, perhaps, brief and vulnerable enough.

Cadfael lost sight of him, plodding modestly ahead with his own efforts. It is perfectly possible to be spiritually involved in private prayer while working hard at gathering apples, but he was only too well aware that he himself was fully absorbed in the sensuous pleasure of the day, and from what he had seen of Brother Meriet's face, so was that young man. And very well it suited him.

It was unfortunate that the heaviest and most ungainly of the novices should choose to climb the very tree beneath which the sickle was lying, and still more unfortunate that he should venture to lean out too far in his efforts to reach one cluster of fruit. The tree was of the tip-bearing variety, and the branches weakened by a weighty crop. A limb broke under the strain, and down came the climber in a flurry of falling leaves and crackling twigs, straight on to the upturned blade of the sickle.

It was a spectacular descent, and half a dozen of his fellows heard the crashing fall and came running, Cadfael among the first. The young man lay motionless in the tangle of his habit, arms and legs thrown broadcast, a long gash in the left side of his gown, and a bright stream of blood dappling his sleeve and the grass under him. If ever a man presented the appearance of sudden and violent death, he did. No wonder the unpractised young stood aghast with cries of dismay on seeing him.

Brother Meriet was at some distance, and had not heard the fall. He came in innocence between the trees, hefting a great basket of fruit towards the riverside path. His gaze, for once open and untroubled, fell upon the sprawled figure, the slit gown, the gush of blood. He baulked like a shot horse, starting back with heels stuttering in the turf. The basket fell from his hands and spilled apples all about the sward.

He made no sound at all, but Cadfael, who was kneeling beside the fallen novice, looked up, startled by the rain of fruit, into a face withdawn from life and daylight into the clay-stillness of death. The fixed eyes were green glass with no flame behind them. They stared and stared unblinking at what seemed a stabbed man, dead in the grass. All the lines of the mask shrank, sharpened, whitened, as though they would never move or live again.

'Fool boy!' shouted Cadfael, furious at being subjected to such alarm and shock when he already had one fool boy on his hands. 'Pick up your apples and get them and yourself out of here, and out of my light, if you can do nothing better to help. Can you not see the lad's done no more than knock his few wits out of his head against the bole, and skinned his ribs on the sickle? If he does bleed like a stuck pig, he's well alive, and will be.'

And indeed, the victim proved it by opening one dazed eye, staring round him as if in search of the enemy who had done this to him, and becoming voluble in complaint of his injuries. The relieved circle closed round him, offering aid, and Meriet was left to gather what he had spilled, in stiff obedience, still without word or sound. The frozen mask was very slow to melt, the green eyes were veiled before ever the light revived behind them.

The sufferer's wound proved to be, as Cadfael had said, a messy but shallow graze, soon staunched and bound close with a shirt sacrificed by one of the novices, and the stout linen band from the repaired handle of one of the fruit-baskets. His knock on the head had raised a bump and given him a headache, but no worse than that. He was despatched back to the abbey as soon as he felt inclined to rise and test his legs, in the company of two of his fellows big enough and brawny enough to make a chair for him with their interlaced hands and wrists if he foundered. Nothing was left of the incident but the trampling

200

of many feet about the patch of drying blood in the grass, and the sickle which a frightened boy came timidly to reclaim. He hovered until he could approach Cadfael alone, and was cheered and reassured at being told there was no great harm done, and no blame being urged against his father for an unfortunate oversight. Accidents will happen, even without the assistance of forgetful goat-keepers and clumsy and overweight boys.

As soon as everyone else was off his hands, Cadfael looked round for the one remaining problem. And there he was, one black-habited figure among the rest, working away steadily; just like the others, except that he kept his face averted, and while all the rest were talking shrilly about what had happened, the subsiding excitement setting them twittering like starlings, he said never a word. A certain rigour in his movements, as if a child's wooden doll had come to life; and always the high shoulder turned if anyone came near. He did not want to be observed; not, at least, until he recovered the mastery of his own face.

They carried their harvest home, to be laid out in trays in the lofts of the great barn in the grange court, for these later apples would keep until Christmas. On the way back, in good time for Vespers, Cadfael drew alongside Meriet, and kept pace with him in placid silence most of the way. He was adept at studying people while seeming to have no interest in them beyond a serene acceptance that they were in the same world with him.

'Much ado, back there,' said Cadfael, essaying a kind of apology, which might have the merit of being surprising, 'over a few inches of skin. I spoke you rough, brother, in haste. Bear with me! He might as easily have been what you thought him. I had that vision before me as clear as you had. Now we can both breathe the freer.'

The head bent away from him turned ever so swiftly and warily to stare along a straight shoulder. The flare of the green-gold eyes was like very brief lightning, sharply snuffed out. A soft, startled voice said, 'Yes, thank God! And thank you, brother!' Cadfael thought the 'brother' was a dutiful but belated afterthought, but valued it none the less. 'I was small use, you were right. I ... am not accustomed ...' said Meriet lamely.

'No, lad, why should you be? I'm well past double your age, and came late to the cowl, not like you. I have seen death in many shapes, I've been soldier and sailor in my time; in the

201

east, in the Crusade, and for ten years after Jerusalem fell. I've seen men killed in battle. Come to that, I've killed men in battle. I never took joy in it, that I can remember, but I never drew back from it, either, having made my vows.' Something was happening there beside him, he felt the young body braced to sharp attention. The mention, perhaps, of vows other than the monastic, vows which had also involved the matter of life and death? Cadfael, like a fisherman with a shy and tricky bite on his line, went on paying out small-talk, easing suspicion, engaging interest, exposing, as he did not often do, the past years of his own experience. The silence favoured by the Order ought not to be allowed to stand in the way of its greater aims, where a soul was tormenting itself on the borders of conviction. A garrulous old brother, harking back to an adventurous past, ranging half the known world – what could be more harmless, or more disarming?

'I was with Robert of Normandy's company, and a mongrel lot we were, Britons, Normans, Flemings, Scots, Bretons – name them, they were there! After the city was settled and Baldwin crowned, the most of us went home, over a matter of two or three years, but I had taken to the sea by then, and I stayed. There were pirates ranged those coasts, we had always work to do.'

The young thing beside him had not missed a word of what had been said, he quivered like an untrained but thoroughbred hound hearing the horn, though he said nothing.

'And in the end I came home, because it was home and I felt the need of it,' said Cadfael. 'I served here and there as a free man-at-arms for a while and then I was ripe, and it was time. But I had had my way through the world.'

'And now, what do you do here?' wondered Meriet.

'I grow herbs, and dry them, and make remedies for all the ills that visit us. I physic a great many souls besides those of us within.'

'And that satisfies you?' It was a muted cry of protest; it would not have satisfied him.

'To heal men, after years of injuring them? What could be more fitting? A man does what he must do,' said Cadfael carefully, 'whether the duty he has taken on himself is to fight, or to salvage poor souls from the fighting, to kill, to die or to heal. There are many will claim to tell you what is due from you, but only one who can shear through the many, and reach the truth. And that is you, by what light falls for you to show

202

the way. Do you know what is hardest for me here of all I have vowed? Obedience. And I am old.'

And have had my fling, and a wild one, was implied. And what am I trying to do now, he wondered, to warn him off pledging too soon what he cannot give, what he has not got to give?

'It is true!' said Meriet abruptly. 'Every man must do what is laid on him to do and not question. If that is obedience?' And suddenly he turned upon Brother Cadfael a countenance altogether young, devout and exalted, as though he had just kissed, as once Cadfael had, the crossed hilt of his own poniard, and pledged his life's blood to some cause as holy to him as the deliverance of the city of God.

Cadfael had Meriet on his mind the rest of that day, and after Vespers he confided to Brother Paul the uneasiness he felt in recalling the day's disaster; for Paul had been left behind with the children, and the reports that had reached him had been concerned solely with Brother Wolstan's fall and injuries, not with the unaccountable horror they had aroused in Meriet.

'Not that there's anything strange in shying at the sight of a man lying in his blood, they were all shaken by it. But he – what he felt was surely extreme.'

Brother Paul shook his head doubtfully over his difficult charge. 'Everything he feels is extreme. I don't find in him the calm and the certainty that should go with a true vocation. Oh, he is duty itself, whatever I ask of him he does, whatever task I set him he performs, he's greedy to go faster than I lead him. I never had a more diligent student. But the others don't like him, Cadfael. He shuns them. Those who have tried to approach him say he turns from them, and is rough and short in making his escape. He'd rather go solitary. I tell you, Cadfael, I never knew a postulate pursue his novitiate with so much passion, and so little joy. Have you once seen him smile since he entered here?'

Yes, once, thought Cadfael; this afternoon before Wolstan fell, when he was picking apples in the orchard, the first time he's left the enclave since his father brought him in.

'Do you think it would be well to bring him to chapter?' he wondered dubiously.

'I did better than that, or so I hoped. With such a nature, I would not seem to be complaining where I have no just cause for complaint. I spoke to Father Abbot about him. "Send him to me," says Radulfus, "and reassure him," he says, "that I am here to be open to any who need me, the youngest boy as surely as any of my obedientiaries, and he may approach me as his own father, without fear." And send him I did, and told him he could open his thoughts with every confidence. And what came of it? "Yes, Father, no, Father, I will, Father!" And never a word blurted out from the heart. The only thing that opens his lips freely is the mention that he might be mistaken in coming here, and should consider again. That brings him to his knees fast enough. He begs to have his probation shortened, to be allowed to take his vows soon. Father Abbot read him a lecture on humility and the right use of the year's novitiate, and he took it to heart, or seemed to, and promised patience. But still he presses. Books he swallows faster than I can feed them to him, he's bent on hurrying to his vows at all costs. The slower ones resent him. Those who can keep pace with him, having the start of him by two months or more, say he scorns them. That he avoids them I've seen for myself. I won't deny I'm troubled for him.'

So was Cadfael, though he did not say how deeply.

'I couldn't but wonder ...' went on Paul thoughtfully. 'Tell him he may come to me as to his father, without fear, says the abbot. What sort of reassurance should that be to a young fellow new from home? Did you see them, Cadfael, when they came? The pair of them together?'

'I did,' said Cadfael cautiously, 'though only for moments as they lighted down and shook off the rain, and went within.'

'When did you need more than moments?' said Brother Paul. 'As to his own father, indeed! I was present throughout, I saw them part. Without a tear, with few words and hard, his sire went hence and left him to me. Many, I know, have done so before, fearing the parting as much as their young could fear it, perhaps more.' Brother Paul had never engendered, christened, nursed, tended young of his own, and yet there had been some quality in him that the old Abbot Heribert, no subtle nor very wise man, had rightly detected, and confided to him the boys and the novices in a trust he had never betrayed. 'But I never saw one go without the kiss,' said Paul. 'Never before. As Aspley did.'

In the darkness of the long dortoir, almost two hours past Compline, the only light was the small lamp left burning at the head of the night stairs into the church, and the only sound the occasional sigh of a sleeper turning, or the uneasy shifting of a wakeful brother. At the head of the great room Prior Robert had his cell, commanding the whole length of the open corridor between the two rows of cells. There had been times when some of the younger brothers, not yet purged of the old Adam, had been glad of the fact that the prior was a heavy sleeper. Sometimes Cadfael himself had been known to slip out by way of the night stairs, for reasons he considered good enough. His first encounters with Hugh Beringar, before that young man won his Aline or achieved his office, had been by night, and without leave. And never regretted! What Cadfael did not regret, he found grave difficulty in remembering to confess. Hugh had been a puzzle to him then, an ambiguous young man who might be either friend or enemy. Proof upon proof since then sealed him friend, the closest and dearest.

In the silence of this night after the apple-gathering, Cadfael lay awake and thought seriously, not about Hugh Beringar, but about Brother Meriet, who had recoiled with desperate revulsion from the image of a stabbed man lying dead in the grass. An illusion! The injured novice lay sleeping in his bed now, nor more than three or four cells from Meriet, uneasily, perhaps, with his ribs swathed and sore, but there was not a sound from where he lay, he must be fathoms deep. Did Meriet sleep half as well? And where had he seen, or why had he so vividly imagined, a dead man in his blood?

The quiet, with more than an hour still to pass before midnight, was absolute. Even the restless sleepers had subsided into peace. The boys, by the abbot's orders separated from their elders, slept in a small room at the end of the dortoir, and Brother Paul occupied the cell that shielded their private place. Abbot Radulfus knew and understood the unforeseen dangers that lurked in ambush for celibate souls, however innocent.

Brother Cadfael slept without quite sleeping, much as he had done many a time in camp and on the battlefield, or wrapped in his sea-cloak on deck, under the stars of the Midland Sea. He had talked himself back into the east and the past, alerted to danger, even where no danger could possibly be.

The scream came rendingly, shredding the darkness and the silence, as if two demoniac hands had torn apart by force the slumbers of all present here, and the very fabric of the night. It rose into the roof, and fluttered ululating against the beams of

205

the ceiling, starting echoes wild as bats. There were words in it, but no distinguishable word, it gabbled and stormed like a malediction, broken by sobbing pauses to draw in breath.

Cadfael was out of his bed before it rose to its highest shriek, and groping into the passage in the direction from which it came. Every soul was awake by then, he heard a babble of terrified voices and a frantic gabbling of prayers, and Prior Robert, slow and sleepy, demanding querulously who dared so disturb the peace. Beyond where Brother Paul slept, children's voices joined in the cacophony; the two youngest boys had been startled awake and were wailing their terror, and no wonder. Never had their sleep here been so rudely shattered, and the youngest was no more than seven years old. Paul was out of his cell and flying to comfort them. The clamour and complaint continued, loud and painful, by turns threatening and threatened. Saints converse in tongues with God. With whom did this fierce, violent voice converse, against whom did it contend, and in what language of pain, anger and defiance?

Cadfael had taken his candle out with him, and made for the lamp by the night-stairs to kindle it, thrusting his way through the quaking darkness and shoving aside certain aimless, agitated bodies that blundered about in the passage, blocking the way. The din of shouting, cursing and lamenting, still in the incoherent tongue of sleep, battered at his ears all the way, and the children howled piteously in their small room. He reached the lamp, and his taper flared and burned up steadily, lighting staring faces, open-mouthed and wide-eyed, and the lofty beams of the roof above. He knew already where to look for the disturber of the peace. He elbowed aside those who blundered between, and carried his candle into Meriet's cell. Less confident souls came timidly after, circling and staring, afraid to approach too near.

Brother Meriet sat bolt upright in his bed, quivering and babbling, hands clenched into fists in his blanket, head reared back and eyes tight-closed. There was some reassurance in that, for however tormented, he was still asleep, and if the nature of his sleep could be changed, he might wake unscathed. Prior Robert was not far behind the starers now, and would not hesitate to seize and shake the rigid shoulder readiest to his hand, in peremptory displeasure. Cadfael eased an arm cautiously round the braced shoulders instead and held him close. Meriet shuddered and the rhythm of this distressful crying hiccuped and faltered. Cadfael set down his candle, and

206

spread his palm over the young man's forehead, urging him gently down to his forsaken pillow. The wild crying subsided into a child's querulous whimper, stuttered and ceased. The stiff body yielded, softened, slid down into the bed. By the time Prior Robert reached the bedside, Meriet lay in limp innocence, fast asleep and free of his incubus.

Brother Paul brought him to chapter next day, as needing guidance in the proper treatment of one so clearly in dire spiritual turmoil. For his own part, Paul would have been inclined to content himself with paying special attention to the young man for a day or two, trying to draw from him what inward trouble could have caused him such a nightmare, and accompanying him in special prayers for his peace of mind. But Prior Robert would have no delays. Granted the novice had suffered a shocking and alarming experience the previous day, in the accident to his fellow, but so had all the rest of the labourers in the orchard, and none of them had awakened the whole dortoir with his bellowings in consequence. Robert held that such manifestations, even in sleep, amounted to wilful acts of self-display, issuing from some deep and tenacious demon within, and the flesh could be best eased of its devil by the scourge. Brother Paul stood between him and the immediate use of discipline in this case. Let the matter go to the abbot.

Meriet stood in the centre of the gathering with eyes cast down and hands folded, while his involuntary offence was freely discussed about his ears. He had awakened like the rest, such as had so far recovered their peace as to sleep again after the disturbance, when the bell roused them for Matins, and because of the enjoined silence as they filed down the night-stairs he had known of no reason why so many and such wary eyes should be turned upon him, or why his companions should so anxiously leave a great gap between themselves and him. So he had pleaded when finally enlightened about his misbehaviour, and Cadfael believed him.

'I bring him before you, not as having knowingly committed any offence,' said Brother Paul, 'but as being in need of help which I am not fitted to attempt alone. It is true, as Brother Cadfael has told us – for I myself was not with the party yesterday – that the accident to Brother Wolstan caused great alarm to all, and Brother Meriet came upon the scene without warning, and suffered a severe shock, fearing the poor young man was dead. It may be that this alone preyed upon his mind, and came as a dream to disturb his sleep, and no more is needed now than calm and prayer. I ask for guidance.'

'Do you tell me,' Radulfus, with a thoughtful eye on the submissive figure before him, 'that he was asleep throughout? Having roused the entire dortoir?'

'He slept through all,' said Cadfael firmly. 'To have shaken him awake in that state might have done him great harm, but he did not wake. When persuaded, with care, he sank into a deeper level of sleep, and was healed from his distress. I doubt if he recalls anything of his dream, if he did dream. I am sure he knew nothing of what had happened, and the flurry he had caused, until he was told this morning.'

'That is true, Father,' said Meriet, looking up briefly and anxiously. 'They have told me what I did, and I must believe it, and God knows I am sorry. But I swear I knew nothing of my offence. If I had dreams, evil dreams, I recall nothing of them. I know no reason why I should so disturb the dortoir. It is as much a mystery to me as to any. I can but hope it will not happen again.'

The abbot frowned and pondered. 'It is strange that so violent a disturbance should arise in your mind without cause. I think, rather, that the shock of seeing Brother Wolstan lying in his blood does provide a source of deep distress. But that you should have so little power to accept, and to control your own spirit, does that bode well, son, for a true vocation?'

It was the one suggested threat that seemed to alarm Meriet. He sank to his knees, with an abrupt and agitated grace that brought the ample habit swirling about him like a cloak, and lifted a strained face and pleading hands to the abbot.

'Father, help me, believe me! All my wish is to enter here and be at peace, to do all that the Rule asks of me, to cut off all the threads that bind me to my past. If I offend, if I transgress, willingly or no, wittingly or no, medicine me, punish me, lay on me whatever penance you see fit, only don't cast me out!'

'We do not easily despair of a postulant,' said Radulfus, 'or turn our backs on one in need of time and help. There are medicines to soothe a too-fevered mind. Brother Cadfael has such. But they are aids that should be used only in grave need, while you seek better cures in prayer, and in the mastery of yourself.'

'I could better come to terms,' said Meriet vehemently, 'if you would but shorten the period of my probation, and let me in to the fullness of this life. Then there would be no more doubt or fear ...'

Or hope? wondered Cadfael, watching him; and went on to wonder if the same thought had not entered the abbot's mind.

'The fullness of this life,' said Radulfus sharply, 'must be deserved. You are not ready yet to take vows. Both you and we must practise patience some time yet before you will be fit to join us. The more hotly you hasten, the more will you fall behind. Remember that, and curb your impetuosity. For this time, we will wait. I accept that you have not offended willingly, I trust that you may never again suffer or cause such disruption. Go now, Brother Paul will tell you our will for you.'

Meriet cast one flickering glance round all the considering faces, and departed, leaving the brothers to debate what was best to be done with him. Prior Robert, on his mettle, and quick to recognize a humility in which there was more than a little arrogance, felt that the mortification of the flesh, whether by hard labour, a bread and water diet, or flagellation, might help to concentrate and purify a troubled spirit. Several took the simplest line: since the boy had never intended wrong, and yet was a menace to others, punishment was undeserved, but segregation from his fellows might be considered justified, in the interests of the general peace. Yet even that might seem to him a punishment, Brother Paul pointed out.

'It may well be,' said the abbot finally, 'that we trouble ourselves needlessly. How many of us have never had one ill night, and broken it with nightmares? Once is but once. We have none of us come to any harm, not even the children. Why should we not trust that we have seen both the first and the last of it? Two doors can be closed between the dortoir and the boys, should there again be need. And should there again be need, then further measures can be taken.'

Three nights passed peacefully, but on the fourth there was another commotion in the small hours, less alarming than on the first occasion, but scarcely less disturbing. No wild outcry this time, but twice or thrice, at intervals, there were words spoken loudly and in agitation, and such as were distinguishable were deeply disquieting, and caused his fellow-novices to hold off from him with even deeper suspicion.

'He cried out, "No, no, no!" several times,' reported his nearest neighbour, complaining to Brother Paul next morning. 'And then he said, "I will, I will!" and something about obedience and duty ... Then after all was quiet again he

209

suddenly cried out, "Blood!" And I looked in, because he had started me awake again, and he was sitting up in bed wringing his hands. After that he sank down again, there was nothing more. But to whom was he talking? I dread there's a devil has hold of him. What else can it be?'

Brother Paul was short with such wild suppositions, but could not deny the words he himself had heard, nor the disquiet they aroused in him. Meriet again was astonished and upset at hearing that he had troubled the dortoir a second time, and owned to no recollection of any bad dream, or even so small and understandable a thing as a belly-ache that might have disrupted his own rest.

'No harm done this time,' said Brother Paul to Cadfael, after High Mass, 'for it was not loud, and we had the door closed on the children. And I've damped down their gossip as best I can. But for all that, they go in fear of him. They need their peace, too, and he's a threat to it. They say there's a devil at him in his sleep, and it was he brought it here among them, and who knows which of them it will prey on next? The devil's novice, I've heard him called. Oh, I put a stop to that, at least aloud. But it's what they're thinking.'

Cadfael himself had heard the tormented voice, however subdued this time, had heard the pain and desperation in it, and was assured beyond doubt that for all these things there was a human reason. But what wonder if these untravelled young things, credulous and superstitious, dreaded a reason that was not human?

That was well into October and the same day that Canon Eluard of Winchester, on his journey south from Chester, came with his secretary and his groom to spend a night or two for repose in Shrewsbury. And not for simple reasons of religious policy or courtesy, but precisely because the novice Meriet Aspley was housed within the walls of Saint Peter and Saint Paul.

210

Chapter Three

LUARD OF Winchester was a black canon of
considerable learning and several masterships, some
from French schools. It was this wide scholarship and
breadth of mind which had recommended him to
Bishop Henry of Blois, and raised him to be one of the three
highest ranking and best trusted of that great prelate's
household clergy, and left him now in charge of much of the
bishop's pending business while his principal was absent in
France.

Brother Cadfael ranked too low in the hierarchy to be
invited to the abbot's table when there were guests of such
stature. That occasioned him no heart-burning, and cost him
little in first-hand knowledge of what went on, since it was
taken for granted that Hugh Beringar, in the absence of the
sheriff, would be present at any meeting involving political
matters, and would infallibly acquaint his other self with
whatever emerged of importance.

Hugh came to the hut in the herb garden, yawning, after
accompanying the canon to his apartment in the guest-hall.

'An impressive man, I don't wonder Bishop Henry values
him. Have you seen him, Cadfael?'

'I saw him arrive.' A big, portly, heavily built man who
nonetheless rode like a huntsman from his childhood and a
warrior from puberty; a rounded, bushy tonsure on a round,
solid head, and a dark shadow about the shaven jowls when he
lighted down in early evening. Rich, fashionable but austere

clothing, his only jewellery a cross and ring, but both of rare artistry. And he had a jaw on him and an authoritative eye, shrewd but tolerant. 'What's he doing in these parts, in his bishop's absence overseas?'

'Why, the very same his bishop is up to in Normandy, soliciting the help of every powerful man he can get hold of, to try and produce some plan that will save England from being dismembered utterly. While he's after the support of king and duke in France, Henry wants just as urgently to know where Earl Ranulf and his brother stand. They never paid heed to the meeting in the summer, so it seems Bishop Henry sent one of his men north to be civil to the pair of them and make sure of their favour, just before he set off for France – one of his own household clerics, a young man marked for advancement, Peter Clemence. And Peter Clemence has not returned. Which could mean any number of things, but with time lengthening out and never a word from him or from either of that pair in the north concerning him, Canon Eluard began to be restive. There's a kind of truce in the south and west, while the two sides wait and watch each other, so Eluard felt he might as well set off in person to Chester, to find out what goes on up there, and what's become of the bishop's envoy.'

'And what *has* become of him?' asked Cadfael shrewdly. 'For his lordship, it seems, is now on his way south again to join King Stephen. And what sort of welcome did he get in Chester?'

'As warm and civil as heart could wish. And for what my judgement is worth, Canon Eluard, however loyal he may be to Bishop Henry's efforts for peace, is more inclined to Stephen's side than to the empress, and is off back to Westminster now to tell the King he might be wise to strike while the iron's hot, and go north in person and offer a few sweetmeats to keep Chester and Roumare as well-disposed to him as they are. A manor or two and a pleasant title – Roumare is as good as earl of Lincoln now, why not call him so? – could secure his position there. So, at any rate, Eluard seems to have gathered. Their loyalty is pledged over and over. And for all his wife is daughter to Robert of Gloucester, Ranulf did stay snug at home when Robert brought over his imperial sister to take the field a year and more ago. Yes, it seems the situation there could hardly be more to the canon's satisfaction, now that it's stated. But as for why it was not stated a month or so ago, by the mouth of Peter Clemence returning … Simple enough! The man never got there, and they never got his embassage.'

'As sound a reason as any for not answering it,' said Cadfael, unsmiling, and eyed his friend's saturnine visage with narrowed attention. 'How far did he get on his way, then?' There were wild places enough in this disrupted England where a man could vanish, for no more than the coat he wore or the horse he rode. There were districts where manors had been deserted and run wild, and forests had been left unmanned, and whole villages, too exposed to danger, had been abandoned and left to rot. Yet the north had suffered less than the south and west by and large, and lords like Ranulf of Chester had kept their lands relatively stable thus far.

'That's what Eluard has been trying to find out on his way back, stage by stage along the most likely route a man would take. For certainly he never came near Chester. And stage by stage our canon has drawn blank until he came into Shropshire. Never a trace of Clemence, hide, hair or horse, all through Cheshire.'

'And none as far as Shrewsbury?' For Hugh had more to tell, he was frowning down thoughtfully into the beaker he held between his thin, fine hands.

'Beyond Shrewsbury, Cadfael, though only just beyond. He's turned back a matter of a few miles to us, for reason enough. The last he can discover of Peter Clemence is that he stayed the night of the eighth day of September with a household to which he's a distant cousin on the wife's side. And where do you think that was? At Leoric Aspley's manor, down in the edge of the Long Forest.'

'Do you tell me!' Cadfael stared, sharply attentive now. The eighth of the month, and a week or so later comes the steward Fremund with his lord's request that the younger son of the house should be received, at his own earnest wish, into the cloister. *Post hoc* is not *propter hoc*, however. And in any case, what connection could there possibly be between one man's sudden discovery that he felt a vocation, and another man's overnight stay and morning departure? 'Canon Eluard knew he would make one of his halts there? The kinship was known?'

'Both the kinship and his intent, yes, known both to Bishop Henry and to Eluard. The whole manor saw him come, and have told freely how he was entertained there. The whole manor, or very near, saw him off on his journey next morning.

Aspley and his steward rode the first mile with him, with the household and half the neighbours to see them go. No question, he left there whole and brisk and well-mounted.'

'How far to his next night's lodging? And was he expected there?' For if he had announced his coming, then someone should have been enquiring for him long since.

'According to Aspley, he intended one more halt at Whitchurch, a good halfway to his destination, but he knew he could find easy lodging there and had not sent word before. There's no trace to be found of him there, no one saw or heard of him.'

'So between here and Whitchurch the man is lost?'

'Unless he changed his plans and his route, for which, God knows, there could be reasons, even here in my writ,' said Hugh ruefully, 'though I hope it is not so. We keep the best order anywhere in this realm, or so I claim, challenge me who will, but even so I doubt it good enough to make passage safe everywhere. He may have heard something that caused him to turn aside. But the bleak truth of it is, he's lost. And all too long!'

'And Canon Eluard wants him found?'

'Dead or alive,' said Hugh grimly. 'For so will Henry want him found, and an account paid by someone for his price, for he valued him.'

'And the search is laid upon you?' said Cadfael.

'Not in such short terms, No. Eluard is a fair-minded man, he takes a part of the load upon him, and doesn't grudge. But this shire is my business, under the sheriff, and I pick up my share of the burden. Here is a scholar and a cleric vanished where my writ runs. That I do not like,' said Hugh, in the ominously soft voice that had a silver lustre about it like bared steel.

Cadfael came to the question that was uppermost in his mind. 'And why, then, having the witness of Aspley and all his houses at his disposal, did Canon Eluard feel it needful to turn back these few miles to Shrewsbury?' But already he knew the answer.

'Because, my friend, you have here the younger son of that house, new in his novitiate. He is thorough, this Canon Eluard. He wants word from even the stray from that tribe. Who knows which of all that manor may not have noticed the one thing needful?'

It was a piercing thought; it stuck in Cadfael's mind,

214

quivering like a dart. Who knows, indeed? 'He has not questioned the boy yet?'

'No, he would not disrupt the evening offices for such a matter – nor his good supper, either,' added Hugh with a brief grin. 'But tomorrow he'll have him into the guests' parlour and go over the affair with him, before he goes on southward to join the king at Westminster, and prompt him to go and make sure of Chester and Roumare, while he can.'

'And you will be present at that meeting,' said Cadfael with certainty.

'I shall be present. I need to know whatever any man can tell me to the point, if a man has vanished by foul means within my jurisdiction. This is now as much my business as it is Eluard's.'

'You'll tell me,' said Cadfael confidently, 'what the lad has to say, and how he bears himself?'

'I'll tell you,' said Hugh, and rose to take his leave.

As it turned out, Meriet bore himself with stoical calm during that interview in the parlour, in the presence of Abbot Radulfus, Canon Eluard and Hugh Beringar, the powers here of both church and state. He answered questions simply and directly, without apparent hesitation.

Yes, he had been present when Master Clemence came to break his journey at Aspley. No, he had not been expected, he came unheralded, but the house of his kinsmen was open to him whenever he would. No, he had not been there more than once before as a guest, some years ago, he was now a man of affairs, and kept about his lord's person. Yes, Meriet himself had stabled the guest's horse, and groomed, watered and fed him, while the women had made Master Clemence welcome within. He was the son of a cousin of Meriet's mother, who was some two years dead now – the Norman side of the family. And his entertainment? The best they could lay before him in food and drink, music after the supper, and one more guest at the table, the daughter of the neighbouring manor who was affianced to Meriet's elder brother Nigel. Meriet spoke of the occasion with wide-open eyes and clear, still countenance.

'Did Master Clemence say what his errand was?' asked Hugh suddenly. 'Tell where he was bound and for what purpose?'

'He said he was on the bishop of Winchester's business. I don't recall that he said more than that while I was there. But there was music after I left the hall, and they were still seated. I

215

went to see that all was done properly in the stable. He may have said more to my father.'

'And in the morning?' asked Canon Eluard.

'We had all things ready to serve him when he rose, for he said he must be in the saddle early. My father and Fremund, our steward, with two grooms, rode with him the first mile of his way, and I, and the servants, and Isouda ...'

'Isouda?' said Hugh, pricking his ears at a new name. Meriet had passed by the mention of his brother's betrothed without naming her.

'She is not my sister, she is heiress to the manor of Foriet, that borders ours on the southern side. My father is her guardian and manages her lands, and she lives with us.' A younger sister of small account, his tone said, for once quite unguarded. 'She was with us to watch Master Clemence from our doors with all honour, as is due.'

'And you saw no more of him?'

'I did not go with them. But my father rode a piece more than is needful, for courtesy, and left him on a good track.'

Hugh had still one more question. 'You tended his horse. What like was it?'

'A fine beast, not above three years old, and mettlesome.' Meriet's voice kindled into enthusiasm. 'A tall dark bay, with white blaze on his face from forehead to nose, and two white forefeet.'

Noteworthy enough, then, to be readily recognized when found, and moreover, to be a prize for someone. 'If somebody wanted the man out of this world, for whatever reason,' said Hugh to Cadfael afterwards in the herb garden, 'he would still have a very good use for such a horse as that. And somewhere between here and Whitchurch that beast must be, and where he is there'll be threads to take up and follow. If the worst comes to it, a dead man can be hidden, but a live horse is going to come within some curious soul's sight, sooner or later, and sooner or later I shall get wind of it.'

Cadfael was hanging up under the eaves of his hut the rustling bunches of herbs newly dried out at the end of the summer, but he was giving his full attention to Hugh's report at the same time. Meriet had been dismissed without, on the face of it, adding anything to what Canon Eluard had already elicited from the rest of the Aspley household. Peter Clemence had come and gone in good health, well-mounted, and with the protection of the bishop of Winchester's formidable name

216

about him. He had been escorted civilly a mile on his way. And vanished.

'Give me, if you can, the lad's answers in his very words,' requested Cadfael. 'Where there's nothing of interest to be found in the content, it's worth taking a close look at the manner.'

Hugh had an excellent memory, and reproduced Meriet's replies even to the intonation. 'But there's nothing there, barring a very good description of the horse. Every question he answered and still told us nothing, since he knows nothing.'

'Ah, but he did not answer every question,' said Cadfael. 'And I think he may have told us a few notable things, though whether they have any bearing on Master Clemence's vanishing seems dubious. Canon Eluard asked him, "And you saw no more of him?" And the lad said, "*I did not go with them.*" But he did not say he had seen no more of the departed guest. And again, when he spoke of the servants and this Foriet girl, all gathered to speed the departure with him, he did not say "and my brother". Nor did he say that his brother had ridden with the escort.'

'All true,' agreed Hugh, not greatly impressed. 'But none of these need mean anything at all. Very few of us watch every word, to leave no possible detail in doubt.'

'That I grant. Yet it does no harm to note such small things, and wonder. A man not accustomed to lying, but brought up against the need, will evade if he can. Well, if you find your horse in some stable thirty miles or more from here, there'll be no need for you or me to probe behind every word young Meriet speaks, for the hunt will have outrun him and all his family. And they can forget Peter Clemence – barring the occasional Mass, perhaps, for a kinsman's soul.'

Canon Eluard departed for London, secretary, groom, baggage and all, bent on urging King Stephen to pay a diplomatic visit to the north before Christmas, and secure his interest with the two powerful brothers who ruled there almost from coast to coast. Ranulf of Chester and William of Roumare had elected to spend the feast at Lincoln with their ladies, and a little judicious flattery and the dispensing of a modest gift or two might bring in a handsome harvest. The canon had paved the way already, and meant to make the return journey in the king's party.

'And on the way back,' he said, taking leave of Hugh in the

great court of the abbey, 'I shall turn aside from his Grace's company and return here, in the hope that by then you will have some news for me. The bishop will be in great anxiety.'

He departed, and Hugh was left to pursue the search for Peter Clemence, which had now become, for all practical purposes, the search for his bay horse. And pursue it he did, with vigour, deploying as many men as he could muster along the most frequented ways north, visiting lords of manors, invading stables, questioning travellers. When the more obvious halting places yielded nothing, they spread out into wilder country. In the north of the shire the land was flatter, with less forest but wide expanses of heath, moorland and scrub, and several large tracts of peat-moss, desolate and impossible to cultivate, though the locals who knew the safe dykes cut and stacked fuel there for their winter use.

The manor of Alkington lay on the edge of this wilderness of dark-brown pools and quaking mosses and tangled bush, under a pale, featureless sky. It was sadly run down from its former value, its ploughlands shrunken, no place to expect to find, grazing in the tenant's paddock, a tall bay thoroughbred fit for a prince to ride. But it was there that Hugh found him, white-blazed face, white forefeet and all, grown somewhat shaggy and ill-groomed, but otherwise in very good condition.

There was as little concealment about the tenant's behaviour as about his open display of his prize. He was a free man, and held as subtenant under the lord of Wem, and he was willing and ready to account for the unexpected guest in his stable.

'And you see him, my lord, in better fettle than he was when he came here, for he'd run wild some time, by all accounts, and devil a man of us knew whose he was or where he came from. There's a man of mine has an assart west of here, an island on the moss, and cuts turf there for himself and others. That's what he was about when he caught sight of yon creature wandering loose, saddle and bridle and all, and never a rider to be seen, and he tried to catch him, but the beast would have none of it. Time after time he tried, and began to put out feed for him, and the creature was wise enough to come for his dinner, but too clever to be caught. He'd mired himself to the shoulder, and somewhere he tore loose the most of his bridle, and had the saddle ripped round half under his belly before ever we got near him. In the end I had my mare fit, and we staked her out there and she fetched him. Quiet enough, once we had him, and glad to shed what was left of his harness, and

218

feel a currier on his sides again. But we'd no notion whose he was. I sent word to my lord at Wem, and here we keep him till we know what's right.'

There was no need to doubt a word, it was all above board here. And this was but a mile or two out of the way to Whitchurch, and the same distance from the town.

'You've kept the harness? Such as he still had?'

'In the stable, to hand when you will.'

'But no man. Did you look for a man afterwards?' The mosses were no place for a stranger to go by night, and none too safe for a rash traveller even by day. The peat-pools, far down, held bones enough.

'We did, my lord. There are fellows hereabouts who know every dyke and every path and every island that can be trodden. We reckoned he'd been thrown, or foundered with his beast, and only the beast won free. It has been known. But never a trace. And that creature there, though soiled as he was, I doubt if he'd been in above the hocks, and if he'd gone that deep, with a man in the saddle, it would have been the man who had the better chance.'

'You think,' said Hugh, eyeing him shrewdly, 'he came into the mosses riderless?'

'I do think so. A few miles south there's woodland. If there were footpads there, and got hold of the man, they'd have trouble keeping their hold of this one. I reckon he made his own way here.'

'You'll show my sergeant the way to your man on the mosses? He'll be able to tell us more, and show the places where the horse was straying. There's a clerk of the bishop of Winchester's household lost,' said Hugh, electing to trust a plainly honest man, 'and maybe dead. This was his mount. If you learn of anything more send to me, Hugh Beringar, at Shrewsbury castle, and you shan't be the loser.'

'Then you'll be taking him away. God knows what his name was, I called him Russet.' The free lord of this poor manor leaned over his wattle fence and snapped his fingers, and the bay came to him confidently and sank his muzzle into the extended palm. 'I'll miss him. His coat has not its proper gloss yet, but it will come. At least we got the burrs and the rubble of heather out of it.'

'We'll pay you his price,' said Hugh warmly. 'It's well earned. And now I'd best look at what's left of his accoutrements, but I doubt they'll tell us anything more.'

219

It was pure chance that the novices were passing across the
great court to the cloister for the afternoon's instruction when
Hugh Beringar rode in at the gatehouse of the abbey, leading
the horse, called for convenience Russet, to the stable-yard for
safe-keeping. Better here than at the castle, since the horse
was the property of the bishop of Winchester, and at some
future time had better be delivered to him.

Cadfael was just emerging from the cloister on his way to the
herb garden, and was thus brought face to face with the novices
entering. Late in the line came Brother Meriet, in good time to
see the lofty young bay that trotted into the courtyard on a
leading-rein, and arched his copper neck and brandished his
long, narrow white blaze at strange surroundings, shifting
white-sandalled forefeet delicately on the cobbles.

Cadfael saw the encounter clearly. The horse tossed its
narrow, beautiful head, stretched neck and nostril, and
whinnied softly. The young man blanched white as the
blazoned forehead, and jerked strongly back in his careful
stride, and brief sunlight found the green in his eyes. Then he
remembered himself and passed hurriedly on, following his
fellows into the cloister.

In the night, an hour before Matins, the dortoir was shaken by
a great, wild cry of: 'Barbary ... Barbary ...' and then a single
long, piercing whistle, before Brother Cadfael reached
Meriet's cell, smoothed an urgent hand over brow and cheek
and pursed lips, and eased him back, still sleeping, to his
pillow. The edge of the dream, if it was a dream, was abruptly
blunted, the sounds melted into silence. Cadfael was ready to
frown and hush away the startled brothers when they came,
and even Prior Robert hesitated to break so perilous a sleep,
especially at the cost of inconveniencing everyone else's
including his own. Cadfael sat by the bed long after all was
silence and darkness again. He did not know quite what he had
been expecting, but he was glad he had been ready for it. As
for the morrow, it would come, for better or worse.

Chapter Four

ERIET AROSE for Prime heavy-eyed and sombre, but seemingly quite innocent of what had happened during the night, and was saved from the immediate impact of the brothers' seething dread, disquiet and displeasure by being summoned forth, immediately the office was over, to speak with the deputy-sheriff in the stables. Hugh had the torn and weathered harness spread on a bench in the yard, and a groom was walking the horse called Russet appreciatively about the cobbles to be viewed clearly in the mellow morning light.

'I hardly need to ask,' said Hugh pleasantly, smiling at the way the white-fired brow lifted and the wide nostrils dilated at sight of the approaching figure, even in such unfamiliar garb. 'No question but he knows *you* again, I must needs conclude that you know him just as well.' And, as Meriet volunteered nothing, but continued to wait to be asked: 'Is this the horse Pèter Clemence was riding when he left your father's house?'

'Yes, my lord, the same.' He moistened his lips and kept his eyes lowered, but for one spark of a glance for the horse; he did not ask anything.

'Was that the only occasion when you had to do with him? He comes to you readily. Fondle him if you will, he's asking for your recognition.'

'It was I stabled and groomed and tended him, that night,' said Meriet, low-voiced and hesitant. 'And I saddled him in the

221

morning. I never had his like to care for until then. I ... I am good with horses.'

'So I see. Then you have also handled his gear.' It had been rich and fine, the saddle inlaid with coloured leathers, the bridle ornamented with silver-work now dinted and soiled. 'All this you recognize?'

Meriet said, 'Yes. This was his.' And at last he did ask, almost fearfully, 'Where did you find Barbary?'

'Was that his name? His master told you? A matter of twenty miles and more north of here, on the peat-hags near Whitchurch. Very well, young sir, that's all I need from you. You can go back to your duties now.'

Round the water-troughs in the lavatorium, over their ablutions, Meriet's fellows were making the most of his absence. Those who went in dread of him as a soul possessed, those who resented his holding himself apart, those who felt his silence to be nothing short of disdain for them, all raised their voices clamorously to air their collective grievance. Prior Robert was not there, but his clerk and shadow, Brother Jerome, was, and with ears pricked and willing to listen.

'Brother, you heard him yourself! He cried out again in the night, he awoke us all ...'

'He howled for his familiar. I heard the demon's name, he called him Barbary! And his devil whistled back to him ... we all know it's devils that hiss and whistle!'

'He's brought an evil spirit in among us, we're not safe for our lives. And we get no rest at night ... Brother, truly, we're afraid!'

Cadfael, tugging a comb through the thick bush of grizzled hair ringing his nut-brown dome, was in two minds about intervening, but thought better of it. Let them pour out everything they had stored up against the lad, and it might be seen more plainly how little it was. Some genuine superstitious fear they certainly suffered, such night alarms do shake simple minds. If they were silenced now they would only store up their resentment to breed in secret. Out with it all, and the air might clear. So he held his peace, but he kept his ears pricked.

'It shall be brought up again in chapter,' promised Brother Jerome, who thrived on being the prime channel of appeal to the prior's ears. 'Measures will surely be taken to secure rest at nights. If necessary, the disturber of the peace must be segregated.'

'But, brother,' bleated Meriet's nearest neighbour in the dortoir, 'if he's set apart in a separate cell, with no one to watch him, who knows what he may not get up to? He'll have greater freedom there, and I dread his devil will thrive all the more and take hold on others. He could bring down the roof upon us or set fire to the cellars under us ...'

'That is want of trust in divine providence,' said Brother Jerome, and fingered the cross on his breast as he said it. 'Brother Meriet has caused great trouble, I grant, but to say that he is possessed of the devil –.'

'But, brother, it's true! He has a talisman from his demon, he hides it in his bed. I know! I've seen him slip some small thing under his blanket, out of sight, when I looked in upon him in his cell. All I wanted was to ask him a line in the psalm, for you know he's learned, and he had something in his hand, and slipped it away very quickly, and stood between me and the bed, and wouldn't let me in further. He looked black as thunder at me, brother, I was afraid! But I've watched since. It's true, I swear, he has a charm hidden there, and at night he takes it to him to his bed. Surely this is the symbol of his familiar, and it will bring evil on us all!'

'I cannot believe ...' began Brother Jerome, and broke off there, reconsidering the scope of his own credulity. 'You have *seen* this? In his *bed*, you say? Some alien thing hidden away? That is not according to the Rule.' For what should there be in a dortoir cell but cot and stool, a small desk for reading, and the books for study? These, and the privacy and quiet which can exist only by virtue of mutual consideration, since mere token partitions of wainscot separate cell from cell. 'A novice entering here must give up all worldly possessions,' said Jerome, squaring his meagre shoulders and scenting a genuine infringement of the approved order of things. Grist to the mill! Nothing he loved better than an occasion for admonition. 'I shall speak to Brother Meriet about this.'

Half a dozen voices, encouraged, urged him to more immediate action. 'Brother, go now, while he's away, and see if I have not told you truth! If you take away his charm the demon will have no more power over him.'

'And we shall have quiet again ...'

'Come with me!' said Brother Jerome heroically, making up his mind. And before Cadfael could stir, Jerome was off, out of the lavatorium and surging towards the dortoir stairs, with a flurry of novices hard on his heels.

223

Cadfael went after them hunched with resigned disgust, but not foreseeing any great urgency. The boy was safely out of this, hobnobbing with Hugh in the stables, and of course they would find nothing in his cell to give them any further hold on him, malice being a great stimulator of the imagination. The flat disappointment might bring them down to earth. So he hoped! But for all that, he made haste on the stairs.

But someone else was in an even greater hurry. Light feet beat a sharp drum-roll on the wooden treads at Cadfael's back, and an impetuous body overtook him in the doorway of the long dortoir, and swept him several yards down the tiled corridor between the cells. Meriet thrust past with long, indignant strides, his habit flying.

'I heard you! I heard you! Let my things alone!'

Where was the low, submissive voice now, the modestly lowered eyes and folded hands? This a furious young lordling peremptorily ordering hands off his possessions, and homing on the offenders with fists clenched and eyes flashing. Cadfael, thrust off-balance for a moment, made a grab at a flying sleeve, but only to be dragged along in Meriet's wake.

The covey of awed, inquisitive novices gathered round the opening of Meriet's cell, heads thrust cautiously within and rusty black rumps protruding without, whirled in alarm at hearing this angry apparition bearing down on them, and broke away with agitated clucking like so many flurried hens. In the very threshold of his small domain Meriet came nose to nose with Brother Jerome emerging.

On the face of it it was a very uneven confrontation: a mere postulant of a month or so, and one who had already given trouble and been cautioned, facing a man in authority, the prior's right hand, a cleric and confessor, one of the two appointed for the novices. The check did give Meriet pause for one moment, and Cadfael leaned to his ear to whisper breathlessly, 'Hold back, you fool! He'll have your hide!' He might have saved the breath of which he was short, for Meriet did not even hear him. The moment when he might have come to his senses was already past, for his eye had fallen on the small, bright thing Jerome dangled before him from outraged fingers, as though it were unclean. The boy's face blanched, not with the pallor of fear, but the blinding whiteness of pure anger, every line of bone in a strongly-boned countenance chiselled in ice.

'That is mine,' he said with soft and deadly authority, and held out his hand. 'Give it to me!'

Brother Jerome rose on tiptoe and swelled like a turkey-cock at being addressed in such tones. His thin nose quivered with affronted rage. 'And you openly avow it? Do you not know, impudent wretch, that in asking for admittance here you have forsworn "mine", and may not possess property of any kind? To bring in any personal things here without the lord abbot's permission is flouting the Rule. It is a sin! But wilfully to bring with you this – *this!* – is to offend foully against the very vows you say you desire to take. And to cherish it in your bed is a manner of fornication. Do you dare? Do you dare? You shall be called to account for it!'

All eyes but Meriet's were on the innocent cause of offence; Meriet maintained a burning stare upon his adversary's face. And all the secret charm turned out to be was a delicate linen ribbon, embroidered with flowers in blue and gold and red, such a band as a girl would use to bind her hair, and knotted into its length a curl of that very hair, reddish gold.

'Do you so much as know the meaning of the vows you say you wish to take?' fumed Jerome. 'Celibacy, poverty, obedience, stability – is there any sign in you of any of these? Take thought now, while you may, renounce all thought of such follies and pollutions as this vain thing implies, or you cannot be accepted here. Penance for this backsliding you will not escape, but you have time to amend, if there is any grace in you.'

'Grace enough, at any rate,' said Meriet, unabashed and glittering, 'to keep my hands from prying into another man's sheets and stealing his possessions. Give me,' he said through his teeth, very quietly, 'what is mine!'

'We shall see, insolence, what the lord abbot has to say of your behaviour. Such a vain trophy as this you may not keep. And as for your insubordination, it shall be reported faithfully. Now let me pass!' ordered Jerome, supremely confident still of his dominance and his rightness.

Whether Meriet mistook his intention, and supposed that it was simply a matter of sweeping the entire issue into chapter for the abbot's judgement, Cadfael could never be sure. The boy might have retained sense enough to accept that, even if it meant losing his simple little treasure in the end; for after all, he had come here of his own will, and at every check still insisted that he wanted with all his heart to be allowed to remain and take his vows. Whatever his reason, he did step back, though with a frowning and dubious face, and allowed Jerome to come forth into the corridor.

Jerome turned towards the night-stairs, where the lamp was still burning, and all his mute myrmidons followed respectfully. The lamp stood in a shallow bowl on a bracket on the wall, and was guttering towards its end. Jerome reached it, and before either Cadfael or Meriet realized what he was about, he had drawn the gauzy ribbon through the flame. The tress of hair hissed and vanished in a small flare of gold, the ribbon fell apart in two charred halves, and smouldered in the bowl. And Meriet, without a sound uttered, launched himself like a hound leaping, straight at Brother Jerome's throat. Too late to grasp at his cowl and try to restrain him, Cadfael lunged after.

No question but Meriet meant to kill. This was no noisy brawl, all bark and no bite, he had his hands round the scrawny throat, bringing Jerome crashing to the floor-tiles under him, and kept his grip and held to his purpose though half a dozen of the dismayed and horrified novices clutched and clawed and battered at him, themselves ineffective, and getting in Cadfael's way. Jerome grew purple, heaving and flapping like a fish out of water, and wagging his hands helplessly against the tiles. Cadfael fought his way through until he could stoop to Meriet's otherwise oblivious ear, and bellow inspired words into it.

'For shame, son! An old man!'

In truth, Jerome lacked twenty of Cadfael's own sixty years, but the need justified the mild exaggeration. Meriet's ancestry nudged him in the ribs. His hands relaxed their grip, Jerome gasped in breath noisily and cooled from purple to brick-red, and a dozen hands hauled the culprit to his feet and held him, still breathing fire and saying no word, just as Prior Robert, tall and awful as though he wore the mitre already, came sailing down the tiled corridor, blazing like a bolt of the wrath of God.

In the bowl of the lamp, the two ends of flowered ribbons smouldered, giving off a dingy and ill-scented smoke, and the stink of the burned ringlet still hung upon the air.

Two of the lay servants, at Prior Robert's orders, brought the manacles that were seldom used, shackled Meriet's wrists, and led him away to one of the punishment cells isolated from all the communal uses of the house. He went with them, still wordless, too aware of his dignity to make any resistance, or put them to any anxiety on his account. Cadfael watched him go with particular interest, for it was as if he saw him for the first time. The habit no longer hampered him, he strode

226

disdainfully, held his head lightly erect, and if it was not quite a sneer that curled his lips and his still-roused nostrils, it came very close to it. Chapter would see him brought to book, and sharply, but he did not care. In a sense he had had his satisfaction.

As for Brother Jerome, they picked him up, put him to bed, fussed over him, brought him soothing draughts which Cadfael willingly provided, bound up his bruised throat with comforting oils, and listened dutifully to the feeble, croaking sounds he soon grew wary of assaying, since they were painful to him. He had taken no great harm, but he would be hoarse for some while, and perhaps for a time he would be careful and civil in dealing with the still unbroken sons of the nobility who came to cultivate the cowl. Mistakenly? Cadfael brooded over the inexplicable predilection of Meriet Aspley. If ever there was a youngster bred for the manor and the field of honour, for horse and arms, Meriet was the man.

'For shame, son! An old man!' And he had opened his hands and let his enemy go, and marched off the field prisoner, but with all the honours.

The outcome at chapter was inevitable; there was nothing to be done about that. Assault upon a priest and confessor could have cost him excommunication, but that was set aside in clemency. But his offence was extreme, and there was no fitting penalty but the lash. The discipline, there to be used only in the last resort, was nevertheless there to be used. It was used upon Meriet. Cadfael had expected no less. The criminal, allowed to speak, had contented himself with saying simply that he denied nothing of what was alleged against him. Invited to plead in extenuation, he refused, with impregnable dignity. And the scourge he endured without a sound.

In the evening, before Compline, Cadfael went to the abbot's lodging to ask leave to visit the prisoner, who was confined to his solitary cell for some ten days of penance.

'Since Brother Meriet would not defend himself,' said Cadfael, 'and Prior Robert, who brought him before you, came on the scene only late, it is as well that you should know all that happened, for it may bear on the manner in which this boy came to us.' And he recounted his sad history of the keepsake Meriet had concealed in his cell and fondled by night. 'Father, I don't claim to know. But the elder brother of our most troublous postulant is affianced, and is to marry soon, as I understand.'

227

'I take your meaning,' said Radulfus heavily, leaning linked hands upon his desk, 'and I, too, have thought of this. His father is a patron of our house, and the marriage is to take place here in December. I had wondered if the younger son's desire to be out of the world ... It would, I think, account for him.' And he smiled wryly for all the plagued young who believe that frustration in love is the end of their world, and there is nothing left for them but to seek another. 'I have been wondering for a week or more,' he said, 'whether I should not send someone with knowledge to speak with his sire, and examine whether we are not all doing this youth a great disservice, in allowing him to take vows very ill-suited to his nature, however much he may desire them now.'

'Father,' said Cadfael heartily, 'I think you would be doing right.'

'The boy has qualities admirable in themselves, even here,' said Radulfus half-regretfully, 'but alas, not at home here. Not for thirty years, and after satiety with the world, after marriage, and child-getting and child-rearing, and the transmission of a name and a pride of birth. We have our ambience, but they – they are necessary to continue both what they know, and what we can teach them. These things you understand, as do all too few of us who harbour here and escape the tempest. Will you go to Aspley in my behalf?'

'With all my heart, Father,' said Cadfael.

'Tomorrow?'

'Gladly, if you so wish. But may I, then, go now and see both what can be done to settle Brother Meriet, mind and body, and also what I can learn from him?'

'Do so, with my goodwill,' said the abbot.

In his small stone penal cell, with nothing in it but a hard bed, a stool, a cross hung on the wall, and the necessary stone vessel for the prisoner's bodily needs, Brother Meriet looked curiously more open, easy and content than Cadfael had yet seen him. Alone, unobserved and in the dark, at least he was freed from the necessity of watching his every word and motion, and fending off all such as came too near. When the door was suddenly unlocked, and someone came in with a tiny lamp in hand, he certainly stiffened for a moment, and reared his head from his folded arms to stare; and Cadfael took it as a compliment and an encouragement that on recognizing him the young man just as spontaneously sighed, softened, and laid his cheek back on his forearms, though in such a way that he could watch the newcomer. He was lying on his belly on the pallet, shirtless, his habit stripped down to the waist to leave his weals open to the air. He was defiantly calm, for his blood was still up. If he had confessed to all that was charged against him, in perfect honesty, he had regretted nothing.

'What do they want of me now?' he demanded directly, but without noticeable apprehension.

'Nothing. Lie still, and let me put this lamp somewhere steady. There, you hear? We're locked in together. I shall have to hammer at the door before you'll be rid of me again.' Cadfael set his light on the bracket below the cross, where it would shine upon the bed. 'I've brought what will help you to a night's sleep, within and without. If you choose to trust my medicines, there's a draught can dull your pain and put you to sleep, if you want it.'

'I don't,' said Meriet flatly, and lay watchful with his chin on his folded arms. His body was brown and lissom and sturdy, the bluish welts on his back were not too gross a disfigurement. Some lay servant had held his hand; perhaps he himself had no great love for Brother Jerome. 'I want to be wakeful. This is quiet here.'

'Then at least keep still and let me salve this copper hide of yours. I told you he would have it!' Cadfael sat down on the edge of the narrow pallet, opened his jar, and began to anoint the slender shoulders that rippled and twitched to his touch. 'Fool boy,' he said chidingly, 'you could have spared yourself.'

'Oh, that!' said Meriet indifferently, nevertheless passive under the soothing fingers. 'I've had worse,' he said, lax and easy on his spread arms. 'My father, if he was roused, could teach them something here.'

'He failed to teach you much sense, at any rate. Though I won't say,' admitted Cadfael generously, 'that I haven't sometimes wanted to strangle Brother Jerome myself. But on the other hand, the man was only doing his duty, if in a heavy-handed fashion. He is a confessor to the novices, of whom I hear – can I believe it? – you are one. And if you do so aspire, you are held to be renouncing all ado with women, my friend, and all concern with personal property. Do him justice, he had grounds for complaint of you.'

'He had no grounds for stealing from me,' flared Meriet hotly.

'He had a right to confiscate what is forbidden here.'

229

'I still call it stealing. And he had no right to destroy it before my eyes – nor to speak as though women were unclean!'

'Well, if you've paid for your offences, so has he for his,' said Cadfael tolerantly. 'He has a sore throat will keep him quiet for a week yet, and for a man who likes the sound of his own sermons that's no mean revenge. But as for you, lad, you've a long way to go before you'll ever make a monk, and if you mean to go through with it, you'd better spend your penance here doing some hard thinking.'

'Another sermon?' said Meriet into his crossed arms, and for the first time there was almost a smile in his voice, if a rueful one.

'A word to the wise.'

That caused him to check and hold his breath, lying utterly still for one moment, before he turned his head to bring one glittering, anxious eye to bear on Cadfael's face. The dark-brown hair coiled and curled agreeably in the nape of his summer-browned neck, and the neck itself had still the elegant, tender shaping of boyhood. Vulnerable still to all manner of wounds, on his own behalf, perhaps, but certainly on behalf of others all too fiercely loved. The girl with the red-gold hair?

'They have not said anything?' demanded Meriet, tense with dismay. 'They don't mean to cast me out? He wouldn't do that – the abbot? He would have told me openly!' He turned with a fierce, lithe movement, drawing up his legs and rising on one hip, to seize Cadfael urgently by the wrist and stare into his eyes. 'What is it you know? What does he mean to do with me? I can't, I won't, give up now.'

'You've put your own vocation in doubt,' said Cadfael bluntly, 'no other has had any hand in it. If it had rested with me, I'd have clapped your pretty trophy back in your hand, and told you to be off out of here, and find either her or another as like her as one girl is to another equally young and fair, and stop plaguing us who ask nothing more than a quiet life. But if you still want to throw your natural bent out of door, you have that chance. Either bend your stiff neck, or rear it, and be off!'

There was more to it than that, and he knew it. The boy sat bolt upright, careless of his half-nakedness in a cell stony and chill, and held him by the wrist with strong, urgent fingers, staring earnestly into his eyes, probing beyond into his mind, and not afraid of him, or even wary.

230

'I will bend it,' he said. 'You doubt if I can, but I can, I will. Brother Cadfael, if you have the abbot's ear, help me, tell him I have not changed, tell him I do want to be received. Say I will wait, if I must, and learn and be patient, but I will deserve! In the end he shall not be able to complain of me. Say so to him! He won't reject me.'

'And the gold-haired girl?' said Cadfael, purposely brutal.

Meriet wrenched himself away and flung himself down again on his breast. 'She is spoken for,' he said no less roughly, and would not say one word more of her.

'There are others,' said Cadfael. 'Take thought now or never. Let me tell you, child, as one old enough to have a son past your age, and with a few regrets in his own life, if he had time to brood on them – there's many a young man has got his heart's dearest wish, only to curse the day he ever wished for it. By the grace and good sense of our abbot, you will have time to make certain before you're bound past freeing. Make good use of your time, for it won't return once you're pledged.'

A pity, in a way, to frighten a young creature so, when he was already torn many ways, but he had ten days and nights of solitude before him now, a low diet, and time both for prayer and thought. Being alone would not oppress him, only the pressure of uncongenial numbers around him had done that. Here he would sleep without dreams, not starting up to cry out in the night. Or if he did, there would be no one to hear him and add to his trouble.

'I'll come and bring the salve in the morning,' said Cadfael, taking up his lamp. 'No, wait!' He set it down again. 'If you lie so, you'll be cold in the night. Put on your shirt, the linen won't trouble you too much, and you can bear the brychan over it.'

'I'm well enough,' said Meriet, submitting almost shame-facedly, and subsiding with a sigh into his folded arms again. 'I ... I do thank you – brother!' he ended as an awkward afterthought, and very dubiously, as if the form of address did no justice to what was in his mind, though he knew it to be the approved one here.

'That came out of you doubtfully,' remarked Cadfael judiciously, 'like biting on a sore tooth. There are other relationships. Are you still sure it's a brother you want to be?'

'I *must*,' blurted Meriet, and turned his face morosely away.

Now why, wondered Cadfael, banging on the door of the cell for the porter to open and let him out, why must the one thing of meaning he says be said only at the end, when he's settled and eased, and it would be shame to plague him further? Not: I do! or: I will! but: I must! Must implies a resolution enforced, either by another's will, or by an overwhelming necessity. Now who has willed this sprig into the cloister, or what force of circumstance has made him choose this way as the best, the only one left open to him?

Cadfael came out from Compline that night to find Hugh waiting for him at the gatehouse.

'Walk as far as the bridge with me. I'm on my way home, but I hear from the porter here that you're off on an errand for the lord abbot tomorrow, so you'll be out of my reach day-long. You'll have heard about the horse?'

'That you've found him, yes, nothing more. We've been all too occupied with our own miscreants and crimes this day to have much time or thought for anything outside,' owned Cadfael ruefully. 'No doubt you've been told about that.' Brother Albin, the porter, was the most consummate gossip in the enclave. 'Our worries go side by side and keep pace, it seems, but never come within touch of each other. That's strange in itself. And now you find the horse miles away to the north, or so I heard.'

They passed through the gate together and turned left towards the town, under a chill, dim sky of driving clouds, though on the ground there was no more than a faint breeze, hardly enough to stir the moist, sweet, rotting smells of autumn. They absorbed the darkness of trees on the right of the road, the flat metallic glimmer of the mill-pond on their left, and the scent and sound of the river ahead, between them and the town.

'Barely a couple miles short of Whitchurch,' said Hugh, 'where he had meant to pass the night, and have an easy ride to Chester next day.' He recounted the whole of it; Cadfael's thoughts were always a welcome illumination from another angle. But here their two minds moved as one.

'Wild enough woodland short of the place,' said Cadfael sombrely, 'and the mosses close at hand. If it was done there, whatever was done, and the horse, being young and spirited, broke away and could not be caught, then the man may be fathoms deep. Past finding. Not even a grave to dig.'

'It's what I've been thinking myself,' agreed Hugh grimly. 'But if I have such footpads living wild in my shire, how is it I've heard no word of them until now?'

232

'A venture south out of Cheshire? You know how fast they can come and go. And even where your writ runs, Hugh, the times breed changes. But if these were masterless men, they were no skilled hands with horses. Any outlaw worth his salt would have torn out an arm by the shoulder rather than lose a beast like that one. I went to have a look at him in the stables,' owned Cadfael, 'when I was free. And the silver on his harness … only a miracle could have got it away from them once they clapped eyes on it. What the man himself had on him can hardly have been worth more than horse and harness together.'

'If they're preying on travellers there,' said Hugh, 'they'll know just where to slide a weighted man into the peat-hags, where they're hungriest. But I've men there searching, whether or no. There are some among the natives there can tell if a pool has been fed recently – will you believe it? But I doubt, truly I doubt, if even a bone of Peter Clemence will ever be seen again.'

They had reached the near end of the bridge. In the half-darkness the Severn slid by at high speed, close to them and silent, like a great serpent whose scales occasionally caught a gleam of starlight and flashed like silver, before that very coil had passed and was speeding downstream far too fast for overtaking. They halted to take leave.

'And you are bound for Aspley,' said Hugh. 'Where the man lay safely with his kin, a single day short of his death. If indeed he is dead! I forget we are no better than guessing. How if he had good reasons to vanish there and be written down as dead? Men change their allegiance these days as they change their shirts, and for every man for sale there are buyers. Well, use your eyes and your wits at Aspley for your lad – I can tell by now when you have a wing spread over a fledgling – but bring me back whatever you can glean about Peter Clemence, too, and what he had in mind when he left them and rode north. Some innocent there may be nursing the very word we need, and thinking nothing of it.'

'I will so,' said Cadfael, and turned back in the gloaming towards the gatehouse and his bed.

Chapter Five

AVING THE abbot's authority about him, and
something more than four miles to go, Brother
Cadfael helped himself to a mule from the stables in
preference to tackling the journey to Aspley on foot.
Time had been when he would have scorned to ride, but he was
past sixty years old, and minded for once to take his ease.
Moreover, he had few opportunities now for riding, once a
prime pleasure, and could not afford to neglect such as did
come his way.

He left after Prime, having taken a hasty bite and drink. The
morning was misty and mild, full of the heavy, sweet, moist
melancholy of the season, with a thickly veiled sun showing
large and mellow through the haze. And the way was pleasant,
for the first part on the highway.

The Long Forest, south and south-west of Shrewsbury, had
survived unplundered longer than most of its kind, its assarts
few and far between, its hunting coverts thick and wild, its
open heaths home to all manner of creatures of earth and air.
Sheriff Prestcote kept a weather eye on changes there, but did
not interfere with what reinforced order rather than
challenging it, and the border manors had been allowed to
enlarge and improve their fields, provided they kept the peace
there with a firm enough hand. There were very ancient
holdings along the rim which had once been assarts deep in
woodland, and now had hewn out good arable land from old
upland, and fenced their intakes. The three old neighbour-

manors of Linde, Aspley and Foriet guarded this eastward fringe, half-wooded, half-open. A man riding for Chester from this place would not need to go through Shrewsbury, but would pass it by and leave it to westward. Peter Clemence had done so, choosing to call upon his kinsfolk when the chance offered, rather than make for the safe haven of Shrewsbury abbey. Would his fate have been different, had he chosen to sleep within the pale of Saint Peter and Saint Paul? His route to Chester might even have missed Whitchurch, passing to westward, clear of the mosses. Too late to wonder!

Cadfael was aware of entering the lands of the Linde manor when he came upon well-cleared fields and the traces of grain long harvested, and stubble being culled by sheep. The sky had partially cleared by then, a mild and milky sun was warming the air without quite dispersing the mist, and the young man who came strolling along a headland with a hound at his heel and a half-trained merlin on a creance on his wrist had dew-darkened boots, and a spray of drops on his uncovered light-brown hair from the shaken leaves of some copse left behind him. A young gentleman very light of foot and light of heart, whistling merrily as he rewound the creance and soothed the ruffled bird. A year or two past twenty, he might be. At sight of Cadfael he came bounding down from the headland to the sunken track, and having no cap to doff, gave him a very graceful inclination of his fair head and a blithe:

'Good-day, brother! Are you bound for us?'

'If by any chance your name is Nigel Aspley,' said Cadfael, halting to return the airy greeting, 'then indeed I am.' But this could hardly be the elder son who had five or six years the advantage of Meriet, he was too young, of too markedly different a colouring and build, long and slender and blue-eyed, with rounded countenance and ready smile. A little more red in the fair hair, which had the elusive greenish-yellow of oak leaves just budded in spring, or just turning in autumn, and he could have provided the lock that Meriet had cherished in his bed.

'Then we're out of luck,' said the young man gracefully, and made a pleasant grimace of disappointment. 'Though you'd still be welcome to halt at home for a rest and a cup, if you have the leisure for it? For I'm only a Linde, not an Aspley, and my name is Janyn.'

Cadfael recalled what Hugh had told him of Meriet's replies to Canon Eluard. The elder brother was affianced to the daughter of the neighbouring manor; and that could only be a Linde, since he had also mentioned without much interest the foster-sister who was a Foriet, and heiress to the manor that bordered Aspley on the southern side. Then this personable and debonair young creature must be a brother of Nigel's prospective bride.

'That's very civil of you,' said Cadfael mildly, 'and I thank you for the goodwill, but I'd best be getting on about my business. For I think I must have only a mile or so still to go.'

'Barely that, sir, if you take the left-hand path below here where it forks. Through the copse, and you're into their fields, and the track will bring you straight to their gate. If you're not in haste I'll walk with you and show you.'

Cadfael was more than willing. Even if he learned little from his companion about this cluster of manors all productive of sons and daughters of much the same age, and consequently brought up practically as one family, yet the companionship itself was pleasant. And a few useful grains of knowledge might be dropped like seed, and take root for him. He let the mule amble gently, and Janyn Linde fell in beside him with a long, easy stride.

'You'll be from Shrewsbury, brother?' Evidently he had his share of human curiosity. 'Is it something concerning Meriet? We were shaken, I can tell you, when he made up his mind to take the cowl, and yet, come to think, he went always his own ways, and would follow them. How did you leave him? Well, I hope?'

'Passably well,' said Cadfael cautiously. 'You must know him a deal better than we do, as yet, being neighbours, and much of an age.'

'Oh, we were all raised together from pups, Nigel, Meriet, my sister and me – especially after both our mothers died – and Isouda, too, when she was left orphan, though she's younger. Meriet's our first loss from the clan, we miss him.'

'I hear there'll be a marriage soon that will change things still more,' said Cadfael, fishing delicately.

'Roswitha and Nigel?' Janyn shrugged lightly and airily. 'It was a match our fathers planned long ago – but if they hadn't, they'd have had to come round to it, for those two made up their own minds almost from children. If you're bound for Aspley you'll find my sister somewhere about the place. She's more often there than here, now. They're deadly fond!' He sounded tolerantly amused, as brothers still unsmitten

236

frequently are by the eccentricities of lovers. Deadly fond! Then if the red-gold hair had truly come from Roswitha's head, surely it had not been given? To a besotted younger brother of her bridegroom? Clipped on the sly, more likely, and the ribbon stolen. Or else it came, after all, from some very different girl.

'Meriet's mind took another way,' said Cadfael, trailing his line. 'How did his father take it when he chose the cloister? I think were I a father, and had but two sons, I should take no pleasure in giving up either of them.'

Janyn laughed, briefly and gaily. 'Meriet's father took precious little pleasure in anything Meriet ever did, and Meriet took precious little pains to please him. They waged one long battle. And yet I dare swear they loved each other as well as most fathers and sons do. Now and then they come like that, oil and water, and nothing they can do about it.'

They had reached a point below the headland where the fields gave place to a copse, and a broad ride turned aside at a slight angle to thread the trees.

'There lies your best way,' said Janyn, 'straight to their manor fence. And if you should have time to step in at our house on your way back, brother, my father would be glad to welcome you.'

Cadfael thanked him gravely, and turned into the green ride. At a turn of the path he looked back. Janyn was strolling jauntily back towards his headland and the open fields, where he could fly the merlin on his creance without tangling her in trees to her confusion and displeasure. He was whistling again as he went, very melodiously, and his fair head had the gloss and rare colour of young oak foliage, Meriet's contemporary, but how different by nature! This one would have no difficulty in pleasing the most exacting of fathers, and would certainly never vex his by electing to remove from a world which obviously pleased him very well.

The copse was open and airy, the trees had shed half their leaves, and let in light to a floor still green and fresh. There were brackets of orange fungus jutting from the tree-boles, and frail bluish toadstools in the turf. The path brought Cadfael out, as Janyn had promised, to the wide, striped fields of the Aspley manor, carved out long ago from the forest, and enlarged steadily ever since, both to westward, into the forest land, and eastward, into richer, tamed country. The sheep had been turned into the stubble here, too, in greater numbers, to

237

crop what they could from the aftermath, and leave their droppings to manure the ground for the next sowing. And along a raised track between strips the manor came into view, within an enclosing wall, but high enough to be seen over its crest; a long, stone-built house, a windowed hall floor over a squat undercroft, and probably some chambers in the roof above the solar end. It was well built and well kept, worth inheriting, like the land that surrounded it. Low, wide doors made to accommodate carts and wagons opened into the undercroft, a steep stairway led up to the hall door. There were stables and byres lining the inside of the wall on two sides. They kept ample stock.

There were two or three men busy about the byres when Cadfael rode in at the gate, and a groom came out from the stable to take his bridle, quick and respectful at the sight of the Benedictine habit. And out from the open hall door came an elderly, thickset, bearded personage who must, Cadfael supposed rightly, be the steward Fremund who had been Meriet's herald to the abbey. A well-run household. Peter Clemence must have been met with ceremony on the threshold when he arrived unexpectedly. It would not be easy to take these retainers by surprise.

Cadfael asked for the lord Leoric, and was told that he was out in the back fields superintending the grubbing of a tree that had heeled into his stream from a slipping bank, and was fouling the flow, but he would be sent for at once, if Brother Cadfael would wait but a quarter of an hour in the solar, and drink a cup of wine or ale to pass the time. An invitation which Cadfael accepted willingly after his ride. His mule had already been led away, doubtless to some equally meticulous hospitality of its own. Aspley kept up the lofty standards of his forbears. A guest here would be a sacred trust.

Leoric Aspley filled the narrow doorway when he came in, his thick bush of greying hair brushing the lintel. Its colour, before he aged, must have been a light brown. Meriet did not favour him in figure or complexion, but there was a strong likeness in the face. Was it because they were too unbendingly alike that they fought and could not come to terms, as Janyn had said? Aspley made his guest welcome with cool, immaculate courtesy, waited on him with his own hand, and pointedly closed the door upon the rest of the household.

'I am sent,' said Cadfael, when they were seated, facing each other in a deep window embrasure, their cups on the stone beside them, 'by Abbot Radulfus, to consult you concerning your son Meriet.'

'What of my son Meriet? He has now, of his own will, a closer kinship with you, brother, than with me, and has taken another father in the lord abbot. Where is the need to consult me?'

His voice was measured and quiet, making the chill words sound rather mild and reasonable than implacable, but Cadfael knew then that he would get no help here. Still, it was worth trying.

'Nevertheless, it was you engendered him. If you do not wish to be reminded of it,' said Cadfael, probing for a chink in this impenetrable armour, 'I recommend you never look in a mirror. Parents who offer their babes as oblates do not therefore give up loving them. Neither, I am persuaded, do you.'

'Are you telling me he has repented of his choice already?' demanded Aspley, curling a contemptuous lip. 'Is he trying to escape from the Order so soon? Are you sent to herald his coming home with his tail between his legs?'

'Far from it! With every breath he insists on this one wish, to be admitted. All that can help to hasten his acceptance he does, with almost too much fervour. His every waking hour is devoted to achieving the same goal. But in sleep it is no such matter. Then, as it seems to me, his mind and spirit recoil in horror. What he desires, waking, he turns from, screaming, in his bed at night. It is right you should know this.'

Aspley sat frowning at him in silence and surely, by his fixed stillness, in some concern. Cadfael pursued his first advantage, and told him of the disturbances in the dortoir, but for some reason which he himself did not fully understand he stopped short of recounting the attack on Brother Jerome, its occasion and its punishment. If there was a fire of mutual resentment between them, why add fuel? 'When he wakes,' said Cadfael, 'he has no knowledge of what he has done in sleep. There is no blame there. But there is a grave doubt concerning his vocation. Father Abbot asks that you will consider seriously whether we are not, between us, doing Meriet a great wrong in allowing him to continue, however much he may wish it now.'

'That he wants to be rid of him,' said Aspley, recovering his implacable calm, 'I can well understand. He was always an obdurate and ill-conditioned youth.'

'Neither Abbot Radulfus nor I find him so,' said Cadfael, stung.

'Then whatever other difficulties there may be, he is better

239

with you than with me, for I have so found him from a child. And might not I as well argue that we should be doing him a great wrong if we turned him from a good purpose when he inclines to one? He has made his choice, only he can change it. Better for him he should endure these early throes, rather than give up his intent.'

Which was no very surprising reaction from such a man, hard and steadfast in his own undertakings, certainly strict to his word, and driven to pursue his courses to the end as well by obstinacy as by honour. Nevertheless, Cadfael went on trying to find the joints in his armour, for it must be a strangely bitter resentment which could deny a distracted boy a single motion of affection.

'I will not urge him one way or the other,' said Aspley finally, 'nor confuse his mind by visiting him or allowing any of my family to visit him. Keep him, and let him wait for enlightenment, and I think he will still wish to remain with you. He has put his hand to the plough, he must finish his furrow. I will not receive him back if he turns tail.'

He rose to indicate that the interview was over, and having made it plain that there was no more to be got out of him, he resumed the host with assured grace, offered the midday meal, which was as courteously refused, and escorted his guest out to the court.

'A pleasant day for your ride,' he said, 'though I should be the better pleased if you would take meat with us.'

'I would and thank you,' said Cadfael, 'but I am pledged to return and deliver your answer to my abbot. It is an easy journey.'

A groom led forth the mule. Cadfael mounted, took his leave civilly, and rode out at the gate in the low stone wall.

He had gone no more than two hundred paces, just enough to carry him out of sight of those he had left within the pale, when he was aware of two figures sauntering without haste back towards that same gateway. They walked hand in hand, and they had not yet perceived a rider approaching them along the pathway between the fields, because they had eyes only for each other. They were talking by broken snatches, as in a shared dream where precise expression was not needed, and their voices, mellowly male and silverly female, sounded even in the distance like brief peaks of laughter. Or bridle bells, perhaps, but that they came afoot. Two tolerant, well-trained hounds followed them at heel, nosing up the drifted scents

240

from either side, but keeping their homeward line without distraction.

So these must surely be the lovers, returning to be fed. Even lovers must eat. Cadfael eyed them with interest as he rode slowly towards them. They were worth observing. As they came nearer, but far enough from him to be oblivious still, they became more remarkable. Both were tall. The young man had his father's noble figure, but lissome and light-footed with youth, and the light brown hair and ruddy, outdoor skin of the Saxon. Such a son as any man might rejoice in. Healthy from birth, as like as not, growing and flourishing like a hearty plant, with every promise of full harvest. A stocky dark second, following lamely several years later, might well fail to start any such spring of satisfied pride. One paladin is enough, besides being hard to match. And if he strides towards manhood without ever a flaw or a check, where's the need for a second?

And the girl was his equal. Tipping his shoulder, and slender and straight as he, she was the image of her brother, but everything that in him was comely and attractive was in her polished into beauty. She had the same softly rounded, oval face, but refined almost into translucence, and the same clear blue eyes, but a shade darker and fringed with auburn lashes. And there beyond mistake was the reddish gold hair, a thick coil of it, and curls escaping on either side of her temples.

Thus, then, was Meriet explained? Frantic to escape from his frustrated love into a world without women, perhaps also anxious to remove from his brother's happiness the slightest shadow of grief or reproach – did that account for him? But he had taken the symbol of his torment into the cloister with him – was that sensible?

The small sound of the mule's neat hooves in the dry grass of the track and the small stones had finally reached the ears of the girl. She looked up and saw the rider approaching, and said a soft word into her companion's ear. The young man checked for a moment in his stride, and stared with reared head to see a Benedictine monk in the act of riding away from the gates of Aspley. He was very quick to connect and wonder. The light smiled faded instantly from his face, he drew his hand from the girl's hold, and quickened his pace with the evident intention of accosting the departing visitor.

They drew together and halted by consent. The elder son, close to, loomed even taller than his sire, and improbably good to look upon, in a world of imperfection. With a large but shapely hand raised to the mule's bridle, he looked up at Cadfael with clear brown eyes rounded in concern, and gave short greeting in his haste.

'From Shrewsbury, brother? Pardon if I dare question, but you have been to my father's house? There's news? My brother – he has not ...' He checked himself there to make belated reverence, and account for himself. 'Forgive such a rough greeting, when you do not even know me, but I am Nigel Aspley, Meriet's brother. Has something happened to him? He has not done – any foolishness?'

What should be said to that? Cadfael was by no means sure whether he considered Meriet's conscious actions to be foolish or not. But at least there seemed to be one person who cared what became of him, and by the anxiety and concern in his face suffered fears for him which were not yet justified.

'There's no call for alarm on his account,' said Cadfael soothingly. 'He's well enough and has come to no harm, you need not fear.'

'And he is still set – he has not changed his mind?'

'He has not. He is as intent as ever on taking vows.'

'But you've been with my father! What could there be to discuss with him? You are sure that Meriet ...' He fell silent, doubtfully studying Cadfael's face. The girl had drawn near at her leisure and stood a little apart, watching them both with serene composure, and in a posture of such natural grace that Cadfael's eyes could not forbear straying to enjoy her.

'I left your brother in stout heart,' he said, carefully truthful, 'and of the same mind as when he came to us. I was sent by my abbot only to speak with your father about certain doubts which have arisen rather in the lord abbot's mind than in Brother Meriet's. He is still very young to take such a step in haste, and his zeal seems to older minds excessive. You are nearer to him in years than either your sire or our officers,' said Cadfael persuasively. 'Can you not tell me why he may have taken this step? For what reason, sound and sufficient to him, should he choose to leave the world so early?'

'I don't know,' said Nigel lamely, and shook his head over his failure. 'Why do they do so? I never understood.' As why should he, with all the reasons he had for remaining in and of this world? 'He said he wanted it,' said Nigel.

'He says so still. At every turn he insists on it.'

'You'll stand by him? You'll help him to have his will? If that is truly what he wishes?'

'We're all resolved,' said Cadfael sententiously, 'on helping him to his desire. Not all young men pursue the same destiny, as you must know.' His eyes were on the girl; she was aware of it, and he was aware of her awareness. Another coil of red-gold hair had escaped from the band that held it; it lay against her smooth cheek, casting a deep gold shadow.

'Will you carry him my dear remembrances, brother? Say he has my prayers, and my love always.' Nigel withdrew his hand from the bridle, and stood back to let the rider proceed.

'And assure him of my love, also,' said the girl in a voice of honey, heavy and sweet. Her blue eyes lifted to Cadfael's face. 'We have been playfellows many years, all of us here,' she said, certainly with truth. 'I may speak in terms of love, for I shall soon be his sister.'

'Roswitha and I are to be married at the abbey in December,' said Nigel, and again took her by the hand.

'I'll bear your messages gladly,' said Cadfael, 'and wish you both all possible blessing against the day.'

The mule moved resignedly, answering the slight shake of the bridle. Cadfael passed them with his eyes still fixed on the girl Roswitha, whose infinite blue gaze opened on him like a summer sky. The slightest of smiles touched her lips as he passed, and a small, contented brightness flashed in her eyes. She knew that he could not but admire her, and even the admiration of an elderly monk was satisfaction to her. Surely the very motions she had made in his presence, so slight and so conscious, had been made in the knowledge that he was well aware of them, cobweb threads to entrammel one more unlikely fly.

He was careful not to look back, for it had dawned on him that she would confidently expect him to.

Just within the fringe of the copse, at the end of the fields, there was a stone-built sheepfold, close beside the ride, and someone was sitting on the rough wall, dangling crossed ankles and small bare feet, and nursing in her lap a handful of late hazelnuts, which she cracked in her teeth, dropping the fragments of shell into the long grass. From a distance Cadfael had been uncertain whether this was boy or girl, for her gown was kilted to the knee, and her hair cropped just short enough to swing clear of her shoulders, and her dress was the common brown homespun of the countryside. But as he drew nearer it became clear that this was certainly a girl, and moreover, busy

243

about the enterprise of becoming a woman. There were high, firm breasts under the close-fitting bodice, and for all her slenderness she had the swelling hips that would some day make childbirth natural and easy for her. Sixteen, he thought, might be her age. Most curiously of all, it appeared that she was both expecting and waiting for him, for as he rode towards her she turned on her perch to look towards him with a slow, confident smile of recognition and welcome, and when he was close she slid from the wall, brushing off the last nutshells, and shook down her skirts with the brisk movements of one making ready for action.

'Sir, I must talk to you,' she said with firmness, and put up a slim brown hand to the mule's neck. 'Will you light down and sit with me?' She had still her child's face, but the woman was beginning to show through, paring away the puppy-flesh to outline the elegant lines of her cheekbones and chin. She was brown almost as her nutshells, with a warm rose-colour mantling beneath the tanned, smooth skin, and a mouth rose-red, and curled like the petals of a half-open rose. The short, thick mane of curling hair was richly russet-brown, and her eyes one shade darker, and black-lashed. No cottar's girl, if she did choose to go plain and scorning finery. She knew she was an heiress, and to be reckoned with.

'I will, with pleasure,' said Cadfael promptly, and did so. She took a step back, her head on one side, scarcely having expected such an accommodating reception, without explanation asked or given; and when he stood on level terms with her, and barely half a head taller, she suddenly made up her mind, and smiled at him radiantly.

'I do believe we two can talk together properly. You don't question, and yet you don't even know me.'

'I think I do,' said Cadfael, hitching the mule's bridle to a staple in the stone wall. 'You can hardly be anyone else but Isouda Foriet. For all the rest I've already seen, and I was told already that you must be the youngest of the tribe.'

'He told you of me?' she demanded at once, with sharp interest, but no noticeable anxiety.

'He mentioned you to others, but it came to my ears.'

'How did he speak of me?' she asked bluntly, jutting a firm chin. 'Did that also come to your ears?'

'I did gather that you were a kind of young sister.' For some reason, not only did he not feel it possible to lie to this young person, it had no value even to soften the truth for her.

244

She smiled consideringly, like a confident commander weighing up the odds in a threatened field. 'As if he did not much regard me. Never mind! He will.'

'If I had the ruling of him,' said Cadfael with respect, 'I would advise it now. Well, Isouda, here you have me, as you wished. Come and sit, and tell me what you wanted of me.'

'You brothers are not supposed to have to do with women,' said Isouda, and grinned at him warmly as she hoisted herself back on to the wall. 'That makes him safe from *her*, at least, but it must not go too far with this folly of his. May I know your name, since you know mine?'

'My name is Cadfael, a Welshman from Trefriw.'

'My first nurse was Welsh,' she said, leaning down to pluck a frail green thread of grass from the fading stems below her, and set it between strong white teeth. 'I don't believe you have always been a monk, Cadfael, you know too much.'

'I have known monks, children of the cloister from eight years old,' said Cadfael seriously, 'who knew more than I shall ever know, though only God knows how, who made it possible. But no, I have lived forty years in the world before I came to it. My knowledge is limited. But what I know you may ask of me. You want, I think, to hear of Meriet.'

'Not "Brother Meriet"?' she said, pouncing, light as a cat, and glad.

'Not yet. Not for some time yet.'

'*Never!*' she said firmly and confidently. 'It will not come to that. It must not.' She turned her head and looked him in the face with a high, imperious stare. 'He is mine,' she said simply. 'Meriet is mine, whether he knows it yet or no. And no one else will have him.'

245

Chapter Six

 SK ME whatever you wish,' said Cadfael, shifting to find the least spiky position on the stones of the wall. 'And then there are things I have to ask of you.'

'And you'll tell me honestly what I need to know? Every part of it?' she challenged. Her voice had a child's directness and high, clear pitch, but a lord's authority.

'I will.' For she was equal to it, even prepared for it. Who knew this vexing Meriet better?

'How far has he got towards taking vows? What enemies has he made? What sort of fool has he made of himself, with his martyr's wish? Tell me everything that has happened to him since he went from me.' 'From me' was what she said, not 'from us'.

Cadfael told her. If he chose his words carefully, yet he made them tell her the truth. She listened with so contained and armed a silence, nodding her head occasionally where she recognized necessity, shaking it where she deprecated folly, smiling suddenly and briefly where she understood, as Cadfael could not yet fully understand, the proceedings of her chosen man. He ended telling her bluntly of the penalty Meriet had brought upon himself, and even, which was a greater temptation to discretion, about the burned tress that was the occasion of his fall. It did not surprise or greatly dismay her, he noted. She thought about it not more than a moment.

'If you but knew the whippings he has brought on himself

246

before! No one will ever break him that way. And your Brother Jerome has burned her lure – that was well done. He won't be able to fool himself for long, with no bait left him.' She caught, Cadfael thought, his momentary suspicion that he had nothing more to deal with here than women's jealousy. She turned and grinned at him with open amusement. 'Oh, but I saw you meet them! I was watching, though they didn't know it, and neither did you. Did you find her handsome? Surely you did, so she is. And did she not make herself graceful and pleasing for you? Oh, it was for you, be sure – why should she fish for Nigel, she has him landed, the only fish she truly wants. But she cannot help casting her line. *She* gave Meriet that lock of hair, of course! She can never quite let go of any man.'

It was so exactly what Cadfael had suspected, since casting eyes on Roswitha, that he was silenced.

'I'm not afraid of *her*,' said Isouda tolerantly. 'I know her too well. He only began to imagine himself loving her because she belonged to Nigel. He must desire whatever Nigel desires, and he must be jealous of whatever Nigel possesses and he has not. And yet, if you'll trust me, there is no one he loves as he loves Nigel. No one. Not yet!'

'I think,' said Cadfael, 'you know far more than I about this boy who troubles my mind and engages my liking. And I wish you would tell me what he does not, everything about this home of his and how he has grown up in it. For he's in need of your help and mine, and I am willing to be your dealer in this, if you wish him well, for so do I.'

She drew up her knees and wrapped her slender arms around them, and told him. 'I am the lady of a manor, left young, and left to my father's neighbour as his ward, my Uncle Leoric, though he is not my uncle. He is a good man. I know my manor is as well-run as any in England, and my uncle takes nothing out of it. You must understand, this is a man of the old kind, stark upright. It is not easy to live with him, if you are his and a boy, but I am a girl, and he has been always indulgent and good to me. Madam Avota, who died two years back – well, she was his wife first, and only afterwards Meriet's mother. You saw Nigel – what more could any man wish for his heir? They never even needed or wished for Meriet. They did all their duty by him when he came, but they could not even see past Nigel to notice the second one. And he was so different.'

She paused to consider the two, and probably had her finger on the very point where they went different ways.

'Do you think,' she asked doubtfully, 'that small children know when they are only second best? I think Meriet knew it early. He was different even to look at, but that was the least part. I think he always went the opposing way, whatever they wished upon him. If his father said white, Meriet said black; wherever they tried to turn him, he dug his heels hard and wouldn't budge. He couldn't help learning, because he was sharp and curious, so he grew lettered, but when he knew they wanted him a clerk, he went after all manner of low company, and flouted his father every way. He's always been jealous of Nigel,' said the girl musing against her raised knees, 'but always worshipped him. He flouts his father purposely, because he knows he's loved less, and that grieves him bitterly, and yet he can't hate Nigel for being loved more. How can he, when *he* loves him so much?'

'And Nigel repays his affection?' asked Cadfael, recollecting the elder brother's troubled face.

'Oh, yes, Nigel's fond of him, too. He always defended him. He's stood between him and punishment many a time. And he always would keep him with him, whatever they were about, when they all played together.'

'They?' said Cadfael. 'Not "we"?'

Isouda spat out her chewed stem of late grass, and turned a surprised and smiling face. 'I'm the youngest, three years behind even Meriet, I was the infant struggling along behind. For a little while, at any rate. There was not much I did not see. You know the rest of us? Those two boys, with six years between them, and the two Lindes, midway between. And me, come rather late and too young. You've seen Roswitha. I don't know if you've seen Janyn?'

'I have,' said Cadfael, 'on my way here. He directed me.'

'They are twins. Had you guessed that? Though I think he got all the wits that were meant for both. She is only clever one way,' said Isouda judicially, 'in binding men to her and keeping them bound. She was waiting for you to turn and look after her, and she would have rewarded you with one quick glance. And now you think I am only a silly girl, jealous of one prettier,' she said disconcertingly, and laughed at seeing him bridle. 'I would like to be beautiful, why not? But I don't envy Roswitha. And after our cross-grained fashion we have all been very close here. Very close! All those years must count for something.'

'It seems to me,' said Cadfael, 'that you of all people best know this young man. So tell me, if you can, why did he ever take a fancy for the cloistered life? I know as well as any, now, how he clings to that intent, but for my life I do not see why? Are you any wiser?'

She was not. She shook her head vehemently. 'It goes counter to all I know of him.'

'Tell me, then, everything you recall about the time when this resolve was made. And begin,' said Cadfael, 'with the visit to Aspley of the bishop's envoy, this Peter Clemence. You'll know by now – who does not! – that the man never got to his next night's lodging. And has not been seen since.'

She turned her head sharply to stare. 'And his horse is found, so they're saying now. Found near the Cheshire border. You don't think Meriet's whim has anything to do with that? How could it? And yet ...' She had a quick and resolute mind, she was already making disquieting connections. 'It was the eighth night of September that he slept at Aspley. There was nothing strange, nothing to remark. He came alone, very early in the evening. Uncle Leoric came out to greet him, and I took his cloak indoors and had the maids make ready a bed for him, and Meriet cared for his horse. He always makes easy friends with horses. We made good cheer for the guest. They were keeping it up in hall with music after I went to my bed. And the next morning he broke his fast, and Uncle Leoric and Fremund and two grooms rode with him the first part of his way.'

'What like was he, this clerk?'

She smiled, between indulgence and mild scorn. 'Very fine, and knew it. Only a little older than Nigel, I should guess, but so travelled and sure of himself. Very handsome and courtly and witty, not like a clerk at all. Too courtly for Nigel's liking! You've seen Roswitha, and what she is like. This young man was just as certain all women must be drawn to him. They were two who matched like hand and glove, and Nigel was not best pleased. But he held his tongue and minded his manners, at least while I was there. Meriet did not like their by-play, either, he took himself off early to the stable, he liked the horse better than the man.'

'Did Roswitha bide overnight, too?'

'Oh, no, Nigel walked home with her when it was growing dark. I saw them go.'

'Then her brother was not with her that night?'

'Janyn? No, Janyn has no interest in the company of lovers. He laughs at them. No, he stayed at home.'

249

'And the next day ... Nigel did not ride with the guest departing? Nor Meriet? What were they about that morning?'

She frowned over that, thinking back. 'I think Nigel must have gone quite early back to the Lindes. He is jealous of her, though he sees no wrong in *her*. I believe he was away most of the day, I don't think he even came home to supper. And Meriet – I know he was with us when Master Clemence left, but after that I didn't see him until late in the afternoon. Uncle Leoric had been out with hounds after dinner, with Fremund and the chaplain and his kennelman. I remember Meriet came back with them, though he didn't ride out with them. He had his bow – he often went off solitary, especially when he was out of sorts with all of us. They went in, all. I don't know why, it was a very quiet evening, I supposed because the guest was gone, and there was no call for ceremony. I don't believe Meriet came to supper in hall that day. I didn't see him again all the evening.'

'And after? When was it that you first heard of his wish to enter with us at Shrewsbury?'

'It was Fremund who told me, the night following. I hadn't seen Meriet all that day to speak for himself. But I did the next day. He was about the manor as usual then, he did not look different, not in any particular. He came and helped me with the geese in the back field,' said Isouda, hugging her knees, 'and I told him what I had heard, and that I thought he was out of his wits, and asked him why he should covet such a fruitless life ...' She reached a hand to touch Cadfael's arm, and a smile to assure herself of his understanding, quite unperturbed. 'You are different, you've had one life already, a new one halfway is a fresh blessing for you, but what has he had? But he stared me in the eye, straight as a lance, and said he knew what he was doing, and it was what he wanted to do. And lately he had outgrown me and gone away from me, and there was no possible reason he should pretend with me, or scruple to tell me what I asked. And I have none to doubt what he did tell me. He wanted this. He wants it still. But why? That he never told me.'

'That,' said Brother Cadfael ruefully, 'he has not told anyone, nor will not if he can evade it. What is to be done, lady, with this young man who wills to destroy himself, shut like a wild bird in cage?'

'Well, he's not lost yet,' said Isouda resolutely. 'And I shall see him again when we come for Nigel's marriage in

250

December, and after that Roswitha will be out of his reach utterly, for Nigel is taking her north to the manor near Newark, which Uncle Leoric is giving to them to manage. Nigel was up there in midsummer, viewing his lordship and making ready, Janyn kept him company on the visit. Every mile of distance will help. I shall look for you, Brother Cadfael, when we come. I'm not afraid, now I've talked to you. Meriet is mine, and in the end I shall have him. It may not be me he dreams of now, but his dreams now are devilish, I would not be in those. I want him well awake. If you love him, you keep him from the tonsure, and I will do the rest!'

If I love him – and if I love you, faun, thought Cadfael, riding very thoughtfully homeward after leaving her. For you may very well be the woman for him. And what you have told me I must sort over with care, for Meriet's sake, and for yours.

He took a little bread and cheese on his return, and a measure of beer, having forsworn a midday meal with a household where he felt no kinship; and that done, he sought audience with Abbot Radulfus in the busy quiet of the afternoon, when the great court was empty, and most of the household occupied in cloister or gardens or fields.

The abbot had expected him, and listened with acute attention to everything he had to recount.

'So we are committed to caring for this young man, who may be misguided in his choice, but still persists in it. There is no course open to us but to keep him, and give him every chance to win his way in among us. But we have also his fellows to care for, and they are in real fear of him, and of the disorders of his sleep. We have yet the nine remaining days of his imprisonment, which he seems to welcome. But after that, how can we best dispose of him, to allow him access to grace, and relieve the dortoir of its trouble?'

'I have been thinking of that same question,' said Cadfael. 'His removal from the dortoir may be as great a benefit to him as to those remaining, for he is a solitary soul, and if ever he takes the way of withdrawal wholly I think he will be hermit rather than monk. It would not surprise me to find that he has gained by being shut in a penal cell, having that small space and great silence to himself, and able to fill it with his own meditations and prayers, as he could not do in a greater place shared by many others. We have not all the same image of brotherhood.'

251

'True! But we are a house of brothers sharing in common, and not so many desert fathers scattered in isolation,' said the abbot drily. 'Nor can the young man be left for ever in a punishment cell, unless he plans to attempt the strangling of my confessors and obedientiaries one by one to ensure it. What have you to suggest?'

'Send him to serve under Brother Mark at Saint Giles,' said Cadfael. 'He'll be no more private there, but he will be in the company and the service of creatures manifestly far less happy then himself, lepers and beggars, the sick and maimed. It may be salutary. In them he can forget his own troubles. There are advantages beyond that. Such a period of absence will hold back his instruction, and his advance towards taking vows, but that can only be good, since clearly he is in no fit mind to take them yet. Also, though Brother Mark is the humblest and simplest of us all, he has the gift of many such innocent saints, of making his way into the heart. In time Brother Meriet may open to him, and be helped from his trouble. At least it would give us all a breathing-space.'

Keep him from the tonsure, said Isouda's voice in his mind, and I will do the rest.

'So it would,' agreed Radulfus reflectively. 'The boys will have time to forget their alarms, and as you say, ministering to men worse blessed than himself may be the best medicine for him. I will speak with Brother Paul, and when Brother Meriet has served out his penance he shall be sent there.'

And if some among us take it that banishment to work in the lazar-house is a further penance, thought Cadfael, going away reasonably content, let them take satisfaction from it. For Brother Jerome was not the man to forget an injury, and any sop to his revenge might lessen his animosity towards the offender. A term of service in the hospice at the far edge of the town might also serve more turns than Meriet's, for Brother Mark, who tended the sick there, had been Cadfael's most valued assistant until a year or so ago, and he had recently suffered the loss of his favourite and much-indulged waif, the little boy Bran, taken into the household of Joscelin and Iveta Lucy on their marriage, and would be somewhat lost without a lame duck to cosset and care for. It wanted only a word in Mark's ear concerning the tormented record of the devil's novice, and his ready sympathy would be enlisted on Meriet's behalf. If Mark could not reach him, no one could; but at the same time he might also do much for Mark. Yet another

252

advantage was that Brother Cadfael, as supplier of the many medicines, lotions and ointments that were in demand among the sick, visited Saint Giles every third week, and sometimes oftener, to replenish the medicine cupboard, and could keep an eye on Meriet's progress there.

Brother Paul, coming from the abbot's parlour before Vespers, was clearly relieved at the prospect of enjoying a lengthened truce even after Meriet was released from his prison.

'Father Abbot tells me the suggestion came from you. It was well thought of, there's need of a long pause and a new beginning, though the children will easily forget their terrors. But that act of violence – that will not be so easily forgotten.'

'How is your penitent faring?' asked Cadfael. 'Have you visited him since I was in there early this morning?'

'I have. I am not so sure of his penitence,' said Brother Paul dubiously, 'but he is very quiet and biddable, and listens to exhortation patiently. I did not try him too far. We are failing sadly if he is happier in a cell than out among us. I think the only thing that frets him is having no work to do, so I have taken him the sermons of Saint Augustine, and given him a better lamp to read by, and a little desk he can set on his bed. Better far to have his mind occupied, and he is quick at letters. I suppose you would rather have given him Palladius on agriculture,' said Paul, mildly joking. 'Then you could make a case for taking him into your herbarium, when Oswin moves on.'

It was an idea that had occurred to Brother Cadfael, but better the boy should go clean away, into Mark's gentle stewardship, 'I have not asked leave again,' he said, 'but if I may visit him before bed, I should be glad. I did not tell him of my errand to his father, I shall not tell him now, but there are two people there have sent him messages of affection which I have promised to deliver.' There was also one who had not, and perhaps she knew her own business best.

'Certainly you may go in before Compline,' said Paul. 'He is justly confined, but not ostracized. To shun him utterly would be no way to bring him into our family, which must be the end of our endeavours.'

It was not the end of Cadfael's but he did not feel it necessary or timely to say so. There is a right place for every soul under the sun, but it had already become clear to him that the cloister was no place for Meriet Aspley, however feverishly he demanded to be let in.

253

*

Meriet had his lamp lighted, and so placed as to illumine the leaves of Saint Augustine on the head of his cot. He looked round quickly but tranquilly when the door opened, and knowing the incomer, actually smiled. It was very cold in the cell, the prisoner wore habit and scapular for warmth, and by the careful way he turned his body, and the momentary wincing halt to release a fold of his shirt from a tender spot, his weals were stiffening as they healed.

'I'm glad to see you so healthily employed,' said Cadfael. 'With a small effort in prayer, Saint Augustine may do you good. Have you used the balm since this morning? Paul would have helped you, if you had asked him.'

'He is good to me,' said Meriet, closing his book and turning fully to his visitor. And he meant it, that was plain.

'But you did not choose to condescend to ask for sympathy or admit to need – I know! Let me have off the scapular and drop your habit.' It had certainly not yet become a habit in which he felt at home, he moved naturally in it only when he was aflame, and forgot he wore it. 'There, lie down and let me at you.'

Meriet presented his back obediently, and allowed Cadfael to draw up his shirt and anoint the fading weals that showed only here and there a dark dot of dried blood. 'Why do I do what you tell me?' he wondered, mildly rebelling. 'As though you were no brother at all, but a father?'

'From all I've heard of you,' said Cadfael, busy with his balm, 'you are by no means known for doing what your own father tells you.'

Meriet turned in his cradling arms and brought to bear one bright green-gold eye upon his companion. 'How do you know so much of me? Have you been there and talked with my father?' He was ready to bristle in distrust, the muscles of his back had tensed. 'What are they trying to do? What business is there needs my father's words now? I am here! If I offend, I pay. No one else settles my debts.'

'No one else has offered,' said Cadfael placidly. 'You are your own master, however ill you master yourself. Nothing is changed. Except that I have to bring you messages, which do not meddle with your lordship's liberty to save or damn yourself. Your brother sends you his best remembrances and bids me say he holds you in his love always.'

254

Meriet lay very still, only his brown skin quivered very faintly under Cadfael's fingers.

'And the lady Roswitha also desires you to know that she loves you as befits a sister.'

Cadfael softened in his hands the stiffened folds of the shirt, where they had dried hard, and drew the linen down over fading lacerations that would leave no scar. Roswitha might be far more deadly. 'Draw up your gown now, and if I were you I'd put out the lamp and leave your reading, and sleep.' Meriet lay still on his face, saying never a word. Cadfael drew up the blanket over him, and stood looking down at the mute and rigid shape in the bed.

It was no longer quite rigid, the wide shoulders heaved in a suppressed and resented rhythm, the braced forearms were stiff and protective, covering the hidden face. Meriet was weeping. For Roswitha or for Nigel? Or for his own fate?

'Child,' said Cadfael, half-exasperated and half-indulgent, 'you are nineteen years old, and have not even begun to live, and you think in the first misery of your life that God has abandoned you. Despair is deadly sin, but worse it is mortal folly. The number of your friends is legion, and God is looking your way as attentively as ever he did. And all you have to do to deserve is to wait in patience, and keep up your heart.'

Even through his deliberate withdrawal and angrily suppressed tears Meriet was listening, so much was clear by his tension and stillness.

'And if you care to know,' said Cadfael, almost against his will, and sounding still more exasperated in consequence, 'yes, I am, by God's grace, a father. I have a son. And you are the only one but myself who knows it.'

And with that he pinched out the wick of the lamp, and in the darkness went to thump on the door to be let out.

It was a question, when Cadfael visited next morning, which of them was the more aloof and wary with the other, each of them having given away rather more than he had intended. Plainly there was to be no more of that. Meriet had put on an austere and composed face, not admitting to any weakness, and Cadfael was gruff and practical, and after a look at the little that was still visible of the damage to his difficult patient, pronounced him in no more need of doctoring, but very well able to concentrate on his reading and make the most of his penitential time for the good of his soul.

'Does that mean,' asked Meriet directly, 'that you are washing your hands of me?'

'It means I have no more excuse for demanding entry here, when you are supposed to be reflecting on your sins in solitude.'

Meriet scowled briefly at the stones of the wall, and then said stiffly, 'It is not that you fear I'll take some liberty because of what you were so good as to confide to me? I shall never say word, unless to you and at your instance.'

'No such thought ever entered my mind,' Cadfael assured him, startled and touched. 'Do you think I would have said it to a blabbermouth who would not know a confidence when one was offered him? No, it's simply that I have no warranty to go in and out here without good reason, and I must abide by the rules as you must.'

The fragile ice had already melted. 'A pity, though,' said Meriet, unbending with a sudden smile which Cadfael recalled afterwards as both startlingly sweet and extraordinarily sad. 'I reflect on my sins much better when you are here scolding. In solitude I still find myself thinking how much I would like to make Brother Jerome eat his own sandals.'

'We'll consider that a confession in itself,' said Cadfael, 'and one that had better not be made to any other ears. And your penance will be to make do without me until your ten days of mortification are up. I doubt you're incorrigible and past praying for, but we can but try.'

He was at the door when Meriet asked anxiously: 'Brother Cadfael ...?' And when he turned at once: 'Do you know what they mean to do with me afterwards?'

'Not to discard you, at all events,' said Cadfael, and saw no reason why he should not tell him what was planned for him. It seemed that nothing was changed. The news that he was in no danger of banishment from his chosen field calmed, reassured, placated Meriet; it was all that he wanted to hear. But it did not make him happy.

Cadfael went away discouraged, and was cantankerous with everyone who came in his path for the rest of the day.

Chapter Seven

UGH CAME south from the peat-hags empty-handed to his house in Shrewsbury, and sent an invitation to Cadfael to join him at supper on the evening of his return. To such occasional visits Cadfael had the most unexceptionable claim, since Giles Beringar, now some ten months old, was his godson, and a good godfather must keep a close eye on the welfare and progress of his charge. Of young Giles's physical wellbeing and inexhaustible energy there could be little question, but Hugh did sometimes express doubts about his moral inclinations, and like most fathers, detailed his son's ingenious villainies with respect and pride.

Aline, having fed and wined her menfolk, and observed with a practised eye the first droop of her son's eyelids, swept him off out of the room to be put to bed by Constance, who was his devoted slave, as she had been loyal friend and servant to his mother from childhood. Hugh and Cadfael were left alone for a while to exchange such information as they had. But the sum of it was sadly little.

'The men of the moss,' said Hugh, 'are confident that not one of them has seen hide or hair of a stranger, whether victim or malefactor. Yet the plain fact is that the horse reached the moss, and the man surely cannot have been far away. It still seems to me that he lies somewhere in those peat-pools, and we are never likely to see or hear of him again. I have sent to Canon Eluard to try and find out what he carried on him. I

257

gather he went very well-presented and was given to wearing jewels. Enough to tempt footpads. But if that was the way of it, it seems to be a first venture from farther north, and it may well be that our scourings there have warned off the marauders from coming that way again for a while. There have been no other travellers molested in those parts. And indeed, strangers in the moss would be in some peril themselves. You need to know the safe places to tread. Still, for all I can see, that is what happened to Peter Clemence. I've left a sergeant and a couple of men up there, and the natives are on the watch for us, too.'

Cadfael could not but agree that this was the likeliest answer to the loss of a man. 'And yet ... you know and I know that because one event follows another, it is not necessary the one should have caused the other. And yet the mind is so constructed, it cannot break the bond between the two. And here were two events, both unexpected; Clemence visited and departed – for he did depart, not one but four people rode a piece with him and said farewell to him in goodwill – and two days later the younger son of the house declares his intent to take the cowl. There is no sensible connection, and I cannot reeve the two apart.'

'Does that mean,' demanded Hugh plainly, 'that you think this boy may have had a hand in a man's death and be taking refuge in the cloister?'

'No,' said Cadfael decidedly. 'Don't ask what is in my mind, for all I find there is mist and confusion, but whatever lies behind the mist, I feel certain it is not that. What his motive is I dare not guess, but I do not believe it is blood-guilt.' And even as he said and meant it, he saw again Brother Wolstan prone and bleeding in the orchard grass, and Meriet's face fallen into a frozen mask of horror.

'For all that – and I respect what you say – I would like to keep a hand on this strange young man. A hand I can close at any moment if ever I should so wish,' said Hugh honestly. 'And you tell me he is to go to Saint Giles? To the very edge of town, close to woods and open heaths!'

'You need not fret,' said Cadfael, 'he will not run. He has nowhere to run to, for whatever else is true, his father is utterly estranged from him and would refuse to take him in. But he will not run because he does not wish to. The only haste he still nurses is to rush into his final vows and be done with it, and beyond deliverance.'

'It's perpetual imprisonment he's seeking, then? Not escape?' said Hugh, with his dark head on one side, and a rueful and affectionate smile on his lips.

'Not escape, no. From all I have seen,' said Cadfael heavily, 'he knows of no way of escape, anywhere, for him.'

At the end of his penance Meriet came forth from his cell, blinking even at the subdued light of a November morning after the chill dimness within, and was presented at chapter before austere, unrevealing faces to ask pardon for his offences and acknowledge the justice of his penalty, which he did, to Cadfael's relief and admiration, with a calm and dignified bearing and a quiet voice. He looked thinner for his low diet, and his summer brown, smooth copper when he came, had faded into dark, creamy ivory, for though he tanned richly, he had little colour beneath the skin except when enraged. He was docile enough now, or had discovered how to withdraw into himself so far that curiosity, censure and animosity should not be able to move him.

'I desire,' he said, 'to learn what is due from me and to deliver it faithfully. I am here to be disposed of as may best be fitting.'

Well, at any rate he knew how to keep his mouth shut, for evidently he had never let out, even to Brother Paul, that Cadfael had told him what was intended for him. By Isouda's account he must have been keeping his own counsel ever since he began to grow up, perhaps even before, as soon as it burned into his child's heart that he was not loved like his brother, and goaded him to turn mischievous and obdurate to get a little notice from those who undervalued him. Thus setting them ever more against him, and rendering himself ever more outrageously exiled from grace.

And I dared trounce him for succumbing to the first misery of his life, thought Cadfael, remorseful, when half his life has been a very sharp misery.

The abbot was austerely kind, putting behind them past errors atoned for, and explaining to him, what was now asked of him. 'You will attend with us this morning,' said Radulfus, 'and take your dinner in refectory among your brothers. This afternoon Brother Cadfael will take you to the hospice at Saint Giles, since he will be going there to refill the medicine cupboard.' And that, at least three days early, was news also to Cadfael, and a welcome indication of the abbot's personal

259

concern. The brother who had shown a close interest in this troubled and troublesome young novice was being told plainly that he had leave to continue his surveillance.

They set forth from the gatehouse side by side in the early afternoon, into the common daily traffic of the high road through the Foregate. Not a great bustle at this hour on a soft, moist, melancholy November day, but always some evidence of human activity, a boy jog-trotting home with a bag on his shoulder and a dog at his heels, a carter making for the town with a load of coppice-wood, an old man leaning on his staff, two sturdy housewives of the Foregate bustling back from the town with their purchases, one of Hugh's officers riding back towards the bridge at a leisurely walk. Meriet opened his eyes wide at everything about him, after ten days of close stone walls and meagre lamplight. His face was solemn and still, but his eyes devoured colour and movement hungrily. From the gatehouse to the hospice of Saint Giles was barely half a mile's walk, alongside the enclave wall of the abbey, past the open green of the horse-fair, and along the straight road between the houses of the Foregate, until they thinned out with trees and gardens between, and gave place to the open countryside. And there the low roof of the hospital came into view, and the squat tower of its chapel, on a slight rise to the left of the highway, where the road forked.

Meriet eyed the place as they approached, with purposeful interest but no eagerness, simply as the field to which he was assigned.

'How many of these sick people can be housed here?'

'There might be as many as five and twenty at a time, but it varies. Some of them move on, from lazar-house to lazar-house, and make no long stay anywhere. Some come here too ill to go further. Death thins the numbers, and newcomers fill the gaps again. You are not afraid of infection?'

Meriet said, 'No,' so indifferently that it was almost as if he had said, 'Why should I be? What threat can disease possibly be to me?'

'Your Brother Mark is in charge of all?' he asked.

'There is a lay superior, who lives in the Foregate, a decent man and a good manager. And two other helpers. But Mark looks after the inmates. You could be a great help to him if you choose,' said Cadfael, 'for he's barely older than you, and your company will be very welcome to him. Mark was my right hand and comfort in the herbarium, until he felt it his need to come here and care for the poor and the strays, and now I doubt I shall ever win him back, for he has always some soul here that he cannot leave, and as he loses one he finds another.'

He drew in prudently from saying too much in praise of his most prized disciple; but still it came as a surprise to Meriet when they climbed the gentle slope that lifted the hospital clear of the highway, passed through wattled fence and low porch, and came upon Brother Mark sitting at his little desk within. He was furrowing his high forehead over accounts, his lips forming figures silently as he wrote them down on his vellum. His quill needed retrimming, and he had managed to ink his fingers, and by scrubbing bewilderedly in his spiky, straw-coloured fringe of hair had left smudges on both his eyebrow and his crown. Small and slight and plain of face, himself a neglected waif in his childhood, he looked up at them, when they entered the doorway, with a smile of such disarming sweetness that Meriet's firmly shut mouth fell open, like his guarded eyes, and he stood staring in candid wonder as Cadfael presented him. This little, frail thing, meagre as a sixteen-year-old, and a hungry one at that, was minister to twenty or more sick, maimed, poor, verminous and old!

'I've brought you Brother Meriet,' said Cadfael, 'as well as this scrip full of goods. He'll be staying with you a while to learn the work here, and you can rely on him to do whatever you ask of him. Find him a corner and a bed, while I fill up your cupboard for you. Then you can tell me if there's anything more you need.'

He knew his way here. He left them studying each other and feeling without haste for words, and went to unlock the repository of his medicines, and fill up the shelves. He was in no hurry; there was something about those two, utterly separate through they might be, the one son to a lord of two manors, the other a cottar's orphan, that had suddenly shown them as close kin in his eyes. Neglected and despised both, both of an age, and with such warmth and humility on the one side, and such passionate and impulsive generosity on the other, how could they fail to come together?

When he had unloaded his scrip, and noted any depleted places remaining on the shelves, he went to find the pair, and followed them at a little distance as Mark led his new helper through hospice and chapel and graveyard, and the sheltered patch of orchard behind, where some of the abler in body sat for part of the day outside, to take the clean air. A household

261

of the indigent and helpless, men, women, even children, forsaken or left orphans, dappled by skin diseases, deformed by accident, leprosy and agues; and a leaven of reasonably healthy beggars who lacked only land, craft, a place in the orders, and the means to earn their bread. In Wales, thought Cadfael, these things are better handled, not by charity but by blood-kinship. If a man belongs to a kinship, who can separate him from it? It acknowledges and sustains him, it will not let him be outcast or die of need. Yet even in Wales, the outlander without a clan is one man against the world. So are these runaway serfs, dispossessed cottagers, crippled labourers thrown out when they lose their working value. And the poor, drab, debased women, some with children at skirt, and the fathers snug and far, those that are not honest but dead.

He left them together, and went away quietly with his empty scrip and his bolstered faith. No need to say one word to Mark of his new brother's history, let them make what they could of each other in pure brotherhood, if that term has truly any meaning. Let Mark make up his own mind, unprejudiced, unprompted, and in a week we may learn something positive about Meriet, not filtered through pity.

The last he saw of them they were in the little orchard where the children ran to play; four who could run, one who hurtled on a single crutch, and one who at nine years old scuttled on all fours like a small dog, having lost the toes of both feet through a gangrene after being exposed to hard frost in a bad winter. Mark had the littlest by the hand as he led Meriet round the small enclosure. Meriet had as yet no armoury against horror, but at least horror in him was not revulsion. He was stooping to reach a hand to the dog-boy winding round his feet, and finding him unable to rise, and therefore unwilling to attempt it, he did not hoist the child willy-nilly, but suddenly dropped to his own nimble haunches to bring himself to a comparable level, and squatted there distressed, intent, listening.

It was enough. Cadfael went away content and left them together.

He let them alone for some days, and then made occasion to have a private word with Brother Mark, on the pretext of attending one of the beggars who had a persistent ulcer. Not a word was said of Meriet until Mark accompanied Cadfael out to the gate, and a piece of the way along the road towards the abbey wall.

'And how is your new helper doing?' asked Cadfael then, in the casual tone in which he would have enquired of any other beginner in this testing service.

'Very well,' said Mark, cheerful and unsuspicious. 'Willing to work until he drops, if I would let him.' So he might, of course; it is one way of forgetting what cannot be escaped. 'He's very good with the children, they follow him round and take him by the hand when they can.' Yes, that also made excellent sense. The children would not ask him questions he did not wish to answer, or weigh him up in the scale as grown men do, but take him on trust and if they liked him, cling to him. He would not need his constant guard with them. 'And he does not shrink from the worst disfigurement or the most disgusting tasks,' said Mark, 'though he is not inured to them as I am, and I know he suffers.'

'That's needful,' said Cadfael simply. 'If he did not suffer he ought not to be here. Cold kindness is only half a man's duty who tends the sick. How do you find him with you – does he speak of himself ever?'

'Never,' said Mark, and smiled, feeling no surprise that it should be so. 'He has nothing he wishes to say. Not yet.'

'And there is nothing you wish to know of him?'

'I'll listen willingly,' said Mark, 'to anything you think I *should* know of him. But what most matters I know already: that he is by nature honest and sweet clean through, whatever manner of wreck he and other people and ill circumstances may have made of his life. I only wish he were happier. I should like to hear him laugh.'

'Not for your need, then,' said Cadfael, 'but in case of his, you had better know all of him that I know.' And forthwith he told it.

'Now I understand,' said Mark at the end of it, 'why he *would* take his pallet up into the loft. He was afraid that in his sleep he might disturb and frighten those who have more than enough to bear already. I was in two minds about moving up there with him, but I thought better of it. I knew he must have his own good reasons.'

'Good reasons for everything he does?' wondered Cadfael.

'Reasons that seem good to him, at any rate. But they might not always be wise,' conceded Mark very seriously.

Brother Mark said no word to Meriet about what he had learned, certainly made no move to join him in his self-exile in the loft over the barn, nor offered any comment on such a choice; but he did, on the following three nights, absent himself very quietly from his own bed when all was still, and go softly into the barn to listen for any sound from above. But there was nothing but the long, easy breathing of a man peacefully asleep, and the occasional sigh and rustle as Meriet turned without waking. Perhaps other, deeper sighs at times, seeking to heave away a heavy weight from a heart; but no outcry. At Saint Giles Meriet went to bed tired out and to some consoling degree fulfilled, and slept without dreams.

Among the many benefactors of the leper hospital, the crown was one of the greatest through its grants to the abbey and the abbey's dependencies. There were other lords of manors who allowed certain days for the gathering of wild fruits or dead wood, but in the nearby reaches of the Long Forest the lazar-house had the right to make forays for wood, both for fuel and fencing or other building uses, on four days in the year, one in October, one in November, one in December, whenever the weather allowed, and one in February or March to replenish stocks run down by the winter.

Meriet had been at the hospice just three weeks when the third of December offered a suitably mild day for an expedition to the forest, with early sun and comfortably firm and dry earth underfoot. There had been several dry days, and might not be many more. It was ideal for picking up dead wood, without the extra weight of damp to carry, and even stacked coppice-wood was fair prize under the terms. Brother Mark sniffed the air and declared what was to all intents a holiday. They marshalled two light hand-carts, and a number of woven slings to bind faggots, put on board a large leather bucket of food, and collected all the inmates capable of keeping up with a leisurely progress into the forest. There were others who would have liked to come, but could not manage the way and had to wait at home.

From Saint Giles the highway led south, leaving aside to the left the way Brother Cadfael had taken to Aspley. Some way past that divide they kept on along the road, and wheeled right into the scattered copse-land which fringed the forest, following a good, broad ride which the carts could easily negotiate. The toeless boy went with them, riding one of the carts. His weight, after all, was negligible, and his joy beyond price. Where they halted in a clearing to collect fallen wood, they set him down in the smoothest stretch of grass, and let him play while they worked.

Meriet had set out as grave as ever, but as the morning progressed, so did he emerge from his hiding-place into muted sunlight, like the day. He sniffed the forest air, and trod its sward, and seemed to expand, as a dried shoot does after rain, drawing in sustenance from the earth on which he strode. There was no one more tireless in collecting the stouter boughs of fallen wood, no one so agile in binding and loading them. When the company halted to take meat and drink, emptying the leather bucket, they were well into the border areas of the forest, where their pickings would be best, and Meriet ate his bread and cheese and onion, and drank his ale, and lay down flat as ground-ivy under the trees, with the toeless boy sprawled in one arm. Thus deep-drowned in the last pale grass, he looked like some native ground-growth burgeoning from the earth, half-asleep towards the winter, half-wakeful towards another growing year.

They had gone no more than ten minutes deeper into the woodland, after their rest, when he checked to look about him, at the slant of the veiled sun between the trees, and the shape of the low, lichened outcrop of rocks on their right.

'Now I know just where we are. When I had my first pony I was never supposed to come further west than the highroad from home, let alone venture this far south-west into the forest, but I often did. There used to be an old charcoal-burner had a hearth somewhere here, it can't be far away. They found him dead in his hut a year and more ago, and there was no son to take on after him, and nobody wanted to live as lone as he did. He may have left a cord or two of coppice-wood stacked to season, that he never lived to burn. Shall we go and see, Mark? We could do well there.'

It was the first time he had ever volunteered even so innocuous a recollection of his childhood, and the first time he had shown any eagerness. Mark welcomed the suggestion gladly.

'Can you find it again? We have a fair load already, but we can very well cart the best out to the roadside, and send for it again when we've unloaded the rest. We have the whole day.'

'This way it should be,' said Meriet, and set off confidently to the left between the trees, lengthening his step to quest ahead of his charges. 'Let them follow at their own pace. I'll go forward and find the place. A hollow clearing it was – the stacks must have shelter ...' His voice and his striding figure dwindled among the trees. He was out of sight for a few minutes before they heard him call, a hail as near pleasure as Mark had ever heard from him.

When Mark reached him he was standing where the trees thinned and fell back, leaving a shallow bowl perhaps forty or fifty paces across, with a level floor of beaten earth and old ash. At the rim, close to them, the decrepit remains of a rough hut of sticks and bracken and earth sagged over its empty log doorway, and on the far side of the arena there were stacked logs of coppice-wood, left in the round, and now partially overgrown at the base of the stack with coarse grass and mosses. There was room enough on the prepared floor for two hearths some five long paces each in diameter, and their traces were still plain to be seen, though grass and herbage were encroaching from the edges of the plain, invading even the dead circles of ash with defiant green shoots. The nearer hearth had been cleared after its last burning, and no new stack built there, but on the more distant ring a mound of stacked logs, half burned out and half still keeping its form beneath the layers of grass and leaves and earth, lay flattened and settling.

'He had built his last stack and fired it,' said Meriet, gazing, 'and then never had time to build its fellow while the first was burning, as he always used to do, nor even to tend the one he had lighted. You see there must have been a wind, after he was dead, and no one by to dress the gap when it began to burn through. All the one side is dead ash, look, and the other only charred. Not much charcoal to be found there, but we might get enough to fill the bucket. And at least he left us a good stock of wood, and well seasoned, too.'

'I have no skill in this art,' said Mark curiously. 'How can such a great hill of wood be got to burn without blazing, so that it may be used as fuel over again?'

'They begin with a tall stake in the middle, and stack dry split logs round it, and then the whole logs, until the stack is made. Then you must cover it with a clean layer, leaves or grass or bracken, to keep out the earth and ash that goes over all to seal it. And to light it, when it's ready, you hoist out the stake to leave a chimney, and drop your first red-hot coals down inside, and good dry sticks after, until it's well afire. Then you cover up the vent, and it burns very slow and hot, sometimes as long as ten days. If there's a wind you must watch it all the while, for if it burns through the whole stack goes up in flames. If there's danger you must patch the place and keep it sealed. There was no one left to do that here.'

266

Their slower companions were coming up through the trees. Meriet led the way down the slight incline into the hearth, with Mark close at his heels.

'It seems to me,' said Mark, smiling, 'that you're very well versed in the craft. How did you learn so much about it?'

'He was a surly old man and not well liked,' said Meriet, making for the stacked cordwood, 'but he was not surly with me. I was here often at one time, until I once helped him to rake down a finished burn, and went home dirtier than even I could account for. I got my tail well leathered, and they wouldn't let me have my pony again until I promised not to venture over here to the west. I suppose I was about nine years old – it's a long time ago.' He eyed the piled wood with pride and pleasure, and rolled the topmost log from its place, sending a number of frightened denizens scuttling for cover.

They had left one of their hand-carts, already well filled, in the clearing where they had rested at noon. Two of the sturdiest gleaners brought the second weaving between the trees, and the whole company fell gleefully upon the logs and began to load them.

'There'll be half-burned wood still in the stack,' said Meriet, 'and maybe some charcoal, too, if we strip it.' And he was off to the tumbledown hut, and emerged with a large wooden rake, with which he went briskly to attack the misshapen mound left by the last uncontrolled burning. 'Strange,' he said, lifting his head and wrinkling his nose, 'there's still the stink of old burning, who would have thought it could last so long?'

There was indeed a faint stench such as a woodland fire might leave after it had been damped by rain and dried out by wind. Mark could distinguish it, too, and came to Meriet's side as the broad rake began to draw down the covering of earth and leaves from the windward side of the mound. The moist, earthy smell of leaf-mould rose to their nostrils, and half-consumed logs heeled away and rolled down with the rake. Mark walked round to the other side, where the mound had sunk into a weathered mass of grey ash, and the wind had carried its fine dust as far as the rim of the trees. There the smell of dead fire was sharper, and rose in waves as Mark's feet stirred the debris. And surely on this side the leaves still left on the nearest trees were withered as though by scorching.

'Meriet!' called Mark in a low but urgent tone. 'Come here to me!'

Meriet looked round, his rake locked in the covering of soil.

Surprised but undisturbed, he skirted the ring of ash to come to where Mark stood, but instead of relinquishing the rake he tugged the head after him across the low crest of the mound, and tore down with it a tumble of half-burned logs, rolling merrily down into the ashen grass. It occurred to Mark that this was the first time he had seen his new helper look almost happy, using his body energetically, absorbed in what he was doing and forgetful of his own concerns. 'What is it? What have you seen?'

The falling logs, charred and disintegrating, settled in a flurry of acrid dust. Something rolled out to Meriet's feet, something that was not wood. Blackened, cracked and dried, a leathern shape hardly recognisable at first sight for a long-toed riding shoe, with a tarnished buckle to fasten it across the instep; and protruding from it, something long and rigid, showing gleams of whitish ivory through fluttering, tindery rags of calcined cloth.

There was a long moment while Meriet stood staring down at it without comprehension, his lips still shaping the last word of his blithe enquiry, his face still animated and alert. Then Mark saw the same shocking and violent change Cadfael had once seen, as the brightness of the hazel eyes seemed to collapse inward into total darkness, and the fragile mask of content shrank and froze into horror. He made a very small sound in his throat, a harsh rattle like a man dying, took one reeling step backwards, stumbled in the uneven ground, and dropped cowering into the grass.

Chapter Eight

T WAS no more than an instant's withdrawal from the unbearable, recoiling into his enfolding arms, shutting out what nevertheless he could not choose but go on seeing. He had not swooned. Even as Mark flew to him, with no outcry to alarm the busy party dismantling the stack of cordwood, he was already rearing his head and doubling his fists grimly into the soil to raise himself. Mark held him with an arm about his body, for he was trembling still when he got to his feet.

'Did you see? Did you see it?' he asked in a whisper. What remained of the half-burned stack was between them and their charges, no one had turned to look in their direction.

'Yes, I saw. I know! We must get them away,' said Mark. 'Leave this pile as it is, touch nothing more, leave the charcoal. We must just load the wood and start them back for home. Are you fit to go? Can you be as always, and keep your face before them?'

'I can,' said Meriet, stiffening, and scrubbed a sleeve over a forehead dewed with a chilly sweat. 'I will! But, Mark, if you saw what I saw – we must *know* ...'

'We do know,' said Mark, 'you and I both. It's not for us now, this is the law's business, and we must let ill alone for them to see. Don't even look that way again. I saw, perhaps, more than you. I know what is there. What we must do is get our people home without spoiling their day. Now, come and see to loading the cart with me. Can you, yet?'

For answer, Meriet braced his shoulders, heaved in a great breath, and withdrew himself resolutely from the thin arm that still encircled him. 'I'm ready!' he said, in a fair attempt at the cheerful, practical voice with which he had summoned them to the hearth, and was off across the level floor to plunge fiercely into the labour of hoisting logs into the cart.

Mark followed him watchfully, and against all temptation contrived to obey his own order, and give no single glance to that which had been uncovered among the ashes. But he did, as they worked, cast a careful eye about the rim of the hearth, where he had also noticed certain circumstances which gave him cause for thought. What he had been about to say to Meriet when the rake fetched down its avalanche was never said.

They loaded their haul, stacking the wood so high that there was no room for the toeless boy to ride on top for the return journey. Meriet carried him on his back, until the arms that clasped him round the neck fell slack with sleepiness, and he shifted his burden to one arm, so that the boy's tow-coloured head could nod securely on his shoulder. The load on his arm was light enough, and warm against his heart. What else he carried unseen, thought Mark watching him with reticent attention, weighed more heavily and struck cold as ice. But Meriet's calm continued rock-firm. The one moment of recoil was over, and there would be no more such lapses.

At Saint Giles Meriet carried the boy indoors, and returned to help haul the carts up the slight slope to the barn, where the wood would be stacked under the low eaves, to be sawn and split later as it was needed.

'I am going now into Shrewsbury,' said Mark, having counted all his chicks safely into the coop, tired and elated from their successful foray.

'Yes,' said Meriet, without turning from the neat stack he was building, end-outwards between two confining buttresses of wood. 'I know someone must.'

'Stay here with them. I'll come back as soon as I can.'

'I know,' said Meriet. 'I will. They're happy enough. It was a good day.'

Brother Mark hesitated when he reached the abbey gatehouse, for his natural instinct was to take everything first to Brother Cadfael. It was plain that his errand now was to the officers of the king's law in the shire, and urgent, but on the other hand it was Cadfael who had confided Meriet to him, and he was certain in his own mind that the grisly discovery in the charcoal hearth was in some way connected with Meriet. The shock he had felt was genuine, but extreme, his wild recoil too intense to be anything but personal. He had not known, had not dreamed, what he was going to find, but past any doubt he knew it when he found it.

While Mark was hovering irresolute in the arch of the gatehouse Brother Cadfael, who had been sent for before Vespers to an old man in the Foregate who had a bad chest ailment, came behind and clapped him briskly on the shoulder. Turning to find the clemency of heaven apparently presenting him with the answer to his problem, Mark clutched him gratefully by the sleeve, and begged him, 'Cadfael, come with me to Hugh Beringar. We've found something hideous in the Long Forest, business for him, surely. I was just by way of praying for you. Meriet was with me – this somehow touches Meriet ...'

Cadfael fixed him with an acute stare, took him by the arm and turned him promptly towards the town. 'Come on then and save your breath to tell the tale but once. I'm earlier back than anyone will expect me, I can stretch my licence an hour or two, for you and for Meriet.'

So they were two who arrived at the house near Saint Mary's, where Hugh had settled his family. By luck he was home before supper, and free of his labours for the day. He haled them in warmly, and had wit enough not to offer Brother Mark respite or refreshment until he had heaved his whole anxiety off his narrow chest. Which he did very consideringly, measuring words. He stepped meticulously from fact to fact, as on sure stepping-stones through a perilous stream.

'I called him round to me because I had seen that on the side of that stack where I was, and where the pile was burned out, the wind had carried fine ash right into the trees, and the near branches of the trees were scorched, the leaves browned and withered. I meant to call his attention to these things, for such a fire was no long time ago. Those were this year's leaves scorched brown, that was ash not many weeks old still showing grey. And he came readily, but as he came he held on to the rake and tugged it with him, to bring down the top of the stack, where it had not burned out. So he brought down a whole fall of wood and earth and leaves, and this thing rolled down between, at our feet.'

271

'You saw it plainly,' said Hugh gently, 'tell us as plainly.'

'It is a fashionable long-toed riding shoe,' said Mark steadily, 'shrunk and dried and twisted by fire, but not consumed. And in it a man's leg-bone, in the ashes of hose.'

'You are in no doubt,' said Hugh, watching him with sympathy.

'None. I saw projecting from the pile the round knee-joint from which the shin-bone had parted,' said Brother Mark, pale but tranquil. 'It so happened I saw it break away. I am sure the man is there. The fire broke through on the other side, a strong wind drove it, and left him, it may be, almost for Christian burial. At least we may collect his bones.'

'That shall be done with all reverence,' said Hugh, 'if you are right. Go on, you have more to tell. Brother Meriet saw what you had seen. What then?'

'He was utterly stricken and shocked. He had spoken of coming there as a child, and helping the old charcoal-burner. I am certain he knew of nothing worse there than what he remembered. I told him first we must get our people home undisturbed, and he did his part valiantly,' said Brother Mark. 'We have left all as we found it – or as we disturbed it unwitting. In the morning light I can show you the place.'

'I think, rather,' said Hugh with deliberation, 'Meriet Aspley shall do that. But now you have told us what you had to tell, now you may sit down with me and eat and drink a morsel, while we consider this matter.'

Brother Mark sat down obediently, sighing away the burden of his knowledge. Grateful for the humblest of hospitality, he was equally unawed by the noblest, and having no pride, he did not know how to be servile. When Aline herself brought him meat and drink, and the same for Cadfael, he received it gladly and simply, as saints accept alms, perpetually astonished and pleased, perpetually serene.

'You said,' Hugh pressed him gently over the wine, 'that you had cause, in the blown ash and the scorching of the trees, to believe that the fire was of this season, and not from a year ago, and that I accept. Had you other reasons to think so?'

'I had,' said Mark simply, 'for though we have brought home, to our gain, a whole cord of good coppice-wood, yet not far aside from ours there were two other flattened and whitened shapes in the grass, greener than the one we have now left, but still clear to be seen, which I think must have been bared when the wood was used for this stack. Meriet told

272

me the logs must be left to season. These would have seasoned more than a year, dried out, it may be, too far for what was purposed. No one was left to watch the burning, and the over-dried wood burned through and burst into a blaze. You will see the shapes where the wood lay. You will judge better than I how long since it was moved.'

'That I doubt,' said Hugh, smiling, 'for you seem to have done excellently well. But tomorrow we shall see. There are those can tell to a hair, by the burrowing insects and the spiders, and the tinder fringing the wood. Sit and take your ease a while, before you must return, for there's nothing now can be done before morning.'

Brother Mark sat back, relieved, and bit with astonished pleasure into the game pasty Aline had brought him. She thought him underfed, and worried about him because he was so meagre; and indeed he may very well have been underfed, through forgetting to eat while he worried about someone else. There was a great deal of the good woman in Brother Mark, and Aline recognized it.

'Tomorrow morning,' said Hugh, when Mark rose to take his leave and make his way back to his charges, 'I shall be at Saint Giles with my men immediately after Prime. You may tell Brother Meriet that I shall require him to come with me and show me the place.'

That, of course, should occasion no anxiety to an innocent man, since he had been the cause of the discovery in the first place, but it might bring on a very uneasy night for one not entirely innocent, at least of more knowledge than was good for him. Mark could not object to the oblique threat, since his own mind had been working in much the same direction. But in departing he made over again his strongest point in Meriet's defence.

'He led us to the place, for good and sensible reasons, seeing it was fuel we were after. Had he known what he was to find there, he would never have let us near it.'

'That shall be borne in mind,' said Hugh gravely. 'Yet I think you found something more than natural in his horror when he uncovered a dead man. You, after all, are much of his age, and have had no more experience of murder and violence than has he. And I make no doubt you were shaken to the soul – yet not as he was. Granted he knew nothing of this unlawful burial, still the discovery meant to him something more, something worse, than it meant to you. Granted he did not know a body had been so disposed of, may he not, nevertheless, have had knowledge of a body in need of secret disposal, and recognized it when he uncovered it?'

'That is possible,' said Mark simply. 'It is for you to examine all these things.' And he took his leave, and set off alone on the walk back to Saint Giles.

'There's no knowing, as yet,' said Cadfael, when Mark was gone, 'who or what this dead man may be. He may have nothing to do with Meriet, with Peter Clemence or with the horse straying in the mosses. A live man missing, a dead man found – they need not be one and the same. There's every reason to doubt it. The horse more than twenty miles north of here, the rider's last night halt four miles south-east, and this burning hearth another four miles south-west from there. You'll have hard work linking those into one sequence and making sense of it. He left Aspley travelling north, and one thing's certain by a number of witnesses, he was man alive then. What should he be doing now, not north, but south of Aspley? And his horse miles north, and on the right route he would be taking, bar a little straying at the end?'

'I don't know but I'll be the happier,' owned Hugh, 'if this turns out to be some other traveller fallen by thieves some-where, and nothing to do with Clemence, who may well be down in the peat-pools this moment. But do you know of any other gone missing in these parts? And another thing, Cadfael, would common thieves have left him his riding shoes? Or his hose, for that matter? A naked man has nothing left that could benefit his murderers, and nothing by which he may be easily known, two good reasons for stripping him. And again, since he wore long-toed shoes, he was certainly not going far afoot. No sane man would wear them for walking.'

A rider without a horse, a saddled horse without a rider, what wonder if the mind put the two together?

'No profit in racking brains,' said Cadfael, sighing, 'until you've viewed the place, and gathered what there is to be gathered there.'

'*We*, old friend1 I want you with me, and I think Abbot Radulfus will give me leave to take you. You're better skilled than I in dead men, in how long they may have been dead, and how they died. Moreover, he'll want a watching eye on all that affects Saint Giles, and who better than you? You're waist-deep in the whole matter already, you must either sink or haul clear.'

'For my sins!' said Cadfael, somewhat hypocritically. 'But I'll gladly come with you. Whatever devil it is that possesses young Meriet is plaguing me by contagion, and I want it exorcised at all costs.'

Meriet was waiting for them when they came for him next day, Hugh and Cadfael, a sergeant and two officers, equipped with crows and shovels, and a sieve to sift the ashes for every trace and every bone. In the faint mist of a still morning, Meriet eyed all these preparations with a face stonily calm, braced for everything that might come, and said flatly, 'The tools are still there, my lord, in the hut. I fetched the rake from there, Mark will have told you – a corrack, the old man called it.' He looked at Cadfael, with the faintest softening in the set of his lips. 'Brother Mark said I should be needed. I'm glad he need not go back himself.' His voice was in as thorough control as his face; whatever confronted him today, it would not take him by surprise.

They had brought a horse for him, time having its value. He mounted nimbly, perhaps with the only impulse of pleasure that would come his way that day, and led the way down the high road. He did not glance aside when he passed the turning to his own home, but turned on the other hand into the broad ride, and within half an hour had brought them to the shallow bowl of the charcoal hearth. Ground mist lay faintly blue over the shattered mound as Hugh and Cadfael walked round the rim and halted where the log that was no log lay tumbled among the ashes.

The tarnished buckle on the perished leather strap was of silver. The shoe had been elaborate and expensive. Slivers of burned cloth fluttered from the almost fleshless bone.

Hugh looked from the foot to the knee, and on above among the exposed wood for the joint from which it had broken free. 'There he should be lying, aligned thus. Whoever put him there did not open a deserted stack, but built this new, and built him into the centre. Someone who knew the method, though perhaps not well enough. We had better take this apart carefully. You may rake off the earth covering and the leaves,' he said to his men, 'but when you reach the logs we'll hoist them off one by one where they're whole. I doubt he'll be little but bones, but I want all there is of him.'

They went to work, raking away the covering on the unburned side, and Cadfael circled the mound to view the

275

quarter from which the destroying wind must have been blowing. Low to the ground a small, arched hole showed in the roots of the pile. He stooped to look more closely, and ran a hand under the hanging leaves that half-obscured it. The hollow continued inward, swallowing his arm to the elbow. It had been built in as the stack was made. He went back to where Hugh stood watching.

'They knew the method, sure enough. There's a vent built in on the windward side to let in a draught. The stack was meant to burn out. But they overdid it. They must have had the vent covered until the stack was well alight, and then opened and left it. It blew too fiercely, and left the windward half hardly more than scorched while the rest blazed. These things have to be watched day and night.'

Meriet stood apart, close to where they had tethered the horses, and watched this purposeful activity with an impassive face. He saw Hugh cross to the edge of the arena, where three paler, flattened oblongs in the herbage showed where the wood had been stacked to season. Two of them showed greener than the third, as Mark had said, where new herbage had pierced the layer of dead grass and risen to the light. The third, the one which had supplied such a harvest for the inmates of Saint Giles, lay bleached and flat.

'How long,' asked Hugh, 'to make this much new growth, and at this season?'

Cadfael pondered, digging a toe into the soft mat of old growth below. 'A matter of eight to ten weeks, perhaps. Difficult to tell. And the blown ash might show as long as that. Mark was right, the heat reached the trees. If this floor had been less bare and hard, the fire might have reached them, too, but there was no thick layer of roots and leaf-mould to carry it along the ground.'

They returned to where the covering of earth and leaves now lay drawn aside, and the ridged surfaces of logs showed, blackened but keeping their shape. The sergeant and his men laid down their tools and went to work with their hands, hoisting the logs off one by one and stacking them aside out of the way. Slow work; and throughout Meriet stood watching, motionless and mute.

The dead man emerged from his coffin of timber piecemeal after more than two hours of work. He had lain close to the central chimney on the leeward side, and the fire had been fierce enough to burn away all but a few tindery flakes of his clothing, but had passed by too rapidly to take all the flesh from his bones, or even the hair from his head. Laboriously they brushed away debris of charcoal and ash and half-consumed wood from him, but could not keep him intact. The collapse of part of the stack had started his joints and broken him apart. They had to gather up his bones as best they could, and lay them out on the grass until they had, if not the whole man, all but such small bones of finger and wrist as would have to be sifted from the ashes. The skull still retained, above the blackened ruin of a face, the dome of a naked crown fringed with a few wisps and locks of brown hair, cropped short.

But there were other things to lay beside him. Metal is very durable. The silver buckles on his shoes, blackened as they were, kept the form a good workman had given them. There was the twisted half of a tooled leather belt, with another silver buckle, large and elaborate, and traces of silver ornamenting in the leather. There was a broken length of tarnished silver chain attached to a silver cross studded with what must surely be semi-precious stones, though now they were blackened and encrusted with dirt. And one of the men, running fine ash from close to the body through the sieve, came to lay down for examination a finger-bone and the ring it had loosely retained while the flesh was burned from between. The ring bore a large black stone engraved with a design fouled by clotted ash, but which seemed to be a decorative cross. There was also something which had lain within the shattered rib-cage, burned almost clean by the fire, the head of the arrow that had killed him.

Hugh stood over the remnants of a man and his death for a long while, staring down with a grim face. Then he turned to where Meriet stood, rigid and still at the rim of the decline.

'Come down here, come and see if you cannot help us further. We need a name for this murdered man. Come and see if by chance you know him.'

Meriet came, ivory-faced, drew close as he was ordered, and looked at what lay displayed. Cadfael held off, but at no great distance, and watched and listened. Hugh had not only his work to do, but his own wrung senses to avenge, and if there was some resultant savagery in his handling of Meriet, at least it was not purposeless. For now there was very little doubt of the identity of this dead man they had before them, and the chain that drew Meriet to him was contracting.

277

'You observe,' said Hugh, quite gently and coldly, 'that he wore the tonsure, that his own hair was brown, and his height, by the look of his bones, a tall man's. What age would you say, Cadfael?'

'He's straight, and without any of the deformities of ageing. A young man. Thirty he might be, I doubt more.'

'And a priest,' pursued Hugh mercilessly.

'By the ring, the cross and the tonsure, yes, a priest.'

'You perceive our reasoning, Brother Meriet. Have you knowledge of such a man lost hereabouts?'

Meriet continued to stare down at the silent relics that had been a man. His eyes were huge in a face blanched to the palest ivory. He said in a level voice: 'I see your reasoning. I do not know the man. How can anyone know him?'

'Not by his visage, certainly. But by his accoutrements, perhaps? The cross, the ring, even the buckles – these could be remembered, if a priest of such years, and so adorned, came into your acquaintance? As a guest, say, in your house?'

Meriet lifted his eyes with a brief and restrained flash of green, and said, 'I understand you. There was a priest who came and stayed the night over in my father's house, some weeks ago, before I came into the cloister. But that one travelled on the next morning, northwards, not this way. How could he be here? And how am I, or how are you, to tell the difference between one priest and another, when they are brought down to this?'

'Not by the cross? The ring? If you can say positively that this is *not* the man,' said Hugh insinuatingly, 'you would be helping me greatly.'

'I was of no such account in my father's house,' said Meriet with chill bitterness, 'to be so close to the honoured guest. I stabled his horse – to that I have testified. To his jewellery I cannot swear.'

'There will be others who can,' said Hugh grimly. 'And as to the horse, yes, I have seen in what comfortable esteem you held each other. You said truly that you are good with horses. If it became advisable to convey the mount some twenty miles or more away from where the rider met his death, who could manage the business better? Ridden or led, he would not give any trouble to you.'

'I never had him in my hands but one evening and the morning after,' said Meriet, 'nor saw him again until you brought him to the abbey, my lord.' And though sudden angry

278

colour flamed upward to his brow, his voice was ready and firm, and his temper well in hand.

'Well, let us first find a name for our dead man,' said Hugh, and turned to circle the dismembered mound once more, scanning the littered and fouled ground for any further detail that might have some bearing. He pondered what was left of the leather belt, all but the buckle end burned away, the charred remnant extending just far enough to reach a lean man's left hip. 'Whoever he was, he carried sword or dagger, here is the loop of the strap by which it hung – a dagger, too light and elegant for a sword. But no sign of the dagger itself. That should be somewhere here among the rubble.'

They raked through the debris for a further hour, but found no more of metal or clothing. When he was certain there was nothing more to be discovered, Hugh withdrew his party. They wrapped the recovered bones and the ring and cross reverently in a linen cloth and a blanket, and rode back with them to Saint Giles. There Meriet dismounted, but halted in silence to know what was the deputy-sheriff's will with him.

'You will be remaining here at the hospice?' asked Hugh, eyeing him impartially. 'Your abbot has committed you to this service?'

'Yes, my lord. Until or unless I am recalled to the abbey, I shall be here.' It was said with emphasis, not merely stating a fact, but stressing that he felt himself to have taken vows already, and not only his duty of obedience but his own will would keep him here.

'Good! So we know where to find you at need. Very well, continue your work here without hindrance, but subject to your abbot's authority, hold yourself also at my disposal.'

'So I will, my lord. So I do,' said Meriet, and turned on his heel with a certain drear dignity, and stalked away up the incline to the gate in the wattle fence.

'And now, I suppose,' sighed Hugh, riding on towards the Foregate with Cadfael beside him, 'you will be at odds with me for being rough with your fledgling. Though I give you due credit, you held your tongue very generously.'

'No,' said Cadfael honestly, 'he's none the worse for goading. And there's no blinking it, suspicion drapes itself round him like cobwebs on an autumn bush.'

'It *is* the man, and he knows that it is. He knew it as soon as he raked out the shoe and the foot within it. That, and not the

279

mere matter of some unknown man's ugly death, was what shook him almost out of his wits. He knew – quite certainly he knew – that Peter Clemence was dead, but just as certainly he did *not* know what had been done with the body. Will you go with me so far?'

'So far,' said Cadfael ruefully, 'I have already gone. An irony, indeed, that he led them straight to the place, when for once he was thinking of nothing but finding his poor folk fuel for the winter. Which is on the doorstep this very evening, unless my nose for weather fails me.'

The air had certainly grown still and chill, and the sky was closing down upon the world in leaden cloud. Winter had delayed, but was not far away.

'First,' pursued Hugh, harking back to the matter in hand, 'we have to affix a name to these bones. That whole household at Aspley saw the man, spent an evening in his company, they must all know these gems of his, soiled as they may be now. It might put a rampaging cat among pigeons if I sent to summon Leoric here to speak as to his guest's cross and ring. When the birds fly wild, we may pick up a feather or two.'

'But for all that,' said Cadfael earnestly, 'I should not do it. Say never a probing word to any, leave them lulled. Let it be known we've found a murdered man, but no more. If you let out too much, then the one with guilt to hide will be off and out of reach. Let him think all's well, and he'll be off his guard. You'll not have forgotten, the older boy's marriage is set for the twenty-first of this month, and two days before that the whole clan of them, neighbours, friends and all, will be gathering in our guest-halls. Bring them in, and you have everyone in your hand. By then we may have the means to divine truth from untruth. And as for proving that this is indeed Peter Clemence – not that I'm in doubt! – did you not tell me that Canon Eluard intends to come back to us on the way south from Lincoln, and let the king go without him to Westminster?'

'True, so he said he would. He's anxious for news to take back to the bishop at Winchester, but it's no good news we have for him.'

'If Stephen means to spend his Christmas in London, then Canon Eluard may very well be here before the wedding party arrives. He knew Clemence well, they've both been close about Bishop Henry. He should be your best witness.'

'Well, a couple of weeks can hardly hurt Peter Clemence

now,' agreed Hugh wryly. 'But have you noticed, Cadfael, the strangest thing in all this coil? Nothing was stolen from him, everything burned with him. Yet more than one man, more than two, worked at building that pyre. Would you not say there was a voice in authority there, that would not permit theft though it had been forced to conceal murder? And those who took his orders feared him – or at the least minded him – more than they coveted rings and crosses.'

It was true. Whoever had decreed that disposal of Peter Clemence had put it clean out of consideration that his death could be the work of common footpads and thieves. A mistake, if he hoped to set all suspicion at a distance from himself and his own people. That rigid honesty had mattered more to him, whoever he was, than safety. Murder was within the scope of his understanding, if not of his tolerance; but not theft from the dead.

Chapter Nine

ROST SET in that night, heralding a week of hard weather. No snow fell, but a blistering east wind scoured the hills, wild birds ventured close to human habitations to pick up scraps of food, and even the woodland foxes came skulking a mile closer to the town. And so did some unknown human predator who had been snatching the occasional hen from certain outlying runs, and now and then a loaf of bread from a kitchen. Complaints began to be brought in to the town provost of thefts from the garden stores outside the walls, and to the castle of poultry taken from homesteads at the edge of Foregate, and not by foxes or other vermin. One of the foresters from the Long Forest brought in a tale of a gutted deer lost a month ago, with evidence enough that the marauder was in possession of a good knife. Now the cold was driving someone living wild nearer to the town, where nights could be spent warmer in byre or barn than in the bleak woods.

King Stephen had detained his sheriff at Shropshire in attendance about his person that autumn, after the usual Michaelmas accounting, and taken him with him in the company now paying calculated courtesies to the earl of Chester and William of Roumare in Lincoln, so that this matter of the henhouse marauder, along with all other offences against the king's peace and good order, fell into Hugh's hands. 'As well!' said Hugh. 'For I'd just as lief keep the

Clemence affair mine without interference, now it's gone so far.'

He was well aware that he had not too much time left in which to bring it to a just end single-handed, for if the king meant to be back in Westminster for Christmas, then the sheriff might return to his shire in a very few days. And certainly this wild man's activities seemed to be centred on the eastern fringe of the forest, which was engaging Hugh's interest already for a very different reason.

In a country racked by civil war, and therefore hampered in keeping ordinary law and order, everything unaccountable was being put down to outlaws living wild; but for all that, now and then the simplest explanation turns out to be the true one. Hugh had no such expectations in this case, and was greatly surprised when one of his sergeants brought in to the castle wards in triumph the thief who had been living off the more unwary inhabitants of the Foregate. Not because of the man himself, who was very much what might have been expected, but because of the dagger and sheath which had been found on him, and were handed over as proof of his villainies. There were even traces of dried blood, no doubt from someone's pullet or goose, engrained in the grooved blade.

It was a very elegant dagger, with rough gems in the hilt, so shaped as to be comfortable to the hand, and its sheath of metal covered with tooled leather had been blackened and discoloured by fire, the leather frayed away for half its length from the tip. An end of thin leather strap still adhered to it. Hugh had seen the loop from which it, or its fellow, should have depended.

In the bleak space of the inner ward he jerked his head towards the anteroom of the hall, and said, 'Bring him within.' There was a good fire in there, and a bench to sit on. 'Take off his chains,' said Hugh, after one look at the wreck of a big man, 'and let him sit by the fire. You may keep by him, but I doubt if he'll give you any trouble.'

The prisoner could have been an imposing figure, if he had still had flesh and sinew on his long, large bones, but he was shrunken by starvation, and with nothing but rags on him in this onset of winter. He could not be old, his eyes and his shock of pale hair were those of a young man, his bones, however starting from his flesh, moved with the live vigour of youth. Close to the fire, warmed after intense cold, he flushed and dilated into something nearer approaching his proper growth.

283

But his face, blue-eyed, hollow-cheeked, stared in mute terror upon Hugh. He was like a wild thing in a trap, braced taut, waiting for a bolthole. Ceaselessly he rubbed at his wrists, just loosed from the heavy chains.

'What is your name?' asked Hugh, so mildly that the creature stared and froze, afraid to understand such a tone.

'What do men call you?' repeated Hugh patiently.

'Harald, my lord. I'm named Harald.' The large frame produced a skeletal sound, deep but dry and remote. He had a cough that perforated his speech uneasily, and a name that had once belonged to a king, and that within the memory of old men still living, men of his own fair colouring.

'Tell me how you came by this thing, Harald. For it's a rich man's weapon, as you must know. See the craftsmanship of it, and the jeweller's work. Where did you find such a thing?'

'I didn't steal it,' said the wretch, trembling. 'I swear I didn't! It was thrown away, no one wanted it ...'

'Where did you find it?' demanded Hugh more sharply.

'In the forest, my lord. There's a place where they burn charcoal.' He described it, stammering and blinking, voluble to hold off blame. 'There was a dead fire there, I took fuel from it sometimes, but I was afraid to stay so near the road. The knife was lying in the ashes, lost or thrown away. Nobody wanted it. And I needed a knife ...' He shook, watching Hugh's impassive face with frightened blue eyes. 'It was not stealing ... I never stole but to keep alive, my lord, I swear it.'

He had not been a very successful thief, even so, for he had barely kept body and soul together. Hugh regarded him with detached interest, and no particular severity.

'How long have you been living wild?'

'Four months it must be, my lord. But I never did violence, nor stole anything but food. I needed a knife for my hunting ...'

Ah, well, thought Hugh, the king can afford a deer here and there. This poor devil needs it more than Stephen does, and Stephen in his truest mood would give it to him freely. Aloud he said, 'A hard life for a man, come wintertime. You'll do better indoors with us for a while, Harald, and feed regularly, if not on venison.' He turned to the sergeant, who was standing warily by. 'Lock him away. Let him have blankets to wrap him. And see to it he eats – but none too much to start with or he'll gorge and die on us.' He had known it happen among the wretched creatures in flight the previous winter from the storming of Worcester, starving on the road and eating themselves to death when they came to shelter. 'And use him well!' said Hugh sharply as the sergeant hauled up his prisoner. 'He'll not stand rough handling, and I want him. Understood?'

The sergeant understood it as meaning this was the wanted murderer, and must live to stand his trial and take his ceremonial death. He grinned, and abated his hold on the bony shoulder he gripped. 'I take your meaning, my lord.'

They were gone, captor and captive, off to a securely locked cell where the outlaw Harald, almost certainly a runaway villein, and probably with good reason, could at least be warmer than out in the woods, and get his meals, rough as they might be, brought to him without hunting.

Hugh completed his daily business about the castle, and then went off to find Brother Cadfael in his workshop, brewing some aromatic mixture to soothe aching throats through the first chills of the winter. Hugh sat back on the familiar bench against the timber wall, and accepted a cup of one of Cadfael's better wines, kept for his better acquaintances.

'Well, we have our murderer safely under lock and key,' he announced, straight-faced, and recounted what had emerged. Cadfael listened attentively, for all he seemed to have his whole mind on his simmering syrup.

'Folly!' he said then, scornfully. His brew was bubbling too briskly, he lifted it to the side of the brazier.

'Of course folly,' agreed Hugh heartily. 'A poor wretch without a rag to his covering or a crust to his name, kill a man and leave him his valuables, let alone his clothes? They must be about of a height, he would have stripped him naked and been glad of such cloth. And build the clerk single-handed into that stack of timber? Even if he knew how such burnings are managed, and I doubt if he does .... No, it is beyond belief. He found the dagger, just as he says. What we have here is some poor soul pushed so far by a heavy-handed lord that he's run for it. And too timid, or too sure of his lord's will to pursue him, to risk walking into the town and seeking work. He's been loose four months, picking up what food he could where he could.'

'You have it all clear enough, it seems,' said Cadfael, still brooding over his concoction, though it was beginning to settle in the pot, gently hiccuping. 'What is it you want of me?'

'My man has a cough, and a festered wound on his forearm, I judge a dog's bite, somewhere he lifted a hen. Come and sain it for him, and get out of him whatever you can, where he came from, who is his master, what is his trade. We've room for good craftsmen of every kind in the town, as you know, and have taken in several, to our gain and theirs. This may well be another as useful.'

'I'll do that gladly,' said Cadfael, turning to look at his friend with a very shrewd eye. 'And what has he to offer you in exchange for a meal and a bed? And maybe a suit of clothes, if you had his inches, as by your own account you have not. I'd swear Peter Clemence could have topped you by a hand's length.'

'This fellow certainly could,' allowed Hugh, grinning. 'Though sidewise even I could make two of him as he is now. But you'll see for yourself, and no doubt be casting an eye over all your acquaintance to find a man whose cast-offs would fit him. As for what use I have for him, apart from keeping him from starving to death – my sergeant is already putting it about that our wild man is taken, and I've no doubt he won't omit the matter of the dagger. No need to frighten the poor devil worse than he's been frightened already by charging him, but if the world outside has it on good authority that our murderer is safe behind bars, so much the better. Everyone can breathe more freely – notably the murderer. And a man off his guard, as you said, may make a fatal slip.'

Cadfael considered and approved. So desirable an ending, to have an outlaw and a stranger, who mattered to nobody, blamed for whatever evil was done locally; and one week now to pass before the wedding party assembled, all with minds at ease.

'For that stubborn lad of yours at Saint Giles,' said Hugh very seriously, 'knows what happened to Peter Clemence, whether he had any hand in it, or no.'

'Knows,' said Brother Cadfael, equally gravely, 'or thinks he knows.'

He went up through the town to the castle that same afternoon, bespoken by Hugh from the abbot as healer even to prisoners and criminals. He found the prisoner Harald in a cell at least dry with a stone bench to lie on, and blankets to soften it and wrap him from the cold, and that was surely Hugh's doing. The opening of the door upon his solitude occasioned instant mute alarm, but the appearance of a Benedictine habit both astonished and soothed him, and to be asked to show his

286

hurts was still deeper bewilderment, but softened into wonder and hope. After long loneliness, where the sound of a voice could mean nothing but threat, the fugitive recovered his tongue rustily but gratefully, and ended in a flood of words like floods of tears, draining and exhausting him. After Cadfael left him he stretched and eased into prodigious sleep.

Cadfael reported to Hugh before leaving the castle wards.

'He's a farrier, he says a good one. It may well be true, it is the only source of pride he has left. Can you use such? I've dressed his bite with a lotion of hound's-tongue, and anointed a few other cuts and grazes he has. I think he'll do well enough. Let him eat little but often for a day or two or he'll sicken. He's from some way south, by Gretton. He says his lord's steward took his sister against her will, and he tried to avenge her. He was not good at murder,' said Cadfael wryly, 'and the ravisher got away with a mere graze. He may be better at farriery. His lord sought his blood and he ran – who could blame him?'

'Villein?' asked Hugh resignedly.

'Surely.'

'And sought, probably vindictively. Well, they'll have a vain hunt if they hunt him into Shrewsbury castle, we can hold him securely enough. And you think he tells truth?'

'He's too far gone to lie,' said Cadfael. 'Even if lying came easily, and I think this is a simple soul who leans to truth. Besides, he believes in my habit. We have still a reputation, Hugh, God send we may deserve it.'

'He's within a charter town, if he is in prison,' said Hugh with satisfaction, 'and it would be a bold lord who would try to take him from the king's hold. Let his master rejoice in thinking the poor wretch held for murder, if that gives him pleasure. We'll put it about, then, that our murderer's taken, and watch for what follows.'

The news went round, as news does, from gossip to gossip, those within the town parading their superior knowledge to those without, those who came to market in town or Foregate carrying their news to outer villages and manors. As the word of Peter Clemence's disappearance had been blown on the wind, and after it news of the discovery of his body in the forest, so did every breeze spread abroad the word that his killer was already taken and in prison in the castle, found in possession of the dead man's dagger, and charged with his murder. No more mystery to be mulled over in taverns and on street-corners, no further sensations to be hoped for. The town made do with what it had, and made the most of it. More distant and isolated manors had to wait a week or more for the news to reach them.

The marvel was that it took three whole days to reach Saint Giles. Isolated though the hospice was, since its inmates were not allowed nearer the town for fear of contagion, somehow they usually seemed to get word of everything that was happening almost as soon as it was common gossip in the streets; but this time the system was slow in functioning. Brother Cadfael had given anxious thought to consideration of what effect the news was likely to have upon Meriet. But there was nothing to be done about that but to wait and see. No need to make a point of bringing the story to the young man's ear's deliberately, better let it make its way to him by the common talk, as to everyone else.

So it was not until two lay servants came to deliver the hospital's customary loaves from the abbey bakery, on the third day, that word of the arrest of the runaway villein Harald came to Meriet's ears. By chance it was he who took in the great basket and unloaded the bread in the store, helped by the two bakery hands who had brought it. For his silence they made up in volubility.

'You'll be getting more and more beggars coming in for shelter, brother, if this cold weather sets in in earnest. Hard frost and an east wind again, no season to be on the roads.'

Civil but taciturn, Meriet agreed that winter came hard on the poor.

'Not that they're all honest and deserving,' said the other, shrugging. 'Who knows what you're taking in sometimes? Rogues and vagabonds as likely as not, and who's to tell the difference?'

'There's one you might have got this week past that you can well do without,' said his fellow, 'for you might have got a throat cut in the night, and whatever's worth stealing made away with. But you're safe from him, at any rate, for he's locked up in Shrewsbury castle till he comes to his trial for murder.'

'For killing a priest, at that! He'll pay for it with his own neck, surely, but that's poor reparation for a priest.'

Meriet had turned, stiffly attentive, staring at them with frowning eyes. 'For killing a priest? What priest? Who is this you speak of?'

288

'What, have you not heard yet? Why, the bishop of Winchester's chaplain that was found in the Long Forest. A wild man who's been preying on the houses outside the town killed him. It's what I was saying, with winter coming on sharp now you might have had him shivering and begging at your door here, and with the priest's own dagger under his ragged coat ready for you.'

'Let me understand you,' said Meriet slowly. 'You say a man is taken for that death? Arrested and charged with it?'

'Taken, charged, gaoled, and as good as hanged,' agreed his informant cheerfully. 'That's one you need not worry your head about, brother.'

'What man is he? How did this come about?' asked Meriet urgently.

They told him, in strophe and antistrophe, pleased to find someone who had not already heard the tale.

'And waste of time to deny, for he had the dagger on him that belonged to the murdered man. Found it, he said, in the charcoal hearth there, and a likely tale that makes.'

Staring beyond them, Meriet asked, low-voiced, 'What like is he, this fellow? A local man? Do you know his name?'

That they could not supply, but they could describe him. 'Not from these parts, some runaway living rough, a poor starving wretch, swears he's never done worse than steal a little bread or an egg to keep himself alive, but the foresters say he's taken their deer in his time. Thin as a fence-pale, and in rags, a desperate case ...'

They took their basket and departed, and Meriet went about his work in dead, cold silence all that day. A desperate case – yes, so it sounded. As good as hanged! Starved and runaway and living wild, thin to emaciation ...

He said no word to Brother Mark, but one of the brightest and most inquisitive of the children had stretched his ears in the kitchen doorway and heard the exchanges, and spread the news through the household with natural relish. Life in Saint Giles, however sheltered, could be tedious, it was none the worse for an occasional sensation to vary the routine of the day. The story came to Brother Mark's ears. He debated whether to speak or not, watching the chill mask of Meriet's face, and the inward state of his hazel eyes. But at last he did venture a word.

'You have heard, they have taken up a man for the killing of Peter Clemence?'

'Yes,' said Meriet, leaden-voiced, and looked through him and far away.

'If there is no guilt in him,' said Mark emphatically, 'then will no harm come to him.'

But Meriet had nothing to say, nor did it seem fitting to Mark to add anything more. Yet he did watch his friend from that moment with unobtrusive care, and fretted to see how utterly he had withdrawn into himself with this knowledge that seemed to work in him like poison.

In the darkness of the night Mark could not sleep. It was some time now since he had stolen across to the barn by night, to listen intently at the foot of the ladder stair that led up into the loft, and take comfort in the silence that meant Meriet was deeply asleep; but on this night he made that pilgrimage again. He did not know the true cause and nature of Meriet's pain, but he knew that it was heart-deep and very bitter. He rose with careful quietness, not to disturb his neighbours, and made his way out to the barn.

The frost was not so sharp that night, the air had a stillness and faint haze instead of the piercing starry glitter of past nights. In the loft there would be warmth enough, and the homely scents of timber, straw and grain, but also great loneliness for that inaccessible sleeper who shrank from having neighbours, for fear of frightening them. Mark had wondered lately whether he might not appeal to Meriet to come down and rejoin his fellowmen, but it would not have been easy to do without alerting that austere spirit to the fact that his slumbers had been spied upon, however benevolently, and Mark had never quite reached the point of making the assay.

He knew his way in pitch darkness to the foot of the steep stairway, a mere step-ladder unprotected by any rail. He stood there and held his breath, nose full of the harvest-scent of the barn. Above him the silence was uneasy, stirred by slight tremors of movement. He thought first that sleep was shallow, and the sleeper turning in his bed to find a posture from which he could submerge deeper into peace. Then he knew that he was listening to Meriet's voice, withdrawn into a strange distance but unmistakable, without distinguishable words, a mere murmur, but terrible in its sustained argument between one need and another need, equally demanding – like some obdurate soul drawn apart by diverse horses, torn limb from limb. And yet so slight and faint a sound, he had to strain his ears to follow it.

Brother Mark stood wretched, wondering whether to go up and either awake this sleeper, if indeed he slept, or lie by him and refuse to leave him if he was awake. There is a time to let well or ill alone, and a time to go forward into forbidden places with banners flying and trumpets sounding, and demand a surrender. But he did not know if they were come to that extreme. Brother Mark prayed, not with words, but by somehow igniting a candle-flame within him that burned immensely tall, and sent up the smoke of his entreaty, which was all for Meriet.

Above him in the darkness a foot stirred in the small, dry dust of chaff and straw, like mice venturing forth by night. Soft steps moved overhead, even and slow. In the dimness below, softened now by filtering starlight, Mark stared upward, and saw the darkness stir and swirl. Something suave and pale dipped from the yawning trap, and reached for the top rung of the ladder; a naked foot. Its fellow followed, stooping a rung lower. A voice, still drawn back deep into the body that leaned at the head of the stair, said distantly but clearly, 'No I will not suffer it!'

He was coming down, he was seeking help. Brother Mark breathed gratitude, and said softly into the dimness above him: 'Meriet! I am here!' Very softly, but it was enough.

The foot seeking its rest on the next tread baulked and stepped astray. There was a faint, distressed cry , weak as a bird's and then an awakened shriek, live and indignant in bewilderment. Meriet's body folded sidelong and fell, hurtling, half into Brother Mark's blindly extended arms, and half askew from him with a dull, deflating thud to the floor of the barn. Mark clung desperately to what he held, borne down by the weight, and lowered it as softly as he might, feeling the limbs fold together to lie limp and still. There was a silence but for his own labouring breath.

With anguished hands he felt about the motionless body, stooped his ear to listen for breathing and the beat of the heart, touched a smooth cheek and the thick thatch of dark hair, and drew his fingers away warm and sticky with blood. 'Meriet!' he urged, whispering close to a deaf ear, and knew that Meriet was far out of reach.

Mark ran for lights and help, but even at this pass was careful not to alarm the whole dortoir, but only to coax out of their sleep two of the most able-bodied and willing of his flock, who slept close to the door, and could withdraw without

291

disturbing the rest. Between them they brought a lantern, and examined Meriet on the floor of the barn, still out of his senses. Mark had partially broken his fall, but his head had struck the sharp edge of the step-ladder, and bore a long graze that ran diagonally across his right temple and into his hair which bled freely, and he had fallen with his right foot twisted awkwardly beneath him.

'My fault, my fault!' whispered Mark wretchedly, feeling about the limp body for broken bones. 'I startled him awake. I didn't know he was asleep, I thought he was coming to me of his own will ...'

Meriet lay oblivious and let himself be handled as they would. There seemed to be no fractures, but there might well be sprains, and his head wound bled alarmingly. To move him as little as need be they brought down his pallet from the loft, and set it below in the barn where he lay, so that he might have quiet from the rest of the household. They bathed and dressed his head and lifted him gently into his cot with an added brychan for warmth, injury and shock making him very cold to the touch. And all the while his face, beneath the swathing bandage, was remote and peaceful and pale as Mark had never seen it before, his trouble for these few hours stricken out of him.

'Go now and get your own rest,' said Brother Mark to his concerned helpers. 'There's nothing more we can do at this moment. I shall sit with him. If I need you I'll call you.'

He trimmed the lantern to burn steadily, and sat beside the pallet all the rest of the night. Meriet lay mute and motionless until past the dawn, though his breathing perceptibly lengthened and grew calmer as he passed from senselessness into sleep, but his face remained bloodless. It was past Prime when his lips began to twitch and his eyelids to flutter, as if he wished to open them, but had not the strength. Mark bathed his face, and moistened the struggling lips with water and wine.

'Lie still,' he said, with a hand cupping Meriet's cheek. 'I am here – Mark. Be troubled by nothing, you are safe here with me.' He was not aware that he had meant to say that. It was promising infinite blessing, and what right had he to claim any such power? And yet the words had come to him unbidden.

The heavy eyelids heaved, fought for a moment with the unknown weight holding them closed, and parted upon a reflected flame in desperate green eyes. A shudder passed through Meriet's body. He worked a dry mouth and got out faintly: 'I must go – I must tell them ... Let me up!'

The effort he made to rise was easily suppressed by a hand on his breast; he lay helpless but shaking.

'I must go! Help me!'

'There is nowhere you need go,' said Mark, leaning over him. 'If there is any message you wish sent to any man, lie still, and only tell me. You know I will do it faithfully. You had a fall, you must lie still and rest.'

'Mark ... It is you?' He felt outside his blankets blindly, and Mark took the wandering hand and held it. 'It *is* you,' said Meriet, sighing. 'Mark – the man they've taken ... for killing the bishop's clerk ... I must tell them ... I must go to Hugh Beringar ...'

'Tell me,' said Mark, 'and you have done all. I will see done whatever you want done, and you may rest. What is it I am to tell Hugh Beringar?' But in his heart he already knew.

'Tell him he must let this poor soul go ... Say he never did that slaying. Tell him I *know*! Tell him,' said Meriet, his dilated eyes hungry and emerald-green on Mark's attentive face, 'that I confess my mortal sin ... that it was I who killed Peter Clemence. I shot him down in the woods, three miles and more from Aspley. Say I am sorry so to shame my father's house.'

He was weak and dazed, shaking with belated shock, the tears sprang from his eyes, startling him with their unexpected flood. He gripped and wrung the hand he held. 'Promise! Promise you will tell him so ...'

'I will, and bear the errand myself, no other shall,' said Mark, stooping low to straining, blinded eyes to be seen and believed. 'Every word you give me I will deliver. If you will also do a good and needful thing for yourself and for me, before I go. Then you may sleep more peacefully.'

The green eyes cleared in wonder, staring up at him. 'What thing is that?'

Mark told him, very gently and firmly. Before he had the words well out, Meriet had wrenched away his hand and heaved his bruised body over in the bed, turning his face away. 'No!' he said in a low wail of distress. 'No, I will not! No ...'

Mark talked on, quietly urging what he asked, but stopped when it was still denied, and with ever more agitated rejection. 'Hush!' he said then placatingly. 'You need not fret so. Even without it, I'll do your errand, every word. You be still and sleep.'

He was instantly believed; the body stiff with resistance softened and eased. The swathed head turned towards him again; even the dim light within the barn caused his eyes to narrow and frown. Brother Mark put out the lantern and drew the brychans close. Then he kissed his patient and penitent, and went to do his errand.

Brother Mark walked the length of the Foregate and across the stone bridge into the town, exchanging the time of day with all he met, enquired for Hugh Beringar at his house by Saint Mary's, and walked on undismayed and unwearied when he was told that the deputy-sheriff was already at the castle. It was by way of a bonus that Brother Cadfael happened to be there also, having just emerged from applying another dressing to the festered wound in the prisoner's forearm. Hunger and exposure are not conducive to ready healing, but Harald's hurts were showing signs of yielding to treatment. Already he had a little more flesh on his long, raw bones, and a little more of the texture of youth in his hollow cheeks. Solid stone walls, sleep without constant fear, warm blankets and three rough meals a day were a heaven to him.

Against the stony ramparts of the inner ward, shut off from even what light there was in this muted morning, Brother Mark's diminutive figure looked even smaller, but his grave dignity was in no way diminished. Hugh welcomed him with astonishment, so unexpected was he in this place, and haled him into the anteroom of the guard, where there was a fire burning, and torchlight, since full daylight seldom penetrated there to much effect.

'I'm sent with a message,' said Brother Mark, going directly to his goal, 'to Hugh Beringar, from Brother Meriet. I've promised to deliver it faithfully word for word, since he cannot do it himself, as he wanted to do. Brother Meriet learned only yesterday, as did we all at Saint Giles, that you have a man held here in prison for the murder of Peter Clemence. Last night, after he had retired, Meriet was desperately troubled in his sleep, and rose and walked. He fell from the loft, sleeping, and is now laid in his bed with a broken head and many bruises, but he has come to himself, and I think with care he'll take no grave harm. But if Brother Cadfael would come and look at him I should be easier in my mind.'

'Son, with all my heart!' said Cadfael, dismayed. 'But what was he about, wandering in his sleep? He never left his bed before in his fits. And men who do commonly tread very skilfully, even where a waking man would not venture.'

294

'So he might have done,' owned Mark, sadly wrung, 'if I had not spoken to him from below. For I thought he was well awake, and coming to ask comfort and aid, but when I called his name he stepped at fault, and cried out and fell. And now he is come to himself. I know where he was bound, even in his sleep, and on what errand. For that errand he has committed to me, now he is helpless, and I am here to deliver it.'

'You've left him safe?' asked Cadfael anxiously, but half-ashamed to doubt whatever Brother Mark thought fit to do.

'There are two good souls keeping an eye on him, but I think he will sleep. He has unloaded his mind upon me, and here I discharge the burden,' said Brother Mark, and he had the erect and simple solitude of a priest, standing small and plain between them and Meriet. 'He bids me say to Hugh Beringar that he must let this prisoner go, for he never did that slaying with which he is charged. He bids me say that he speaks of his own knowledge, and confesses to his own mortal sin, for it was he who killed Peter Clemence. Shot him down in the woods, says Meriet, more than three miles north of Aspley. And he bids me say also that he is sorry so to have disgraced his father's house.'

He stood fronting them, wide-eyed and open-faced as was his nature, and they stared back at him with withdrawn and thoughtful faces. So simple an ending! The son, passionate of nature and quick to act, kills, the father, upright and austere yet jealous of his ancient honour, offers the sinner a choice between the public contumely that will destroy his ancestral house, or the lifelong penance of the cloister, and his father's son prefers his personal purgatory to shameful death, and the degradation of his family. And it could be so! It could answer every question.

'But of course,' said Brother Mark, with the exalted confidence of angels and archangels, and the simplicity of children, 'it is not true.'

'I need not quarrel with what you say,' said Hugh mildly, after a long and profound pause for thought, 'if I ask you whether you speak only on belief in Brother Meriet – for which you may feel you have good cause – or from knowledge by proof? How do you know he is lying?'

'I do know by what I know of him,' said Mark firmly, 'but I have tried to put that away. If I say he is no such person to shoot down a man from ambush, but rather to stand square in his way and challenge him hand to hand, I am saying what I strongly believe. But I was born humble, out of this world of honour, how should I speak to it with certainty? No, I have tested him. When he told me what he told me, I said to him that for his soul's comfort he should let me call our chaplain, and as a sick man make his confession to him and seek absolution. And he would not do it,' said Mark, and smiled upon them. 'At the very thought he shook and turned away. When I pressed him, he was in great agitation. For he can lie to me and to you, to the king's law itself, for a cause that seems to him good enough,' said Mark, 'but he will not lie to his confessor, and through his confessor to God.'

Chapter Ten

FTER LONG and sombre consideration, Hugh said:
'For the moment, it seems, this boy will keep,
whatever the truth of it. He is in his bed with a
broken head, and not likely to stir for a while, all the
more if he believes we have accepted what, for whatever cause,
he wishes us to believe. Take care of him, Mark, and let him
think he has done what he set out to do. Tell him he can be
easy about this prisoner of ours, he is not charged, and no
harm will come to him. But don't let it be put abroad that we're
holding an innocent man who is in no peril of his life. Meriet
may know it. Not a soul outside. For the common ear, we have
our murderer safe in hold.'

One deceit partnered another deceit, both meant to some
good end; and if it seemed to Brother Mark that deceit ought
not to have any place in the pilgrimage after truth, yet he
acknowledged the mysterious uses of all manner of improbable
devices in the workings of the purposes of God, and saw the
truth reflected even in lies. He would let Meriet believe his
ordeal was ended and his confession accepted, and Meriet
would sleep without fears or hopes, without dreams, but with
the drear satisfaction of his voluntary sacrifice, and grow well
again to a better, an unrevealed world.

'I will see to it,' said Mark, 'that only he knows. And I will
be his pledge that he shall be at your disposal whenever you
need him.'

'Good! Then go back now to your patient. Cadfael and I will

297

follow you very shortly.'

Mark departed, satisfied, to trudge back through the town and out along the Foregate. When he was gone, Hugh stood gazing eye to eye with Brother Cadfael, long and thoughtfully. 'Well?'

'It's a tale that makes excellent sense,' said Cadfael, 'and a great part of it most likely true. I am of Mark's way of thinking, I do not believe the boy has killed. But the rest of it? The man who caused that fire to be built and kindled had force enough to get his men to do his will and keep his secret. A man well-served, well-feared, perhaps even well-loved. A man who would neither steal anything from the dead himself, nor allow any of his people to do so. All committed to the fire. Those who worked for him respected and obeyed him. Leoric Aspley is such a man, and in such a manner he might behave, if he believed a son of his had murdered from ambush a man who had been a guest in his house. There would be no forgiveness. If he protected the murderer from the death due, it might well be for the sake of his name, and only to serve a lifetime's penance.'

He was remembering their arrival in the rain, father and son, the one severe, cold and hostile, departing without the kiss due between kinsmen, the other submissive and dutiful, but surely against his nature, at once rebellious and resigned. Feverish in his desire to shorten his probation and be imprisoned past deliverance, but in his sleep fighting like a demon for his liberty. It made a true picture. But Mark was absolute that Meriet had lied.

'It lacks nothing,' said Hugh, shaking his head. 'He has said throughout that it was his own wish to take the cowl – so it might well be; good reason, if he was offered no other alternative but the gallows. The death came there, soon after leaving Aspley. The horse was taken far north and abandoned, so that the body should be sought only well away from where the man was killed. But whatever else the boy knows, he did not know that he was leading his gleaners straight to the place where the bones would be found, and his father's careful work undone. I take Mark's word for that, and by God, I am inclined to take Mark's word for the rest. But if Meriet did not kill the man, why should he so accept condemnation and sentence? Of his own will!'

'There is but one possible answer,' said Cadfael. 'To protect someone else.'

'Then you are saying that he knows who the murderer is.'

'Or thinks he knows,' said Cadfael. 'For there is veil on veil here hiding these people one from another, and it seems to me that Aspley, if he has done this to his son, believes he knows beyond doubt that the boy is guilty. And Meriet, since he has sacrificed himself to a life against which his whole spirit rebels, and now to shameful death, must be just as certain of the guilt of that other person whom he loves and desires to save. But if Leoric is so wildly mistaken, may not Meriet also be in error?'

'Are we not all?' said Hugh, sighing. 'Come, let's go and see this sleep-walking penitent first, and – who knows? – if he's bent on confession, and has to lie to accomplish it, he may let slip something much more to our purpose. I'll say this for him, he was not prepared to let another poor devil suffer in his place, or even in the place of someone dearer to him than himself. Harald has fetched him out of his silence fast enough.'

Meriet was sleeping when they came to Saint Giles. Cadfael stood beside the pallet in the barn, and looked down upon a face strangely peaceful and childlike, exorcised of its devil. Meriet's breathing was long and deep and sweet. It was believable that here was a tormented sinner who had made confession and cleansed his breast, and found all thing hereafter made easy. But he would not repeat his confession to a priest. Mark had a very powerful argument there.

'Let him rest,' said Hugh, when Mark, though reluctantly, would have awakened the sleeper. 'We can wait.' And wait they did, the better part of an hour, until Meriet stirred and opened his eyes. Even then Hugh would have him tended and fed and given drink before he consented to sit by him and hear what he had to say. Cadfael had looked him over, and found nothing wrong that a few days of rest would not mend, though he had turned an ankle and foot under him in falling, and would find it difficult and painful to put any weight upon it for some time. The blow on the head had shaken his wits sadly, and his memory of recent days might be hazy, though he held fast to the one more distant memory which he so desired to declare. The gash crossing his temple would soon heal; the bleeding had already stopped.

His eyes, in the dim light within the barn, shone darkly green, staring up dilated and intent. His voice was faint but resolute, as he repeated with slow emphasis the confession he had made to Brother Mark. He was bent on convincing, very willing and patient in dredging up details. Listening, Cadfael had to admit to himself, with dismay, that Meriet was indeed utterly convincing. Hugh must also be thinking so.

He questioned, slowly and evenly, 'You watched the man ride away, with your father in attendance, and made no demur. Then you went out with your bow – mounted or afoot?'

'Mounted,' said Meriet with fiery readiness; for if he had gone on foot, how could he have circled at speed, and been ahead of the rider after his escort had left him to return home? Cadfael remembered Isouda saying that Meriet had come home late that afternoon with his father's party, though he had not ridden out with them. She had not said whether he was mounted when he returned or walking; that was something worth probing.

'With murderous intent?' Hugh pursued mildly. 'Or did this thing come on you unawares? For what can you have had against Master Clemence to warrant his death?'

'He had made far too free with my brother's bride,' said Meriet. 'I did hold it against him – a priest, playing the courtier, and so sure of his height above us. A manorless man, with only his learning and his patron's name for lands and lineage, and looking down upon us, as long rooted as we are. On grievance for my brother ...'

'Yet your brother made no move to take reparation,' said Hugh.

'He was gone to the Lindes, to Roswitha ... He had escorted her home the night before, and I am sure he had quarrelled with her. He went out early, he did not even see the guest leave, he went to make good whatever was ill between those two ... He never came home,' said Meriet, clearly and firmly, 'until late in the evening, long after all was over.'

True, by Isouda's account, thought Cadfael. After all was over, and Meriet brought home a convicted murderer, to reappear only after he had chosen of his own will to ask admittance to the cloister, and was prepared to go forth on his parole, and so declare himself, an oblate to the abbey, fully aware of what he was doing. So he had told his very acute and perceptive playmate, in calm control of himself. He was doing what he wished to do.

'But you, Meriet, you rode ahead of Master Clemence. With murder in mind?'

'I had not thought,' said Meriet, hesitating for the first time. 'I went alone ... But I was angry.'

300

'You went in haste,' said Hugh, pressing him, 'if you overtook the departing guest, and by a roundabout way, if you passed and intercepted him, as you say.'

Meriet stretched and stiffened in his bed, large eyes straining on his questioner. He set his jaw. 'I did hasten, though not for any deliberate purpose. I was in thick covert when I was aware of him riding towads me, in no hurry. I drew and loosed upon him. He fell ...' Sweat broke on the pallid brow beneath his bandages. He closed his eyes.

'Let be!' said Cadfael, quiet at Hugh's shoulder. 'He has said enough.'

'No,' said Meriet strongly. 'Let me make an end. He was dead when I stooped over him. I had killed him. And my father took me so, red-handed. The hounds – he had hounds with him – they scented me and brought him down upon me. He has covered up for my sake, and for the sake of an honoured name, what I did, but for whatever he may have done that is unlawful, to keep me man alive, I take the blame upon me, for I am the cause of it. But he would not condone. He promised me cover for my forfeit life, if I would accept banishment from the world and take myself off into the cloister. What was done afterwards no one ever told me. I did by my own will and consent accept my penalty. I even hoped ... and I have tried ... But set down all that was done to my account, and let me pay all.'

He thought he had done, and heaved a great sigh out of him. Hugh also sighed and stirred as if about to rise, but then asked carelessly, 'At what hour was this, Meriet, that your father happened upon you in the act of murder?'

'About three in the afternoon,' said Meriet indifferently, falling headlong into the trap.

'And Master Clemence set out soon after Prime? It took him a great while,' said Hugh with deceptive mildness, 'to ride somewhat over three miles.'

Meriet's eyes, half-closed in weariness and release from tension, flared wide open in consternation. It cost him a convulsive struggle to master voice and face, but he did it, hoisting up out of the well of his resolution and dismay a credible answer. 'I cut my story too short, wanting it done. When this thing befell it cannot have been even mid-morning. But I ran from him and let him lie, and wandered the woods in dread of what I'd done. But in the end I went back. It seemed better to hide him in the thick coverts off the pathways, where he could lie undiscovered, and I might come by night and bury

301

him. I was in terror, but in the end I went back. I am not sorry,' said Meriet at the end, so simply that somewhere in those last words there must be truth. But he had never shot down any man. He had come upon a dead man lying in his blood, just as he had baulked and stood aghast at the sight of Brother Wolstan bleeding at the foot of the apple tree. A three-mile ride from Aspley, yes, thought Cadfael with certainty, but well into the autumn afternoon, when his father was out with hawk and hound. 'I am not sorry,' said Meriet again, quite gently. 'It's good that I was taken so. Better still that I have now told you all.'

Hugh rose, and stood looking down at him with an unreadable face. 'Very well! You should not yet be moved, and there is no reason you should not remain here in Brother Mark's care. Brother Cadfael tells me you would need crutches if you tried to walk for some days yet. You'll be secure enough where you are.'

'I would give you my parole,' said Meriet sadly, 'but I doubt if you would take it. But Mark will, and I will submit myself to him. Only – the other man – you will see he goes free?'

'You need not fret, he is cleared of all blame but a little thieving to fill his belly, and that will be forgotten. It is to your own case you should be giving thought,' said Hugh gravely. 'I would urge you receive a priest and make your confession.'

'You and the hangman can be my priests,' said Meriet, and fetched up from somewhere a wry and painful smile.

'He is lying and telling truth in the selfsame breath,' said Hugh with resigned exasperation on the way back along the Foregate. 'Almost surely what he says of his father's part is truth, so he was caught, and so he was both protected and condemned. That is how he came to you, willing-unwilling. It accounts for all the to-and-fro you have had with him, waking and sleeping. But it does not give us our answer to who killed Peter Clemence, for it's as good as certain Meriet did not. He had not even thought of that glaring error in the time of day, until I prodded him with it. And considering the shock it gave him, he did pretty well at accounting for it. But far too late. To have made that mistake was enough. Now what is our best way? Supposing we should blazon it abroad that young Aspley has confessed to the murder, and put his neck in a noose? If he is indeed sacrificing himself for someone else, do you think that person would come forward and loose the knot and slip his own neck in it, as Meriet has for him?'

302

With bleak conviction Cadfael said, 'No. If he let him go unredeemed into one hell to save his own sweet skin, I doubt if he'd lift a hand to help him down the gallows. God forgive me if I misjudge him, but on that conscience there'll be no relying. And you would have committed yourself and the law to a lie for nothing, and brought the boy deeper into grief. No. We have still a little time, let things be. In two or three days more this wedding party will be with us in the abbey, and Leoric Aspley could be brought to answer for his own part, but since he's truly convinced Meriet is guilty, he can hardly help us to the real murderer. Make no move to bring him to account, Hugh, until after the marriage. Let me have him to myself until then. I have certain thoughts concerning this father and son.'

'You may have him and welcome,' said Hugh, 'for as things are I'm damned if I know what to do with him. His offence is rather against the church than against any law I administer. Depriving a dead man of Christian burial and the proper rites due to him is hardly within my writ. Aspley is a patron of the abbey, let the lord abbot be his judge. The man I want is the murderer. You, I know, want to hammer it into that old tyrant's head that he knows his younger son so poorly that mere acquaintances of a few weeks have more faith in the lad, and more understanding of him, than his sire has. And I wish you success. As for me, Cadfael, I'll tell you what troubles me most. I cannot for my life see what cause anyone in these parts, Aspley or Linde or Foriet or who you will, had to wish Peter Clemence out of the world. Shoot him down for being too bold and too ingratiating with the girl? Foolery! The man was leaving, none of them had seen much of him before, none need ever see him again, and the bridegroom's only concern, it seems, was to make his peace with his bride after too sharp reproaches. Kill for such a cause? Not unless a man ran utterly mad. You tell me the girl will flutter her lashes at every admirer, but none has ever died for it. No, there is, there must be, another cause, but for my life I cannot see what it can be.'

It had troubled Cadfael, too. Minor brawls of one evening over a girl, and over too assiduous compliments to her, not affronts, a mere bubble in one family's hitherto placid life – no, men do not kill for such trivial causes. And no one had ever yet suggested a deeper quarrel with Peter Clemence. His distant kinsmen knew him but slightly, their neighbours not at all. If you find a new acquaintance irritating, but know he remains for only one night, you bear with him tolerantly, and wave him away from your doorsill with a smile, and breathe the more easily thereafter. But you do not skulk in woods where he must pass, and shoot him down.

But if it was not the man himself, what else could there be to bring him to his death? His errand? He had not said what it was, at least while Isouda was by to hear. And even if he had, what was there in that to make it necessary to halt him? A civil diplomatic mission to two northern lords, to secure their allegiance to Bishop Henry's efforts for peace. A mission Canon Eluard had since pursued successfully, to such happy effect that he had now conducted his king thither to seal the accord, and by this time was accompanying him south again to keep his Christmas in high content. There could be nothing amiss there. Great men have their private plans, and may welcome at one time a visit they repel at another, but here was the proof of the approach, and a reasonably secure Christmas looming.

Back to the man, and the man was harmless, a passing kinsman expanding and preening himself under a family roof, then passing on.

No personal grudge, then. So what was left but the common hazard of travel, the sneak-thief and killer loose in the wild places, ready to pull a man from his horse and bludgeon his head to pulp for the clothes he wore, let alone a splendid horse and a handful of jewellery? And that was ruled out, because Peter Clemence had not been robbed, not of a silver buckle, not of a jewelled cross. No one had benefited in goods or gear from his death, even the horse had been turned loose in the mosses with his harness untouched.

'I have wondered about the horse,' said Hugh, as though he had been following Cadfael's thoughts.

'I, too. The night after you brought the beast back to the abbey, Meriet called him in his sleep. Did they ever tell you that? Barbary, Barbary – and he whistled after him. His devil whistled back to him, the novices said. I wonder if he came, there in the woods, or if Leoric had to send out men after him later? I think he would come to Meriet. When he found the man dead, his next thought would be for the beast, he went calling him.'

'The hounds may well have picked up his voice,' said Hugh ruefully, 'before ever they got his scent. And brought his father down on him.'

'Hugh, I have been thinking. The lad answered you very

valiantly when you fetched him up hard against that error in time. But I do not believe it had dawned on him at all what it meant. See, if Meriet had simply blundered upon a lone body dead in the forest, with no sign to turn his suspicions towards any man, all he would then have known was that Clemence had ridden but a short way before he was shot. Then how could the boy know or even guess by whom? But if he chanced upon some other soul trapped as he was, stooped over the dead, or trying to drag him into hiding – someone close and dear to him – then he has not realized, even now, that this someone else came to this spot in the forest, even as he himself did, at least six hours too late to be the murderer!'

On the eighteenth day of December Canon Eluard rode into Shrewsbury in very good conceit of himself, having persuaded his king into a visit which had turned out conspicuously well, and escorted him thus far south again towards his customary London Christmas, before leaving him in order to diverge westward in search of news of Peter Clemence. Chester and Lincoln, both earls now in name as well as in fact, had made much of Stephen, and pledged him their unshakeable loyalty, which he in turn had recognized with gifts of land as well as titles. Lincoln castle he retained in his own hand, well-garrisoned, but the city and the shire were open to his new earl. The atmosphere in Lincoln had been of holiday and ease, aided by clement weather for December. Christmas in the north-east bade fair to be a carefree festival.

Hugh came down from the castle to attend on the canon and exchange the news with him, though it was a very uneven exchange. He had brought with him the relics of Peter Clemence's jewels and harness, cleaned of their encrusted filth of ash and soil, but discoloured by the marks of fire. The dead man's bones reposed now in a lead-lined coffin in the mortuary chapel of the abbey, but the coffin was not yet sealed. Canon Eluard had it opened for him, and gazed upon the remains within, grim-faced but unwincing.

'Cover him,' he said, and turned away. There was nothing there that could ever again be known as any man. The cross and ring were a very different matter.

'This I do know. This I have commonly seen him wearing,' said Eluard, with the cross in the palm of his hand. Over the silver surface the coloured sheen of tarnish glimmered, but the gems shone clear. 'This is certainly Clemence,' said Eluard heavily. 'It will be grievous news for my bishop. And you have some fellow in hold for this crime?'

'We have a man in prison, true,' said Hugh, 'and have let it be noised abroad that he is the man, but in truth I must tell you that he is not charged, and almost certainly never will be. The worst known of him is a little thieving here and there, from hunger, and on that I continue to hold him. But a murderer I am sure he is not.' He told the story of his search, but said no word of Meriet's confession. 'If you intend to rest here two or three days before riding on, there may yet be more news to take with you.'

It was in his mind as he said it that he was a fool to promise any such thing, but his thumbs had pricked, and the words were out. Cadfael had business with Leoric Aspley when he came, and the imminent gathering here of all those closest about Peter Clemence's last hours seemed to Hugh like the thickening and lowering of a cloud before the storm breaks and the rain falls. If the rain refused to fall, then after the wedding Aspley should be made to tell all that he knew, and probed after what he did not know, taking into account such small matters as those six unrecorded hours, and the mere three miles Clemence had ridden before he met his death.

'Nothing can restore the dead,' said Canon Eluard sombrely, 'but it is only just and right that his murderer should be brought to account. I trust that may yet be done.'

'And you'll be here yet a few days? You're not in haste to rejoin the king?'

'I go to Winchester, not Westminster. And it will be worth waiting a few days to have somewhat more to tell the bishop concerning this grievous loss. I confess to being in need of a brief rest, too, I am not so young as once I was. Your sheriff still leaves you to carry the cares of the shire alone, by the way. King Stephen wishes to retain him in his company over the feast, they go directly to London.'

That was by no means unwelcome news to Hugh. The business he had begun he was strongly minded to finish, and two minds bent to the same task, the one more impatient than the other, do not make for good results. 'And you are content with your visit,' he said. 'Something, at least, has gone well.'

'It was worth all the travelling,' said Eluard with satisfaction. 'The king can be easy in his mind about the north, Ranulf and William between them have every mile of it well in hand, it would be a bold man who would meddle with their order. His

Grace's castellan in Lincoln is on the best of terms with the earls and their ladies. And the messages I bear to the bishop are gracious indeed. Yes, it was well worth the miles I've ridden to secure it.'

On the following day the wedding party arrived in modest manorial state at apartments prepared for them in the abbey guest-halls: the Aspleys, the Lindes, the heiress of Foriet, and a great rout of their invited guests from all the neighbouring manors down the fringes of the forest. All but the common hall and dortoir for the pedlars and pilgrims and birds of passage was given over to the party. Canon Eluard, the abbot's guest, took a benevolent interest in the bright bustle from his privileged distance. The novices and the boys looked on in eager curiosity, delighted at any distraction in their ordered lives. Prior Robert allowed himself to be seen about the court and the cloisters at his most benign and dignified, always at his best where there were ceremonies to be patronized and a patrician audience to appreciate and admire him; and Brother Jerome made himself even more than usually busy and authoritative among the novices and lay servants. In the stable-yard there was great activity, and all the stalls were filled. Brothers who had kin among the guests were allowed to receive them in the parlour. A great wave of admiration and interest swept through the courts and the gardens, all the more gaily because the weather, though crisp and very cold, was clear and fine, and daylight lasted late towards evening.

Cadfael stood with Brother Paul at the corner of the cloister and watched them ride in in their best travelling array, with pack-ponies bringing their wedding finery. The Lindes came first. Wulfric Linde was a fat, flabby, middle-aged man of amiable, lethargic face, and Cadfael could not choose but wonder what his dead lady must have been like, to make it possible for the pair of them to produce two such beautiful children. His daughter rode a pretty, cream-coloured palfrey, smilingly aware of all the eyes upon her, and keeping her own eyes tantalizingly lowered, in an appearance of modesty which gave exaggerated power to every flashing sidelong glance. Swathed warmly in a fine blue cloak that concealed all but the rosy oval of her face, she still knew how to radiate beauty, and oh, she knew, how well she knew, that she had at least forty pairs of innocent male eyes upon her, marvelling at what strange delights were withheld from them. Women of all ages, practical and purposeful, went in and out regularly at these gates, with complaint, appeal, request and gift, and made no stir and asked no tribute. Roswitha came armed in knowledge of her power, and delighted in the disquiet she brought with her. There would be some strange dreams among Brother Paul's novices.

Close behind her, and for a moment hard to recognize, came Isouda Foriet on a tall, spirited horse. Groomed and shod and well-mounted, her hair netted and uncovered to the light, a bright russet like autumn leaves, with her hood tossed back on her shoulders and her back straight and lissome as a birch-tree, Isouda rode without artifice, and needed none. As good as a boy! As good as the boy who rode beside her, with a hand stretched out to her bridle-hand, lightly touching. Neighbours, each with a manor to offer, would it be strange if Janyn's father and Isouda's guardian planned to match them? Excellently matched in age, in quality, having known each other from children, what could be more suitable? But the two most concerned still chattered and wrangled like brother and sister, very easy and familiar together. And besides, Isouda had other plans.

Janyn carried with him, here as elsewhere, his light, comely candour, smiling round him with pleasure on all he saw. Sweeping a bright glance round all the watching faces, he recognized Brother Cadfael, and his face lit up engagingly as he gave him a marked inclination of his fair head.

'He knows you,' said Brother Paul, catching the gesture.

'The bride's brother – her twin. I encountered him when I went to talk with Meriet's father. The two families are close neighbours.'

'A great pity,' said Paul sympathetically, 'that Brother Meriet is not well enough to be here. I am sure he would wish to be present when his brother marries, and to wish them God's blessing. He cannot walk yet?'

All that was known of Meriet among these who had done their best for him was that he had had a fall, and was laid up with a lingering weakness and a twisted foot.

'He hobbles with a stick,' said Cadfael.' 'I would not like him to venture far as he is. In a day or two we shall see how far we may let him try his powers.'

Janyn was down from his saddle with a bound, and attentive at Isouda's stirrup as she made to descend. She laid a hand heartily on his shoulder and came down like a feather, and they laughed together, and turned to join the company already assembled. After them came the Aspleys, Leoric as Cadfael had imagined and seen him, bolt-upright body and soul, appearing tall as a church column in his saddle; an irate, intolerant, honourable man, exact to his responsibilities, absolute on his privileges. A demi-god to his servants, and one to be trusted provided they in turn were trustworthy; a god to his sons. What he had been to his dead wife could scarcely be guessed, or what she had felt towards her second boy. The admirable firstborn, close at his father's elbow, vaulted out of his tall saddle like a bird lighting, large, vigorous and beautiful. At every move Nigel did honour to his progenitors and his name. Cloistered young men watching him murmured admiration, and well they might.

'Difficult,' said Brother Paul, always sensitive to youth and its obscure torments, 'to be second to such a one.'

'Difficult indeed,' said Cadfael ruefully.

Kinsmen and neighbours followed, small lords and their ladies, self-confident folk, commanding limited realms, perhaps, but absolute within them, and well able to guard their own. They alighted, their grooms led away the horses and ponies, the court gradually emptied of the sudden blaze of colour and animation, and the fixed and revered order continued unbroken, with Vespers drawing near.

Brother Cadfael went to his workshop in the herbarium after supper to fetch certain dried herbs needed by Brother Petrus, the abbot's cook, for the next day's dinner, when the Aspleys and the Lindes were to dine with Canon Eluard at the abbot's table. Frost was setting in again for the night, the air was crisp and still and the sky starry, and even the smallest sound rang like a bell in the pure darkness. The footsteps that followed him along the hard earth path between the pleached hedges were very soft, but he heard them; someone small and light of foot, keeping her distance, one sharp ear listening for Cadfael's guiding steps ahead, the other pricked back to make sure no others followed behind. When he opened the door of his hut and passed within, his pursuer halted, giving him time to strike a spark from his flint and light his little lamp. Then she came into the open doorway, wrapped in a dark cloak, her hair loose on her neck as he had first seen her, the cold stinging her cheeks into rose-red, and the flame of the lamp making stars of her eyes.

309

'Come in, Isouda,' said Cadfael placidly, rustling the bunches of herbs that dangled from the beams above. 'I've been hoping to find a means of talking with you. I should have known you would make your own occasion.'

'But I mustn't stay long,' she said, coming in and closing the door behind her. 'I am supposed to be lighting a candle and putting up prayers in the church for my father's soul.'

'Then should you not be doing that?' said Cadfael, smiling. 'Here, sit and be easy for the short time you have, and whatever you want of me, ask.'

'I have lit my candle,' she said, seating herself on the bench by the wall, 'it's there to be seen, but my father was a fine man, and God will take good care of his soul without any interference from me. And I need to know what is really happening to Meriet.'

'They'll have told you that he had a bad fall, and cannot walk as yet?'

'Brother Paul told us so. He said it would be no lasting harm. Is it so? Will he be well again surely?'

'Surely he will. He got a gash on the head in his fall, but that's already healed, and his wrenched foot needs only a little longer rest, and it will bear him again as well as ever. He's in good hands, Brother Mark is taking care of him, and Brother Mark is his staunch friend. Tell me, how did his father take the word of his fall?'

'He kept a severe face,' she said, 'though he said he grieved to hear it, so coldly, who would believe him? But for all that, he does grieve.'

'He did not ask to visit him?'

She made a disdainful face at the obstinacy of men. 'Not he! He has given him to God, and God must fend for him. He will not go near him. But I came to ask you if you will take *me* there to see him.'

Cadfael stood earnestly considering her for a long moment, and then sat down beside her and told her all that had happened, all that he knew or guessed. She was shrewd, gallant and resolute, and she knew what she wanted and was ready to fight for it. She gnawed a calculating lip when she heard that Meriet had confessed to murder, and glowed in proud acknowledgement when Cadfael stressed that she was the sole privileged person, besides himself and Mark and the law, to be apprised of it, and to know, to her comfort, that it was not believed.

'Sheer folly!' she said roundly. 'I thank God you see through him as through gauze. And his fool of a father *believes* it? But he never has known him, he never has valued or come close to him, from the day Meriet was born. And yet he's a fair-minded man, I own it, he would not knowingly do any man wrong. He must have urgent cause to believe this. And Meriet cause just as grave to leave him in the mistake – even while he certainly must be holding it against him that he's so ready to believe evil of his own flesh and blood. Brother Cadfael, I tell you, I never before saw so clearly how like those two are, proud and stubborn and solitary, taking to themselves every burden that falls their way, shutting out kith and kin and liegemen and all. I could knock their two fool crowns together. But what good would that do, without an answer that would shut both their mouths – except on penitence?'

'There will be such an answer,' said Cadfael, 'and if ever you do knock their heads together, I promise you both shall be unshaven. And yes, tomorrow I will take you to practise upon the one of them, but after dinner – for before it, I aim to bring your Uncle Leoric to visit his son, whether he will or no. Tell me, if you know, what are their plans for the morrow? They have yet one day to spare before the marriage.'

'They mean to attend High Mass,' she said, sparkling hopefully, 'and then we women will be fitting gowns and choosing ornaments, and putting a stitch in here and there to the wedding clothes. Nigel will be shut out of all that, until we go to dine with the lord abbot, and I think he and Janyn intend to go into town for some last trifles. Uncle Leoric may be left to himself after Mass. You might snare him then, if you catch your time.'

'I shall be watching for it,' Cadfael assured her. 'And after the abbot's dinner, if you can absent yourself, then I will take you to Meriet.'

She rose joyfully when she thought it high time to leave, and she went forth valiantly, certain of herself and her stars, and her standing with the powers of heaven. And Cadfael went to deliver his selected herbs to Brother Petrus, who was already brooding over the masterpieces he would produce the next day at noon.

After High Mass on the morning of the twentieth of December the womenfolk repaired to their own apartments, to make careful choice of the right array for dining with the abbot.

Leoric's son and his son's bosom friend went off on foot into the town, his guests dispersed to pay local visits for which this was rare opportunity, and make purchases of stores for their country manors while they were close to the town, or to burnish their own finery for the morrow. Leoric walked briskly in the frosty air the length of the gardens, round fish-ponds and fields, down to the Meole brook, fringed with delicate frost like fine lace, and after that as decisively vanished. Cadfael had waited to give him time to be alone, as plainly he willed to be, and then lost sight of him, to find him again in the mortuary chapel where Peter Clemence's coffin, closed now and richly draped, waited for Bishop Henry's word as to its disposal. Two new, fine candles burned on a branched candlestick at the head, and Leoric Aspley was on his knees on the flagstones at the foot. His lips moved upon silent, methodical prayers, his open eyes were fixed unflinchingly upon the bier. Cadfael knew then that he was on firm ground. The candles might have been simply any courtly man's offering to a dead kinsman, however distant, but the grim and grievous face, silently acknowledging a guilt not yet confessed or atoned for, confirmed the part he had played in denying this dead man burial, and pointed plainly at the reason.

Cadfael withdrew silently, and waited for him to come forth. Blinking as he emerged into daylight again, Leoric found himself confronted by a short, sturdy, nut-brown brother who stepped into his path and addressed him ominously, like a warning angel blocking the way:

'My lord, I have an urgent errand to you. I beg you to come with me. You are needed. Your son is mortally ill.'

It came so suddenly and shortly, it struck like a lance. The two young men had been gone half an hour, time for the assassin's stroke, for the sneak-thief's knife, for any number of disasters. Leoric heaved up his head and snuffed the air of terror, and gasped aloud: 'My son ...?'

Only then did he recognize the brother who had come to Aspley on the abbot's errand. Cadfael saw hostile suspicion flare in the deep-set, arrogant eyes, and forestalled whatever his antagonist might have had to say.

'It's high time,' said Cadfael, 'that you remembered you have two sons. Will you let one of them die uncomforted?'

Chapter Eleven

EORIC WENT with him; striding impatiently, suspiciously, intolerantly, yet continuing to go with him. He questioned, and was not answered. When Cadfael said simply, 'Turn back, then, if that's your will, and make your own peace with God and him!' Leoric set his teeth and his jaw, and went on.

At the rising path up the grass slope to Saint Giles he checked, but rather to take stock of the place where his son served and suffered than out of any fear of the many contagions that might be met within. Cadfael brought him to the barn, where Meriet's pallet was still laid, and Meriet at this moment was seated upon it, the stout staff by which he hobbled about the hospice braced upright in his right hand, and his head leaned upon its handle. He would have been about the place as best he might since Prime, and Mark must have banished him to an interval of rest before the midday meal. He was not immediately aware of them, the light within the barn being dim and mellow, and subject to passing shadows. He looked several years older than the silent and submissive youth Leoric had brought to the abbey a postulant, almost three months earlier.

His sire, entering with the light sidelong, stood gazing. His face was closed and angry, but the eyes in it stared in bewilderment and grief, and indignation, too, at being led here in this fashion when the sufferer had no mark of death upon

313

him, but leaned resigned and quiet, like a man at peace with his fate.

'Go in,' said Cadfael at Leoric's shoulder, 'and speak to him.'

It hung perilously in the balance whether Leoric would not turn, thrust his deceitful guide out of the way, and stalk back by the way he had come. He did cast a black look over his shoulder and make to draw back from the doorway; but either Cadfael's low voice or the stir of movement had reached and startled Meriet. He raised his head and saw his father. The strangest contortion of astonishment, pain, and reluctant and grudging affection twisted his face. He made to rise respectfully and fumbled it in his haste. The crutch slipped out of his hand and thudded to the floor, and he reached for it, wincing.

Leoric was before him. He crossed the space between in three long, impatient strides, pressed his son back to the pallet with a brusque hand on his shoulder, and restored the staff to his hand, rather as one exasperated by clumsiness than considerate of distress. 'Sit!' he said gruffly. 'No need to stir. They tell me you have had a fall, and cannot yet walk well.'

'I have come to no great harm,' said Meriet, gazing up at him steadily. 'I shall be fit to walk very soon. I take it kindly that you have come to see me, I did not expect a visit. Will you sit, sir?'

No, Leoric was too disturbed and too restless; he gazed about him at the furnishings of the barn, and only by rapid glimpses at his son. 'This life – the way you consented to – they tell me you have found it hard to come to terms with it. You put your hand to the plough, you must finish the furrow. Do not expect me to take you back again.' His voice was harsh but his face was wrung.

'My furrow bids fair to be a short one, and I daresay I can hold straight to the end of it,' said Meriet sharply. 'Or have they not told you, also, that I have confessed the thing I did, and there is no further need for you to shelter me?'

'You have confessed ...' Leoric was at a loss. He passed a long hand over his eyes, and stared, and shook. The boy's dead calm was more confounding than any passion could have been.

'I am sorry to have caused you so much labour and pain to no useful end,' said Meriet. 'But it was necessary to speak. They were making a great error, they had charged another man, some poor wretch living wild, who had taken food here

314

and there. You had not heard that? Him, at least, I could deliver. Hugh Beringar has assured me no harm will come to him. You would not have had me leave him in his peril? Give your blessing to this act, at least.'

Leoric stood speechless some minutes, his tall body palsied and shaken as though he struggled with his own demon, before he sat down abruptly beside his son on the creaking pallet, and clamped a hand over Meriet's hand; and though his face was still marble-hard, and the very gesture of his hand like a blow, and his voice when he finally found words still severe and harsh, Cadfael nevertheless withdrew from them quietly, and drew the door to after him. He went aside and sat in the porch, not so far away that he could not hear the tones of the two voices within, though not their words, and so placed that he could watch the doorway. He did not think he would be needed any more, though at times the father's voice rose in helpless rage, and once or twice Meriet's rang with a clear and obstinate asperity. That did not matter, they would have been lost without the sparks they struck from each other.

After this, thought Cadfael, let him put on indifference as icily as he will, I shall know better.

He went back when he judged it was time, for he had much to say to Leoric for his own part before the hour of the abbot's dinner. Their rapid and high-toned exchanges ceased as he entered, what few words they still had to say came quietly and lamely.

'Be my messenger to Nigel and to Roswitha. Say that I pray their happiness always. I should have liked to be there to see them wed,' said Meriet steadily, 'but that I cannot expect now.'

Leoric looked down at him and asked awkwardly, 'You are cared for here? Body and soul?'

Meriet's exhausted face smiled, a pale smile but warm and sweet. 'As well as ever in my life. I am very well-friended, here among my peers. Brother Cadfael knows!'

And this time, at parting, it fell out not quite as once before. Cadfael had wondered. Leoric turned to go, turned back, wrestled with his unbending pride a moment, and then stooped almost clumsily and very briefly, and bestowed on Meriet's lifted cheek a kiss that still resembled a blow. Fierce blood mantled at the smitten cheekbone as Leoric straightened up, turned, and strode from the barn.

He crossed towards the gate mute and stiff, his eyes looking inwards rather than out, so that he struck shoulder and hip

315

against the gatepost, and hardly noticed the shock.

'Wait!' said Cadfael. 'Come here with me into the church, and say whatever you have to say, and so will I. We still have time.'

In the little single-aisled church of the hospice, under its squat tower, it was dim and chill, and very silent. Leoric knotted veined hands and wrung them, and turned in formidable quiet anger upon his guide. 'Was this well done, brother? Falsely you brought me here! You told me my son was mortally ill.'

'So he is,' said Cadfael. 'Have you not his own word for it how close he feels his death? So are you, so are we all. The disease of mortality is in us from the womb, from the day of our birth we are on the way to our death. What matters is how we conduct the journey. You heard him. He has confessed to the murder of Peter Clemence. Why have you not been told that, without having to hear it from Meriet? Because there was no one to tell you else but Brother Mark, or Hugh Beringar, or myself, for no one else knows. Meriet believes himself to be watched as a committed felon, that barn his prison. Now *I* tell you, Aspley, that it is not so. There is not one of us three who have heard his avowal, but is heart-sure he is lying. You are the fourth, his father, and the only one to believe in his guilt.'

Leoric was shaking his head violently and wretchedly. 'I wish it were so, but I know better. Why do you say he is lying? What proof can you have for your trust, compared with that I have for my certainty?'

'I will give you one proof for my trust,' said Cadfael, 'in exchange for all your proofs of your certainty. As soon as he heard there was another man accused, Meriet made his confession of guilt to the law, which can destroy his body. But resolutely he refused then and refuses still to repeat that confession to a priest, and ask penance and absolution for a sin he has not committed. That is why I believe him guiltless. Now show me, if you can, as strong a reason why you should believe him guilty.'

The lofty, tormented grey head continued its anguished motions of rejection. 'I wish to God you were right and I wrong, but I know what I saw and what I heard. I never can forget it. Now that I must tell it openly, since there's an innocent man at stake, and Meriet to his honour has cleansed his breast, why should I not tell it first to you? My guest was gone on his way safely, it was a day like any other day. I went

316

out for exercise with hawk and hounds, and three besides, my chaplain and huntsman, and a groom, honest men all, they will bear me out. There's thick woodland three miles north from us, a wide belt of it. It was the hounds picked up Meriet's voice, no more than a distant call to me until we got nearer and I knew him. He was calling Barbary and whistling for him – the horse that Clemence rode. It may have been the whistle the hounds caught first, and went eager but silent to find Meriet. By the time we came on him he had the horse tethered – you'll have heard he has a gift. When we burst in on him, he had the dead man under the arms, and was dragging him deep into a covert off the path. An arrow in Peter's breast, and bow and quiver on Meriet's shoulder. Do you want more? When I cried out on him, what had he done? – he never said word to deny. When I ordered him to return with us, and laid him under lock and key until I could consider such a shame and horror, and know my way, he never said nay to it, but submitted to all. When I told him I would keep him man alive and cover up his mortal sin, but on conditions, he accepted life and withdrawal, I do believe, as much for our name's sake as for his own life, but he chose.'

'He did choose, he did far more than accept,' said Cadfael, 'for he told Isouda what he told us all, later, that he came to us of his own will, at his own desire. Never has he said that he was forced. But go on, tell me your own part.'

'I did what I had promised him, I had the horse led far to the north, by the way Clemence should have ridden, and there turned loose in the mosses, where it might be thought his rider had foundered. And the body we took secretly, with all that was his, and my chaplain read the rites over him with all reverence, before we laid him within a new stack on the charcoal-burner's old hearth, and fired it. It was ill-done and against my conscience, but I did it. Now I will answer for it. I shall not be sorry to pay whatever is due.'

'Your son has taken care,' said Cadfael hardly, 'to claim to himself, along with the death, all that you have done to conceal it. But he will not confess lies to his confessor, as mortal a sin as hiding truth.'

'But why?' demanded Leoric wildly. 'Why should he so yield and accept all, if he had an answer for me? Why?'

'Because the answer he had for you would have been too hard for you to bear, and unbearable also to him. For love, surely,' said Brother Cadfael. 'I doubt if he has had his proper

317

fill of love all his life, but those who most hunger for it do most and best deliver it.'

'I have loved him,' protested Leoric, raging and writhing, 'though he has been always so troublous a soul, for ever going contrary.'

'Going contrary is one way of getting your notice,' said Cadfael ruefully, 'when obedience and virtue go unregarded. But let that be. You want instances. This spot where you came upon him, it was hardly more than three miles from your manor – what, forty minutes' ride? And the hour when you came there was well on in the afternoon. How many hours had Clemence lain there dead? And suddenly there is Meriet toiling to hide the dead body, and whistling up the straying horse left riderless. Even if he had run in terror, and wandered the woods fevered over his deed, would he not have dealt with the horse before he fled? Either lashed him away to ride wild, or caught and ridden him far off. What was he doing there calling and tethering the horse, and hiding the body, all those hours after the man must have died? Did you never think of that?'

'I thought,' said Leoric, speaking slowly now, wide-eyed, urgent upon Cadfael's face, 'as you have said, that he had run in terror from what he had done, and come back, late in the day, to hide it from all eyes.'

'So he has said now, but it cost him a great heave of the heart and mind to fetch that excuse up out of the well.'

'Then what,' whispered Leoric, shaking now with mingled hope and bewilderment, and very afraid to trust, 'what has moved him to accept so dreadful a wrong? How could he do such an injury to me and to himself?'

'For fear, perhaps, of doing you a greater. And for love of someone he had cause to doubt, as you found cause to doubt him. Meriet has a great store of love to give,' said Brother Cadfael gravely, 'and you would not allow him to give much of it to you. He has given it elsewhere, where it was not repelled, however it may have been undervalued. Have I to say to you again, that you have two sons?'

'No!' cried Leoric in a muted howl of protest and outrage, towering taller in his anger, head and shoulders above Cadfael's square, solid form. 'That I will not hear! You presume! It is impossible!'

'Impossible for your heir and darling, yet instantly believable in his brother? In this world all men are fallible, and all things are possible.'

318

'But I tell you I saw him hiding his dead man, and sweating over it. If he had happened on him innocently by chance he would not have had cause to conceal the death, he would have come crying it aloud.'

'Not if he happened innocently on someone dear to him as brother or friend stooped over the same horrid task. You believe what you saw, why should not Meriet also believe what he saw? You put your own soul in peril to cover up what you believed he had done, why should not he do as much for another? You promised silence and concealment at a price – and that protection offered to him was just as surely protection for another – only the price was still to be exacted from Meriet. And Meriet did not grudge it. Of his own will he paid it – that was no mere consent to your terms, he wished it and tried to be glad of it, because it bought free someone he loved. Do you know of any other creature breathing that he loves as he loves his brother?'

'This is madness!' said Leoric, breathing hard like a man who has run himself half to death. 'Nigel was the whole day with the Lindes, Roswitha will tell you, Janyn will tell you. He had a falling-out to make up with the girl, he was off to her early in the morning, and came home only late in the evening. He knew nothing of that day's business, he was aghast when he heard of it.'

'From Linde's manor to that place in the forest is no long journey for a mounted man,' said Cadfael relentlessly. 'How if Meriet found him busy and bloodied over Clemence's body, and said to him: Go, get clean away from here, leave him to me – go and be seen elsewhere all this day. I will do what must be done. What then?'

'Are you truly saying,' demanded Leoric in hoarse whisper, 'that Nigel killed the man? Such a crime against hospitality, against kinship, against his nature?'

'No,' said Cadfael. 'But I am saying that it may be true that Meriet did so find him, just as you found Meriet. Why should what was such plain proof to you be any less convincing to Meriet? Had he not overwhelming reason to believe his brother guilty, to fear him guilty, or no less terrible, to dread that he might be convicted in innocence? For bear this ever in mind, if you could be mistaken in giving such instant credence to what you saw, so could Meriet. For those lost six hours still stick in my craw, and how to account for them I don't yet know.'

'Is it possible?' whispered Leoric, shaken and wondering. 'Have I so wronged him? And my own part – must I not go straight to Hugh Beringar and let him judge? In God's name, what are we to do, to set right what can be righted?'

'You must go, rather, to Abbot Radulfus's dinner,' said Cadfael, 'and be such a convivial guest as he expects, and tomorrow you must marry your son as you have planned. We are still groping in the dark, and have no choice but to wait for enlightenment. Think of what I have said, but say no word of it to any other. Not yet. Let them have their wedding day in peace.'

But for all that he was certain then, in his own mind, that it would not be in peace.

Isouda came to find him in his workshop in the herbarium. He took one look at her, forgot his broodings, and smiled. She came in the austere but fine array she had thought suitable for dining with abbots, and catching the smile and the lighting of Cadfael's eyes, she relaxed into her impish grin and opened her cloak wide, putting off the hood to let him admire her.

'You think it will do?'

Her hair, too short to braid, was bound about her brow by an embroidered ribbon fillet, just such a one as Meriet had hidden in his bed in the dortoir, and below the confinement it clustered in a thick mane of curls on her neck. Her dress was an over-tunic of deep blue, fitting closely to the hip and there flowing out in gentle folds, over a long-sleeved and high-necked cotte of a pale rose-coloured wool. Exceedingly grown-up, not at all the colours or the cut to which a wild child would fly, allowed for once to dine with the adults. Her bearing, always erect and confident, had acquired a lordly dignity to go with the dress, and her gait as she entered was princely. The close necklace of heavy natural stones, polished but not cut, served beautifully to call the eye to the fine carriage of her head. She wore no other ornaments.

'It would do for me,' said Cadfael simply, 'if I were a green boy expecting a hoyden known from a child. Are you as unprepared for him, I wonder, as he will be for you?'

Isouda shook her head until the brown curls danced, and settled again into new and distracting patterns on her shoulders. 'No! I've thought of all you've told me, and I know my Meriet. Neither you nor he need fear. I can deal!'

'Then before we go,' said Cadfael, 'you had better be armed

320

with everything I have gleaned in the meantime.' And he sat down with her and told. She heard him out with a serious but tranquil face, unshaken.

'Listen, Brother Cadfael, why should he *not* come to see his brother married, since things are as you say? I know it would not be a kindness, not yet, to tell him he's *known* as an innocent and deceives nobody, it would only set him agonizing for whoever it is he's hiding. But you know him now. If he's given his parole, he'll not break it, and he's innocent enough, God knows, to believe that other men are as honest as he, and will take his word as simply as he gives it. He would credit it if Hugh Beringar allowed even a captive felon to come to see his brother married.'

'He could not yet walk so far,' said Cadfael, though he was captivated by the notion.

'He need not. I would send a groom with a horse for him. Brother Mark could come with him. Why not? He could come early, and cloaked, and take his place privately where he could watch. Whatever follows,' said Isouda with grave determin- ation, 'for I am not such a fool as to doubt there's grief here somehow for their house – whatever follows, I want *him* brought forth into daylight, where he belongs. Or whatever faces may be fouled! For his is fair enough, and so I want it shown.'

'So do I,' said Cadfael heartily, 'so do I!'

'Then ask Hugh Beringar if I may send for him to come. I don't know – I feel there may be need of him, that he has the right to be there, that he should be there.'

'I will speak to Hugh,' said Cadfael. 'And now, come, let's be off to Saint Giles before the light fails.'

They walked together along the Foregate, veered right at the bleached grass triangle of the horse-fair, and out between scattered houses and green fields to the hospice. The shadowy, skeleton trees made lace patterns against a greenish, pallid sky thinning to frost.

'This is where even lepers may go for shelter?' she said, climbing the gentle grassy slope to the boundary fence. 'They medicine them here, and do their best to heal? That is noble!'

'They even have their successes,' said Cadfael. 'There's never any want of volunteers to serve here, even after a death. Mark may have gone far to heal your Meriet, body and soul.'

'When I have finished what he has begun,' she said with a sudden shining smile, 'I will thank him properly. Now where must we go?'

Cadfael took her directly to the barn, but at this hour it was empty. The evening meal was not yet due, but the light was too far gone for any activity outdoors. The solitary low pallet stood neatly covered with its dun blanket.

'This is his bed?' she asked, gazing down at it with a meditative face.

'It is. He had it up in the loft above, for fear of disturbing his fellows if he had bad dreams, and it was here he fell. By Mark's account he was on his way in his sleep to make confession to Hugh Beringar, and get him to free his prisoner. Will you wait for him here? I'll find him and bring him to you.'

Meriet was seated at Brother Mark's little desk in the anteroom of the hall, mending the binding of a service book with a strip of leather. His face was grave in concentration on his task, his fingers patient and adroit. Only when Cadfael informed him that he had a visitor waiting in the barn was he shaken by sudden agitation. Cadfael he was used to, and did not mind, but he shrank from showing himself to others, as though he carried a contagion.

'I had rather no one came,' he said, torn between gratitude for an intended kindness and reluctance to have to make the effort of bearing the consequent pain. 'What good can it do, now? What is there to be said? I've been glad of my quietness here.' He gnawed a doubtful lip and asked resignedly, 'Who is it?'

'No one you need fear,' said Cadfael, thinking of Nigel, whose brotherly attentions might have proved too much to bear, had they been offered. But they had not. Bridegrooms have some excuse for putting all other business aside, certainly, but at least he should have asked after his brother. 'It is only Isouda.'

Only Isouda! Meriet drew relieved breath. 'Isouda has thought of me? That was kind. But – does she know? That I am a confessed felon. I would not have her in a mistake …'

'She does know. No need to say word of that, and neither will she. She would have me bring her because she has a loyal affection for you. It won't cost you much to spend a few minutes with her, and I doubt if you'll have to do much talking, for she will do the most of it.'

Meriet went with him, still a little reluctantly, but not greatly disturbed by the thoughts of having to bear the regard, the sympathy, the obstinate championship, perhaps, of a child playmate. The children among his beggars had been good for him, simple, undemanding, accepting him without question.

322

Isouda's sisterly fondness he could meet in the same way, or so he supposed.

She had helped herself to the flint and tinder in the box beside the cot, struck sparks, and kindled the wick of the small lamp, setting it carefully on the broad stone placed for it, where it would be safe from contact with any drifting straw, and shed its mellow, mild light upon the foot of the bed, where she had seated herself. She had put back her cloak to rest only upon her shoulders and frame the sober grandeur of her gown, her embroidered girdle, and the hands folded in her lap. She lifted upon Meriet as he entered the discreet, age-old smile of the Virgin in one of the more worldly paintings of the Annunciation, where the angel's embassage is patently superfluous, for the lady has known it long before.

Meriet caught his breath and halted at gaze, seeing this grown lady seated calmly and expectantly upon his bed. How could a few months so change anyone? He had meant to say gently but bluntly, 'You should not have come here,' but the words were never uttered. There she sat in possession of herself and of place and time, and he was almost afraid of her, and of the sorry changes she might find in him, thin, limping, outcast, no way resembling the boy who had run wild with her no long time ago. But Isouda rose, advanced upon him with hands raised to draw his head down to her, and kissed him soundly.

'Do you know you've grown almost handsome? I'm sorry about your broken head,' she said, lifting a hand to touch the healed wound, 'but this will go, you'll bear no mark. Someone did good work closing that cut. You may surely kiss me, you are not a monk yet.'

Meriet's lips, still and chill against her cheek, suddenly stirred and quivered, closing in helpless passion. Not for her as a woman, not yet, simply as a warmth, a kindness, someone coming with open arms and no questions or reproaches. He embraced her inexpertly, wavering between impetuosity and shyness of this transformed being, and quaked at the contact.

'You're still lame,' she said solicitously. 'Come and sit down with me. I won't stay too long, to tire you, but I couldn't be so near without coming to see you again. Tell me about this place,' she ordered, drawing him down to the bed beside her. 'There are children here, too, I heard their voices. Quite young children.'

Spellbound, he began to tell her in stumbling, broken

phrases about Brother Mark, small and fragile and indestructible, who had the signature of God upon him and longed to become a priest. It was not hard to talk about his friend, and the unfortunates who were yet fortunate in falling into such hands. Never a word about himself or her, while they sat shoulder to shoulder, turned inwards towards each other, and their eyes ceaselessly measured and noted the changes wrought by this season of trial. He forgot that he was a man self-condemned, with only a brief but strangely tranquil life before him, and she a young heiress with a manor double the value of Aspley, and grown suddenly beautiful. They sat immured from time and unthreatened by the world; and Cadfael slipped away satisfied, and went to snatch a word with Brother Mark, while there was time. She had her finger on the pulse of the hours, she would not stay too long. The art was to astonish, to warm, to quicken an absurd but utterly credible hope, and then to depart.

When she thought fit to go, Meriet brought her from the barn by the hand. They had both a high colour and bright eyes, and by the way they moved together they had broken free from the first awe, and had been arguing as of old; and that was good. He stooped his cheek to be kissed when they separated, and she kissed him briskly, gave him a cheek in exchange, said he was a stubborn wretch as he always had been, and yet left him exalted almost into content, and herself went away cautiously encouraged.

'I have as good as promised him I will send my horse to fetch him in good time tomorrow morning,' she said, when they were reaching the first scattered houses of the Foregate.

'I have as good as promised Mark the same,' said Cadfael. 'But he had best come cloaked and quietly. God, he knows if I have any good reason for it, but my thumbs prick and I want him there, but unknown to those closest to him in blood.'

'We are troubling too much,' said the girl buoyantly, exalted by her own success. 'I told you long ago, he is mine, and no one else will have him. If it is needful that Peter Clemence's slayer must be taken, to give Meriet to me, then why fret, for he will be taken.'

'Girl,' said Cadfael, breathing in deeply, 'you terrify me like an act of God. And I do believe you will pull down the thunderbolt.'

In the warmth and soft light in their small chamber in the guest-hall after supper, the two girls who shared a bed sat brooding over their plans for the morrow. They were not sleepy, they had far too much on their minds to wish for sleep. Roswitha's maid-servant, who attended them both, had gone to her bed an hour ago; she was a raw country girl, not entrusted with the choice of jewels, ornaments and perfumes for a marriage. It would be Isouda who would dress her friend's hair, help her into her gown, and escort her from guest-hall to church and back again, withdrawing the cloak from her shoulders at the church door, in this December cold, restoring it when she left on her lord's arm, a new-made wife.

Roswitha had spread out her wedding gown on the bed, to brood over its every fold, consider the set of the sleeves and the fit of the bodice, and wonder whether it would not be the better still for a closer clasp to the gilded girdle.

Isouda roamed the room restlessly, replying carelessly to Roswitha's dreaming comments and questions. They had the wooden chests of their possessions, leather-covered, stacked against one wall, and the small things they had taken out were spread at large on every surface; bed, shelf and chest. The little box that held Roswitha's jewels stood upon the press beside the guttering lamp. Isouda delved a hand idly into it, plucking out one piece after another. She had no great interest in such adornments.

'Would you wear the yellow mountain stones?' asked Roswitha, 'To match with this gold thread in the girdle?'

Isouda held the amber pebbles to the light and let them run smoothly through her fingers. 'They would suit well. But let me see what else you have here. You've never shown me the half of these.' She was fingering them curiously when she caught the buried gleam of coloured enamels, and unearthed from the very bottom of the box a large brooch of the ancient ring-and-pin kind, the ring with its broad, flattened terminals intricately ornamented with filigree shapes of gold framing the enamels, sinuous animals that became twining leaves if viewed a second time, and twisted back into serpents as she gazed. The pin was of silver, with a diamond-shaped head engraved with a formal flower in enamels, and the point projected the length of her little finger beyond the ring, which filled her palm. A princely thing, made to fasten the thick folds of a man's cloak. She had begun to say: 'I've never seen this ...' before she had it out and saw it clearly. She broke off then, and the sudden silence caused Roswitha to look up. She rose quickly, and came to plunge her own hand into the box and thrust the brooch to the bottom

325

again, out of sight.

'Oh, not that!' she said with a grimace. 'It's too heavy, and so old-fashioned. Put them all back, I shall need only the yellow necklace and the silver hair-combs.' She closed the lid firmly, and drew Isouda back to the bed, where the gown lay carefully outspread. 'See here, there are a few frayed stitches in the embroidery, could you catch them up for me? You are a better needlewoman than I.'

With a placid face and steady hand Isouda sat down and did as she was asked, and refrained from casting another glance at the box that held the brooch. But when the hour of Compline came, she snapped off her thread at the final stitch, laid her work aside and announced that she was going to attend the office. Roswitha, already languidly undressing for bed, made no move to dissuade, and certainly none to join her.

Brother Cadfael left the church after Compline by the south porch, intending only to pay a brief visit to his workshop to see that the brazier, which Brother Oswin had been using earlier, was safely out, everything securely stoppered, and the door properly closed to conserve what warmth remained. The night was starry and sharp with frost, and he needed no other light to see his way by such familiar paths. But he had got no further than the archway into the court when he was plucked urgently by the sleeve, and a breathless voice whispered in his ear, 'Brother Cadfael, I must talk to you!'

'Isouda! What is it? Something has happened?' He drew her back into one of the carrels of the scriptorium; no one else would be stirring there now, and in the darkness the two of them were invisible, drawn back into the most sheltered corner. Her face at his shoulder was intent, a pale oval afloat above the darkness of her cloak.

'Happened, indeed! You *said* I might pull down the thunderbolt. I have found something,' she said, rapid and low in his ear, 'in Roswitha's jewel box. Hidden at the bottom. A great ring-brooch, very old and fine, in gold and silver and enamels, the kind men made long before ever the Normans came. As big as the palm of my hand, with a long pin. When she saw what I had, she came and thrust it back into the box and closed the lid, saying that was too heavy and old-fashioned to wear. So I let it pass, and never said word of what I knew. I doubt if she understands what it is, or how whoever gave it to her came by it, though I think he must have warned her not to

326

wear or show it, not yet ... Why else should she be so quick to put it out of my sight? Or else simply she doesn't like it – I suppose it might be no more than that. But *I* know what it is and where it came from, and so will you when I tell you ...' She had run out of breath in her haste, and panted soft warmth against his cheek, leaning close. 'I have seen it before, as she may not have done. It was I who took the cloak from him and carried it within, to the chamber we made ready for him. Fremund brought in his saddle-bags, the cloak I carried ... and this brooch was pinned in the collar.'

Cadfael laid a hand over the small hand that gripped his sleeve, and asked, half-doubting, half-convinced already, 'Whose cloak? Are you saying this thing belonged to Peter Clemence?'

'I *am* saying it. I will swear it.'

'You are sure it must be the same?'

'I am sure. I tell you I carried it in, I touched, I admired it.'

'No, there could not well be two such,' he said, and drew breath deep. 'Of such rare things I doubt there were ever made two alike.'

'Even if there were, why should both wander into this shire? But no, surely every one was made for a prince or a chief and never repeated. My grandsire had such a brooch, but not near so fine and large; he said it came from Ireland, long ago. Besides, I remember the very colours and the strange beasts. It is the same. And she has it!' She had a new thought, and voiced it eagerly. 'Canon Eluard is still here, he knew the cross and ring, he will surely know this, and he can swear to it. But if that fails, so can I, and I will. Tomorrow – how must we deal tomorrow? For Hugh Beringar is not here to be told, and the time so short. It rests with us. Tell me what I can best do?'

'So I will,' said Cadfael slowly, his hand firm over hers, 'when you have told me one more most vital thing. This brooch – it is whole and clean? No stain, no discolouration anywhere upon it, on metals or enamels? Not even thin edges where such discolourings may have been cleaned away?'

'No!' said Isouda after a sudden brief silence, and drew in understanding breath. 'I had not thought of that! No, it is as it was made, bright and perfect. Not like the others ... No, *this* has *not* been through the fire.'

Chapter Twelve

HE WEDDING day dawned clear, bright and very cold. A flake or two of frozen snow, almost too fine to be seen but stinging on the cheek, greeted Isouda as she crossed the court for Prime, but the sky was so pure and lofty that it seemed there would be no fall. Isouda prayed earnestly and bluntly, rather demanding help from heaven than entreating it. From the church she went to the stable-yard, to give orders that her groom should go with her horse and bring Meriet at the right time, with Mark in attendance, to see his brother married. Then she went to dress Roswitha, braid her hair and dress it high with the silver combs and gilt net, fasten the yellow necklace about her throat, walk round her and twitch every fold into place. Uncle Leoric, whether avoiding this cloistered abode of women or grimly preoccupied with the divergent fortunes of his two sons, made no appearance until it was time for him to proceed to his place in the church, but Wulfric Linde hovered in satisfied admiration of his daughter's beauty, and did not seem to find this over-womaned air hard to breathe. Isouda had a mild, tolerant regard for him; a silly, kind man, competent at getting good value out of a manor, and reasonable with his tenants and villeins, but seldom looking beyond, and always the last to know what his children or neighbours were about.

Somewhere, at this same time, Janyn and Nigel were certainly engaged in the same archaic dance, making the bridegroom ready for what was at the same time triumph and sacrifice.

Wulfric studied the set of Roswitha's bliaut, and turned her about fondly to admire her from every angle. Isouda withdrew to the press, and let them confer contentedly, totally absorbed, while she fished up by touch, from the bottom of the casket, the ancient ring-brooch that had belonged to Peter Clemence, and secured it by the pin in her wide over-sleeve.

The young groom Edred arrived at Saint Giles with two horses, in good time to bring Meriet and Brother Mark to the dim privacy within the church before the invited company assembled. In spite of his natural longing to see his brother wed, Meriet had shrunk from being seen to be present, an accused felon as he was, and a shame to his father's house. So he had said when Isouda promised him access, and assured him that Hugh Beringar would allow the indulgence and accept his prisoner's sworn word not to take advantage of such clemency; the scruple had suited Isouda's purpose then and was even more urgently welcome now. He need not make himself known to anyone, and no one should recognize or even notice him. Edred would bring him early, and he could be safely installed in a dim corner of the choir before ever the guests came in, some withdrawn place where he could see and not be seen. And when the married pair left, and the guests after them, then he could follow unnoticed and return to his prison with his gentle gaoler, who was necessary as friend, prop in case of need, and witness, though Meriet knew nothing of the need there might well be of informed witnesses.

'And the lady of Foriet orders me,' said Edred cheerfully, 'to tether the horses outside the precinct, ready for when you want to return. Outside the gatehouse I'll hitch them until the rest have gone in, if you so please. You won't mind, brothers, if I take an hour or so free while you're within? There's a sister of mine has a house along the Foregate, a small cot for her and her man.' There was also a girl he fancied in the hovel next door, but that he did not feel it necessary to say.

Meriet came forth from the barn strung taut like an overtuned lute, his cowl drawn forward to hide his face. He had discarded his stick, except when overtired at the end of the day, but he still went a little lame on his sprained foot. Mark kept close at his elbow, watching the sharp, lean profile that was honed even finer by the dark backcloth of the cowl, a face lofty-browed, high-nosed, fastidious.

'Should I so intrude upon him?' wondered Meriet, his voice thin with pain. 'He has not asked after me,' he said, aching, and turned his face away, ashamed of so complaining.

'You should and you must,' said Mark firmly. 'You promised the lady, and she has put herself out to make your visit easy. Now let her groom mount you, you have not yet the full use of that foot, you cannot spring.'

Meriet gave way, consenting to borrow a hand to get into the saddle. 'And that's her own riding horse you have there,' said Edred, looking up proudly at the tall young gelding. 'And a stout little horsewoman she is, and thinks the world of him. There's not many she'd let into a saddle on *that* back, I can tell you.'

It occurred to Meriet, somewhat late, to wonder if he was not trying Brother Mark too far, in enforcing him to clamber aboard a beast strange and possibly fearsome to him. He knew so little of this small, tireless brother, only what he was, not at all what he had been aforetime, nor how long he had worn the habit; there were those children of the cloister who had been habited from infancy. But Brother Mark set foot briskly enough in the stirrup, and hoisted his light weight into the saddle without either grace or difficulty.

'I grew up on a well-farmed yardland,' he said, noting Meriet's wide eye. 'I have had to do with horses from an infant, not your high-bred stock, but farm-drudges. I plod like them, but I can stay up, and I can get my beast where he must go. I began very early,' he said, remembering long hours half-asleep and sagging in the fields, a small hand clutching the stones in his bag, to sling at the crows along the furrow.

They went out along the Foregate thus, two mounted brothers of the Benedictines with a young groom trotting alongside. The winter morning was young, but the human traffic was already brisk, husbandmen out to feed their winter stock, housewives shopping, late packmen humping their packs, children running and playing, everybody quick to make use of a fine morning, where daylight was in any case short, and fine mornings might be few. As brothers of the abbey, they exchanged greetings and reverences all along the way.

They lighted down before the gatehouse, and left the horses with Edred to bestow as he had said. Here in the precinct where he had sought entry, for whatever reason of his own and counter-reason of his father's, Meriet hung irresolute, trembling, and would have stayed, if Mark had not taken him by the arm and drawn him within. Through the great court, busy enough but engrossed, they made their way into the blessed dimness and chill of the church, and if any noticed them they never wondered at two brothers going cowled and in a hurry on such a frosty morning.

Edred, whistling, tethered the horses as he had said he would, and went off to visit his sister and the girl next door.

Hugh Beringar, not a wedding guest, was nevertheless as early on the scene as were Meriet and Mark, nor did he come alone. Two of his officers loitered unobtrusively among the shifting throng in the great court, where a number of the curious inhabitants of the Foregate had added themselves to the lay servants, boys and novices, and the various birds of passage lodged in the common hall. Cold though it might be, they intended to see all there was to be seen. Hugh kept out of sight in the anteroom of the gatehouse, where he could observe without himself being observed. Here he had within his hand all those who had been closest to the death of Peter Clemence. If this day's ferment did not cast up anything fresh, then both Leoric and Nigel must be held to account, and made to speak out whatever they knew.

In compliment to a generous patron of the abbey, Abbot Radulfus himself had elected to conduct the marriage service, and that ensured that his guest Canon Eluard should also attend. Moreover, the sacrament would be at the high altar, not the parish altar, since the abbot was officiating, and the choir monks would all be in their places. That severed Hugh from any possibility of a word in advance with Cadfael. A pity, but they knew each other well enough by now to act in alliance even without pre-arrangement.

The leisurely business of assembly had begun already, guests crossed from hall to church by twos and threes, in their best. A country gathering, not a court one, but equally proud and of lineage as old or older. Compassed about with a great cloud of witnesses, equally Saxon and Norman, Roswitha Linde would go to her bridal. Shrewsbury had been given to the great Earl Roger almost as soon as Duke William became king, but many a manor in the outlying countryside had remained with its old lord, and many a come-lately Norman lordling had had the sense to take a Saxon wife, and secure his gains through blood older than his own, and a loyalty not due to himself.

331

The interested crowd shifted and murmured, craning to get the best view of the passing guests. There went Leoric Aspley, and there his son Nigel, that splendid young man, decked out to show him at his best, and Janyn Linde in airy attendance, his amused and indulgent smile appropriate enough in a good-natured bachelor assisting at another young man's loss of liberty. That meant that all the guests should now be in their places. The two young men halted at the door of the church and took their stand there.

Roswitha came from the guest-hall swathed in her fine blue cloak, for her gown was light for a winter morning. No question but she was beautiful, Hugh thought, watching her sail down the stone steps on Wulfric's plump, complacent arm. Cadfael had reported her as quite unable to resist drawing all men after her, even elderly monks of no attraction or presence. She had the audience of her life now, lined up on either side of her unhurried passage to the church, gaping in admiration. And in her it seemed as innocent and foolish as an over-fondness for honey. To be jealous of her would be absurd.

Isouda Foriet, demure in eclipse behind such radiance, walked after the bride, bearing her gilded prayer-book and ready to attend on her at the church door, where Wulfric lifted his daughter's hand from his own arm, and laid it in the eager hand Nigel extended to receive it. Bride and groom entered the church porch together, and there Isouda lifted the warm mantle from Roswitha's shoulders and folded it over her own arm, and so followed the bridal pair into the dim nave of the church.

Not at the parish altar of Holy Cross, but at the high altar of Saint Peter and Saint Paul, Nigel Aspley and Roswitha Linde were made man and wife.

Nigel made his triumphal way from the church by the great west door which lay just outside the enclave of the abbey, close beside the gatehouse. He had Roswitha ceremoniously by the hand, and was so blind and drunk with his own pride of possession that it was doubtful if he was aware even of Isouda herself standing in the porch, let alone of the cloak she spread in her hands and draped over Roswitha's shoulders, as bride and groom reached the chill brightness of the frosty noon outside. After them streamed the proud fathers and gratified guests; and if Leoric's face was unwontedly grey and sombre

332

for such an occasion, no one seemed to remark it; he was at all times an austere man.

Nor did Roswitha notice the slight extra weight on her left shoulder of an ornament intended for a man's wear. Her eyes were fixed only on the admiring crowd that heaved and sighed with approbation at sight of her. Here outside the wall the throng had grown, since everyone who had business or a dwelling along the Foregate had come to stare. Not here, thought Isouda, following watchfully, not here will there be any response, here all those who might recognize the brooch are walking behind her, and Nigel is as oblivious as she. Only when they turn in again at the gatehouse, having shown themselves from the parish door, will there be anyone to take heed. And if Canon Eluard fails me, she thought resolutely, then *I* shall speak out, my word against hers or any man's.

Roswitha was in no hurry; her progress down the steps, across the cobbles of the forecourt to the gateway and so within to the great court, was slow and stately, so that every man might stare his fill. That was a blessed chance, for in the meantime Abbot Radulfus and Canon Eluard had left the church by transept and cloister, and stood to watch benevolently by the stair to the guest-hall, and the choir monks had followed them out to disperse and mingle with the fringes of the crowd, aloof but interested.

Brother Cadfael made his way unobtrusively to a post close to where the abbot and his guest stood, so that he could view the advancing pair as they did. Against the heavy blue cloth of Roswitha's cloak the great brooch, aggressively male, stood out brilliantly. Canon Eluard had broken off short in the middle of some quiet remark in the abbot's ear, and his beneficent smile faded, and gave place to a considering and intent frown, as though at this slight distance his vision failed to convince him he was seeing what indeed he saw.

'But that ...', he murmured, to himself rather than to any other. 'But no, how can it be?'

Bride and groom drew close, and made dutiful reverence to the dignitaries of the church. Behind them came Isouda, Leoric, Wulfric, and all the assembly of their guests. Under the arch of the gatehouse Cadfael saw Janyn's fair head and flashing blue eyes, as he loitered to exchange a word with someone in the Foregate crowd known to him, and then came on with his light, springing step, smiling.

Nigel was handing his wife to the first step of the stone

333

stairway when Canon Eluard stepped forward and stood between, with an arresting motion of his hand. Only then, following his fixed gaze, did Roswitha look down at the collar of her cloak, which swung loose on her shoulders, and see the glitter of enamelled colours and the thin gold outlines of fabulous beasts, entwined with sinuous leaves.

'Child,' said Eluard, 'may I look more closely?' He touched the raised threads of gold, and the silver head of the pin. She watched in wary silence, startled and uneasy, but not yet defensive or afraid. 'That is a beautiful and rare thing you have there,' said the canon, eyeing her with a slight, uncertain frown. 'Where did you get it?'

Hugh had come forth from the gatehouse and was watching and listening from the rear of the crowd. At the corner of the cloister two habited brothers watched from a distance. Pinned here between the watchers round the west door and the gathering now halted inexplicably here in the great court, and unwilling to be noticed by either, Meriet stood stiff and motionless in shadow, with Brother Mark beside him, and waited to return unseen to his prison and refuge.

Roswitha moistened her lips, and said with a pale smile, 'It was a gift to me from a kinsman.'

'Strange!' said Eluard, and turned to the abbot with a grave face. 'My lord abbot, I know this brooch well, too well ever to mistake it. It belonged to the bishop of Winchester, and he gave it to Peter Clemence – to that favoured clerk of his household whose remains now lie in your chapel.'

Brother Cadfael had already noted one remarkable circumstance. He had been watching Nigel's face ever since that young man had first looked down at the adornment that was causing so much interest, and until this moment there had been no sign whatever that the brooch meant anything to him. He was glancing from Canon Eluard to Roswitha, and back again, a puzzled frown furrowing his broad forehead and a faint, questioning smile on his lips, waiting for someone to enlighten him. But now that its owner had been named, it suddenly had meaning for him, and a grim and frightening meaning at that. He paled and stiffened, staring at the canon, but though his throat and lips worked, either he found no words or thought better of those that he had found, for he remained mute. Abbot Radulfus had drawn close on one side, and Hugh Beringar on the other.

'What is this? You recognize this gem as belonging to Master

334

Clemence? You are certain?'

'As certain as I was of those possessions of his which you have already shown me, cross and ring and dagger, which had gone through the fire with him. This he valued in particular as the bishop's gift. Whether he was wearing it on his last journey I cannot say, but it was his habit, for he prized it.'

'If I may speak, my lord,' said Isouda clearly from behind Roswitha's should, 'I *do* know that he was wearing it when he came to Aspley. The brooch was in his cloak when I took it from him at the door and carried it to the chamber prepared for him, and it was in his cloak also when I brought it out to him the next morning when he left us. He did not need the cloak for riding, the morning was warm and fine. He had it slung over his saddle-bow when he rode away.'

'In full view, then,' said Hugh sharply. For cross and ring had been left with the dead man and gone to the fire with him. Either time had been short and flight imperative, or else some superstitious awe had deterred the murderer from stripping a priest's gems of office from his very body, though he had not scrupled to remove this one fine thing which lay open to his hand. 'You observe, my lords,' said Hugh, 'that this jewel seems to show no marks of damage. If you will allow us to handle and examine it ...?'

Good, thought Cadfael, reassured, I should have known Hugh would need no nudging from me. I can leave all to him now.

Roswitha made no move either to allow or prevent, as Hugh unpinned the great brooch from its place. She looked on with a blanched and apprehensive face, but said never a word. No, Roswitha was not entirely innocent in the matter; whether she had known what this gift was and how come by or not, she had certainly understood that it was perilous and not to be shown – not yet! Perhaps not here? And after their marriage they were bound for Nigel's northern manor. Who was likely to know it there?

'This has never seen the fire,' said Hugh, and handed it to Canon Eluard for confirmation. 'Everything else the man had was burned with him. Only this one thing was taken from him before ever those reached him who built him into his pyre. And only one person, last to see him alive, first to see him dead, can have taken this from his cloak as he lay, and that was his murderer.' He turned to Roswitha, who stood pale to translucency, like a woman of ice, staring at him with wide and

335

horrified eyes.

'Who gave it to you?'

She cast one rapid glance around her, and then as suddenly took heart, and drawing breath deep, she answered loudly and clearly, 'Meriet!'

Cadfael awoke abruptly to the realization that he possessed knowledge which he had not yet confided to Hugh, and if he waited for the right challenge to this bold declaration from other lips he might wait in vain, and lose what had already been gained. For most of those here assembled, there was nothing incredible in this great lie she had just told, nothing even surprising, considering the circumstances of Meriet's entry into the cloister, and the history of the devil's novice within these walls. And she had clutched at the brief general hush as encouragement, and was enlarging boldly, 'He was always following me with his dog's eyes. I didn't want his gifts, but I took it to be kind to him. How could I know where he got it?'

'*When*?' demanded Cadfael loudly, as one having authority. '*When* did he give you this gift?'

'When?' She looked round, hardly knowing where the question had come from, but hasty and positive in answering it, to hammer home conviction. 'It was the day after Master Clemence left Aspley – the day after he was killed – in the afternoon. He came to me in our paddock at Linde. He pressed me so to take it ... I did not want to hurt him ...' From the tail of his eye Cadfael saw that Meriet had come forth from his shadowy place and drawn a little nearer, and Mark had followed him anxiously though without attempting to restrain him. But the next moment all eyes were drawn to the tall figure of Leoric Aspley, as he came striding and shouldering forward to tower over his son and his son's new wife.

'Girl,' cried Leoric, 'think what you say! Is it well to lie? *I know* this cannot be true.' He swung about vehemently, encountering in turn with his grieved, grim eyes abbot and canon and deputy-sheriff. 'My lords all, what she says is false. My part in this I will confess, and accept gladly whatever penalty is due from me. For this I know, I brought home my son Meriet, that same day that I brought home the dead body of my guest and kinsman, and having cause, or so I thought, to believe my son the slayer, I laid him under lock and key from that hour, until I had considered, and he had accepted, the fate

336

I decreed for him. From late afternoon of the day Peter Clemence died, all the next day, and until noon of the third, my son Meriet was close prisoner in my house. He never visited this girl. He never gave her this gift, for he never had it in his possession. Nor did he ever lift hand against my guest and his kinsman, now it is shown! God forgive me that ever I credited it!'

'I am not lying!' shrilled Roswitha, struggling to recover the belief she had felt within her grasp. 'A mistake only – I mistook the day! It was the third day he came ...'

Meriet had drawn very slowly nearer. From deep within his shadowing cowl great eyes stared, examining in wonder and anguish his father, his adored brother and his first love, so frantically busy twisting knives in him. Roswitha's roving, pleading eyes met his, and she fell mute like a songbird shot down in flight, and shrank into Nigel's circling arms with a wail of despair.

Meriet stood motionless for a long moment, then he turned on his heel and limped rapidly away. The motion of his lame foot was as if at every step he shook off dust.

'Who gave it to you?' asked Hugh, with pointed and relentless patience.

All the crowd had drawn in close, watching and listening, they had not failed to follow the logic of what had passed. A hundred pairs of eyes settled gradually and remorselessly upon Nigel. He knew it, and so did she.

'No, no, no!' she cried, turning to wind her arms fiercely about her husband. 'It was not my lord – not Nigel! It was my brother gave me the brooch!'

On the instant everyone present was gazing round in haste, searching the court for the fair head, the blue eyes and light-hearted smile, and Hugh's officers were burrowing through the press and bursting out at the gate to no purpose. For Janyn Linde had vanished silently and circumspectly, probably by cool and unhurried paces, from the moment Canon Eluard first noticed the bright enamels on Roswitha's shoulder. And so had Isouda's riding-horse, the better of the two hitched outside the gatehouse for Meriet's use. The porter had paid no attention to a young man sauntering innocently out and mounting without haste. It was a youngster of the Foregate, bright-eyed and knowing, who informed the sergeants that a young gentleman had left by the gate, as long as a quarter of an hour earlier, unhitched his horse, and ridden off along the Foregate, not towards the town. Modestly enough to start with said the shrewd urchin, but he was into a good gallop by the time he reached the corner at the horse-fair and vanished.

From the chaos within the great court, which must be left to sort itself out without his aid, Hugh flew to the stables, to mount himself and the officers he had with him, send for more men, and pursue the fugitive; if such a word might properly be applied to so gay and competent a malefactor as Janyn.

'But why, in God's name, why?' groaned Hugh, tightening girths in the stable-yard, and appealing to Brother Cadfael, busy at the same task beside him. 'Why should he kill? What can he have had against the man? He had never so much as seen him, he was not at Aspley that night. How in the devil's name did he even know the looks of the man he was waiting for?

'Someone had pictured him for him – and he knew the time of his departure and the road he would take, that's plain.' But all the rest was still obscure, to Cadfael as to Hugh.

Janyn was gone, he had plucked himself gently out of the law's reach in excellent time, foreseeing that all must come out. By fleeing he had owned to his act, but the act itself remained inexplicable.

'Not the man,' fretted Cadfael to himself, puffing after Hugh as he led his saddled horse at a trot up to the court and the gatehouse. 'Not the man, then it must have been his errand, after all. What else is there? But why should anyone wish to prevent him from completing his well-intentioned ride to Chester, on the bishop's business? What harm could there be to any man in that?'

The wedding party had scattered indecisively about the court, the involved families taking refuge in the guest-hall, their closest friends loyally following them out of sight, where wounds could be dressed and quarrels reconciled without witnesses from the common herd. More distant guests took counsel, and some withdrew discreetly, preferring to be at home. The inhabitants of the Foregate, pleased and entertained and passing dubiously reliable information hither and yon and adding to it as it passed, continued attentive about the gatehouse.

Hugh had his men mustered and his foot in the stirrup when the furious pounding of galloping hooves, rarely heard in the Foregate, came echoing madly along the enclave wall, and

338

clashed in over the cobbles of the gateway. An exhausted rider, sweating on a lathered horse, reined to a slithering, screaming stop on the frosty stones, and fell rather than dismounted into Hugh's arms, his knees giving under him. All those left in the court, Abbot Radulfus and Prior Robert among them, came closing in haste about the newcomer, foreseeing desperate news.

'Sheriff Prestcote,' panted the reeling messenger, 'or who stands here for him – from the lord bishop of Lincoln, in haste, and pleads for haste ...'

'I stand here for the sheriff,' said Hugh. 'Speak out! What's the lord bishop's urgent word for us?'

'That you should call up all the king's knight-service in the shire,' said the messenger, bracing himself strongly, 'for in the north-east there's black treason, in despite of his Grace's head. Two days after the lord king left Lincoln, Ranulf of Chester and William of Roumare made their way into the king's castle by a subterfuge and have taken it by force. The citizens of Lincoln cry out to his Grace to rescue them from an abominable tyranny, and the lord bishop has contrived to send out a warning, through tight defences, to tell his Grace of what is done. There are many of us now, riding every way with the word. It will be in London by nightfall.'

'King Stephen was there but a week or more ago,' cried Canon Eluard, 'and they pledged their faith to him. How is this possible? They promised a strong chain of fortresses across the north.'

'And that they have,' said the envoy, heaving at breath, 'but not for King Stephen's service, nor the empress's neither, but for their own bastard kingdom in the north. Planned long ago, when they met and called all their castellans to Chester in September, with links as far south as here, and garrisons and constables ready for every castle. They've been gathering young men about them everywhere for their ends ...'

So that was the way of it! Planned long ago, in September, at Chester, where Peter Clemence was bound with an errand from Henry of Blois, a most untimely visitor to intervene where such a company was gathered in arms and such a plot being hatched. No wonder Clemence could not be allowed to ride on unmolested and complete his embassy. And with links as far south as here!

Cadfael caught at Hugh's arm. 'They were two in it together, Hugh. Tomorrow this newly wed pair were to be on their way

339

north to the very borders of Lincolnshire – it's Aspley has the manor there, not Linde. Secure Nigel, while you can! If it's not already too late!'

Hugh turned to stare for an instant only, grasped the force of it, dropped his bridle and ran, beckoning his sergeants after him to the guest-hall. Cadfael was close at his heels when they broke in upon a demoralized wedding party, bereft of gaiety, appetite or spirits, draped about the untouched board in burdened converse more fitting a wake than a wedding. The bride wept desolately in the arms of a stout matron, with three or four other women clucking and cooing around her. The bridegroom was nowhere to be seen.

'He's away!' said Cadfael. 'While we were in the stable-yard, no other chance. And without her! The bishop of Lincoln got his message out of a tightly sealed city at least a day too soon.'

There was no horse tethered outside the gatehouse, when they recalled the possibility and ran to see. Nigel had taken the first opportunity of following his fellow-conspirator towards the lands, offices and commands William of Roumare had promised them, where able young men of martial achievements and small scruples could carve out a fatter future than in two modest Shropshire manors on the edge of the Long Forest.

Chapter Thirteen

HERE WAS new and sensational matter for gossip now, and the watchers in the Foregate, having taken in all that stretched ears and sharp eyes could command, went to spread the word further, that there was planned rebellion in the north, a bid to set up a private kingdom for the earls of Chester and Lincoln, that the fine young men of the wedding company were in the plot from long since, and were fled because the matter had come to light before they could make an orderly withdrawal as planned. The lord bishop of Lincoln, no very close friend of King Stephen, had nevertheless found Chester and Roumare still more objectionable, and bestirred himself to smuggle out word to the king and implore rescue, for himself and his city.

The comings and goings about bridge and abbey were watched avidly. Hugh Beringar, torn two ways, had delegated the pursuit of the traitors to his sergeants, while he rode at once to the castle to send out the call to the knight-service of the shire to be ready to join the force which King Stephen would certainly be raising to besiege Lincoln, to begin commandeering mounts enough for his force, and see that all that was needed in the armoury was in good order. The bishop's messenger was lodged at the abbey, and his message sped on its way by another rider to the castles in the south of the shire. In the guest-hall the shattered company and the deserted bride remained invisible, shut in with the ruins of their celebration.

All this, and the twenty-first day of December barely past two in the afternoon! And what more was to happen before night, who could guess, when things were rushing along at such a speed?

Abbot Radulfus had reasserted his domestic rule, and the brothers went obediently to dinner in the refectory at his express order, somewhat later than usual. The horarium of the house could not be altogether abandoned even for such devastating matters as murder, treason and man-hunt. Besides, as Brother Cadfael thoughtfully concluded, those who had survived this upheaval to gain, instead of lose, might safely be left to draw breath and think in peace, before they must encounter and come to new terms. And those who had lost must have time to lick their wounds. As for the fugitives, the first of them had a handsome start, and the second had benefited by the arrival of even more shocking news to gain a limited breathing-space, but for all that, the hounds were on their trail, well aware now what route to take, for Aspley's northern manor lay somewhere south of Newark, and anyone making for it must set forth by the road to Stafford. Somewhere in the heathland short of that town, dusk would be closing on the travellers. They might think it safe to lodge overnight in the town. They might yet be overtaken and brought back.

On leaving the refectory Cadfael made for his normal destination during the afternoon hours of work, the hut in the herb garden where he brewed his mysteries. And they were there, the two young men in Benedictine habits, seated quietly side by side on the bench against the end wall. The very small spark of the brazier glowed faintly on their faces. Meriet leaned back against the timbers in simple exhaustion, his cowl thrust back on his shoulders, his face shadowy. He had been down into the very profound of anger, grief and bitterness, and surfaced again to find Mark still constant and patient beside him; and now he was at rest, without thought or feeling, ready to be born afresh into a changed world, but not in haste. Mark looked as he always looked, mild, almost deprecatory, as though he pleaded a fragile right to be where he was, and yet would stand to it to the death.

'I thought I might find you here,' said Brother Cadfael, and took the little bellows and blew the brazier into rosy life, for it was none too warm within there. He closed and barred the door to keep out even the draught that found its way through

342

the chinks. 'I doubt if you'll have eaten,' he said, feeling along
the shelf behind the door. 'There are oat cakes here and some
apples, and I think I have a morsel of cheese. You'll be the
better for a bite. And I have a wine that will do you no harm
either.'

And behold, the boy was hungry! So simple it was. He was
not long turned nineteen, and physically hearty, and he had
eaten nothing since dawn. He began listlessly, docile to
persuasion, but at the first bite he was alive again and
ravenous, his eyes brightening, the glow of the blown brazier
gilding and softening hollow cheeks. The wine, as Cadfael had
predicted, did him no harm at all. Blood flowed through him
again, with new warmth and urgency.

He said not one word of brother, father or lost love. It was
still too early. He had heard himself falsely accused by one of
them, falsely suspected by another, and what by the third? Left
to pursue his devoted and foolish self-sacrifice, without a word
to absolve him. He had a great load of bitterness still to shake
from his heart. But praise God, he came to life for food and ate
like a starved schoolboy. Brother Cadfael was greatly
encouraged.

In the mortuary chapel, where Peter Clemence lay in his sealed
coffin on his draped bier, Leoric Aspley had chosen to make
his confession, and entreated Abbot Radulfus to be the priest
to hear it. On his knees on the flagstones, by his own choice, he
set forth the story as he had known it, the fearful discovery of
his younger son labouring to drag a dead man into cover and
hide him from all eyes, Meriet's tacit acceptance of the guilt,
and his own reluctance to deliver up his son to death, or let him
go free.

'I promised him I would deal with his dead man, even at the
peril of my soul, and he should live, but in perpetual penance
out of the world. And to that he agreed and embraced his
penalty, as I now know or fear that I now know, for love of his
brother, whom he had better reason for believing a murderer
than ever I had for crediting the same guilt to Meriet. I am
afraid, father, that he accepted his fate as much for my sake as
for his brother's, having cause, to my shame, to believe – no, to
know! – that I built all on Nigel and all too little upon him, and
could live on after writing him out of my life, though the loss of
Nigel would be my death. As now he is lost indeed, but I can
and I will live. Therefore my grievous sin against my son

343

Meriet is not only this doubt of him, this easy credence of his crime and his banishment into the cloister, but stretches back to his birth in lifelong misprizing.

'And as to my sin against you, father, and against this house, that also I confess and repent, for so to dispose of a suspect murderer and so to enforce a young man without a true vocation, was vile towards him and towards this house. Take that also into account, for I would be free of all my debts.

'And as to my sin against Peter Clemence, my guest and my kinsman, in denying him Christian burial to protect the good name of my own house, I am glad now that the hand of God made use of my own abused son to uncover and undo the evil I have done. Whatever penance you decree for me in that matter, I shall add to it an endowment to provide Masses for his soul for as long as my own life continues ...'

As proud and rigid in confessing faults as in correcting them in his son, he unwound the tale to the end, and to the end Radulfus listened patiently and gravely, decreed measured terms by way of amends, and gave absolution.

Leoric arose stiffly from his knees, and went out in unaccustomed humility and dread, to look for the one son he had left.

The rapping at the closed and barred door of Cadfael's workshop came when the wine, one of Cadfael's three-year-old brews, had begun to warm Meriet into a hesitant reconciliation with life, blurring the sharp memories of betrayal. Cadfael opened the door, and into the mellow ring of light from the brazier stepped Isouda in her grown-up wedding finery, crimson and rose and ivory, a silver fillet round her hair, her face solemn and important. There was a taller shape behind her in the doorway, shadowy against the winter dusk.

'I thought we might find you here,' she said, and the light gilded her faint, secure smile. 'I am a herald. You have been sought everywhere. Your father begs you to admit him to speech with you.'

Meriet had stiffened where he sat, knowing who stood behind her. 'That is not the way I was ever summoned to my father's presence,' he said, with a fading spurt of malice and pain. 'In his house things were not conducted so.'

'Very well then,' said Isouda, undisturbed. 'Your father *orders* you to admit him here, or I do in his behalf, and you had better be sharp and respectful about it.' And she stood aside,

344

eyes imperiously beckoning Brother Cadfael and Brother Mark, as Leoric came into the hut, his tall head brushing the dangling bunches of dried herbs swinging from the beams.

Meriet rose from the bench and made a slow, hostile but punctilious reverence, his back stiff as pride itself, his eyes burning. But his voice was quiet and secure as he said, 'Be pleased to come in. Will you sit, sir?'

Cadfael and Mark drew away one on either side, and followed Isouda into the chill of the dusk. Behind them they heard Leoric say, very quietly and humbly, 'You will not now refuse *me* the kiss?'

There was a brief and perilous silence; then Meriet said hoarsely, 'Father ...' and Cadfael closed the door.

In the high and broken heathland to the south-west of the town of Stafford, about this same hour, Nigel Aspley rode headlong into a deep copse, over thick, tussocky turf, and all but rode over his friend, neighbour and fellow-conspirator, Janyn Linde, cursing and sweating over a horse that went deadly lame upon a hind foot after treading askew and falling in the rough ground. Nigel cried recognition with relief, for he had small appetite for venturesome enterprises alone, and lighted down to look what the damage might be. But Isouda's horse limped to the point of foundering, and manifestly could go no further.

'You?' cried Janyn. 'You broke through, then? God curse this damned brute, he's thrown me and crippled himself.' He clutched at his friend's arm. 'What have you done with my sister? Left her to answer for all? She'll run mad!'

'She's well enough and safe enough, we'll send for her as soon as we may ... *You* to cry out on me!' flared Nigel, turning on him hotly. '*You* made your escape in good time, and left the pair of us in mire to the brows. Who sank us in this bog in the first place? Did *I* bid you kill the man? All I asked was that you send a rider ahead to give warning, have them put everything out of sight quickly before he came. They could have done it! How could *I* send? The man was lodged there in our house, I had no one to send who would not be missed ... But you – *you* had to shoot him down ...'

'I had the hardihood to make all certain, where you would have flinched,' spat Janyn, curling a contemptuous lip. 'A rider would have got there too late. I made sure the bishop's lackey should never get there.'

'And left him lying! Lying in the open ride!'

'For you to be fool enough to run there as soon as I told you!' Janyn hissed derisive scorn at such weakness of will and nerve. 'If you'd let him lie, who was ever to know who struck him down? But you must take fright, and rush to try and hide him, who was far better not hidden. And fetch your poor idiot brother down on you, and your father after him! That ever I broached such high business to such a broken reed!'

'Or I ever listened to such a plausible tempter!' fretted Nigel wretchedly. 'Now here we are helpless. This creature cannot go – you see it! And the town above a mile distant, and night coming ...'

'And I had a head start,' raged Janyn, stamping the thick, blanched grass, 'and fortune ahead of me, and the beast had to founder! And you'll be off to pick up the prizes due to both of us – you who crumple at the first threat! God's curse on the day!'

'Hush your noise!' Nigel turned his back despairingly, stroking the lame horse's sweating flank. 'I wish to God I'd never in life set eyes on you, to come to this pass, but I'll not leave you. If you must be dragged back – you think they'll be far behind us now? – we'll go back together. But let's at least *try* to reach Stafford. Let's leave this one tethered to be found, and ride and run by turns with the other ...'

His back was still turned when the dagger slid in between his ribs from behind, and he sagged and folded, marvelling, not yet feeling any pain, but only the withdrawal of his life and force, that laid him almost softly in the grass. Blood streamed out from his wound and warmed his side, flowing round to fire the ground beneath him. He tried to raise himself, and could not stir a hand.

Janyn stood a moment looking down at him dispassionately. He doubted if the wound itself was fatal, but judged it would take less than half an hour for his sometime friend to bleed to death, which would do as well. He spurned the motionless body with a careless foot, wiped his dagger on the grass, and turned to mount the horse Nigel had ridden. Without another glance behind he dug in his heels and set off at a rapid canter towards Stafford, between the darkening trees.

Hugh's officers, coming at speed some ten minutes later, found half-dead man and lamed horse and, divided their forces, two men riding on to try to overtake Janyn, while the remaining pair salvaged both man and beast, bestowed Isouda's horse at the nearest holding, and carried Nigel back to Shrewsbury, pallid, swathed and senseless, but alive.

'... he promised us advancement, castles and commands – William of Roumare. It was when Janyn went north with me at midsummer to view my manor – it was Janyn persuaded me.' Nigel brought out the sorry, broken fragments of his confession late in the dusk of the following day, in his wits again and half-wishing he were not. So many eyes round his bed, his father erect and ravaged of face at the foot, staring upon his heir with grieved eyes, Roswitha kneeling at his right side, tearless now, but bloated with past weeping, Brother Cadfael and Brother Edmund the infirmarer watchful from the shadows in case their patient tried his strength too far too soon. And on his left Meriet, back in cotte and hose, stripped of the black habit which had never fitted or suited him, and looking strangely taller, leaner and older than when he had first put it on. His eyes, aloof and stern as his father's, were the first Nigel's waking, wandering stare had encountered. There was no knowing what went on in the mind behind them.

'We have been his men from that time on ... We knew the time set for the strike at Lincoln. We meant to ride north after our marriage, Janyn with us – but Roswitha did not know! And now we have lost. Word came through too soon ...'

'Come to the death-day,' said Hugh, standing at Leoric's shoulder.

'Yes – Clemence. At supper he let out what his business was. And they were there in Chester, all their constables and castellans ... in the act! When I took Roswitha home I told Janyn, and begged him to send a rider ahead at once, through the night, to warn them. He swore he would ... I went there next morning early, but he was not there, he never came until past noon, and when I asked if all was well, he said, very well! For Peter Clemence was dead in the forest, and the gathering in Chester safe enough. He laughed at me for being in dread. Let him lie, he said, who'll be the wiser, there are footpads everywhere ... But I was afraid! I went to find him, to hide him away until night ...'

'And Meriet happened upon you in the act,' said Hugh, quietly prompting.

'I had cut away the shaft, the better to move him. There was blood on my hands – what else could he think? I swore it was

347

not my work, but he did not believe me. He told me, go quickly, wash off the blood, go back to Roswitha, stay the day out, I will do what must be done. For our father's sake, he said ... he sets such store on you, he said, it would break his heart ... And I did as he said! A jealous killing, he must have thought ... he never knew what I had – what we had – to cover up. I went from him and left him to be taken in guilt that was none of his ...'

Tears sprang in Nigel's eyes. He groped out blindly for any hand that would comfort him with a touch, and it was Meriet who suddenly dropped to his knees and took it. His face remained obstinately stern and ever more resembling his father's, but still he accepted the fumbling hand and held it firmly.

'Only late at night, when I went home, then I heard ... How could I speak? It would have betrayed all ... all ... When Meriet was loosed out to us again, when he had given his pledge to take the cowl, then I did go to him,' pleaded Nigel feebly. 'I did offer ... He would not let me meddle. He said he was resolved and willing, and I must let things be ...'

'It is true,' said Meriet. 'I did so persuade him. Why make bad worse?'

'But he did not know of treason ... I repent me,' said Nigel, wringing at the hand he held in his, and subsiding into his welcome weakness, refuge from present harassment. 'I do repent of what I have done to my father's house ... and most of all to Meriet ... If I live, I will make amends ...'

'He'll live,' said Cadfael, glad to escape from that dolorous bedside into the frosty air of the great court, and draw deep breaths to breathe forth again in silver mist. 'Yes, and make good his present losses by mustering for King Stephen, if he can bear arms by the time his Grace moves north. It cannot be till after the feast, there's an army to raise. And though I'm sure young Janyn meant murder, for it seems to come easily to him as smiling, his dagger went somewhat astray, and has done no mortal harm. Once we've fed and rested him, and made good the blood he's lost, Nigel will be his own man again, and do his devoir for whoever can best vantage him. Unless you see fit to commit him for this treason?'

'In this mad age,' said Hugh ruefully, 'what is treason? With two monarchs in the field, and a dozen petty kings like Chester riding the tide, and even such as Bishop Henry hovering between two or three loyalties? No, let him lie, he's small chaff, only a half-hearted traitor, and no murderer at all – that I believe, he would not have the stomach.'

Behind them Roswitha emerged from the infirmary, huddling her cloak about her against the cold, and crossed with a hasty step towards the guest-hall. Even after abasement, abandonment and grief she had the resilience to look beautiful, though these two men, at least, she could now pass by hurriedly and with averted eyes.

'Handsome is as handsome does,' said Brother Cadfael somewhat morosely, looking after her. 'Ah, well, they deserve each other. Let them end or mend together.'

Leoric Aspley requested audience of the abbot after Vespers of that day.

'Father, there are yet two matters I would raise with you. There is this young brother of your fraternity at Saint Giles, who has been brother indeed to my son Meriet, beyond his brother in blood. My son tells me it is the heart's wish of Brother Mark to be a priest. Surely he is worthy. Father, I offer whatever moneys may be needed to provide him the years of study that will bring him to his goal. If you will guide, I will pay all, and be his debtor still.'

'I have myself noted Brother Mark's inclination,' said the abbot, 'and approved it. He has the heart of the matter in him. I will see him advanced, and take your offer willingly.'

'And the second thing,' said Leoric, 'concerns my sons, for I have learned by good and by ill that I have two, as a certain brother of this house has twice found occasion to remind me, and with good reason. My son Nigel is wed to a daughter of a manor now lacking another heir, and will therefore inherit through his wife, if he makes good his reparation for faults confessed. Therefore I intend to settle my manor of Aspley to my younger son Meriet. I mean to make my intent known in a charter, and beg you to be one of my witnesses.'

'With my goodwill,' said Radulfus, gravely smiling, 'and part with him gladly, to meet him in another fashion, outside this pale which never was meant to contain him.'

Brother Cadfael betook himself to his workshop that night before Compline, to make his usual nightly check that all was in order there, the brazier fire either out or so low that it presented no threat, all the vessels not in use tidied away, his

349

current wines contentedly bubbling, the lids on all his jars and the stoppers in all his flasks and bottles. He was tired but tranquil, the world about him hardly more chaotic than it had been two days ago, and in the meantime the innocent delivered, not without great cost. For the boy had worshipped the easy, warm, kind brother so much more pleasing to the eye and so much more gifted in graces and physical accomplishments than ever he could be, so much more loved, so much more vulnerable and frail, if only the soul showed through. Worship was over now, but compassion and loyalty, even pity, can be just as enchanting. Meriet had been the last to leave Nigel's sick-room. Strange to think that it must have cost Leoric a great pang of jealousy to leave him there so long, fettered to his brother and letting his father go. They had still some fearful lunges of adjustment to make between those three before all would be resolved.

Cadfael sat down with a sigh in his dark hut, only a glowing spark in the brazier to keep him company. A quarter of an hour yet before Compline. Hugh was away home at last, shutting out for tonight the task of levying men for the king's service. Christmas would come and go, and Stephen would move almost on its heels – that mild, admirable, lethargic soul of generous inclinations, stung into violent action by a blatantly treasonous act. He could move fast when he chose, his trouble was that his animosities died young. He could not really hate. And somewhere in the north, far towards his goal now, rode Janyn Linde, no doubt still smiling, whistling, light of heart, with his two unavoidable dead men behind him, and his sister, who had been nearer to him than any other human creature, nonetheless shrugged off like a split glove. Hugh would have Janyn Linde in his levelled eye, when he came with Stephen to Lincoln. A light young man with heavy enormities to answer for, and all to be paid, here or hereafter. Better here.

As for the villein Harald, there was a farrier on the town side of the western bridge willing to take him on, and as soon as the flighty public mind had forgotten him he would be quietly let out to take up honest work there. A year and a day in a charter borough, and he would be a free man.

Unwittingly Cadfael had closed his eyes for a few drowsing moments, leaning well back against his timber wall, with legs stretched out before him and ankles comfortably crossed. Only the momentary chill draught penetrated his half-sleep, and caused him to open his eyes. And they were there before him, standing hand in hand, very gravely smiling, twin images of indulgence to his age and cares, the boy become a man and the girl become what she had always been in the bud, a formidable woman. There was only the glow-worm spark of the dying brazier to light them, but they shone most satisfactorily.

Isouda loosed her playfellow's hand and came forward to stoop and kiss Cadfael's furrowed russet cheek.

'Tomorrow early we are going home. There may be no chance then to say farewell properly. But we shall not be far away. Roswitha is staying with Nigel, and will take him home with her when he is well.'

The secret light played on the planes of her face, rounded and soft and strong, and found frets of scarlet in her mane of hair. Roswitha had never been as beautiful as this, the burning heart was wanting.

'We do love you!' said Isouda impulsively, speaking for both after her confident fashion, 'You and Brother Mark!' She swooped to cup his sleepy face in her hands for an instant, and quickly withdrew to surrender him generously to Meriet.

He had been out in the frost with her, and the cold had stung high colour into his cheeks. In the warmer air within the hut his dark, thick thatch of hair, still blessedly untonsured, dangled thawing over his brow, and he looked somewhat as Cadfael had first seen him, lighting down in the rain to hold his father's stirrup, stubborn and dutiful, when those two, so perilously alike, had been at odds over a mortal issue. But the face beneath the damp locks was mature and calm now, even resigned, acknowledging the burden of a weaker brother in need of loyalty. Not for his disastrous acts, but for his poor, faulty flesh and spirit.

'So we've lost you,' said Cadfael. 'If ever you'd come by choice I should have been glad of you, we can do with a man of action to leaven us. Brother Jerome needs a hand round his over-voluble throat now and again.'

Meriet had the grace to blush and the serenity to smile. 'I've made my peace with Brother Jerome, very civilly and humbly, you would have approved. I *hope* you would! He wished me well, and said he would continue to pray for me.'

'Did he, indeed!' In one who might grudgingly forgive an injury to his person, but seldom one to his dignity, that was handsome, and should be reckoned as credit to Jerome. Or was it simply that he was heartily glad to see the back of the devil's novice, and giving devout thanks after his own fashion?

'I was very young and foolish,' said Meriet, with a sage's indulgence for the green boy he had been, hugging to his grieving heart the keepsake of a girl he would live to hear unload upon him shamelessly the guilt of murder and theft. 'Do you remember,' asked Meriet, 'the few times I've ever called you "brother"? I was trying hard to get into the way of it. But it was not what I felt, or what I wanted to say. And now in the end it seems it's Mark I shall have to call "father", though he's the one I shall always think of as a brother. I was in need of fathering, more ways than one. This once, will you let me so claim and so call you as ... as I would have liked to then ...?'

'Son Meriet,' said Cadfael, rising heartily to embrace him and plant the formal kiss of kinship resoundingly on a cheek frostily cool and smooth, 'you're of my kin and welcome to whatsoever I have whenever you need it. And bear in mind, I'm Welsh, and that's a lifelong tie. There, are you satisfied?'

His kiss was returned, very solemnly and fervently, by cold lips that burned into ardent heat as they touched. But Meriet had yet one more request to make, and clung to Cadfael's hand as he advanced it.

'And will you, while he's here, extend the same goodness to my brother? For his need is greater than mine ever was.'

Withdrawn discreetly into shadow, Cadfael thought he heard Isouda utter a brief, soft spurt of laughter, and after it heave a resigned sigh; but if so, both escaped Meriet's ears.

'Child,' said Cadfael, shaking his head over such obstinate devotion, but very complacently, 'you are either an idiot or a saint, and I am not in the mood at present to have much patience with either. But for the sake of peace, yes, I will, I will! What I can do, I'll do. There, be off with you! Take him away, girl, and let me put out the brazier and shut up my workshop or I shall be late for Compline!'

Dead Man's Ransom

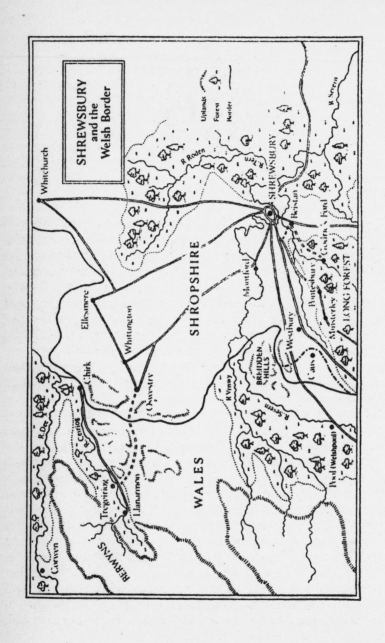

SHREWSBURY
and the
Welsh Border

Whitchurch

Uplands
Forest
Border

R. Roden

R. Tern

SHREWSBURY

R. Severn

Ellesmere

SHROPSHIRE

Whittington

Reabill

Condor Pool

Montford

Pontesbury

LONG FOREST

Chirk

Oswestry

Minsterley

R. Dee

Ceiriog

R. Vyrnwy

Westbury

BREIDDEN
HILLS

R. Ceiriog

Caus

Trefriw

R. Severn

Llansilin

Corwen

BERWYNS

WALES

Pool (Welshpool)

Chapter One

N THAT day, which was the seventh of February of
the year of Our Lord 1141, they had offered special
prayers at every office, not for the victory of one
party or the defeat of another in the battlefields of
the north, but for better counsel, for reconciliation, for the
sparing of blood-letting and the respect of life between men of
the same country – all desirable consummations, as Brother
Cadfael sighed to himself even as he prayed, but very unlikely
to be answered in this torn and fragmented land with any but a
very dusty answer. Even God needs some consideration and
support from his material to make reasoning and benign
creatures of men.

Shrewsbury had furnished King Stephen with a creditable
force to join his muster for the north, where the earls of
Chester and Lincoln, ambitious half-brothers, had flouted the
king's grace and moved to set up their own palatine, and with
much in their favour, too. The parish part of the great church
was fuller than usual even at the monastic offices, with anxious
wives, mothers and grandsires fervent in praying for their
menfolk. Not every man who had marched with Sheriff Gilbert
Prestcote and his deputy, Hugh Beringar, would come home
again unscathed to Shrewsbury. Rumours flew, but news was
in very poor supply. Yet word had filtered through that
Chester and Lincoln, long lurking in neutrality between rival
claimants for the crown, having ambitious plans of their own in
defiance of both, had made up their minds in short order when

355

menaced by King Stephen's approach, and sent hotfoot for help from the champions of his antagonist, the Empress Maud. Thus committing themselves for the future, perhaps, so deep that they might yet live to regret it.

Cadfael came out from Vespers gloomily doubting the force, and even the honesty of his own prayers, however he had laboured to give them heart. Men drunk with ambition and power do not ground their weapons, nor stop to recognise the fellow-humanity of those they are about to slay. Not here – not yet. Stephen had gone rampaging north with his muster, a huge, gallant, simple, swayable soul roused to rage by Chester's ungrateful treachery, and drawn after him many, and many a wiser and better-balanced man who could have done his reasoning for him, had he taken a little more time for thought. The issue hung in the balance and the good men of Shropshire were committed with their lord. So was Cadfael's close friend, Hugh Beringar of Maesbury, deputy sheriff of the shire, and his wife must be anxiously waiting there in the town for news. Hugh's son, a year old now, was Cadfael's godson, and he had leave to visit him whenever he wished, a godfather's duties being important and sacred. Cadfael turned his back on supper in the refectory, and made his way out of the abbey gates, along the highway between the abbey mill and mill-pond on his left, and the belt of woodland sheltering the main abbey gardens of the Gaye on his right, over the bridge that spanned the Severn, glimmering in the wintry, starlit frost, and in through the great town gate.

There were torches burning at the door of Hugh's house by Saint Mary's church and beyond, at the High Cross, it seemed to Cadfael that there were more folk abroad and stirring than was usual at this hour of a winter evening. The faintest shiver of excitement hung in the air, and as soon as his foot touched the doorstone Aline came flying to the doorway with open arms. When she knew him her face remained pleased and welcoming, but nonetheless lost in an instant its special burning brightness.

'Not Hugh!' said Cadfael ruefully, knowing for whom the door had been thus thrown wide. 'Not yet. Is there news, then? Are they homing?'

'Will Warden sent word an hour ago, before the light was quite gone. They sighted steel from the towers, a good way off then, but by now they must be in the castle foregate. The gate's open for them. Come in to the fire, Cadfael, and stay for him.'

She drew him in by the hands, and closed the door resolutely on the night and her own aching impatience. 'He is there,' she said, catching in Cadfael's face the reflection of her own partisan love and anxiety. 'They caught his colours. And the array in good order. Yet it cannot be quite as it went forth, that I know.'

No, never that. Those who go forth to the battle never return without holes in their ranks, like gaping wounds. Pity of all pities that those who lead never learn, and the few wise men among those who follow never quite avail to teach. But faith given and allegiance pledged are stronger than fear, thought Cadfael, and that, perhaps, is virtue, even in the teeth of death. Death, after all, is the common expectation from birth. Neither heroes nor cowards can escape it.

'He's sent no word ahead,' he asked, 'of how the day went?'

'None. But the rumour is it did not go well.' She said it firmly and freely, putting back with a small hand the pale gold hair from her forehead. A slender girl, still only twenty-one years old and mother of a year-old son and as fair as her husband was black-avised. The shy manner of her girlhood years had matured into a gentle dignity. 'This is a very wanton idea that flows and carries us all, here in England,' she said. 'It cannot always run one way, there must be an ebb.' She was brisk and practical about it, whatever that firm face cost her. 'You haven't eaten, you can't have stayed for supper,' she said, the housewife complete. 'Sit there and nurse your godson a little while, and I'll bring you meat and ale.'

The infant Giles, formidably tall for a year old when he was reared erect by holding to benches and trestles and chests to keep his balance, made his way carefully but with astonishing rapidity round the room to the stool by the fireside, and clambered unaided into Cadfael's rusty black lap. He had a flow of words, mostly of his own invention, though now and then a sound made sudden adult sense. His mother talked to him much, so did her woman Constance, his devoted slave, and this egg of the nobility listened and made voluble response. Of lordly scholars, thought Cadfael, rounding his arms to cradle the solid weight comfortably, we can never have too many. Whether he takes to the church or the sword, he'll never be the worse for a quick and ready mind. Like a pair of hound puppies nursed in the lap, Hugh's heir gave off glowing warmth, and the baked-bread scent of young and untainted flesh.

357

'He won't sleep,' said Aline, coming with a wooden tray to set it on the chest close to the fire, 'for he knows there's something in the wind. Never ask me how, I've said no word to him, but he knows. There, give him to me now, and take your meal. We may have a long wait, for they'll see all provided at the castle before ever Hugh comes to me.'

It was more than an hour before Hugh came. By then Constance had whisked away the remains of Cadfael's supper, and carried off a drooping princeling, who could not keep his eyes open any longer for all his contrivances, but slept in sprawled abandon in her arms as she lifted him. For all Cadfael's sharp hearing, it was Aline who first pricked up her head and rose, catching the light footsteps in the doorway. Her radiant smile faltered suddenly, for the feet trod haltingly.

'He's hurt!'

'Stiff from a long ride,' said Cadfael quickly. 'His legs serve him. Go, run, whatever's amiss will mend.'

She ran, and Hugh entered into her arms. As soon as she had viewed him from head to foot, weary and weather-stained as he was, and found him whole, whatever lesser injuries he might be carrying, she became demure, brisk and calm, and would make no extravagant show of anxiety, though she watched him every moment from behind the fair shield of her wifely face. A small man, lightly built, not much taller than his wife, black-haired, black-browed. His movements lacked their usual supple ease, and no wonder after so long in the saddle, and his grin was brief and wry as he kissed his wife, drove a fist warmly into Cadfael's shoulder, and dropped with a great, hoarse sigh on to the cushioned bench beside the fire, stretching out his booted feet gingerly, the right decidedly with some pain. Cadfael kneeled, and eased off the stiff, ice-rimmed boots that dripped melting rivulets into the rushes.

'Good Christian soul!' said Hugh, leaning to clap a hand on his friend's tonsure. 'I could never have reached them myself. God, but I'm weary! No matter, that's the first need met – they're home and so am I.'

Constance came sailing in with food and a hot posset of wine, Aline with his gown and to rid him of his leather coat. He had ridden light the last stages, shedding his mail. He scrubbed with both hands at cheeks stiffened from the cold, twitched his shoulders pleasurably in the warmth of the fire, and drew in a great, easing breath. They watched him eat and drink with hardly a word spoken. Even the voice stiffens and baulks after

358

long exertion and great weariness. When he was ready the cords of his throat would soften and warm, and words find their way out without creaking.

'Your man-child held open his eyelids,' said Aline cheerfully, eyeing his every least move as he ate and warmed, 'until he could prop them up no longer, even with his fingers. He's well and grown even in this short while – Cadfael will tell you. He goes on two feet now and makes nothing of a fall or two.' She did not offer to wake and bring him; clearly there was no place here tonight for matters of childhood, however dear.

Hugh sat back from his meal, yawned hugely, smiled upwards suddenly at his wife, and drew her down to him in his arm. Constance bore away the tray and refilled the cup, and closed the door quietly on the room where the boy slept.

'Never fret for me, love,' said Hugh, clasping Aline to his side. 'I'm saddle-sore and bruised, but nothing worse. But a fall or two we have certainly taken. No easy matter to rise, either. Oh, I've brought back most of the men we took north with us, but not all – not all! Not the chief – Gilbert Prestcote's gone. Taken, not dead, I hope and think, but whether it's Robert of Gloucester or the Welsh that hold him – I wish I knew.'

'The Welsh?' said Cadfael, pricking his ears. 'How's that? Owain Gwynedd has never put his hand in the fire for the empress? After all his careful holding off, and the gains it's brought him? He's no such fool! Why should he aid either of his enemies? He'd be more like to leave them free to cut each other's throats.'

'Spoke like a good Christian brother,' said Hugh, with a brief, grey smile, and fetched a grunt and a blush out of Cadfael to his small but welcome pleasure. 'No, Owain has judgement and sense, but alas for him, he has a brother. Cadwaladr was there with a swarm of his archers, and Madog ap Meredith of Powys with him, hot for plunder, and they've sunk their teeth into Lincoln and swept the field clear of any prisoner who promises the means of ransom, even the half-dead. And I doubt they've got Gilbert among the rest.' He shifted, easing his stiff, sore body in the cushions. 'Though it's not the Welsh,' he said grimly, 'that have got the greatest prize. Robert of Gloucester is halfway to his own city this night with a prisoner worth this kingdom to deliver up to the Empress Maud. God knows what follows now, but I know

359

what my work must be. My sheriff is out of the reckoning, and there's none now at large to name his successor. This shire is mine to keep, as best I may, and keep it I will, till fortune turns her face again. King Stephen is taken at Lincoln, and carried off prisoner to Gloucester.'

Once his tongue was loosed he had need to tell the whole of it, for his own enlightenment as much as theirs. He was the sole lord of a county now, holding and garrisoning it on the behalf of a king in eclipse, and his task was to nurse and guard it inviolate within its boundaries, until it could serve again beyond them for an effective lord.

'Ranulf of Chester slipped out of Lincoln castle and managed to get out of a hostile town before ever we got near, and off to Robert of Gloucester in a great hurry, with pledges of allegiance to the empress in exchange for help against us. And Chester's wife is Robert's daughter, when all's said, and he'd left her walled up in the castle with the earl of Lincoln and his wife, and the whole town in arms and seething round them. That was a welcome indeed, when Stephen got his muster there, the city fawned on him. Poor wretches, they've paid for it since. Howbeit, there we were, the town ours and the castle under siege, and winter on our side, any man would have said, with the distance Robert had to come, and the snow and the floods to hold him. But the man's none so easily held.'

'I never was there in the north,' said Cadfael, with a glint in his eye and a stirring in his blood that he had much ado to subdue. His days in arms were over, forsworn long since, but he could not help prickling to the sting of battle, when his friends were still venturing. 'It's a hill city, Lincoln, so they say. And the garrison penned close. It should have been easy to hold the town, Robert or no Robert. What went astray?'

'Why, granted we under-valued Robert, as always, but that need not have been fatal. The rains there'd been up there, the river round the south and west of the town was up in flood, the bridge guarded, and the ford impassable. But Robert passed it, whether or no! Into the flood with him, and what could they do but come after? "A way forward, but no way back!" he says – so one of our prisoners told us. And what with the solid wall of them, they got across with barely a man swept away. Oh, surely they still had the uphill way, out of that drowned plain to our hilltop – if Stephen were not Stephen! With the mass of them camped below in the wet fields and all the omens at Mass against him – you know he half-regards such warnings – what say you he'll do? Why, with that mad chivalry of his, for which God knows I love him though I curse him, he orders his array down from the height into the plain, to meet his enemy on equal terms.'

Hugh heaved his shoulders back against the solid brace of the wall, hoisted his agile brows and grinned, torn between admiration and exasperation.

'They'd drawn up on the highest and driest bit of land they could find, in what was a half-frozen marsh. Robert had all the disinherited, Maud's liegemen who had lost lands eastward for her sake, drawn up in the first line, horsed, with nothing to lose and all to gain, and vengeance the first of all. And our knights had every man his all to lose and nothing to gain, and felt themselves far from their homes and lands, and aching to get back and strengthen their own fences. And there were these hordes of Welsh, hungry for plunder, and their own goods and gear safe as sanctuary in the west, with no man threatening. What should we look for? When the disinherited hit our horse five earls broke under the shock and ran. On the left Stephen's Flemings drove the Welshmen back; but you know their way, they went but far enough and easily enough to mass again without loss, and back they came, archers almost to a man, able to pick their ground and their prey, and when the Flemish footmen ran, so did their captains – William of Ypres and Ten Eyck and all. Stephen was left unhorsed with us, the remnant of his horse and foot, around him. They rolled over us. It was then I lost sight of Gilbert. No marvel, it was hand to hand chaos, no man saw beyond the end of his sword or dagger, whatever he had in his hand to keep his head. Stephen still had his sword then. Cadfael, I swear to you, you never saw such a man in battle once roused, for all his easy goodwill takes so much rousing. It was rather the siege of a castle than the overcoming of a man. There was a wall round him of the men he had slain, those coming had to clamber over it, and went to build it higher. Chester came after him – give him his due, there's not much can frighten Ranulf – and he might have been another stone in the rampart, but that the king's sword shattered. There was one somewhere close to him thrust a Danish axe into his hand in its place, but Chester had leaped back out of reach. And then someone clear of the mêlée grubbed a great stone out of the ground, and hurled it at Stephen from aside. It struck him down flatlings, clean out of his wits, and they swarmed over him and pinned him hand and foot while he was senseless. And I went down under another wave,' said Hugh ruefully, 'and was trampled below better men's bodies, to come to myself in the best time to make vantage of it, after they'd dragged the king away and swarmed into the town to strip it bare, and before they came back to comb the battlefield for whatever was worth picking up. So I mustered what was left of our own, more than ever I expected, and hauled them off far enough to be out of reach, while I and one or two with me looked for Gilbert. We did not find him and when they began to come back sated out of the city, scavenging, we drew off to bring back such as we had. What else could we have done?'

'Nothing to any purpose,' said Cadfael firmly. 'And thanks to God you were brought out man alive to do so much. If there's a place Stephen needs you now, it's here, keeping this shire for him.'

He was talking to himself, Hugh knew that already, or he would never have withdrawn from Lincoln. As for the slaughter there, no word was said. Better to make sure of bringing back all but a few of the solid townsfolk of Shrewsbury, his own special charge, and so he had done.

'Stephen's queen is in Kent and mistress of Kent, with a strong army, all the south and the east she holds,' said Hugh. 'She will shift every stone between her and London, but she'll get Stephen out of captivity somehow. It is not an ending. A reverse can be reversed. A prisoner can be loosed from prison.'

'Or exchanged,' said Cadfael, but very dubious. 'There's no great prize taken on the king's side? Though I doubt if the empress would let go of Stephen for any three of her best lords, even Robert himself, helpless as she'd be without him. No, she'll keep a fast hold of her prisoner, and make headlong for the throne. And do you see the princes of the church standing long in her way?'

'Well,' said Hugh, stretching his slight body wincingly, discovering new bruises, 'my part at least I know. It's my writ that runs here in Shropshire now as the king's writ, and I'll see to it this shire, at least, is kept for the king.'

He came down to the abbey, two days later, to attend the Mass Abbot Radulfus had decreed for the souls of all those dead at Lincoln, on both parts, and for the healing of England's raw and festering wounds. In particular there were prayers to be offered for the wretched citizens of the northern city, prey to vengeful armies and plundered of all they had, many even of their lives, and many more fled into the wilds of the winter countryside. Shropshire stood nearer to the fighting now than it had been for three years, being neighbour to an earl of Chester elated by success and greedy for still more lands. Every one of Hugh's depleted garrison stood to arms, ready to defend its threatened security.

They were out from Mass, and Hugh had lingered in speech with the abbot in the great court, when there was sudden bustle in the arch of the gatehouse, and a small procession entered from the Foregate. Four sturdy countrymen in homespun came striding confidently, two with bows strung and slung ready for action, one shouldering a billhook, and the fourth a long-handled pikel. Between them, with two of her escort on either side, rode a plump middle-aged woman on a diminutive mule, and wearing the black habit of a Benedictine nun. The white bands of her wimple framed a rounded rosy face, well-fleshed and well-boned, and lit by a pair of bright brown eyes. She was booted like a man, and her habit kilted for riding, but she swung it loose with one motion of a broad hand as she dismounted, and stood alert and discreet, looking calmly about her in search of someone in authority.

'We have a visiting sister,' said the abbot mildly, eyeing her with interest, 'but one that I do not know.'

Brother Cadfael, crossing the court without haste towards the garden and the herbarium, had also marked the sudden brisk bustle at the gate, and checked at the sight of a well-remembered figure. He had encountered this lady once before, and found her well worth remembering. And it seemed that she, also, recalled their meeting with pleasure, for the moment her eyes lit upon him the spark of recognition flashed in them, and she came at once towards him. He went to meet her gladly. Her rustic bodyguard, satisfied at having delivered her successfully where she would be, stood by the gatehouse, straddling the cobbles complacently, and by no means intimidated or impressed by their surroundings.

'I thought I should know that gait,' said the lady with satisfaction. 'You are Brother Cadfael, who came once on business to our cell. I'm glad to have found you to hand, I know no one else here. Will you make me known to your abbot?'

'Proudly,' said Cadfael, 'and he's regarding you this minute from the corner of the cloister. It's two years now ... Am I to tell him he's honoured by a visit from Sister Avice?'

'Sister Magdalen,' she said demurely and faintly smiled; and when she smiled, however briefly and decorously, the sudden dazzling dimple he remembered flashed like a star in her weathered cheek. He had wondered then whether she had not better find some way of exorcising it in her new vocation, or whether it might not still be the most formidable weapon in her armoury. He was aware that he blinked, and that she noted it. There was always something conspiratorial in Avice of Thornbury that made every man feel he was the only one in whom she confided. 'And my errand,' she said practically, 'is really to Hugh Beringar, for I hear Gilbert Prestcote did not come back from Lincoln. They told us in the Foregate we should find him here, or we were bound up to the castle to look for him.'

'He is here,' said Cadfael, 'fresh from Mass, and talking with Abbot Radulfus. Over my shoulder you'll see them both.'

She looked, and by the expression of her face she approved. Abbot Radulfus was more than commonly tall, erect as a lance, and sinewy, with a lean hawk-face and a calmly measuring eye; and Hugh, if he stood a whole head shorter and carried but light weight, if he spoke quietly and made no move to call attention to himself, nevertheless seldom went unnoticed. Sister Magdalen studied him from head to heel with one flash of her brown eyes. She was a judge of a man, and knew one when she saw him.

'Very well so!' she said, nodding. 'Come, and I'll pay my respects.'

Radulfus marked their first move towards him and went to meet them, with Hugh at his shoulder.

'Father Abbot,' said Cadfael, 'here is come Sister Magdalen of our order, from the cell of Polesworth which lies some miles to the south-west, in the forest at Godric's Ford. And her business is also with Hugh Beringar as sheriff of this shire.'

She made a very graceful reverence and stooped to the abbot's hand. 'Truly, what I have to tell concerns all here who have to do with order and peace, Father. Brother Cadfael here has visited our cell, and knows how we stand in these troublous times, solitary and so close to Wales. He can advise and explain, if I fall short.'

'You are welcome, sister,' said Radulfus, measuring her as shrewdly as she had measured him. 'Brother Cadfael shall be

of our counsel; I trust you will be my guest for dinner. And for
your guards – for I see they are devoted in attendance on you –
I will give orders for their entertainment. And if you are not so
far acquainted, here at my side is Hugh Beringar, whom you
seek.'

Though that cheek was turned away from him, Cadfael was
certain that her dimple sparkled as she turned to Hugh and
made her formal acknowledgement. 'My lord, I was never so
happy,' she said – and whether that was high courtesy or
mischief might still be questioned – 'as to meet with you
before, it was with your sheriff I once had some speech. As I
have heard he did not return with you and may be prisoner,
and for that I am sorry.'

'I, too,' said Hugh. 'As I hope to redeem him, if chance
offers. I see from your escort, sister, that you have had cause to
move with caution through the forest. I think that is also my
business, now I am back.'

'Let us go into my parlour,' said the abbot, 'and hear what
Sister Magdalen has to tell us. And, Brother Cadfael, will you
bear word to Brother Denis that the best of our house is at the
disposal of our sister's guards? And then come to join us, for
your knowledge may be needed.'

She was seated a little withdrawn from the fire when Cadfael
entered the abbot's parlour some minutes later, her feet drawn
trimly under the hem of her habit, her back erect against the
panelled wall. The more closely and the longer he viewed her,
the more warmly did he remember her. She had been for many
years, from her beautiful youth, a baron's mistress, accepting
that situation as an honest business agreement, a fair return for
her body to give her escape from her poverty and cultivation
for her mind. And she had held to her bargain loyally, even
affectionately, as long as her lord remained alive. The loss of
one profession offering scope for her considerable talents had
set her looking about, with her customary resolution, for
another as rewarding, at an age when such openings may be
few indeed. The superior at Godric's Ford, first, and the
prioress of Polesworth after, however astonished they might
have been at being confronted with such a postulant, must
have seen something in Avice of Thornbury well worth
acquiring for the order. A woman of her word, ungrudging, to
her first allegiance, she would be as good as her word now to
this new attachment. Whether it could have been called a

vocation in the first place might seem very doubtful, but with application and patience she would make it so.

'When this matter of Lincoln blazed up as it did in January,' she said, 'we got rumour that certain of the Welsh were ready to rise in arms. Not, I suppose, for any partisan loyalty, but for plunder to be had when these two powers collided. Prince Cadwaladr of Gwynedd was mustering a war-band, and the Welsh of Powys rose to join him, and it was said they would march to aid the earl of Chester. So before the battle we had our warning.'

It was she who had heeded it. Who else, in that small nest of holy women, could have sensed how the winds blew between claimants for the crown, between Welsh and English, between ambitious earl and greedy tribesman?

'Therefore, Father, it was no great surprise to us, some four days ago, when a lad from an assart west of us came running in haste to tell us how his father's cot and holding was laid waste, his family fled eastward, and how a Welsh raiding party was drinking its fill in what remained of his home, and boasting how it would disembowel the nunnery of Godric's Ford. Huntsmen on their way home will not despise a few stray head of game to add to their booty. We had not the news of the defeat of Lincoln then,' she said, meeting Hugh's attentive gaze, 'but we made our judgements accordingly and took heed. Cadwaladr's shortest way home with his plunder to his castle at Aberystwyth skirts Shrewsbury close. Seemingly he still feared to come too near the town, even with the garrison thinned as he knew it must be. But he felt safer with us in the forest. And with only a handful of women to deal with, it was worth his while to spend a day in sport, and strip us bare.'

'And this was four days ago?' asked Hugh, sharply intent.

'Four when the boy came. He's safe enough, and so is his sire, but their cattle are gone, driven off westward. Three days, when they reached us. We had a day to prepare.'

'This was a despicable undertaking,' said Radulfus with anger and disgust, 'to fasten like cowards upon a household of defenceless women. Great shame to the Welsh or any others who attempt such infamies. And we here knowing nothing of your need!'

'Never fear, Father, we have weathered this storm well enough. Our house yet stands, and has not been plundered, nor harm come to any of our women, and barely a scratch or two among the forest menfolk. And we were not quite

366

defenceless. They came on the western side, and our brook runs between. Brother Cadfael knows the lie of the land there.'

'The brook would be a very frail barrier most of the year,' said Cadfael doubtfully. 'but we have had great rains this winter season. But there's both the ford and the bridge to guard.'

'True, but it takes no time there among good neighbours to raise a very fair muster. We are well thought of among the forest folk, and they are stout men.' Four of the stout men of her army were regaling themselves in the gatehouse with meat and bread and ale at this moment, proud and content, set up in their own esteem, very properly, by their own exploits. 'The brook was high in flood already, but we contrived to pit the ford, in case they should still venture it, and then John Miller opened up all his sluices to swell the waters. As for the bridge, we sawed through the wood of the piers, leaving them only the last holt, and fastened ropes from them into the bushes. You'll recall the banks are well treed both sides. We could pluck the piers loose from cover whenever we saw fit. And all the men of the forest came with bills and dung-forks and bows to line our bank, and deal with any who did get over.'

No question who had generalled that formidable reception. There she sat, solid, placid and comely, like a well-blessed village matron talking of the doings of her children and grandchildren, fond and proud of their precocious achievements, but too wise to let them see it.

'The foresters,' she said, 'are as good archers as you will find anywhere, we had them spaced among the trees, all along our bank. And the men of the other bank were drawn aside in cover, to speed the enemy's going when he ran.'

The abbot was regarding her with a warily respectful face, and brows that signalled his guarded wonder. 'I recall,' he said, 'that Mother Mariana is old and frail. This attack must have caused her great distress and fear. Happy for her that she had you, and could delegate her powers to so stout and able a deputy.'

Sister Magdalen's benign smile might, Cadfael thought, be discreet cover for her memory of Mother Mariana distracted and helpless with dread at the threat. But all she said was, 'Our superior was not well at that time, but praise be, she is now restored. We entreated her to take with her the elder sisters, and shut themselves up in the chapel, with such sacred

367

valuables as we have, and there to pray for our safe deliverance. Which doubtless availed us above our bills and bows, for all passed without harm to us.'

'Yet their prayers did not turn the Welsh back short of the planned attempt, I doubt,' said Hugh, meeting her guileless eyes with an appreciative smile. 'I see I shall have to mend a few fences down there. What followed? You say all fell out well. You used those ropes of yours?'

'We did. They came thick and fast, we let them load the bridge almost to the near bank, and then plucked the piers loose. Their first wave went down into the flood, and a few who tried the ford lost their footing in our pits, and were swept away. And after our archers had loosed their first shafts, the Welsh turned tail. The lads we had in cover on the other side took after them and sped them on their way. John Miller has closed his sluices now. Give us a couple of dry weeks, and we'll have the bridge up again. The Welsh left three men dead, drowned in the brook, the rest they hauled out half-sodden, and dragged them away with them when they ran. All but one, and he's the occasion for this journey of mine. There's a very fine young fellow,' she said, 'was washed downstream, and we pulled him out bloated with water and far gone, if we had not emptied him, and pounded him alive to tell the tale. You may send and take him off our hands whenever you please. Things being as it seems they are, you may well have a use for him.'

'For any Welsh prisoner,' said Hugh, glowing. 'Where have you stowed him?'

'John Miller has him under lock and key and guarded. I did not venture to try and bring him to you, for good reason. He's sudden as a kingfisher and slippery as a fish, and short of tying him hand and foot I doubt if we could have held him.'

'We'll undertake to bring him away safely,' said Hugh heartily. 'What manner of man do you make of him? And has he given you a name?'

'He'll say no word but in Welsh, and I have not the knowledge of that tongue, nor has any of us. But he's young, princely provided, and lofty enough in his manner to be princely born, no common kern. He may prove valuable if it comes to an exchange.'

'I'll come and fetch him away tomorrow,' promised Hugh, 'and thank you for him heartily. By morning I'll have a company ready to ride. As well I should look to all that border, and if you can bide overnight, sister, we can escort you home in safety.'

'Indeed it would be wise,' said the abbot. 'Our guest-hall and all we have is open to you, and your neighbours who have done you such good service are equally welcome. Far better return with the assurance of numbers and arms. Who knows if there may not be marauding parties still lurking in the forest, if they're grown so bold?'

'I doubt it,' she said. 'We saw no sign of it on the way here. It was the men themselves would not let me venture alone. But I will accept your hospitality, Father, with pleasure, and be as grateful for your company, my lord,' she said, smiling thoughtfully at Hugh, 'on the way home.'

'Though, faith,' said Hugh to Cadfael, as they crossed the court together, leaving Sister Magdalen to dine as the abbot's guest, 'it would rather become me to give her the generalship of all the forest than offer her any protection of mine. We should have had her at Lincoln, where our enemies crossed the floods, as hers failed to do. Riding south with her tomorrow will certainly be pleasure, it might well be profit. I'll bend a devout ear to any counsel that lady chooses to dispense.'

'You'll be giving pleasure as well as receiving it,' said Cadfael frankly. 'She may have taken vows of chastity, and what she swears she'll keep. But she has not sworn never to take delight in the looks and converse and company of a proper man. I doubt they'll ever bring her to consent to that, she'd think it a waste and a shame, so to throw God's good gifts in his teeth.'

The party mustered after Prime next morning, Sister Magdalen and her four henchmen, Hugh and his half-dozen armed guards from the castle garrison. Brother Cadfael stood to watch them gather and mount, and took a warmly appreciative leave of the lady.

'I doubt I shall be hard put to it, though,' he admitted, 'to learn to call you by your new name.'

At that her dimple dipped and flashed, and again vanished. 'Ah, that! You are thinking that I never yet repented of anything I did – and I confess I don't recall such a thing myself. No, but it was such a comfort and satisfaction to the women. They took me to their hearts so joyfully, the sweet things, a fallen sister retrieved. I couldn't forbear giving them what they wanted and thought fitting. I am their special pride, they boast of me.'

369

'Well they may,' said Cadfael, 'seeing you just drove back pillage, ravishment and probable murder from their nest.'

'Ah, that they feel to be somewhat unwomanly, though glad enough of the result. The doves were all aflutter – but then, I was never a dove,' said Sister Magdalen, 'and it's only the men truly admire the hawk in me.'

And she smiled, mounted her little mule and rode off homeward surrounded by men who already admired her, and men who were more than willing to offer admiration. In the court or in the cloister, Avice of Thornbury would never pass by without turning men's heads to follow her.

Chapter Two

EFORE NIGHTFALL Hugh was back with his prisoner, having prospected the western fringe of the Long Forest and encountered no more raiding Welshmen and no masterless men living wild. Brother Cadfael saw them pass by the abbey gatehouse on their way up through the town to the castle, where this possibly valuable Welsh youth could be held in safe-keeping and, short of a credible parole, doubtless under lock and key in some sufficiently impenetrable cell. Hugh could not afford to lose him.

Cadfael caught but a passing glimpse of him as they rode by in the early dusk. It seemed he had given some trouble on the way, for his hands were tied, his horse on a leading rein, his feet roped into the stirrups and an archer rode suggestively close at his rear. If these precautions were meant to secure him, they had succeeded, but if to intimidate, as the young man himself appeared to suppose, they had signally failed, for he went with a high, disdainful impudence, stretching up tall and whistling as he went, and casting over his shoulder at the archer occasional volleys of Welsh, which the man might not have endured so stolidly had he been able to understand their purport as well as Cadfael did. He was, in fact, a very forward and uppish young fellow, this prisoner, though it might have been partly bravado.

He was also a very well-looking young man, middling tall for a Welshman, with the bold cheekbones and chin and the ruddy

371

colouring of his kind, and a thick tangle of black curls that fell very becomingly about his brow and ears, blown by the south-west wind, for he wore no cap. Tethered hands and feet did not hamper him from sitting his horse like a centaur, and the voice that teased his guards in insolent Welsh was light and clear. Sister Magdalen had said truly that his gear was princely, and his manner proclaimed him certainly proud and probably, thought Cadfael, spoiled to the point of ruin. Not a particularly rare condition in a well-made, personable and probably only son.

They passed, and the prisoner's loud, melodious whistle of defiance died gradually along the Foregate and over the bridge. Cadfael went back to his workshop in the herbarium, and blew up his brazier to boil a fresh elixir of horehound for the winter coughs and colds.

Hugh came down from the castle next morning with a request to borrow Brother Cadfael on his captive's behalf, for it seemed the boy had a raw gash in his thigh, ripped against a stone in the flood, and had gone to some pains to conceal it from the nuns.

'Ask me,' said Hugh, grinning, 'he'd have died rather than bare his hams for the ladies to poultice. And give him his due, though the tear is none so grave, the few miles he rode yesterday must have cost him dear in pain, and he never gave a sign. And blushed like a girl when we did notice him favouring the raw cheek, and made him strip.'

'And left his sore undressed overnight? Never tell me! So why do you need me?' asked Cadfael shrewdly.

'Because you speak good Welsh, and Welsh of the north, and he's certainly from Gwynedd, one of Cadwaladr's boys – though you may as well make the lad comfortable while you're about it. We speak English to him, and he shakes his head and answers with nothing but Welsh, but for all that, there's a saucy look in his eye that tells me he understands very well, and is having a game with us. So come and speak English to him, and trip the bold young sprig headlong when he thinks his Welsh insults can pass for civilities.'

'He'd have had short shrift from Sister Magdalen,' said Cadfael thoughtfully, 'if she'd known of his hurt. All his blushes wouldn't have saved him.' And he went off willingly enough to see Brother Oswin properly instructed as to what needed attention in the workshop, before setting out with

Hugh to the castle. A fair share of curiosity, and a little over-measure, was one of the regular items of his confessions. And, after all, he was a Welshman; somewhere in the tangled genealogies of his nation, this obdurate boy might be his distant kin.

They had a healthy respect for their prisoner's strength, wit and ingenuity, and had him in a windowless cell, though decently provided. Cadfael went in to him alone, and heard the door locked upon them. There was a lamp, a floating wick in a saucer of oil, sufficient for seeing, since the pale stone of the walls reflected the light from all sides. The prisoner looked askance at the Benedictine habit, unsure what this visit predicted. In answer to what was clearly a civil greeting in English, he replied as courteously in Welsh, but in answer to everything else he shook his dark head apologetically, and professed not to understand a word of it. He responded readily enough, however, when Cadfael unpacked his scrip and laid out his salves and cleansing lotions and dressings. Perhaps he had found good reason in the night to be glad of having submitted his wound to tending, for this time he stripped willingly, and let Cadfael renew the dressing. He had aggravated his hurt with riding, but rest would soon heal it. He had pure, spare flesh, lissome and firm. Under the skin the ripple of muscles was smooth as cream.

'You were foolish to bear this,' said Cadfael in casual English, 'when you could have had it healed and forgotten by now. Are you a fool? In your situation you'll have to learn discretion.'

'From the English,' said the boy in Welsh, and still shaking his head to show he understood no word of this, 'I have nothing to learn. And no, I am not a fool, or I should be as talkative as you, old shaven-head.'

'They would have given you good nursing at Godric's Ford,' went on Cadfael innocently. 'You wasted your few days there.'

'A parcel of silly women,' said the boy, brazen-faced, 'and old and ugly into the bargain.'

That was more than enough. 'A parcel of women,' said Cadfael in loud and indignant Welsh, 'who pulled you out of the flood and squeezed your lordship dry, and pummelled the breath back into you. And if you cannot find a civil word of thanks to them, in a language they'll understand, you are the most ungrateful brat who ever disgraced Wales. And that you

373

may know it, my fine paladin, there's nothing older nor uglier than ingratitude. Nor sillier, either, seeing I'm minded to rip that dressing off you and let you burn for the graceless limb you are.'

The young man was bolt upright on his stone bench by this time, his mouth fallen open, his half-formed, comely face stricken into childishness. He stared and swallowed, and slowly flushed from breast to brow.

'Three times as Welsh as you, idiot child,' said Cadfael, cooling, 'being three times your age, as I judge. Now get your breath and speak, and speak English, for I swear if you ever speak Welsh to me again, short of extremes, I'll off and leave you to your own folly, and you'll find that cold company. Now, have we understood each other?'

The boy hovered for an instant on the brink of humiliation and rage, being unaccustomed to such falls, and then as abruptly redeemed himself by throwing back his head and bursting into a peal of laughter, both rueful for his own folly and appreciative of the trap into which he had stepped so blithely. Blessedly, he had the native good-nature that prevented his being quite spoiled.

'That's better,' said Cadfael disarmed. 'Fair enough to whistle and swagger to keep up your courage, but why pretend you know no English? So close to the border, how long before you were bound to be smoked out?'

'Even a day or two more,' sighed the young man resignedly, 'and I might have found out what's in store for me.' His command of English was fluent enough, once he had consented to use it. 'I'm new to this, I wanted to get my bearings.'

'And the impudence was to stiffen your sinews, I suppose. Shame to miscall the holy women who saved your saucy life for you.'

'No one was meant to hear and understand,' protested the prisoner, and in the next breath owned magnanimously: 'But I'm not proud of it, either. A bird in a net, pecking every way, as much for spite as for escape. And then I didn't want to give away any word of myself until I had my captor's measure.'

'Or to admit to your value,' Cadfael hazarded shrewdly, 'for fear you should be held against a high ransom. No name, no rank, no way of putting a price on you?'

The black head nodded. He eyed Cadfael, and visibly debated within himself how much to concede, even now he was found out, and then as impulsively flung open the floodgates and let the words come hurtling out. 'To tell truth, long before ever we made that assault on the nunnery I'd grown very uneasy about the whole wild affair. Owain Gwynedd knew nothing of his brother's muster, and he'll be displeased with us all, and when Owain's displeased I mind my walking very carefully. Which is what I did *not* do when I went with Cadwaladr. I wish heartily that I had, and kept out of it. I never wanted to do harm to your ladies, but how could I draw back once I was in? And then to let myself be taken! By a handful of old women and peasants! I shall be in black displeasure at home, if not a laughing-stock.' He sounded disgusted rather than downcast, and shrugged and grinned good-naturedly at the thought of being laughed at, but for all that, the prospect was painful. 'And if I'm to cost Owain high, there's another black stroke against me. He's not the man to take delight in paying out gold to buy back idiots.'

Certainly this young man improved upon acquaintance. He turned honestly and manfully from wanting to kick everyone else to acknowledging that he ought to be kicking himself. Cadfael warmed to him.

'Let me drop a word in your ear. The higher your value, the more welcome will you be to Hugh Beringar, who holds you here. And not for gold, either. There's a lord, the sheriff of this shire, who is most likely prisoner in Wales as you are here, and Hugh Beringar wants him back. If you can balance him, and he is found to be there alive, you may well be on your way home. At no cost to Owain Gwynedd, who never wanted to dip his fingers into that trough, and will be glad to show it by giving Gilbert Prestcote back to us.'

'You mean it?' The boy had brightened and flushed, wide-eyed. 'Then I should speak? I'm in a fair way to get my release and please both Welsh and English? That would be better deliverance than ever I expected.'

'Or deserved!' said Cadfael roundly, and watched the smooth brown neck stiffen in offence, and then suddenly relax again, as the black curls tossed and the ready grin appeared. 'Ah, well, you'll do! Tell your tale now, while I'm here, for I'm mightily curious, but tell it once. Let me fetch in Hugh Beringar, and let's all come to terms. Why lie here on stone and all but in the dark, when you could be stretching your legs about the castle wards?'

'I'm won!' said the boy, hopefully shining. 'Bring me to confession, and I'll hold nothing back.'

Once his mind was made up he spoke up cheerfully and volubly, an outward soul by nature, and very poorly given to silence. His abstention must have cost him prodigies of self-control. Hugh listened to him with an unrevealing face, but Cadfael knew by now how to read every least twitch of those lean, live brows and every glint in the black eyes.

'My name is Elis ap Cynan, my mother was cousin to Owain Gwynedd. He is my overlord, and he has over-watched me in the fosterage where he placed me when my father died. That is with my uncle Griffith ap Meilyr, where I grew up with my cousin Eliud as brothers. Griffith's wife is also distant kin to the prince, and Griffith ranks high among his officers. Owain values us. He will not willingly leave me in captivity,' said the young man sturdily.

'Even though you hared off after his brother to a battle in which he wanted no part?' said Hugh, unsmiling but mild of voice.

'Even so,' persisted Elis firmly. 'Though if truth must out, I wish I never had, and am like to wish it even more earnestly when I must go back and face him. He'll have my hide, as like as not.' But he did not sound particularly depressed at the thought, and his sudden grin, tentative here in Hugh's untested presence, nevertheless would out for a moment. 'I was a fool. Not for the first time and I daresay not the last. Eliud had more sense. He's grave and deep, he thinks like Owain. It was the first time we ever went different ways. I wish now I'd listened to him. I never knew him to be wrong when it came to it. But I was greedy to see action, and pig-headed, and I went.'

'And did you like the action you saw?' asked Hugh drily.

Elis gnawed a considering lip. 'The battle, that was fair fight, all in arms on both parts. You were there? Then you know yourself it was a great thing we did, crossing the river in flood, and standing to it in that frozen marsh as we were, sodden and shivering ...' That exhilarating memory had suddenly recalled to him the second such crossing attempted, and its less heroic ending, the reverse of the dream of glory. Fished out like a drowning kitten, and hauled back to life face-down in muddy turf, hiccuping up the water he had swallowed, and being squeezed between the hands of a brawny forester. He caught Hugh's eye, and saw his own recollection reflected there, and had the grace to grin. 'Well, flood-water is on no man's side, it gulps down Welsh as readily as English. But I was not sorry then, not at Lincoln. It was a good fight. Afterwards – no – the town turned my stomach. If I'd known before, I should not have been there. But I was there, and I couldn't undo it.'

'You were sick at what was done to Lincoln,' Hugh pointed out reasonably, 'yet you went with the raiders to sack Godric's Ford.'

'What was I to do? Draw out against the lot of them, my own friends and comrades, stick my nose in the air and tell them what they intended was vile? I'm no such hero!' said Elis openly and heartily. 'Still, you'll allow I did no harm there to anyone, as it fell out. I was taken, and if it please you to say, serve me right, I'll take no offence. The end of it is, here I am and at your disposal. And I'm kin to Owain and when he knows I'm living he'll want me back.'

'Then you and I may very well come to a sensible agreement,' said Hugh, 'for I think it very likely that my sheriff, whom I want back just as certainly, is prisoner in Wales as you are here, and if that proves true, an exchange should be no great problem. I've no wish to keep you under lock and key in a cell, if you'll behave yourself seemly and wait the outcome. It's your quickest way home. Give me your parole not to attempt escape, or to go outside the wards here, and you may have the run of the castle.'

'With all my heart!' said Elis eagerly. 'I pledge you my word to attempt nothing, and set no foot outside your gates, until you have your man again, and give me leave to go.'

Cadfael paid a second visit next day, to make sure that his dressing had drawn the Welsh boy's ragged scratch together with no festering; but that healthy young flesh sprang together like the matching of lovers, and the slash would vanish with barely a scar.

He was an engaging youth, this Elis ap Cynan, readable like a book, open like a daisy at noon. Cadfael lingered to draw him out, which was easy enough, and brought a lavish and guileless harvest. All the more with nothing now to lose, and no man listening but a tolerant elder of his own race, he unfolded his leaves in garrulous innocence.

'I fell out badly with Eliud over this caper,' he said ruefully. 'He said it was poor policy for Wales, and whatever booty we might bring back with us, it would not be worth half the damage done. I should have known he'd be proved right, he always is. And yet no offence in it, that's the marvel! A man can't be angry with him – at least I can't.'

'Kin by fostering can be as close as brothers by blood, I know,' said Cadfael.

'Closer far than most brothers. Like twins, as we almost could be. Eliud had half an hour's start of me into the world, and has acted the elder ever since. He'll be half out of his wits over me now, for all he'll hear is that I was swept away in the brook. I wish we might make haste with this exchange, and let him know I'm still alive to plague him.'

'No doubt there'll be others besides your friend and cousin,' said Cadfael, 'fretting over your absence. No wife as yet?'

Elis made an urchin's grimace. 'No more than threatened. My elders betrothed me long ago as a child, but I'm in no haste. The common lot, it's what men do when they grow to maturity. There are lands and alliances to be considered.' He spoke of it as of the burden of the years, accepted but not welcomed. Quite certainly he was not in love with the lady. Probably he had known and played with her from infancy, and scarcely gave her a thought now, one way or the other.

'She may yet be a deal more troubled for you than you are for her,' said Cadfael.

'Ha!' said Elis on a sharp bark of laughter. 'Not she! If I had drowned in the brook they'd have matched her with another of suitable birth, and he would have done just as well. She never chose me, nor I her. Mind, I don't say she makes any objections, more than I do, we might both of us do very much worse.'

'Who is this fortunate lady?' Cadfael wondered drily.

'Now you grow prickly, because I am honest,' Elis reproved him airily. 'Did I ever say I was any great bargain? The girl is very well, as a matter of fact, a small, sharp, dark creature, quite handsome in her way, and if I must, then she'll do. Her father is Tudur ap Rhys, the lord of Tregeiriog in Cynllaith – a man of Powys, but close friend to Owain and thinks like him, and her mother was a woman of Gwynedd. Cristina, the girl is called. Her hand is regarded as a great prize,' said the proposed beneficiary without enthusiasm. 'So it is, but one I could have done without for a while yet.'

They were walking the outer ward to keep warm, for though the weather had turned fine it was also frosty, and the boy was loth to go indoors until he must. He went with his face turned up to the clear sky above the towers, and his step as light and springy as if he trod turf already.

378

'We could save you yet a while,' suggested Cadfael slyly, 'by spinning out this quest for our sheriff, and keeping you here single and snug as long as you please.'

'Oh, no!' Elis loosed a shout of laughter. 'Oh, no, not that! Better a wife in Wales than that fashion of freedom here. Though best of all Wales and no wife,' admitted the reluctant bridegroom, still laughing at himself. 'Marry or avoid, I suppose, it's all one in the end. There'll still be hunting and arms and friends.'

A poor lookout, thought Cadfael, shaking his head, for that small, sharp, dark creature, Cristina daughter of Tudur, if she required more of her husband than a good-looking adolescent boy, willing to tolerate and accommodate her, but quite indisposed to love. Though many a decent marriage has started on no better ground, and burned into a glow later.

They had reached the archway into the inner ward in their circlings, and the slanting sunlight, chill and bright, shone through across their path. High in the corner tower within there, Gilbert Prestcote had made his family apartments, rather than maintain a house in the town. Between the merlons of the curtain wall the sun just reached the narrow doorway that led to the private rooms above, and the girl who emerged stepped full into the light. She was the very opposite of small, sharp and dark, being tall and slender like a silver birch, delicately oval of face, and dazzlingly fair. The sun in her uncovered, waving hair glittered as she hesitated an instant on the doorstone, and shivered lightly at the embrace of the frosty air.

Elis had seen her shimmering pallor take the light, and stood stock-still, gazing through the archway with eyes rounded and fixed, and mouth open. The girl hugged her cloak about her, closed the door at her back, and stepped out briskly across the ward towards the arch on her way out to the town. Cadfael had to pluck Elis by the sleeve to bring him out of his daze, and draw him onward out of her path, recalling him to the realisation that he was staring with embarrassing intensity, and might well give her offence if she noticed him. He moved obediently, but in a few more paces his chin went round on to his shoulder, and he checked again and stood, and could not be shifted further.

She came through the arch, half-smiling for pleasure in the fine morning, but still with something grave, anxious and sad in her countenance. Elis had not removed himself far enough to pass unobserved, she felt a presence close, and turned her head sharply. There was a brief moment when their eyes met, hers darkly blue as periwinkle flowers. The rhythm of her gait was broken, she checked at his gaze, and it almost seemed that she smiled at him hesitantly, as at someone recognised. Fine rose-colour mounted softly in her face, before she recollected herself, tore her gaze away, and went on more hurriedly towards the barbican.

Elis stood looking after her until she had passed through the gate and vanished from sight. His own face had flooded richly red.

'Who was that lady?' he asked, at once urgent and in awe.

'That lady,' said Cadfael, 'is daughter to the sheriff, that very man we're hoping to find somewhere alive in Welsh hold, and buy back with your captive person. Prestcote's wife is come to Shrewsbury on that very matter, and brought her step-daughter and her little son with her, in hopes soon to greet her lord again. This is his second lady. The girl's mother died without bringing him a son.

'Do you know her name? The girl?'

'Her name,' said Cadfael, 'is Melicent.'

'Melicent!' the boy's lips shaped silently. Aloud he said, to the sky and the sun rather than to Cadfael: 'Did you ever see such hair, like sun silver, finer than gossamer! And her face all milk and rose … How old can she be?'

'Should I know? Eighteen or so by the look of her. Much the same age as your Cristina, I suppose,' said Brother Cadfael, dropping a none too gentle reminder of the reality of things. 'You'll be doing her a great service and grace if you send her father back to her. And as I know, you're just as eager to get home yourself,' he said with emphasis.

Elis removed his gaze with an effort from the corner where Melicent Prestcote had disappeared and blinked uncomprehendingly, as though he had just been startled out of a deep sleep. 'Yes,' he said uncertainly, and walked on still in a daze.

In the middle of the afternoon, while Cadfael was busy about replenishing his stock of winter cordials in his workshop in the herb-garden, Hugh came in bringing a chilly draught with him before he could close the door against the east wind. He warmed his hands over the brazier, helped himself uninvited to a beaker from Cadfael's wine-flask, and sat down on the broad bench against the wall. He was at home in this dim, timber-scented, herb-rustling miniature world where Cadfael spent so much of his time, and did his best thinking.

'I've just come from the abbot,' said Hugh, 'and borrowed you from him for a few days.'

'And he was willing to lend me?' asked Cadfael with interest, busy stoppering a still-warm jar.

'In a good cause and for a sound reason, yes. In the matter of finding and recovering Gilbert he's as earnest as I am. And the sooner we know whether such an exchange is possible, the better for all.'

Cadfael could not but agree with that. He was thinking, uneasily but not too anxiously as yet, about the morning's visitation. A vision so far from everything Welsh and familiar might well dazzle young, impressionable eyes. There was a prior pledge involved, the niceties of Welsh honour, and the more bitter consideration that Gilbert Prestcote had an old and flourishing hatred against the Welsh, which certain of that race heartily reciprocated.

'I have a border to keep and a garrison to conserve,' said Hugh, nursing his beaker in both hands to warm it, 'and neighbours across the border drunk on their own prowess, and all too likely to be running wild in search of more conquests. Getting word through to Owain Gwynedd is a risky business and we all know it. I would be dubious of letting a captain loose on that mission who lacks Welsh, for I might never see hide nor hair of him again. Even a well-armed party of five or six could vanish. You're Welsh, and have your habit for a coat of mail, and once across the border you have kin everywhere. I reckon you a far better hazard than any battle party. With a small escort, in case of masterless men, and your Welsh tongue and net of kindred to tackle any regular company that crosses you. What do you say?'

'I should be ashamed, as a Welshman,' said Cadfael comfortably, 'if I could not recite my pedigree back sixteen degrees, and some of my kin are here across the border of this shire, a fair enough start towards Gwynedd.'

'Ah, but there's word that Owain may not be so far distant as the wilds of Gwynedd. With Ranulf of Chester so set up in his gains, and greedy for more, the prince has come east to keep an eye on his own. So the rumours say. There's even a whisper he may be our side of the Berwyns, in Cynllaith or Glyn Ceiriog, keeping a close watch on Chester and Wrexham.'

'It would be like him,' agreed Cadfael. 'He thinks large and forwardly. What is the commission? Let me hear it?'

381

'To ask of Owain Gwynedd whether he has, or can take from his brother, the person of my sheriff, taken at Lincoln. And if he has him, or can find and possess him, whether he will exchange him for this young kinsman of his, Elis ap Cynan. You know, and can report best of any, that the boy is whole and well. Owain may have whatever safeguards he requires, since all men know that he's a man of his word, but regarding me he may not be certain of the same. He may not so much as know my name. Though he shall know me better, if he will have dealings over this. Will you go?'

'How soon?' asked Cadfael, putting his jar aside to cool, and sitting down beside his friend.

'Tomorrow, if you can delegate all here.'

'Mortal man should be able and willing to delegate at any moment,' said Cadfael soberly, 'since mortal he is. Oswin is grown wonderfully deft and exact among the herbs, more than I ever hoped for when he first came to me. And Brother Edmund is master of his own realm, and well able to do without me. If Father Abbot frees me, I'm yours. What I can, I'll do.'

'Then come up to the castle in the morning, after Prime, and you shall have a good horse under you.' He knew that would be a lure and a delight, and smiled at seeing it welcomed. 'And a few picked men for your escort. The rest is in your Welsh tongue.'

'True enough,' said Cadfael complacently, 'a fast word in Welsh is better than a shield. I'll be there. But have your terms drawn up fair on a parchment. Owain has a legal mind, he likes a bill well drawn.'

After Prime in the morning – a greyer morning than the one that went before – Cadfael donned boots and cloak, and went up through the town to the castle wards, and there were the horses of his escort already saddled, and the men waiting for him. He knew them all, even to the youngster Hugh had chosen as a possible hostage for the desired prisoner, should all go well. He spared a few moments to say farewell to Elis, and found him sleepy and mildly morose at this hour in his cell.

'Wish me well, boy, for I'm away to see what can be done about this exchange for you. With a little goodwill and a morsel of luck, you may be on your way home within a couple of weeks. You'll be mightily glad to be back in your own country and a free man.'

Elis agreed that he would, since it was obviously expected of him, but it was a very lukewarm agreement. 'But it's not yet certain, is it, that your sheriff is there to be redeemed? And even if he is, it may take some time to find him and get him out of Cadwaladr's hands.'

'In that case,' said Cadfael, 'you will have to possess your soul in patience and in captivity a while longer.'

'If I must, I can,' agreed Elis, all too cheerfully and continently for one surely not hitherto accomplished at possessing his soul in patience. 'But I do trust you may go and return safe,' he said dutifully.

'Behave yourself, while I'm about your affairs,' Cadfael advised resignedly and turned to leave him. 'I'll bear your greetings to your foster-brother Eliud, if I should encounter him, and leave him word you've come to no harm.'

Elis embraced that offer gladly enough, but crassly failed to add another name that might fittingly have been linked with the same message. And Cadfael refrained from mentioning it in his turn. He was at the door when Elis suddenly called after him, 'Brother Cadfael ...'

'Yes?' said Cadfael, turning.

'That lady ... the one we saw yesterday, the sheriff's daughter ...'

'What of her?'

'Is she spoken for?'

Ah well, thought Cadfael, mounting with his mission well rehearsed in his head, and his knot of light-armed men about him, soon on, soon off, no doubt, and she has never spoken word to him and most likely never will. Once home, he'll soon forget her. If she had not been so silver-fair, so different from the trim, dark Welsh girls, he would never have noticed her.

Cadfael had answered the enquiry with careful indifference, saying he had no notion what plans the sheriff had for his daughter, and forbore from adding the blunt warning that was on the tip of his tongue. With such a springy lad as this one, to put him off would only put him on the more resolutely. With no great obstacles in the way, he might lose interest. But the girl certainly had an airy beauty, all the more appealing for being touched with innocent gravity and sadness on her father's account. Only let this mission succeed, and the sooner the better!

They left Shrewsbury by the Welsh bridge, and made good

383

speed over the near reaches of their way, north-west towards Oswestry.

Sybilla, Lady Prestcote, was twenty years younger than her husband, a pretty, ordinary woman of good intentions towards all, and notable chiefly for one thing, that she had done what the sheriff's first wife could not do, and borne him a son. Young Gilbert was seven years old, the apple of his father's eye and the core of his mother's heart. Melicent found herself indulged but neglected, but in affection to a very pretty little brother she felt no resentment. An heir is an heir; an heiress is a much lesser achievement.

The apartments in the castle tower, when the best had been done to make them comfortable, remained stony, draughty and cold, no place to bring a young family, and it was exceptional indeed for Sybilla and her son to come to Shrewsbury, when they had six far more pleasant manors at their disposal. Hugh would have offered the hospitality of his own town house on this anxious occasion, but the lady had too many servants to find accommodation there, and preferred the austerity of her bleak but spacious dwelling in the tower. Her husband was accustomed to occupying it alone, when his duties compelled him to remain with the garrison. Wanting him and fretting over him, she was content to be in the place which was his by right, however Spartan its appointments.

Melicent loved her little brother, and found no fault with the system which would endow him with all their father's possessions, and provide her with only a modest dowry. Indeed, she had had serious thoughts of taking the veil, and leaving the Prestcote inheritance as good as whole, having an inclination towards altars, relics and devotional candles, though she had just sense enough to know that what she felt fell far short of a vocation. It had not that quality of overwhelming revelation it should have had.

The shock of wonder, delight and curiosity, for instance, that stopped her, faltering, in her steps when she sailed through the archway into the outer ward and glanced by instinct towards the presence she felt close and intent beside her, and met the startled dark eyes of the stranger, the Welsh prisoner. It was not even his youth and comeliness, but the spellbound stare he fixed on her, that pierced her to the heart.

She had always thought of the Welsh with fear and distrust, as uncouth savages; and suddenly here was this trim and personable young man whose eyes dazzled and whose cheeks flamed at meeting her gaze. She thought of him much. She asked questions about him, careful to dissemble the intensity of her interest. And on the same day that Cadfael set out to hunt for Owain Gwynedd, she saw Elis from an upper window, half-accepted already among the young men of the garrison, stripped to the waist and trying a wrestling-bout with one of the best pupils of the master-at-arms in the inner ward. He was no match for the English youth, who had the advantage in weight and reach, and he took a heavy fall that made her catch her breath in distressed sympathy, but he came to his feet laughing and blown, and thumped the victor amiably on the shoulder.

There was nothing in him, no movement, no glance, in which she did not find generosity and grace.

She took her cloak and slipped away down the stone stair, and out to the archway by which he must pass to his lodging in the outer ward. It was beginning to be dusk, they would all be putting away their work and amusement, and making ready for supper in hall. Elis came through the arch limping a little from his new bruises, and whistling, and the same quiver of awareness which had caused her to turn her head now worked the like enchantment upon him.

The tune died on his parted lips. He stood stock-still, holding his breath. Their eyes locked, and could not break free, nor did they try very hard.

'Sir,' she said, having marked the broken rhythm of his walk, 'I fear you are hurt.'

She saw the quiver that passed through him from head to foot as he breathed again. 'No,' he said, hesitant as a man in a dream, 'no, never till now. Now I am wounded to death.'

'I think,' she said, shaken and timorous, 'you do not yet know me ...'

'I do know you,' he said. 'You are Melicent. It is your father I must buy back for you – at a price ...'

At a price, at a disastrous price, at the price of tearing asunder this marriage of eyes that drew them closer until they touched hands, and were lost.

Chapter Three

ADWALADR MIGHT have had his frolics on his way back to his castle at Aberystwyth with his booty and his prisoners, but to the north of his passage Owain Gwynedd had kept a fist clamped down hard upon disorder. Cadfael and his escort had had one or two brushes with trouble, after leaving Oswestry on their right and plunging into Wales, but on the first occasion the three masterless men who had put an arrow across their path thought better of it when they saw what numbers they had challenged, and took themselves off at speed into the brush; and on the second, an unruly patrol of excitable Welsh warmed into affability at Cadfael's unruffled Welsh greeting, and ended giving them news of the prince's movements; Cadfael's numerous kinsfolk, first and second cousins and shared forebears, were warranty enough over much of Clwyd and part of Gwynedd.

Owain, they said, had come east out of his eyrie to keep a weather eye upon Ranulf of Chester, who might be so blown up with his success as to mistake the mettle of the prince of Gwynedd. He was patrolling the fringes of Chester territory, and had reached Corwen on the Dee. So said the first informants. The second, encountered near Rhiwlas, were positive that he had crossed the Berwyns and come down into Glyn Ceiriog, and might at that moment be encamped near Llanarmon, or else with his ally and friend, Tudur ap Rhys, at his maenol at Tregeiriog. Seeing it was winter, however merciful at this moment, and seeing that Owain Gwynedd was considerably saner than most Welshmen, Cadfael chose to make for Tregeiriog. Why camp, when there was a close ally at hand, with a sound roof and a well-stocked larder, in a comparatively snug valley among these bleak central hills?

Tudur ap Rhys's maenol lay in a cleft where a mountain brook came down into the river Ceiriog, and his boundaries were well but unobtrusively guarded in these shaken days, for a two-man patrol came out on the path, one on either side, before Cadfael's party were out of the scrub forest above the valley. Shrewd eyes weighed up this sedate company, and the mind behind the eyes decided that they were harmless even before Cadfael got out his Welsh greeting. That and his habit were enough warranty. The young man bade his companion run ahead and acquaint Tudur that he had visitors, and himself conducted them at leisure the rest of the way. Beyond the river, with its fringes of forest and the few stony fields and huddle of wooden cots about the maenol, the hills rose again brown and bleak below, white and bleak above, to a round snow-summit against a leaden sky.

Tudur ap Rhys came out to welcome them and exchange the civilities; a short, square man, very powerfully built, with a thick thatch of brown hair barely touched with grey, and a loud, melodious voice that ranged happily up and down the cadences of song rather than speech. A Welsh Benedictine was a novelty to him; a Welsh Benedictine sent as negotiator from England to a Welsh prince even more so, but he suppressed his curiosity courteously, and had his guest conducted to a chamber in his own house, where presently a girl came to him bearing the customary water for his feet, by the acceptance or rejection of which he would signify whether or not he intended to spend the night there.

It had not occurred to Cadfael, until she entered, that this same lord of Tregeiriog was the man of whom Elis had talked, when he poured out the tale of his boyhood betrothal to a little, sharp, dark creature who was handsome enough in her way, and who, if he must marry at all, would do. Now there she stood, with the gently steaming bowl in her hands, demure before her father's guest, by her dress and her bearing manifestly Tudur's daughter. Little she certainly was, but trimly made and carried herself proudly. Sharp? Her manner was brisk and confident, and though her approach was deferent and proper, there was an assured spark in her eyes. Dark,

387

assuredly. Both eyes and hair fell just short of raven black by the faint, warm tint of red in them. And handsome? Not remarkably so in repose, her face was irregular in feature, tapering from wide-set eyes to pointed chin, but as soon as she spoke or moved there was such flashing life in her that she needed no beauty.

'I take your service very kindly,' said Cadfael, 'and thank you for it. And you, I think, must be Cristina, Tudur's daughter. And if you are, then I have word for you and for Owain Gwynedd that should be heartily welcome to you both.'

'I am Cristina,' she said, burning into bright animation, 'but how did a brother of Shrewsbury learn my name?'

'From a young man by the name of Elis ap Cynan, whom you may have been mourning for lost, but who is safe and well in Shrewsbury castle this moment. What may you have heard of him, since the prince's brother brought his muster and his booty home again from Lincoln?'

Her alert composure did not quiver, but her eyes widened and glowed. 'They told my father he was left behind with some that drowned near the border,' she said, 'but none of them knew how he had fared. Is it true? He is alive? And prisoner?'

'You may be easy,' said Cadfael, 'for so he is, none the worse for the battle of the brook, and can be bought free very simply, to come back to you and make you, I hope, a good husband.'

You may cast your bait, he told himself watching her face, which was at once eloquent and unreadable, as though she even thought in a strange language, but you'll catch no fish here. This one has her own secrets, and her own way of taking events into her hands. What she wills to keep to herself you're never like to get out of her. And she looked him full in the eyes and said: 'Eliud will be glad. Did he speak of him, too?' But she knew the answer.

'A certain Eliud was mentioned,' Cadfael admitted cautiously, feeling shaky ground under them. 'A cousin, I gathered, but brought up like brothers.'

'Closer than brothers,' said the girl. 'Am I permitted to tell him this news? Or should it wait until you have supped with my father and told him your errand?'

'Eliud is here?'

'Not here at this moment, but with the prince, somewhere north along the border. They'll come with the evening. They are lodged here, and Owain's companies are encamped close by.'

'Good, for my errand is to the prince, and it concerns the exchange of Elis ap Cynan for one of comparable value to us, taken, as we believe, by Prince Cadwaladr at Lincoln. If that is as good news to Eliud as it is to you, it would be a Christian act to set his mind at rest for his cousin as soon as may be.'

She kept her face bright, mute and still as she said, 'I will tell him as soon as he alights. It would be a great pity to see such a comradely love blighted a moment longer than it need be.' But there was acid in the sweet, and her eyes burned. She made her courteous obeisance, and left him to his ablutions before the evening meal. He watched her go, and her head was high and her step fierce but soundless, like a hunting cat.

So that was how it went, here in this corner of Wales! A girl betrothed, and with a girl's sharp eye on her rights and privileges, while the boy went about whistling and obtuse, child to her woman, and had his arm about another youth's neck, sworn pair from infancy, oftener than he even paid a compliment to his affianced wife. And she resented with all her considerable powers of mind and heart the love that made her only a third, and barely half-welcome.

Nothing here for her to mourn, if she could but know it. A maid is a woman far before a boy is a man, leaving aside the simple maturity of arms. All she need do was wait a little, and use her own arts, and she would no longer be the neglected third. But she was proud and fierce and not minded to wait.

Cadfael made himself presentable, and went to the lavish but simple table of Tudur ap Rhys. In the dusk torches flared at the hall door and up the valley from the north, from the direction of Llansantffraid, came a brisk bustle of horsemen back from their patrol. Within the hall the tables were spread and the central fire burned bright, sending up fragrant wood-smoke into the blackened roof, as Owain Gwynedd, lord of North Wales and much country beside, came content and hungry to his place at the high table.

Cadfael had seen him once before, a few years past, and he was not a man to be easily forgotten, for all he made very little ado about state and ceremony, barring the obvious royalty he bore about in his own person. He was barely thirty-seven years old, in his vigorous prime; very tall for a Welshman, and fair, after his grandmother Ragnhild of the Danish kingdom of Dublin, and his mother Angharad, known for her flaxen hair among the dark women of the south. His young men, reflecting his solid self-confidence, did it with a swagger of which their prince had no need. Cadfael wondered which of all these boisterous boys was Eliud ap Griffith, and whether Cristina had yet told him of his cousin's survival, and in what terms, and with what jealous bitterness at being still a barely regarded hanger-on in this sworn union.

'And here is Brother Cadfael of the Shrewsbury Benedictines,' said Tudur heartily, placing Cadfael close at the high table, 'with an embassage to you, my lord, from that town and shire.'

Owain weighed and measured the stocky figure and weathered countenance with a shrewd blue gaze, and stroked his close-trimmed golden beard. 'Brother Cadfael is welcome, and so is any motion of amity from that quarter, where I can do with an assured peace.'

'Some of your countrymen and mine,' said Cadfael bluntly, 'paid a visit recently to Shropshire's borders with very little amity in mind, and left our peace a good deal less assured, even, than it could be said to be after Lincoln. You may have heard of it. Your princely brother did not come raiding himself, it may even be that he never sanctioned the frolic. But he left a few drowned men in one of our brooks in flood whom we have buried decently. And one,' he said, 'whom the good sisters took out of the water living, and whom your lordship may wish to redeem, for by his own tale he's of your kinship.'

'Do you tell me!' The blue eyes had widened and brightened. 'I have not been so busy about fencing out the earl of Chester that I have failed to go into matters with my brother. There was more than one such frolic on the way home from Lincoln, and every one a folly that will cost me some pains to repair. Give your prisoner a name.'

'His name,' said Cadfael, 'is Elis ap Cynan.'

'Ah!' said Owain on a long, satisfied breath, and set down his cup ringing on the board. 'So the fool boy's alive yet to tell the tale, is he? I'm glad indeed to hear it, and thank God for the deliverance and you, brother, for the news. There was not a man of my brother's company could swear to how he was lost or what befell him.'

'They were running too fast to look over their shoulders,' said Cadfael mildly.

'From a man of our own blood,' said Owain grinning, 'I'll take that as it's meant. So Elis is live and prisoner! Has he come to much harm?'

'Barely a scratch. And he may have come by a measure of sense into the bargain. Sound as a well-cast bell, I promise you, and my mission is to offer an exchange with you, if by any chance your brother has taken among his prisoners one as valuable to us as Elis is to you. I am sent,' said Cadfael, 'by Hugh Beringar of Maesbury, speaking for Shropshire, to ask of you the return of his chief and sheriff, Gilbert Prestcote. With all proper greetings and compliments to your lordship, and full assurance of our intent to maintain the peace with you as hitherto.'

'The time's ripe for it,' acknowledged Owain drily, 'and it's to the vantage of both of us, things being as they are. Where is Elis now?'

'In Shrewsbury castle, and has the run of the wards on his parole.'

'And you want him off your hands?'

'No haste for that,' said Cadfael. 'We think well enough of him to keep him yet a while. But we do want the sheriff, if he lives, and if you have him. For Hugh looked for him after the battle, and found no trace, and it was your brother's Welsh who overran the place where he fought.'

'Bide here a night or two,' said the prince, 'and I will send to Cadwaladr, and find out if he holds your man. And if so, you shall have him.'

There was harping after supper, and singing, and drinking of good wine long after the prince's messenger had ridden out on the first stage of his long journey to Aberystwyth. There was also a certain amount of good-natured wrestling and horse-play between Owain's young cockerels and the men of Cadfael's escort, though Hugh had taken care to choose some who had Welsh kin to recommend them, no very hard task in Shrewsbury at any time.

'Which of all these,' asked Cadfael, surveying the hall, smoky now from the fire and the torches, and loud with voices, 'is Eliud ap Griffith?'

'I see Elis has chattered to you as freely as ever,' said Owain smiling, 'prisoner or no. His cousin and foster-brother is hovering this moment at the end of the near table, and eyeing you hard, waiting his chance to have speech with you as soon as I withdraw. The long lad in the blue coat.'

No mistaking him, once noticed, though he could not have been more different from his cousin: such a pair of eyes fixed upon Cadfael's face in implacable determination and eagerness and such a still, braced body waiting for the least encouragement to fly to respond. Owain, humouring him, lifted a beckoning finger, and he came like a lance launched, quivering. A long lad he was, and thin and intense, with bright hazel eyes in a grave oval face, featured finely enough for a woman, but with good lean bones in it, too. There was a quality of devotional anxiety about him that must be for Elis ap Cynan at this moment, but at another might be for Wales, for his prince, some day, no doubt, for a woman, but whatever its object it would always be there. This one would never be quite at rest.

He bent the knee eagerly to Owain, and Owain clouted him amiably on the shoulder and said: 'Sit down here with Brother Cadfael, and have out of him everything you want to know. Though the best you know already. Your other self is alive and can be bought back for you at a price.' And with that he left them together and went to confer with Tudur.

Eliud sat down willingly and spread his elbows on the board to lean ardently close. 'Brother, it *is* true, what Cristina told me? You have Elis safe in Shrewsbury? They came back without him ... I sent to know, but there was no one could tell me where he went astray or how. I have been hunting and asking everywhere and so has the prince, for all he makes a light thing of it. He is my father's fostering – you're Welsh yourself, so you know. We grew up together from babes, and there are no more brothers, either side ...'

'I do know,' agreed Cadfael, 'and I say again, as Cristina said to you, he is safe enough, man alive and as good as new.'

'You've seen him? Talked to him? You're sure it's Elis and no other? A well-looking man of his company,' explained Eliud apologetically, 'if he found himself a prisoner, might award himself a name that would stead him better than his own ...'

Cadfael patiently described this man, and told over the whole tale of the rescue from the flooded brook and Elis's obstinate withdrawal into the Welsh tongue until a Welshman challenged him. Eliud listened, his lips parted and his eyes intent, and was visibly eased into conviction.

'And was he so uncivil to those ladies who saved him? Oh, now I do know him for Elis, he'd be so shamed, to come back to life in such hands – like a babe being thumped into breathing!' No mistake, the solemn youth could laugh, and laughter lit up his grave face and made his eyes sparkle. It was no blind love he had for his twin who was no twin, he knew him through and through, scolded, criticised, fought with him, and

392

loved him none the less. The girl Cristina had a hard fight on her hands. 'And so you got him from the nuns. And had he no hurts at all, once he was wrung dry?'

'Nothing worse than a gash in his hinder end, got from a sharp rock in the brook, while he was drowning. And that's salved and healed. His worst trouble was that you would be mourning him for dead, but my journey here eases him of that anxiety, as it does you of yours. No need to fret about Elis ap Cynan. Even in an English castle he is soon and easily at home.'

'So he would be,' agreed Eliud in the soft, musing voice of tolerant affection. 'So he always was and always will be. He has the gift. But so *free* with it, sometimes I fret for him indeed!'

Always, rather than sometimes, thought Cadfael, after the young man had left him, and the hall was settling down for the night round the turfed and quiet fire. Even now, assured of his friend's safety and well-being, and past question or measure glad of that, even now he goes with locked brows and inward-gazing eyes. He had a troubled vision of those three young creatures bound together in inescapable strife, the two boys linked together from childhood, locked even more securely by the one's gravity and the other's innocent rashness, and the girl betrothed in infancy to half of an inseparable pair. Of the three the prisoner in Shrewsbury seemed to him the happiest by far, since he lived in the day, warming in its sunlight, taking cover from its storms, in every case finding by instinct the pleasant corner and the gratifying entertainment. The other two burned like candles, eating their own substance and giving an angry and vulnerable light.

He said prayers for all three before he slept, and awoke in the night to the uneasy reflection that somewhere, shadowy as yet, there might be a fourth to be considered and prayed for.

The next day was clear and bright, with light frost that lost its powdery sparkle as soon as the sun came up; and it was pleasure to have a whole day to spend in his own Welsh countryside with a good conscience and in good company. Owain Gwynedd again rode out eastward upon another patrol with a half-dozen of his young men, and again came back in the evening well content. It seemed that Ranulf of Chester was lying low for the moment, digesting his gains.

As for Cadfael, since word could hardly be expected to come back from Aberystwyth until the following day, he gladly accepted the prince's invitation to ride with them, and see for himself the state of readiness of the border villages that kept watch on England. They returned to the courtyard of Tudur's maenol in the early dusk, and beyond the flurry and bustle of activity among the grooms and the servants, the hall door hung open, and sharp and dark against the glow of the fire and the torches within stood the small, erect figure of Cristina, looking out for the guests returning, in order to set all forward for the evening meal. She vanished within for a few moments only, and then came forth to watch them dismount, her father at her side.

It was not the prince Cristina watched. Cadfael passed close by her as he went within, and saw by the falling light of the torches how her face was set, her lips taut and unsmiling, and her eyes fixed insatiably upon Eliud as he alighted and handed over his mount to the waiting groom. The glint of dark red that burned in the blackness of hair and eyes seemed by this light to have brightened into a deep core of anger and resentment.

What was no less noticeable, when Cadfael looked back in sheer human curiosity, was the manner in which Eliud, approaching the doorway, passed by her with an unsmiling face and a brief word, and went on his way with averted eyes. For was not she as sharp a thorn in his side as he in hers?

The sooner the marriage, the less the mischief, and the better prospect of healing it again, thought Cadfael, departing to his Vespers office, and instantly began to wonder whether he was not making far too simple a matter of this turmoil between three people, of whom only one was simple at all.

The prince's messenger came back late in the afternoon of the following day, and made report to his master, who called in Cadfael at once to hear the result of the quest.

'My man reports that Gilbert Prestcote is indeed in my brother's hands, and can and shall be offered in exchange for Elis. There may be a little delay, for it seems he was badly wounded in the fighting at Lincoln, and is recovering only slowly. But if you will deal directly with me, I will secure him as soon as he is fit to be moved, and have him brought by easy stages to Shrewsbury. We'll lodge him at Montford on the last night, where Welsh princes and English earls used to meet for parley, send Hugh Beringar word ahead, and bring him to the town. There your garrison may hand over Elis in exchange.'

'Content, indeed!' said Cadfael heartily, 'And so will Hugh Beringar be.'

'I shall require safeguards,' said Owain, 'and am willing to give them.'

'As for your good faith, nowhere in this land of Wales or my foster-land of England is it in question. But *my* lord you do not know, and he is content to leave with you a hostage, to be his guarantee until you have Elis safe in your hands again. From you he requires none. Send him Gilbert Prestcote, and you may have Elis ap Cynan, and send back the guarantor at your pleasure.'

'No,' said Owain firmly. 'If I ask warranty of a man, I also give it. Leave me your man here and now, if you will, and if he has his orders and is ready and willing, and when my men bring Gilbert Prestcote home I will send Eliud with him to remain with you as surety for his cousin's honour and mine until we again exchange hostages halfway – on the border dyke by Oswestry, shall we say, if I am still in these parts? – and conclude the bargain. There is virtue, sometimes, in observing the forms. And besides, I should like to meet your Hugh Beringar, for he and I have a common need to be on our guard against others you wot of.'

'The same thought has been much in Hugh's mind,' agreed Cadfael fervently, 'and trust me, he will take pleasure in coming to meet you wherever may be most suited to the time. He shall bring you Eliud again, and you shall restore him a young man who is his cousin on his mother's side, John Marchmain. You noted him this morning, the tallest among us. John came with me ready and willing to remain if things went well.'

'He shall be well entertained,' said Owain.

'Faith, he's been looking forward to it, though his knowledge of Welsh is small. And since we are agreed,' said Cadfael, 'I'll see him instructed in his duty tonight, and make an early start back to Shrewsbury in the morning with the rest of my company.'

Before sleeping that night he went out from the smoke and warmth of the hall to take a look at the weather. The air was on the softer edge of frost, no wind stirring. The sky was clear and full of stars, but they had not the blaze and bite of extreme cold. A beautiful night, and even without his cloak he was tempted to go as far as the edge of the maenol, where a copse

395

of bushes and trees sheltered the gate. He drew in deep, chill breaths, scented with timber, night and the mysterious sweetness of turf and leaf sleeping but not dead, and blew the smokiness of withindoors out of his nose.

He was about to turn back and compose his mind for the night prayers when the luminous darkness quickened around him, and two people came up from the shadowy buildings of the stables towards the hall, softly and swiftly, but with abrupt pauses that shook the air more than their motion. They were talking as they came, just above the betraying sibilance of whispers, and their conference had an edge and an urgency that made him freeze where he stood, covered by the bulk and darkness of the trees. By the time he was aware of them they were between him and his rest, and when they drew close enough he could not choose but hear. But man being what he is, it cannot be avowed that he would so have chosen, even if he could.

'–mean me no harm!' breathed the one, bitter and soft. 'And do you not harm me, do you not rob me of what's mine by right, with every breath you draw? And now you will be off to him, as soon as this English lord can be moved ...'

'Have I a choice,' protested the other, 'when the prince sends me? And he is my foster-brother, can you change that? Why can you not let well alone?'

'It is *not* well, it is very ill! Sent, indeed!' hissed the girl's voice viciously. 'Ha! And you would murder any who took the errand from you, and well you know it. And I to sit here! While you will be together again, his arm around your neck, and never a thought for me!'

The two shadows glared in the muted gleam from the dying fire within, black in the doorway. Eliud's voice rose perilously. The taller shadow, head and shoulders taller, wrenched itself away.

'For God's love, woman, will you not hush, and let me be!'

He was gone, casting her off roughly, and vanishing into the populous murmur and hush of the hall. Cristina plucked her skirts about her with angry hands, and followed slowly, withdrawing to her own retiring place.

And so did Cadfael, as soon as he was sure there was none to be discomposed by his going. There went two losers in this submerged battle. If there was a winner, he slept with a child's abandon, as seemed to be his wont, in a stone cell that was no prison, in Shrewsbury castle. One that would always fall on his feet. Two that probably made a practice of falling over theirs, from too intense peering ahead, and too little watching where they trod.

Nevertheless, he did not pray for them that night. He lay long in thought instead, pondering how so complex a knot might be disentangled.

In the early morning he and his remaining force mounted and rode. It did not surprise him that the devoted cousin and foster-brother should be there to see him go, and send by him all manner of messages to his captive friend, to sustain him until his release. Most fitting that the one who was older and wiser should stand proxy to rescue the younger and more foolish. If folly can be measured so.

'I was not clever,' owned Eliud ruefully, holding Cadfael's stirrup as he mounted, and leaning on his horse's warm shoulder when he was up. 'I made too much of it that he should not go with Cadwaladr. I doubt I drove him the more firmly into it. But I *knew* it was mad!'

'You must grant him one grand folly,' said Cadfael comfortably. 'Now he's lived through it, and knows it was folly as surely as you do. He'll not be so hot after action again. And then,' he said, eyeing the grave oval countenance close, 'I understand he'll have other causes for growing into wisdom when he comes home. He's to be married, is he not?'

Eliud faced him a moment with great hazel eyes shining like lanterns. Then: 'Yes!' he said very shortly and forbiddingly, and turned his head away.

Chapter Four

HE NEWS went round in Shrewsbury – abbey, castle and town – almost before Cadfael had rendered account of his stewardship to Abbot Radulfus, and reported his success to Hugh. The sheriff was alive, and his return imminent, in exchange for the Welshman taken at Godric's Ford. In her high apartments in the castle, Lady Prestcote brightened and grew buoyant with relief. Hugh rejoiced not only in having found and recovered his chief, but also in the prospect of a closer alliance with Owain Gwynedd, whose help in the north of the shire, if ever Ranulf of Chester did decide to attack, might very well turn the tide. The provost and guildsmen of the town, in general, were well pleased. Prestcote was a man who did not encourage close friendships, but Shrewsbury had found him a just and well-intentioned officer of the crown, if heavy-handed at times, and was well aware that it might have fared very much worse. Not everyone, however, felt the same simple pleasure. Even just men make enemies.

Cadfael returned to his proper duties well content, and having reviewed Brother Oswin's stewardship in the herbarium and found everything in good order, his next charge was to visit the infirmary and replenish the medicine-cupboard there.

'No new invalids since I left?'

'None. And two have gone out, back to the dortoir, Brother Adam and Brother Everard. Strong constitutions they have, both, in spite of age, and it was no worse than a chest cold, and has cleared up well. Come and see how they all progress. If only we could send out Brother Maurice with the same satisfaction as those two,' said Edmund sadly. 'He's eight years younger, strong and able, and barely sixty. If only he was as sound in mind as in body! But I doubt we'll never dare let him loose. It's the bent his madness has taken. Shame that after a blameless life of devotion he now remembers only his grudges, and seems to have no love for any man. Great age is no blessing, Cadfael, when the body's strength outlives the mind.'

'How do his neighbours bear with him?' asked Cadfael with sympathy.

'With Christian patience! And they need it. He fancies now that every man is plotting some harm against him. And says so, outright, besides any real and ancient wrongs he's kept in mind all too clearly.'

They came into the big, bare room where the beds were laid, handy to the private chapel where the infirm might repair for the offices. Those who could rise to enjoy the brighter part of the day sat by a large log fire, warming their ancient bones and talking by fits and starts, as they waited for the next meal, the next office or the next diversion. Only Brother Rhys was confined to his bed, though most of those within here were aged, and spent much time there. A generation of brothers admitted in the splendid enthusiasm of an abbey's founding also comes to senility together, yielding place to the younger postulants admitted by ones and twos after the engendering wave. Never again, thought Cadfael, moving among them, would a whole chapter of the abbey's history remove thus into retirement and decay. From this time on they would come one by one, and be afforded each a death-bed reverently attended, single and in solitary dignity. Here were four or five who would depart almost together, leaving even their attendant brothers very weary, and the world indifferent.

Brother Maurice sat installed by the fire, a tall, gaunt, waxen-white old man of elongated patrician face and irascible manner. He came of a noble house, an oblate since his youth, and had been removed here some two years previously, when after a trivial dispute he had suddenly called out Prior Robert in a duel to the death, and utterly refused to be distracted or reconciled. In his more placid moments he was gracious, accommodating and courteous, but touch him in his pride of family and honour and he was an implacable enemy. Here in his old age he called up from the past, vivid as when they happened, every affront to his line, every lawsuit waged against them, back to his own birth and beyond, and brooded over every one that had gone unrevenged.

It was a mistake, perhaps, to ask him how he did, but his enthroned hauteur seemed to demand it. He raised his narrow hawk-nose, and tightened his bluish lips. 'None the better for what I hear, if it be true. They're saying that Gilbert Prestcote is alive and will soon be returning here. Is that truth?'

'It is,' said Cadfael. 'Owain Gwynedd is sending him home in exchange for the Welshman captured in the Long Forest a while since. And why should you be none the better for good news of a decent Christian man?'

'I had thought justice had been done,' said Maurice loftily, 'after all too long a time. But however long, divine justice should not fail in the end. Yet once again it has glanced aside and spared the malefactor.' The glitter of his eyes was grey as steel.

'You'd best leave divine justice to its own business,' said Cadfael mildly, 'for it needs no help from us. And I asked you how *you* did, my friend, so never put me off with others. How is it with that chest of yours, this wintry weather? Shall I bring you a cordial to warm you?'

It was no great labour to distract him, for though he was no complainer as to his health, he was open to the flattery of concerned attention and enjoyed being cosseted. They left him soothed and complacent, and went out to the porch very thoughtful.

'I knew he had these hooks in him,' said Cadfael when the door was closed between, 'but not that he had such a barb from the Prestcote family. What is it he holds against the sheriff?'

Edmund shrugged, and drew resigned breath. 'It was in his father's time, Maurice was scarcely born! There was a lawsuit over a piece of land and long arguments either side, and it went Prestcote's way. For all I know, as sound a judgement as ever was made, and Maurice was in his cradle, and Gilbert's father, good God, was barely a man, but here the poor ancient has dredged it up as a mortal wrong. And it is but one among a dozen he keeps burnished in his memory, and wants blood for them all. Will you believe it, he has never set eyes on the sheriff? Can you hate a man you've never seen or spoken to, because his grandsire beat your father at a suit at law? Why should old age lose everything but the all-present evil?'

A hard question, and yet sometimes it went the opposite

way, kept the good, and let all the malice and spite be washed away. And why one old man should be visited by such grace, and another by so heavy a curse, Cadfael could not fathom. Surely a balance must be restored elsewhere.

'Not everyone, I know,' said Cadfael ruefully, 'loves Gilbert Prestcote. Good men can make as devoted enemies as bad men. And his handling of law has not always been light or merciful, though it never was corrupt or cruel.'

'There's one here has somewhat better cause than Maurice to bear him a grudge,' said Edmund. 'I am sure you know Anion's history as well as I do. He's on crutches, as you'll have seen before you left us on this journey, and getting on well, and we like him to go forth when there's no frost and the ground's firm and dry, but he's still bedded with us, within there. He says nothing, while Maurice says too much, but you're Welsh, and you know how a Welshman keeps his counsel. And one like Anion, half-Welsh, half-English, how do you read such a one?'

'As best you can,' agreed Cadfael, 'bearing in mind both are humankind.'

He knew the man Anion, though he had never been brought close to him, since Anion was a lay servant among the livestock, and had been brought into the infirmary in late autumn from one of the abbey granges, with a broken leg that was slow to knit. He was no novelty in the district about Shrewsbury, offspring of a brief union between a Welsh wool-trader and an English maid-servant. And like many another of his kind, he had kept touch with his kin across the border, where his father had a proper wife, and had given her a legitimate son no long time after Anion was conceived.

'I do remember now,' said Cadfael, enlightened. 'There were two young fellows came to sell their fleeces that time, and drank too deep and got into a brawl, and one of the gate-keepers on the bridge was killed. Prestcote hanged them for it. I did hear tell at the time the one had a half-brother this side the border.'

'Griffri ap Griffri, that was the young man's name. Anion had got to know him, the times he came into town, they were on good terms. He was away among the sheep in the north when it happened or he might well have got his brother to bed without mischief. A good worker and honest, Anion, but a surly fellow and silent, and never forgets a benefit nor an injury.'

401

Cadfael sighed, having seen in his time a long line of decent men wiped out in alternate savageries as the result of just such a death. The blood-feud could be a sacred duty in Wales.

'Ah, well, it's to be hoped the English half of him can temper his memories. That must be two years ago now. No man can bear a grudge for ever.'

In the narrow, stone-cold chapel of the castle by the meagre light of the altar lamp, Elis waited in the gloom of the early evening, huddled into his cloak in the darkest corner, biting frost without and gnawing fire within. It was a safe place for two to meet who could otherwise never be alone together. The sheriff's chaplain was devout, but within limits, and preferred the warmth of the hall and the comforts of the table, once Vespers was disposed of, to this cold and draughty place.

Melicent's step on the threshold was barely audible, but Elis caught it, and turned eagerly to draw her in by both hands, and swing the heavy door closed to shut out the rest of the world.

'You've heard?' she said, hasty and low. 'They've found him, they're bringing him back. Owain Gwynedd has promised it …'

'I know!' said Elis, and drew her close, folding the cloak about them both, as much to assert their unity as to shield her from the chill and the trespassing wind. For all that, he felt her slipping away like a wraith of mist out of his hold. 'I'm glad you'll have your father back safely.' But he could not sound glad, no matter how manfully he lied. 'We knew it must be so if he lived …' His voice baulked there, trying not to sound as if he wished her father dead, one obstacle out of the way from between them, and himself still a prisoner, unransomed. Her prisoner, for as long as might be, long enough to work the needful miracle, break one tie and make another possible, which looked all too far out of reach now.

'When he comes back,' she said, her cold brow against his cheek, 'then you will have to go. How shall we bear it!'

'Don't I know it! I think of nothing else. It will all be vain, and I shall never see you again. I won't, I can't accept that. There *must* be a way …'

'If you go,' she said, 'I shall die.'

'But I must go, we both know it. How else can I even do this one thing for you, to buy your father back?' But neither could he bear the pain of it. If he let her go now he was for ever lost, there would be no other to take her place. The little dark creature in Wales, so faded from his mind he could hardly recall her face, she was nothing, she had no claim on him. Rather a hermit's life, if he could not have Melicent. 'Do you not *want* him back?'

'Yes!' she said vehemently, torn and shivering, and at once took it back again: '*No*! Not if I must lose you! Oh, God, do I know what I want? I want both you and him – *but you most*! I do love my father, but as a father. I must love him, love is due between us, but ... Oh, Elis, I hardly know him, he never came near enough to be loved. Always duty and affairs taking him away, and my mother and I lonely, and then my mother dead ... He was never unkind, always careful of me, but always a long way off. It is a kind of love, but not like this ... not as I love you! It's no fair exchange ...'

She did not say, 'Now if he had died ...' but it was there stark at the back of her mind, horrifying her. If they had failed to find him, or found him dead, she would have wept for him, yes, but her stepmother would not have cared too much where she chose to marry. What would have mattered most to Sybilla was that her son should inherit all, and her husband's daughter be content with a modest dowry. And so she would have been content, yes, with none.

'But it must not be an end!' vowed Elis fiercely. 'Why should we submit to it? I won't give you up, I can't, I won't part from you.'

'Oh, foolish!' she said, her tears gushing against his cheek, 'The escort that brings him home will take you away. There's a bargain struck, and no choice but to keep it. You must go, and I must stay, and that will be the end. Oh, if he need never reach here ...' Her own voice uttering such things terrified her, she buried her lips in the hollow of his shoulder to smother the unforgivable words.

'No, but listen to me, my heart, my dear! Why should I not go to him and offer for you? Why should he not give me fair hearing? I'm born princely, I have lands, I'm his equal, why should he refuse to let me have you? I can endow you well, and there's no man could ever love you more.'

He had never told her, as he had so light-heartedly told Brother Cadfael, of the girl in Wales, betrothed to him from childhood. But that agreement had been made over their heads, by consent of others, and with patience and goodwill it could be honourably dissolved by the consent of all. Such a reversal might be a rarity in Gwynedd, but it was not unheard of. He had done no wrong to Cristina, it was not too late to withdraw.

'Sweet fool innocent!' she said, between laughter and rage. 'You do not know him! Every manor he holds is a border manor, he has had to sweat and fight for them many a time. Can you not see that after the empress, his enemy is Wales? And he as good a hater as ever was born! He would as soon marry his daughter to a blind leper in St Giles as to a Welshman, if he were the prince of Gwynedd himself. Never go near him, you will but harden him, and he'll rend you. Oh, trust me, there's no hope there.'

'Yet I will not let you go,' vowed Elis into the cloud of her pale hair, that stirred and stroked against his face with a life of its own, in nervous, feathery caresses. 'Somehow, somehow, I swear I'll keep you, no matter what I must do to hold you, no matter how many I must fight to clear the way to you. I'll kill whoever comes between us, my love, my dear ...'

'Oh, hush!' she said. 'Don't talk so. That's not for you. There must, there must be some way for us ...'

But she could see none. They were caught in an inexorable process that would bring Gilbert Prestcote home, and sweep Elis ap Cynan away.

'We have still a little time,' she whispered, taking heart as best she could. 'They said he is not well, he had wounds barely healed. They'll be a week or two yet.'

'And you'll still come? You *will* come? Every day? How should I bear it if I could no longer see you?'

'I'll come,' she said, 'these moments are my life, too. Who knows, something may yet happen to save us.'

'Oh God, if we could but stop time! If we could hold back the days, make him take for ever on the journey, and never, never reach Shrewsbury!'

It was ten days before the next word came from Owain Gwynedd. A runner came in on foot, armed with due authorisation from Einon ab Ithel, who ranked second only to Owain's own *penteulu*, the captain of his personal guard. The messenger was brought to Hugh in the castle guardroom early in the afternoon; a border man, with some business dealings into England, and well acquainted with the language.

'My lord, I bring greetings from Owain Gwynedd through the mouth of his captain, Einon ab Ithel. I am to tell you that the party lies tonight at Montford, and tomorrow we shall bring you our charge, the lord Gilbert Prestcote. But there is more. The lord Gilbert is still very weak from his wounds and hardships, and for most of the way we have carried him in a litter. All went well enough until this morning, when we had hoped to reach the town and discharge our task in one day. Because of that, the lord Gilbert would ride the last miles, and not be carried like a sick man into his own town.'

The Welsh would understand and approve that, and not presume to deter him. A man's face is half his armour, and Prestcote would venture any discomfort or danger to enter Shrewsbury erect in the saddle, a man master of himself even in captivity.

'It was like him and worthy of him,' said Hugh, but scenting what must follow. 'And he tried himself too far. What has happened?'

'Before we had gone a mile he swooned and fell. Not a heavy fall, but a healed wound in his side has started open again, and he lost some blood. It may be that there was some manner of fit or seizure, more than the mere exertion, for when we took him up and tended him he was very pale and cold. We wrapped him well – Einon ab Ithel swathed him further in his own cloak – and laid him again in the litter, and have carried him back to Montford.'

'Has he his senses? Has he spoken?' asked Hugh anxiously.

'As sound in his wits as any man, once he opened his eyes, and speaks clearly, my lord. We would keep him at Montford longer, if need be, but he is set to reach Shrewsbury now, being so near. He may take more harm, being vexed, than if we carry him here as he wishes, tomorrow.'

So Hugh thought, too, and gnawed his knuckles a while pondering what was best. 'Do you think this setback may be dangerous to him? Even mortal?'

The man shook his head decidedly. 'My lord, though you'll find him a sick man and much fallen and aged, I think he needs only rest and time and good care to be his own man again. But it will not be a quick or an easy return.'

'Then it had better be here, where he desires to be,' Hugh decided, 'but hardly in these cold, harsh chambers. I would take him to my own house, gladly, but the best nursing will surely be at the abbey, and there you can just as well bear him, and he may be spared being carried helpless through the town. I will bespeak a bed for him in the infirmary there, and see his wife and children into the guest-hall to be near him. Go back

405

now to Einon ab Ithel with my greetings and thanks, and ask him to bring his charge straight to the abbey. I will see Brother Edmund and Brother Cadfael prepared to receive him, and all ready for his rest. At what hour may we expect your arrival? Abbot Radulfus will wish to have your captains be his guests before they leave again.'

'Before noon,' said the messenger, 'we should reach the abbey.'

'Good! Then there shall be places at table for all, for the midday meal, before you set forth with Elis ap Cynan in exchange for my sheriff.'

Hugh carried the news to the tower apartments, to Lady Prestcote, who received them with relief and joy, though tempered with some uneasiness when she heard of her husband's collapse. She made haste to collect her son and her maid, and make ready to move to the greater comfort of the abbey guest-hall, ready for her lord's coming, and Hugh conducted them there and went to confer with the abbot about the morrow's visit. And if he noted that one of the party went with them mute and pale, brilliant-eyed as much with tears as with eagerness, he thought little of it then. The daughter of the first wife, displaced by the son of the second, might well be the one who missed her father most, and had worn her courage so threadbare with the grief of waiting that she could not yet translate her exhaustion into joy.

Meantime, there was hum and bustle about the great court. Abbot Radulfus issued orders, and took measures to furnish his own table for the entertainment of the representatives of the prince of Gwynedd. Prior Robert took counsel with the cooks concerning properly lavish provision for the remainder of the escort, and room enough in the stables to rest and tend their horses. Brother Edmund made ready the quietest enclosed chamber in the infirmary, and had warm, light covers brought, and a brazier to temper the air, while Brother Cadfael reviewed the contents of his workshop with the broken wound in mind, and the suggestion of something more than a swoon. The abbey had sometimes entertained much larger parties, even royalty, but this was the return of a man of their own, and the Welsh who had been courteous and punctilious in providing him his release and his safe-conduct must be honoured like princes, as they stood for a prince.

In his cell in the castle Elis ap Cynan lay face-down on his pallet, the heart in his breast as oppressive as a hot and heavy stone. He had watched her go, but from hiding, unwilling to cause her the same suffering and despair he felt. Better she should go without a last reminder, able at least to try to turn all her thoughts towards her father, and leave her lover out of mind. He had strained his eyes after her to the last, until she vanished down the ramp from the gatehouse, the silver-gold of her coiled hair the only brightness in a dull day. She was gone, and the stone that had taken the place of his heart told him that the most he could hope for now was a fleeting glimpse of her on the morrow, when they released him from the castle wards and conducted him down to the abbey, to be handed over to Einon ab Ithel; for after the morrow, unless a miracle happened, he might never see her again.

Chapter Five

ROTHER CADFAEL was ready with Brother
Edmund in the porch of the infirmary to see them
ride in, as they did in the middle of the morning, just
after High Mass was ended. Owain's trusted captain
in the lead with Eliud ap Griffith, very solemn of face, close
behind him as body-squire and two older officers following,
and then the litter, carefully slung between two strong hill
ponies, with attendants on foot walking alongside to steady the
ride. The long form in the litter was so cushioned and swathed
that it looked bulky, but the ponies moved smoothly and
easily, as if the weight was very light.

Einon ab Ithel was a big, muscular man in his forties,
bearded, with long moustaches and a mane of brown hair. His
clothing and the harness of the fine horse under him spoke his
wealth and importance. Eliud leaped down to take his lord's
bridle, and walked the horse aside as Hugh Beringar came to
greet the arrivals and after him, with welcoming dignity, Abbot
Radulfus himself. There would be a leisurely and ceremonious
meal in the abbot's lodging for Einon and the elder officers of
his party, together with Lady Prestcote and her daughter and
Hugh himself, as was due when two powers came together in
civilised agreement. But the most urgent business fell to
Brother Edmund and his helpers.

The litter was unharnessed, and carried at once into the
infirmary, to the room already prepared and warmed for the
sick man's reception. Edmund closed the door even against

Lady Prestcote, who was blessedly delayed by the civilities, until they should have unwrapped, unclothed and installed the invalid, and had some idea of his state.

They unfastened from the high, close-drawn collar of the clipped sheepskin cloak that was his outer wrapping a long pin with a large, chased gold head, secured by a thin gold chain. Everyone knew there was gold worked in Gwynedd, probably this came from Einon's own land for certainly this must be his cloak, added to pillow and protect his sacred charge. Edmund laid it aside, folded, on a low chest beside the bed, the great pin showing clearly, for fear someone should run his hand on to the point if it were hidden. Between them they unwound Gilbert Prestcote from the layers in which he was swathed, and as they handled him his eyes opened languidly, and his long, gaunt body made some feeble moves to help them. He was much fallen in flesh, and bore several scars, healed but angry, besides the moist wound in his flank which had gaped again with his fall. Carefully Cadfael dressed and covered the place. Even being handled exhausted the sick man. By the time they had lifted him into the warmed bed and covered him his eyes were again closed. As yet he had not tried to speak.

A marvel how he had ever ridden even a mile before foundering, thought Cadfael, looking down at the figure stretched beneath the covers, and the lean, livid face, all sunken blue hollows and staring, blanched bones. The dark hair of his head and beard was thickly sown with grey, and lay lank and lifeless. Only his iron spirit, intolerant of any weakness, most of all his own, had held him up in the saddle, and when even that failed he was lost indeed.

But he drew breath, he had moved to assert his rights over his own body, however weakly, and again he opened the dulled and sunken eyes and stared up into Cadfael's face. His grey lips formed, just audibly: 'My son?' Not: 'My wife?' Nor yet: 'My daughter?' Cadfael thought with rueful sympathy, and stooped to assure him: 'Young Gilbert is here, safe and well.' He glanced at Edmund, who signalled back agreement. 'I'll bring him to you.'

Small boys are very resilient, but for all that Cadfael said some words, both of caution and reassurance, as much for the mother as the child, before he brought them in and drew aside into a corner to leave them the freedom of the bedside. Hugh came in with them. Prestcote's first thought was naturally for his son, the second, no less naturally, would be for his shire.

And his shire, considering all things, was in very good case to encourage him to live, mend and mind it again.

Sybilla wept, but quietly. The little boy stared in some wonder at a father hardly recognised, but let himself be drawn close by a gaunt, cold hand, and stared at hungrily by eyes like firelit caverns. His mother leaned and whispered to him, and obediently he stooped his rosy, round face and kissed a bony cheek. He was an accommodating child, puzzled but willing, and not at all afraid. Prestcote's eyes ranged beyond, and found Hugh Beringar.

'Rest content,' said Hugh, leaning close and answering what need not be asked, 'your borders are whole and guarded. The only breach has provided you your ransom, and even there the victory was ours. And Owain Gwynedd is our ally. What is yours to keep is in good order.'

The dulling glance faded beneath drooping lids, and never reached the girl standing stark and still in the shadows near the door. Cadfael had observed her, from his own retired place, and watched the light from brazier and lamp glitter in the tears flowing freely and mutely down her cheeks. She made no sound at all, she hardly drew breath. Her wide eyes were fixed on her father's changed, aged face, in the most grievous and desperate stare.

The sheriff had understood and accepted what Hugh said. Brow and chin moved slightly in a satisfied nod. His lips stirred to utter almost clearly, 'Good!' And to the boy, awed but curious, hanging over him: 'Good boy! Take care ... of your mother ...'

He heaved a shallow sigh and his eyes drooped closed. They held still for some time, watching and listening to the heave and fall of the covers over his sunken breast and the short, harsh in and out of his breath, before Brother Edmund stepped softly forward and said in a cautious whisper. 'He's sleeping. Leave him so, in quiet. There is nothing better or more needed any man can do for him.'

Hugh touched Sybilla's arm, and she rose obediently and drew her son up beside her. 'You see him well cared for,' said Hugh gently. 'Come to dinner, and let him sleep.'

The girl's eyes were quite dry, her cheeks pale but calm, when she followed them out to the great court, and down the length of it to the abbot's lodging, to be properly gracious and grateful to the Welsh guests, before they left again for Montford and Oswestry.

410

Over their midday meal, which was served before the brothers ate in the refectory, the inhabitants of the infirmary laid their ageing but inquisitive heads together to make out what was causing the unwonted stir about their retired domain. The discipline of silence need not be rigorously observed among the old and sick, and just as well, since they tend to be incorrigibly garrulous, from want of other active occupation.

Brother Rhys, who was bedridden and very old indeed, but sharp enough in mind and hearing even if his sight was filmed over, had a bed next to the corridor, and across from the retired room where some newcomer had been brought during the morning, with unusual to-do and ceremony. He took pleasure in being the member who knew what was going on. Among so few pleasures left to him, this was the chief, and not to be lightly spent. He lay and listened. Those who sat at the table, as once in the refectory, and could move around the infirmary and sometimes the great court if the weather was right, nevertheless were often obliged to come to him for knowledge.

'Who should it be,' said Brother Rhys loftily, 'but the sheriff himself, brought back from being a prisoner in Wales.'

'Prestcote?' said Brother Maurice, rearing his head on its stringy neck like a gander giving notice of battle. 'Here? In our infirmary? Why should they bring him here?'

'Because he's a sick man, what else? He was wounded in the battle, and in no shape to shift for himself yet, or trouble any other man. I heard their voices in there – Edmund, Cadfael and Hugh Beringar – and the lady, too, and the child. It's Gilbert Prestcote, take my word.'

'There is justice,' said Maurice with sage satisfaction, and the gleam of vengeance in his eye, 'though it be too long delayed. So Prestcote is brought low, neighbour to the unfortunate. The wrong done to my line finds a balance at last, I repent that ever I doubted.'

They humoured him, being long used to his obsessions. They murmured variously, most saying reasonably enough that the shire had not fared badly in Prestcote's hands, though some had old grumbles to vent and reservations about sheriffs in general, even if this one of theirs was not by any means the worst of his kind. On the whole they wished him well. But Brother Maurice was not to be reconciled.

'There was a wrong done,' he said implacably, 'which even now is not fully set right. Let the false pleader pay for his offence, I say, to the bitter end.'

The stockman Anion, at the end of the table, said never a word, but kept his eyes lowered to his trencher, his hip pressed against the crutch he was almost ready to discard, as though he needed a firm contact with the reality of his situation, and the reassurance of a weapon to hand in the sudden presence of his enemy. Young Griffri had killed, yes, but in drink, in hot blood, and in fair fight man against man. He had died a worse death, turned off more casually than wringing a chicken's neck. And the man who had made away with him so lightly lay now barely twenty yards away, and at the very sound of his name every drop of blood in Anion ran Welsh, and cried out to him of the sacred duty of *galanas*, the blood-feud for his brother.

Eliud led Einon's horse and his own down the great court into the stable-yard, and the men of the escort followed with their own mounts, and the shaggy hill ponies that had carried the litter. An easy journey those two would have on the way back to Montford. Einon ab Ithel, when representing his prince on a ceremonial occasion, required a squire in attendance, and Eliud undertook the grooming of the tall bay himself. Very soon now he would be changing places with Elis, and left to chafe here while his cousin rode back to his freedom in Wales. In silence he hoisted off the heavy saddle, lifted aside the elaborate harness, and draped the saddle-cloth over his arm. The bay tossed his head with pleasure in his freedom, and blew great misty breaths. Eliud caressed him absently; his mind was not wholly on what he was doing, and his companions had found him unusually silent and withdrawn all that day. They eyed him cautiously and let him alone. It was no great surprise when he suddenly turned and tramped away out of the stable-yard, back to the open court.

'Gone to see whether there's any sign of his cousin yet,' said his neighbour tolerantly, rubbing down one of the shaggy ponies. 'He's been like a man maimed and out of balance ever since the other one went off to Lincoln. He can hardly believe it yet that he'll turn up here without a scratch on him.'

'He should know his Elis better than that,' grunted the man beside him. 'Never yet did that one fall anywhere but on his feet.'

Eliud was away perhaps ten minutes, long enough to have

412

been all the way to the gatehouse and peered anxiously along the Foregate towards the town, but he came back in dour silence, laid aside the saddle-cloth he was still carrying, and went to work without a word or a look aside.

'Not come yet?' asked his neighbour with careful sympathy.

'No,' said Eliud shortly, and continued working vigorously on the bright bay hide.

'The castle's the far side of the town, they'll have kept him there until they were sure of our man. They'll bring him. He'll be at dinner with us.'

Eliud said nothing. At this hour the monks themselves were at their meal in the refectory, and the abbot's guests with him at his own table in his lodging. It was the quietest hour of the day; even the comings and goings about the guest-hall were few at this time of year, though with the spring the countryside would soon be on the move again.

'Never show him so glum a face,' said the Welshman, grinning, 'even if you must be left here in his place. Ten days or so, and Owain and this young sheriff will be clasping hands on the border, and you on your way home to join him.'

Eliud muttered a vague agreement, and turned a forbidding shoulder on further talk. He had Einon's horse stalled and glossy and watered by the time Brother Denis the hospitaller came to bid them to the refectory, newly laid and decked for them after the brothers had ended their repast, and dispersed to enjoy their brief rest before the afternoon's work began. The resources of the house were at their disposal, warmed water brought to the lavatorium for their hands, towels laid out and their table, when they entered the refectory, graced with more dishes than the brothers had enjoyed. And there waiting, somewhat in the manner of a nervous host, was Elis ap Cynan, freshly brushed and spruced for the occasion, and on his most formal behaviour.

The awe of the exchange, himself the unwise cause of it and to some extent already under censure for his unwisdom, or something else of like weight, had had its effect upon Elis, for he came with stiff bearing and very sombre face, who was known rather for his hearty cheerfulness in and out of season. Certainly his eyes shone at the sight of Eliud entering, and he came with open arms to embrace him, but thereafter shoved free again. The grip of his hand had some unaccountable tension about it, and though he sat down to table beside his cousin, the talk over that meal was general and restrained. It

413

caused some mild wonder among their companions. There were these two inseparables, together again after long and anxious separation, and both as mute as blocks, and as pale and grave of face as men arraigned for their lives.

It was very different when the meal was over, the grace said, and they were free to go forth into the court. Elis caught his cousin by the arm and hauled him away into the cloister, where they could take refuge in one of the carrels where no monk was working or studying, and go to earth there like hunted foxes, shoulder warm for comfort against shoulder, as when they were children and fled into sanctuary from some detected misdeed. And now Eliud could recognise his foster-brother as he had always been, as he always would be, and marvelled fondly what misdemeanour or misfortune he could have to pour out here, where he had been so loftily on his dignity.

'Oh, Eliud!' blurted Elis, hugging him afresh in arms which had certainly lost none of their heedless strength. 'For God's sake, what am I to do? How shall I tell you! I can't go back! If I do, I've lost all. Oh, Eliud, I must have her! If I lose her I shall die! You haven't seen her? Prestcote's daughter?'

'His daughter?' whispered Eliud, utterly dazed. 'There was a lady, with a grown girl and a young boy ... I hardly noticed.'

'For God's sake, man, how could you *not* notice her? Ivory and roses, and her hair all pale, like spun silver ... I love her!' proclaimed Elis in high fever. 'And she is just as fain, I swear it, and we've pledged ourselves. Oh, Eliud, if I go now I shall never have her. If I leave her now, I'm lost. And he's an enemy, she warned me, he hates the Welsh. Never go near him, she said ...'

Eliud, who had sat stunned and astray, roused himself to take his friend by the shoulders and shake him furiously until he fell silent for want of breath, staring astonished.

'*What* are you telling me? You have a girl here? You *love* her? You no longer want to make any claim on Cristina? Is *that* what you're saying?'

'Were you not listening? Haven't I told you?' Elis, unsubdued and unchastened, heaved himself free and grappled in his turn. 'Listen, let me tell you how it fell. What pledge did I myself ever give Cristina? Is it her fault or mine if we're tied like tethered cattle? She cares no more for me than I for her. I'd brother the girl and dance at her wedding, and kiss her and wish her well heartily. But this ... this is another matter! Oh, Eliud, hush and hear me!'

It poured forth like music, the whole story from his first glimpse of her, the silver maiden at the door, blue-eyed, magical. Plenty of bards had issued from the stock to which Elis belonged, he had both the gift of words and the eloquent tune. Eliud sat stricken mute, gaping at him in blanched astonishment and strange dismay, his hands gripped and wrung in Elis's persuading hands.

'And I was frantic for you!' he said softly and slowly, almost to himself. 'If I had but known …'

'But Eliud, he's here!' Elis held him by the arms, peering eagerly into his face. 'He *is* here? You brought him, you must know. She says, don't go, but how can I lose this chance? I'm noble, I pledge the girl my whole heart, all my goods and lands, where will he find a better match? And she is not spoken for. I can, I must win him, he must listen to me … why should he not?' He flashed one sweeping glance about the most vacant court. 'They're not yet ready, they haven't called us. Eliud, you know where he's laid. I'm going to him! I must, I will! Show me the place!'

'He's in the infirmary.' Eliud was staring at him with open mouth and wide, shocked eyes. 'But you can't, you mustn't … He's sick and weary, you can't trouble him now.'

'I'll be gentle, humble, I'll kneel to him. I'll put my life in his hands. The infirmary – which is it? I never was inside these walls until now. Which door?' He caught Eliud by the arm and dragged him to the archway that looked out on the court. 'Show me, quickly!'

'*No*! Don't go! Leave him be! For shame to rush in on his rest …'

'*Which door*?' Elis shook him fiercely. 'You brought him, you saw!'

'There! The building drawn back to the precinct wall, to the right from the gatehouse. But don't do it! Surely the girl knows her father best. Wait, don't harry him now – an old, sick man!'

'You think I'd offer any hardihood to *her father*? All I want is to tell him my heart, and that I have her favour. If he curses me, I'll bear it. But I must put it to the test. What chance shall I ever have again?' He made to pull clear, and Eliud held him convulsively, then as suddenly heaved a great sigh and loosed his hold.

'Go, then, try your fortune! I can't keep you.'

Elis was away, without the least caution or dissembling, out into the court and straight as an arrow across it to the door of

415

the infirmary. Eliud stood in shadow to watch him vanish within, and leaned his forehead against the stone and waited with eyes closed some while before he looked again.

The abbot's guests were just emerging from the doorway of his lodging. The young man who was now virtually sheriff set off with the lady and her daughter, to conduct them again to the porch of the guest-hall. Einon ab Ithel lingered in talk with the abbot, his two companions, having less English, waited civilly a pace aside. Very soon he would be ordering the saddling of the horses, and the ceremonious leave-taking.

From the doorway of the infirmary two figures emerged, Elis first, stiffly erect, and after him one of the brothers. At the head of the few stone steps the monk halted, and stood to watch Elis stalk away across the great court, taut with offence, quenched in despair, like our first forefather expelled from Eden.

'He's sleeping,' he said, coming in crestfallen. 'I couldn't speak with him, the infirmarer turned me away.'

Barely half an hour now, and they would be on their way back to Montford, there to spend the first night of their journey into Wales. In the stables Eliud led out Einon's tall bay, and saddled and bridled him, before turning his attention to the horse he himself had ridden, which now Elis must ride in his place, while he lingered here.

The brothers had roused themselves after their customary rest, and were astir about the court again, on their way to their allotted labours. Some days into March, there was already work to be done in field and garden, besides the craftsmen who had their workshops in cloister and scriptorium. Brother Cadfael, crossing at leisure towards the garden and the herbarium, was accosted suddenly by an Eliud evidently looking about him for a guide, and pleased to recognise a face he knew.

'Brother, if I may trouble you – I've been neglecting my duty, there's something I had forgotten. My lord Einon left his cloak wrapping the lord Gilbert in the litter, for an extra covering. Of sheared sheepskins – you'll have seen it? I must reclaim it, but I don't want to disturb the lord Gilbert. If you will show me the place, and hand it forth to me ...'

'Very willingly,' said Cadfael, and led the way briskly. He eyed the young man covertly as they walked together. That passionate, intense face was closed and sealed, but trouble

416

showed in his eyes. He would always be carrying half the weight of that easy foster-brother of his who went so light through the world. And a fresh parting imminent, after so brief a reunion; and that marriage waiting to make parting inevitable and lifelong. 'You'll know the place,' said Cadfael, 'though not the room. He was deep asleep when we all left him. I hope he is still. Sleep in his own town, with his family by and his charge in good heart, is all he needs.'

'There was no mortal harm, then?' asked Eliud, low-voiced.

'None that time should not cure. And here we are. Come in with me. I remember the cloak. I saw Brother Edmund fold it aside on the chest.'

The door of the narrow chamber had been left ajar, to avoid the noise of the iron latch, but it creaked on being opened far enough to admit entrance. Cadfael slipped through the opening sidewise, and paused to look attentively at the long, still figure in the bed, but it remained motionless and oblivious. The brazier made a small, smokeless eye of gold in the dimness within. Reassured, Cadfael crossed to the chest on which the clothes lay folded and gathered up the sheepskin cloak. Unquestionably it was the one Eliud sought, and yet even at this moment Cadfael was oddly aware that it did not answer exactly to his recollection of it, though he did not stop to try and identify what was changed about it. He had turned back to the door, where Eliud hovered half-in, half-out, peering anxiously, when the young man made a step aside to let him go first into the passage, and knocked over the stool that stood in the corner. It fell with a loud wooden clap and rolled. Eliud bent to arrest its flight and snatch it up from the tiled floor and Cadfael, waving a hand furiously at him for silence, whirled round to see if the noise had startled the sleeper awake.

Not a movement, not a sharp breath, not a sigh. The long body, scarcely lifting the bedclothes, lay still as before. Too still. Cadfael went close, and laid a hand to draw down the brychan that covered the grizzled beard and hid the mouth. The bluish eyelids in their sunken hollows stared up like carven eyes in a tomb sculpture. The lips were parted and drawn a little back from clenched teeth, as if in some constant and customary pain. The gaunt breast did not move at all. No noise could ever again disturb Gilbert Prestcote's sleep.

'What is it?' whispered Eliud, creeping close to gaze.

'Take this,' ordered Cadfael, thrusting the folded cloak into the boy's hands. 'Come with me to your lord and Hugh

417

Beringar, and God grant the women are safe indoors.'

He need not have been in immediate anxiety for the women, he saw as he emerged into the open court with Eliud mute and quivering at his heels. It was chilly out there, and this was men's business now the civilities were properly attended to, and Lady Prestcote had made her farewells and withdrawn with Melicent into the guest-hall. The Welsh party were waiting with Hugh in an easy group near the gatehouse, ready to mount and ride, the horses saddled and tramping the cobbles with small, ringing sounds. Elis stood docile and dutiful at Einon's stirrup, though he did not look overjoyed at being on his way home. His face was overcast like the sky. At the sound of Cadfael's rapid steps approaching, and the sight of his face, every eye turned to fasten on him.

'I bring black news,' said Cadfael bluntly. 'My lord, your labour has been wasted, and I doubt your departure must wait yet a while. We are just come from the infirmary. Gilbert Prestcote is dead.'

Chapter Six

HEY WENT with him, Hugh Beringar and Einon ab Ithel, jointly responsible here for this exchange of prisoners which had suddenly slithered away out of their control. They stood beside the bed in the dim, quiet room, the little lamp a mild yellow eye on one side, the brazier a clear red one on the other. They gazed and touched, and held a bright, smooth blade to the mouth and nose, and got no trace of breath. The body was warm and pliable, no long time dead; but dead indeed.

'Wounded and weak, and exhausted with travelling,' said Hugh wretchedly. 'No blame to you, my lord, if he had sunk too far to climb back again.'

'Nevertheless, I had a mission,' said Einon. 'My charge was to bring you one man, and take another back from you in exchange. This matter is void, and cannot be completed.'

'So you did bring him, living, and living you delivered him over. It is in our hands his death came. There is no bar but you should take your man and go, according to the agreement. Your part was done, and done well.'

'Not well enough. The man is dead. My prince does not countenance the exchange of a dead man for one living,' said Einon haughtily. 'I split no hairs, and will have none split in my favour. Nor will Owain Gwynedd. We have brought you, however innocently, a dead man. I will not take a live one for him. This exchange cannot go forward. It is null and void.'

Brother Cadfael, though with one ear pricked and aware of

419

these meticulous exchanges, which were no more than he had foreseen, had taken up the small lamp, shielding it from draughts with his free hand, and held it close over the dead face. No very arduous or harsh departure. The man had been deeply asleep, and very much enfeebled, to slip over a threshold would be all too easy. Not, however, unless the threshold were greased or had too shaky a doorstone. This mute and motionless face, growing greyer as he gazed, was a face familiar to him for some years, fallen and aged though it might be. He searched it closely, moving the lamp to illumine every plane and every cavernous hollow. The pitted places had their bluish shadows, but the full lips, drawn back a little, should not have shown the same livid tint, nor the pattern of the large, strong teeth within, and the staring nostrils should not have gaped so wide and shown the same faint bruising.

'You will do what seems to you right,' said Hugh at his back, 'but I, for my part, make plain that you are free to depart in company as you came, and take both your young men with you. Send back mine, and I consider the terms will have been faithfully observed. Or if Owain Gwynedd still wants a meeting, so much the better, I will go to him on the border, wherever he may appoint, and take my hostage from him there.'

'Owain will speak his own mind,' said Einon, 'when I have told him what has happened. But without his word I must leave Elis ap Cynan unredeemed, and take Eliud back with me. The price due for Elis has not been paid, not to my satisfaction. He stays here.'

'I am afraid,' said Cadfael, turning abruptly from the bed, 'Elis will not be the only one constrained to remain here.' And as they fixed him with two blank and questioning stares: 'There is more here than you know. Hugh said well, there was no mortal harm to him, all he needed was time, rest and peace of mind, and he would have come back to himself. An older self before his time, perhaps, but he would have come. This man did not simply drown in his own weakness and weariness. There was a hand that held him under.'

'You are saying,' said Hugh, after a bleak silence of dismay and doubt, 'that this was murder?'

'I am saying so. There are the signs on him clear.'

'Show us,' said Hugh.

He showed them, one intent face stooped on either side to follow the tracing of his finger. 'It would not take much

420

pressure, there would not be anything to be called a struggle. But see what signs there are. These marks round nose and mouth, faint though they are, are bruises he had not when we bedded him. His lips are plainly bruised, and if you look closely you will see the shaping of his teeth in the marks on the upper lip. A hand was clamped over his face to cut off breath. I doubt if he awoke, in his deep sleep and low state it would not take long.'

Einon looked at the furnishings of the bed, and asked, low-voiced, 'What was used to muffle nose and mouth, then? These covers?'

'There's no knowing yet. I need better light and time enough. But as sure as God sees us, the man was murdered.'

Neither of them raised a word to question further. Einon had experience of many kinds of dying, and Hugh had implicit trust by now in Brother Cadfael's judgement. They looked wordlessly at each other for a long, thinking while.

'The brother here is right,' said Einon then, 'I cannot take away any of my men who may by the very furthest cast have any part in this killing. Not until truth is shown openly can they return home.'

'Of all your party,' said Hugh, 'you, my lord, and your two captains are absolutely clear of any slur. You never entered the infirmary until now, they have not entered it at all, and all three have been in my company and in the abbot's company every minute of this visit, besides the witness of the women. There is no one can keep you, and it is well you should return to Owain Gwynedd, and let him know what has happened here. In the hope that truth may out very soon and set all the guiltless free.'

'I will so return, and they with me. But for the rest ...' They were both considering that, recalling how the party had separated to its several destinations, the abbot's guests with him to his lodging, the rest to the stables to tend their horses, and after that to wander where they would and talk to whom they would until they were called to the refectory for their dinner. And that half-hour before the meal saw the court almost empty.

'There is not one other among us,' said Einon, 'who could not have entered here. Six men of my own, and Eliud. Unless some of them were in company with men of this household, or within sight of such, throughout. That I doubt, but it can be examined.'

421

'There are also all within here to be considered. Of all of us, surely your Welshmen had the least cause to wish him dead, having carried and cared for him all this way. It is madness to think it. Here are the brothers, such wayfarers as they have within the precinct, the lay-servants, myself, though I have been with you the whole while, my men who brought Elis from the castle ... Elis himself ...'

'He was taken straight to the refectory,' said Einon. 'However, he above all stays here. We had best be about sifting out any of mine who can be vouched for throughout, and if there are such I will have them away with me, for the sooner Owain Gwynedd knows of this, the better.'

'And I,' said Hugh ruefully, 'must go break the news to his widow and daughter, and make report to the lord abbot, and a sorry errand that will be. Murder in his own enclave!'

Abbot Radulfus came, grimly composed, looked long and grievously at the dead face, heard what Cadfael had to tell, and covered the stark visage with a linen cloth. Prior Robert came, jolted out of his aristocratic calm, shaking his silver head over the iniquity of the world and the defilement of holy premises. There would have to be ceremonies of re-consecration to make all pure again, and that could not be done until truth was out and justice vindicated. Brother Edmund came, distressed beyond all measure at such a happening in his province and under his devoted and careful rule, as though the guilt of it fouled his own hands and set a great black stain against his soul. It was hard to comfort him. Over and over he lamented that he had not placed a constant watch by the sheriff's bed, but how could any man have known that there would be need? Twice he had looked in, and found all quiet and still, and left it so. Quietness and stillness, time and rest, these were what the sick man most required. The door had been left ajar, any brother passing by could have heard if the sleeper had awakened and wanted for any small service.

'Hush you, now!' said Cadfael sighing. 'Take to yourself no more than your due, and that's small enough. There's no man takes better care of his fellows, as well you know. Keep your balance, for you and I will have to question all those within here, if they heard or saw anything amiss.'

Einon ab Ithel was gone by then, with only his two captains to bear him company, his hill ponies on a leading rein, back to Montford for the night, and then as fast as might be to

422

wherever Owain Gwynedd now kept his border watch in the north. There was not one of his men could fill up every moment of his time within here, and bring witnesses to prove it. Here or in the closer ward of the castle they must stay, until Prestcote's murderer was found and named.

Hugh, wisely enough, had gone first to the abbot, and only after speeding the departing Welsh did he go to perform the worst errand of all.

Edmund and Cadfael withdrew from the bedside when the two women came in haste and tears from the guest-hall, Sybilla stumbling blindly on Hugh's arm. The little boy they had managed to leave in happy ignorance with Sybilla's maid. There would be a better time than this to tell him he was fatherless.

Behind him, as he drew the door quietly to, Cadfael heard the widow break into hard and painful weeping, as quickly muffled in the coverings of her husband's bed. From the girl not a sound. She had walked into the room stiffly, with blanched, icy face and eyes fallen empty with shock.

In the great court the little knot of Welshmen hung uneasily together, with Hugh's guards unobtrusive but watchful on all sides, and in particular between them and the closed wicket in the gate. Elis and Eliud, struck silent and helpless in this disaster, stood a little apart, not touching, not looking at each other. Now for the first time Cadfael could see a family resemblance in them, so tenuous that in normal times it would never be noticed, while the one went solemn and thoughtful, and the other as blithe and untroubled as a bird. Now they both wore the same shocked visage, the one as lost as the other, and they could almost have been twin brothers.

They were still standing there waiting to be disposed of, and shifting miserably from foot to foot in silence, when Hugh came back across the court with the two women. Sybilla had regained a bleak but practical control over her tears, and showed more stiffening in her backbone than Cadfael, for one, had expected. Most likely she had already turned a part of her mind and energy to the consideration of her new situation, and what it meant for her son, who was now the lord of six valuable manors, but all of them in this vulnerable border region. He would need either a very able steward or a strong and well-disposed step-father. Her lord was dead, his overlord the king a prisoner; there was no one to force her into an unwelcome match. She was many years younger than her lost husband, and had a dower of her own, and good enough looks to make her a fair bargain. She would live, and do well enough.

The girl was another matter. Within her frosty calm a faint fire had begun to burn again, deep sparks lurked in the quenched eyes. She turned one unreadable glance upon Elis, and then looked straight before her.

Hugh checked for a moment to commit the Welshmen of the escort to his sergeants, and have them led away to the security of the castle, with due civility, since all of them might be entirely innocent of wrong, but into close and vigilant guard. He would have passed on to see the women into their apartments before attempting any further probing, but Melicent suddenly laid a hand upon his arm.

'My lord, since Brother Edmund is here, may I ask him a question, before we leave this in your hands?' She was very still but the fire in her was beginning to burn through, and her pallor to show sharp edges of steel. 'Brother Edmund, you best know your own domain, and I know you watch over it well. There is no blame falls upon you. But tell us, who, if anyone, entered my father's chamber after he was left there asleep?'

'I was not constantly by,' said Edmund unhappily. 'God forgive me, I never dreamed there could be any need. Anyone could have gone in to him.'

'But you know of one who certainly did go in?'

Sybilla had plucked her step-daughter by the sleeve, distressed and reproving, but Melicent shook her off without a glance. 'And only one?' she said sharply.

'To my knowledge, yes,' agreed Edmund, uncomprehendingly, 'but surely no harm. It was shortly before you all returned from the abbot's lodging. I had time then to make a round, and I saw the sheriff's door opened, and found a young man beside the bed, as though he meant to disturb his sleep. I could not have that, so I took him by the shoulder and turned him about, and pointed him out of the room. And he went obediently and made no protest. There was no word spoken,' said Edmund simply, 'and no harm done. The patient had not awakened.'

'No,' said Melicent, her voice shaken at last out of its wintry calm, 'nor never did again, nor never will. Name him, this *one*.'

And Edmund did not even know the boy's name, so little had he had to do with him. He indicated Elis with a hesitant hand. 'It was our Welsh prisoner.'

424

Melicent let out a strange, grievous sound of anger, guilt and pain, and whirled upon Elis. Her marble whiteness had become incandescent, and the blue of her eyes was like the blinding fire sunlight strikes from ice. 'Yes, *you*! None but you! None but you went in there. Oh, God, what have you and I done between us! And I, fool, fool, I never believed you could mean it, when you told me, many times over, you'd kill for me, kill whoever stood between us. Oh, God, and I *loved* you! I may even have invited you, urged you to the deed. I never understood. Anything, you said, to keep us together a while longer, anything to prevent your being sent away, back to Wales. *Anything*! You said you would kill, and now you have killed, and God forgive me, I am guilty along with you.'

Elis stood facing her, the poor lucky lad suddenly most unlucky and defenceless as a babe. He stared with dropped jaw and startled, puzzled, terrified face, struck clean out of words and wits, open to any stab. He shook his head violently from side to side, as if dreamers who use their fingers to prise open eyelids beset by unbearable dreams. He could not get out a word or a sound.

'I take back every evidence of love,' raged Melicent, her voice like a cry of pain. 'I hate you, I loathe you ... I hate myself for ever loving you. You have so mistaken me, you have killed my father.'

He wrenched himself out of his stupor then, and made a wild move towards her. 'Melicent! For God's sake, what are you saying?'

She drew back violently out of his reach. 'No, don't touch me, don't come near me. Murderer!'

'This shall end,' said Hugh, and took her by the shoulders and put her into Sybilla's arms. 'Madam, I had thought to spare you any further distress today, but you see this will not wait. Bring her! And sergeant, have these two put into the gatehouse, where we may be private. Edmund and Cadfael, go with us, we may well need you.'

'Now,' said Hugh, when he had herded them all, accused, accuser and witnesses, into the anteroom of the gatehouse out of the cold and out of the public eye, 'now let us get to the heart of this. Brother Edmund, you say you found this man in the sheriff's chamber, standing beside his bed. How did you read it? Did you think, by appearances, he had been long in there? Or that he had but newly come?'

425

'I thought he had but just crept in,' said Edmund. 'He was close to the foot of the bed, a little stooped, looking down as though he wondered whether he dared wake the sleeper.'

'Yet he could have been here longer? He could have been standing over a man he had smothered, to assure himself it was thoroughly done?'

'It might be interpretable so,' agreed Edmund very dubiously, 'but the thought did not enter my mind. If there had been anything so sinister in him, would it not have shown? It's true he started when I touched him, and looked guilty – but I mean as a boy caught in mischief, nothing that caused me an ill thought. And he went, when I ordered him, as biddable as a child.'

'Did you look again at the bed, after he was gone? Can you say if the sheriff was still breathing then? And the coverings of the bed, were they disarranged?'

'All was smooth and quiet as when we left him sleeping. But I did not look more closely,' said Edmund sadly. 'I wish to God I had.'

'You knew of no cause, and his best cure was to be let alone to sleep. One more thing – had Elis anything in his hands?'

'No, nothing. Nor had he on the cloak he has on his arm now.' It was of a dark red cloth, smooth-surfaced and close-woven.

'Very well. And you have no knowledge of any other who may have made his way into the room?'

'No knowledge, no. But at any time entry was possible. There may well have been others.'

Melicent said with deadly bitterness, 'One was enough! And that one we do know.' She shook Sybilla's hand from her arm, refusing any restraint but her own. 'My lord Beringar, hear me speak. I say again, he has killed my father. I will not go back from that.'

'Have your say,' said Hugh shortly.

'My lord, you must know that this Elis and I learned to know each other in your castle where he was prisoner, but with the run of the wards on his parole, and I was with my mother and brother in my father's apartments waiting for news of him. We came to see and touch – my bitter regret that I am forced to say it, we loved. It was not our fault, it happened to us, we had no choice. We came to extreme dread that when my father came home we must be parted, for then Elis must leave in his place. And you, my lord, who best knew my father, know that he would never countenance a match with a Welshman. Many a time we talked of it, many a time we despaired. And he said – I swear he said so, he dare not deny it! – he said he would kill for me if need be, kill any man who stood between us. Anything, he said, to hold us together, even murder. In love men say wild things. I never thought of harm, and yet I am to blame, for I was as desperate for love as he. And now he has done what he threatened, for he has surely killed my father.'

Elis got his breath, coming out of his stunned wretchedness with a heave that almost lifted him out of his boots. 'I did not! I swear to you I never laid hand on him, never spoke word to him. I would not for any gain have hurt your father, even though he barred you from me. I would have reached you somehow, there would have been a way ... You do me terrible wrong!'

'But you did go to the room where he lay?' Hugh reminded him equably. 'Why?'

'To make myself known to him, to plead my cause with him, what else? It was the only present hope I had, I could not let it slip through my fingers. I wanted to tell him that I love Melicent, that I am a man of lands and honour, and desire nothing better than to serve her with all my goods and gear. He might have listened! I knew, she had told me, that he was sworn enemy to the Welsh, I knew it was a poor hope, but it was all the hope I had. But I never got the chance to speak. He was deep asleep, and before I ventured to disturb him the good brother came and banished me. This is the truth, and I will swear to it on the altar.'

'It *is* truth!' Eliud spoke up vehemently for his friend. He stood close, since Elis had refused a seat, his shoulder against Elis's shoulder for comfort and assurance. He was as pale as if the accusation had been made against him, and his voice was husky and low. 'He was with me in the cloister, he told me of his love, and said he would go to the lord Gilbert and speak to him man to man. I thought it unwise, but he would go. It was not many minutes before I saw him come forth, and Brother Infirmarer making sure he departed. And there was no manner of stealth in his dealings,' insisted Eliud stoutly, 'for he crossed the court straight and fast, not caring who might see him go in.'

'That may well be true,' agreed Hugh thoughtfully, 'but for all that, even if he went in with no ill intent, and no great hope, once he stood there by the bedside it might come into his mind how easy, and how final, to remove the obstacle – a man sleeping and already very low.'

'He never would!' cried Eliud. 'His is no such mind.'

427

'I did not,' said Elis, and looked helplessly at Melicent, who stared back at him stonily and gave him no aid. 'For God's sake, believe me! I think I could not have touched or roused him, even if there had been no one to send me away. To see a fine, strong man so – quite defenceless ...'

'Yet no one entered there but you,' she said mercilessly.

'That cannot be proved!' flashed Eliud. 'Brother Infirmarer has said that the way was open, anyone might have gone in.'

'Nor can it be proved that anyone did,' she said with aching bitterness.

'But I think it can,' said Brother Cadfael.

He had all eyes on him in an instant. All this time some morsel of his memory had been worrying at the flaw he could not quite identify. He had picked up the folded sheepskin cloak from the chest, where he had watched Edmund lay it, and there had been something different about it, though he could not think what it could be. And then the encounter with death had driven the matter to the back of his mind, but it had lodged there ever since, like chaff in the throat after eating porridge. And suddenly he had it. The cloak was gone now, gone with Einon ab Ithel back to Wales, but Edmund was there to confirm what he had to say. And so was Eliud, who would know his lord's belongings.

'When we disrobed and bedded Gilbert Prestcote,' he said, 'the cloak that wrapped him, which belonged to Einon ab Ithel, was folded and laid by – Brother Edmund will remember it – in such case as to leave plain to be seen in the collar a great gold pin that fastened it. When Eliud, here, came to ask me to show him the room and hand out his lord's cloak to him and I did so, the cloak was folded as before, but the pin was gone. Small wonder if we forgot the matter, seeing what else we found. But I knew there was something I should have noted, and now I have recalled what it was.'

'It is truth!' cried Eliud, his face brightening eagerly. 'I never thought! And I have let my lord go without it, never a word said. I fastened the collar of the cloak with it myself, when we laid him in the litter, for the wind blew cold. But with this upset, I never thought to look for it again. Here is Elis and has never been out of men's sight since he came from the infirmary – ask all here! If he took it, he has it on him still. And if he has it not, then someone else has been in there before him and taken it. My foster-brother is no thief and no murderer – but if you doubt, you have your remedy.'

'What Cadfael says is truth,' said Edmund. 'The pin was there plain to be seen. If it is gone, then someone went in and took it.'

Elis had caught the fierce glow of hope, in spite of the unchanging bitterness and grief of Melicent's face. 'Strip me!' he demanded, glittering. 'Search my body! I won't endure to be thought thief and murderer both.'

In justice to him, rather than having any real doubts in the matter, Hugh took him at his word, but allowed only Cadfael and Edmund to be witnesses with him in the borrowed cell where Elis, with sweeping, arrogant, hurt gestures, tore off his clothes and let them fall about him, until he stood naked with braced feet astride and arms outspread, and dragged disdainful fingers painfully through his thick thatch of curls and shook his head violently to show there was nothing made away there. Now that he was safe from the broken, embittered stare of Melicent's eyes the tears he had defied came treacherously into his own, and he blinked and shook them proudly away.

Hugh let him cool gradually and in considerate silence.

'Are you content?' the boy demanded stiffly, when he had his voice well in rein.

'Are *you*?' said Hugh, and smiled.

There was a brief, almost consoling silence. Then Hugh said mildly, 'Cover yourself, then. Take your time.' And while Elis was dressing, with hands that shook now in reaction: 'You do understand that I must hold you in close guard, you and your foster-brother and the others alike. As at this moment, you are no more in suspicion than many who belong here within the pale, and will not be let out of it until I know to the last moment where they spent this morn and noon. This is no more than a beginning, and you but one of many.'

'I do understand,' said Elis and wavered, hesitant to ask a favour. 'Need I be separated from Eliud?'

'You shall have Eliud,' said Hugh.

When they went out again to those who still waited in the anteroom, the two women were on their feet, and plainly longing to withdraw. Sybilla had but half her mind here in support of her step-daughter, the better half was with her son; and if she had been a faithful and dutiful wife to her older husband and mourned him truly now after her fashion, love was much too large a word for what she had felt for him and

429

barely large enough for what she felt for the boy he had given her. Sybilla's thoughts were with the future, not the past.

'My lord,' she said, 'you know where we may be found for the days to come. Let me take my daughter away now, we have things which must be done.'

'At your pleasure, madam,' said Hugh. 'You shall not be troubled more than is needful.' And he added only: 'But you should know that the matter of this missing pin remains. There has been more than one intruder into your husband's privacy. Bear it in mind.'

'Very gladly I leave it all in your hands,' said Sybilla fervently. And forth she went, her hand imperative at Melicent's elbow. They passed close by Elis in the doorway, and his starving stare fastened on the girl's face. She passed him by without a glance, she even drew aside her skirts for fear they should brush him in departing. He was too young, too open, too simple to understand that more than half the hatred and revulsion she felt for him belonged rather to herself, and her dread that she had gone far towards desiring the death she now so desperately repented.

Chapter Seven

N THE death-chamber, with the door closed fast, Hugh Beringar and Brother Cadfael stood beside Gilbert Prestcote's body and turned back the brychan and sheet to the sunken breast. They had brought in lamps to set close where they would burn steadily and cast a strong light on the dead face. Cadfael took the smaller saucer lamp in his hand and moved it slowly across the bruised mouth and nostrils and the grizzled beard, to catch every angle of vision and pick out every mote of dust or thread.

'No matter how feeble, no matter how deep asleep, a man will fight as best as he can for his breath, and whatever is clamped over his face, unless so hard and smooth it lacks any surface pile, he will inhale. And so did this one.' The dilated nostrils had fine hairs within, a trap for tiny particles of thread. 'Do you see colour there?'

In an almost imperceptible current of air a gossamer wisp quivered, taking the light. 'Blue,' said Hugh, peering close, and his breath caused the cobweb strand to dance. 'Blue is a difficult and expensive dye. And there's no such tint in these brychans.'

'Let's have it forth,' said Cadfael, and advanced his small tweezers, used for extracting thorns and splinters from unwary labouring fingers, to capture a filament almost too delicate to be seen. There was more of it, however, when it emerged, two or three fine strands that had the springy life of wool.

'Hold your breath,' said Cadfael, 'till I have this safe under a

431

lid from being blown away.' He had brought one of the containers in which he stored his tablets and lozenges when he had moulded and dried them, a little polished wooden box, almost black in colour, and against the glossy dark surface the shred of wool shone brightly, a full, clear blue. He shut the lid upon it carefully, and probed again with the tweezers. Hugh shifted the lamp to cast its light at a new angle, and there was a brief gleam of red, the soft pale red of late summer roses past their prime. It winked and vanished. Hugh moved the light to find it again. Barely two frail, curling filaments of the many that must have made up this wool that had woven the cloth, but wool carries colour bravely.

'Blue and rose. Both precious colours, not for the furnishings of a bed.' Cadfael captured the elusive thing after two or three casts, and imprisoned it with the blue. The light, carefully deployed, found no more such traces in the stretched nostrils. 'Well, he also wore a beard. Let us see!'

There was a clear thread of the blue fluttering in the greying beard. Cadfael extracted it, and carefully combed the grizzled strands out into order to search for more. When he shook and stroked out the dust and hairs from the comb into his box, two or three points of light glimmered and vanished, like motes of dust lit by the sun. He tilted the box from side to side to recover them, for they were invisible once dimmed, and one single gold spark rewarded him. He found what he sought caught between the clenched teeth. One strand had frayed from age or use, and the spasm of death had bitten and held it. He drew it forth and held it to the light in his tweezers. A first finger-joint long, brittle and bright, glinting in the lamplight, the gold thread that had shed those invisible, scintillating particles.

'Expensive indeed!' said Cadfael, shutting it carefully into his box. 'A princely death, to be smothered under cloth of fine wool embroidered with thread of gold. Tapestry? Altar-cloth? A lady's brocaded gown? A piece from a worn vestment? Certainly nothing here within the infirmary, Hugh. Whatever it may have been, some man brought it with him.'

'So it would seem,' agreed Hugh, brooding.

They found nothing more, but what they had found was puzzling enough.

'So where is the cloth that smothered him?' wondered Cadfael, fretting. 'And where is the gold pin that fastened Einon ab Ithel's cloak?'

'Search for the cloth,' said Hugh, 'since it has a richness that could well be found somewhere within the abbey walls. And I will search for the pin. I have six Welshmen of the escort and Eliud yet to question and strip, and if that fails, we'll burrow our way through the entire enclave as best we can. If they are here, we'll find them.'

They searched, Cadfael for a cloth, any cloth which could show the rich colours and the gold thread he was seeking, Hugh for the gold pin. With the abbot's leave and the assistance of Prior Robert, who had the most comprehensive knowledge of the riches of the house and demonstrated its treasures with pride, Cadfael examined every hanging, tapestry and altar-cloth the abbey possessed, but none of them matched the quivering fragments he brought to the comparison. Shades of colour are exact and consistent. This rose and this blue had no companions here.

Hugh, for his part, thoroughly searched the clothing and harness of all the Welshmen made prisoner by this death, and Prior Robert, though with disapproval, sanctioned the extension of the search into the cells of the brothers and novices, and even the possessions of the boys, for children may be tempted by a bright thing, without realising the gravity of what they do. But nowhere did they find any trace of the old and massive pin that had held the collar of Einon's cloak close to keep the cold away from Gilbert Prestcote on his journey.

The day was spent by then and the evening coming on, but after Vespers and supper Cadfael returned to the quest. The inhabitants of the infirmary were quite willing to talk; they had not often so meaty a subject on which to debate. Yet neither Cadfael nor Edmund got much information out of them. Whatever had happened had happened during the half-hour or more when the brothers were at dinner in the refectory, and at that time the infirmary, already fed, was habitually asleep. There was one, however, who, being bedridden, slept a great deal at odd times, and was well able to remain wakeful if something more interesting than usual was going on.

'As for seeing,' said Brother Rhys ruefully, 'I'm as little profit to you, brother, as I am to myself. I know if another inmate passes by me and I know which of them it is, and I know light from dark, but little more. But my ears, I dare swear, have grown sharper as my eyes have grown dimmer. I heard the door of the chamber opposite, where the sheriff lay,

433

open twice, now you ask me to cudgel my memory. You know it creaks, opening. Closing, it's silent.'

'So someone entered there or at least opened the door. What more did you hear? Did anyone speak?'

'No, but I heard a stick tapping – very lightly – and then the door creaked. I reckoned it must be Brother Wilfred, who helps here when he's needed, for he's the only brother who walks with a stick, being lame from a young man.'

'Did he go in?'

'That you may better ask him, for I can't tell you. All was quiet a while, and then I heard him tap away along the passage to the outer door. He may only have pushed the door open to look and listen if all was well in there.'

'He must have drawn the door to again after him,' said Cadfael, 'or you would not have heard it creak again the second time. When was it Brother Wilfred paid his visit?'

But Rhys was vague about time. He shook his head and pondered. 'I did drowse for a while after my dinner. How should I know for how long? But they must have been still in the refectory some time after that, for it wasn't until later that Brother Edmund came back.'

'And the second time?'

'That must have been some while later, it might be as much as a quarter-hour. The door creaked again. He had a light step, whoever came, I just caught the fall of his foot on the threshold, and then nothing. The door making no sound, drawn to, I don't know how long he was within there, but I fancy he did go in. Brother Wilfred might have a proper call to peer inside to see all was well, but this other one had none.'

'How long was he within there? How long *could* he have been? Did you hear him leave?'

'I was in a doze again,' admitted Rhys regretfully. 'I can't tell you. And he did tread very soft, a young man's tread.'

So the second could have been Elis, for there had been no word spoken when Edmund followed him in and expelled him, and Edmund from long sojourning among the sick trod as silently as a cat. Or it might have been someone else, someone unknown, coming and going undisturbed and deadly, before ever Elis intruded with his avowedly harmless errand.

Meantime, he could at least find out if Brother Wilfred had indeed been left here to keep watch, for Cadfael had not numbered the brothers in the refectory at dinner, or noticed who was present and who absent. He had another thought.

434

'Did anyone from within here leave this room during all that time? Brother Maurice, for one, seldom sleeps much during the day, and when others are sleeping he may well be restless, wanting company.'

'None of them passed by me to the door while I was waking,' said Rhys positively. 'And I was not so deep asleep but I think I should have awakened if they had.'

Which might very well be true, yet could not be taken for granted. But of what he had heard he was quite certain. Twice the door had creaked open wide enough to let somebody in.

Brother Maurice had spoken up for himself without even being asked, as soon as the sheriff's death was mentioned, as daily it would be now until the truth was known and the sensation allowed to fade away into oblivion. Brother Edmund reported it to Cadfael after Compline, in the half-hour of repose before bed.

'I had prayers said for his soul, and told them tomorrow we should say a Mass for him – an honourable officer who died here among us and had been a good patron of our house. Up stands Maurice and says outright that he will faithfully put up prayers for the man's salvation, for now at last his debts are fully paid, and divine justice has been done. I asked him by whose hand, seeing he knew so much,' said Edmund with uncharacteristic bitterness, but even more resignation, 'and he reproved me for doubting that the hand was God's. Sometimes I question whether his ailment of the mind is misfortune or cunning. But try to pin him down and he'll slip through your fingers every time. He is certainly very content with this death. God forgive us all our backslidings and namely those into which we fall unwitting.'

'Amen!' said Cadfael fervently. 'And he's a strong, able man, and always in the right, even if it came to murder. But where would he lay hands on such a cloth as I have in mind?' He remembered to ask: 'Did you leave Brother Wilfred to keep a close eye on things here, when you went to dinner in the refectory?'

'I wish I had,' owned Edmund sadly. 'There might have been no such evil then. No, Wilfred was at dinner with us, did you never see him? I wish I had set a watch, with all my heart. But that's hindsight. Who was ever to suppose that murder would walk in and let loose chaos on us? There was nothing to give me warning.'

'Nothing,' agreed Cadfael and brooded, considering. 'So

435

Wilfred is out of the reckoning. Who else among us walks with a stick? None that I know of.'

'There's Anion is still on a crutch,' said Edmund, 'though he's about ready to discard it. He rather flies with it now than hobbles, but for the moment it's grown a habit with him, after so stubborn a break. Why, are you looking for a man with a prop?'

Now there, thought Cadfael, going wearily to his bed at last, is a strange thing. Brother Rhys, hearing a stick tapping, looks for the source of it only among the brothers; and I, making my way round the infirmary, never give a thought to any but those who are brothers, and am likely to be blind and deaf to what any other may be up to even in my presence. For it had only now dawned on him that when he and Brother Edmund entered the long room, already settling for the evening, one younger and more active soul had risen from the corner where he sat and gone quietly out by the door to the chapel, the leather-shod tip of his crutch so light upon the stones that it seemed he hardly needed it, and could only have taken it away with him, as Edmund said, out of habit or in order to remove it from notice.

Well, Anion would have to wait until tomorrow. It was too late to trouble the repose of the ageing sick tonight.

In a cell of the castle, behind a locked door, Elis and Eliud shared a bed no harder than many they had shared before and slept like twin babes, without a care in the world. They had care enough now. Elis lay on his face, sure that his life was ended, that he would never love again, that nothing was left to him, even if he escaped this coil alive, but to go on Crusade or take the tonsure or undergo some barefoot pilgrimage to the Holy Land from which he would certainly never return. And Eliud lay patient and agonising at his back, with an arm wreathed over the rigid, rejecting shoulders, fetching up comfort from where he himself had none. This cousin-brother of his was far too vehemently alive to die for love, or to succumb for grief because he was accused of an infamy he had not committed. But his pain, however curable, was extreme while it lasted.

'She never loved me,' lamented Elis, tense and quivering under the embracing arm. 'If she had, she would have trusted me, she would have known me better. If ever she'd loved me, how could she believe I would do murder?' As indignantly as if he had never in his transports sworn that he would! That or *anything*.

'She's shocked to the heart for her father,' pleaded Eliud stoutly. 'How can you ask her to be fair to you? Only wait, give her time. If she loved you, then she still does. Poor girl, she can't choose. It's for her you should be sorry. She takes this death to her own account – have you not told me? You've done no wrong and so it will be proved.'

'No, I've lost her, she'll never let me near her again, never believe a word I say.'

'She will, for it will be proven you're blameless. I swear to you it will! Truth will come out, it must, it will.'

'If I don't win her back,' Elis vowed, muffled in his cradling arms, 'I shall die.'

'You won't die, you won't fail to win her back,' promised Eliud in desperation. 'Hush, hush and sleep!' He reached out a hand and snuffed out the flailing flame of their tiny lamp. He knew the tensions and releases of this body he had slept beside from childhood, and knew that sleep was already a weight on Elis's smarting eyelids. There are those who come brand-new into the new day and have to rediscover their griefs. Eliud was no such person. He nursed his griefs, unsleeping into the small hours, with the chief of them fathoms deep under his protecting arm.

Chapter Eight

ANION THE cattle-man, for want of calf or lamb to keep his hand in within the abbey enclave, had taken to spending much of his time in the stables, where at least there was horseflesh to be tended and enjoyed. Very soon now he would be fit to be sent back to the grange where he served, but he could not go until Brother Edmund discharged him. He had a gifted hand with animals, and the grooms were on familiar and friendly terms with him.

Brother Cadfael approached him somewhat sidelong, unwilling to startle or dismay him too soon. It was not difficult. Horses and mules had their sicknesses and injuries, as surely as men, and called frequently for remedies from Cadfael's store. One of the ponies the lay servants used as pack-horses had fallen lame and was in need of Cadfael's rubbing oils to treat the strain, and he brought the flask himself to the stable-yard, as good as certain he would find Anion there. It was easy enough to entice the practised stockman into taking over the massage, and to linger to watch and admire as he worked his thick but agile fingers into the painful muscles. The pony stood like a statue for him, utterly trusting. That in itself had something eloquent to say.

'You spend less and less time in the infirmary now,' said Cadfael, studying the dour, dark profile under the fall of straight black hair. 'Very soon we shall be losing you at this rate. You're as fast on a crutch as many of us are with two sturdy legs that never suffered a break. I fancy you could throw

438

the prop away anytime you pleased.'

'I'm told to wait,' said Anion shortly. 'Here I do what I'm told. It's some men's fate in life, brother, to take orders.'

'Then you'll be glad to be back with your cattle again, where they do obedience to you for a change.'

'I tend and care for them and mean them well,' said Anion, 'and they know it.'

'So does Edmund to you, and you know it.' Cadfael sat down on a saddle beside the stooping man, to come down to his level and view him on equal terms. Anion made no demur, it might even have been the faint shadow of a smile that touched his firmly closed mouth. Not at all an ill-looking man, and surely no more than twenty-seven or twenty-eight years old. 'You know the thing that happened there in the infirmary,' said Cadfael. 'You may well have been the most active man in there that dinner time. Though I doubt if you stayed long after you'd eaten. You're over-young to be shut in there with the ailing old. I've asked them all, did they hear or see any man go in there, by stealth or any other way, but they slept after they'd eaten. That's for the aged, not for you. You'd be up and about while they drowsed.'

'I left them snoring,' said Anion, turning the full stare of his deep-set eyes on Cadfael. He reached for a rag to wipe his hands, and rose nimbly enough, the still troublesome leg drawn up after him.

'Before we were all out of the refectory? And the Welsh lads led in to their repast?'

'While it was all quiet. I reckon you brothers were in the middle of your meal. Why?' demanded Anion pointblank.

'Because you might be a good witness, what else? Do you know of anyone who made his way into the infirmary about that time that you left it? Did you see or hear aught to give you pause? Any man lurking who should not have been there? The sheriff had his enemies,' said Cadfael firmly, 'like the rest of us mortals, and one of them deadly. Whatever he owed is paid now, or shortly to pay. God send none of us may take with him a worse account.'

'Amen!' said Anion. 'When I came forth from the infirmary, brothers, I met no man, I saw no man, friend or enemy, anywhere near that door.'

'Where were you bound? Down here to view the Welsh horses? If so,' explained Cadfael easily, warding off the sharp glance Anion gave him, 'you'd be a witness if any of those lads went off and left his fellows about that time.'

Anion shrugged that off disdainfully. 'I never came near the stables, not then. I went through the garden and down to the brook. With a west wind it smells of the hills down there,' said Anion. 'I grow sick of the shut-in smell of tired old men, and their talk that goes round and round.'

'Like mine!' said Cadfael tolerantly, and rose from the saddle. His eye lingered upon the crutch that was laid carelessly aside against the open door of a stall, a good fifty paces from where its owner was working. 'Yes, I see you're about ready to throw it away. You were still using it yesterday, though, unless Brother Rhys was mistaken. He heard you tap your way out for your walk in the garden, or thought he did.'

'He well might,' said Anion, and shook back his shaggy black mane from his round brown forehead. 'It's habit with me, after so long, even after the need's gone. But when there's a beast to see to, I forget, and leave it behind me in corners.'

He turned deliberately, laid an arm over the pony's neck, and led him slowly round on the cobbles, to mark his gait. And that was the end of the colloquy.

Brother Cadfael was fully occupied with his proper duties all that day, but that did not prevent him from giving a great deal of thought to the matter of Gilbert Prestcote's death. The sheriff had long ago requested space for his tomb in the abbey church of which he had been a steady patron and benefactor, and the next day was to see him laid to rest there. But the manner of his death would not allow any rest to those who were left behind him. From his distracted family to the unlucky Welsh suspects and prisoners in the castle, there was no one who did not find his own life disrupted and changed by this death.

The news was surely making its way about the countryside by this time, from village to village and assart to manor round the shire, and no doubt men and women in the streets of Shrewsbury were busily allotting the blame to this one and that one, with Elis ap Cynan their favourite villain. But they had not seen the minute, bright fragments Cadfael nursed in his little box, or hunted in vain through the precinct for any cloth that could show the identical tints and the twisted gold thread. They knew nothing about the massive gold pin that had vanished from Gilbert's death-chamber and could not be found within the pale.

Cadfael had caught glimpses of Lady Prestcote about the court, moving between the guest-hall and the church, where her husband lay in the mortuary chapel, swathed for his burial. But the girl had not once shown her face. Gilbert the younger, a little bewildered but oblivious of misfortune, played with the child oblates and the two young pupils, and was tenderly shepherded by Brother Paul, the master of the children. At seven years old he viewed with untroubled tolerance the eccentricities of grown-up people, and could make himself at home wherever his mother unaccountably conveyed him. As soon as his father was buried she would certainly take him away from here, to her favourite among her husband's manors, where his life would resume its placid progress untroubled by bereavement.

A few close acquaintances of the sheriff had begun to arrive and take up residence ready for the morrow. Cadfael lingered to watch them, and fit noble names to the sombre faces. He was thus occupied, on his way to the herbarium, when he observed one unexpected but welcome face entering. Sister Magdalen, on foot and alone, stepped briskly through the wicket, and looked about her for the nearest known face. To judge by her brightening eye and prompt advice, she was pleased that it should be Cadfael's.

'Well, well!' said Cadfael, going to meet her with equal pleasure. 'We had no thought of seeing you again so soon. Is all well in your forest? No more raiders?'

'Not so far,' said Sister Magdalen cautiously, 'but I would not say they might not try again, if ever they see Hugh Beringar looking the other way. It must have gone much against the grain with Madog ap Meredith to be bested by a handful of foresters and cottars, he may well want his revenge when he feels it safe to bid for it. But the forest men are keeping a good watch. It's not we who are in turmoil now, it seems. What's this I've been hearing in the town? Gilbert Prestcote dead, and that Welsh youngster I sent you blamed for the deed?'

'You've been in the town, then? And no stout escort with you this time?'

'Two,' she said, 'but I've left them up in the Wyle, where we shall lie overnight. If it's true the sheriff is to be buried tomorrow I must stay to do him honour among the rest. I'd no thought of such a thing when we set out this morning. I came on quite different business. There's a great-niece of Mother

Mariana, daughter to a cloth-merchant here in Shrewsbury, who's coming to take the veil among us. A plain child, none too bright, but willing, and knows she has small hopes of a pleasing marriage. Better with us than sold off like an unpromising heifer to the first that makes a grudging offer for her. I've left my men and horses in their yard, where I heard tell of what had happened here. Better to get the tale straight – there are any number of versions up there in the streets.'

'If you have an hour to spare,' said Cadfael heartily, 'come and share a flask of wine of my own making in the herb-garden, and I'll tell you the whole truth of it, so far as any man knows what's truth. Who knows, you may find a pattern in it that I have failed to find.'

In the wood-scented dimness of the workshop in the herbarium he told her, at leisure and in detail, everything he knew or had gathered concerning the death of Gilbert Prestcote, everything he had observed or thought concerning Elis ap Cynan. She listened, seated with spread knees and erect back on the bench against the wall, with her cup nursed in both hands to warm it, for the wine was red and full. She no longer exerted herself to be graceful, if ever she had, but her composed heaviness had its own impressive grace.

'I would not say but that boy *might* kill,' she said at the end of it. 'They act before they think and regret only too late. But I don't think he would kill his girl's father. Very easy, you say, and I believe it, to ease the man out of the world, so that even one not given to murder might do it before ever he realised. Yes, but those a man kills easily are commonly strangers to him. Hardly people at all. But this one would be armoured in identity – her father, no less, the man that begot her. And yet,' she owned, shaking her head, 'I may be wrong about him. He may be the one of his kind who does what his kind does not do. There is always one.'

'The girl believes absolutely that he is guilty,' said Cadfael thoughtfully, 'perhaps because she is all too well aware of what she feels to be her own guilt. The sire returns and the lovers are to be torn apart – no great step to dream of his failure to return, and only one more leap to see death as the final and total cause of that failure. But dreams they surely were, never truly even wished. The boy is on firmer ground when he swears he went to try and win her father to look kindly on his suit. For if ever I saw a lad sunlit and buoyed up with hope by nature, Elis is the one.'

'And this girl?' wondered Sister Magdalen, twirling her wine-cup between nursing palms. 'If they're of an age, then she must be the more mature by some years. So it goes! Is it anyway possible that *she* ...?'

'No,' said Cadfael with certainty. 'She was with the lady, and Hugh, and the Welsh princelings, throughout. I know she left her father living, and never came near him again until he was dead, and then in Hugh's company. No, she torments herself vainly. If you had her in your hands,' said Cadfael with conviction, 'you would soon find her out for the simple, green child she is.'

Sister Magdalen was in the act of saying philosophically, 'I'm hardly likely to get the chance,' when the tap on the door came. So light and tentative a sound, and yet so staunchly repeated, they fell silent and still to make sure of it.

Cadfael rose to open it and peer out through the narrowest possible chink, convinced there was no one there; and there she stood, her hand raised to knock again, pallid, wretched and resolute, half a head taller than he, the simple, green child of his description, with a steely core of Norman nobility forcing her to transcend herself. Hastily he flung the door wide. 'Come within from the cold. How can I serve you?'

'The porter told me,' said Melicent, 'that the sister from Godric's Ford came a while ago, and might be here wanting remedies from your store. I should like to speak with her.'

'Sister Magdalen is here,' said Cadfael. 'Come, sit with her by the brazier, and I'll leave you to talk with her in private.'

She came in half afraid, as though this small, unfamiliar place held daunting secrets. She stepped with fastidious delicacy, almost inch by inch, and yet with that determination in her that would not let her turn back. She looked at Sister Magdalen eye to eye, fascinated, doubtless having heard her history both ancient and recent, and found some difficulty in reconciling the two.

'Sister,' said Melicent, going arrow-straight to the point, 'when you go back to Godric's Ford, will you take me with you?'

Cadfael, as good as his word, withdrew softly and with alacrity, drawing the door to after him, but not so quickly that he did not hear Sister Magdalen reply simply and practically, 'Why?'

She never did or said quite what was expected of her, and it was a good question. It left Melicent in the delusion that this

443

formidable woman knew little or nothing about her, and necessitated the entire re-telling of the disastrous story, and in the re-telling it might fall into truer proportion, and allow the girl to reconsider her situation with somewhat less desperate urgency. So, at any rate, Brother Cadfael hoped, as he trotted away through the garden to go and spend a pleasant half-hour with Brother Anselm, the precentor, in his carrel in the cloister, where he would certainly be compiling the sequence of music for the burial of Gilbert Prestcote.

'I intend', said Melicent, rather grandly because of the jolt the blunt question had given her, 'to take the veil, and I would like it to be among the Benedictine sisters of Polesworth.'

'Sit down here beside me,' said Sister Magdalen comfortably, 'and tell me what has turned you to this withdrawal, and whether your family are in your confidence and approve your choice. You are very young, and have the world before you …'

'I am done with the world,' said Melicent.

'Child, as long as you live and breathe you will not have done with this world. We within the pale live in the same world as all poor souls without. Come, you have your reasons for wishing to enter the conventual life. Sit and tell me, let me hear them. You are young and fair and nobly born, and you wish to abandon marriage, children, position, honours, all … Why?'

Melicent, yielding, sank beside her on the bench, hugged her slenderness in the warmth of the brazier, and let fall the barriers of her bitterness to loose the flood. What she had vouchsafed to the preoccupied ears of Sybilla was no more than the thread on which this confession was strung. All that heady dream of minstrels' love-tales poured out of her.

'Even if you are right in rejecting one man,' said Magdalen mildly, 'you may be most unjust in rejecting all. Let alone the possibility that you mistake even this Elis ap Cynan. For until it is proved he lies, you must bear in mind he *may* be telling truth.'

'He said he would kill for me,' said Melicent, relentless, 'he went to where my father lay, and my father is dead. There was no other known to have gone near. As for me, I have no doubts. I wish I had never seen his face, and I pray I never may again.'

'And you will not wait to make your peace with one betrayal, and still show your countenance to others who do not betray?'

'At least I do know,' said Melicent bitterly, 'that God does not betray. And I am done with men.'

'Child,' said Sister Magdalen, sighing, 'not until the day of your death will you have done with men. Bishops, abbots, priests, confessors, all are men, blood-brothers to the commonest of sinful mankind. While you live, there is no way of escape from your part in humanity.'

'I have finished, then, with love,' said Melicent, all the more vehemently because a morsel of her heart cried out to her that she lied.

'Oh, my dear soul, love is the one thing with which you must never dispense. Without it, what use are you to us or to any? Granted there are ways and ways of loving,' said the nun come late to her celibacy, recalling what at the time she had hardly recognised as deserving the title, but knew now for one aspect of love, 'yet for all there is a warmth needed, and if that fire goes out it cannot be rekindled. Well,' she said, considering, 'if your stepmother approve your going with me, then you may come, and welcome. Come and be quiet with us for a while, and we shall see.'

'Will you come with me to my mother, then, and hear me ask her leave?'

'I will,' said Sister Magdalen, and rose and plucked her habit about her ready to set forth.

She told Brother Cadfael the gist of it when she stayed to attend Vespers before going back to the cloth-merchant's house in the town.

'She'll be better out of here, away from the lad, but left with the image of him she already carries about with her. Time and truth are what the pair of them most need, and I'll see she takes no vows until this whole matter is resolved. The boy is better left to you, if you can keep an eye on him now and then.'

'You don't believe,' said Cadfael with certainty, 'that he ever did violence to her father.'

'Do I know? Is there man or woman who might not kill given the driving need? A proper, upstanding, impudent, open-hearted lad, though,' said Sister Magdalen, who had never repented anything she did, 'one that I might have fancied, when my fancying days were.'

Cadfael went to supper in the refectory, and then to Collations in the chapter-house, which he often missed if he had vulnerable

445

preparations brewing in his workshop. In thinking over such slight gains as he had made in his quest for the truth, he had got nowhere, and it was good to put all that aside and listen with good heart to the lives of saints who had shrugged off the cares of the world to let in the promises of a world beyond and viewed earthly justice as no more than a futile shadow-play obscuring the absolute justice of heaven, for which no man need wait longer than the life-span of mortality.

They were past St Gregory and approaching St Edward the Confessor and St Benedict himself – the middle days of March, and the blessed works of spring beginning, with everything hopeful and striving ahead. A good time. Cadfael had spent the hours before Sister Magdalen came digging and clearing the fresh half of his mint-bed, to give it space to proliferate new and young and green, rid of the old and debilitated. He emerged from the chapter-house feeling renewed, and it came at first as no more than a mild surprise when Brother Edmund came seeking him before Compline, looking almost episcopal as he brandished in one hand what at first sight might have been a crozier but when lowered to the ground reached no higher than his armpit, and was manifestly a crutch.

'I found it lying in a corner of the stable-yard. Anion's! Cadfael, he did not come for his supper tonight and he is nowhere in the infirmary – neither in the common room, nor in his bed, nor in the chapel. Have you seen him anywhere this day?'

'Not since morning,' said Cadfael, thinking back with something of an effort from the peace of the chapter-house. 'He came to dinner at midday?'

'So he did, but I find no man who has seen him since. I've looked for him everywhere, asked every man, and found nothing more of him than this, discarded. Anion is gone! Oh, Cadfael, I doubt he has fled his mortal guilt. Why else should he run from us?'

It was well past Compline when Hugh Beringar entered his own hall, empty-handed and disconcerted from his enquiries among the Welshmen, and found Brother Cadfael sitting by the fireside with Aline, waiting for him with a clouded brow.

'What brings you here so late?' wondered Hugh. 'Out without leave again?' It had been known to happen, and the recollection of one such expedition, before the austere days of Abbot Radulfus, was an old and private joke between them.

'That I am not,' said Cadfael firmly. 'There's a piece of unexpected news even Prior Robert thought had better come to your ears as soon as possible. We had in our infirmary, with a broken leg mending and all but ready to leave us, a fellow named Anion. I doubt if the name means much to you, it was not you had to do with his brother. But do you remember a brawl in the town, two years ago now, when a gate-keeper on the bridge was knifed? Prestcote hanged the Welshman that did it – well, whether he did it or not, and naturally he'd say he didn't, but he was blind drunk at the time and probaby never knew the truth of it himself. However it was, he was hanged for it. A young fellow who used to trade in fleeces to the town market from somewhere in Mechain. Well, this Anion is his brother born the wrong side of the brychan, when the father was doing the trading, and there was no bad blood between the two. They got to know each other and there was a fondness.'

'If ever I knew of this,' said Hugh, drawing up to the fire with him, 'I had forgot it.'

'So had not Anion. He's said little, but it's known he nursed his grudge, and there's enough Welsh in him to make him look upon revenge as a duty, if ever the chance came his way.'

'And what of him now?' Hugh was studying his friend's face intently, foreseeing what was to come. 'Are you telling me this fellow was within the pale now, when the sheriff was brought there helpless?'

'He was, and only a door ajar between him and his enemy – if so he held him, as rumour says he did. Not the only one with a grudge, either, so that's no proof of anything more than this, that the opportunity was there. But tonight there's another mark against him. The man's gone. He did not come for his supper, he's not in his bed, and no man has seen him since dinner. Edmund missed him at the meal and has been looking for him ever since, but never a sign. And the crutch he was still using, though more from habit than need, was lying in the stable-yard. Anion has taken to his heels. And the blame, if blame there is,' said Cadfael honestly, 'is mine. Edmund and I have been asking every man in the infirmary if he saw or heard anything of note about the sheriff's chamber, any traffic in or out. It was but the same asking with Anion, indeed I was more cautious with him than with any when I spoke with him this morning in the stables. But for all that, no question, I've frightened him away.'

'Not necessarily a proof of guilt, to take fright and run,' said

447

Hugh reasonably. 'Men without privilege are apt to suppose they'll be blamed for whatever's done amiss. Is it certain he's gone? A man just healed of a broken leg? Has he taken horse or mule? Nothing stolen?'

'Nothing. But there's more to tell. Brother Rhys, whose bed is by the door, across the passage from where the sheriff lay, heard the door creak twice and the first time he says someone entered, or at least pushed the door open, who walked with a stick. The second time came later, and may have been the time the Welsh boy went in there. Rhys is hazy about time, and slept before and after, but both visitors came while the court was quiet – he says, while we of the house were in the refectory. With that, and now he's run – even Edmund is taking it for granted Anion is your murderer. They'll be crying his guilt in the town by morning.'

'But you are not so sure,' said Hugh, eyeing him steadily.

'Something he had on his mind, surely, something he saw as guilt, or knew others would call guilt, or he would not have run. But murderer …? Hugh, I have in that pill-box of mine certain proof of dyed wools and gold thread in whatever cloth was used to kill. *Certain* – whereas flight is uncertain proof of anything worse than fear. You know as I know that there was no such woven cloth anywhere in that room, or in the infirmary, or in the entire pale so far as we can discover. Whoever used it brought it with him. Where would Anion get hold of any such rich material? He can never have handled anything better than drab homespun and unbleached flax in his life. It casts great doubt on his guilt, though it does not utterly rule it out. It's why I did not press him too far – or thought I had not!' he added ruefully.

Hugh nodded guarded agreement, and put the point away in his mind. 'But for all that, tomorrow at dawn I must send out search parties between here and Wales, for surely that's the way he'll go. A border between him and his fear will be his first thought. If I can take him, I must and will. Then we may get out of him whatever it is he does know. A lame man cannot yet have got very far.'

'But remember the cloth. For those threads do not lie, though a mortal man may, guilty or innocent. The instrument of death is what we have to find.'

The hunt went forth at dawn, in small parties filtering through the woods by all the paths that led most directly to Wales, but they came back with the dark, empty-handed. Lame or no,

Anion had contrived to vanish within half a day.

The tale had gone forth through the town and the Foregate by then, every shop had it and every customer, the ale-houses discussed it avidly, and the general agreement was that neither Hugh Beringar nor any other man need look further for the sheriff's murderer. The dour cattle-man with a grudge had been heard going into and leaving the death-chamber, and on being questioned had fled. Nothing could be simpler.

And that was the day when they buried Gilbert Prestcote, in the tomb he had had made for himself in a transept of the abbey church. Half the nobility of the shire was there to do him honour, and Hugh Beringar with an escort of his officers, and the provost of Shrewsbury, Geoffrey Corviser, with his son Philip and his son's wife Emma, and all the solid merchants of the town guild. The sheriff's widow came in deep mourning, with her small son round-eyed and awed at the end of her arm. Music and ceremony, and the immensity of the vault, and the candles and the torches, all charmed and fascinated him, he was good as gold throughout the service.

And whatever personal enemies Gilbert Prestcote might have had, he had been a fair and trusted sheriff to this county in general, and the merchant princes were well aware of the relative security and justice they had enjoyed under him, where much of England suffered a far worse fate.

So in his passing Gilbert had his due, and his people's weighty and deserved intercession for him with his God.

'No,' said Hugh, waiting for Cadfael as the brothers came out from Vespers that evening, 'nothing as yet. Crippled or not, it seems young Anion has got clean away. I've set a watch along the border, in case he's lying in covert this side till the hunt is called off, but I doubt he's already over the dyke. And whether to be glad or sorry for it, that's more than I know. I have Welsh in my own manor, Cadfael, I know what drives them, and the law that vindicates them where ours condemns. I've been a frontiersman all my life, tugged two ways.'

'You must pursue it,' said Cadfael with sympathy. 'You have no choice.'

'No, none. Gilbert was my chief,' said Hugh, 'and had my loyalty. Very little we two had in common, I don't know that I even liked him overmuch. But respect – yes, that we had. His wife is taking her son back to the castle tonight, with what little she brought here. I'm waiting now to conduct her.' Her step-daughter was already departed with Sister Magdalen and the cloth-merchant's daughter, to the solitude of Godric's Ford. 'He'll miss his sister,' said Hugh, diverted into sympathy for the little boy.

'So will another,' said Cadfael, 'when he hears of her going. And the news of Anion's flight could not change her mind?'

'No, she's marble, she's damned him. Scold if you will,' said Hugh, wryly smiling, 'but I've let fall the word in his ear already that she's off to study the nun's life. Let him stew for a while – he owes us that, at least. And I've accepted his parole, his and the other lad's, Eliud. Either one of them has gone bail for himself *and* his cousin, not to stir a foot beyond the barbican, not to attempt escape, if I let them have the run of the wards. They've pledged their necks, each for the other. Not that I want to wring either neck, they suit very well as they are, untwisted, but no harm in accepting their pledges.'

'And I make no doubt,' said Cadfael, eyeing him closely, 'that you have a very sharp watch posted on your gates, and a very alert watchman on your walls, to see whether either of the two, or which of the two, breaks and runs for it.'

'I should be ashamed of my stewardship,' said Hugh candidly, 'if I had not.'

'And do they know, by this time, that a bastard Welsh cowman in the abbey's service has cast his crutch and run for his life?'

'They know it. And what do they say? They say with one voice, Cadfael, that such a humble soul and Welsh into the bargain, without kin or privilege here in England, would run as soon as eyes were cast on him, sure of being blamed unless he could show he was a mile from the matter at the fatal time. And can you find fault with that? It's what I said myself when you brought me the same news.'

'No fault,' said Cadfael thoughtfully. 'Yet matter for consideration, would you not say? From the threatened to the threatened, that's large grace.'

Chapter Nine

WAIN GWYNEDD sent back his response to the events at Shrewsbury on the day after Anion's flight, by the mouth of young John Marchmain, who had remained in Wales to stand surety for Gilbert Prestcote in the exchange of prisoners. The half-dozen Welsh who had escorted him home came only as far as the gates of the town, and there saluted and withdrew again to their own country.

John, son to Hugh's mother's younger sister, a gangling youth of nineteen, rode into the castle stiff with the dignity of the embassage with which he was entrusted, and reported himself ceremoniously to Hugh.

'Owain Gwynedd bids me to say that in the matter of a death so brought about, his own honour is at stake, and he orders his men here to bear themselves in patience and give all possible aid until the truth is known, the murderer uncovered, and they vindicated and free to return. He sends me back as freed by fate. He says he has no other prisoner to exchange for Elis ap Cynan, nor will he lift a finger to deliver him until both guilty and innocent are known.'

Hugh, who had known him from infancy, hoisted impressed eyebrows into his dark hair, whistled and laughed. 'You may stoop now, you're flying too high for me.'

'I speak for a high-flying hawk,' said John, blowing out a great breath and relaxing into a grin as he leaned back against the guard-room wall. 'Well, you've understood him. That's the elevated tenor of it. He says hold them and find your man. But there's more. How recent is the news you have from the south? I fancy Owain has his eyes and ears alert up and down the borders, where your writ can hardly go. He says that the empress is likely to win her way and be crowned queen, for Bishop Henry has let her into Winchester cathedral, where the crown and the treasure are guarded, and the archbishop of Canterbury is dilly-dallying, putting her off with – he can't well acknowledge her until he's spoken with the King. And by God, so he has, for he's been to Bristol and taken a covey of bishops with him, and been let in to speak with Stephen in his prison.'

'And what says King Stephen?' wondered Hugh.

'He told them, in that large way of his, that they kept their own consciences, that they must do, of course, what seemed to them best. And so they will, says Owain, what seems to them best for their own skins! They'll bend their necks and go with the victor. But here's what counts and what Owain has in mind. Ranulf of Chester is well aware of all this, and knows by now that Gilbert Prestcote is dead and this shire, he thinks, is in confusion, and the upshot is he's probing south, towards Shropshire and over into Wales, pouring men into his forward garrisons and feeling his way ahead by easy stages.'

'And what does Owain ask of us?' questioned Hugh, with kindling brightness.

'He says, if you will come north with a fair force, show your hand all along the Cheshire border, and reinforce Oswestry and Whitchurch and every other fortress up there, you will be helping both yourself and him, and he will do as much for you against the common enemy. And he says he'll come to the border at Rhyd-y-Croesau by Oswestry two days from now, about sunset, if you're minded to come and speak with him there.'

'Very firmly so minded!' said Hugh heartily, and rose to embrace his glowing cousin round the shoulders and haul him out about the business of meeting Owain's challenge and invitation, with the strongest force possible from a beleaguered shire.

That Owain had given them only two and a half days in which to muster, provide cover for the town and castle with a depleted garrison, and get their host into the north of the shire in time for the meeting on the border, was rather an earnest of the ease and speed with which Owain could move about his own mountainous land than a measure of the urgency of their mutual watch. Hugh spent the rest of that day making his dispositions in Shrewsbury and sending out his call for men to those who owed service. At dawn the next day his advance party would leave, and he himself with the main body by noon. There was much to be done in a matter of hours.

Lady Prestcote was also marshalling her servants and possessions in her high, bleak apartments, ready to leave next morning for the most easterly and peaceful of her manors. She had already sent off one string of pack-ponies with three of her men-servants. But while she was in town it was sensible to purchase such items as she knew to be in short supply where she was bound, and among other commodities she had requested a number of dried herbs from Cadfael's store. Her lord might be dead and in his tomb, but she had still an honour to administer, and for her son's sake had every intention of proving herself good at it. Men might die, but the meats necessary to the living would still require preservatives, salts and spices to keep them good and palatable. The boy was given, also, to a childish cough in spring, and she wanted a jar of Cadfael's herbal rub for his chest. Between them, Gilbert Prestcote the younger and domestic cares would soon fill up the gap, already closing, where Gilbert Prestcote the elder had been.

There was no real need for Cadfael to deliver the herbs and medicines in person, but he took advantage of the opportunity as much to satisfy his curiosity as to enjoy the walk and the fresh air on a fine, if blustery, March day. Along the Foregate, over the bridge spanning a Severn muddied and turgid from the thaw in the mountains, in through the town gate, up the long, steep curve of the Wyle, and gently downhill from the High Cross to the castle gatehouse, he went with eyes and ears alert, stopping many times to exchange greetings and pass the time of day. And everywhere men were talking of Anion's flight, and debating whether he would get clean away or be hauled back before night in a halter.

Hugh's muster was not yet common gossip in the town, though by nightfall it surely would be. But as soon as Cadfael entered the castle wards it was plain, by the purposeful bustle everywhere, that something of importance was in hand. The smith and the fletchers were hard at work, so were the grooms, and store-wagons were being loaded to follow stolidly after the faster horse- and foot-men. Cadfael delivered his herbs to the maid who came down to receive them, and went looking for Hugh. He found him directing the stalling of commandeered horses in the stables.

'You're moving, then? Northward?' said Cadfael, watching without surprise. 'And making quite a show, I see.'

'With luck, it need be only a show,' said Hugh, breaking his concentration to give his friend a warm sidelong smile.

'Is it Chester feeling his oats?'

Hugh laughed and told him. 'With Owain one side of the border and me the other, he should think twice. He's no more than trying his arm. He knows Gilbert is gone, but me he does not know. Not yet!'

'High time he should know Owain,' observed Cadfael. 'Men of sense have measured and valued him some while since, I fancy. And Ranulf is no fool, though I wouldn't say he's not capable of folly, blown up by success as he is. The wisest man in his cups may step too large and fall on his face.' And he asked, alert to all the sounds about him, and all the shadows that patterned the cobbles, 'Do your Welsh pair know where you're bound, and why, and who sent you word?'

He had lowered his voice to ask it, and Hugh, without need of a reason, did the same. 'Not from me. I've had no time to spare for civilities. But they're at large. Why?' He did not turn his head; he had noted where Cadfael was looking.

'Because they're bearing down on us, the pair in harness. And in anxiety.'

Hugh made their approach easier, waving into the groom's hands the thickset grey he had been watching about the cobbles, and turning naturally to withdraw from the stables as from a job finished for the present. And there they were, Elis and Eliud, shoulders together as though they had been born in one linked birth, moving in on him with drawn brows and troubled eyes.

'My lord Beringar ...' It was Eliud who spoke for them, the quiet, the solemn, the earnest one. 'You're moving to the border? There's threat of war? Is it with Wales?'

'To the border, yes,' said Hugh easily, 'there to meet with the prince of Gwynedd. The same that bade you and all your company here bear your souls in patience and work with me for justice concerning the matter you know of. No, never fret! Owain Gwynedd lets me know that both he and I have a common interest in the north of this shire, and a common enemy trying his luck there. Wales is in no danger from me and my shire, I believe, in no danger from Wales. At least,' he added, reconsidering briskly, 'not from Gwynedd.'

The cousins looked along wide, straight shoulders at each other, measuring thoughts. Elis said abruptly, 'My lord, but keep an eye to Powys. They ... *we*,' he corrected in a gasp of disgust, '*we* went to Lincoln under the banner of Chester. If it's Chester now, they'll know in Caus as soon as you move north. They may think it time ... think it safe ... The ladies there at Godric's Ford ...'

'A parcel of silly women,' said Cadfael musingly into his cowl, but audibly, 'and old and ugly into the bargain.'

The round, ingenuous face under the tangle of black curls flamed from neck to brow, but did not lower its eyes or lose its fixed intensity. 'I'm confessed and shriven of all manner of follies,' said Elis sturdily, 'that among them. Only do keep a watch on them! I mean it! That failure will rankle, they may still venture.'

'I had thought of it,' said Hugh patiently. 'I have no mind to strip this border utterly of men.'

The boy's blush faded and flamed anew. 'Pardon!' he said. 'It is your field. Only I do know ... It will have gone deep, that rebuff.'

Eliud plucked at his cousin's arm, drawing him back. They withdrew some paces without withdrawing their twin, troubled gaze. At the gate of the stables they turned, still with one last glance over their shoulders, and went away still linked, as one disconsolate creature.

'Christ!' said Hugh on a blown breath, looking after them. 'And I with less men than I should like, if truth be told, and that green child to warn me! As if I do not know I take chances now with every breath I draw and every archer I move. Should I ask him how a man spreads half a company across three times a company's span?'

'Ah, but he would have your whole force drawn up between Godric's Ford and his own countrymen,' said Cadfael tolerantly. 'The girl he fancies is there. I doubt if he cares so much what happens to Oswestry or Whitchurch, provided the Long Forest is left undisturbed. They've neither of them given you any trouble?'

'Good as gold! Not a step even into the shadow of the gate.' It was said with casual certainty. Cadfael drew his own conclusions. Hugh had someone commissioned to watch every move the two prisoners made, and knew all that they did, if not all that they said, from dawn to dark, and if ever one of them did advance a foot over the threshold, his toes would be promptly and efficiently trampled on. Unless, of course, it was more important to follow, and find out with what intent he broke his parole. But when Hugh was in the north, who was to say his deputy would maintain the same unobtrusive watch?

'Who is it you're leaving in charge here?'

'Young Alan Herbard. But Will Warden will have a hand on his shoulder. Why, do you expect a bolt for it as soon as my back's turned?' By the tone of his voice Hugh was in no great anxiety on that score. 'There's no absolute certainty in any man, when it comes to it, but those two have been schooled under Owain, and measure themselves by him, and by and large I'd take their word.'

So thought Cadfael, too. Yet it's truth that to any man may come the one extreme moment when he turns his back on his own nature and goes the contrary way. Cadfael caught one more glimpse of the cousins as he turned for home and passed through the outer ward. They were up on the guard-walk of the curtain wall, leaning together in one of the wide embrasures between the merlons, and gazing clean across the busy wards of the castle into the hazy distance beyond the town, on the road to Wales. Eliud's arm was about Elis's shoulders, to settle them comfortably into the space, and the two faces were close together and equally intent and reticent. Cadfael went back through the town with that dual likeness before his mind's eye, curiously memorable and deeply disturbing. More than ever they looked to him like mirror images, where left and right were interchangeable, the bright side and the dark side of the same being.

Sybilla Prestcote departed, her son on his stout brown pony at her elbow, her train of servants and pack-horses stirring the March mire which the recent east winds were drying into fine dust. Hugh's advance party had left at dawn, he and his main body of archers and men-at-arms followed at noon, and the commissariat wagons creaked along the northern road between the two groups, soon overhauled and left behind on the way to Oswestry. In the castle a somewhat nervous Alan Herbard, son of a knight and eager for office, mounted scrupulous guard and made every round of his responsibilities twice, for fear he had missed something the first time. He was athletic, fairly skilled in arms, but of small experience as yet, and well aware that any one of the sergeants Hugh had left behind was better equipped for the task in hand than he. They knew it, too, but spared him the too obvious demonstration of it.

A curious quiet descended on town and abbey with the departure of half the garrison, as though nothing could now happen here. The Welsh prisoners were condemned to boredom in captivity, the quest for Gilbert's murderer was at a standstill, there was nothing to be done but go on with the daily routine of work and leisure and worship, and wait.

And think, since action was suspended. Cadfael found himself thinking all the more steadily and deeply about the two missing pieces that held the whole puzzle together. Einon ab Ithel's gold pin, which he remembered very clearly, and that mysterious cloth which he had never seen, but which had stifled a man and urged him out of the world.

But was it so certain that he had never seen it? Never consciously, yet it had been here, here within the enclave, within the infirmary, within that room. It had been here, and now was not. And the search for it had been begun the same day, and the gates had been closed to all men attempting departure from the moment the death was discovered. How long an interval did that leave? Between the withdrawal of the brothers into the refectory and the finding of Gilbert dead, any man might have walked out by the gatehouse unquestioned. A matter of nearly two hours. That was one possibility.

The second possibility, thought Cadfael honestly, is that both cloth and pin are still here, somewhere within the enclave, but so well hidden that all our searching has not uncovered them.

And the third – he had been mulling it over in his mind all day, and repeatedly discarding it as a pointless aberration, but still it came back insistently, the one loophole. Yes, Hugh had put a guard on the gate from the moment the crime was known, but three people had been let out, all the same, the three who could not possibly have killed, since they had been in the abbot's company and Hugh's throughout. Einon ab Ithel and his two captains had ridden back to Owain Gwynedd. They had not taken any particle of guilt with them, yet they might unwittingly have taken evidence.

Three possibilities, and surely it might be worth examining even the third and most tenuous. He had lived with the other two for some days, and pursued them constantly, and all to no purpose. And for those countrymen of his penned in the castle, and for abbot and prior and brothers here, and for the dead man's family, there would be no true peace of mind until the truth was known.

Before Compline Cadfael took his trouble, as he had done many times before, to Abbot Radulfus.

'Either the cloth is still here among us, Father, but so well hidden that all our searching has failed to find it, or else it has been taken out of our walls by someone who left it in the short time between the hour of dinner and the discovery of the sheriff's death, or by someone who left, openly and with sanction, after that discovery. From that time Hugh Beringar has had a watch kept on all who left the enclave. For those who may have passed through the gates before the death was known, I think they must be few indeed, for the time was short, and the porter did name three, all good folk of the Foregate on parish business, and all have been visited and are clearly blameless. That there may be others I do concede, but he has called no more to mind.'

'We know,' said the abbot thoughtfully, 'of three who left that same afternoon, to return to Wales, being by absolute proof clear of all blame. Also of one, the man Anion, who fled after being questioned. It is known to you, as it is to me, that for most men Anion's guilt is proven by his flight. It is not so to you?'

'No, Father, or at least not that mortal guilt. Something he surely knows, and fears, and perhaps has cause to fear. But not that. He has been in our infirmary for some weeks, his every possession is known to all those within – he has little enough, the list is soon ended – and if ever he had had in his hands such a cloth as I seek, it would have been noticed and questioned.'

Radulfus nodded agreement. 'You have not mentioned, though that also is missing, the gold pin from the lord Einon's cloak.'

'That,' said Cadfael, understanding the allusion, 'is possible. It would account for his flight. And he has been sought, and still is. But if he took the one thing, he did not bring the other. Unless he had in his hands such a cloth as I have shadowed for you, Father, then he is no murderer. And that little he had, many men here have seen and known. Nor, so far as ever we can discover, had this house ever such a weave within its store, to be pilfered and so misused.'

'Yet if this cloth came and went in that one day,' said

Radulfus, 'are you saying it went hence with the Welsh lords? We know they did no wrong. If they had cause to think anything in their baggage, on returning, had to do with this matter, would they not have sent word?'

'They would have no such cause, Father, they would not know it had any importance to us. Only after they were gone did we recover those few frail threads I have shown you. How should they know we were seeking such a thing? Nor have we had any word from them, nothing but the message from Owain Gwynedd to Hugh Beringar. If Einon ab Ithel valued and has missed his jewel, he has not stopped to think he may have lost it here.'

'And you think,' asked the abbot, considering, 'that it might be well to speak with Einon and his officers, and examine these things?'

'At your will only,' said Cadfael. 'There is no knowing if it will lead to more knowledge than we have. Only, it *may*! And there are so many souls who need for their comfort to have this matter resolved. Even the guilty.'

'He most of all,' said Radulfus, and sat a while in silence. There in the parlour the light was only now beginning to fade. A cloudy day would have brought the dusk earlier. About this time, perhaps a little before, Hugh would have been waiting on the great dyke at Rhyd-y-Croesau by Oswestry for Owain Gwynedd. Unless, of course, Owain was like him in coming early to any meeting. Those two would understand each other without too many words. 'Let us go to Compline,' said the abbot, stirring, 'and pray for enlightenment. Tomorrow after Prime we will speak again.'

The Welsh of Powys had done very well out of their Lincoln venture, undertaken rather for plunder than out of any desire to support the earl of Chester, who was more often enemy than ally. Madog ap Meredith was quite willing to act in conjunction with Chester again, provided there was profit in it for Madog, and the news of Ranulf's probes into the borders of Gwynedd and Shropshire alerted him to pleasurable possibilities. It was some years since the men of Powys had captured and partially burned the castle of Caus, after the death of William Corbett and in the absence of his brother and heir, and they had held on to this advanced outpost ever since, a convenient base for further incursions. With Hugh Beringar gone north, and half the Shrewsbury garrison with him, the time seemed ripe for action.

The first thing that happened was a lightning raid from Caus along the valley towards Minsterley, the burning of an isolated farmstead and the driving off of a few cattle. The raiders drew off as rapidly as they had advanced, when the men of Minsterley mustered against them, and vanished into Caus and through the hills into Wales with their booty. But it was indication enough that they might be expected back and in greater strength, since this first assay had passed off so easily and without loss. Alan Herbard sweated, spared a few men to reinforce Minsterley, and waited for worse.

News of this tentative probe reached the abbey and the town next morning. The deceptive calm that followed was too good to be true, but the men of the borders, accustomed to insecurity as the commonplace of life, stolidly picked up the pieces and kept their billhooks and pitchforks ready to hand.

'It would seem, however,' said Abbot Radulfus, pondering the situation without surprise or alarm, but with concern for a shire threatened upon two fronts, 'that this conference in the north would be the better informed, on both parts, if they knew of this raid. There is a mutual interest. However short-lived it may prove,' he added drily, and smiled. A stranger to the Welsh, he had learned a great deal since his appointment in Shrewsbury. 'Gwynedd is close neighbour to Chester, as Powys is not, and their interests are very different. Moreover, it seems the one is to be trusted to be both honourable and sensible. The other – no, I would not say either wise or stable by our measure. I do not want these western people of ours harried and plundered, Cadfael. I have been thinking of what we said yesterday. If you return once again to Wales, to find these lords who visited us, you will also be close to where Hugh Beringar confers with the prince.'

'Certainly,' said Cadfael, 'for Einon ab Ithel is next in line to Owain Gwynedd's *penteulu*, the captain of his own guard. They will be together.'

'Then if I send you, as my envoy, to Einon, it would be well if you should also go to the castle, and make known to this young deputy there that you intend this journey, and can carry such messages as he may wish to Hugh Beringar. You know, I think,' said Radulfus with his dark smile, 'how to make such a contact discreetly. The young man is new to office.'

'I must, in any case, pass through the town,' said Cadfael mildly, 'and clearly I ought to report my errand to the authorities at the castle, and have their leave to pass. It is a good opportunity, where men are few and needed.'

'True,' said Radulfus, thinking how acutely men might shortly be needed down the border. 'Very well! Choose a horse to your liking. You have leave to deal as you think best. I want this death reconciled and purged, I want God's peace on my infirmary and within my walls, and the debt paid. Go, do what you can.'

There was no difficulty at the castle. Herbard needed only to be told that an envoy from the abbot was bound into Oswestry and beyond, and he added an embassage of his own to his sheriff. Raw and uneasy though he might be, he was braced and steeled to cope with whatever might come, but it was an additional shell of armour to have informed his chief. He was frightened but resolute; Cadfael thought he shaped well, and might be a useful man to Hugh, once blooded. And that might be no long way off.

'Let the lord Beringar know,' said Herbard, 'that I intend a close watch on the border by Caus. But I desire he should know the men of Powys are on the move. And if there are further raids, I will send word.'

'He shall know,' said Cadfael, and forthwith rode back a short spell through the town, down from the high cross to the Welsh bridge, and so north-west for Oswestry.

It was two days later that the next thrust came. Madog ap Meredith had been pleased with his first probe, and brought more men into the field before he launched his attack in force. Down the Rea valley to Minsterley they swarmed, burned and looted, wheeled both ways round Minsterley, and flowed on towards Pontesbury.

In Shrewsbury castle Welsh ears, as well as English, stretched and quivered to the bustle and fever of rumours.

'They are out!' said Elis, tense and sleepless beside his cousin in the night. 'Oh God, and Madog with this grudge to pay off! And *she* is there! Melicent is there at Godric's Ford. Oh, Eliud, if he should take it into his head to take revenge!'

'You're fretting for nothing,' Eliud insisted passionately. 'They know what they're doing here, they're on the watch, they'll not let any harm come to the nuns. Besides, Madog is not aiming there, but along the valley, where the pickings are best. And you saw yourself what the forest men can do. Why should he try that a second time? It wasn't his own nose was

461

put out of joint there, either, you told me who led that raid. What plunder is there at Godric's Ford for such as Madog, compared with the fat farms in the Minsterley valley? No, surely she's safe there.'

'*Safe*! How can you say it? Where is there any safety? They should never have let her go.' Elis ground angry fists in the rustling straw of their palliasse, and heaved himself round in the bed. 'Oh, Eliud, if only I were out of here and free ...'

'But you're not,' said Eliud, with the exasperated sharpness of one racked by the same pain, 'and neither am I. We're bound, and nothing we can do about it. For God's sake, do some justice to these English, they're neither fools nor cravens, they'll hold their city and their ground, and they'll take care of their women, without having to call on you or me. What right have you to doubt them? And you to talk so, who went raiding there yourself!'

Elis subsided with a defeated sigh and a drear smile. 'And got my come-uppance for it! Why did I ever go with Cadwaladr? God knows how often and how bitterly I've repented it since.'

'You would not be told,' said Eliud sadly, ashamed at having salted the wound. 'But she will be safe, you'll see, no harm will come to her, no harm will come to the nuns. Trust these English to look after their own. You must! There's nothing else we can do.'

'If I were free,' Elis agonised helplessly, 'I'd fetch her away from there, take her somewhere out of all danger ...'

'She would not go with you,' Eliud reminded him bleakly. 'You, of all people! Oh, God, how did we ever get into this quagmire, and how are we ever to get out of it?'

'If I could reach her, I could persuade her. In the end she would listen. She'll have remembered me better by now, she'll know she wrongs me. She'd go with me. If only I could reach her ...'

'But you're pledged, as I am,' said Eliud flatly. 'We've given our word, and it was freely accepted. Neither you nor I can stir a foot out of the gates without being dishonoured.'

'No,' agreed Elis miserably, and fell silent and still, staring into the darkness of the shallow vault over them.

Chapter Ten

ROTHER CADFAEL arrived in Oswestry by evening, to find town and castle alert and busy, but Hugh Beringar already departed. He had moved east after his meeting with Owain Gwynedd, they told him, to Whittington and Ellesmere, to see his whole northern border stiffened and call up fresh levies as far away as Whitchurch. While Owain had moved north on the border to meet the constable of Chirk and see that corner of the confederacy secure and well-manned. There had been some slight brushes with probing parties from Cheshire, but so tentative that it was plain Ranulf was feeling his way with caution, testing to see how well organised the opposition might prove to be. So far he had drawn off at the first encounter. He had made great gains at Lincoln and had no intention of endangering them now, but a very human desire to add to them if he found his opponents unprepared.

'Which he will not,' said the cheerful sergeant who received Cadfael into the castle and saw his horse stabled and the rider well entertained. 'The earl is no madman to shove his fist into a hornets' nest. Leave him one weak place he can gnaw wider and he'd be in, but we're leaving him none. He thought he might do well, knowing Prestcote was gone. He thought our lad would be green and easy. He's learning different! And if these Welsh of Powys have an ear pricked this way, they should also take the omens. But who's to reason what the Welsh will do? This Owain, now, he's a man on his own.

Straw-gold like a Saxon, and big! What's such a one doing in Wales?'

'He came here?' asked Cadfael, feeling his Cambrian blood stir in welcome.

'Last night, to sup with Beringar, and rode for Chirk at dawn. Welsh and English will man that fortress instead of fighting over it. There's a marvel!'

Cadfael pondered his errands and considered time. 'Where would Hugh Beringar be this night, do you suppose?'

'At Ellesmere, most like. And tomorrow at Whitchurch. The next day we should look for him back here. He means to meet again with Owain, and make his way down the border after, if all goes well here.'

'And if Owain lies at Chirk tonight, where will he be bound tomorrow?'

'He has his camp still at Tregeiriog, with his friend Tudur ap Rhys. It's there he's called whatever new levies come in to his border service.'

So he must keep touch there always, in order to deploy his forces wherever they might be needed. And if he returned there the next night, so would Einon ab Ithel.

'I'll sleep the night here,' said Cadfael, 'and tomorrow I'll also make for Tregeiriog. I know the maenol and its lord. I'll wait for Owain there. And do you let Hugh Beringar know that the Welsh of Powys are in the field again, as I've told you. Small harm yet, and should there be worse, Herbard will send word here. But if this border holds fast, and bloodies Chester's nose wherever he ventures it, Madog ap Meredith will also learn sense.'

This extreme border castle of Oswestry, with its town, was the king's, but the manor of Maesbury, of which it had become the head, was Hugh's own native place, and there was no man here who did not hold with him and trust him. Cadfael felt the solid security of Hugh's name about him, and a garrison doubly loyal – to Stephen and to Hugh. It was a good feeling, all the more now that Owain Gwynedd spread the benign shadow of his hand over a border that belonged by location to Powys. Cadfael slept well after hearing Compline in the castle chapel, rose early, took food and drink, and crossed the great dyke into Wales.

He had all but ten miles to go to Tregeiriog, winding all the way through the enclosing hills, always with wooded slopes one side or the other or both, and in open glimpses the bald grass summits leaning to view, and a sky veiled and still and mild overhead. Not mountain country, not the steel-blue rocks of the north-west, but hill-country always, with limited vistas, leaning hangers of woodland, closed valleys that opened only at the last moment to permit another curtained view. Before he drew too close to Tregeiriog the expected pickets heaved out of the low brush, to challenge, recognise and admit him. His Welsh tongue was the first safe-conduct, and stood him in good stead.

All the colours had changed since last he rode down the steep hillside into Tregeiriog. Round the brown, timbered warmth of maenol and village beside the river, the trees had begun to soften their skeletal blackness with a delicate pale-green froth of buds, and on the lofty, rounded summits beyond the snow was gone, and the bleached pallor of last year's grass showed the same elusive tint of new life. Through the browned and rotting bracken the first fronds uncurled. Here it was already Spring.

At the gate of Tudur's maenol they knew him, and came readily to lead him in and take charge of his horse. Not Tudur himself, but his steward, came to welcome the guest and do the honours of the house. Tudur was with the prince, doubtless at this hour on his way back from Chirk. In the cleft of the tributary brook behind the maenol the turfed camp-fires of his border levies gave off blue wisps of smoke on the still air. By evening the hall would again be Owain's court, and all his chief captains in this border patrol mustered about his table.

Cadfael was shown to a small chamber within the house, and offered the ceremonial water to wash off the dust of travel from his feet. This time it was a maid-servant who waited upon him, but when he emerged into the court it was to see Cristina advancing upon him in a flurry of blown skirts and flying hair from the kitchens.

'Brother Cadfael ... it *is* you! They told me,' she said, halting before him breathless and intent, 'there was a brother come from Shrewsbury, I hoped it might be you. You know them – you can tell me the truth ... about Elis and Eliud ...'

'What have they already told you?' asked Cadfael. 'Come within, where we can be quiet, and what I can tell you, that I will, for I know you must have been in bitter anxiety.' But for all that, he thought ruefully, as she turned willingly and led the way into the hall, if he made that good, and told all he knew, it

465

would be little to her comfort. Her betrothed, for whom she was contending so fiercely with so powerful a rival, was not only separated from her until proven innocent of murder, but disastrously in love with another girl as he had never been with her. What can you say to such a misused lady? Yet it would be infamous to lie to Cristina, just as surely as it would be cruel to bludgeon her with the blunt truth. Somewhere between the two he must pick his way.

She drew him with her into a corner of the hall, remote and shadowed at this hour when most of the men were out about their work, and there they sat down together against smoky tapestries, her black hair brushing his shoulder as she poured out what she knew and begged for what she needed to know.

'The English lord died, that I know, before ever Einon ab Ithel was ready to leave, and they are saying it was no simple death from his wounds, and all those who are not proven blameless must stay there as prisoners and suspect murderers, until the guilt is proven on some one man – English or Welsh, lay or brother, who knows? And here we must wait also. But what is being done to set them free? How are you to find the guilty one? Is all this true? I know Einon came back and spoke with Owain Gwynedd, and I know the prince will not receive his men back until they are cleared of all blame. He says he sent back a dead man, and a dead man cannot buy back one living. And moreover, that your dead man's ransom must be a life – the life of his murderer. Do *you* believe any man of ours owes that debt?'

'I dare not say there is any man who might not kill, given some monstrous, driving need,' said Cadfael honestly.

'Or any woman, either,' she said with a fierce, helpless sigh. 'But you have not fixed on any one man for this deed? No finger has been pointed? Not yet?'

No, of course she did not know. Einon had left before ever Melicent cried out both her love and her hatred, accusing Elis. No further news had yet reached these parts. Even if Hugh had now spoken of this matter with the prince, no such word had yet found its way back here to Tregeiriog. But surely it would, when Owain returned. In the end she would hear how her betrothed had fallen headlong in love with another woman, and been accused by her of her father's murder, murder for love that put an end to love. And where did that leave Cristina? Forgotten, eclipsed, but still in tenuous possession of a bridegroom who did not want her, and could not have the

466

bride he did want! Such a tangled coil enmeshing all these four hapless children!

'Fingers have been pointed, more than one way,' said Cadfael, 'but there is no proof against one man more than another. No one is yet in danger of his life, and all are in health and well enough treated, even if they must be confined. There is no help for it but to wait and believe in justice.'

'Believing in justice is not always so easy,' she said tartly. 'You say they are well? And they are together, Elis and Eliud?'

'They are. They have that comfort. And within the castle wards they have their liberty. They have given their word not to try to escape, and it has been accepted. They are well enough, you may believe that.'

'But you can give me no hope, set me no period, when he will come home?' She sat confronting Cadfael with great, steady eyes, and in her lap her fingers were knotted so tightly that the knuckles shone white as naked bone. 'Even if he does come home, living and justified,' she said.

'That I can tell no more than you,' Cadfael owned wryly. 'But I will do what I can to shorten the time. This waiting is hard upon you, I know it.' But how much harder would the return be, if ever Elis came back vindicated, only to pursue his suit for Melicent Prestcote, and worm his way out of his Welsh betrothal. It might even be better if she had warning now, before the blow fell. Cadfael was pondering what he could best do for her, and with only half an ear tuned to what she was saying.

'At least I have purged my own soul,' she said, as much to herself as to him. 'I have always known how well he loves me, if only he did not love his cousin as well or better. Fosterlings are like that – you are Welsh, you know it. But if he could not bring himself to undo what was done so ill, I have done it for him now. I tired of silence. Why should we bleed without a cry? I have done what had to be done. I've spoken with my father and with his. In the end I shall have my way.'

She rose, giving him a pale but resolute smile. 'We shall be able to speak again, brother, before you leave us. I must go and see how things fare in the kitchen, they'll be home with the evening.'

He gave her an abstracted farewell, and watched her cross the hall with her free, boy's stride and straight, proud carriage. Not until she had reached the door did he realise the meaning of what she had said. 'Cristina!' he called in startled enlightenment, but the door had closed and she was gone.

467

There was no error, he had heard aright. *She knew how well he loved her, if only he did not love his cousin as well or better, in the way of fosterlings!* Yes, all that he had known before, he had seen it manifested in their warring exchanges, and misread it utterly. How a man can be deceived, where every word, every aspect, confirms him in his blindness! Not a single lie spoken or intended, yet the sum total a lie.

She had spoken with her father – *and with his!*

Cadfael heard in his mind's ear Elis ap Cynan's blithe voice accounting for himself when first he came to Shrewsbury. Owain Gwynedd was his overlord, and had overseen him in the fosterage where he had placed him when his father died …

' … with my uncle Griffith ap Meilyr, where I grew up with my cousin Eliud as brothers …'

Two young men, close as twins, far too close to make room for the bride destined for one of them. Yes, and she fighting hard for what she claimed as her rights, and knowing there was love deep enough and wild enough to match her love, *if only* … If only a mistaken bond made in infancy could be honourably dissolved. If only those two could be severed, that dual creature staring into a mirror, the left-handed image and the right-handed, and which of them the reality? How is a stranger to tell?

But now he knew. She had not used the word loosely, of the kinsman who had reared them both. No, she meant just what she had said. An uncle may also be a foster-father, but only a natural father is a father.

They came, as before, with the dusk. Cadfael was still in a daze when he heard them come, and stirred himself to go out and witness the torchlit bustle in the court, the glimmer on the coats of the horses, the jingle of harness, bit and spur, the cheerful and purposeful hum of entwining voices, the hissing and crooning of the grooms, the trampling of hooves and the very faint mist of warm breath in the chilling but frostless air. A grand, vigorous pattern of lights and shadows, and the open door of the hall glowing warmly for welcome.

Tudur ap Rhys was the first down from the saddle, and himself strode to hold his prince's stirrup. Owain Gwynedd's fair hair gleamed uncovered in the ruddy light of the torches as he sprang down, a head taller than his host. Man after man they came, chieftain after chieftain, the princelings of Gwynedd's nearer commoes, the neighbours of England. Cadfael stood to survey each one as he dismounted, and lingered until all were on foot, and their followers dispersed into the camps beyond the maenol. But he did not find among them Einon ab Ithel, whom he sought.

'Einon?' said Tudur, questioned. 'He's following, though he may come late to table. He had a visit to pay in Llansantffraid, he has a daughter married there, and his first grandson is come new into the world. Before the evening's out he'll be with us. You're heartily welcome to my roof again, brother, all the more if you bring news to please the prince's ear. It was an ill thing that happened there with you, he feels it as a sad stain on a clean acquaintance.'

'I'm rather seeking than bringing enlightenment,' Cadfael confessed. 'But I trust one man's ill deed cannot mar these meetings between your prince and our sheriff. Owain Gwynedd's goodwill is gold to us in Shropshire, all the more since Madog ap Meredith is showing his teeth again.'

'Do you tell me so? Owain will want to hear of it, but after supper will be the fitting time. I'll make you a place at the high table.'

Since he had in any case to wait for the arrival of Einon, Cadfael sat back to study and enjoy the gathering in Tudur's hall over supper, the warmth of the central fire, the torches, the wine, and the harping. A man of Tudur's status was privileged to possess a harp and maintain his own harper, in addition to his duty to be a generous patron to travelling minstrels. And with the prince here to praise and be praised, they had a rivalry of singers that lasted throughout the meal. There was still a deal of coming and going in the courtyard, late-comers riding in, officers from the camps patrolling their bounds and changing pickets, and the womenfolk fetching and carrying, and loitering to talk to the archers and men-at-arms. For the time being this was the court of Gwynedd, where petitioners, bringers of gifts, young men seeking office and favour, all must come.

The dishes had been removed, and the mead and wine were circulating freely, when Tudur's steward came into the hall and made for the high table.

'My lord, there's one here asks leave to present to you his natural son, whom he has acknowledged and admitted to his kinship only two days ago. Griffri ap Llywarch, from close by Meifod. Will you hear him?'

469

'Willingly,' said Owain, pricking up his fair head to stare down through the smoke and shadows of the hall with some curiosity. 'Let Griffri ap Llywarch come in and be welcome.'

Cadfael had not paid due attention to the name, and might not even have recognised it if he had, nor was he likely to recognise a man he had never seen before. The newcomer followed the steward into the hall, and up between the tables to the high place. A lean, sinewy man, perhaps fifty years old, balding and bearded, with a hillman's gait, and the weathered face and wrinkled, far-seeing eyes of the shepherd. His clothing was plain and brown, but good homespun. He came straight to the dais, and made the Welshman's brisk, unservile reverence to the prince.

'My lord Owain, I have brought you my son, that you may know and approve him. For the only son I had by my wife is two years and more dead, and I was without children, until this my son by another woman came to me declaring his birth and proving it. And I have acknowledged him mine and brought him into my kinship, and as mine he is accepted. Now I ask your countenance also.'

He stood proudly, glad of what he had to say and of the young man he had to present; and Cadfael would have had neither eyes nor ears for any other man present, if it had not been for the courteous silence that had followed him up the hall, and the one clear sound that carried in it. Shadows and smoke veiled the figure that followed respectfully at some yards distance, but the sound of its steps was plainly audible, and went haltingly, lighter and faster upon one foot. Cadfael's eyes were upon the son when he came hesitantly into the torchlight from the high table. This one he knew, though the black hair was trimmed and thrown proudly back from a face not now sullen and closed, but open, hopeful and eager, and there was no longer a crutch under the leaning armpit.

Cadfael looked back from Anion ap Griffri to Griffri ap Llywarch, to whose drear and childless middle age this unlooked-for son had suddenly supplied a warm heart of hope and content. The homespun cloak hanging loose upon Griffri's shoulders bore in its folds a long pin with a large, chased gold head secured with a thin gold chain. And that, too, Cadfael had seen before, and knew only too well.

So did another witness. Einon ab Ithel had come in, as one familiar with the household and desirous of making no inconvenient stir, by the high door from the private chamber, and emerged behind the prince's table unnoticed. The man who was holding all attention naturally drew his. The red of torchlight flashed from the ornament worn openly and proudly. Its owner had the best reason to know there could not be two such, not of that exact and massive size and ornamentation.

'God's breath!' swore Einon ab Ithel in a great bellow of astonishment and indignation. 'What manner of thief have we here, wearing my gold under my very eyes?'

Silence fell as ominously as thunder, and every head whirled from prince and petitioner to stare at this loud accuser. Einon came round the high table in a few long strides, dropped from the dais so close as to send Griffri lurching back in alarm, and stabbed a hard brown finger at the pin that glowed in the drab cloak.

'My lord, *this* – is mine! Gold out of my earth, I had it mined, I had it made for me, there is not another exactly like it in this or any land. When I came back from Shrewsbury, on that errand you know of, it was not in my collar, nor have I seen it since that day. I thought it fallen somewhere on the road, and made no ado about it. What is it to mourn for, gold! Now I see it again and marvel. My lord, it is in your hands. Demand of this man how he comes to be wearing what is mine.'

Half the hall was on its feet, and rumbling with menace, for theft, unmitigated by circumstances, was the worst crime they acknowledged, and the thief caught red-handed could be killed on sight by the wronged man. Griffri stood stricken dumb, staring in bewilderment. Anion flung himself with stretched arms and braced body between his father and Einon.

'My lord, my lord, I gave it, I brought it to my father. I did not steal … I took a price! Hold my father blameless, if there is blame it is mine only …'

He was sweating with terror, great sudden gouts that ran on his forehead and were snared in his thick brows. And if he knew a little Welsh, in this extremity it did not serve him, he had cried out in English. That gave them all a moment of surprise. And Owain swept a hand over the hall and brought silence.

They murmured, but they obeyed. In the ensuing hush Brother Cadfael rose unobtrusively to his feet and made his way round the table and down to the floor of the hall. His movements, however discreet, drew the prince's eye.

'My lord,' said Cadfael deprecatingly, 'I am of Shrewsbury, I know and am known to this man Anion ap Griffri. He was raised

English, no fault of his. Should he need one to interpret, I can do that service, so that he may be understood by all here.'

'A fair offer,' said Owain, and eyed him thoughtfully. 'Are you also empowered, brother, to speak for Shrewsbury, since it seems this accusation goes back to that town, and the business of which we know? And if so, for shire and town or for abbey?'

'Here and now,' said Cadfael boldly, 'I will venture for both. And if you find fault hereafter, let it fall on me.'

'You are here, I fancy,' said Owain, considering, 'over this very matter.'

'I am. In part to look for this same jewel. For it vanished from Gilbert Prestcote's chamber in our infirmary on the day that he died. The cloak that had been added to the sick man's wrappings in the litter was handed back to Einon ab Ithel without it. Only after he had left did we remember and look for the brooch. And only now do I see it again.'

'From the room where a man died by murder,' said Einon. 'Brother, you have found more than the gold. You may send our men home.'

Anion stood fearful but steadfast between his father and the accusing stare of a hall full of eyes. He was white as ice, translucent, as though all the blood had left his veins. 'I did not kill,' he said hoarsely, and heaved hard to get breath enough to speak. 'My lord, I never knew … I thought the pin was his, Prestcote's. I took it from the cloak, yes –'

'After you had killed him,' said Einon harshly.

'No! I swear it! I never touched the man.' He turned in desperate appeal to Owain, who sat listening dispassionately at the table, his fingers easy round the stem of his wine-cup, but his eyes very bright and aware. 'My lord, only hear me! And hold my father clear of all, for all he knows is what I have told him, and the same I shall tell you, and as God sees me, I do not lie.'

'Hand up to me,' said Owain, 'that pin you wear.' And as Griffri hurried with trembling fingers to detach it, and reached up to lay it in the prince's hand: 'So! I have known this too long and seen it worn too often to be in any doubt whose it is. From you, Brother, as from Einon here, I know how it came to be lying open to hand by the sheriff's bed. Now you may tell, Anion, how you came by it. English I can follow, you need not fear being misunderstood. And Brother Cadfael will put what you say into Welsh, so that all here may understand you.'

Anion gulped air and found a creaky voice had contracted his throat, but the flow of words washed constraint away. 'My lord, until these last days I never saw my father, nor he me, but I had a brother, as he has said, and by chance I got to know him when he came into Shrewsbury with wool to sell. There was a year between us, and I am the elder. He was my kin, and I valued him. And once when he visited the town and I was not by, there was a fight, a man was killed and my brother was blamed for it. Gilbert Prestcote hanged him!'

Owain glanced aside at Cadfael, and waited until this speech had been translated for the Welshmen. Then he asked, 'You know of this case? Was it fairly done?'

'Who knows which hand did the killing?' said Cadfael. 'It was a street brawl, the young men were drunk. Gilbert Prestcote was hasty by nature, but just. But this is certain, here in Wales the young man would not have hanged. A blood-price would have paid it.'

'Go on,' said Owain.

'I carried that grudge on my heart from that day,' said Anion, gathering passion from old bitterness. 'But when did I ever come within reach of the sheriff? Never until your men brought him into Shrewsbury wounded and housed him in the infirmary. And I was there with this broken leg of mine all but healed, and that man only twenty paces from me, only a wall between us, my enemy at my mercy. While it was all still and the brothers at dinner, I went into the room where he was. He owed my house a life – even if I was mongrel, I felt Welsh then, and I meant to take my due revenge – I meant to kill! The only brother ever I had, and he was merry and good to look upon, and then to hang for an unlucky blow when he was full of ale! I went in there to kill. But I could not do it! When I saw my enemy brought down so low, so old and weary, hardly blood or breath in him ... I stood by him and watched, and all I could feel was sadness. It seemed to me that there was no call there for vengeance, for all was already avenged. So I thought on another way. There was no court to set a blood-price or enforce payment, but there was the gold pin in the cloak beside him. I thought it was his. How could I know? So I took it as *galanas*, to clear the debt and the grudge. But by the end of that day I knew, we all knew, that Prestcote was dead and dead by murder, and when they began to question even me, I knew that if ever it came out what I had done it would be said I had also killed him. So I ran. I meant, in any case, to come and

473

seek my father some day, and tell him my brother's death was paid for, but because I was afraid I had to run in haste.'

'And come to me he did,' said Griffri earnestly, his hand upon his son's shoulder, 'and showed me by way of warranty the yellow mountain stone I gave his mother long ago. But by his face I knew him, for he's like the brother he lost. And he gave me that thing you hold, my lord, and told me that young Griffri's death was requited, and this was the token price exacted, and the grudge buried, for our enemy was dead. I did not well understand him then, for I told him if he had slain Griffri's slayer, then he had no right to take a price as well. But he swore to me by most solemn oath that it was not he who had killed and I believe him. And judge if I am glad to have a son restored me in my middle years, to be the prop of my old age. For God's sake, my lord, do not take him from me now!'

In the dour, considering hush that followed Cadfael completed his translation of what Anion had said, and took his time about it to allow him to study the prince's impassive face. At the end of it the silence continued still for a long minute, since no one would speak until Owain made it possible. He, too, was in no hurry. He looked at father and son, pressed together there below the dais in apprehensive solidarity, he looked at Einon, whose face was as unrevealing as his own, and last at Cadfael.

'Brother, you know more of what has gone forward in Shrewsbury abbey than any of us here. You know this man. How do you say? Do you believe his story?'

'Yes,' said Cadfael, with grave and heartfelt gratitude, 'I do believe it. It fits with all I know. But I would ask Anion one question.'

'Ask it.'

'You stood beside the bed, Anion, and watched the sleeper. Are you sure that he was then alive?'

'Yes, surely,' said Anion wondering. 'He breathed, he moaned in his sleep. I saw and heard. I know.'

'My lord,' said Cadfael, watching Owain's enquiring eye, 'there was another heard to enter and leave that room, some little while later, someone who went not haltingly, as Anion did, but lightly. That one did not take anything, unless it was a life. Moreover, I believe what Anion has told us because there is yet another thing I have to find before I shall have found Gilbert Prestcote's murderer.'

Owain nodded comprehension, and mused for a while in

silence. Then he picked up the gold pin with a brisk movement, and held it out to Einon. 'How say you? Was this theft?'

'I am content,' said Einon and laughed, releasing the tension in the hall. In the general stir and murmur of returning ease, the prince turned to his host.

'Make a place below there, Tudur, for Griffri ap Llywarch, and his son Anion.'

Chapter Eleven

O THERE went Shrewsbury's prime suspect, the man gossip had already hanged and buried, down the hall on his father's heels, stumbling a little and dazed like a man in a dream, but beginning to shine as though a torch had been kindled within him; down to a place with his father at one of the tables, equal among equals. From a serving-maid's by-blow, without property or privilege, he was suddenly become a free man, with a rightful place of his own in a kindred, heir to a respected sire, accepted by his prince. The threat that had forced him to take to his heels had turned into the greatest blessing of his life and brought him to the one place that was his by right in Welsh law, true son to a father who acknowledged him proudly. Here Anion was no bastard.

Cadfael watched the pair of them to their places, and was glad that something good, at least, should have come out of the evil. Where would that young man have found the courage to seek out his father, distant, unknown, speaking another language, if fear had not forced his hand, and made it easy to leap across a frontier? The ending was well worth the terror that had gone before. He could forget Anion now. Anion's hands were clean.

'At least you've sent me one man,' observed Owain, watching thoughtfully as the pair reached their places, 'in return for my eight still in bond. Not a bad figure of a man, either. But no training in arms, I doubt.'

'An excellent cattle-man,' said Cadfael. 'He has an

understanding with all animals. You may safely put your horses in his care.'

'And you lose, I gather, your chief contender for a halter. You have no after-thoughts concerning him?'

'None. I am sure he did as he says he did. He dreamed of avenging himself on a strong and overbearing man, and found a broken wreck he could not choose but pity.'

'No bad ending,' said Owain. 'And now I think we might withdraw to some quieter place, and you shall tell us whatever you have to tell, and ask whatever you need to ask.'

In the prince's chamber they sat about the small, wire-guarded brazier, Owain, Tudur, Einon ab Ithel and Cadfael. Cadfael had brought with him the little box in which he had preserved the wisps of wool and gold thread. Those precise shades of deep blue and soft rose could not be carried accurately in the mind, but must continually be referred to the eye, and matched against whatever fabric came to light. He had the box in the scrip at his girdle, and was wary of opening it where there might be even the faintest draught, for fear the frail things within would be blown clean away. A breath from a loophole could whisk his ominous treasures out of reach in an instant.

He had debated within himself how much he should tell, but in the light of Cristina's revelation, and since her father was here in conference, he told all he knew, how Elis in his captivity had fallen haplessly in love with Prestcote's daughter, and how the pair of them had seen no possible hope of gaining the sheriff's approval for such a match, hence providing reason enough why Elis should attempt to disturb the invalid's rest – whether to remove by murder the obstacle to his love, as Melicent accused, or to plead his forlorn cause, as Elis himself protested.

'So that was the way of it,' said Owain, and exchanged a straight, hard look with Tudur, unsurprised, and forbearing from either sympathy or blame. Tudur was on close terms of personal friendship with his prince, and had surely spoken with him of Cristina's confidences. Here was the other side of the coin. 'And this was after Einon had left you?'

'It was. It came out that the boy had tried to speak with Gilbert, and been ordered out by Brother Edmund. When the girl heard of it, she turned on him for a murderer.'

'But you do not altogether accept that. Nor, it seems, has Beringar accepted it.'

477

'There is no more proof of it than that he was there, beside the bed, when Edmund came and drove him out. It could as well have been for the boy's declared purpose as for anything worse. And then, you'll understand, there was the matter of the gold pin. We never realised it was missing, my lord, until you had ridden for home. But very certainly Elis neither had it on him, nor had had any opportunity to hide it elsewhere before he was searched. Therefore someone else had been in that room, and taken it away.'

'But now that we know what befell my pin,' said Einon, 'and are satisfied Anion did not murder, does not that leave that boy again in danger of being branded for the killing of a sick and sleeping man? Though it sorts very poorly,' he added, 'with what I know of him.'

'Which of us,' said Owain sombrely, 'has never been guilty of some unworthiness that sorts very ill with what our friends know of us? Even with what we know, or think we know of ourselves! I would not rule out any man from being capable once in his life of a gross infamy.' He looked up at Cadfael. 'Brother, I recall you said, within there, that there was yet one more thing you must find, before you would have found Prestcote's murderer. What is that thing?'

'It is the cloth that was used to smother Gilbert. By its traces it will be known, once found. For it was pressed down over his nose and mouth, and he breathed it into his nostrils and drew it into his teeth, and a thread or two of it we found in his beard. No ordinary cloth. Elis had neither that nor anything else in his hands when he came from the infirmary. Once I had found and preserved the filaments from it, we searched for it throughout the abbey precincts, for it could have been a hanging or an altar-cloth, but we have found nothing to match these fragments. Until we know what it was, and what became of it, we shall not know who killed Gilbert Prestcote.'

'This is certain?' asked Owain. 'You drew these threads from the dead man's nostrils and mouth? You think you will know, when you find it, the very cloth that was used to stifle him?'

'I do think so, for the colours are clear, and not common dyes. I have the box here. But open it with care. What's within is fine as cobweb.' Cadfael handed the little box across the brazier. 'But not here. The up-draught from the warmth could blow them away.'

Owain took the box aside, and held it low under one of the lamps, where the light would play into it. The minute threads

478

quivered faintly, and again were still. 'Here's gold thread, that's plain, a twisted strand. The rest – I see it's wool, by the many hairs and the live texture. A darker colour and a lighter.' He studied them narrowly, but shook his head. 'I could not say what tints are here, only that the cloth had a good gold thread woven into it. And I fancy it would be thick, a heavy weave, by the way the wool curls and crimps. Many more such fine hairs went to make up this yarn.'

'Let me see,' said Einon, and narrowed his eyes over the box. 'I see the gold, but the colours … No, it means nothing to me.'

Tudur peered, and shook his head. 'We have not the light for this, my lord. By day these would show very differently.'

It was true, by the mellow light of these oil-lamps the prince's hair was deep harvest-gold, almost brown. By daylight it was the yellow of primroses. 'It might be better', agreed Cadfael, 'to leave the matter until morning. Even had we better vision, what could be done at this hour?'

'This light foils the eye,' said Owain. He closed the lid over the airy fragments. 'Why did you think you might find what you seek here?'

'Because we have not found it within the pale of the abbey, so we must look outside, wherever men have dispersed from the abbey. The lord Einon and two captains beside had left us before ever we recovered these threads; it was a possibility, however frail, that unknowingly this cloth had gone with them. By daylight the colours will show for what they truly are. You may yet recall seeing such a weave.'

Cadfael took back the box. It had been a fragile hope at best, but the morrow remained. There was a man's life, a man's soul's health, snared in those few quivering hairs, and he was their custodian.

'Tomorrow,' said the prince emphatically, 'we will try what God's light can show us, since ours is too feeble.'

In the deep small hours of that same night Elis awoke in the dark cell in the outer ward of Shrewsbury castle, and lay with stretched ears, struggling up from the dullness of sleep and wondering what had shaken him out of so profound a slumber. He had grown used to all the daytime sounds native to this place, and to the normal unbroken silence of the night. This night was different, or he would not have been heaved so rudely out of the only refuge he had from his daytime miseries.

Something was not as it should have been, someone was astir at a time when there was always silence and stillness. The air quivered with soft movements and distant voices.

They were not locked in, their word had been accepted without question, bond enough to hold them. Elis raised himself cautiously on an elbow, and leaned to listen to Eliud's breathing in the bed beside him. Deep asleep, if not altogether at peace. He twitched and turned without awaking, and the measure of his breathing changed uneasily, shortening and shallowing sometimes, then easing into a long rhythm that promised better rest. Elis did not want to disturb him. It was all due to him, to his pig-headed folly in joining Cadwaladr, that Eliud was here a prisoner beside him. He must not be drawn still deeper into question and danger, whatever happened to Elis.

There were certainly voices, at some small distance but muffled and made to sound infinitely more distant by the thick stone walls. And though at this remove there could not possibly be distinguishable words, yet there was an indefinable agitation about the exchanges, a quiver of panic on the air. Elis slid carefully from the bed, halted and held his breath a moment to make sure that Eliud had not stirred, and felt for his coat, thankful that he slept in shirt and hose, and need not fumble in the dark to dress. With all the grief and anxiety he carried about with him night and day, he must discover the reason of this added and unforeseen alarm. Every divergence from custom was a threat.

The door was heavy but well hung, and swung without a sound. Outside the night was moonless but clear, very faint starlight patterned the sky between the walls and towers that made a shell of total darkness. He drew the door closed after him, and eased the heavy latch into its socket gingerly. Now the murmur of voices had body and direction, it came from the guard-room within the gatehouse. And that crisp, brief clatter that struck a hidden spark on the ground was hooves on the cobbles. A rider at this hour?

He felt his way along the wall towards the sound, at every angle flattening himself against the stones to listen afresh. The horse shifted and blew. Shapes grew gradually out of the solid darkness, the twin turrets of the barbican showed their teeth against a faintly lighter sky, and the flat surface of the closed gate beneath had a tall, narrow slit of pallor carved through it, tall as a man on horse-back, and wide enough for a horse to pass in haste. The rider's wicket was open. Open because someone had entered by it with urgent news only minutes since, and no one had yet thought to close it.

Elis crept nearer. The door of the guard-room was ajar, a long sliver of light from torches within quivered across the dark cobbles. The voices emerged by fits and starts, as they were raised and again lowered, but he caught words clearly here and there.

' ... burned a farm west of Pontesbury,' reported a messenger, still breathless from his haste, 'and never withdrew ... They're camped overnight ... and another party skirting Minsterley to join them.'

Another voice, sharp and clear, most likely one of the experienced sergeants: 'What numbers?'

'In all ... if they foregather ... I was told it might be as many as a hundred and fifty ...'

'Archers? Lancers? Foot or horse?' That was not the sergeant, that was a young voice, a shade higher than it should have been with alarm and strain. They had got Alan Herbard out of bed. This was a grave matter.

'My lord, far the greater part on foot. Lancers and archers both. They may try to encircle Pontesbury ... they know Hugh Beringar is in the north ...'

'Halfway to Shrewsbury!' said Herbard's voice, taut and jealous for his first command.

'They'll not dare that,' said the sergeant. 'Plunder's the aim. Those valley farms ... with new lambs ...'

'Madog ap Meredith has a grudge to settle,' ventured the messenger, still short of breath, 'for that raid in February. They're close ... but the pickings are smaller, there in the forest ... I doubt ...'

Halfway to Shrewsbury was more than halfway to the ford in the forest where that grudge had come to birth. And the pickings ... Elis turned his forehead into the chill of the stone against which he leaned and swallowed terror. A parcel of women! He was more than paid for that silly flaunt, who had a woman of his own there to sweat and bleed for, young, beautiful, fair as flax, tall like a willow. The square dark men of Powys would come to blows over her, kill one another for her, kill her when they were done.

He had started out of his shelter under the wall before he even knew what he intended. The patient, drooping horse might have given him away, but there was no groom holding it,

481

and it stood its ground silently, unstartled, as he stole past, a hand raised to caress and beseech acceptance. He did not dare take it, the first clatter of hooves would have brought them out like hornets disturbed, but as least it let him pass unbetrayed. The big body steamed gently, he felt its heat. The tired head turned and nuzzled his hand. He drew his fingers away with stealthy gentleness, and slid past towards the elongated wicket that offered a way out into the night.

He was through, he had the descent to the castle Foregate on his right, and the way up into the town on his left. But he was out of the castle, he who had given his word not to pass the threshold, he who was forsworn from this moment, false to his word, outcast. Not even Eliud would speak for him when he knew.

The town gates would not open until dawn. Elis turned left, into the town, and groped his way by unknown lanes and passages to find some corner where he could hide until the morning. He was none too sure of his best way out, and did not stop to wonder if he would ever manage to pass unnoticed. All he knew was that he had to get to Godric's Ford before his countrymen reached it. He got his bearings by instinct, blundering blindly round towards the eastward gates. In Saint Mary's churchyard, though he did not know it for that, he shrank into the shelter of a porch from the chill of the wind. He had left his cloak behind in his dishonoured cell, he was half-naked to shame and the night, but he was free and on his way to deliver her. What was his honour, more than his life, compared to her safety.

The town woke early. Tradesmen and travellers rose and made their way down to the gates before full daylight, to be out and about their proper business betimes. So did Elis ap Cynan, going with them discreetly down the Wyle, cloakless, weaponless, desperate, heroic and absurd, to the rescue of his Melicent.

Eliud put out his hand, before he was fully awake, to feel for his cousin, and sat up in abrupt shock to find Elis's side of the bed empty and cold. But the dark red cloak was still draped over the foot of the bed, and Eliud's sense of loss was utterly irrational. Why should not Elis rise early and go out into the wards before his bedfellow was awake? Without his cloak he could not be far away. But for all that, and however brief the separation, it troubled Eliud like a physical pain. Here in their imprisonment they had hardly been a moment out of each other's company, as if for each of them faith in a final happy delivery depended upon the presence of the other.

Eliud rose and dressed, and went out to the trough by the well, to wash himself fully awake in the shock of the cold water. There was an unusual stir about the stables and the armoury, but he saw no sign of Elis anywhere in either place, nor was he brooding on the walls with his face towards Wales. The want of him began to ache like an amputation.

They took their meals in hall among their English peers, but on this clear morning Elis did not come to break his fast. And by this time others had remarked his absence.

One of the sergeants of the garrison stopped Eliud as he was leaving the hall. 'Where is your cousin? Is he sick?'

'I know no more than you,' said Eliud. 'I've been looking for him. He was out before I awoke, and I've seen nothing of him since.' And he added in jealous haste, seeing the man frown and give him the first hard stare of suspicion, 'But he can't be far. His cloak is still in the cell. There's so much stirring here, I thought he might have risen early to find out what was all the to-do.'

'He's pledged not to set foot out of the gates,' said the sergeant. 'But do you tell me he's given up eating? You must know more than you pretend.'

'No! But he's here within, he must be. He would not break his word, I promise you.'

The man eyed him hard, and turned abruptly on his heel to make for the gatehouse and question the guards. Eliud caught him entreatingly by the sleeve. 'What is brewing here? Is there news? Such activity in the armoury and the archers drawing arrows … What's happened overnight?'

'What's happened? Your countrymen are swarming in force along the Minsterley valley, if you want to know, burning farmsteads and moving in on Pontesbury. Three days ago it was a handful, it's past a hundred tribesmen now.' He swung back suddenly to demand, 'Did you hear aught in the night? Is that it? Has that cousin of yours run, broke out to join his ragamuffin kin and help in the killing? The sheriff was not enough for him?'

'No!' cried Eliud. 'He would not! It's impossible!'

'It's how we got him in the first place, a murdering, looting raid the like of these. It suited him then, it comes very timely for him now. His neck out of a noose and his friends close by to bring him off safely.'

'You cannot say so! You don't yet know but he's here within, true to his word.'

'No, but soon we shall,' said the sergeant grimly, and took Eliud firmly by the arm. 'Into your cell and wait. The lord Herbard must know of this.'

He flung away at speed and Eliud, in desolate obedience, trudged back to his cell and sat there upon the bed with only Elis's cloak for company. By then he was certain what the result of any search must be. Only an hour or two of daylight gone and there were endless places a man could be, if he felt no appetite either for food or for the company of his fellowmen, and yet the castle felt empty of Elis, as cold and alien as if he had never been there. And a courier had come in the night, it seemed, with news of stronger forces from Powys plundering closer to Shrewsbury, and closer still to the forest grange of the abbey of Polesworth at Godric's Ford. Where all this heavy burden had begun and where, perhaps, it must end. If Elis had heard that nocturnal arrival and gone out to discover the cause – yes, then he might in desperation forget oath and honour and all. Eliud waited wretchedly until Alan Herbard came, with two sergeants at his heels. A long wait it had been. They would have scoured the castle by now. By their grim faces it was clear they had not found Elis.

Eliud rose to his feet to face them. He would need all his powers and all his dignity now if he was to speak for Elis. This Alan Herbard was surely no more than a year or two his senior, and being as harshly tested as he.

'If you know the manner of your cousin's flight,' said Herbard bluntly, 'you would be wise to speak. You shared this narrow space. If he rose in the night, surely you would know. For I tell you plainly, he is gone. He has run. In the night the wicket was opened for a man to enter. It's no secret now that it let out a man-renegade, forsworn, self-branded murderer. Why else should he so seize this chance?'

'No!' said Eliud. 'You wrong him and in the end it will be shown you wrong him. He is no murderer. If he has run, that is not the reason.'

'There is no *if*. He is gone. You know nothing of it? You slept through his flight?'

'I missed him when I awoke,' said Eliud. 'I know nothing of how he went or when. But I know *him*. If he rose in the night because he heard your man arriving and if he heard then – is it so? – that the Welsh of Powys are coming too close and in dangerous numbers, then I swear to you he had fled only out of dread for Gilbert Prestcote's daughter. She is there with the sisters at Godric's Ford and Elis loves her. Whether she has discarded him or no, he has not ceased to love her, and if she is in danger, he will venture life, yes and his honour with it, to bring her to safety. And when that is done,' said Eliud passionately, 'he will return here, to suffer whatever fate may await him. He is no renegade! He has broken his oath only for Melicent's sake. He will come back and give himself up. I pledge my own honour for him! My own life!'

'I would remind you,' said Herbard grimly, 'you have already done so. Either one of you gave his word for both. At this moment you stand attainted as his surety for his treachery. I could hang you, and be fully justified.'

'Do so!' said Eliud, blanched to the lips, his eyes dilated into a blaze of green. 'Here am I, still his warranty. I tell you, this neck is yours to wring if Elis proves false. I give you leave freely. You are mustering to ride, I've seen it. You go against these Welsh of Powys. Take me with you! Give me a horse and a weapon, and I will fight for you, and you may have an archer at my back to strike me dead if I make a false step, and a halter about my neck ready for the nearest tree after the Powys men are hammered, if Elis does not prove to you the truth of every word I say.'

He was shaking with fervour, strung taut like a bowstring. Herbard opened his eyes wide at such open passion, and studied him in wary surprise a long moment. 'So be it!' he said then abruptly, and turned to his men. 'See to it! Give him a horse and a sword, and a rope about his neck, and have your best shot follow him close and be ready to spit him if he plays false. He says he is a man of his word, that even this defaulting fellow of his is such. Very well, we'll take him at his word.'

He looked back from the doorway. Eliud had taken up Elis's red cloak and was holding it in his arms. 'If your cousin had been half the man you are,' said Herbard, 'your life would be safe enough.'

Eliud whirled, hugging the folded cloak to him as if applying balm to an unendurable ache. 'Have you not understood even yet? He is *better* than I, a thousand times better!'

485

Chapter Twelve

N TREGEIRIOG, too, they were up with the first blush of light, barely two hours after Elis's flight through the wicket at Shrewsbury. For Hugh Beringar had ridden through half the night, and arrived with the dove-grey hush of pre-dawn. Sleepy grooms rose, blear-eyed, to take the horses of their English guests, a company of twenty men. The rest Hugh had left distributed across the north of the shire, well armed, well supplied, and so far proof against the few and tentative tests to which they had been subjected.

Brother Cadfael, as sensitive to nocturnal arrivals as Elis, had started out of sleep when he caught the quiver and murmur on the air. There was much to be said for the custom of sleeping in the full habit, apart from the scapular, a man could rise and go, barefoot or staying to reclaim his sandals, as complete and armed as in the middle of the day. No doubt the discipline had originated where monastic houses were located in permanently perilous places, and time had given it the blessing of tradition. Cadfael was out, and halfway to the stables, when he met Hugh coming thence in the pearly twilight, and Tudur equally wide awake and alert beside his guest.

'What brings you so early?' asked Cadfael. 'Is there fresh news?'

'Fresh to me, but for all I know stale already in Shrewsbury.' Hugh took him by the arm, and turned him back with them

486

towards the hall. 'I must make my report to the prince, and then we're off down the border by the shortest way. Madog's castellan from Caus is pouring more men into the Minsterley valley. There was a messenger waiting for me when we rode into Oswestry or I'd meant to stay the night there.'

'Herbard sent the word from Shrewsbury?' asked Cadfael. 'It was no more than a handful of raiders when I left, two days ago.'

'It's a war-party of a hundred or more now. They hadn't moved beyond Minsterley when Herbard got wind of the muster, but if they've brought out such a force as that, they mean worse mischief. And you know them better than I – they waste no time. They may be on the move this very dawn.'

'You'll be needing fresh horses,' said Tudur practically.

'We got some remounts at Oswestry, they'll be fit for the rest of the way. But I'll gladly borrow from you for the rest, and thank you heartily. I've left all quiet and every garrison on the alert across the north, and Ranulf seems to have pulled back his advance parties towards Wrexham. He made a feint at Whitchurch and got a bloody nose, and it's my belief he's drawn in his horns for this while. Whether or no, I must break off to attend to Madog.'

'You may make your mind easy about Chirk,' Tudur assured him. 'We'll see to that. Have your men in for a meal, at least, and give the horses a breather. I'll get the womenfolk out of their beds to see to the feeding of you, and have Einon rouse Owain, if he's not already up.'

'What do you intend?' Cadfael asked. 'Which way shall you head?'

'For Llansilin and down the border. We'll pass to east of the Breiddens, and down by Westbury to Minsterley, and cut them off, if we can, from getting back to their base in Caus. I tire of having men of Powys in that castle,' said Hugh, setting his jaw. 'We must have it back and make it habitable, and keep a garrison there.'

'You'll be few for such a muster as you report,' said Cadfael. 'Why not aim at getting to Shrewsbury first for more men, and westward to meet them from there?'

'The time's too short. And besides, I credit Alan Herbard with sense and stomach enough to field a good force of his own to mind the town. If we move fast enough we may take them between the two prongs and crack them like a nut.'

They had reached the hall. Word had gone before, the

487

sleepers within were rolling out of the rushes in haste, servants were setting tables, and the maids ran with new loaves from the bakery, and great pitchers of ale.

'If I can finish my business here,' said Cadfael tempted, 'I'll ride with you, if you'll have me.'

'I will so and heartily welcome.'

'Then I'd best be seeing to what's left undone here, when Owain Gwynedd is free. While you're closeted with him, I'll see my own horse readied for the journey.'

He was so preoccupied with thoughts of the coming clash, and of what might already be happening in Shrewsbury, that he turned back towards the stables without at first noticing the light footsteps that came flying after him from the direction of the kitchens, until a hand clutched at his sleeve, and he turned to find Cristina confronting him and peering intently up into his face with dilated dark eyes.

'Brother Cadfael, is it true, what my father says? He says I need fret no longer, for Elis has found some girl in Shrewsbury, and wants nothing better now than to be rid of me. He says it can be ended with goodwill on both sides. That I'm free, and Eliud is free! Is it true?' She was grave, and yet she glowed. Elis's desertion was hope and help to her. The tangled knot could indeed be undone by consent, without grudges.

'It is true,' said Cadfael. 'But beware of building too high on his prospects as yet, for it's no way certain he'll get the lady he wants. Did Tudur also tell you it is she who accuses Elis of being her father's murderer? No very hopeful way to set up a marriage.'

'But he's in earnest? He loves the girl? Then he'll not turn back for me, whether he wins his way with her or no. He never wanted me. Oh, I would have done well enough for him,' she said, hoisting eloquent shoulders and curling a tolerant lip, 'as any girl his match in age and rank would have done, but all I ever was to him was a child he grew up with, and was fond of after a fashion. Now,' she said feelingly, 'he knows what it is to want. God knows I wish him his happiness as I hope for mine.'

'Walk with me down to the stables,' said Cadfael, 'and keep me company, these few minutes we have. For I'm away with Hugh Beringar as soon as his men have broken their fast and rested their horses, and I've had a word again with Owain Gwynedd and Einon ab Ithel. Come, and tell me plainly how things stand between you and Eliud, for once before when I saw you together I misread you utterly.'

488

She went with him gladly, her face clear and pure in the pearly light just flushing into rose. Her voice was tranquil as she said, 'I loved Eliud from before I knew what love was. All I knew was how much it hurt, that I could not endure to be away from him, that I followed and would be with him, and he would not see me, would not speak with me, put me roughly from his side as often as I clung. I was already promised to Elis, and Elis was more than half Eliud's world, and not for anything would he have touched or coveted anything that belonged to his foster-brother. I was too young then to know that the measure of his rejection of me was the measure of how much he wanted me. But when I came to understand what it was that tortured me, then I knew that Eliud went daily in the selfsame pain.'

'You are quite sure of him,' said Cadfael, stating, not doubting.

'I am sure. From the time I understood, I have tried to make him acknowledge what I know and he knows to be truth. The more I pursue and plead, the more he turns away and will not speak or listen. But ever the more he wants me. I tell you truth, when Elis went away, and was made prisoner, I began to believe I had almost won Eliud, almost brought him to admit to love and join with me to break this threatened marriage, and speak for me himself. Then he was sent to be surety for this unhappy exchange and all went for nothing. And now it's Elis who cuts the knot and frees us all.'

'Too early yet to speak of being free,' warned Cadfael seriously. 'Neither of those two is yet out of the wood – none of us is, until the matter of the sheriff's death is brought to a just end.'

'I can wait,' said Cristina.

Pointless, thought Cadfael, to attempt to cast any doubt over this new radiance of hers. She had lived in shadow far too long to be intimidated. What was a murder unsolved to her? He doubted if guilt or innocence would make any difference. She had but one aim, nothing would deflect her from it. No question but from childhood she had read her playfellows rightly, known the one who contained the gnawing grief of loving her and knowing her to be pledged to the foster-brother he loved only a little less. Perhaps no less at all, until he grew into the pain of manhood. Girl children are always years older than their brothers at the same age in years, and see more accurately and jealously.

'Since you are going back,' said Cristina, viewing the activity in the stables with a kindling eye, 'you will see him again. Tell him I am my own woman now, or soon shall be, and can give myself where I will. And I will give myself to no one but him.'

'I will tell him so,' said Cadfael.

The yard was alive with men and horses, harness and gear slung on every staple and trestle down the line of stalls. The morning light rose clear and pale over the timber buildings, and the greens of the valley forest were stippled with the pallor of new leaf-buds like delicate green veils among the darkness of fir. There was a small wind, enough to refresh without troubling. A good day for riding.

'Which of these horses is yours?' she asked.

Cadfael led him forth to be seen, and surrendered him to the groom who came at once to serve.

'And that great raw-boned grey beast? I never saw him before. He should go well, even under a man in armour.'

'That is Hugh Beringar's favourite,' said Cadfael, recognising the dapple with pleasure. 'And a very ill-conditioned brute towards any other rider. Hugh must have left him resting in Oswestry, or he would not be riding him now.'

'I see they're saddling up for Einon ab Ithel, too,' she said. 'I fancy he'll be going back to Chirk, to keep an eye on your Beringar's northern border while he's busy elsewhere.'

A groom had come out across their path with a draping of harness on one arm and a saddle-cloth over the other, and tossed them over a rail while he went back to lead out the horse that would wear them. A very handsome beast, a tall, bright bay that Cadfael remembered seeing in the great court at Shrewsbury. He watched its lively gait with pleasure as the groom hoisted the saddle-cloth and flung it over the broad, glossy back, so taken with the horse that he barely noticed the quality of its gear. Fringes to the soft leather bridle, and a tooled brow-band with tiny studs of gold. There was gold on Einon's land, he recalled. And the saddle-cloth itself ...

He fixed and stared, motionless, for an instant holding his breath. A thick, soft fabric of dyed woollens, woven from heavy yarns in a pattern of twining, blossomy sprays, muted red roses, surely faded to that gentle shade, and deep blue irises. Through the centre of the flowers and round the border ran thick, crusted gold threads. It was not new, it had seen considerable wear, the wool had rubbed into tight balls here and there, some threads had frayed, leaving short, fine strands quivering.

490

No need even to bring out for comparison the little box in which he kept his captured threads. Now that he saw these tints at last he knew them past any doubt. He was looking at the very thing he had sought, too well known here, too often seen and too little regarded, to stir any man's memory.

He knew, moreover, instantly and infallibly, the meaning of what he saw.

He said never a word to Cristina of what he knew, as they walked back together. What could he say? Better by far keep all to himself until he could see his way ahead, and knew what he must do. Not one word to any, except to Owain Gwynedd, when he took his leave.

'My lord,' he said then, 'I have heard it reported of you that you have said, concerning the death of Gilbert Prestcote, that the only ransom for a murdered man is the life of the murderer. Is that truly reported? Must there be another death? Welsh law allows for the paying of a blood-price, to prevent the prolonged bloodshed of a feud. I do not believe you have forsaken Welsh for Norman law.'

'Gilbert Prestcote did not live by Welsh law,' said Owain, eyeing him very keenly. 'I cannot ask him to die by it. Of what value is a payment in goods or cattle to his widow and children?'

'Yet I think *galanas* can be paid in other mintage,' said Cadfael. 'In penitence, grief and shame, as high as the highest price judge ever set. What then?'

'I am not a priest,' said Owain, 'nor any man's confessor. Penance and absolution are not within my writ. Justice is.'

'And mercy also,' said Cadfael.

'God forbid I should order any death wantonly. Deaths atoned for, whether by goods or grief, pilgrimage or prison, are better far than deaths prolonged and multiplied. I would keep alive all such as have value to this world and to those who rub shoulders with them here in this world. Beyond that it is God's business.' The prince leaned forward, and the morning light through the embrasure shone on his flaxen head. 'Brother,' he said gently, 'had you not something we should have looked at again this morning by a better light? Last night we spoke of it.'

'That is of small importance now,' said Brother Cadfael, 'if you will consent to leave it in my hands some brief while. There shall be account rendered.'

'I will well!' said Owain Gwynedd, and suddenly smiled, and

491

the small chamber was filled with the charm of his presence. 'Only, for my sake – and others, doubtless? – carry it carefully.'

Chapter Thirteen

LIS HAD more sense than to go rushing straight to the enclosure of the Benedictine sisters, all blown and mired as he was from his run, and with the dawn only just breaking. So few miles from Shrewsbury here, and yet so lonely and exposed! Why, he had wondered furiously as he ran, why had those women chosen to plant their little chapel and garden in so perilous a place? It was provocation! The abbess at Polesworth should be brought to realise her error and withdraw her threatened sisters. This present danger could be endlessly repeated, so near so turbulent a border.

He made rather for the mill on the brook, upstream, where he had been held prisoner, under guard by a muscular giant named John, during those few February days. He viewed the brook with dismay, it was so fallen and tamed, for all its gnarled and stony bed, no longer the flood he remembered. But if they came they would expect to wade across merrily where the bed opened out into a smooth passage, and would scarcely wet them above the knee. Those stretches, at least, could be pitted and sown with spikes or caltrops. And the wooded banks at least still offered good cover for archers.

John Miller, sharpening stakes in the mill-yard, dropped his hatchet and reached for his pitch-fork when the hasty, stumbling feet thudded on the boards. He whirled with astonishing speed and readiness for a big man, and gaped to see his sometime prisoner advancing upon him empty-handed and purposeful, and to be greeted in loud, demanding English by one who had professed total ignorance of that language only a few weeks previously.

'The Welsh of Powys – a war-party not two hours away! Do the women know of it? We could still get them away towards the town – they're surely mustering there, but *late* ...'

'Easy, easy!' said the miller, letting his weapon fall, and scooping up his pile of murderous, pointed poles. 'You've found your tongue in a hurry, seemingly! And whose side may you be on this time, and who let you loose? Here, carry these, if you're come to make yourself useful.'

'The women must be got away,' persisted Elis feverishly. 'It's not too late, if they go at once ... Get me leave to speak to them, surely they'll listen. If *they* were safe, we could stand off even a war-band. I came to warn them ...'

'Ah, but they know. We've kept good watch since the last time. And the women won't budge, so you may spare your breath to make one man more, and welcome,' said the miller, 'if you're so minded. Mother Mariana holds it would be want of faith to shift an ell, and Sister Magdalen reckons she can be more use where she is, and most of the folks hereabouts would say that's no more than truth. Come on, let's get these planted – the ford's pitted already.'

Elis found himself running beside the big man, his arms full. The smoothest stretch of the brook flanked the chapel wall of the grange, and he realised as he fed out stakes at the miller's command that there was a certain amount of activity among the bushes and coppice-woods on both sides of the water. The men of the forest were well aware of the threat, and had made their own preparations, and by her previous showing, Sister Magdalen must also be making ready for battle. To have Mother Mariana's faith in divine protection is good, but even better if backed by the practical assistance heaven has a right to expect from sensible mortals. But a war-party of a hundred or more – and with one ignominious rout to avenge! Did they understand what they were facing?

'I need a weapon,' said Elis, standing aloft on the bank with feet solidly spread and black head reared towards the north-west, from which the menace must come. 'I can use sword, lance, bow, whatever's to spare ... That hatchet of yours, on a long haft ...' He had another chance weapon of his own, he had just realised it. If only he could get wind in time, and be the first to face them when they came, he had a loud

Welsh tongue where they would be looking only for terrified English, he had the fluency of bardic stock, all the barbs of surprise, vituperation and scarifying mockery, to loose in a flood against the cowardly paladins who came preying on holy women. A tongue like a whip-lash! Better still drunk, perhaps, to reach the true heights of scalding invective, but even in this state of desperate sobriety, it might still serve to unnerve and delay.

Elis waded into the water, and selected a place for one of his stakes, hidden among the water-weed with its point sharply inclined to impale anyone crossing in unwary haste. By the careful way John Miller was moving, the ford had been pitted well out in midstream. If the attackers were horsed, a step astray into one of those holes might at once lame the horse and toss the rider forward on to the pales. If they came afoot, at least some might fall foul of the pits, and bring down their fellows with them, in a tangle very vulnerable to archery.

The miller, knee-deep in midstream, stood to look on critically as Elis drove in his murderous stake, and bedded it firmly through the tenacious mattress of weed into the soil under the bank. 'Good lad!' he said with mild approval. 'We'll find you a pikel, or the foresters may have an axe to spare among them. You shan't go weaponless if your will's good.'

Sister Magdalen, like the rest of the household, had been up since dawn, marshalling all the linens, scissors, knives, lotions, ointments and stunning draughts that might be needed within a matter of hours, and speculating how many beds could be made available with decorum and where, if any of the men of her forest army should be too gravely hurt to be moved. Magdalen had given serious thought to sending away the two young postulants eastward to Beistan, but decided against it, convinced in the end that they were safer where they were. The attack might never come. If it did, at least here there was readiness, and enough stout-hearted forest folk to put up a good defence. But if the raiders moved instead towards Shrewsbury, and encountered a force they could not match, then they would double back and scatter to make their way home, and two girls hurrying through the woods eastward might fall foul of them at any moment on the way. No, better hold together here. In any case, one look at Melicent's roused and indignant face had given her due warning that that one, at any rate, would not go even if she was ordered.

495

'I am not afraid,' said Melicent disdainfully.

'The more fool you,' said Sister Magdalen simply. 'Unless you're lying, of course. Which of us doesn't, once challenged with being afraid! Yet it's generations of being afraid, with good reason, that have caused us to think out these defences.'

She had already made all her dispositions within. She climbed the wooden steps into the tiny bell-turret and looked out over the exposed length of the brook and the rising bank beyond, thickly lined with bushes, and climbing into a slope once coppiced but now run to neglected growth. Countrymen who have to labour all the hours of daylight to get their living cannot, in addition, keep up a day-and-night vigil for long. Let them come today, if they're coming at all, thought Sister Magdalen, now that we're at the peak of resolution and readiness, can do no more, and can only grow stale if we must wait too long.

From the opposite bank she drew in her gaze to the brook itself, the deep-cut and rocky bed smoothing out under her walls to the broad stretch of the ford. And there John Miller was just wading warily ashore, the water turgid after his passage and someone else, a young fellow with a thatch of black curls, was bending over the last stake, vigorous arms and shoulders driving it home, low under the bank and screened by reeds. When he straightened up and showed a flushed face, she knew him.

She descended to the chapel very thoughtfully. Melicent was busy putting away, in a coffer clamped to the wall and strongly banded, the few valuable ornaments of the altar and the house. At least it should be made as difficult as possible to pillage this modest church.

'You have not looked out to see how the men progress?' said Sister Magdalen mildly. 'It seems we have one ally more than we knew. There's a young Welshman of your acquaintance and mine hard at work out there with John Miller. A change of allegiance for him, but by the look of him he relishes this cause more than when he came the last time.'

Melicent turned to stare, her eyes very wide and solemn. '*He*?' she said, in a voice brittle and low. 'He was prisoner in the castle. How can he be here?'

'Plainly he has slipped his collar. And been through a bog or two on his way here,' said Sister Magdalen placidly, 'by the state of his boots and hose, and I fancy fallen in at least one by his dirty face.'

'But why make this way? If he broke loose ... what is he doing here?' demanded Melicent feverishly.

'By all the signs he's making ready to do battle with his own countrymen. And since I doubt if he remembers me warmly enough to break out of prison in order to fight for me,' said Sister Magdalen with a small, reminiscent smile, 'I take it he's concerned with *your* safety. But you may ask him by leaning over the fence.'

'No!' said Melicent in sharp recoil, and closed down the lid of the coffer with a clash. 'I have nothing to say to him.' And she folded her arms and hugged herself tightly as if cold, as if some traitor part of her might break away and scuttle furtively into the garden.

'Then if you'll give me leave,' said Sister Magdalen serenely, 'I think I have.' And out she went, between newly dug beds and first salad sowings in the enclosed garden, to mount the stone block that made her tall enough to look over the fence. And suddenly there was Elis ap Cynan almost nose to nose with her, stretching up to peer anxiously within. Soiled and strung and desperately in earnest, he looked so young that she, who had never borne children, felt herself grandmotherly rather than merely maternal. The boy recoiled, startled, and blinked as he recognised her. He flushed beneath the greenish smear the marsh had left across his cheek and brow, and reached a pleading hand to the crest of the fence between them.

'Sister, is she – is Melicent within there?'

'She is, safe and well,' said Sister Magdalen, 'and with God's help and yours, and the help of all the other stout souls busy on our account like you, safe she'll remain. How you got here I won't enquire, boy, but whether let out or broken out you're very welcome.'

'I wish to God,' said Elis fervently, 'that she was back in Shrewsbury this minute.'

'So do I, but better here than astray in between. And besides, she won't go.'

'Does she know', he asked humbly, 'that I am here?'

'She does, and what you're about, too.'

'Would she not – could you not persuade her? – to speak to me?'

'That she refuses to do. But she may think the more,' said Sister Magdalen encouragingly. 'If I were you, I'd let her alone to think the while. She knows you're here to fight for us –

there's matter for thought there. Now you'd best go to ground soon and keep in cover. Go and sharpen whatever blade they've found for you and keep yourself whole. These flurries never take long,' she said, resigned and tolerant, 'but what comes after lasts a lifetime, yours and hers. You take care of Elis ap Cynan, and I'll take care of Melicent.'

Hugh and his twenty men had skirted the Breidden hills before the hour of Prime, and left those great, hunched outcrops on the right as they drove on towards Westbury. A few remounts they got there, not enough to relieve all the tired beasts. Hugh had held back to a bearable pace for that very reason, and allowed a halt to give men and horses time to breathe. It was the first opportunity there had been even to speak a word, and now that it came no man had much to say. Not until the business on which they rode was tackled and done would tongues move freely again. Even Hugh, lying flat on his back for ease beside Cadfael under the budding trees, did not question him concerning his business in Wales.

'I'll ride with you, if I can finish my business here,' Cadfael had said. Hugh had asked him nothing then, and did not ask him now. Perhaps because his mind was wholly engrossed in what had to be done to drive the Welsh of Powys back into Caus and beyond. Perhaps because he considered this other matter to be very much Cadfael's business, and was willing to wait for enlightenment until it was offered, as at the right time it would be.

Cadfael braced his aching back against the bole of an oak just forming its tight leaf-buds, eased his chafed feet in his boots, and felt his sixty-one years. He felt all the older because all these troubled creatures pulled here and there through this tangle of love and guilt and anguish were so young and vulnerable. All but the victim, Gilbert Prestcote, dead in his helpless weakness – for whom Hugh would, because he must, take vengeance. There could be no clemency, there was no room for it. Hugh's lord had been done to death, and Hugh would exact payment. In iron duty, he had no choice.

'Up!' said Hugh, standing over him, smiling the abstracted but affectionate smile that flashed like a reflection from the surface of his mind when his entire concern was elsewhere. 'Get your eyes open! We're off again.' And he reached a hand to grip Cadfael's wrist and hoist him to his feet, so smoothly and carefully that Cadfael was minded to take offence. He was

498

not so old as all that, nor so stiff! But he forgot his mild grievance when Hugh said, 'A shepherd from Pontesbury brought word. They're up from their night camp and making ready to move.'

Cadfael was wide awake instantly. 'What will you do?'

'Hit the road between them and Shrewsbury and turn them back. Alan will be up and alert, we may meet him along the way.'

'Dare they attempt the town?' wondered Cadfael, astonished.

'Who knows? They're blown up with success, and I'm thought to be far off. And our man says they've avoided Minsterley but brought men round it by night. It seems they may mean a foray into the suburbs, at least, even if they draw off after. Town pickings would please them. But we'll be faster, we'll make for Hanwood or thereabouts and be between.'

Hugh made a gentle joke of hoisting Cadfael into the saddle, but for all that, Cadfael set the pace for the next mile, ruffled at being humoured and considered like an old man. Sixty-one was not old, only perhaps a little past a man's prime. He had, after all, done a great deal of hard riding these last few days, he had a right to be stiff and sore.

They came over a hillock into view of the Shrewsbury road, and beheld, thin and languid in the air above the distant trees beyond, a faint column of smoke rising. 'From their doused fires,' said Hugh, reining in to gaze. 'And I smell older burning than that. Somewhere near the rim of the forest, someone's barns have gone up in flames.'

'More than a day old and the smoke gone,' said Cadfael, sniffing the air. 'Better make straight for them, while we know where they are, for there's no telling which way they'll strike next.'

Hugh led his party down to the road and across it, where they could deploy in the fringes of woodland, going fast but quietly in thick turf. For a while they kept within view of the road, but saw no sign of the Welsh raiders. It began to seem that their present thrust was not aimed at the town after all, or even the suburbs, and Hugh led his force deeper into the woodland, striking straight at the deserted night camp. Beyond that trampled spot there were traces enough for eyes accustomed to reading the bushes and grass. A considerable number of men had passed through here on foot, and not so long ago, with a few ponies among them to leave droppings and brush off budding twigs from the tender branches. The ashen, blackened ruin of a cottage and its clustering sheds showed where their last victim had lost home, living and all, if not his life, and there was blood dried into the soil where a pig had been slaughtered. They spurred fast along the trail the Welsh had left, sure now where they were bound, for the way led deeper into the northern uplands of the Long Forest, and it could not be two miles now to the cell at Godric's Ford.

That ignominious rout at the hands of Sister Magdalen and her rustic army had indeed rankled. The men of Caus were not averse to driving off a few cattle and burning a farm or two by the way, but what they wanted above all, what they had come out to get, was revenge.

Hugh set spurs to his horse and began to thread the open woodland at a gallop, and after him his company spurred in haste. They had gone perhaps a mile more when they heard before them, distant and elusive, a voice raised high and bellowing defiance.

It was almost the hour of High Mass when Alan Herbard got his muster moving out of the castle wards. He was hampered by having no clear lead as to which way the raiders planned to move, and there was small gain in careering aimlessly about the western border hunting for them. For want of knowledge he had to stake on his reasoning. When the company rode out of the town they aimed towards Pontesbury itself, prepared to swerve either northward, to cut across between the raiders and Shrewsbury, or south-west towards Godric's Ford, according as they got word on the way from scouts sent out before daylight. And this first mile they took at speed, until a breathless countryman started out of the bushes to arrest their passage, when they were scarcely past the hamlet of Beistan.

'My lord, they've turned away from the road. From Pontesbury they're making eastward into the forest towards the high commons. They've turned their backs on the town for other game. Bear south at the fork.'

'How many?' demanded Herbard, already wheeling his horse in haste.

'A hundred at least. They're holding all together, no rogue stragglers left loose behind. They expect a fight.'

'They shall have one!' promised Herbard and led his men

south down the track, at a gallop wherever the going was fairly open.

Eliud rode among the foremost, and found even that pace too slow. He had in full all the marks of suspicion and shame he had invited, the rope to hang him coiled about his neck for all to see, the archer to shoot him down if he attempted escape close at his back, but also he had a borrowed sword at his hip, a horse under him and was on the move. He fretted and burned, even in the chill of the March morning. Here Elis had at least the advantage of having ridden these paths and penetrated these woodlands once before. Eliud had never been south of Shrewsbury, and though the speed they were making seemed to his anxious heart miserably inadequate, he could gain nothing by breaking away, for he did not know exactly where Godric's Ford lay. The archer who followed him, however good a shot he might be, was no very great horseman, it might be possible to put on speed, make a dash for it and elude him, but what good would it do? Whatever time he saved he would inevitably waste by losing himself in these woods. He had no choice but to let them bring him there, or at least near enough to the place to judge his direction by ear or eye. There would be signs. He strained for any betraying sound as he rode, but there was nothing but the swaying and cracking of brushed branches, and the thudding rumble of their hooves in the deep turf, and now and again the call of a bird, undisturbed by this rough invasion, and startlingly clear.

The distance could not be far now. They were threading rolling uplands of heath, to drop lower again into thick woodland and moist glades. All this way Elis must have run afoot in the night hours, splashing through these hollows of stagnant green and breasting the sudden rises of heather and scrub and outcrop rock.

Herbard checked abruptly in open heath, waving them all to stillness. 'Listen! Ahead on our right – men on the move.'

They sat straining their ears and holding their breath. Only the softest and most continuous whisper of sounds, compounded of the swishing and brushing of twigs, the rustle of last autumn's leaves under many feet, the snap of a dead stick, the brief and soft exchange of voices, a startled bird rising from underfoot in shrill alarm and indignation. Signs enough of a large body of men moving through woods almost stealthily, without noise or haste.

'Across the brook and very near the ford,' said Herbard

sharply. And he shook his bridle, spurred and was away, his men hard on his heels. Before them a narrow ride opened between well-grown trees, a long vista with a glimpse of low timber buildings, weathered dark brown, distant at the end of it, and a sudden lacework of daylight beyond, between the trees, where the channel of the brook crossed.

They were halfway down the ride when the boiling murmur of excited men breaking out of cover eddied up from the invisible waterside, and then, soaring loudly above, a single voice shouting defiance, and even more strangely, an instant's absolute hush after the sound.

The challenge had meant nothing to Herbard. It meant everything to Eliud. For the words were Welsh, and the voice was the voice of Elis, high and imperious, honed sharp by desperation, bidding his fellow-countrymen, 'Stand and turn! For shame on your fathers, to come whetting your teeth on holy women! Go back where you came from and find a fight that does you some credit!' And higher and more peremptorily: 'The first man ashore I spit on this pikel, Welsh or no, he's no kinsman of mine!'

This to a war-band roused and happy and geared for killing!

'Elis!' cried Eliud in a great howl of anger and dismay, and he lay forward over his horse's neck and drove in his heels, shaking the bridle wild. He heard the archer at his back shout an order to halt, heard and felt the quivering thrum of the shaft as it skimmed his right shoulder, tore away a shred of cloth, and buried itself vibrating in the turf beyond. He paid no heed, but plunged madly ahead, down the steep green ride and out on to the bank of the brook.

They had come by way of the thicker cover a little downstream, to come at the grange and the ford before they were detected, and leave aimless and out of range any defenders who might be stationed at the mill, where there was a better field for archery. The little footbridge had not yet been repaired, but with a stream so fallen from its winter spate there was no need of a bridge. From stone to stone the water could be leaped in two or three places, but the attackers favoured the ford, because so many could cross there shoulder to shoulder and bring a battering-ram of lances in one sweep to drive along the near bank. The forest bowmen lay in reeds and bushes, dispersed along the brink, but such a spearhead, with men and weight enough behind it, could cleave through and past them and be into the precinct within moments.

They were deceived if they thought the forest men had not detected their approach, but there was no sign of movement as the attackers threaded their way quietly between the trees to mass and sweep across the brook. Perhaps twenty cottars, woodsmen and hewers of laborious assarts from the forest lay in cover against more than a hundred Welsh, and every man of the twenty braced himself, and knew only too well how great a threat he faced. They knew how to keep still until the proper moment to move. But as the lurkers in the trees signalled along their half-seen ranks and closed all together in a sudden surge into the open at the edge of the ford, one man rose out of the bushes opposite and bestrode the grassy shelf of the shore, brandishing a long, two-tined pikel lashed to a six-foot pole, and sweeping the ford with it at breast-height.

That was enough to give them an instant's pause out of sheer surprise. But what stopped them mid-stride and set them back on their heels was the indignant Welsh trumpet blaring: 'Stand and turn! For shame on your fathers, to come whetting your teeth on holy women!'

He had not done, there was more, rolling off the inspired tongue in dread of a pause, or in such flight as to be unable to pause. 'Cowards of Powys, afraid to come north and meddle with men! They'll sing you in Gwynedd for this noble venture, how you jumped a brook and showed yourselves heroes against women older than your mothers, and a world more honest. Even your drabs of dams will disown you for this. You and your mongrel pedigrees shall be known for ever by the songs we'll make ...'

They had begun to stir out of their astonishmnent, to scowl and to grin. And still the hidden bowmen in the bushes held their hands, willing to wait the event, though their shafts were fitted and their bows partly drawn, ready to brace and loose. If by some miracle this peril might dissolve in withdrawal and conciliation, why lose arrows or blunt blades?

'*You*, is it?' shouted a Welshman scornfully. 'Cynan's pup, that we left spewing water and being pumped dry by the nuns. He, to halt us! A lickspit of the English now!'

'A match for you and better!' flashed Elis, and swung the pikel towards the voice. 'And with grace enough to let the sisters here alone, and to be grateful to them, too, for a life they could as well have let go down the stream, for all they owed me. What are you looking for here? What plunder is there, here among the willing poor? And for God's sake and your Welsh fathers' sake, what glory?'

He had done all he could, perhaps provided a few minutes of time, but he could do little more, and it was not enough. He knew it. He even saw the archer in the fringe of the trees opposite fit his shaft without haste, and draw very steadily and deliberately. He saw it out of the corner of his eye, while he continued to confront the lances levelled against him, but there was nothing he could do to deflect or elude, he was forced to stand and hold them as long as he could, shifting neither foot nor eye.

Behind him there was a rush of hooves, stamping deep into the turf, and someone flung himself sobbing out of the saddle in one vaulting bound, and along the shelf of grass above the water, just as the forest bowmen drew and loosed their first shafts, every man for himself, and the archer on the opposite shore completed his easy draw, and loosed full at Elis's breast. Welsh of Powys striking coldly at Welsh of Gwynedd. Eliud vented a scream of anger and defiance, and hurled himself between, embracing Elis breast to breast and covering him with his own body, sending them both reeling a pace backwards into the turf, to crash against a corner of the sisters' garden fence. The pikel with its long handle was jerked out of Elis's hand, and slashed into the stream in a great fan of water. The Welshman's arrow jutted from under Eliud's right shoulder-blade, transfixing his body and piercing through the under-flesh of Elis's upper arm, pinning the two together inseparably. They slid down the fence and lay in the grass locked in each other's arms, and their blood mingled and made one, closer even than fostering.

And then the Welsh were over and ashore, floundering in the pits of the ford, ripped on the stakes among the reeds, trampling the two fallen bodies, and battle was joined along the banks of the brook.

Almost at the same moment, Alan Herbard deployed his men along the eastern bank and waded into the fighting, and Hugh Beringar swept through the trees on the western bank, and drove the Welsh outposts into the churned and muddied ford.

The clang of hammer on anvil, with themselves cracked between, demoralised the Welsh of Powys, and the battle of Godric's Ford did not last long. The din and fury was out of

504

proportion to the damage done, when once they had leisure to assess it. The Welsh were ashore when their enemies struck from both sides, and had to fight viciously and hard to get out of the trap and melt away man by man into cover, like the small forest predators whose kinship with the earth and close understanding of it they shared. Beringar, once he had shattered the rear of the raiders, herded them like sheep but held his hand from unnecessary killing as soon as they fled into cover and made for home. Alan Herbard, younger and less experienced, gritted his teeth and thrust in with all his weight, absolute to make a success of his first command, and perhaps did more execution than was needful out of pure anxiety.

However it was, within half an hour it was over.

What Brother Cadfael most keenly remembered, out of all that clash, was the apparition of a tall girl surging out of the fenced enclosure of the grange, her black habit kilted in both hands, the wimple torn from her head and her fair hair streaming silvery in sudden sunlight, a long, fighting scream of defiance trailing like a bannerole from her drawn-back lips, as she evaded a greedy Welsh hand grasping at her, and flung herself on her knees beside the trampled, bruised, bleeding bodies of Elis and Eliud, still clamped in each other's arms against the bloodied fence.

Chapter Fourteen

T WAS done, they were gone, vanishing very rapidly and quietly, leaving only the rustling of bushes behind them on the near side of the brook, to make for some distant place where they could cross unseen and unpursued. On the further side, where the bulk of their numbers fled, the din of their flight subsided gradually into the depths of the neglected coppices, seeking thicker cover into which they could scatter and be lost. Hugh was in no haste, he let them salvage their wounded and hustle them away with them, several among them who might, indeed, be dead. There would be cuts and grazes and wounds enough among the defenders, by all means let the Welsh tend their own and bury their own. But he deployed his men, and a dozen or so of Herbard's party, like beaters after game, to herd the Welshmen back methodically into their own country. He had no wish to start a determined blood-feud with Madog ap Meredith, provided this lesson was duly learned.

The defenders of the grange came out of hiding, and the nuns out of their chapel, all a little dazed, as much by the sudden hush as by the violence that had gone before. Those who had escaped hurt dropped their bows and forks and axes, and turned to help those who were wounded. And Brother Cadfael turned his back on the muddy ford and the bloodied stakes, and knelt beside Melicent in the grass.

'I was in the bell-turret,' she said in a dry whisper. 'I saw how splendid ... He for us and his friend for him. They will live,

506

they *must* live, both … we can't lose them. Tell me what I must do.'

She had done well already, no tears, no shaking, no outcry after that first scream that had carried her through the ranks of the Welsh like the passage of a lance. She had slid an arm carefully under Elis's shoulders to raise him, and prevent the weight of the two of them from falling on the head of the arrow that had pinned them together. That spared them at least the worst agony and aggravated damage of being impaled. And she had wrapped the linen of her wimple round the shaft beneath Elis's arm to stem the bleeding as best she could.

'The iron is clean through,' she said. 'I can raise them more, if you can reach the shaft.'

Sister Magdalen was at Cadfael's shoulder by then, as sturdy and practical as ever, but having taken a shrewd look at Melicent's intent and resolute face she left the girl the place she had chosen, and went off placidly to salve others. Folly to disturb either Melicent or the two young men she nursed on her arm and her braced knee, when shifting them would only be worse pain. She went, instead, to fetch a small saw and the keenest knife to be found, and linen enough to stem the first bursts of bleeding when the shaft should be withdrawn. It was Melicent who cradled Elis and Eliud as Cadfael felt his way about the head of the shaft, sawed deeply into the wood, and then braced both hands to snap off the head with the least movement. He brought it out, barely dinted from its passage through flesh and bone, and dropped it aside in the grass.

'Lay them down now – so! Let them lie a moment.' The solid slope, cushioned by turf, received the weight gently as Melicent lowered her burden. 'That was well done,' said Cadfael. She had bunched the blood-stained wimple and held it under the wound as she drew aside, freeing a cramped and aching arm. 'Now do you rest, too. The one of these is shorn through the flesh of his arm, and has let blood enough, but his body is sound, and his life safe. The other – no blinking it, his case is grave.'

'I know it,' she said, staring down at the tangled embrace that bound the pair of them fast. 'He made his body a shield,' she said softly, marvelling. 'So much he loved him!'

And so much *she* loved him, Cadfael thought, that she had blazed forth out of shelter in much the same way, shrieking defiance and rage. To the defence of her father's murderer? Or had she long since discarded that belief, no matter how heavily

507

circumstances might tell against him? Or had she simply forgotten everything else, when she heard Elis yelling his solitary challenge? Everything but his invited peril and her anguish for him?

No need for her to have to see and hear the worst moment of all. 'Go fetch my scrip from the saddle yonder,' said Cadfael, 'and bring more cloth, padding and wrapping both, we shall need plenty.'

She was gone long enough for him to lay firm hold on the impaling shaft, rid now of its head, and draw it fast and forcefully out from the wound, with a steadying hand spread against Eliud's back. Even so it fetched a sharp, whining moan of agony, that subsided mercifully as the shaft came free. The spurt of blood that followed soon flowed; the wound was neat, a mere slit, and healthy flesh closes freely over narrow lesions, but there was no certainty what damage had been done within. Cadfael lifted Eliud's body carefully aside, to let both breathe more freely, though the entwined arms relinquished their hold very reluctantly. He enlarged the slit the arrow had made in the boy's clothing, wadded a clean cloth against the wound, and turned him gently on his back. By that time Melicent was back with all that he had asked; a wild, soiled figure with a blanched and resolute face. There was blood drying on her hands and wrists, the skirts of her habit at the knee were stiffening into a hard, dark crust, and her wimple lay on the grass, a stained ball of red. It hardly mattered. She was never going to wear that or any other in earnest.

'Now, we'd best get these two indoors, where I can strip and cleanse their injuries properly,' said Cadfael, when he was assured the worst of the bleeding was checked. 'Go and ask Sister Magdalen where we may lay them, while I find some stout men to help me carry them in.'

Sister Magdalen had made provision for more than one cell to be emptied within the grange, and Mother Mariana and the nuns of the house were ready to fetch and carry, heat water and bandage minor injuries with very good will, relieved now of the fear of outrage. They carried Elis and Eliud within and lodged them in neighbouring cells, for the space was too small to allow free movement to Cadfael and those helping him, if both cots were placed together. All the more since John Miller, who had escaped without a scratch from the mêlée, was one of the party. The gentle giant could not only heft sturdy young

508

men as lightly as babies, he also had a deft and reassuring hand with injuries.

Between the two of them they stripped Eliud, slitting the clothes from him to avoid racking him with worse pain, washed and dressed the wounds in back and breast, and laid him in the cot with his right arm padded and cradled to lie still. He had been trampled in the rush of the Welshmen crossing to shore, bruises were blackening on him, but he had no other wound, and it seemed the trampling feet had broken no bones. The arrowhead had emerged well to the right, through his shoulder, to pierce the flesh of Elis's upper arm. Cadfael considered the line the shot had taken, and shook his head doubtfully but not quite hopelessly over the chances of life and death. With this one he would stay, sit with him the evening through – the night if need be – wait the return of sense and wit. There were things they had to say to each other, whether the boy was to live or die.

Elis was another matter. He would live, his arm would heal, his honour would be vindicated, his name cleared, and for all Cadfael could see, there was no reason in the world why he should not get his Melicent. No father to deny him, no overlord at liberty to assert his rights in the girl's marriage, and Lady Prestcote would be no bar at all. And if Melicent had flown to his side before ever the shadow was lifted from him, how much more joyfully would she accept him when he emerged sunlit from head to foot. Happy innocent, with nothing left to trouble him but a painful arm, some weakness from loss of blood, a wrenched knee that gave him pain at an incautious movement, and a broken rib from being trampled. Troubles that might keep him from riding for some time, but small grievances indeed, now he had opened dazed dark eyes on the unexpected vision of a pale, bright face stooped close to his, and heard a remembered voice, one hard and cold as ice, saying very softly and tenderly, 'Elis … Hush, lie still! I'm here, I won't leave you.'

It was another hour and more before Eliud opened his eyes, unfocussed and feverish, glittering greenly in the light of the lamp beside his bed, for the cell was very dim. Even then he roused to such distress that Cadfael eased him out of it again with a draught of poppy syrup, and watched the drawn lines of pain gradually smooth out from the thin, intense face, and the large eyelids close again over the distracted gleam. No point in adding further trouble to one so troubled in body and soul. When he revived so far as to draw the garment of his own dignity about him, then his time would come.

Others came in to look down at him for a moment, and as quietly depart. Sister Magdalen came to bring Cadfael food and ale, and stood a while in silence watching the shallow, painful heave and fall of Eliud's breast, and the pinched flutter of his nostrils on whistling breath. All her volunteer army of defenders had dispersed about its own family business, every hurt tended, the stakes uprooted from the ford, the pitted bed raked smooth again, a day's work very well done. If she was tired, she gave no sign of it. Tomorrow there would be a number of the injured to visit again, but there had been few serious hurts, and no deaths. Not yet! Not unless this boy slipped through their fingers.

Hugh came back towards evening, and sought out Cadfael in the silent cell. 'I'm off back to the town now,' he said in Cadfael's ear. 'We've shepherded them more than halfway home, you'll see no more of them here. You'll be staying?'

Cadfael nodded towards the bed.

'Yes – a great pity! I'll leave you a couple of men, send by them for whatever you need. And after this,' said Hugh grimly, 'we'll have them out of Caus. They shall know whether there's still a sheriff in the shire.' He turned to the bedside and stood looking down sombrely at the sleeper. 'I saw what he did. Yes, a pity ...' Eliud's soiled and dismembered clothing had been removed; he retained nothing but the body in which he had been born into the world, and the means by which he had demanded to be ushered out of it, if Elis proved false to his word. The rope was coiled and hung over the bracket that held the lamp. 'What is this?' asked Hugh, as his eye lit upon it, and as quickly understood. 'Ah! Alan told me. This I'll take away, let him read it for a sign. This will never be needed. When he wakes, tell him so.'

'I pray God!' said Cadfael, so low that not even Hugh heard.

And Melicent came, from the cell where Elis lay sore with trampling, but filled and overfilled with unexpected bliss. She came at his wish, but most willingly, saw Cadfael to all appearances drowsing on his stool against the wall, signed Eliud's oblivious body solemnly with the cross, and stooped suddenly to kiss his furrowed forehead and hollow cheek before stealing silently away to her own chosen vigil.

510

Brother Cadfael opened one considerate eye to watch her draw the door to softly after her, and could not take great comfort. But with all his heart he hoped and prayed that God was watching with him.

In the pallid first light before dawn Eliud stirred and quivered, and his eyelids began to flutter stressfully as though he laboured hard to open them and confront the day, but had not yet the strength. Cadfael drew his stool close, leaning to wipe the seamed brow and working lips, and having an eye to the ewer he had ready to hand for when the tormented body needed it. But that was not the unease that quickened Eliud now, rousing out of his night's respite. His eyes opened wide, staring into the wooden roof of the cell and beyond, and shortened their range only when Cadfael leaned down to him braced to speak, seeing desperate intelligence in the hazel stare, and having something ripe within him that must inevitably be said.

He never needed to say it. It was taken out of his mouth.

'I have got my death,' said the thread of a voice that issued from Eliud's dry lips, 'get me a priest. I have sinned – I must deliver all those who suffer doubt ...'

Not his own deliverance, not that first, only the deliverance of all who laboured under the same suspicion.

Cadfael stooped closer. The gold-green eyes were straining too far, they had not recognised him. They did so now and lingered, wondering. 'You are the brother who came to Tregeiriog. Welsh?' Something like a sorrowful smile mellowed the desperation of his face. 'I do remember. It was you brought word of him ... Brother, I have my death in my mouth, whether he take me now of this grief or leave me for worse ... A debt ... I pledged it ...' He essayed, briefly, to raise his right hand, being strongly right-handed, and gave up the attempt with a whining intake of breath at the pain it cost him and shifted, pitiless, to the left, feeling at his neck where the coiled rope should have been. Cadfael laid a hand to the lifted wrist, and eased it back into the covers of the bed.

'Hush, lie still! I am here to command, there's no haste. Rest, take thought, ask of me what you will, bid me whatever you will. I'm here, I shan't leave you.'

He was believed. The slight body under the brychans seemed to sink and slacken in one great sigh. There was a small silence. The hazel eyes hung upon him with a great weight of

511

trust and sorrow, but without fear. Cadfael offered a drop of wine laced with honey, but the braced head turned aside. 'I want confession,' said Eliud faintly but clearly, 'of my mortal sin. Hear me!'

'I am no priest,' said Cadfael. 'Wait, he shall be brought to you.'

'I cannot wait. Do I know my time? If I live,' he said simply, 'I will tell it again and again – as long as there's need – I am done with all conceal.'

They had neither of them observed the door of the cell slowly opening, it was done so softly and shyly, by one troubled with dawn voices, but as hesitant to disturb those who might wish to be private as unwilling to neglect those who might be in need. In her own as yet unreasoned and unquestioned happiness Melicent moved as one led by angelic inspiration, exalted and humbled, requiring to serve. Her bloodied habit was shed, she had a plain woollen gown on her. She hung in the half-open doorway, afraid to advance or withdraw, frozen into stillness and silence because the voice from the bed was so urgent and uncomforted.

'I have killed,' said Eliud clearly. 'God knows I am sorry! I had ridden with him, cared for him, watched him founder and urged his rest ... And if ever he came home alive, then Elis was free ... to go back to Cristina, to marry ...' A great shudder went through him from head to foot, and fetched a moan of pain out of him. 'Cristina ... I loved her always ... from when we were children, but I did not, I did not speak of it, never, never ... She was promised to him before ever I knew her, in her cradle. How could I touch, how could I covet what was his?'

'She also loved,' said Cadfael, nursing him along the way. 'She let you know of it ...'

'I would not hear, I dared not, I had no right ... And all the while she was so dear, I could not bear it. And when they came back without Elis, and we thought him lost ... Oh, God, can you conceive such trouble as was mine, half-praying for his safe return, half wishing him dead, for all I loved him, so that at last I might speak out without dishonour, and ask for my love ... And then – you know it, it was you brought word ... and I was sent here, my mouth stopped just when it was so full of words ... And all that way I thought, I could not stop thinking, the old man is so sick, so frail, if he dies there'll be none to exchange for Elis ... If he dies I can return and Elis must stay ... Even a little time and I could still speak ... All I needed was a little time, now I was resolved. And that last day when he foundered ... I did all I could, I kept him man alive, and all the time, all the time it was clamouring in me, let him die! I did not do it, we brought him still living ...'

He lay still for a minute to draw breath, and Cadfael wiped the corners of the lips that laboured against exhaustion to heave the worst burden from heart and conscience. 'Rest a little. You try yourself too hard.'

'No, let me end it. Elis ... I loved him, but I loved Cristina more. And he would have wed her, and been content, but she ... He did not know the burning we knew. He knows it now. I never willed it ... it was not planned, what I did. All I did was to remember the lord Einon's cloak and I went, just as I was, to fetch it. I had his saddle-cloth on my arm –.' He closed his eyes against what he remembered all too clearly, and tears welled out from under the bruised lids and ran down on either cheek. 'He was so still, hardly breathing at all – so like death. And in an hour Elis would have been on his way home and I left behind in his place. So short a step to go! I did the thing I wish to God I had cut off my hands rather than do, I held the saddle-cloth over his face. There has not been a waking moment since when I have not wished it undone,' whispered Eliud, 'but to undo is not so easy as to do. As soon as I understood my own evil I snatched my hands away, but he was gone. And I was cowardly afraid and left the cloak lying, for if I'd taken it, it would have been known I'd been there. And that was the quiet hour and no one saw me, going or coming.'

Again he waited, gathering strength with a terrible, earnest patience to continue to the end. 'And all for nothing – for nothing! I made myself a murderer for nothing. For Elis came and told me how he loved the lord Gilbert's daughter and willed to be released from his bond with Cristina, as bitterly as she willed it, and I also. And he would go to make himself known to her father ... I tried to stop him ... I needed someone to go there and find my dead man, and cry it aloud, but not Elis, oh, not Elis! But he would go. And even then they still thought the lord Gilbert alive, only sleeping. So I had to fetch the cloak, if no one else would cry him dead – but not alone ... a witness, to make the discovery. I still thought Elis would be held and I should go home. He longed to stay and I to go ... This knot some devil tied,' sighed Eliud, 'and only I have deserved it. All they three suffer because of me. And you, brother, I did foully by you ...'

513

'In choosing me to be your witness?' said Cadfael gently. 'And you had to knock over the stool to make me look closely enough, even then. Your devil still had you by the hand, for if you had chosen another there might never have been the cry of murder that kept you both prisoners.'

'It was my angel, then, no devil. For I am glad to be rid of all lies and known for what I am. I would never have let it fall on Elis – nor on any other man. But I am human and fearful,' he said inflexibly, 'and I hoped to go free. Now that is solved. One way or another, I shall give a life for a life. I would not have let Elis bear it ... Tell her so!'

There was no need, she already knew. But the head of the cot was towards the door, and Eliud had seen nothing but the rough vault of the cell, and Cadfael's stooping face. The lamp had not wavered, and did not waver now, as Melicent withdrew from the threshold very softly and carefully, drawing the door to by inches after her.

'They have taken away my halter,' said Eliud, his eyes wandering languidly over the bare little room. 'They'll have to find me another one now.'

When it was all told he lay drained, very weak and utterly biddable, eased of hope and grateful for contrition. He let himself be handled for healing, though with a drear smile that said Cadfael wasted his pains on a dead man. He did his best to help the handling, and bore pain without a murmur when his wounds were probed and cleansed and dressed afresh. He tried to swallow the draughts that were held to his lips, and offered thanks for even the smallest service. When he drifted into an uneasy sleep, Cadfael went to find the two men Hugh had left to run his errands, and sent one of them riding to Shrewsbury with the news that would bring Hugh back again in haste. When he returned into the precinct, Melicent was waiting for him in the doorway. She read in his face the mixture of dismay and resignation he felt at having to tell over again what had been ordeal enough to listen to in the first place, and offered instant and firm reassurance.

'I know. I heard. I heard you talking, and his voice ... I thought you might need someone to fetch and carry for you, so I came to ask, I heard what Eliud said. What is to be done now?' For all her calm, she was bewildered and lost between father killed and lover saved, and the knowledge of the fierce affection those two foster-brothers had for each other, and

514

every way was damage and every escape was barred. 'I have told Elis,' she said. 'Better we should all know what we are about. God knows I am so confused now, I doubt if I know right from wrong. Will you come to Elis? He's fretting for Eliud.'

Cadfael went with her in perplexity as great as hers. Murder is murder, but if a life can pay the debt for a life, there was Elis to level the account. Was yet another life demanded? Another death justifiable? He sat down with her beside the bed, confronted by an Elis wide awake and in full possession of his senses, for all he hesitated on the near edge of fever.

'Melicent has told me,' said Elis, clutching agitatedly at Cadfael's sleeve. '*But is it true*? You don't know him as I do! Are you sure he is not making up this story, because he fears I may yet be charged? May he not even believe I did it? It would be like him to shoulder all to cover me. So he has done in old times when we were children, so he might even now. You saw, you saw what he has already done for me! Should I be here alive now but for Eliud? I can't believe so easily …'

Cadfael went about hushing him the most practical way, by examining the dressing on his arm and finding it dry, unstained and causing him no pain, let well alone for the time being. The tight binding round his damaged rib had caused him some discomfort and shortness of breath, and might be slightly slackened to ease him. And whatever dose was offered him he swallowed almost absently, his eyes never shifting from Cadfael's face, demanding answers to desperate questions. And there would be small comfort for him in the naked truth.

'Son,' said Cadfael, 'there's no virtue in fending off truth. The tale Eliud has told fits in every particular and it is truth. Sorry I am to say it, but true it is. Put all doubts out of your head.'

They received that with the same white calm and made no further protest. After a long silence Melicent said, 'I think you knew it before.'

'I did know it, from the moment I set eyes on Einon ab Ithel's brocaded saddle-cloth. That, and nothing else, could have killed Gilbert, and it was Eliud whose duty it was to care for Einon's horse and harness. Yes, I knew. But he made his confession willingly, eagerly, before I could question or accuse him. That must count to him for virtue, and speak on his side.'

'God knows,' said Melicent, shutting her pale face hard between her hands, as if to hold her wits together, 'on what

515

side I dare speak, who am so torn. All I know is that Eliud cannot, does not carry all the guilt. In this matter, which of us is innocent?'

'*You* are!' said Elis fiercely. 'How did you fail? But if I had taken a little thought to see how things were with him and with Cristina ... I was too easy, too light, too much in love with myself to take heed. I'd never dreamed of such a love, I didn't know ... I had all to learn.' It had been no easy lesson for him, but he had it by heart now.

'If only I had had more faith in myself and my father,' said Melicent, 'we could have sent word honestly into Wales, to Owain Gwynedd and to my father, that we two loved and entreated leave to marry ...'

'If only I had been as quick to see what ailed Eliud as he always was to put trouble away from me ...'

'If none of us ever fell short, or put a foot astray,' said Cadfael sadly, 'everything would be good in this great world, but we stumble and fall, every one. We must deal with what we have. He did it, and all we must share the gall.'

Out of a drear hush Elis asked, 'What will become of him? Will there be mercy? Surely he need not die?'

'It rests with the law, and with the law I have no weight.'

'Melicent relented to me,' said Elis, 'before ever she knew I was clean of her father's blood ...'

'Ah, but I did know!' she said quickly. 'I was sick in mind that ever I doubted.'

'And I love her the more for it. And Eliud has made confession when no man was accusing, and that must count for virtue to him, as you said, and speak on his side.'

'That and all else that speaks for him,' promised Cadfael fervently, 'shall be urged in his defence, I will see to that.'

'But you are not hopeful,' said Elis bleakly, watching his face with eyes all too sharp.

He would have liked to deny it, but to what end, when Eliud himself had accepted and embraced, with resignation and humility, the inevitable death? Cadfael made what comfort he could, short of lying, and left them together. The last glimpse, as he closed the door, was of two braced, wary faces following his going with a steady, veiled stare, their minds shuttered and secret. Only the fierce alliance of hand clasping hand on the brychan betrayed them.

Hugh Beringar came next day in a hurry, listened in dour silence

516

as Eliud laboured with desolate patience through the story yet again, as he had already done for the old priest who said Mass for the sisters. As Eliud's soul faced humbly toward withdrawal from the world, Cadfael noted his misused body began to heal and find ease, very slowly, but past any doubt. His mind consented to dying, his body resolved to live. The wounds were clean, his excellent youth and health fought hard, whether for or against him who could say?

'Well, I am listening,' said Hugh somewhat wearily, pacing the bank of the brook with Cadfael at his side. 'Say what you have to say.' But Cadfael had never seen his face grimmer.

'He made full and free confession,' said Cadfael, 'before ever a finger was pointed at him, as soon as he felt he might die. He was in desperate haste to do justice to all, not merely Elis, who might lie under the shadow of suspicion because of him. You know me, I know you. I have said honestly, I was about to tell him that I knew he had killed. I swear to you he took that word clean out of my mouth. He wanted confession, penance, absolution. Most of all he wanted to lift the threat from Elis and any other who might be overcast.'

'I take your word absolutely,' said Hugh, 'and it is something. But enough? This was no hot-blood squall blown up in a moment before he could think, it was an old man, wounded and sick, sleeping in his bed.'

'It was not planned. He went to reclaim his lord's cloak. That I am sure is true. But if you think the blood was cold, dear God, how wrong you are! The boy was half-mad with the long bleeding of hopeless love, and had just come to the point of rebellion, and the thread of a life – one he had been nursing in duty! – cut him off from the respite his sudden courage needed. God forgive him, he had hoped Gilbert would die! He has said so honestly. Chance showed him a thread so thin it could be severed by a breath, and before ever he took thought, he blew! He says he has repented of it every moment that has passed since that moment, and I believe it. Did you never, Hugh, do one unworthy thing on impulse, that grieved and shamed you ever after?'

'Not to the length of killing an old man in his bed,' said Hugh mercilessly.

'No! Nor nothing to match it,' said Cadfael with a deep sigh and briefer smile. 'Pardon me, Hugh! I am Welsh and you are English. We Welsh recognise degrees. Theft, theft absolute, without excuse, is our most mortal offence, and therefore we hedge it about with degrees, things which are not theft absolute – taking openly by force, taking in ignorance, taking without leave, providing the offender owns to it, and taking to stay alive, where a beggar has starved three days – no man hangs in Wales for these. Even in dying, even in killing, we acknowledge degrees. We make a distinction between homicide and murder, and even the worst may sometimes be compounded for a lesser price than hanging.'

'So might I make distinctions,' said Hugh, brooding over the placid ford. 'But this was my lord, into whose boots I step, for want of my king to give orders. He was no close friend of mine, but he was fair to me always, he had an ear to listen, if I was none too happy with some of his more austere judgments. He was an honourable man and did his duty by this shire of mine as he best knew, and his death fetters me.'

Cadfael was silent and respectful. It was a discipline removed now from his, but once there had been such a tie, such a fealty, and he remembered it, and they were none so far apart.

'God forbid,' said Hugh, 'that I should hurl out of the world any but such as are too vile to be let live in it. And this is no such monster. One mortal error, one single vileness, and a creature barely – what's his age? Twenty-one? And driven hard, but which of us is not? He shall have his trial and I shall do what I must,' said Hugh hardly. 'But I would to God it was taken out of my hands!'

Chapter Fifteen

EFORE HE left that evening he made his will clear for the others. 'Owain may be pressed, if Chester moves again, he wants his men. I have sent to say that all who are clear now shall leave here the day after tomorrow. I have six good men-at-arms belonging to him in Shrewsbury. They are free, and I shall equip them for their journey home. The day after tomorrow as early as may be, around dawn, they will be here to take Elis ap Cynan with them, back to Tregeiriog.'

'Impossible,' said Cadfael flatly. 'He cannot yet ride. He has a twisted knee and a cracked rib, besides the arm wound, though that progresses well. He will not ride in comfort for three or four weeks. He will not ride hard or into combat for longer.'

'He need not,' said Hugh shortly. 'You forget we have horses borrowed from Tudur ap Rhys, rested and ready for work now, and Elis can as well ride in a litter as could Gilbert in far worse condition. I want all the men of Gwynedd safely out of here before I move against Powys, as I mean to. Let's have one trouble finished and put by before we face another.'

So that was settled and no appeal. Cadfael had expected the order to be received with consternation by Elis, both on Eliud's account and his own, but after a brief outcry of dismay, suddenly checked, there was a longer pause for thought, while Elis put the matter of his own departure aside, not without a hard, considering look, and turned only to confirm that there

519

was no chance of Eliud escaping trial for murder and very little of any sentence but death being passed upon him. It was a hard thing to accept, but in the end it seemed Elis had no choice but to accept it. A strange, embattled calm had taken possession of the lovers, they had a way of looking at each other as though they shared thoughts that needed no words to be communicated, but were exchanged in a silent code no one else could read. Unless, perhaps, Sister Magdalen understood the language. She herself went about in thoughtful silence and with a shrewd eye upon them both.

'So I am to be fetched away early, the day after tomorrow,' said Elis. He cast one brief glance at Melicent and she at him. 'Well, I can and will send in proper form from Gwynedd, it's as well the thing should be done openly and honestly when I pay my suit to Melicent. And there will be things to set right at Tregeiriog before I shall be free.' He did not speak of Cristina, but the thought of her was there, desolate and oppressive in the room with them. To win her battle, only to see the victory turn to ash and drift through her fingers. 'I'm a sound sleeper,' said Elis with a sombre smile, 'they may have to roll me in my blankets and carry me out snoring, if they come too early.' And he ended with abrupt gravity: 'Will you ask Hugh Beringar if I may have my bed moved into the cell with Eliud these last two nights? It is not a great thing to ask of him.'

'I will,' said Cadfael, after a brief pause to get the drift of that, for it made sense more ways than one. And he went at once to proffer the request. Hugh was already preparing to mount and ride back to the town, and Sister Magdalen was in the yard to see him go. No doubt she had been deploying for him, in her own way, all the arguments for mercy which Cadfael had already used, and perhaps others of which he had not thought. Doubtful if there would be any harvest even from her well-planted seed, but if you never sow you will certainly never reap.

'Let them be together by all means,' said Hugh, shrugging morosely, 'if it can give them any comfort. As soon as the other one is fit to be moved I'll take him off your hands, but until then let him rest. Who knows, that Welsh arrow may yet do the solving for us, if God's kind to him.'

Sister Magdalen stood looking after him until the last of the escort had vanished up the forested ride.

'At least,' she said then, 'it gives him no pleasure. A pity to proceed where nobody's the gainer and every man suffers.'

'A great pity! He said himself,' reported Cadfael, equally thoughtfully, 'he wished to God it could be taken out of his hands.' And he looked along his shoulder at Sister Magdalen, and found her looking just as guilelessly at him. He suffered a small, astonished illusion that they were even beginning to resemble each other, and to exchange glances in silence as eloquently as did Elis and Melicent.

'Did he so?' said Sister Magdalen in innocent sympathy. 'That might be worth praying for, I'll have a word said in chapel at every office tomorrow. If you ask for nothing, you deserve nothing.'

They went in together, and so strong was this sense of an agreed understanding between them, though one that had better not be acknowledged in words, that he went so far as to ask her advice on a point which was troubling him. In the turmoil of the fighting and the stress of tending the wounded he had had no chance to deliver the message with which Cristina had entrusted him, and after Eliud's confession he was divided in mind as to whether it would be a kindness to do so now, or the most cruel blow he could strike.

'This girl of his in Tregeiriog – the one for whom he was driving himself mad – she charged me with a message to him and I promised her he should be told. But now, with this hanging over him ... Is it well to give him everything to live for, and when there may be no life for him? Should we make the world, if he's to leave it, a thousand times more desirable? What sort of kindness would that be?'

He told her, word for word, what the message was. She pondered, but not long.

'Small choice if you promised the girl. And truth should never be feared as harm. But besides – from all I see, he is willing himself to die, though his body is determined on life, and without every spur he may win the fight over his body, turn his face to the wall, and slip away. As well, perhaps, if the only other way is the gallows. But if – I say *if* – the times relent and let him live, then pity not to give him every armour and every weapon to survive to hear the good news.' She turned her head and looked at him again with the deep, calculating glance he had observed before, and then she smiled. 'It is worth a wager,' she said.

'I begin to think so, too,' said Cadfael and went in to see the wager laid.

521

They had not yet moved Elis and his cot into the neighbouring cell; Eliud still lay alone. Sometimes, marking the path the arrow had taken clean through his right shoulder, but a little low, Cadfael doubted if he would ever draw bow again, even if at some future time he could handle a sword. That was the least of his threatened harms now. Let him be offered as counter-balance the greatest promised good.

Cadfael sat down beside the bed, and told how Elis had asked leave to join him and been granted what he asked. That brought a strange, forlorn brightness to Eliud's thin, vulnerable face. Cadfael refrained from saying a word about Elis's imminent departure, however, and wondered briefly why he kept silent on that matter, only to realise hurriedly that it was better not even to wonder, much less question. Innocence is an infinitely fragile thing and thought can sometimes injure, even destroy it.

'And there is also a word I promised to bring you and have had no quiet occasion until now. From Cristina when I left Tregeiriog.' Her name caused all the lines of Eliud's face to contract into a tight, wary pallor, and his eyes to dilate in sudden bright green like stormy sunlight through June leaves. 'Cristina sends to tell you, by me, that she has spoken with her father and with yours and soon, by consent, she will be her own woman to give herself where she will. And she will give herself to none but you.'

An abrupt and blinding flood drowned the green and sent the sunlight sparkling in sudden fountains, and Eliud's good left hand groped lamely after anything human he might hold by for comfort, closed hungrily on the hand Cadfael offered, and drew it down against his quivering face, and lower into the bed, against his frantically beating heart. Cadfael let him alone thus for some moments, until the storm passed. When the boy was still again, he withdrew his hand gently.

'But she does not know,' whispered Eliud wretchedly, 'what I am ... what I have done ...'

'What she knows of you is all she needs to know, that she loves you as you love her, and there is not nor ever could be any other. I do not believe that guilt or innocence, good or evil can change Cristina towards you. Child, by the common expectation of man you have some thirty years at least of your life to live, which is room for marriage, children, fame,

522

atonement, sainthood. What is done matters, but what is yet to do matters far more. Cristina has that truth in her. When she does know all, she will be grieved, but she will not be changed.'

'My expectation,' said Eliud faintly through the covers that hid his ravaged face, 'is in weeks, months at most, not thirty years.'

'It is God fixes the term,' said Cadfael, 'not men, not kings, not judges. A man must be prepared to face life, as well as death, there's no escape from either. Who knows the length of the penance, or the magnitude of the reparation, that may be required of you?'

He rose from his place then, because John Miller and a couple of other neighbours, nursing the small scars of the late battle, carried in Elis, cot and all, from the next cell and set him down beside Eliud's couch. It was a good time to break off, the boy had the spark of the future already alive in him, however strongly resignation prompted him to quench it, and now this reunion with the other half of his being came very aptly, Cadfael stood by to see them settled and watch John Miller strip down the covers from Eliud and lift and replace him bodily, as lightly as an infant and as deftly as if handled by a mother. John had been closeted with Elis and Melicent, and was grown fond of Elis as of a bold and promising small boy from among his kin. A useful man, with his huge and balanced strength, able to pick up a sick man from his sleep – provided he cared enough for the man! – and carry him hence without disturbing his rest. And devoted to Sister Magdalen, whose writ ran here firm as any king's.

Yes, a useful ally.

Well …

The next day passed in a kind of deliberate hush, as if every man and every woman walked delicately, with bated breath, and kept the ritual of the house with particular awe and reverence warding off all mischance. Never had the horarium of the order been more scrupulously observed at Godric's Ford. Mother Mariana, small, wizened and old, presided over a sisterhood of such model devotion as to disarm fate. And her enforced guests in their twin cots in one cell were quiet and private together, and even Melicent, now a lay guest of the house and no postulant, went about the business of the day with a pure, still face, and left the two young men to their own measures.

523

Brother Cadfael observed the offices, made some fervent prayers of his own, and went out to help Sister Magdalen tend the few injuries still in need of supervision among the neighbours.

'You're worn out,' said Sister Magdalen solicitously, when they returned for a late bite of supper and Compline. 'Tomorrow you should sleep until Prime, you've had no real rest for three nights now. Say your farewell to Elis tonight, for they'll be here at first light in the morning. And now I think of it,' she said, 'I could do with another flask of that syrup you brew from poppies, for I've emptied my bottle, and I have one patient to see tomorrow who gets little sleep from pain. Will you refill the flask if I bring it?'

'Willingly,' said Cadfael, and went to fetch the jar he had had sent from Brother Oswin in Shrewsbury after the battle. She brought a large green glass flask, and he filled it to the brim without comment.

Nor did he rise early in the morning, though he was awake in good time; he was as good at interpreting a nudge in the ribs as the next man. He heard the horsemen when they came, and the voice of the portress and other voices, Welsh and English both, and among them, surely, the voice of John Miller. But he did not rise and go out to speed them on their way.

When he came forth for Prime, the travellers, he reckoned, must be two hours gone on their way into Wales, armed with Hugh's safe-conduct to cover the near end of the journey, well mounted and provided. The portress had conducted them to the cell where their charge, Elis ap Cynan, would be found in the nearer bed, and John Miller had carried him out in his arms, warmly swathed, and bestowed him in the litter sent to bear him home. Mother Mariana herself had risen to witness and bless their going.

After Prime Cadfael went to tend his remaining patient. As well to continue just as in the previous days. Two clear hours should be ample start, and someone had to be the first to go in – no, not the first, for certainly Melicent was there before him, but the first of the others, the potential enemy, the uninitiated.

He opened the door of the cell, and halted just within the threshold. In the dim light two roused, pale faces confronted him, almost cheek to cheek. Melicent sat on the edge of the bed, supporting the occupant in her arms, for he had raised himself to sit upright, with a cloak draped round his naked shoulders, to meet this moment erect. The bandage swathing

524

his cracked rib heaved to a quickened and apprehensive heart-beat, and the eyes that fixed steadily upon Cadfael were not greenish hazel, but almost as dark as the tangle of black curls.

'Will you let the lord Beringar know,' said Elis ap Cynan, 'that I have sent away my foster-brother out of his hands, and am here to answer for all that may be held against him. He put his neck in a noose for me, so do I now for him. Whatever the law wills can be done to me in his place.'

It was said. He drew a deep breath, and winced at the stab it cost him, but the sharp expectancy of his face eased and warmed now the first step was taken, and there was no more need of any concealment.

'I am sorry I had to deceive Mother Mariana,' he said. 'Say I entreat her forgiveness, but there was no other way in fairness to all here. I would not have any other blamed for what I have done.' And he added with sudden impulsive simplicity, 'I'm glad it was you who came. Send to the town quickly, I shall be glad to have this over. And Eliud will be safe now.'

'I'll do your errand,' said Cadfael gravely, 'both your errands. And ask no questions.' Not even whether Eliud had been in the plot, for he already knew the answer. From all those who had found it necessary to turn a blind eye and a deaf ear, Eliud stood apart in his despairing innocence and lamentable guilt. Some-one among those bearers of his on the road to Wales might have a frantically distressed invalid on his hands when the long, deep sleep drew to a close. But at the end of the enforced flight, whatever measures Owain Gwynedd took in the matter, there was Cristina waiting.

'I have provided as well as I could,' said Elis earnestly. 'They'll send word ahead, she'll come to meet him. It will be a hard enough furrow, but it will be life.'

A deal of growing up seemed to have been done since Elis ap Cynan first came raiding to Godric's Ford. This was not the boy who had avenged his nervous fears in captivity by tossing Welsh insults at his captors with an innocent face, nor the girl who had cherished dreamy notions of taking the veil before ever she knew what marriage or vocation meant.

'The affair seems to have been well managed,' said Cadfael judicially. 'Very well, I'll go and make it known – here and in Shrewsbury.'

He had the door half-closed behind him when Elis called, 'And then will you come and help me do on my clothes? I would like to meet Hugh Beringar decent and on my feet.'

525

And that was what he did, when Hugh came in the afternoon, grim-faced and black-browed, to probe the loss of his felon. In Mother Mariana's tiny parlour, dark-timbered and bare, Elis and Melicent stood side by side to face him. Cadfael had got the boy into his hose and shirt and coat, and Melicent had combed out the tangles from his hair, since he could not do it himself without pain. Sister Magdalen, after one measuring glance as he took his first unsteady steps, had provided him a staff to reinforce his treacherous knee, which would not go fairly under him as yet, but threatened to double all ways to let him fall. When he was ready he looked very young, neat and solemn, and understandably afraid. He stood twisted a little sideways, favouring the knitting rib that shortened his breath. Melicent kept a hand ready, close to his arm, but held off from touching.

'I have sent Eliud back to Wales in my place,' said Elis, stiff as much with apprehension as with resolve, 'since I owe him a life. But here am I, at your will and disposal, to do with as you see fit. Whatever you hold due to him, visit upon me.'

'For God's sake sit down,' said Hugh shortly and disconcertingly. 'I object to being made the target of your self-inflicted suffering. If you're offering me your neck, that's enough. I have no need of your present pains. Sit and take ease. I am not interested in heroes.'

Elis flushed, winced and sat obediently, but he did not take his eyes from Hugh's grim countenance.

'Who helped you?' demanded Hugh with chilling quietness.

'No one. I alone made this plan. Owain's men did as they were ordered by me.' That could be said boldly, they were well away in their own country.

'*We* made the plan,' said Melicent firmly.

Hugh ignored her, or seemed to. 'Who helped you?' he repeated forcibly.

'No one. Melicent knew, but she took no part. The sole blame is mine. Deal with me!'

'So alone you moved your cousin into the other bed. That was marvel enough, for a man crippled himself and unable to walk, let alone lift another man's weight. And as I hear, a certain miller of these parts carried Eliud ap Griffith to the litter.'

'It was dark within, and barely light without,' said Elis steadily, 'and I ...'

'*We*,' said Melicent.

' … I had already wrapped Eliud well, there was little of him to see. John did nothing but lend his strong arms in kindness to me.'

'Was Eliud party to this exchange?'

'*No!*' they said together, loudly and fiercely.

'No!' repeated Elis, his voice shaking with the fervour of his denial. 'He knew nothing. I gave him in his last drink a great draught of the poppy syrup that Brother Cadfael used on us to dull the pain, that first day. It brings on deep sleep. Eliud slept through all. He never knew! He never would have consented.'

'And how did you, bed-held as you were, come by that syrup?'

'*I* stole the flask from Sister Magdalen,' said Melicent. 'Ask her! She will tell you what a great dose has been taken from it.'

So she would, with all gravity and concern. Hugh never doubted it, nor did he mean to put her to the necessity of answering. Nor Cadfael either. Both had considerately absented themselves from this trial, judge and culprits held the whole matter in their hands.

There was a brief, heavy silence that weighed distressfully on Elis, while Hugh eyed the pair of them from under knitted brows, and fastened at last with frowning attention upon Melicent.

'You of all people,' he said, 'had the greatest right to require payment from Eliud. Have you so soon forgiven him? Then who else dare gainsay?'

'I am not even sure,' said Melicent slowly, 'that I know what forgiveness is. Only it seems a sad waste that all a man's good should not be able to outweigh one evil, however great. That is the world's loss. And I wanted no more deaths. One was grief enough, the second would not heal it.'

Another silence, longer than the first. Elis burned and shivered, wanting to hear his penalty, whatever it might be, and know the best and the worst. He quaked when Hugh rose abruptly from his seat.

'Elis ap Cynan, I have no charge to make in law against you. I want no exaction from you. You had best rest here a while yet. Your horse is still in the abbey stables. When you are fit to ride, you may follow your foster-brother home.' And before they had breath to speak, he was out of the room, and the door closing after him.

Brother Cadfael walked a short way beside his friend when

Hugh rode back to Shrewsbury in the early evening. The last days had been mild, and in the long green ride the branches of the trees wore the first green veil of the spring budding. The singing of the birds, likewise, had begun to throb with the yearly excitement and unrest before mating and nesting and rearing the young. A time for all manner of births and beginnings, and for putting death out of mind.

'What else could I have done?' said Hugh. 'This one has done no murder, never owed me that very comely neck he insists on offering me. And if I had hanged him I should have been hanging both, for God alone knows how even so resolute a girl as Melicent – or the one you spoke of in Tregeiriog for that matter – is ever going to part the two halves of that pair. Two lives for one is no fair bargain.' He looked down from the saddle of the raw-boned grey which was his favourite mount, and smiled at Cadfael, and it was the first time for some days that he had been seen to smile utterly without irony or reserve. 'How much did you know?'

'Nothing,' said Cadfael simply. 'I guessed at much, but I can fairly say I knew nothing and never lifted finger.' In silence and deafness and blindness he had connived, but no need to say that, Hugh would know it, Hugh, who could not have connived. Nor was there any need for Hugh ever to say with what secret gratitude he relinquished the judgement he would never have laid down of his own will.

'What will become of them all?' Hugh wondered. 'Elis will go home as soon as he's well enough, I suppose, and send formally to ask for his girl. There's no man of her kin to ask but her own mother's brother, and he's far off with the queen in Kent and out of reach. I fancy Sister Magdalen will advise the girl to go back to her step-mother for the waiting time, and have all done in proper form, and she has sense enough to listen to advice, and the patience to wait for what she wants, now she's assured of getting it in the end. But what of the other pair?'

Eliud and his companions would be well into Wales by this time and need not hurry, to tire the invalid too much. The draught of forgetfulness they had given him might dull his senses for a while even when he awoke, and his fellows would do their best to ease his remorse and grief, and his fear for Elis. But that troubled and passionate spirit would never be quite at rest.

'What will Owain do with him?'

'Neither destroy nor waste him,' said Cadfael, 'provided you cede your rights in him. He'll live, he'll marry his Cristina – there'll be no peace for prince or priest or parent until she gets her way. As for his penance, he has it within him, he'll carry it lifelong. There is nothing but death itself you or any man could lay upon him that he will not lay upon himself. But God willing, he will not have to carry it alone. There is no crime and no failure can drive Cristina from him.'

They parted at the head of the ride. It was premature dusk under the trees, but still the birds sang with the extreme and violent joy that seemed loud enough to shake such fragile instruments into dust or burst the hearts in their breasts. There were windflowers quivering in the grass.

'I go lighter than I came,' said Hugh, reining in for a moment before he took the homeward road.

'As soon as I see that lad walking upright and breathing deep, I shall follow. And glad to be going home.' Cadfael looked back at the low timber roofs of Mother Mariana's grange, where the silvery light through gossamer branches reflected the ceaseless quivering of the brook. 'I hope we have made, between us all, the best of a great ill, and who could do more? Once, I remember, Father Abbot said that our purpose is justice, and with God lies the privilege of mercy. But even God, when he intends mercy, needs tools to his hand.'

THE HEAVEN TREE TRILOGY

Edith Pargeter

Volume 1 THE HEAVEN TREE

England in the reign of King John — a time of beauty
and squalor, of swift treachery and unswerving loyalty.
Against this violent, exciting background the story of
Harry Talvace, master mason, unfolds. Harry and his
foster-brother Adam flee to Paris, where Harry's genius
for carving draws him into friendship with Ralf Isambard,
lord of Parfois, and the incomparably beautiful Madonna
Benedetta, a Venetian courtesan.
'If you do not appreciate this superb novel, I despair of
you'
Illustrated London News

Volume 2 THE GREEN BRANCH

Young Harry Talvace, the son of Ralf Isambard's master-
builder has grown up in the court of Llewelyn, Prince of
North Wales. Deep in his heart he nurses a desire for
vengeance . . .
'A remarkably fine and historical novel'
Books and Bookmen

Volume 3 THE SCARLET SEED

The story reaches a strange and violent climax as the
principal characters are drawn together in the final siege
of Parfois under the towering shadow of the first Harry's
master-work.
'It is immensely readable. A swinging, romantic yarn'
Sunday Telegraph

MOST LOVING
MERE FOLLY

Edith Pargeter

When Suspiria Freeland is charged with poisoning her
artist husband Theo, a scandalised country presumes her
guilty. What could one expect of a woman like that, with
her clever tongue and abrupt manners, those odd-shaped
pots she calls art and her ramshackle house – a woman
who brazenly admits her affair with a garage mechanic
fourteen years her junior?

Dissected in the full limelight of public courts and gutter
press, Dennis and Suspiria's already ill-matched liaison
seems doomed – and Suspiria's acquittal is only the start
of their real problems. Under the weight of popular
sentiment and censure, a world watching, misinterpreting
and taking possession of their every move, expecting and
hoping for disaster, how can their love survive? Worse,
the question the lovers dare not voice – if Suspiria did
not kill Theo, who did?

Eight and a half centuries have passed since Brother Cadfael walked the streets of Shrewsbury but you can still follow in his footsteps.

The Abbey of Saint Peter and Saint Paul and Shrewsbury Council have joined together to create a series of walks round this ancient town that will allow you, literally, to stand in the steps of Brother Cadfael. You can see the castle, the Meole Brook, St Giles' Church and many other locations that have survived from mediaeval times.

These walks have been created by the Abbey Restoration Project, which is dedicated to the upkeep of the Abbey of Saint Peter and Saint Paul and the excavation and preservation of the monastery ruins.

If you would like further details, or even to make a contribution to the horrendous cost of preservation, please contact:

Shrewsbury Abbey Restoration Project,
Project Office,
1 Holy Cross Houses,
Abbey Foregate,
Shrewsbury SY2 6BS

CADFAEL COUNTRY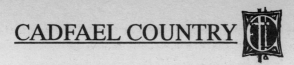

SHROPSHIRE AND THE WELSH BORDERS

Rob Talbot & Robin Whiteman

Introduction by *ELLIS PETERS*

'. . . no ground in the kingdom has been more tramped over by armies, coveted by chieftains, ravaged by battles, sung by poets and celebrated in epics of legend and tragedy' *Ellis Peters*

This beautifully illustrated book is a celebration of Ellis Peters's Shropshire and the world of the medieval sleuth she has created in Brother Cadfael. Robin Whiteman's meticulous and authoritative text, complemented by Rob Talbot's timeless photographs, creates an impression of the Shropshire landscape as it would once have appeared to Brother Cadfael as he travelled its desolate moorlands, dense forests and hidden valleys.

From Salop (Shrewsbury) and the Stiperstones to the remote hills of Clun Forest, from Offas's Dyke to the Devil's Chair, CADFAEL COUNTRY – based on the bestselling *Chronicles of Brother Cadfael* – is an enthralling pilgrimage through this wild and fascinating border country. Informative and comprehensive, it is a must for all fans of Ellis Peters and for those who love the region.

THE CADFAEL COMPANION

Robin Whiteman

Introduction by ELLIS PETERS

Since the publication of A MORBID TASTE FOR
BONES in 1977, millions of readers throughout the world
have been captivated and enthralled by the exploits and
adventures of Brother Cadfael – the twelfth-century Welsh
monk and herbalist of Shrewsbury Abbey who uses his
skills, knowledge and considerable powers of deduction to
solve murder mysteries.

The first book was set in the spring of 1137; the second in
the summer of 1138. Thereafter, the Chronicles have
progressed steadily until they now number eighteen. Set in
England and Wales during the turbulent reign of King
Stephen, the novels are a rich blend of historical fact and
derived fiction: people and places, real and imagined, are
woven with such skill and confidence into the fabric of the
whole that without access to the author's mind or
knowledge of her references it becomes almost impossible
to disentangle. But Cadfael fans, like the good monk
himself, are endlessly curious . . .

While writing and researching CADFAEL COUNTRY,
Robin Whiteman discovered a wealth of fascinating
material relating to Cadfael and his colourful world.
Indexing the mysteries produced a list of over one
thousand characters and locations, factual and fictional –
some appearing in only one story, others recurring again
and again. An encyclopaedic guide to these, and to
Cadfael's plants and herbs, plus a glossary of mediaeval
terms, form THE CADFAEL COMPANION.